The Good Companions

A rediscovery book

GREAT NORTHERN

First published by:
William Heinemann Ltd 1929
This special edition published 2007 by: Great Northern Books
PO Box 213, Ilkley, LS29 9WS
www.greatnorthernbooks.co.uk

Copyright details
Good Companions novel: © J B Priestley
Quotations from other works: © J B Priestley reprinted by permission
of PFD on behalf of the Estate of J B Priestley.

Priestley's 'Happy Daydream' – Biographical Background and
The Good Companions on Stage and Screen: © Lee Hanson

ISBN: 978-1-905080-35-9

Layout and production: David Burrill

Printed in Spain

CIP Data
A catalogue for this book is available from the British Library

For more information about J.B. Priestley and events visit www.jbpriestley.co.uk
and www.jbpriestley-society.com

Contents

The Good
Companions
fills Selfridge's
window,
Oxford Street,
London,
December
1929.
(Special
Collections,
Bradford
University
Library)

A First Word

Barry Cryer

The scene: St. Ives in the early 60s. The kids were small, the sun shone and I was wandering round a bookshop, seeking beach fodder. And there it was – *The Good Companions*. I picked up a Penguin and the die was cast. I'd already dabbled in JB's 'adventures' – *The Doomsday Men, The Shapes of Sleep* etc, but this was the big one, that I'd never read. We went down to the beach. I don't remember the rest of that day – the old maestro had me in his thrall. Embarking, in those quaint pre-Google days on a quest to devour everything I could from his pen. *Bright Day, Lost Empires*, on and on it went. My shelves now groan happily. If JB's work is Trafalgar Square, *The Good Companions* is Nelson's Column. Picaresque, picturesque - but enough of alliteration. It was love at first sight and remains so. If you haven't read *The Good Companions*, I envy you, it lies ahead. If you have, read it again and the old spell will be cast once more.

Foreword

Tom Priestley

On the 5th of January 1928, my father wrote to his stepmother in Bradford: "I am going up to London in a week's time to stay with Walpole so that we can finish our novel, "Farthing Hall", together. I have just begun my long novel, "*The Good Companions*". It begins in the West Riding but wanders all over the place, is comic and deals with some people who run a Pierrot troupe. You'll like it I think". I am sure she did like it, as did many many thousands more.

He had met Hugh Walpole in 1925, when editing a series of books called "*These Diversions*", and they had become close friends, close enough for Walpole to offer to join forces on a book together, and to pass on the advance to my father to allow him sufficient financial security to settle down to his "long novel". He thanked Walpole in his dedication: "To Hugh Walpole for a friendship that has triumphantly survived a collaboration". When I asked him how he came to write "*The Good Companions*", he told me:

"What I needed was a fair time for the writing of it. Circumstances fell out so I just had the time to do a long book". It took him a year to write, beginning in Church Hanborough in Oxfordshire, continuing down in Deal, where he went for a change of air, and finishing in London in the newly bought house in Hampstead. All this was of course before my time; I arrived after the family had moved into our Highgate House, and after the establishment of The Good Companions Trust, which my mother had wisely set up to provide funds for my sisters' education. I am a Trustee now, but alas not a beneficiary!

Then I asked him how he set about writing a novel; did he plan it in his head or work from notes? "I make a certain number of notes, but I probably make fewer than most novelists. I certainly don't work to a plan or a definite synopsis because I think that makes rather dull writing". So I asked if he did much revision; "No none at all; I mean I just go through for elementary mistakes, but not real revision. Quite a number of people have to write something before they know what they want to write; I'm not one of those people – that part I would do in my head so to speak. If you write to a synopsis, then you haven't left the

Tom and his father in the garden of 3 The Grove, Highgate prior to the opening of Priestley House on Athlone Street, Kentish Town, 30th June 1937. Priestley house was a block of flats built to house the needy; it also provided a nursery. Tom was chosen to open the building, hence the key. Today the flats are managed by Camden Council and still provide much needed social housing in the capital. (Special Collections, Bradford University Library)

most important part of your mind free – you've dictated to it so you're never going to be at your best really". And in a novel is it the characters that are more important or the story? "Oh it's chiefly the characters. I think a good novel has to come out of the characters".

And what splendid characters they are here; the three principals: Jess Oakroyd, "a working man between forty-five and fifty years of age, a trifle under medium height but stockily built, neither ugly nor handsome, with a blunt nose, a moustache that may have been once brisk and fair but is now ragged and mousey, and blue eyes that regard the world pleasantly enough"; Miss Elizabeth Trant, "who must be about thirty-seven, though being so straight and slim and fair she does not look it"; and Inigo Jollifant, "now in his twenty-sixth year ..He is a thin loose-limbed youth, a trifle above medium height...A long lock of hair falls perpetually across his right eyebrow; his nose itself is long, wandering, and whimsical, and his grey eyes are set unusually wide apart and have in them a curious gleam". And a host of others, Joby Jackson, Unkerlarthur, Effie and Elsie, Morton Mitcham, Jerry Jerningham, Mr & Mrs Joe, Jimmy Nunn, and of course the ravishing Susie Dean et al, amusing, eccentric and all vividly portrayed, who our principals meet on the journey through their lives, through the story, and through an England my father would truly discover when he came to write "*English Journey*" a few years later.

Interesting to note he is not always precise in his descriptions, Jess Oakroyd is "between 45 and 50", Miss Trant is "about 37"; his favourite suffix is "-ish"; often characters in his novels are thinnish or oldish; perhaps this imprecision encourages the readers to use their imaginations, in the same way he invites them to join him on the journey through the story, which is as much his journey without a synopsis, as the journey of the characters themselves. The journey is a joint adventure, and one feels he is aware of his reader looking over his shoulder as he writes for instance "once more we look down upon English hills".

"*The Good Companions*" combines two of his favourite themes: the emancipation of the individual, escaping from the restraints of dull, ordinary life, and the dynamic of the group where the individual becomes free to join others and form a new unit, and the reader becomes attached to

Priestley stops
to tie his
shoelace.
Photographed
by Tom
Priestley, early
1950s.
(Special
Collections,
Bradford
University
Library)

both, ready to echo with Jess: "I don't like the thowt on us all leavin' one another, I don't ....Eh, we've had wer bit of fun together, three on us". Fun it certainly is, and Jess, like Joe Gargery in *Great Expectations*, finds it all a great "lark". And if the characters are enjoying themselves and the author is enjoying himself, free in his mind from the dull and the boring, how can the readers fail to enjoy themselves too? "You'll like it I think"!

But for him this book was only one milestone of many in his literary journey, and strangely he found its enormous success unbalancing because it attached an unwanted label to him. Our conversation continued:

TP: The Good Companions was a tremendous success, wasn't it? It was a great best seller.
JBP: Yes, I've never been allowed to forget it.
TP: Was that a surprise for you?
JBP: Not really, but it's not one of my favourite books.
TP: Did the success please you in the end, or was it a nuisance?
JBP: Oh no, on the whole it pleased me – yes. But I don't like to be thought of as the author of The Good Companions.

If this seems puzzling at first, reflect on what he wrote to his American publishers in 1940: "By the way my reputation seems to be changing here. A few years ago I was that despised thing, the popular novelist, the best-seller, the rich mountebank, fair game for any young highbrow. But now they are all turning round, perhaps led by Desmond McCarthy, and I receive solemn tributes from the solemn young. I think the autobiographical books and the experimental plays have done this. I believe it might pay you to change your note about me a little, dropping the references to *The Good Companions'* period successes, and rather concentrating on the work of the last three years – rather more emphasis on the philosophical side and less on the pure entertainment side".

The general public only discovered him with *The Good Companions*, ignorant of the seventeen books which preceded it, and even today there are many people who have only read that one book, ignorant of the output of over one hundred books, so his feelings may well be justified; a writer wants to be judged on the work of his maturity, not just one popular book. And, remember, he was a man who liked to experiment and try his hand at a great variety of genres, so the attempts to label him as

a one book author were callously limiting.

But this later grumble cannot diminish the "pure entertainment" of *The Good Companions*. It is one of those books you think you will dip into and suddenly find you have gone several lengths, beckoned forward to meet new characters, and travel to new places, laughing the while. It is a great read, a book to relish and enjoy; a merry journey through the late '20s, through a world of concert parties, grim towns, bedraggled theatres, station waiting rooms, seaside piers, cafés and bars, in the company of such a delightful set of characters you won't want to leave them. And we can sense the pleasure he had in writing it, dipping day after day into the well of his imagination, exercising his skill in vigorous prose, welcoming the characters as they came flooding into his mind, and sharing it all with us his partners in the process, in that special relationship between writer and reader. What larks indeed. You'll like it I think!
Tom Priestley

Tom Priestley is one of Britain's most highly acclaimed film editors. He won a BAFTA in 1967 for his work on the now cult classic *Morgan: A Suitable Case for Treatment* and was Oscar nominated in 1972 for *Deliverance* directed by John Boorman. He has worked on numerous prize-winning films with many talented filmmakers including Karel Reisz, Lindsay Anderson, Bryan Forbes, Michael Radford, Jack Clayton, Blake Edwards and Roman Polanski. He now spends his time more in the world, lecturing on film editing and promoting his father's life and work. He is both President of The Priestley Centre for the Arts and The J.B. Priestley Society.

Dame Judi
Dench
appearing as
Miss Trant in
the 1974 Stage
Musical of the
book at Her
Majesty's
Theatre.
(Photographer
unknown)

Foreword

Dame Judi Dench

The Good Companions is a wonderful story. I played Miss Trant in the 1974 West End stage production, which was adapted by Ronnie Harwood with music by André Previn and lyrics by Johnny Mercer. The show contained the whole essence of the novel and provincial England in the 1920s. It looked absolutely right and I loved doing it; my husband saw it on nine occasions and enjoyed it each time. It ran for eight months at Her Majesty's Theatre and I'm sure it could have run for much longer had it not been for several IRA bomb scares in the West End. Nevertheless it was a wonderfully successful show, with a talented cast.

I met two J.B. Priestleys. The first one came to watch a rehearsal of *The Good Companions* and I remember we were all paralysed with fright. He looked at me rather gravely and I believed he really didn't see me as his idea of Miss Trant. Later, when he saw me in my stage costume with my Marcel wave wig, I found he did approve of me.

The second J.B. Priestley invited my husband, Michael Williams, and me to lunch at his home in Stratford. He wasn't a bit frightening then, and was in very good form. The time passed like a flash, and I found him enormously entertaining. I recall that in one of the windows at Kissing Tree House there was a large carved fish eye which seemed to have a magnifying effect. He did this marvellous thing where he went out into the garden and looked through it. We saw his face through the fish eye beckoning us, and at that moment I saw him as an enchanter, a real magician. It was wonderful, but I still always thought of him as a Yorkshireman first.

I am delighted this wonderful story is returning after a long absence. I believe Priestley would be delighted too. It is one of his finest achievements and a book with which we should all become reacquainted.
Dame Judi Dench

Top:
Priestley's father Jonathan, stepmother Amy and half-sister Winnie on the steps of the family home, 5 Saltburn Place, off Toller Lane, Bradford, circa 1908. Jonathan Priestley was a pioneering teacher, headmaster and socialist who had a profound influence on his son. (Special Collections, Bradford University Library)

Bottom:
Priestley second from the left on the back row in the Saltburn United Football Team, 1906. It was at this time he was beginning to read the novels that would eventually help shape The Good Companions. Football is featured in the opening pages of the novel as Jess Oakroyd returns home from a match. (Special Collections, Bradford University Library)

Priestley's 'Happy Daydream' –

Biographical Background

'Here indeed', said a *Sunday Times* review on the 3rd August 1929, 'is a truly great novel which so far from being dead and forgotten within a season or two, will find more friends as the years pass by.' These words were prophetic and to readers of a certain generation *The Good Companions* is a familiar title, a book stored away in the collective memory – a novel in which both the characters and the story exert a powerful hold on the reader.

To get at the book's origins we must begin in Priestley's boyhood, with his formative reading experiences and the authors who influenced him most. Alone in his front attic bedroom at 5 Saltburn Place, Bradford, he fashioned painted bookshelves from old orange boxes and filled them with choice volumes of *World Classics* and the *Everyman* series. Fielding, Defoe, Lesage, Richardson, Smollett, Sterne and Dickens all found their place and were read avidly. 'The shelves and the books were light enough, but their literary culture weighed tons… sitting close to my angry little gas fire, which could only begin to warm my hands by first roasting my feet, I would spend an hour or so with one of the world's giants, in all the hungry solemnity of a seventeen-year-old'.

It was in this small gas lit room he gained a love for the Picaresque, 'ample tales in which the characters go wandering', and he soon enough had his own favourite realistic tales of travel and adventure: *Moll Flanders, Tom Jones, Humphrey Clinker, Roderick Random, The Pickwick Papers* and above all *Cervantes' Don Quixote* – a book he came to describe as 'one of the most amusing and wisest tales ever written' and its main characters, 'Spain's greatest gifts to the world of Western Man'. The bustle of adventure, grand humour, sense of movement and fantastic characters captivated him. 'I remember first reading it. It was one Christmas, one real snowy Christmas, and I'd had to go to bed with a snivelling cold – and I remember curling up in bed, very cosy, with the snow

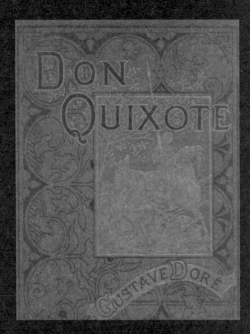

Top:
Don Quixote
illustrated by
Gustave Dore.
This circa 1900
edition by
Cassell, Petter
and Galpin
would have
been similar to
that read by
the young J.B.
Priestley in his
attic bedroom.
(Photographer
unknown)

Bottom:
Priestley
grouped with
his fellow
entrants after
his
matriculation
ceremony into
Trinity Hall,
Cambridge,
1919.
(Photographer
Unknown)

thickening on the window panes and the cold blue daylight dying – and first staring at the pictures…'

Then, in 1914, a giant crack in the world opened and Priestley set out on his own perilous adventure into the unknown, where he was confronted with dangers far removed from the fantastical world of the Don and his earthy Squire. On this decision to join up for the Great War he said 'I went at a signal from the unknown… there came, out of the unclouded blue of that summer a challenge that was almost like a conscription of the spirit. Other men, who had not lived as easily as we had, had drilled and marched and borne arms – couldn't we?'

He was lucky to return, a fact he never lost sight of. Few of his friends made it back to the Bradford streets of his youth. Gone also was the young lad reading tales of adventure in an upstairs room. Life was now a matter of recovery, of carrying on and allowing the scars to heal. After a period of time back in Bradford and some forays into local journalism an ex-servicemen's grant led him away to Cambridge University and after into writing good solid prose as a reviewer, literary critic and in time a brilliant essayist. No tales of glorious adventure on the pages now, just hard graft and his head down.

Cambridge wasn't really to his liking, in his twenties and from the north he felt he didn't fit. Yet despite this he thrived. In his third year he delivered his own lectures and even turned down the security of several overseas academic posts in the pursuit of his dream to be a writer. Cambridge also provided him with his greatest friend and confidant, the poet and editor Edward Davison. The two men formed a close bond and corresponded with each other for the rest of their lives. He also gained a wife at this time, Pat Tempest, a Bradford girl he'd known since boyhood and who had written to him throughout the war. On a visit home he plucked her from behind the counter of Bradford Central Library, married her without fuss and set up home, first in Cambridge and then in London where they shared a flat with Davison.

Forever fretful about where money would come from, Priestley worked almost non-stop through the early twenties to gain a footing in the literary world. Then, just when success was signalling tragedy struck. After the birth of their second daughter, Pat was diagnosed with an inoperable bladder

Top left:
Priestley's first wife Pat Tempest seen here with daughter Barbara, 1923. (Special Collections, Bradford University Library)

Top right:
Gerald Bullett, Teddy Davison and Priestley in the garden of the house at Chinnor Hill, 1922. Davison became Priestley's greatest lifelong friend and confidant. (Special Collections, Bradford University Library)

Bottom:
The only surviving picture of Jack Priestley and Pat Tempest together. (Special Collections, Bradford University Library)

cancer. Having survived the horrors of the trenches Priestley now endured the slow and painful death of his young wife. Not long after this news he also lost his much loved and influential father at the age of only 56. What the war had started these hammer blows finished: his youth was now lost forever.

Out of his mind with worry Priestley took Pat and the family away from London to the cleaner air of Chinnor Hill in Buckinghamshire. Hopeful the countryside might aid her recovery he shuttled back and forth to London, writing whenever he could to meet the rising cost of medical bills. Work became not only a necessity, but his main source of solace. Everyday he sat at his typewriter and wrote himself out of misery. Other support came from Edward Davison, Chinnor Hill neighbours Gerald and Rosemary Bullett, and his relationship with Jane Wyndham Lewis who he met at a literary function. They married in September 1926, ten months after Pat's untimely death at the age of 29. Jane immediately took responsibility for Priestley's daughters treating them as her own and becoming a wonderful step-mother. She also came to have three children of her own with her new husband.

By now Priestley had published four successful volumes of essays and some commissioned biography and criticism. With a rising reputation and the regular habit of hard work at his disposal his thoughts turned to fiction. Supported by a growing band of literary friends that included Arnold Bennett, H.G. Wells, Rose Macauley and J.M. Barrie, he sent up two trial balloons in *Adam in Moonshine*, (1927) and *Benighted*, (1928). When considering his next attempt he turned to the novels that had nourished him in his far away attic bedroom and the idea of a contemporary picaresque long novel emerged. But one look at his perilous finances told him that buying the time to write it was impossible. It was here that his close friend, the novelist Hugh Walpole, intervened and suggested they collaborate on a novel to be called *Farthing Hall*. Once the book was underway Walpole donated his share of the advance royalties – a huge generous act that changed Priestley's life forever.

'I saw no reason why the picaresque novel should vanish with the stagecoach. Why not one about my own England of the twenties? The England I knew and presenting it quite realistically.' His publisher, agent and

Top:
Priestley and second wife Jane Wyndham Lewis early 1930s. (Special Collections, Bradford University Library)

Bottom Left:
With Hugh Walpole in the garden of Walpole's house, Brackenburn, in The Lake District. Walpole's generosity changed Priestley's life forever. (Special Collections, Bradford University Library)

Bottom Right:
Hugh Walpole and Rose Macauley as godparents at Rachel Priestley's christening, 1930. (Special Collections, Bradford University Library)

some friends saw things differently. He was told the picaresque was definitely out, as was the long novel. Such books were hard to print and even harder to sell. And didn't he know there was depression sweeping across the country with unemployment and misery rife?

Faced with this opposition Priestley shrugged and carried on, all the time knowing the reason he had to write it. 'I had had the war, in which almost every man I had known and liked had been killed. Then, just as life was opening out, there came a period of anxiety, overwork, constant strain, ending tragically. Later, when that time was further away, I would be able to face it, not only in memory but in work... But first I had to find some release, give myself a holiday of the spirit while writing this novel of 250,000 words. So I gave myself a holiday from anxiety and strain and tragic circumstance, shaping and colouring a long happy daydream.' Quite simply, it was the only book Priestley wanted to write and therefore the only book he could write at the time.

His next move made things even worse: he chose to build his story around a travelling concert party. 'This, I was told, was fatal. The monster I was planning would now be a back stage novel, which readers, it appeared, had always disliked. That was not all. I had found a title that was no good. 'No, old boy; think again.' I did, once I had finished the book, so that my desk was littered with sheets on which I had scribbled possible alternatives. But it was no use, the white elephant would have to be called *The Good Companions*'

Still Priestley held fast. When the book was completed Heinemann got a lukewarm response of only 3,000 advance sales and printed 10,000 only because of the cost of setting up such a long book. Priestley's 'happy daydream' arrived in bookstores in July, 1929. Good reviews such as that in the *Sunday Times* followed, but sales were only moderate. For a couple of months Heinemann's apprehension appeared correct. Then, in the autumn, to the sudden amazement of the publisher and Priestley the balloon went up. The reading public decided that a long realistically depicted picaresque novel was definitely in fashion. The book became a complete and unexpected triumph.

By Christmas, Heinemann were sending

In his study at Well Walk, Hampstead, where he finished The Good Companions. (Special Collections, Bradford University Library)

out 5,000 a day. A year later it still sold more than a thousand copies a week and was reprinted fifteen times. The book swept across the nation and the world and found a vast audience not aware of fiction before it encountered his work, a similar audience to that Dickens captured. The story created light in a world still recovering from a devastating war and experiencing one of the worst depressions of the century.

The Good Companions contains all Priestley's great strengths as a novelist: narrative that moves at a fine, controlled pace; vigorous and pure writing, free from artistic deception; immense power of place with exact social realism and observation; characters whose thoughts and words and actions reveal to us our own hidden intuitions; and finally, rich and powerful humour.

Certain comparisons with Dickens are sound. Like the master he adapts the conventions of stage drama to serious literature, and as a result the book radiates theatrical energy. Also like Dickens it plunges from one adventure to another and is at times an effortless expression of a comic view of life. Like *The Pickwick Papers* some episodes are supremely funny and unforgettable.

Inigo's high tea with the Second Resurrectionists is a brilliant example.

Not that the book is entirely consolatory in tone, it also something more complex. There is an undertone of sadness in the failed ambitions of some of the characters; and the loneliness of the decaying provisional towns, dingy lodging houses and crumbling theatres reveal an England never before seen. An England Priestley knew better than any author of his day and an England that still exists in forgotten corners of the country.

'Tewborough was like an engine with a burst boiler lying on the side of the road; it was a money-making machine that had almost stopped working, for only a wheel here and there shakily revolved or a pulley gave a groan or two; it was a factory that could now show you nothing but broken windows and litter and mouldering ledgers and a mumbling caretaker, it was nothing but an old cash-box containing only dust and cobwebs and a few forgotten pence… It was a town of dwindling incomes, terrifying overdrafts, of shopkeepers who lived by stretching one another's credit, of working men who were rapidly becoming waiting men, their chief occupation being to

Top:
Priestley slugs
a punch bag in
a 1930
publicity still.
The now
famous author
was in demand
by
photographers
all over the
world.
(Special
Collections,
Bradford
University
Library)

Bottom:
Priestley
convalescing
after being
wounded in the
First World
War; front row
last on the
right.
(Photographer
unknown)

hang about the doors of buildings that
were known – with fine irony – as
Labour Exchanges.'

So here is Priestley's biggest selling
book, the novel he was told not to
write, but wrote anyway. The book that
helped him emerge from one of the
most difficult periods of his life; his
homage to the authors who weighed
down his hand fashioned teenage
bookshelves; his white elephant that
turned into an enormous balloon. *The
Good Companions* returns in this
special hardback edition after too long
away. Priestley's 'happy daydream' has
lost none of its strength or appeal and
is now ready to once again find new
friends up and down the country and
across the world - people seeking a
break from the stresses, strains and
uncertainties of our own age.

*'Shakespeare's Duke of Athens, sitting
in the audience, said 'The best in this
kind are but shadows'; but we,
knowing a darkness and despair
Athens and Elizabethan England never
knew, can find in these shadows a
wealth of meaning, movement, colour
and living speech, and the faces of our
brothers and sisters.'*
From *The Moments*, 1961.

I knew he had served in France during the First World War and I asked him why he had never written about his experiences either in fact or in fiction. It was clumsy of me. A haunted, doomed look crossed his face. He waved a hand repeatedly to and fro, banishing the subject from our conversation. He stared into the fire as though seeing again the horror, repeatedly biting his bottom lip, fighting the memories that were too painful, too terrible to be allowed to surface. And that, I think, is a clue to the real Jack Priestley.

Ronald Harwood

Another photograph of Priestley in his study at Well Walk, Hampstead around the time when The Good Companions was first published. (Special Collections, Bradford University Library)

September 3, 1930

The Sketch

A news cutting that heralds the birth of Priestley's fourth daughter Rachel. The success of The Good Companions gave him celebrity status. (Source and photographers unknown)

The Author
of
"The Good
Companions"
—With his
Good
Companions.

THE AUTHOR OF "THE GOOD COMPANIONS" AND "ANGEL PAVEMENT" AT HIS TYPEWRITER. MR. J. B. PRIESTLEY—SNAPPED BY MRS. PRIESTLEY.

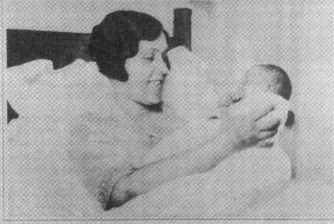

"GOOD COMPANIONS" OF THE AUTHOR OF "THE GOOD COMPANIONS": MRS. J. B. PRIESTLEY AND HER INFANT DAUGHTER.

Mr. J. B. Priestley is the distinguished author of "The Good Companions," the celebrated picaresque novel which enjoyed such an enormous success, and is said to have brought its author in the sum of £16,000—less income tax.! His latest book, "Angel Pavement," has just appeared; and he has also just become the father of a new little daughter. Our photographs show Mrs. Priestley with the infant Miss Priestley, and Mr. Priestley with his typewriter—actually at work on the manuscript of his latest book. Mrs. Priestley took the photograph herself, at their home at Kingsmoor, Devonshire.

PHOTOGRAPH OF MRS. PRIESTLEY BY P. AND N.P.

Other extracts from *Margin Released, Literature and Western Man, Instead of the Trees, Delight* and *Johnson Over Jordan*.

Editors of the Rediscovering Priestley Series and author of the Biographical Background and The Good Companions on Stage and Screen:

Lee Hanson is an expert on J.B. Priestley's life and work. A writer and teacher at Bradford Grammar School he is a member of the J.B. Priestley Society.

David Joy acted as researcher for the anthology J.B. Priestley's Yorkshire. Former editor of the Dalesman he is an acknowledged expert on Yorkshire and the Dales.

A sketch of
Priestley by
Robert Austen,
1925. This is
the earliest
known portrait
of Priestley.

The Good Companions

J.B. Priestley

To
Hugh Walpole
for a friendship that has even
triumphantly survived
collaboration

Contents

CHAPTER ONE
Mr Oakroyd Leaves Home

I

THERE, far below, is the knobbly backbone of England, the Pennine Range. At first, the whole dark length of it, from the Peak to Cross Fell, is visible. Then the Derbyshire hills and the Cumberland fells disappear, for you are descending, somewhere about the middle of the range, where the high moorland thrusts itself between the woollen mills of Yorkshire and the cotton mills of Lancashire. Great winds blow over miles and miles of ling and bog and black rock, and the curlews still go crying in that empty air as they did before the Romans came. There is a glitter of water here and there, from the moorland tarns that are now called reservoirs. In summer you could wander here all day, listening to the larks, and never meet a soul. In winter you could lose your way in an hour or two and die of exposure perhaps, not a dozen miles from where the Bradford trams end or the Burnley trams begin. Here are Bodkin Top and High Greave and Black Moor and Four Gates End, and though these are lonely places, almost unchanged since the Domesday Book was compiled, you cannot understand industrial Yorkshire and Lancashire, the wool trade and the cotton trade and many other things besides, such as the popularity of Handel's *Messiah* or the Northern Union Rugby game, without having seen such places. They hide many secrets. Where the moor thins out are patches of ground called 'Intake', which means that they are land wrested from the grasp of the moor. Over to the right is a long smudge of smoke, beneath which the towns of the West Riding lie buried, and fleeces, tops, noils, yarns, stuffs, come and go, in and out of the mills, down to the railways and canals and lorries. All this too, you may say, is a kind of Intake.

At first the towns only seem a blacker edge to the high moorland, so many fantastic outcroppings of its rock, but now that you are closer you see the host of tall chimneys, the rows and rows of little houses, built of blackening stone, that are like tiny sharp ridges on the hills. These windy moors, these clanging dark valleys, these factories and little stone houses, this business of Intaking, have between them bred a race that has special characteristics. Down there are thousands and thousands of men and women who are stocky and hold themselves very stiffly, who have short upper lips and long chins, who use emphatic consonants and very broad vowels and always sound aggressive, who are afraid of nothing but mysterious codes of etiquette and any display of feeling. If it were night, you would notice strange constellations low down in the sky and little golden beetles climbing up to them. These would be street lamps and lighted tramcars on the hills, for here such things are little outposts in No Man's Land and altogether more adventurous and romantic than ordinary street lamps and tramcars. It is not night, however, but a late September afternoon. Some of its sunshine lights up the nearest of the towns, most of it jammed into a narrow valley running up to the moors. It must be Bruddersford, for there, where so many roads meet, is the Town Hall, and if you know the district at all you must immediately recognize the Bruddersford Town Hall, which has a clock that plays *Tom Bowling* and *The Lass of Richmond Hill.* It has been called 'a noble building in the Italian Renaissance style' and always looks as if it had no right to be there.

Yes, it is Bruddersford. Over there is the enormous factory of Messrs Holdsworth and Co. Ltd, which has never been called a noble building in any style but nevertheless looks as if it had a perfect right to be there. The roof of the Midland Railway Station glitters in the sun, and not very far away is another glitter from the glass roof of the Bruddersford Market Hall, where, securely under cover, you may have a ham tea or buy boots and pans and mint humbugs and dress lengths and comic songs. That squat bulk to the left of the Town Hall is the Lane End Congregational Chapel, a monster that can swallow any two thousand people who happen to be in search of 'hearty singing and a bright service'. That streak of slime must be the Leeds and Liverpool Canal or the Aire and Calder Canal, one of the two. There is a little forest of mill chimneys. Most of them are only puffing meditatively, for it is Saturday afternoon and nearly four hours since the workpeople swarmed out through the big gates. Some of the chimneys show no signs of smoke; they have been quiet for a long time, have stayed there like monuments of an age that has vanished, and all because trade is still bad. Perhaps some of these chimneys have stopped smoking because fashionable women in Paris and London and New York have cried to one another, 'My dear, you can't possibly wear that!' and less fashionable women have repeated it after them, and quite unfashionable women have finally followed their example, and it has all ended in machines lying idle in Bruddersford. Certainly, trade is still very bad. But as you look down on Bruddersford, you feel that it will do something about it, that it is only biding its time, that it will hump its way through somehow: the place wears a grim and resolute look. Yet this afternoon it is not thinking about the wool trade.

Something very queer is happening in that narrow thoroughfare to the west of the town. It is called Manchester Road because it actually leads you to that city, though in order to get there you will have to climb to the windy roof of England and spend an hour or two with the curlews. What is so queer about it now is that the road itself cannot be seen at all. A grey-green tide flows sluggishly down its length. It is a tide of cloth caps.

These caps have just left the ground of the Bruddersford United Association Football Club. Thirty-five thousand men and boys have just seen what most of them call 't'United' play Bolton Wanderers. Many of them should never have been there at all. It would not be difficult to prove by statistics and those mournful little budgets (How a Man May Live - or rather, avoid death - on Thirty-five Shillings a Week) that seem to attract some minds, that these fellows could not afford the entrance fee. When some mills are only working half the week and others not at all, a shilling is a respectable sum of money. It would puzzle an economist to discover where all these shillings came from. But if he lived in Bruddersford, though he might still wonder where they came from, he would certainly understand why they were produced. To say that these men paid their shillings to watch twenty-two hirelings kick a ball is merely to say that a violin is wood and catgut, that *Hamlet* is so much paper and ink. For a shilling the Bruddersford United A.F.C. offered you Conflict and Art; it turned you into a critic, happy in your judgement of fine points, ready in a second to estimate the worth of a well-judged pass, a run down the touch line, a lightning shot, a clearance kick by back or goalkeeper; it turned you into a partisan, holding your breath when the ball came sailing into your own goalmouth, ecstatic when your forwards raced away towards the opposite goal, elated, downcast, bitter, triumphant by turns at the fortunes of your side, watching a ball shape Iliads and Odysseys for you; and, what is more, it turned you into a member of a new community, all brothers together for an hour and a half, for not only had you escaped from the clanking machinery of this lesser life, from work, wages, rent, doles, sick pay, insurance cards, nagging wives, ailing children, bad bosses, idle workmen, but you had escaped with most of your mates and your neighbours, with half the town, and there you were, cheering together, thumping one another on the shoulders, swopping judgements like lords of the earth, having pushed your way through a turnstile into another and altogether more splendid kind of life, hurtling with Conflict and yet passionate and beautiful in its Art. Moreover, it offered you more than a shilling's worth of material for talk during the rest of the week. A man who had missed the last home match of 't'United' had to enter social life on tiptoe in Bruddersford.

Somewhere in the middle of this tide of cloth caps is one that is different from its neighbours. It is neither grey nor green but a rather dirty brown. Then, unlike most of the others, it is not too large for its wearer, but, if anything, a shade too small, though it is true he has pushed it back from his forehead as if he were too hot - as indeed he is. This cap and the head it has almost ceased to decorate are both the property of a citizen of Bruddersford, an old and enthusiastic supporter of the United Football Club, whose name is Jesiah Oakroyd. He owes his curious Christian name to his father, a lanky weaving over-looker who divided his leisure, in alternating periods of sin and repentance, between The Craven Arms and the Lane End Primitive Methodist Chapel, where he chanced to hear the verse from First *Chronicles*, 'Of the sons of Uzziel; Micah the first, and Jesiah the second,' the very day before his second son was born. To all his intimates, however, Mr Oakroyd is known as 'Jess'. He is a working man between forty-five and fifty years of age, a trifle under medium height but stockily built, neither ugly nor handsome, with a blunt nose, a moustache that may have been once brisk and fair but is now ragged and mousey, and blue eyes that regard the world pleasantly enough but with just a trace of either wonder or resentment or of both. He lives almost in the shadow of two great factories, in one of those districts known locally as 'back o' t'mill', to be precise, at 51 Ogden Street. He has lived there these last twenty years, and is known to the whole street as a quiet man and a decent neighbour. He is on his way there now, returning from the match to his Saturday tea, which takes a high rank in the hierarchy of meals, being perhaps second only to Sunday dinner. He has walked this way, home from the match, hundreds of times, but this Saturday in late September is no ordinary day for him - although he does not know it - for it is the very threshold of great events. Chance and Change are preparing an ambush. Only a little way before him there dangles invitingly the end of a thread. He must be followed and watched.

II

As he moved slowly down Manchester Road, the press of fellow-spectators still thick about him, Mr Oakroyd found himself brooding over the hollow vanities of this life. He felt unusually depressed. His physical condition may have had something to do with it, for he was hot, dusty, and tired; there had been a full morning's hard work for him at the mill; he had hurried through his dinner; walked to the ground, and had been on his feet ever since. Manchester Road after a match had never seemed so narrow and airless; a chap could hardly breathe in such a crowd of folk. And what a match it had been! For once he was sorry he had come. No score at all. Not a single goal on either side. Even a goal against the United would have been something, would have wakened them up a bit. The first half had been nothing but exasperation, with the United all round the Wanderers' goal but never able to score; centres clean flung away, open goals missed, crazy football. The second half had not been even that, nothing but aimless kicking about on both sides, a kid's game. During the time that it took him to progress three hundred yards down the crowded road, Mr Oakroyd gave himself up to these bitter reflections. A little farther along, where there was more room, he was able to give them tongue, for he jostled an acquaintance, who turned round and recognized him.

'Na Jess!' said the acquaintance, taking an imitation calabash pipe out of his mouth and then winking mysteriously.

'Na Jim!' returned Mr Oakroyd. This 'Na', which must once have been 'Now', is the recognized salutation in Bruddersford, and the fact that it sounds more like a word of caution than a word of greeting is by no means surprising. You have to be careful in Bruddersford.

'Well,' said Jim, falling into step, 'what did you think on 'em?'

'Think on 'em!' Mr Oakroyd made a number of noises with his tongue to show what he thought of them.

'Ah thowt t'United'd 'a' made rings rahnd 'em,' Jim remarked.

'So they owt to 'a' done,' said Mr Oakroyd, with great bitterness. 'And so they would 'a' done if they'd nobbut tried a bit. I've seen 'em better ner this when they've lost. They were better ner this when they lost to Newcastle t'other week, better bi far.'

'Ay, a seet better,' said the other. 'Did you ivver see sich a match! Ah'd as soon go and see 'tschooil lads at it. A shilling fair thrawn away, ah call it.' And for a moment he brooded over his lost shilling. Then, suddenly changing his tone and becoming very aggressive, he went on: 'Yon new centre-forrard they've getten - MacDermott, or whativver he calls hissen - he'll nivver be owt, nivver. He wer like a great lass on t'job. And what did they pay for him? Wer it two thahsand pahnd?'

'Ay.' Mr Oakroyd made this monosyllable very expressive.

'Two thahsand pahnd. That's abaht a hundred for ivvery goal he missed today. Watson were worth twenty on 'im - ah liked that lad, and if they'd let him alone, he'd 'a' done summat for 'em. And then they go and get this MacDermott and pay two thahsand pahnd for him to kick t'ball ower top!' Jim lit his yellow monster of a pipe and puffed away with an air of great satisfaction. He had obviously found a topic that would carry him comfortably through that evening, in the tap-room of The Hare and Hounds, the next morning, in the East Bruddersford Working Men's Club, and possibly Sunday, Monday, and Tuesday nights.

Mr Oakroyd walked on in silence, quickening his pace now that the crowd was not so thick and there was room to move. At the corner of Manchester Road and Shuttle Street both men halted, for here their paths diverged.

'Ah'll tell tha what it is, Jess,' said his companion, pointing the stem of his pipe and becoming broader in his Yorkshire as he grew more philosophical. 'If t'United had less brass to lake wi', they'd lake better fooitball.' His eyes searched the past for a moment, looking for the team that had less money and had played better football. 'Tha can remember when t'club had nivver set eyes on two thahsand pahnds, when t'job lot wor not worth two thahsand pahnds, pavilion an' all, and what sort o' fooitball did they lake then? We knaw, don't we? They could gi' thee summat worth watching then. Nah, it's all nowt, like t'ale an' baccy they ask so mich for - money fair thrawn away, ah calls it. Well, we mun 'a' wer teas and get ower it. Behave thi-sen, Jess!' And he turned away, for that final word of caution was only one of Bruddersford's familiar good-byes.

'Ay,' replied Mr Oakroyd dispiritedly. 'So long, Jim!'

He climbed to the upper deck of a tram that would carry him through the centre of the town to within a few hundred yards of Ogden Street. There he sat, his little briar pipe, unlit and indeed empty, stuck in the corner of his mouth, his cap still pushed back from his glistening forehead, staring out of a disenchantment. At times the tram jerked him forward, but only to return him, with a bang, against the hard back of the seat. People who were larger than usual, and all parcels and elbows, pushed past or trod on his toes. It is no joke taking a tram on Saturday in Bruddersford.

'I call this two-pennorth o' misery, missis,' he said to a very large woman who wedged herself into the seat beside him. She turned a damp scarlet face, and he saw that it was Mrs Buttershaw, whose husband kept the little shop in Woolgate. Everybody in that district knew Buttershaw's, for it was no ordinary shop. It catered to both body and soul, one half of it being given up to tripe and cow-heels and the other half to music, chiefly sixpenny songs and cheap gramophone records. Strangers frequently stopped in front of Buttershaw's to stare and laugh, but strangers are easily amused: all the people round about recognized that this was a sensible arrangement, for some wanted tripe, some wanted music, and not a few wanted both.

'Eh, well, if it isn't Mr Oakroyd!' Mrs Buttershaw knew him as both a patron (of the tripe counter) and an old neighbour. 'I didn't see yer. And 'ow are yer?'

'Middlin', middlin',' said Mr Oakroyd, with the air of one determined to give nothing away.

'I've been meaning to ask yer for a long time,' she went on, 'only I haven't seen yer - 'ow's your Lily doin' in where's it? - Ameriky?'

'Canada,' Mr Oakroyd announced promptly and rather proudly.

'Canada - that's it. It's all the same, isn't it? Only some calls it one thing, and some calls it another. Well, 'ow's she getting on there? Eh, it doesn't seem more than a week or two since she was a bit of a lass coming in for a pantymine song - she liked a bit o' music, didn't she? - and now she's a married woman in Canada.'

'She's doing all right,' said Mr Oakroyd, vainly trying to appear unconcerned. 'I'd a letter t'other day.' But he did not add that that letter, which began 'My dear Father and Mother, I write these few lines to let you know we are alright as I hope you are,' was reposing in his coat pocket, having been carried there - and brought out and re-read at frequent intervals - these last three days.

'She's settled in, 'as she?' said Mrs Buttershaw, who apparently thought of Canada as a sort of house.

'Ay. She's settling nicely, is Lily. Been there nearly a year.'

'Eh, fancy that! A year! Well, I never did!' Mrs Buttershaw seemed to have these exclamations shaken out of her by the jerky movements of the tram. 'Who was it she married? I owt to know, but I've fergotten. I shall ferget me own name soon, I'm that bad at remembering.'

'Jack Clough, old Sammy's youngest lad,' replied Mr Oakroyd. 'He were a fitter at Sharp's.'

'Eh, of course!' she exclaimed triumphantly. 'I knew 'im well. He were often in, buying a bit of comic song and suchlike. He were a nice lad, an' a lively card. But then your Lily was a lively lass, full o'fun.'

'Ay, lively enough. You knew when she was abaht.' Mr Oakroyd tried to speak off-handedly, but his voice warmed and his eyes were alight with affectionate reminiscence. He had always adored this only daughter of his. She had been the funniest baby, the cleverest child, and the prettiest girl in that part of Bruddersford, or, for that matter, in any other part. There was something wonderful about everything she did and said. Even her naughtiness - and she had always had a will of her own - had seemed to him only a special sort of fun and prettiness, as good as a play.

'Yer must miss 'er. I know I do meself. Even Joe was asking me about 'er t'other day. 'E didn't know she'd got married and gone away, 'e knows nowt, doesn't Joe; 'e's always a year or two be'ind'and.' But she said this in such a way as to hint that Mr Buttershaw, with one eye on his tripe and the other on his music, was rather above this business of knowing things, an absent-minded genius. 'Ther wasn't a nicer little lass came into t'shop, and yer can put that feather in yer cap.'

Mr Oakroyd was so shaken out of his reserve by this praise that he proclaimed very earnestly: 'Ay. I miss her all right. I didn't know ah could miss anybody so much. Place fair seems empty like sometimes.'

For a minute or two nothing more was said. No doubt both of them felt that this last speech had reached the limits to which confession might be pushed. Beyond were extravagance and indecency, and a good Bruddersfordian left such wild regions to actors and Londoners and suchlike. Mr Oakroyd looked out of the window.

The day was just crossing the little magical bridge between afternoon and evening. The early autumn sunlight was bent on working a miracle. A moment of transformation had arrived. It hushed and gilded the moors above, and then, just when Mr Oakroyd's tram reached the centre of the town, passing on one side the Central Free Library and on the other the Universal Sixpenny Bazaar, it touched Bruddersford. All the spaces of the town were filled with smoky gold. Holmes and Hadley's emporium, the Midland Railway Station, the Wool Exchange, Barclays Bank, the Imperial Music Hall, all shone like palaces. Smithson Square was like some quivering Western sea, and the Right Honourable Ebenezer Smithson himself, his marble scroll now a map of the Indies, was conjured into an Elizabethan admiral. The façades of Market Street towered strangely and spread a wealth of carven stone before the sun. Town Hall Square was a vast place of golden light; and its famous clock, as it moved to celebrate the enchanted moments, gave a great whirr and then shook down into the streets its more rapturous chimes, *The Lass of Richmond Hill.*

To all this sudden magic, Mr Oakroyd, sucking at his empty pipe and staring through the window, might have seemed entirely unresponsive. He was not, however. One hand went fumbling up his shabby coat. It would have gone further, would have plunged into the inner pocket, if its owner had not been sharing a seat with Mrs Buttershaw, who was of a breadth beyond the dreams of the Tramways Department. But if the hand could not bring out a letter, it could feel that it was there, and having done so, it dropped, satisfied.

'And 'ow,' said Mrs Buttershaw, looking with disapproval at the warehouse of Messrs Hoggleby, Sons and Co. Ltd, in whose shadow they were, 'is that lad of yours gettin' on?'

Mr Oakroyd's face immediately changed, putting on a grim and satirical expression. 'I can't say. He tells me nowt. I think he'll be all right as long as there's still a good supply o' brilliantine an' fancy socks, and plenty o' young women wi' nowt to do but look for chaps.' Leonard might be the darling of his mother's heart, as indeed he was, but it was clear that his father had no great opinion of him.

Neither, it appeared, had Mrs Buttershaw. 'I seen 'im o' Wednesday,' she said severely, 'standing outside a picture place - I think it were t'Plazzer - and yer'd have thought 'e owned it. "That's Mr Oakroyd's lad," I ses to Joe, but Joe didn't know him. Joe knows nobody, and bin in a shop for thirty year! Nay, I nivver seen such a man. "Yer won't know me next," I tell him. But when I showed 'im your lad,

Joe ses, "Well, if that's Jess Oakroyd's lad, 'e's nowt like his father. 'E looks a bit of a swankpot." "Nay, Joe," I ses, "yer know nowt about t'lad." But I knew what 'e meant. 'E doesn't like to see these lads all toffed up, doesn't Joe. Where's your Leonard workin' now? Is 'e still in t' hair cuttin'?'

'Ay, he's still at Bobsfill's i' Woolgate,' said Mr Oakroyd, who did not seem to resent these remarks.

'Well,' said Mrs Buttershaw, gathering together her assortment of packages and her immense form, "e'll niwer get fat on what old Bobsfill gives 'im. I niwer reckoned nowt o' barbers, and Bobsfill's one o' t' meanest. 'E'd go blind lookin' for a thripenny bit.' And she heaved herself out of the seat and, as the tram slowed up, went waddling down the aisle.

Mr Oakroyd, beginning to expand again into what he felt to be his natural size, fell to thinking of his daughter and her letter. As soon as Lily had gone, 51 Ogden Street had suddenly shrunk and darkened, and there was no family life in it, no real home, only the three of them there, eating and sleeping and sometimes squabbling, with Leonard and his doting mother on one side and him on the other. 'Don't you have it, Dad. Don't you put up with it. You look after yourself,' Lily had whispered just before she went, breaking up an old and happy alliance. Since then he had had a certain mournful pleasure in not putting up with it, in trying to look after himself. But it was a poor sort of business now.

He took the letter out of his pocket, but did not read it again. He had secretly hoped it would contain an invitation to him to go out there. He was ready to go at a word. A handy man like him could easily get work there. Six months' full time at the mill would easily raise the passage money. But no invitation had come, not a word about it. He hoped she had thought of it, had suggested it, and that it was only because Jack Clough, who was a decent young chap but, like the rest, bent on looking after Number One, had put his foot down that she had never said anything. He had mentioned it once or twice when he had written, just making a sort of little joke of it - 'What would your old Father look like in Canada!' - and he did not feel like doing more than that. They had their own way to make, and a baby was coming. He looked down at the letter and then slowly tore it up and slipped the fragments under the seat.

The tram had ground its way to the Black Swan Inn (known locally as 't'Mucky Duck'), and this was his stop. He walked, rather slowly and heavily, the few hundred yards that brought him to Ogden Street.

Nobody could consider Ogden Street very attractive; it was very long and very drab, and contained two rows of singularly ugly black little houses; yet Ogden Street had its boasts, and its residents could claim to have both feet on the social ladder. You could, in fact, have a 'come-down' from Ogden Street, and there were some people who even saw it as a symbol of a prosperity long vanished. To begin with, it was a respectable street, not one of those in which you heard sudden screams in the night or the sound of police whistles. Then too, it was entirely composed of proper houses, all with doors opening on to the street; and in this respect it was unlike its neighbours at the back, Velvet Street and Merino Street, which had nothing but 'passage' or 'back-to-back' houses, the product of an ingenious architectural scheme that crammed four dwelling-places into the space of two and enabled some past citizens to drive a carriage-and-pair and take their wives and daughters to the Paris Exhibition in 1867. When you lived in Ogden Street, you did not disdain to talk to the occupants of 'passage houses', but nevertheless, if you were a woman who knew how to enjoy yourself, you could afford to be sympathetic towards a humble passage-houser or put a presumptuous one in her place. Many of these things had been known to Mr Oakroyd, an old resident, for many years, but he did not entertain himself now with any recollection of them.

The door, which led directly into the single living-room, stood ajar. There was no one in the room, but voices were coming from upstairs. Somebody shouted 'Hello!' as he flung his cap down on the end of the shiny black sofa. He grunted a reply, went through to the scullery, where he hastily washed, returning, with eyes still smarting from the yellow soap, to look very dubiously at the table. What he saw made him shake his head. It was indeed the miserable ruin of a Saturday tea. Three dirty cups, pushed to one end of the table, announced that there had been earlier arrivals, and everything had the air of having been closely examined and then rejected. There were two pieces of bread-and-butter on one plate, half a buttered currant teacake and a squashed lemon-cheese tart on another; and on a third - for the tasty bit, the glory of the meal - were the mere remains, the washy flotsam and jetsam, of a tin of salmon. Mr Oakroyd poked about with a fork in this pink mush, shook his head again, and made little clicking noises. Then he lifted the teapot from the fender, where it had been stewing its contents for some time, sat him down and summoned what was left of a rapidly vanishing appetite.

'You're back, are you!' This was Mrs Oakroyd, who had come downstairs. She was a thin woman, with gleaming eyes, prominent cheek-bones, a pinched nose reddened at the tip, and a long prow of a chin. She had two passions, one for her son, Leonard, and the other for virtuous discomfort. 'I'm house-proud,' she reported of herself; and if she could fill the living-room with steaming clothes a few minutes before her husband arrived home from work, she was happy. She had long regarded him neither as a friend nor as a partner but as a nuisance, somebody who was always coming in to upset the house, always demanding food and drink.

The nuisance gave her one quick glance, and saw at once that she was pleased about something, though ready at any moment to be quarrelsome about it. 'Leonard's in this,' he told himself, gave a nod, then gloomily poured some of the salmon on to his plate.

'We 'ad our teas,' remarked Mrs Oakroyd, coming forward into the room.

'Ay, so I see,' returned her husband dryly. 'I wish I'd been here. Ther seems to ha' been a bit of a party like.'

'Leonard's 'ere, come home this afternoon and brought Albert Tuggridge with 'im, so we all 'ad our teas together.'

'Oh, Leonard's here, is he?' Mr Oakroyd stared rather aggressively at his wife. 'And what's Leonard doing here at this time o' day? I suppose nobody i' Woolgate district wants a shave now o' Saturday.' As this was the only day on which many Woolgate residents ever did want a shave, this remark was the grimmest irony.

There was an added gleam in his wife's eyes. 'Leonard's done wi' Woolgate. Left this morning. *And* not afore 'e told old Bobsfill a thing or two either. Trust 'im,' she added proudly.

Mr Oakroyd laid down his knife and fork. 'Gotten t'sack, has he, or marched out? And what's he going to do now? I call that daft. Lad's got too big for his boots.'

The gleam was really triumphant now. She raised her voice: 'I'll tell yer what he's going to do. He's going to work at Gregson's. There's a chap finishing there today, and our Leonard takes his place o' Monday. Gets two pound and what he makes, and you know what Gregson's is. Now then, what 'ave you got to say to that?'

He had nothing to say to it. He did know what Gregson's was, though he had never been a patron of such a lordly establishment. Gregson's City Toilet Rooms were in the centre of the town, not two hundred yards from Town Hall Square, and heads worth a mint of money were continually being trimmed there. It was impossible to say a word against Gregson's.

'Two pounds and tips galore!' cried Mrs Oakroyd. 'It'll be four pound ten, sometimes five pound, 'e tells me, in a good week, wi' regular customers coming in, wool men and travellers and suchlike. "Well," I tells him, "if it is, it's better money than your poor father ever brought home, and you only fower-and-twenty". Nay, I were that surprised! When I seen 'im walk in wi' Albert Tuggridge, middle o' t'afternoon, you could ha' knocked me down wi' a feather - '

'Ay,' her husband put in, 'an' when I see the way they'd both walked into that salmon, you could 'a' knocked me down wi' t'same feather.'

'Go on, go on! That's right! Go on!' she cried, with the shrillest irony. 'Next time t'lad gets a better job I'll turn 'im and 'is friend out without a bit o' tea. I'll tell him 'e can't 'a' any, tell him it's all for his father. You've got as much there as we'ad. What you wan's a caffy. What we sit down to isn't good enough for a man as can afford a shilling every week for a football match. He ought to 'ave 'am and eggs every night, he ought, steaks and chips every night, he ought, when he's so well off – '

'All right, all right, all right,' growled Mr Oakroyd and tried to look like a man who had had enough of that nonsense. His wife gave a sniff, collected some dirty cups and plates, gave another sniff, then marched the things into the scullery, where she contrived to make an extraordinary clatter. Mr Oakroyd let his features relapse into their ordinary appearance, loudly yet mournfully sucked at a hollow tooth, then took an immense bite of currant teacake and washed it down with a gulp of tea.

'I'll bet t'young women o' Bruddersford will find it hard to keep their heads screwed on tonight,' he observed, when his wife returned. He nodded towards the stairs. 'Is that Albert Tuggridge up there now wi' Leonard?'

'Yes. Leonard's getting ready to go out. They're off to a social an' dance at Shuttle Street Rooms.'

Mr Oakroyd smiled grimly. 'I thought as much. There'll be some 'earts broken i' Shuttle Street tonight. It's fair cruel to let them two loose on t'same night, and a Saturday an' all. It don't give lasses a chance. Them as doesn't prostrate themselves afore Leonard 'ull fall afore the all-conquering Albert. It's an absolute walk-over for the male sex.'

His wife bristled. 'A body'ud think you'd never been young, Jess Oakroyd, the way you go on about them lads.'

'Nay, I've been young. None so old yet, I'm thinking. But I were never so dam' soft as yon two. Lady-killers, I calls 'em - Shuttle Street heart-breakers! Tut-t-t-t!'

It was not a bad description of Leonard and his friend, Albert. With them and their like was perishing, miserably and obscurely, an old tradition. Though they did not know it, they were in truth the last of a long line, the last of the Macaronis, the Dandies, the Swells, the Mashers, the Knuts. Their old home, the West End, knows these figures no longer; their canes and yellow gloves, their pearl-buttoned fawn overcoats, their brilliantine and scent and bouquets, their music-hall promenades, and their hansoms, their ladies, with elaborate golden coiffures, full busts, and naughty frills, all have gone, all went floating to limbo, long ago, on their last tide of champagne; and some foolish and almost forgotten song, in perky six-eight time, of 'Boys and Girls Upon the Spree, In Peek-a-deely or Le-hester Squer-hare', is their requiem. But just as a tide of fashion, raging fiercely in Mayfair for a season, will go rolling on and on, depositing black vases or orange cushions in drawing-rooms more and more remote year after year, so too the tradition of dandyism and lady-killing, after it had forsaken its old home, lingered on in towns like Bruddersford and among such young men as Leonard and Albert. They lived for dress and girls, above all - not having the opportunities of a Brummell - for girls. They ogled and pursued and embraced girls at the Bruddersford dances and socials, in all the local parks and woods, picture theatres and music halls; they followed them on the Bridlington sands, along the Morecambe piers, into the Blackpool ballrooms, and even went as far as Douglas, I.O.M., to treat them to eighteen-penny glasses of champagne and other notorious aphrodisiacs; they knew, and frequently discussed among themselves, the precise difference between the factory girls of Bruddersford and the factory girls of Bradford or Huddersfield, between the tailoresses of Leeds and the shop-girls of Manchester; they were masters of the art of 'picking up' and, young as they were, already veteran strategists in the war against feminine chastity or prudence, and were untiring in the chase, tracking these bright creatures for weeks through the dark jungle of West Riding streets, but apt to be either bored or frightened by the kill. In the end, most of them - as they said - 'got caught', and were to be seen walking out of their old lives, those epics of gallantry, pushing a perambulator.

The two young men now descended the stairs. Leonard walked in first, still patting his purple silk tie. He is a thin youth, with a very elaborate and greasy arrangement of curls and waves in his hair, a hardening eye and a loosening mouth, and an unfortunate habit of becoming spotty about the forehead. His friend, Albert, clerk to Swullans, the noisiest and shadiest auctioneer in the town, is larger and louder, and likes to brighten all social occasions by imitating the public manner of his master. Having no family in Bruddersford, he lives in lodgings, a few streets away, where he says he is very uncomfortable. Already it has been suggested several times, both by Leonard and his mother, that Albert might lodge with them, but Mr Oakroyd, who does not want a lodger and especially does not want to see any more of Albert, rages at the mere hint of such a proceeding.

'My words, Leonard,' cried Mrs Oakroyd, wiping her hands at the scullery door, 'you're a swell tonight all right!' To see him standing there, in his new chocolate-coloured suit, with his purple socks and tie and handkerchief, was as good as an evening out to her, better than the pictures.

'Not so dusty, Mar,' said Leonard, tapping a cigarette against the back of his hand.

'Well, well, well, well!' shouted Albert, winking at Mr Oakroyd, who was pushing his chair back. "Ere we are, 'ere we are! All merry and bright, the old firm! And 'ow many runs did the old United make today?' And he winked at everybody. Mr Oakroyd, who wanted to kick him, bent over his pipe and his packet of Old Salt tobacco, and grunted: 'Drew. Nil, nil.'

'Not much for a bob there then, what do you say, Len?' Albert went to the hearth and straddled there. 'The poor old United will 'ave to do better before they see my money.'

'Rorther, rorther!' said Leonard, who was fond of entertaining company, at times, with an imitation of a musical-comedy duke. This was one of the times.

'Quaite, quaite !' roared Albert, who knew his cue.

Mr Oakroyd, with the air of a man who had heard all this too many times already, very deliberately lit his pipe, then relieved his feelings by blowing out a cloud of smoke. 'Well, they'll 'a' to try and get on without your money, Albert,' he remarked, relishing his irony. 'They'll 'a' to manage somehow, though it'll be a bad lookout for 'em, I can see that. Ha' you told 'em yet, or are you letting 'em find it out for themselves?'

At this moment Mrs Oakroyd and Leonard disappeared into the scullery, where they could be heard whispering. Albert cocked an ear in that direction then opened fire himself. 'You've 'eard the news? Len's new job. Good biz, good biz! Got a rise meself last week. Good biz! We're making money, making money. What d'you say?'

It was plain that Mr Oakroyd had very little to say and that it was not a subject that inspired him. He took out his pipe, looked at it and then looked at Albert, and asked very quietly if Mr Swullans had sold any more mahogany wardrobes lately. This was a malicious question because Mr Swullans had once got into trouble and a half-column report in the *Bruddersford Evening Express* because he sold a certain mahogany wardrobe.

But Albert was not abashed. 'Now then, now then! We all know about that. Tricks in all trades! Did you know I was looking for fresh digs?'

'Ay, I heard summat about it.'

'Well then, what d'you say to having this little drop o' sunshine in the old 'ome? What d'you think of that? Good company and a good payer, right on the nail every Friday night.'

Mr Oakroyd shook his head. 'It won't wash, lad.'

'Right on the nail every Friday,' Albert repeated with gusto. 'And all the family in favour.'

'It won't wash. We don't want no lodgers 'ere. There's plenty as takes 'em without us. We don't want 'em.'

'Oh, we don't, don't we!' This was from Mrs Oakroyd, standing, belligerent, in the scullery doorway.

Her husband gave a steady look, then raised his voice. 'No, we don't.'

'Well, some of us thinks we do.'

'Then you mun think again, and think different,' said Mr Oakroyd, with an air of finality. And before any of them could reply, he had taken his cap from the end of the sofa, clapped it on his head, and walked out.

He told himself that he wanted a little stroll, another ounce of Old Salt an early edition of the *Evening Express Sports*. But he knew he was afraid of what was coming. Having fired, manfully, his one big gun, he felt compelled to retreat. All the way down Ogden Street, he kept repeating to himself, 'Better money than your poor father ever brought home'; and didn't like the look of things at all.

III

The week-end had begun badly for Mr Oakroyd, and it did not improve. The depression of Saturday afternoon could not be shaken off. He could think of nothing to look forward to. He was troubled by a vague foreboding. It was just as if a demoniac black dog went trotting everywhere at his heels. Normally he was happy enough when he was smoking a pipe or two of Old Salt over the *Evening Express Sports*, learning how 'Kelly pushed the ball out to the homesters' left wing and Macdonald shot hard from a fine centre, but the visiting custodian made a great clearance'. But this Saturday night he could not settle down to the welcome pink sheets. It followed him, this black dog, when he tried another stroll later, into the centre of the town, and it even found its way with him into the singing-room of The Boy and Barrel, where he had a half-pint of bitter and listened to a purple-faced tenor, the victim of two passions, one for Doreen, His Darling and His Queen, and the other for Home, Just a Tumble-down Cottage. Nor had it departed when he called, on his return home, at Thwaites' Fish and Chip Shop (it called itself the West End Supper Bar, but nobody took any notice of that), and ate three-pennorth o' chips and a tail while exchanging some remarks on t'United with Sam Thwaites, that excellent critic of the game.

Sunday morning was no better. To begin with, there was a bit of an argument about Albert Tuggridge at breakfast. Then the *Imperial News*, with which, like two million other Britons, he spent Sunday morning, for once gave him no pleasure. Listlessly, he turned from *Secrets of European Courts* to *Dope Dens of Mayfair,* from *What the Husband Saw* to *Scandals of the Boxing Ring*, and the most startling revelations, the most terrible disclosures, failed to brighten his eye. At half past eleven he went to the Woolgate Working Men's Club and sat there over a half-pint, only to learn, to his disgust, that young Maundery had been made secretary of the local branch of his Trade Union, the Textile, Wagon, and Warehouse Workers. Mr Oakroyd had not been on good terms with his Union for some time, and this appointment of Maundery, a hatchet-faced young fanatic who had an unqualified admiration of Russian methods, meant that very soon he would be on even worse terms. He disliked the chap, and only a fortnight ago, in this very club, they had had a long and loud argument, during which Mr Oakroyd had horrified his opponent by calling 'proletariat' - a term that Maundery used in every other sentence and regarded as sacred - 'a bloody daft word'. After that cheerless half-pint, he went home to a dinner that was a sulky silent affair and none too good. This was what he had expected. He knew he had now seen the last of his wife's best efforts in cookery for some time. In the afternoon, he dozed uneasily for an hour or so, suddenly decided to walk to the park, found he had gone far enough when only half-way there, and came back, dusty and gloomy, to a solitary tea. Leonard had gone off for the day, and Mrs Oakroyd was taking tea with some fellow-worshipper at the Woolgate Congregational Chapel. Mr Oakroyd ate and drank a good deal in an absent-minded fashion, then smoked two pipes of Old Salt while he gave himself to a mournful survey of this life.

It was nearly seven o'clock when he finally decided how to spend the evening. He would go and see his friend Sam Oglethorpe out at Wabley. Having arrived at this decision, he immediately felt more cheerful, for to go as far as Wabley, which is four miles out of Bruddersford and almost on the edge of the moors, was something to do, indeed quite a little adventure, and he knew that Sam would be in and ready to welcome him. What he did not know was that this was a most momentous decision, that here was not a little adventure but the beginning of all manner of great adventures, that the thread now dangling in the empty space of his life was almost within reach, that Destiny was hard at work as he had his wash at the scullery sink, walked, took a tram, walked again, out to Wabley.

Yes, Sam was in, and glad to see him, and together they went down to the run and looked at hens. The two had worked side-by-side for years in the wagon department of Higden and Co., but two or three years ago they had parted company, for Sam had come into money, having been left four hundred pounds by an uncle who had kept an off-licence shop, and had boldly walked out of Higden's, never to return. He was now 'on his own' at Wabley, the proud proprietor of a large hen-run, a little cottage, and a sign that said 'Joinery and Jobbing Work Promptly Attended To'. That was why Mr Oakroyd regarded his friend with admiration and envy, for he too would like to walk out of Higden's for the last time, to have done with wages and foremen and the tyrannical buzzer. Deep in his heart was a sign about Joinery and Jobbing Work. The hoisting of that sign, proclaiming Jes. Oakroyd, the independent craftsman, to the world, was one of his constant dreams. And he was a better craftsman than Sam, too; give him a saw, a hammer, a few nails, and he could do anything. But Sam, assisted by the off-licence uncle, had managed to scramble out, while he was still in, in up to the neck, and lucky perhaps to be keeping on at Higden's at all.

Now, the last hen dismissed, they were cosily talking over pipes and a jug of beer. They were not in Mr Oglethorpe's cottage, which was simply a place to eat and sleep in and not meant, as anybody in Wabley would tell you, for social life. No, they were sitting snugly in Mr Oglethorpe's combined henhouse and workshop, with the jug of beer on a bench between them. If you want to know what independent men in Bruddersford and district think about life, you must listen to the talk that comes floating out of hen-houses at night. A man can afford to let himself go in a hen-house. Sam had been letting himself go, enlarging upon his plans and prospects, his hens, his Joinery, his Jobbing, to all of which Mr Oakroyd had been listening with deep and admiring attention. It was now time he had a look in, and Mr Oglethorpe, like the good fellow he was, knew it and gave him his cue.

'Ay,' said Mr Oglethorpe, who had the slow meditative manner that properly belongs to Jobbing Work, 'that's what 'appens i' this sort o' business i' Wabley, ay, and i' Bruddersford too. Did you give it any ittention, Jess, when you was down South? It'll be a bit diff'rent there, I'm thinking.'

Mr Oakroyd's face lit up at once. This 'down South' was the cue. This was where he came in and more than held his own, for if, in this company, Mr Oglethorpe was the independent man, the owner of hens and a sign, the craftsman at large, who could smoke his pipe when he liked, Mr Oakroyd was the travelled man, who had knocked up and down a bit, who could talk of what were to Mr Oglethorpe, who had never been anywhere, foreign parts. It was only in the company of his friend Sam that Mr Oakroyd felt that he really had seen the world. He had not often been away from Bruddersford, though he had had a few little holidays at Morecambe, Blackpool, and Scarborough, had been on football trips to Manchester, Newcastle, Sheffield, and had once gone on a wonderful midnight excursion to London and had actually seen St Paul's and London Bridge before he fell asleep in an eating-house; but it happened that for a whole six months he had worked in Leicester, where his firm had a branch, and ever after he had referred to this exciting period as the time when he was 'down South'. It was another of his dreams, companion to that of the hoisted sign, this happy business of travelling, of knocking about, of seeing this place and that, of telling how you once went there and then moved on somewhere else, and although he knew he had seen nothing much yet and probably never would now, yet he was able, nourished as he was by his secret dream, to capture the manner of the true wanderer. During his six months in Leicester, he had lodged in a street that could hardly be distinguished from his own Ogden Street, had worked in another Higden's mill that was just like the one in Bruddersford except that it was smaller and cleaner. Yet when he said 'down South', he seemed to conjure up a vast journey towards the tropics and at the end of it a life entirely alien; fantastic.

'Ay, it's different there, Sam,' said Mr Oakroyd, puzzling his brains to discover some proof of this difference. 'It's altogether different there, it is.'

''Old on a bit afore you tell me,' the other cried, reaching for the jug. 'There's another sup i' this for both of us, I'm thinking. Nah then!' And he put a match to his pipe and looked across at his friend, his honest red face aglow.

'Well, then you see,' began Mr Oakroyd, but thought better of it and drank some beer instead. Then he reflected a moment. 'Well, what I'd say is this. Yer asking me how this sort o' trade, Joinery and Jobbing, 'ud go down South, aren't yer?'

'That's right, Jess.' And Mr Oglethorpe looked very profound as he said this.

'Well, what I'd say is this; that ther mayn't be so much of it down there but what ther is 'ud be a better class o' thing. D'you follow me, Sam?'

Sam did follow him and looked more profound than ever as he slowly puffed at his short clay pipe. Nothing was said for a minute or two. Then Mr Oglethorpe proceeded to light a very old and evil-smelling paraffin lamp that hung from the roof, and when he had done this, he broke the silence. 'It'll be all different, I'm thinking, Jess. I could nivver settle to it. But I'll bet tha liked it.'

'I like a bit of a change, Sam.'

'I'll bet tha'd like to be off down there ag'in next week,' said Mr Oglethorpe, with an air of great artfulness, as if he had caught his friend at last.

'I might an' I might not,' replied Mr Oakroyd, who was not for giving himself away at once, not even in Sam's hen-house. But then the hour and his mood worked together to fling down his reserve. He leaned forward and looked at once eager and wistful. 'I'll tell you what it is, Sam. I'd give owt to see a bit more afore I'm too old.'

'Yer've seen summat already, Jess.' Mr Oglethorpe spoke proudly, as if his friendship gave him a share in these vast migrations.

'Nowt much when you look at it.'

'Why, look at me,' cried Mr Oglethorpe. 'I've nivver been farther ner Wetherby, to t'races there. Nay, I'm lying; I have. I once went for a day to Southport to see t'sea, but I nivver saw it, not a drop. It were a take-in, that.'

'I'd like to knock up an' down a bit,' Mr Oakroyd went on, 'an' see what there is to see afore I'm too old an' daft. I've gotten fair sick o' Bruddersford lately, Sam, I have that. I'd like to get on t'move.'

'Where d'yer want to go, Jess? Down South ag'in? What is't yer want to see?'

'Nay, I don't know,' said Mr Oakroyd, gloomily. 'I'd like to see summat fresh. I'd like to have a look at - oh, I don't know - Bristol.'

'Ar,' said Mr Oglethorpe knowingly. 'Bristol.'

'Or I'd like to see - yer know - some of them places - Bedfordshire,' he added, at a venture.

The other shook his head at this. 'I nivvr heard tell much o' that place,' he said gravely. 'Is ther owt special i' Bedfordshire, Jess?'

'Nay, I don't know,' replied Mr Oakroyd, a trifle impatiently. 'But it's summat to see. I'd like to go and have a look so I'd know if ther was owt there or not. And I'll tell you another thing, Sam. I'd like to go to Canada.'

'Yer nivver would, yer nivver would, Jess!' Mr Oglethorpe slapped his thigh in appreciation of this audacity. 'An' if yer got there, yer'd want to be back i' no time. Nowt to sup, they tell me, and snaw months and months on end. Plenty o' money, I dare say, but nowt to spend it on. Nay, Jess, I'll nivver believe yer'd go as far as that.'

'I've a lass o' mine there, Sam.'

'Ay, so you have, I'd fergetten. But I'll tell yer what it is. Y'owt to 'a' been a wool-buyer, Jess, and then yer could 'a' gone off all ower t'place and been paid for it. It'ud 'a' suited thee down to t'ground.'

'I dare say,' said Mr Oakroyd grimly. 'An' I owt to have a motor-car and twenty pound a week and nowt to do and plenty o' time to do it in - '

At this moment, a voice cried 'Hello!' and a face appeared in the doorway.

'Who's that? Oh, it's you, is it, Ted? Come in, lad, come in. Yer know my nephew Ted, Jess? And when Ted had sat himself down on an old coop, Mr Oglethorpe went on: 'Now, here's a lad as can tell you a thing or two about knocking up and down. He's nivver at home five minutes. Off wi' t'lorry all ower t'country, aren't yer, Ted?'

Ted, who was part-owner of a lorry that called itself the Wabley Transport Co., admitted that he knocked about a bit and knew a thing or two.

'This lorrying owt to 'a' been your line o' business, Jess,' Mr Oglethorpe continued, winking at his nephew for no particular reason. 'Where d'yer go next, lad?'

'Off tomorrow,' replied Ted, a laconic youth who preferred to talk, like a ventriloquist, with a cigarette in his mouth. 'Load at Bruddersford. Merryweather's Tapp Street. Going to Nuneaton. Shan't get off till late tomorrow night.'

'What time, Ted?' asked his uncle, rather in the manner of counsel in court, as if he already knew the answer himself.

'Ten or eleven. Perhaps twelve. Merryweather's got a rush on. That's how we got the job. Travel all night. Deliver in the morning. Hell of a game.' And Ted, having finished his speech, took out his cigarette to whistle.

'There y'are, Jess. 'Ell of a game,' Mr Oglethorpe repeated triumphantly.

'It 'ud do me,' muttered Mr Oakroyd.

'It 'ud suit 'im,' said Mr Oglethorpe, turning to his nephew. 'Yer'll a' ter give 'im a job on t'lorry, Ted.'

'Nothing doing,' replied Ted. 'Wouldn't thank us if we did. He can have a trip when he likes, of course. See for himself then. Nothing in it. Been all over, Manchester, Liverpool, Newcastle, Leicester, Coventry, even taken it to London twice. Dozens o' smaller places. All over. Nothing in it. Get sick of it. Same old carry-on every time. Places all alike when you come to know 'em.'

'Nay, I'll be damned if they are,' Mr Oakroyd protested. 'You may 'a' seen a sight more ner I have, but you must 'a' given it a funny sort o' look to think that. Places is as different as chalk and cheese. I soon picked that out when I were down South.'

'Ay, that's right,' Mr Oglethorpe observed. 'I've heard Jess 'ere tell many a time 'ow diff'rent it is. I've seen nowt much, but yer can nivver tell me places is all alike. Why, ther's Wabley 'ere is as diff'rent as owt from all t'other small places round Bruddersford. Amazin' it is, fair amazin'! Then Bruddersford's ner more like Leeds or Halifax than

I'm like Billy Baxter.'

'Who's Billy Baxter?' This was from Ted, who ought to have known better.

'What! Nivver heard o' Billy Baxter !' cried Mr Oglethorpe, in great glee. 'Well, well, well! Billy Baxter were the fellow that could nivver stand up without getting on his feet.' And Mr Oglethorpe began to punch himself, and shake and splutter and cough, until at last he was purple and helpless.

'Tha hasn't selled that to anybody for years, Sam,' said Mr Oakroyd approvingly. 'Ted's learned summat tonight, anyway.'

Ted, still with a cigarette in his mouth, was shaking his head and at the same time making a loud tut-tutting noise. He was not abashed - as a man of the world, he could afford to ignore such primitive jests - but he knew that his prestige was gone for the remainder of the evening, and so, after giving his uncle a resounding slap or two on the back, he took his leave.

Mr Oakroyd stayed long enough to smoke another pipe, and was then steered through the darkness - for it was late now - by his host, who accompanied him as far as the tram terminus. The tram that was waiting there, however, only took him to the outskirts of Bruddersford, where it went groaning into its shed. Mr Oakroyd would have to walk the rest of the way. As a rule he liked to go to bed early on Sunday night, but now he was in no mood to consider Monday morning, more especially as he had just left the company of an independent craftsman and a man of travel. The night was fine and he was not tired. Off he went, with his old brown cap at the back of his head, whistling softly, and watching his shadow that grew and then dwindled between one street-lamp and the next. He was walking back into something that was beginning to look like slavery, but the large quiet night was his, and a man might fancy himself anything, proprietor of a Joinery and Jobbing sign, owner of a lorry commanded to go to Bristol or Bedfordshire, even a chap going out to Canada to see his daughter, as he walked in peace through such a night.

He was now in the Merton Park district, Bruddersford's best suburb, where the wool merchants and the manufacturers and the bank managers had their detached villas. These pleasant avenues were full of leafy shadows, for there were trees in the gardens and trees alternating with street-lamps on the pavement itself. Now and then he heard the distant sound of a piano. Two or three cars rolled past. Sometimes from the deeper shadows there came a whispering and sound of kissing, for lovers in Bruddersford favoured the Merton Park district. There were very few of them about now, however; it was too late. Learoyd Avenue, longest and leafiest of these opulent roads, was very quiet. Yet it was in

Learoyd Avenue, nearly at the end, just before it turns into Park Drive, that Mr Oakroyd's adventures really began.

He had just stepped from the lamplit pavement into the shadow of a tree, when he tripped over something and went sprawling.

'What the bl— !' he began, startled and shaken.

'Shush! Shush!' said a voice, close to his ear. 'Naughty! Naughty!'

Mr Oakroyd scrambled to his feet and peered through the gloom at the figure beside him.' 'Ere, Mister, get up.'

The other giggled quietly. 'Can't gerrup,' he said. 'Can't poshibly gerrup.'

'Well, you can't stay there all t'night, Mister,' said Mr Oakroyd, who now understood the situation. 'Can you now?'

'I dunno, I dunno,' said the other meditatively. 'P'raps I can, p'raps I can't. Who knows?' Then in a tone of great melancholy he added: 'Nobody knowsh. And nobody - nobody - caresh. Nobody.' He seemed to be overcome by the pathos of this reflection.

'Well, you've got a load on and no mistake,' said Oakroyd. Then he reached out a hand. 'Come on, come on. This'll nivver do. 'Oist yerself up.'

'That's ri'. Gimme a hand, the hand of frien'ship. Up we go!' And, aided by Mr Oakroyd, he struggled to his feet, clapped Mr Oakroyd on the shoulder, nearly lost his balance again, and finally clung to his companion's arm and began staggering down the road. The lamplight revealed him as a large red-faced man, very smart in a light grey felt hat, check suit, and spats.

'You're a good fella,' he cried. 'A very good fella. And I - I'm a good fella too. Both good fellas. Wass'r name? Mine's George. I've had a mos' extr'or' - extr'or' - 'stonishin' time. Mos' 'stonishin'. Been away nearly a week. Racesh. Yes, I'm a rayshing man. Been to Doncaster - all over. An' lucky ev'ry time, ev'ry ev'ry time. D'you know, d'you know' - and here George separated himself from his companion and stood swaying - 'wha' I made thish week?' He waved a finger at Mr Oakroyd, then repeated, quite sternly: 'D'you know?'

'Nay, I don't know,' replied Mr Oakroyd, good-humouredly. 'But I'll bet it were more ner I did.'

'Well, I'll tell you,' said George, gravely swaying. 'I'll tell you. No, I won't, 'cos I've fergorren. But hundredsh, hundredsh an' hundredsh. Lucky, very very lucky. And now - here I am, here I am, my frien', home again.' And he steadied himself by grasping Mr Oakroyd's arm again.

'But where do you live, Mister?'

'Roun' the corner, roun' the corner. Had mosh 'stonishin' adventures, these lash few days. Came back in car. With palsh, goo' old palsh. But gone, all gone. We had li'l' dishpute. Fact is' - and he lowered his voice and almost rested his head on his companion's shoulder - 'fact is, ol' man, they were drunk, yes, dr'r-unk. An' they dropped me out of the car. Bur I said to them, I says, "I'm berrer without you 'cos you're all drunk and this is reshpec - reshpec'able neighbererer-hood." Thash wor I says, my frien', an' I think you'll agree thar it was well spoken - on my par'.' These three last words came with a rush, for he had suddenly released his hold and had swung round alarmingly.

'Nay, that won't do, Mister,' said Mr Oakroyd, making a grab at him. 'You'll nivver get home at that rate. Now where is it you live?'

'Jus' roun' the corner, roun' the good ol' Johnny Horner,' replied George, with enthusiasm. 'We're all ri', we're all ri'. You're a good fella. You been to racesh thish time?'

'No, I've not, nor nowhere else either for a long time. Hold up, Mister, hold up.'

But George had swung right over and was now slowly collapsing against the railings. His legs slowly slid over the pavement, but he still kept on talking. 'You're a wise man, a wise man - to stay at home.' And he said this several times as his head sank lower and lower.

'Nay, brace up, brace up!' Mr Oakroyd tried to pull him up but the man was heavy and a dead-weight now. For a moment it looked as if he were going to sleep, but Mr Oakroyd gave him a series of nudges and shakings and at last succeeded in arousing him a little. After he had made an effort, and Mr Oakroyd had put out all his strength to assist him, George rose very unsteadily to his feet and staggered one or two paces forward.

''Ere, wha's this?' said Mr Oakroyd, picking up an unusually bulky pocket-book. 'This must be yours.' And he handed it over.

The other waved it in the air. 'My note-case. Full, full to the brim with money. Hundredsh of pounds, hundredsh. Must have dropped ou' pocket.' Then he came closer and held the pocket-book only about two inches from Mr Oakroyd's nose. 'I thank you. I thank you. Knew you were good fella. An honesh man. Come here,' he added, ignoring the fact that it would be impossible for his companion to be any closer than he already was. Indeed, he himself stepped back a pace as he continued: 'Come here. You gave me thish, I give you something. Yes, I do. Fair's fair. Thash George's motto.' He fumbled in the pocket-book. 'Come here. Hold hand out.'

Mr Oakroyd found himself clasping some crisp pieces of paper. They felt like bank-notes, and there were four of them. He did not stop to examine them but held them out to the donor, who was busying himself with the pocket-book. 'Look here, Mister, I can't take these,' he said, for his code demanded that he should help a drunken man if he possibly could and also that he should not take advantage of a man's drunken freaks of generosity.

'Warrer say?' George was still busy fastening his pocket-book and putting it away.

'I say I can't take these,' he repeated, almost pushing the notes in the other's face.

'Warrer mean can't take 'em? I tell you, I give 'em. Li'l' presen' for good boy.'

'If I take these,' said Mr Oakroyd earnestly and somewhat unwisely, 'you'll be sorry in the morning.'

This offended George. 'Warrer mean sorry in the morning?' he cried aggressively. 'Money's mine, isn't it? Do warrer like with it, can't I? Can I or can't I? Ish it mine or ishn't it? Can I or can't I? Answer plain queshuns.' And he brought his face as near as he could.

Mr Oakroyd stepped back and began to feel impatient, but said nothing.

'Come on, come on. Le'sh have answer plain queshuns. Can I or can't I? Have I gorrer ask you warrer do with it?'

'Oh, don't be such a damn fool, Mister,' cried Mr Oakroyd, tired of this daft catechism.

'Damn fool, eh? All ri', all ri'. Thash finish, ab-so-lutely finish.' And he made a sweeping gesture that nearly threw him off his feet. 'You go to hell now, anywhere. Finish. No frien' o' mine.' He turned away and staggered forward at a surprising pace.

Mr Oakroyd, stuffing the notes in his pocket, hurried after him. 'Half a minute, half a minute,' he cried to the swaying figure.

The indignant George stopped for a moment to shout: 'You go to hell. I don't want you. Don't you follow me.' And off he went again, round the corner into Park Drive. A few yards farther on, he stopped again: 'Don't you follow me. You're a bad fella, you are. You leave me alone.' But Mr Oakroyd only increased his pace and was almost up to him, when a large figure stepped out of a shadowy gateway and confronted the pair of them.

'"Ere, 'ere! What's all this about?' said the policeman, flashing his lamp on their faces.

George pulled himself up and saluted. 'Good evening, Conshtable. Jus' going home. You know me, don't you?'

The policeman took another look at him. 'Yes, I think I know you, sir. You live down 'ere, don't you? Well, the sooner you're 'ome the better, if you ask me. And what's all this noise about? Who's this 'ere?'

'Thash the point,' replied George gravely. 'Who is he? I dunno who he is. I've jus' told him he's a bad fella, an' I don't want him following me. You tell him he's a bad fella.' The policeman flashed his lamp over Mr Oakroyd again. 'Now then, what's the game?'

'There's no game,' said Mr Oakroyd, rather sulkily. 'I found him rolling drunk up the road and gave him a hand, that's all.'

'Rollin' drunk!' exclaimed George, horror-stricken. 'You're bad bad fella, an' I told you not to keep following me.'

'You be off,' said the policeman to Mr Oakroyd, 'and leave him alone. And you get off home, sir, afore somebody else starts follering you. You've not far to go.'

'Ay, ay, Cap'en.' And George gave another salute and zig-zagged down the road. Mr Oakroyd moved on after him, but a shout from the policeman behind pulled him up.

'Didn't I tell you to be off?' cried the policeman, who had now caught up to him. 'Get off and leave 'im alone afore you get into trouble.'

'He's not the only chap as is going home.' Mr Oakroyd was indignant. 'I've as much right to walk down this street as he has. I'm going home too. I'm not going to bother with him. He's daft drunk.'

'Where d'you live?'

'Ogden Street.'

'That's a good way from 'ere,' said the policeman suspiciously.

'Ay, but this is nearest way to it, and that's all I care about.'

'Well, walk on the other side then. I shall stand 'ere and watch you. And don't let me see you round 'ere again tonight.'

'I don't want ivver to set eyes on thee agen, lad,' Mr Oakroyd muttered to himself as he crossed the road. He walked as fast as he could now, and took the first possible turning out of Park Drive. 'I wonder who that were,' he said to himself. 'Eh, I've seen some silly drunks in my time, but I nivver saw one sillier.' He had to slow down a little because his heart, which had been given a bump or two by that unpleasant talk with the policeman, kept missing a beat and seemed to make him short of breath. Thus it was very late indeed when he finally arrived at 51 Ogden Street, and even Leonard was obviously in bed.

He found a piece of buttered currant teacake, took a large and comforting bite out of it, and then smoothed out on the table four five-pound notes. Twenty pounds. Only twice before had he ever possessed such a sum, and then it had been scraped together, shilling added to shilling. But here was twenty pounds that had fallen to him out of the blue. What should he do with it? He crept upstairs pondering.

IV

'An' serve 'im right, too,' Mrs Oakroyd muttered. 'I haven't a bit of patience with him.' It was the third time she had turned over this kipper, now blackened on both sides. It awaited, this kipper, the arrival of Mr

Oakroyd from work, being indeed the usual centre-piece of Monday evening's tea; but obviously it had long ceased to care whether he came or not. An hour earlier this kipper might have been said to be wasted on him. Now, as Mrs Oakroyd has suggested, it could only be described as something that served him right. Mr Oakroyd generally arrived home before six, but now it was after seven. His wife, who had been washing all day and had organized a particularly fine display of steaming clothes round the fire at a quarter to six, had lost more and more of her temper with every passing quarter of an hour. Had she known that four five-pound notes had found their way into her husband's pockets, late last night, she might have been alarmed. She knows nothing, however, and has not exchanged a dozen words with her husband, who has to rise very early and take both breakfast and dinner to the mill, since they disposed of the Sunday dinner. She is not alarmed but simply annoyed. 'A body can't get on,' she tells herself fretfully. Very soon she will have to prepare tea for Leonard, who will return from his first day at Gregson's to find a kipper, and a much larger and fatter kipper than the one we have already seen, waiting for him, done to a turn. Meanwhile, his father, like the nuisance he is, must take it into his head - for that is how Mrs Oakroyd saw the matter - to be over an hour late.

'Not 'ome yet!' she cried to Mrs Sugden, who had looked in from next door. 'His tea's been ready nearly an hour and a half. Eh, men's a bother, they are! Is yours 'ome!'

'Long sin',' said Mrs Sugden, a woman of few illusions. 'Been and gone out again. Trust 'im! When 'e's more ner an half-hour late, I know I shan't see 'im afore all pubs an' clubs is closed. But that nivver happens o' Monday 'cos 'e has nowt. They can't be working over at Higden's, can they?'

'Not they!' Mrs Oakroyd knew all about the state of the wool trade. 'They can't get a full week in, and a lot on 'em's been stopped. It's not that, I'm sure. Some piece o' silliness, I'll be bound.'

''E's 'ere,' Mrs Sugden whispered dramatically, then promptly vanished from the doorway.

The next moment he was there, a grimy, hot, and angry man who flung his cap and his bag of joiner's tools down on the sofa, then closed the outer door with a bang.

'Where in the name o' goodness have you been?' his wife demanded. 'And your tea waiting 'ere a full hour and a half!'

'Been on to t'Union office.' he answered shortly.

She glanced at his face and then moderated her tone, 'What d'you want to go there for at this time?'

''Cos I've been stopped.' He bent down and began to unlace his heavy working boots.

'You've been what?' his wife shrieked.

'Stopped, sacked, paid off, whativver you want to call it!' He straightened himself and threw an insurance card and some money on the table. 'I'm not even under notice. Higden's has finished wi' me, and I've finished wi' them. There's a week's money there.' He began to unlace the other boot.

'Well, I nivver did!' cried Mrs Oakroyd. She flopped down into a chair and regarded him with the utmost astonishment. 'What 'a' you been doing?'

'I'll tell you all about it in a minute. I want a wash and summat to eat.' He marched in his stockinged feet towards the scullery. 'Get my tea ready and then you'll soon know what I've been doing,' he added grimly.

In Bruddersford wives do not stand on ceremony at such moments of crisis, and Mrs Oakroyd, without a word of protest, made the tea and released the kipper from its long ordeal.

'If this 'ere fish had 'a' been by t'fire a minute longer,' said Mr Oakroyd, now seated at the table, 'it 'ud 'ave started warping. It's like a bit o' burnt wood.'

'Happen it's last you'll see for a bit,' his wife retorted, having been roused by this gratuitous sally. 'Never mind about that. What 'ave you gotten stopped for?'

'For nowt, just nowt,' he began. 'Or, if you like, for bein' a man and not a damned monkey.' He stopped to take a drink of tea, then, pointing his fork at Mrs Oakroyd, he resumed: 'This morning I hadn't a wagon in, and so were doin' nowt for a bit. Simpson, t'under-manager, comes up an' ses, "What are you on with, Oakroyd?" and I tells him, "Nowt, just now." They're puttin' up a temporary shed for t'wagons, and so Simpson ses, "Well, help wi' t'shed. You can start by getting this into shape." And he points to a beam they pulled out o' t'old shed, and he finds measurements for me. So I borrows an axe an' a big cross-cut saw and gets to work on this 'ere beam. I haven't been at it more ner ten minutes when a chap taps me on t'back. I don't know him but I know he's one t'shop-stewards. "An when did you join t'Carpenters' Union, comrade?" he ses, very nasty. "What d'you mean?" I ses, though I knew what was coming. He pointed to t'beam: "That's a carpenter's job," he ses, "an' you keep off it, comrade." I give him a look. "Comrade!" I ses, "My God!" "I've noticed you once or twice," he ses, "an it's struck me you've got the makings of a blackleg," he ses. "An summat else'll strike you in a minute, mate, if you stay here callin' me names," I ses. "Well, leave that job alone," he ses, an' walks off. And of course I had to.'

He paused for refreshment, and his wife stared at him and said that she didn't know whatever things were coming to.

'Well, let me finish,' said Mr Oakroyd, as if she had been preventing him. 'So I'd nowt to do again. By an' by, Simpson comes round again, this time wi' manager hisself, old Thorley. They're takking a quick look round and seem a bit flustered. Thorley sees me. "What's this man doing?" he asks. "Eh, Oakroyd," Simpson shouts across, "get on wi' that job an' sharp about it." "I can't get on wi' it," I shout back, and moves across to tell 'em. "Go on, man, go on, man, go on !" ses old Thorley, waving his hand at me, and out they goes. At dinner-time I hears that the great man hisself, Sir Joseph Higden, Bart - an' his father were nobbut a weaving over-looker like mine - is on the premises. I knew now why t'managers were so flustered. "I'll bet they're cuttin' summat down," I ses. About three o'clock they lands in our department, Sir Joseph and Thorley, wi' Simpson behind. I see Sir Joseph wave his hand. Then Thorley looks round, an' I see him look at me and then say summat to Simpson. In a minute or two, Simpson comes up an' ses, "I'm sorry, Oakroyd, but you'll 'a' to take a week's notice." "What for?" I ses. "What have I done?" "It's your own fault," he ses, "there's so many to be stopped, an' you shouldn't have let Mr Thorley see you this morning." "It were no fault o' mine," I ses, "an' I'm going to have a word wi' Mr Thorley." And I did have a word wi' him, an' a fat lot o' good it did me. I begins to tell him how long I'd been there, an' he cuts me short an' ses some of us older men is as idle as young uns instead o' setting an example. That were enough for me, and I ses summat I shouldn't ha' said. "Pay 'im off an' give him his card," he ses. "This man's finished wi' Higden's for good an' all."'

'That comes o' not keeping a civil tongue in your head, Jess Oakroyd,' said his wife reproachfully. 'I've warned you afore now.'

'Whatd'you think I'm made of?' demanded Mr Oakroyd. 'When a chap's called a blackleg in t'morning an' an idler i' t'after- noon, he's got to say summat. Well, I gets my week's money and my card at five o'clock, and sets off for t'Union office to tell my tale there. Secretary's not in. That's young Maundery, him as talks so much about the proletariat. I waits about and waits about. By and by in he comes, an' who's with him? That shop-steward, the comrade. In they come, laughing and talking, two bloody comrades together. A fat lot o' good my trying to tell 'em my tale! Started pulling me up right an' left. "Notify this, that, an' t'other." "Oh, you go to Hell," I ses at finish. What wi' one an' another, and being badgered this way an' that, I hadn't a bit o' patience left. "Oh, you go to Hell," I ses, and marches out. And now you know.'

His wife sat there rigid, her eyes fixed on his. For a few moments her face softened and she looked as if she were about to cry. But as she watched him dispose of the remainder of his tea, deal aggressively with a piece of pastry and a second cup, the hard lines came back into her face, the unfriendly gleam into her eyes. 'Well, and what are you going to do now then?' she asked.

Mr Oakroyd pushed aside his cup. It was a little gesture of despair. 'Line up for t'dole till another job turns up.'

'And 'ow long 'ull that be?'

'Don't ask me. You know what it is now. That bag o' tools 'ull be there a long time, I'm thinking.' He stood up now and looked across at his tools, lying on the sofa. Then he glanced down at his dirty old working clothes, and suddenly arrived, he knew not how or why, at a queer little decision. 'I'm off upstairs to change my clothes,' he announced, and departed.

When he came down again, he found his wife preparing Leonard's tea. He saw at a glance that she had made up her mind about something: her lips were tightly folded upon some recent decision. He waited for her to speak, turning, in his misery, to the old-time comfort of Old Salt.

'Well, that settles it,' she began.

'What settles what?' he asked uneasily.

'Albert Tuggridge comes 'ere,' she announced. Then, before he had time to do more than remove his pipe, she charged in, working herself up to a fury of justification. 'Now, don't start on again, don't start on. You've just thrown your job away, you're not going to throw this away an' all, that you're not. If t'lad's still willing to come, 'ere he comes, and sooner the better. If it takes any more work it'll be mine and I'll have it to stand, so it's more my business ner yours, and I say he can come. We've got to live, 'aven't we? You'd got little room to talk when you were in work, and you've less now.'

'You might 'a' let me off Albert for this one night anyhow,' he said quietly.

This only made her angrier. 'It's got to be settled, 'asn't it? An' let me tell you this, if Albert don't come, Leonard might be going. I heard 'em saying summat t'other night. I don't think t'lad would leave his mother, but 'e might, wi' you always on to him. And then where should we be? Just when he's getting a good wage, too!'

So that was it. He was angry too now. 'If Albert comes 'ere,' he said firmly, 'I go.'

'Don't talk so soft. Where are you going? Are you going to live at t'Midland Hotel on your dole money?'

'Not so much about the dole! It's first time it's had to be mentioned in this 'ouse, let me tell you.' He took his wounded pride to the door and there brooded over his pipe. When he swivelled his pipe from one corner of his mouth to the other, his elbow set something rustling in his inside coat pocket. There were four five-pound notes there.

''Ere we are at last, the old firm!' This was Leonard. His father followed him into the living-room. 'Tea ready, Mar?' cried the youth, gaily. 'That's the stuff!'

'Got on all right, Len?' asked his mother, bringing the large fat kipper from the fire.

'Ab-so-lutely! D'you know what I made in tips? Guess. Eight-and-threepence. Eight-shillings-and-threepence. Not so dusty. Good old Gregson's!' His mother poured out a cup of tea for the conquering hero.

'Good job we're gettin' it from somewhere,' she remarked. 'Your father's finished at Higden's.'

'What's this?' A close observer might have noticed a subtle change at once in Leonard's manner.

His father, for once, was a close observer. 'All right, all right,' he said. 'Give it a rest for a minute. Is that t'paper you've got there?' It was, and Mr Oakroyd, claiming it, retired to a corner of the sofa, plodding steadily and miserably down the columns of the *Bruddersford Evening Express* and trying to shut his ears to the whispering of the other two at the table.

Quarter of an hour later, on arriving at the fifth page, it was not necessary for him to try to fix his attention on the paper. His attention was securely riveted there. He stared and stared at a report headed: *Street Robbery. Local Sportsman's Loss*. Phrases leaped up to meet his eye: 'The well-known local sportsman, Mr George Jobley ... returning to his home in Park Drive, Merton Park, Bruddersford, last night ... Mr Jobley had been attending various race-meetings ... had left his friends to walk the short distance to his home ... attacked and robbed .... at least £120 missing ... strange affair ... most important street robbery in Bruddersford for years ... Mr Jobley not injured but some shock.' And the last sentence of all held his eye longest: 'The police announce that they possess a valuable clue to the identity of the assailant.' What was this?

''Ere, who's this chap, George Jobley?' he demanded.

'That's the bookie feller that's been robbed,' replied Leonard. 'I know him well by sight. He's one o' the lads.'

'What's 'e like?'

'Tallish feller with a red face. Always dressed in a check suit and spats. What's up?'

'Nowt!' Mr Oakroyd returned untruthfully. George! He stared at the report again. 'The police announce that they possess a valuable clue ...' Nay, but a hundred and twenty pounds! It had nothing to do with him, nothing at all. There were a thousand things a perfectly innocent citizen might do to clear himself, but now Mr Oakroyd could not consider them, for his little world was shaking, collapsing, and now another prop had been kicked away. One thing coming on top of another!

As if to confirm this, a voice came roaring from the doorway. 'Hello, hello, hello, hello! Ev'rybody at 'ome, and smilin'! Oh, I do like a kipper for my tea! What'o, Len ! 'Evening, Mrs Oakroyd !' And who could this be but Albert?

'Oh, my God!' And groaning thus, Mr Oakroyd flung down his paper and rose to his feet.

'Hello, hello!' cried Albert, still loudly but this time indignantly. 'What 'ave I done wrong?'

'Take no notice of 'im, Albert.' Mrs Oakroyd gave her husband a furious glance, then, with an astonishing quick-change, smiled at her visitor. 'Come in and sit yer down. You know you're welcome. An' another thing, if you want to stay 'ere, you can do.'

'Oh!' cried her husband. 'And who says so?'

'I say so.'

'And so do I,' Leonard added truculently.

Mr Oakroyd took a quick step towards his son, who immediately dropped his truculence and, indeed, seemed to flinch, like a very small boy. But then Mr Oakroyd pulled himself up and stood still, a man at bay, thinking hard. The next moment he had dashed upstairs.

Once there he began looking about him eagerly. 'I must 'a' summat,' he muttered. There was a suitcase, Mrs Oakroyd's pride. No, he wouldn't take that. There was the old round tin trunk. Too heavy and cumbersome. Then he remembered the basket thing, and pulled it out of the corner where it had been for the last fifteen years. It was very light and quite small, only eighteen inches long and a foot deep, and it would hold all he wanted to carry. Into this absurd receptacle - or at least one half of it, for the other half would have to be jammed on as a lid - he stuffed a nightshirt and day shirt, three collars and some handkerchiefs, a muffler, a vest and a pair of pants, and his shaving kit. When he had jammed on the top half, he be-thought him of his old mackintosh, and folded it round the little basket trunk before he fastened it with the strap, which was still intact and boasted of a holder for the hand. Then he put on a pair of strong boots and hurried downstairs, basket in hand, to confront three astonished faces.

'What in the name o' goodness - !' cried his wife.

'I'm off,' he announced.

'Where to?' asked Leonard, still staring. 'Yer can't go like that, Par. Where can you go to?'

'Never mind, never mind!' Mrs Oakroyd was white with temper.

'Let 'im go, let 'im go! Tryin' 'is tricks! 'E won't hear a word from me about stayin'. Let 'im go. 'E'll be in a diff'rent frame o' mind when 'e comes back. And that won't be so long either.'

'You can do what you like wi' t'place now,' said Mr Oakroyd. 'It's yer own. There's a week's money there and no doubt you'll manage after that.'

'Manage!' cried his wife, in a fury of scorn. 'Of course we can manage. Nivver better off. You've been wanting a lesson some time and now you're runnin' to get it. Go on, go on.'

Mr Oakroyd said nothing, but moved over to the sofa and took up his bag of tools, dumping it beside the basket trunk. Then he stuck his old brown cap at the back of his head, and prepared to depart.

''Ere,' said Albert, pointing to the table. 'What about that?'

'That's right,' said Leonard. 'You'll 'ave to 'ave that.' And he held out the insurance card.

Mr Oakroyd stood staring at the greenish-blue card in his hand, staring as if he were in a dream. *Man - Age 16 to 65 .... Failure to surrender this card promptly ... If the Insured Person ... The Insured Person* ... All so familiar and yet so strange. He stood staring, baffled, lost in the dark of a world of notices and notifying, of sneering Comrades and stupid autocratic managers, of buzzers that kept your feet from the road, of signs that could never be hoisted, of daughters that grew up, laughing and singing, and then vanished over the sea. Then something inside him flared and went shooting through this bewildered dark like a rocket, and Mr Oakroyd committed a crime.

'Oh, to hell wi' t'card !' he cried, and tore it across and threw the pieces into the fire. Then, leaving horror-stricken amazement behind him, he picked up his bag of tools and his little basket trunk and made for the door.

'Now you've done it,' they were crying. 'Where yer going?'

'Down South,' he replied, and vanished into the night.

CHAPTER TWO
Miss Trant Takes a Holiday

I

ONCE more we look down upon English hills, lit by the same September sun. But it is another England; the dark Pennines have been left far behind; the grim heights of ling and peat and black rock, the reeking cauldrons that were the valleys, all have vanished. Here are pleasant green mounds, heights of grass for ever stirring to the tune of the south-west winds; clear valleys, each with its gleam of water; grey stone villages, their walls flushing to a delicate pink in the sunlight; parish churches that have rung in and rung out Tudor, Stuart, and Hanoverian kings; manor houses that have waited for news from Naseby and Blenheim and Waterloo and Inkerman and Ypres, then have let their windows blaze through the night or have suddenly grown still and dark, but have kept their stones unchanged; and here and there, in the wider valleys, little woods where you could play *A Midsummer Night's Dream*, and gardens shaped and coloured, to the last inch of lawn cross-gartered with stone paths, from the tallest hollyhock to the smallest rose-bush, for the music and happy folly of *Twelfth Night*. This is, indeed, another England, this green and windy outpost of Arden. Over to the west, beyond the deep channels of the rivers, is the Welsh Border country, a Celtic place, with hills as dark and mysterious as a fragment of Arthurian legend. But here, in the Cotswolds, all is open and pleasant, a Saxon tale of grass and grey stone, wind and clear running water. We have quitted the long war of the north. Here is a place of compromise, for Nature has planed off her sharp summits and laid down green carpets in place of bog and heather and rock, and man has forsworn his mad industrial antics, has settled himself modestly and snugly in the valleys and along the hillsides, has trotted out his sheep and put up a few tiny mills, and has been content. Yes, these two signed a peace here, and it has lasted a thousand years.

Chipping Campden is to the north of us, Cirencester to the south, Burford to the east, and Cheltenham to the west. This grey cluster of roofs, with the square church tower in the middle, is almost equidistant from all those four admirable townships. It is the village of Hitherton-on-the-Wole. Sometimes motorists, hurrying from lunch at Oxford to tea at Broadway or Chipping Campden, lose their way and find themselves at Hitherton, and the little books prepared for their use tell them at once that Hitherton has 855 inhabitants, closes early on Wednesday, empties its letter-box at 5.30 p.m., boasts an hotel, The

Shepherd's Hall (three bedrooms) and a garage, J. Hurley & Son, and has at least one thing worth looking at, for the account closes with the command - *See Church*. Very few of them do stay to see the church, though the rector, the Rev. Thomas J. S. Chillingford, has not only written a short history of it but has also published this history as a pamphlet: *Reprinted from the 'Transactions of the Bristol and Gloucestershire Archaeological Society'*; and any visitor who appreciates an extraordinarily fine rood-screen when he sees one (to say nothing of two possible leper-windows on the north side) cannot fail to obtain a copy of this pamphlet. But away they go, these motorists, and never once turn their heads to remark, with Mr Chillingford, that the church 'from a distance suggests a brooding-mother-bird with head erect'. Thus when any strange and expensive-looking motor-car stops there, everybody in Hitherton, with the exception of Mrs Farley of The Shepherd's Hall and J. Hurley & Son, who are always hopeful, prepares at once to point the way to other and more important places.

There are some days, however, when people do not lose their way and find themselves in Hitherton but deliberately go there and stay there. This is one of the days. For the last three weeks the countryside has been plastered with notices saying that Messrs Medworth, Higgs, and Medworth would sell by auction and without reserve the remaining effects of the Old Hall, Hitherton-on-the-Wole. Well-informed people - and almost everybody in Hitherton is well-informed - have been telling one another ever since old Colonel Trant died, several months ago, that there was sure to be a sale. It was known for certain that the Trants were not so well-off as they used to be. It was known too that Miss Elizabeth Trant, who had looked after her father ever since her mother's death, fifteen years ago, would not live on at the Hall but at the Cottage. Miss Elizabeth had been left everything, it was said, though she was the youngest of the Colonel's three children. But then she well deserved everything the Colonel could leave her - indeed, deserved more than that - for had she not stayed in Hitherton and looked after him in his old age? And in the last years he must have been a trial, too. He had had to miss the last two Flower Shows and could not even hobble to church, the poor old gentleman. It was a blessing when he found his way in the end to the churchyard. And Miss Trant, who must be about thirty-seven, though being so straight and slim and fair she does not look it, had taken care of him year after year and had hardly left the village for more than a night this long time; whereas her brother, who was some sort of judge in India, and her sister, who had married well and lived in London, rarely came near the place. Everybody knew that what with the Colonel's retired pay going and debts to be paid off and one thing and another, Miss Trant would have less than £200 a year for herself.

That was why she intended to live at the Cottage, to which all the things she wanted had already been removed, and why all that remained at the Old Hall, now to be let, was being sold by auction.

It is a long time since Medworth, Higgs, and Medworth last descended upon Hitherton. This is a great day. Any number of cars have gone up to the Old Hall, already Mrs Farley has had to open another bottle of whisky, and J. Hurley & Son have had to mend two punctures and see what they could do with a very queer magneto. People, quite ordinary people, not dealers, have come from as far as Bourton-on-the-Water and Winchcombe and Great Barrington. As for dealers, they have come from the ends of the earth. There are at least two from Cheltenham and three from Oxford and one from Gloucester, all proper antique dealers and not merely grocers and drapers who keep a room upstairs filled with second-hand furniture. Not that there are not any of them here, for of course there are quite a number. And it is said that there is one man, the one with eye-glasses and a pointed beard, who represents some big London firm. He did not come down specially, for it is his business to tour the country, but here he is. Then for every one of these professional buyers there must be at least twenty amateurs, local people who have come to see if they can pick up a bit of china or a bedstead. Last of all, there are people who have not come to buy anything, but to see what the Old Hall looks like inside, to walk round the garden, to turn things over and over, and get in the way, to enjoy themselves. These visitors, many of whom have brought all their children, easily outnumber the others, and just as they were the first to arrive, so they will be the last to go. 'Always the same, always the same!' cried Mr James Medworth to the protesting Miss Trant. 'They *will* come, and there's no stopping 'em.' Mr Medworth has spent years pushing his way through rooms crowded and overheated with these people, and now regards their presence as something inevitable. Still, they laugh at his little jokes, and Mr Medworth has a stock of little jokes. He is a middle-aged man with a very wide mouth and a glitter of large protruding teeth, so that he looks like a jovial shark. Miss Trant does not like him, but is quite willing to believe her solicitor, Mr Truby of Cheltenham, who says: 'Smart man, Medworth. Smart man. Keen people.'

She was there at the Hall this morning, when people began to arrive and look round, but did not stay very long. She is not very sentimental and all her own cherished possessions have been removed to the Cottage, but nevertheless she discovered that the sudden disintegration of a home, however desolating that home might have been sometimes, into a mere jumble of objects, gave her no pleasure. All the things now looked so naked, so helpless. 'Awful lot o' junk here,' she heard one man say to another, dealers every inch of them; and she hurried round the corner, only to run into that familiar steel engraving of Lord Raglan, now Lot 117, and to find that his lordship was glaring into vacancy, cutting her dead. But all the things were like that, either indignant or wistful. She retired, wishing she had taken more of them to the Cottage, though she knew very well that the Cottage was too full already.

She found Mrs Purton putting the Cottage in order, and spent the next hour or two helping her. Mrs Purton had been cook at the Hall, and her husband - and his father before him - had been gardener, and now they had both been transferred, for the time being, to the Cottage. Mrs Purton 'didn't 'old with auctioneering', apparently regarding it as a frivolous pastime, and so she had stayed at home all day. But Purton was up at the Hall, partly because he was a sociable man and had no intention of missing such an event, and partly because he was also very loyal and believed that his presence would put a stop to any thieving, particularly in the kitchen garden. So in order that no vegetables should be taken, he was spending his time following the auctioneer round from room to room, apparently convinced that it was Mr Medworth, his clerks, and the dealers, who would want watching. It was Purton who brought news of the sale.

'Is it all over, Purton?' cried Miss Trant, as soon as she saw him coming down the garden. He came up, touched his cap, then, putting his hands in his trousers pockets, he began swaying back from the hips. This was his favourite attitude when he had anything important to say, so that Miss Trant, who knew her man, realized at once that he was bursting with news. Not that he looked excited. You cannot expect a gardener who for the past six years has won the first prize for onions (Ailsa Craigs) - to say nothing of any number of minor events - at the Hitherton and District Show, to betray his feelings.

'No, Miss, rightly speaking, it isn't over,' he replied. 'But what's left don't amount to much. A lot o' people goin' now. But that thar bit of a sideboard that stood in the 'all, that old un – ' and he stopped talking only to sway more violently.

'You mean the Tudor one. I know. I couldn't find a place for it here, Purton, and they say it's very valuable. What happened to it?'

'A 'undred and forty pound,' announced Purton, staring at her solemnly. 'A 'undred and forty pound, that's just fetched.'

'Isn't that splendid, Purton!' Miss Trant looked at him with shining eyes, and did not seem a day older than twenty.

He stopped swaying, removed one hand from its pocket, and held up three fingers very impressively. 'Three of 'em after it at the finish, that's all - three! Dealers they was. An Oxford feller, and a

Cheltenham feller, and a little chap with a beard that's come from London. Three of 'em! And they 'ardly says a word, 'ardly a word. Never see anything like it!'

'What did they do then?'

'Winks. Just winks.' And Purton produced three of them too, very slow and solemn affairs, to show her how it was done, and then stared at her while she tried hard not to giggle. 'Mr Medworth, 'e says "Goin' at ninety" and then one of 'em winks, and Mr Medworth says "Ninety-five" and looks at another of 'em, gets a wink and 'as it up to a hundred. "And five" says the chap with a beard, and then they starts winkin' again, and then it's winked right up to one 'undred and forty pounds. 'E's done well, 'as that thar sideboard.'

'I never thought it was worth as much as that, Purton.'

'You wouldn't think so, Miss, would you - just a bit of an old sideboard,' said Purton, speaking very confidentially. 'It wouldn't surprise me if it woren't. It's this 'ere competition that does it. Carries you away. You think you must 'ave it. I once found meself landed with ten runner ducks that I no more wanted nor thought o' buying when I went up and 'ad a look at the chap selling 'em than I thought o' buying a ring-tailed monkey. Got carried away. Plenty 'as been carried away this afternoon up at that thar auctioning. Mr Medworth says it's a good Sale. I'll be back thar, Miss, as soon as I've had a bit to eat. I'll 'elp to clear up. There'll be a nasty mess when they've done, I know.'

For the first time that day, Miss Trant began to feel excited about the Sale. Mr Medworth had told her that it was impossible for him to say beforehand what the things would fetch; it all depended on the number of people who came, the sort of people and the mood they were in; and the whole lot might go for less than five hundred pounds, but on the other hand it might realize something like a thousand. It was impossible to doubt anything that Mr Medworth said about such matters. Miss Trant had tried, with some measure of success, to regard the whole proceeding as so much dull routine - one of the innumerable dreary things that had had to be done since her father died - but now she realized that this was a gigantic gamble, a homely Monte Carlo, got up for her benefit. The difference between a good sale and a bad one might mean a difference of several hundred pounds, which in their turn could add a pound or two a month to her income. You could work it out in grades of China tea or silk stockings, that difference. And now it was being decided. She walked up and down the little Cottage garden, her head humming with addition and subtraction as it had done many a time these last few years, when she had had to pay all the bills and keep the accounts for her father. She was poorer now but she did not feel poorer. Actually she felt vaguely rich. 'It's because I've heard so much talk about money,' she told herself, thinking of the discussions she had had with Mr Truby in his Dickens-ish little office, and then, more recently, with Mr Medworth, who was at once too teethy and jovial to be a gentleman.

She saw Purton return to the Hall, but did not follow him. After a restless half-hour or so in the Cottage, mostly spent in picking things up, walking about with them, and then putting them down again, she went to the bottom of the garden. The village below seemed to be full of cars, hooting through the main street and then roaring away to the Oxford or Cheltenham roads. The sale must be all over now. She would walk across and see.

When she approached the Hall, picking her way through a smelly muddle of people and cars and vans, the glorious September afternoon seemed to change at once. Its ripe gold became hot and dusty gilt. The Hall itself seemed smaller in this strange atmosphere, made up of straw and string and petrol and stares and silly jokes and perspiring bargainers. The place gaped vacantly, like a once handsome old idiot. As she skirted the crowd in front and made her way to a side door, she had a glimpse of certain familiar tables and chairs and pictures now being lifted into vans and carts, and that glimpse made her feel, as nothing that had happened before during these last few months had made her feel, that her life indeed was changed, beginning all over again. Those things had seemed more fixed and inevitable than the constellations, and now they were being hurried through the dust. They too were beginning all over again. And before she had reached the side door, she found herself choking a little, close to tears. She brushed past the men who were sweeping up the litter in the passages and made for the hall itself, the glory of the house. There she disturbed the rector, Mr Chillingford, who was peering at the woodwork through a large reading glass.

He looked up, startled. 'Hello! I had to have a look at this panelling at the back, now that I can see it properly. I knew it was different from the rest. I told my wife it was only this morning. Not that she said it wasn't, of course, because she's not interested in this sort of thing.' Then he brought his round red innocent face closer to hers, and said, more gently: 'You look worried, Elizabeth. All this hasn't been very pleasant for you, has it? You shouldn't have come here; you should have kept out of the way, my dear.'

'I suppose I ought,' she replied vaguely. 'But I have kept out of the way most of the time. And I'm not feeling what you think I'm feeling. It's not sentiment about this place that's worrying me.' She stopped, then smiled at him rather wanly.

'You're like Dorothy and all the other young people I know

nowadays,' he said. He always thought of Elizabeth Trant as a contemporary of his daughter and her friend, though actually she was ten years older. He saw her as a tall brisk schoolgirl who would one day become a woman. It was something undeveloped, immature, sexless, in her that fostered such conceptions. 'Yes, you're like the rest,' he continued. 'You think there's something to be ashamed of in sentiment. That's why it seems to be dying out, leaving the world. But I don't see myself that the world will be a better place without it. Not a bit, not a bit! It'll be a worse place. So don't you be ashamed of your feelings, my dear.' And he gave her a little pat or two on the shoulder.

'I'm not. I'm only trying to be honest about them. And it really is something quite different.'

'What is it then?' he inquired indulgently.

'I don't know - quite. It's too complicated.' But she did know, though she had neither the will nor the words at her command to tell him. It was not because something had ended for her but because she had just seen how it ended that she was so troubled, so close to tears. It seemed as if her father's life had not come to its end in the churchyard there, but here and now, in the dust and straw and shouting, had been bargained and frittered away into oblivion this very afternoon. She seemed to have had a sudden terrible glimpse of life as it really was, and was ready to weep at the thought of its strange dusty littleness.

'All the things you really want, of course, have been removed to the Cottage?' Mr Chillingford knew very well they had, but the question seemed to him to have a certain consolatory value.

'Yes, everything,' she told him, and stared at the fantastically empty hall, into which the heavy sunlight came oozing.

'And I'm told it's been a splendid sale, a splendid sale,' he added cheerfully, as they walked together to the front door.

Just outside, Mr Medworth himself was glittering and booming and mopping his brow. At the sight of Miss Trant, he triumphantly raised a hand. 'A very successful afternoon, I'm told,' said Mr Chillingford, opening the subject for him.

'Couldn't be better, couldn't be better,' he cried, and then looked so business-like that Mr Chillingford hurried away at once. 'We're just finishing off now, Miss Trant, the figures, y'know. Over a thousand, I'm confident of that. Yes, over a thousand.'

'Why, that's even more than you thought it would come to, even at the best, isn't it?' Miss Trant felt rich again, in spite of her sober acquaintance with figures.

'Well, I wouldn't say that because I'm never surprised, never,' Mr Medworth said, very judicially. 'But we've been lucky today, very lucky. Some keen men here, real competition. And' - here he lowered his voice and hid his teeth - 'it was lucky you took my advice about the walnut pieces and left them in. Worth far more to these fellows than they are to you. All a fashion!'

'Did they sell very well, then?'

'Fetched ridiculous prices, ridiculous! Knew they would, if we got the right people here. That little bureau went up to thirty-five. Three of 'em after every piece.' And Mr Medworth continued in this strain for the next ten minutes, at the end of which he had to break off because he found a mass of documents thrust under his nose.

'We've got it now,' he announced, five minutes later. 'One thousand and sixty-five pounds, fourteen shillings, and sixpence, that's what we make it. That's less our commission, y'know. All your own, Miss Trant, eh? Yes, all your own. Shall we settle up with Mr Truby? Ah yes, I'll settle with Mr Truby tomorrow. Good!' He turned away as if to depart and swept round again so quickly that he made Miss Trant feel dizzy. 'The house,' he cried, lifting a long fat forefinger. 'We mustn't forget that. They're cleaning it up now, and tomorrow, Miss Trant, perhaps you could get a woman or two in to finish it off. And a gardener to tidy up. You could, eh? I'll tell you why. We're going to get rid of the house sooner than I thought. Inquiry came in yesterday, and I'll send 'em over day after tomorrow. How's that for you? Send someone with 'em, of course, but thought you might like to show 'em round a bit yourself. Sure you don't want to sell? No. Quite right, quite right. Well, we'll stick at a hundred and fifty, not a penny less. Get it easily, best house in the district. Day after tomorrow then, morning if possible. And settle with Mr Truby. Good afternoon, Miss Trant. Go-od afternoon. Here, where's Charlie?' But this last shout was not intended for Miss Trant, and now we have finished with Mr Medworth.

Miss Trant returned to the Cottage, richer by the sum of one thousand and sixty-five pounds, fourteen shillings, and sixpence. She walked quickly and erectly down the lane, then tidied up the Cottage and tidied up herself, dealt justly with an excellent cold supper, wrote a few letters and read a chapter or two before going, rather earlier than usual, to bed; and nobody who saw her could have guessed what she was feeling. Here was the trim, the brisk, the efficient Miss Trant that everybody knew, with not a single hair of that light-brown and unbobbed mass disturbed. Nevertheless, she felt as if she were lost. 'It's weak and silly to feel like this,' she told herself firmly. 'In the morning, I must begin all over again.' Before she could do more than turn over a few vague plans, she was asleep, dreaming perhaps of the long-deferred payment of life to her youth, that youth which the calendar, lying to her bright face, said had slipped by. And now Hitherton was itself again, quiet under the glimmer of stars. There were no cars parked in the main street. The last van had shaken itself from the Hall long ago. J. Hurley & Son had closed the garage and were celebrating their victory over the queer magneto by eating a large late supper of cold potato pie. In the tap-room of The Shepherd's Hall, Purton was finishing his final half-pint and also the whole question of dealers' winks. The dealers themselves, the little buyers, the sight-seers, had long dispersed, and with them all the chairs and tables and chests of drawers and china and guns and books and steel engravings and Indian screens and Burmese gongs, all gone out to strange places; leaving their Colonel resting in the churchyard, and his daughter sleeping under this roof of her own, still in familiar Hitherton and yet perhaps really in a new world.

II

The next morning, Miss Trant, looking through her window at the radiant vapour, decided that the day would be fine and that it should be honoured by her golden-brown jumper suit, a recent and triumphant find in Cheltenham. In the little dining-room, polished and trim and full of sunlight, she found a picture postcard awaiting her. On one side were the Glastonbury ruins. On the other was some equally ruinous and picturesque handwriting : 'Isn't this appalling? Must have been invented for Americans. Can I descend upon you sometime tomorrow, dinner-ish? Love, Hilary.' This was her nephew, the only son of the Indian Judge. He had recently come down from Oxford. Miss Trant looked very thoughtful over this card. She was not sure whether she wanted to entertain Hilary or not.

Before she could make up her mind whether Hilary would be a pleasure or a nuisance, Mrs Purton waddled in, set down a boiled egg, a toast-rack, and a teapot, and then proceeded in a very leisurely fashion to explode a bomb.

'They do say, Miss - ' Mrs Purton began, and then stopped, holding, as it were the smoking bomb in her hand. Miss Trant smiled at her. 'Well, what are they saying now? Don't frighten me, Mrs Purton.'

'They do say - ' she stopped again. Then it came - bang! 'Miss Chillingford, Miss Dorothy, 'as just got herself engaged to be married.'

'What!' Miss Trant nearly shrieked. 'It can't be true. I've never heard anything about it.'

'It come this morning in a letter,' said Mrs Purton, enjoying herself. 'Mrs Chillingford she tells it to Agnes, and Agnes tells it to young Cripps as brings the milk, and young Cripps tells it to me. And she'll 'ave to be married very soon and then go out to Asia or India or Jamaikie or one o' them places, 'cos it's a young gentleman as works there.'

'I wonder who it is?' Miss Trant stared at Mrs Purton's plump red face as if she might find the name written there.

'That I *don't know, Miss.*' Mrs Purton took her tray and turned to go. 'And one o' them cars as come for furniture last night got stuck in a ditch on the Cheltenham road. Drunk, I'll be bound!' And she made her favourite exit, nodding her head like a minor prophet.

Miss Trant cared nothing about the fate of cars on the Cheltenham road, but the news of Dorothy Chillingford's engagement, totally unexpected, left her a little dazed. Her plans, vague as they were, had counted upon Dorothy's companionship or, at least, neighbouring high spirits. She felt hurt, too, at not being told, that is, not being told properly. She debated whether to look in at the Chillingfords', but decided against it. 'If Mrs Chillingford doesn't arrive within an hour,' she told herself, 'I shall know there's nothing in it, just village gossip.' Purton was up at the Hall, restoring order in the big garden, and so she took his place for the morning among the Cottage flower-beds.

She had not very long to wait. As soon as she saw Mrs Chillingford's agile little figure between the grenadier lines of hollyhocks, she knew that she had heard no mere idle rumour. 'Good morning, my dear,' Mrs Chillingford gasped, 'I came round to ask you over to tea this afternoon.' Dorothy's engagement was written all over her.

This was a moment worthy of Mrs Chillingford. She was a small stringy woman, with no shoulders and rheumatic joints but with a fighting face, hooked nose and snapping eyes, and an indomitable spirit. The rector himself, so long as such subjects as leper-windows, the University Commission, and Anglo-Catholicism were avoided, was one of the most placid of mortals, and there are few quieter places in this island than Hitherton. Yet Mrs Chillingford had contrived to turn her life there into a saga. From Monday morning to Saturday night she flung out ultimatums, mobilized, gave battle, and then shot into church on Sunday to hymn her victories and send glances like bayonets to right and left of her while her husband in the pulpit murmured of peace. Visitors newly arrived from the North-western Frontier of the Central American republics found themselves hastily revising their notions of English country life after an hour in her company, and soon returned to London for a rest. There was just one period, lasting about six months, when she lost all her zest for conflict and was very quiet indeed, perhaps because she found it so difficult to understand John Chillingford was in future to be only a name on the village War memorial; and then the good people of Hitherton and neighbourhood discovered a peace that made the subsequent Armistice a mere anti-climax. But it was a disquieting sort of peace, and perhaps they were not altogether sorry when their rector's wife became herself again. When she did come to the end of those six months, buried away that strangely acquiescent little woman in black, there was no holding her at all. Commissioners, recruiting officers, great ladies, even Bishops and Lords Lieutenant, were sent reeling back. And that mild and not unwise man, the Rev. Thomas Chillingford, never uttered a word of reproof but even gently suggested new adversaries and hinted from time to time, he who had never an enemy, that he was in great need of her help, almost at bay. But for a year or two now Mrs Chillingford had had to carry on her saga almost unaided by circumstance, doing what she could with Flower Show Committee meetings and the like; here at last was an event, and it found her worthy.

'Yes, it's true, and I was to tell you at once. His name's Atkinson, Gerald Atkinson - you may have met him; he was down here once, staying with the Horrocks. Dorothy has been seeing him in town, of course, but even then it's rather sudden, but no worse for that, of course, not at all. He has an estate - coffee or something - in Kenya, and they're to be married almost at once because he must go back there very soon. And he's nearly two years younger than Dorothy - not that that matters, of course - and apparently his people, who still command the purse-strings, don't approve - did you ever hear of such a thing!'

Now that Mrs Chillingford stopped for breath, Miss Trant had time to wonder whether Dorothy had not invented this opposition on the part of his family, the slightest mention of which instantly made her mother heart and soul for the match. If she had been told that the Atkinsons approved, she would probably have commanded Dorothy to come home at once. But all Miss Trant said was: 'Yes, I think I remember him. Tall, and fair, wasn't he? He didn't seem at all too young for Dorothy.' As a matter of fact, if it was the youth she was thinking of, he didn't seem too young for anybody. He was a very old youth indeed.

'Of course not!' cried Mrs Chillingford. 'But then, I don't expect to hear any nonsense of that kind. I don't know what I do expect to hear, but I'm going up to town in the morning and shall see for myself. Dorothy can count upon me, if there are fifty thousand Atkinsons there. Some of these people seem to imagine they can keep their children in leading-strings all their lives. They've bought this boy an estate out there - the poor boy has to do something and apparently he's been very successful - the first year - and now they think they can dictate to him about his marriage. Leading-strings!'

'And what has Dorothy decided to do about everything?' Miss Trant asked meekly.

'You mean about the date of the wedding, place, clothes, going out there, and so on? I don't know what the child has decided because she knows better than to announce decisions on such a matter as this to me. I shall go up myself and do the deciding tomorrow. This is a mother's business. There'll be a great deal to do, a great deal, and very little time to do it in, unless of course I decide that the whole thing ought to be postponed. I shan't do that, I think. What are you smiling at, Elizabeth?'

Miss Trant bent down to remove a trowel. 'I was just thinking', she answered, not altogether truthfully, 'how you're going to enjoy yourself.'

'Enjoy myself with all this fuss!' Then Mrs Chillingford met her friend's amused gaze, and laughed. 'Well, perhaps I shall. She's in love with him, I can see that. Don't forget tea.'

Miss Trant sighed as she turned again to her flower-beds. It was not a sentimental sigh. She was certainly not conscious of any desire to be engaged herself. She did not envy her friend, Dorothy; indeed, she felt rather compassionate and at the same time a little irritated, because she remembered Gerald Atkinson now and thought Dorothy was throwing herself away upon him. But then she did not pretend to know a great deal about these affairs of the heart, and really found them rather uninteresting. Her own life had never been disturbed by grand passions, and such relations as she had had with young men had been cool and friendly. There was one exception. It had happened twelve years ago, when she and her father had returned from Malta all the way by boat. She had not been well, and the ship's doctor, a tall bony young Scot, had been called in to examine her. He was gruff and shy at first, with an honesty as plain as daylight, but they soon became friends, trod the upper deck together every morning and quietly explored one another's mind and heart every night. The last two days it had become quite exciting; every glance, every word, became electrical, significant; and then, with the land in sight, he had suddenly changed, turned gruff and shy again, and he had let her go without saying anything, had just given her a handshake that hurt and backed away with a ghastly sort of grin. His name was Hugh McFarlane; his voice was very deep and very Scotch, one of those that bring out huge vowels and smashing consonants; and when he turned his face towards the light there was a fascinating glint of hair about his cheek-bones. There was nothing about him she had forgotten, and though she rarely thought of him, perhaps he served as a secret standard in her judgement of young men. Thus, it suddenly occurred to her that he was worth at least six Gerald Atkinsons.

But the sigh was not for him, nor was it for Dorothy. It was just a breath coming from a kind of emptiness. She was beginning to feel a little lost again. The feeling had not gone when she crossed to the Chillingfords' for tea.

'Elizabeth, you need a change,' said Mr Chillingford, wagging a finger at her. 'I've been keeping my eye on you lately, and you need a change.'

'Take my advice, my dear,' said Mrs Chillingford, 'and leave this place as soon as you can. We shall miss you, of course, but you ought to go.'

'Where?'

'Anywhere. Cheltenham. Oxford. London. It doesn't matter. Sell everything you have - I mean stocks and shares and things - and start in business. That's what I should do in your place. Never hesitate a moment. Go slap into business.' Mrs Chillingford said this with immense gusto, then went slap into a piece of sandwich cake.

'I've thought of it, you know,' said Miss Trant. 'But what could I do? I don't know anything.'

'Of course you do. Try this cake. You could open a shop and sell hats or gowns, like Betty Waltham.'

'Yes, but I've always been told that I haven't very good taste.' This sounded very feeble, she thought, but Miss Trant was nothing if not honest. Nevertheless, she believed in her heart of hearts that she had very good taste.

'Nonsense! You've splendid taste,' cried Mrs Chillingford, who very notoriously had none at all. She went on to discuss other shops and girls who had marched out of the most aristocratic country houses to open them.

'So far as I can see, my dear,' remarked her husband, lighting his pipe, 'it's only myself and this parish and perhaps - er - a certain lack of capital that are preventing you from becoming a second Selfridge or Woolworth.' And he chuckled.

'Perhaps it is,' replied Mrs Chillingford, briskly. 'I know I wish I had Elizabeth's opportunities.'

'Now for my part,' he added, turning to Miss Trant, 'I think the only opportunity you ought to trouble yourself about just now is that of going away for a little rest and change. A little travel, now. What about Italy?'

'Somehow I haven't the slightest desire to go to Italy,' said Miss Trant.

'I should hope not.' Mrs Chillingford was very emphatic. 'Don't, for goodness' sake, Elizabeth, turn yourself into one of those terrible unmarried females who spend their time in Italy. Look at Agatha Spinthorpe and her sister. And the Murrells. No, anything but that.'

'Italy then is condemned. We obliterate the whole peninsula,' said Mr Chillingford, with mild irony. He puffed away dreamily for a few moments, then went on: 'Now if I were in your place, I should do something I've always wanted to do. I should have a little tour - well, perhaps not so very little, when you think of it - visiting all our English cathedrals. You may not be very interested in ecclesiastic architecture - '

'I don't think I am, you know,' Miss Trant murmured.

'Possibly not.' Mr Chillingford was unperturbed. 'But think what a wonderful picture of England you would have. Canterbury, Ely, Norwich, Lincoln, York, supposing you begin at that corner. A wonderful picture! You cross over to this side. Hereford, Gloucester, Wells, Salisbury, and so forth. Wonderful!' His plump face was alight with enthusiasm.

Miss Trant found herself faintly kindled. 'It does sound rather exciting when you think of it like that. And I've hardly seen any of those places.'

'It's been a favourite project of mine for years,' he said gravely.

'It's the first I've ever heard of it,' cried Mrs Chillingford. 'And I must say it sounds very dull to me. If there's one kind of town more like another, it's a cathedral town. Don't take any notice of him, my dear.'

They juggled with cathedrals and shops a few minutes longer, and then Miss Trant went back to the Cottage and spent the next hour and a half with *Redgauntlet*, which she was reading for the fourth time. She had a passion for historical romances, not silly sentimental stories passing themselves off under cover of a few cloaks and daggers and 'halidoms' or 'Odds-fish', but real full-blooded historical tales. These she preferred to any other kind of fiction, and for the last twenty years they had been first her delight and then her solace. She loved to carry a secret message from Louis the Eleventh of France to Charles, Duke of Burgundy; to journey to Blois in foul weather crying vengeance on the Guises; to peep out of a haystack at Ireton's troopers; to hide in the heather after Prince Charlie had taken ship to France; to go thundering over the Rhine with Napoleon and his marshals. To exchange passwords, to rally the Horse on the left, to clatter down the Great North Road, to hammer upon inn doors on nights of wind and sleet, these were the pleasures, strangely boyish, of her imagination. Few people who came upon Miss Trant sitting erectly with a book ever imagined for a moment that she was happily engaged in drinking confusion to the League or firing a matchlock. But such was her taste. Neither the laborious satire nor the luscious sentiment of our present fiction gave her any pleasure. She liked a tale to open at once, in the very first chapter, a little door through which she could escape and have bright sexless adventures. Novels about unmarried women who lived in the country, looking after aged parents or making do in genteel cottages, depressed her so much that she took pains to avoid them.

She had to dine with *Redgauntlet*, and it was after nine when she heard Hilary's car wandering uneasily about the village. It was nearly ten by the time they had put away the two-seater in the Hall garage, walked back to the Cottage, and settled themselves in the little drawing-room.

'Well, Hilary, now you must tell me all the news.' But before he could reply, she went on: 'You know, I think you frighten me.'

'Do I really? How splendid!' cried Hilary, in his high clear voice. He did not ask why he frightened her because he could see innumerable reasons himself.

She replied, however, without being asked. 'Now don't be flattered,' she continued. 'It isn't exactly because you're an important young man from Oxford, though that has something to do with it. It's because I've seen you change so quickly, from a little boy - '

'Oh, it's that!' Hilary was disgusted.

'Yes, I'm afraid it's that. It's like a terrible sort of conjuring trick. I've been here, year after year, going on m the same old way, but almost every time I've seen you, you've been something quite different, nursery, prep, school, public school, Oxford.'

'Yes, I suppose so. But I assure you I've stopped now,' he said, a trifle loftily.

'No, I'm sure you haven't. You'll be getting married or growing a moustache - '

'Heaven forbid!' Hilary shrieked. 'This comes of living in the country, my dear. It's a morbid life. Look at all this rural fiction.'

She looked at him instead. He was now a slim and elegant young man, with a clear-cut and vaguely impertinent profile. Probably he had the most outrageous opinions about everything. His father and her brother, the Indian Judge, who had not seen him for years, would have a surprise when he did see him. The thought gave her pleasure, for it seemed to her that the Judge had never had his share of unpleasant surprises. 'Let me see,' she murmured, 'you're being called to the Bar, aren't you?'

'I'm supposed to be,' he told her. 'That's father's idea, and I'm eating dinners and that sort of thing. But I don't intend to go on with it. Very few fellows do, you know. Most of these barristers-in-embryo, who spend all their time when they're up preparing little speeches for the Union, end as sporting journalists or music-hall agents or something of that sort.' For the next quarter of an hour, she listened to him proving that he was entirely unfitted for the Bar, a contemptible profession to a man of real intellect, and, remembering her somewhat pompous and overbearing brother, she listened with a certain malicious pleasure. When the Bar had been finally demolished, she asked him what his own plans were.

'Well, you've heard, of course, of *The Oxford Static*?' he began.

'No, I haven't. What is it?' And then, noticing his look of pained surprise, she went on: 'I'm sorry. But we never hear about anything down here.'

He brightened. 'No, of course not. You're out of touch, and then Grandfather and everything. *The Oxford Static* was a review we ran. Three of us, Carrera-Brown - most brilliant man up, wonderful brain - and Sturge - he's a poet, you know - and me. It had a tremendous influence, simply tremendous. After a time, all the people who counted up there daren't *move* without it, simply daren't *move*.'

'What was it all about?'

'A review of all the arts, yes, all the arts, even dancing and films. We had a new point of view, you see.' He was so excited now that he rose from his chair and began pacing the room, and his voice got higher and higher. 'We Statics - that's what we call ourselves - awfully good name, isn't it? - believe that Art has got to be beyond emotion. Life and Art have got absolutely choked up with filthy emotion, and we say the time has come for them to be - what shall I say? - feelingless, all calm and clear. Get rid of the feelings, first, we say. We saw the whole thing about two years ago, one night when we were talking in Carrera-Brown's rooms, and we talked and talked until we had settled it. What a night that was!'

'It must have been,' his aunt murmured.

He paced up and down the room, waving his cigarette. 'Then we found the name, and very soon we brought out this review. Now we're thinking of transferring the thing to town, calling it simply *The Static*. A monthly, we think. Lots of important people are interested - Carrera-Brown knows everybody, simply everybody, and Lady Bullard has promised help - and now we're each trying to raise some money to begin. I shall do the Drama and Films and French Literature. Cynthia Grumm, you know, who lives in Paris and has abolished the sentence altogether and makes new words all the time, has promised to write for us. But we've decided that there shan't be any names of contributors in the review, just numbers. I'm to be Static Three. That's a magnificent idea, isn't it? And Oppelworth is going to do some drawings for us, and be Static Six. We soon made a convert of him. He'd been going in for non-representational art - you know, no representation of natural objects but just drawings suggesting the artist's emotions, but now he sees that this won't do and so he's cutting out the emotions and becoming a Static. We're even having music too. Pure form, you know.'

'I'm not so sure that I do know, Hilary,' said Miss Trant, who had enjoyed herself but was beginning to feel very sleepy.

'Well, of course, I simply haven't begun to explain,' he said excitedly. Then he caught sight of her stifling a yawn, and being a well-mannered youth, instantly checked his ardour: 'But look here, you must be awfully tired. I suppose you go to bed about nine, don't you as a rule? Don't let me keep you up. We'll talk about all that in the morning. Are there any books I can read?'

'I shouldn't think so. There are books, but I don't suppose you can read them.'

'Well, I have one or two with me, and I'll scout about, if I may. I shan't be able to sleep for hours yet, hours and hours. And now that I've begun to talk about *The Static*, I feel more wakeful than ever.'

'I can see that it excites you,' said his aunt gravely.

'Yes, doesn't it?' replied the youth innocently. 'I'm tremendously excited about the whole thing. Wouldn't you be? Think of the possibilities and - oh, everything!'

She left him to make himself calm and clear as best he could, and went to bed feeling more cheerful than she had done all day. The fact that any month now *The Static* might arrive to revolutionize the aesthetic doctrines of the world, the fact that she knew nothing whatever about Cynthia Grumm or Oppelworth, to say nothing of Carrera-Brown and Sturge - such matters did not keep her from sleep five minutes. An aunt has her compensations.

III

There was only one letter by Miss Trant's plate the following morning, but it was a very important letter indeed. It ran as follows:

My dear Elizabeth,

Did you know that your father owed me £600? He did, and he gave instructions to Truby that it should be repaid out of his estate. But when Truby settled the debt, he also explained who would be losing the money. If it had been either your brother or sister - who are both well off, or were when I last heard of them - I should have taken it like a shot, but I have no intention of taking it from you, and so have returned the £600 to Truby. Now don't be silly about this. I have as much as I want, and I know what your position is. I feel sure you are sensible enough not to refuse the money. What are you going to do? Twenty years ago, or even ten, I should have advised you to come out here, but the East isn't what it was, ruined by these damned silly student politics. If you can guarantee me something that remotely resembles a summer, I'll pay you a visit, but not before, for the last time I did nothing but shiver and wrap up.

Your affectionate uncle,
George Chatsworth

She had read this once, in a rather dazed fashion, and was beginning again, when Hilary arrived, looking rather more Static than he had done the night before.

'That's my great-uncle, is it, the tea-planter man?' he said, after she had told him the news. 'I saw him once, when I was still at school. He looked like Mark Twain. You'll take the money, of course?'

'I think so,' said Miss Trant, rather slowly and dubiously.

'Why shouldn't you?' Hilary stared. 'As a matter of fact, it's yours, and anyhow you've jolly well earned it. You haven't much money, have you?'

'No, I shall probably have about three hundred a year when I've let the Hall. By the way, some people are coming to look at it today. And I've about a thousand pounds over, from the Sale.'

'Then you'll have a spare sixteen hundred roughly, with this windfall.' Hilary delicately chipped at his egg, then looked across at her with raised eyebrows. 'I suppose you wouldn't like to put some money into *The Static*, would you?'

'I don't think I would, Hilary,' she replied briskly.

'No,' he said, rather gloomily. 'I thought you wouldn't. It's a pity, though, because you'd enjoy the thing so much - I mean really being *in it* - and of course you would probably make something out of it. You didn't mind my asking, did you?'

'Not at all.' She smiled at him, and decided at once not to tell him the real reason why she had refused, which was that she was not going to encourage him to waste his time. 'You see, there may be a family row if you go on with this business - '

'Sure to be,' he put in calmly. 'I haven't written to India yet, but I told Aunt Hilda the other day and she was frightfully down on it. But then she *would* be, you know. She's not like you. Her life's one long orgy of emotionalism, don't you think?'

'And you see,' Miss Trant continued, after an amused glance of the mind at her sister Hilda confronted by the Statics, 'I don't want to be mixed up in it, and I should be at once if I helped you.'

'Couldn't you put the money in anonymously.'

'It would soon come out, I mean my part in it. You know how things do get about.' She herself did not know at all how such things got about, but it sounded convincing.

'Rather,' said Hilary, who knew even less. They looked at one another knowingly, and enjoyed themselves.

'I've got about a hundred that I can spare,' he said, after he had lit the first cigarette. 'But I want about two hundred and fifty. I think I shall sell that two-seater of mine. It's useless in town, anyhow. Only eats its head off. Do you know anybody here who wants a two-seater? It's a Mercia, last year's?'

'No, I don't think I do.' she said slowly, staring at him.

'What's the matter?'

She laughed. 'Nothing. Shall we go out?' But she was still thinking about that two-seater.

He strolled over to the window. 'What shall we do?'

'Anything you like. You're not interested in gardens, are you?'

'Not in the least,' he replied heartily. 'I don't mind sitting in them on warm afternoons, but I simply can't dig them up or talk about them or anything of that kind. We might run round in the car.'

'I should like that. But stop, we can't go until I've shown those people the Hall. They're coming some time today to look at it, and I promised to be here.'

'I think I shall stroll up there myself. I'll have a look at the car, and then if those people come, I shall have a look at them too. I've never seen anybody examine a house.'

'Why, do you want to?' asked Miss Trant, with raised eyebrows.

'I want to see people doing all kinds of things,' he replied very gravely. 'I'm an observer. I want to see but not to feel. That's my duty now, to watch and record. There's rhythm in all these activities and I want to be able to - to detach it. Think of the new films.' After making these enigmatic observations, Static Three looked at her very solemnly, then, with a gesture of farewell, sauntered out of the room.

Miss Trant reached the bottom of the garden in time to see Hurley's ancient and gigantic Daimler, the vehicle for all entrances and exits in Hitherton, come slowly down the lane. Mrs Chillingford was inside, on her way to the station, and she waved as she passed. As the car disappeared, Hitherton and the bright morning seemed to shrink. Mrs Chillingford was on her way to Paddington, to Dorothy, to the embattled Atkinsons, to adventures with the Army and Navy Stores and the shipping offices. 'What are *you* going to *do*, to *do*, to *do*?' the car seemed to roar back at her as it gathered speed down the hill. And she had no answer ready. She thought of the windfall of the morning, six hundred pounds out of the blue, and felt a little quiver of excitement. You could do all manner of things with six hundred pounds, perhaps go all round the world. But she did not want to go all round the world by herself. 'I don't know what I want, that's the trouble,' she told the great staring nodding dahlias. She found, however, that Mrs Purton knew what she wanted, namely, some orders for lunch and dinner, and after consulting with her, Miss Trant went out to shop.

On her way back, she met Purton standing at the entrance to the Hall. 'I was looking for you, Miss,' he said, touching his cap, and then instantly ramming his hands in his pockets. 'They've just come with a young feller from Medworth's. Look like these 'ere profiteers. Come in a car as big as a cottage.'

She had no time to reply because at this moment the young fellow from Medworth's himself suddenly appeared round the corner, raised his hat, and began, in a dramatic whisper: 'We're trying for two hundred.'

He got no further, however, because now another man, very tall, very pale, and with a long drooping moustache, suddenly came round the corner, stared at everybody, took off his hat and forgot to replace it, and mumbled: 'Miss Trant? Yes? Rathbury. Come to look ... Sorry to trouble ... Beautiful morning....'

By this time the familiar entrance to the drive seemed to Miss Trant to have turned itself into a comic stage. She wanted to giggle at everything, but retained sufficient control over herself to tell Mr Rathbury that she hoped he would like the house and that really it was rather charming.

'Just had a glance,' Mr Rathbury murmured. 'Very delightful. Yes, certainly. Just what we're looking for. The very thing, I should think. Most charming.'

'Of course, as you'll see, it's not very big,' said Miss Trant brightly, feeling that she must say something.

'Not very big, no,' the long moustache agreed. 'No worse for that, though. Not at all. Not these days. Just the thing, I fancy.'

'So you're here.'

Everybody jumped. The voice was very loud and stern, and it came from a square woman, with a purplish fat face and two prominent staring grey eyes.

'My wife,' Mr Rathbury muttered, fading out.

'Oh, this is the owner, is it?' shouted Mrs Rathbury, staring away. 'Miss Trant, isn't it? How d'you do?'

'Do you want me to show you round?' Miss Trant felt as if she were addressing a battleship.

'Quite unnecessary, I think, quite unnecessary. We'll just look round ourselves for a few minutes. I don't expect we shall take the house. It's very small, isn't it? We think it will be too small, don't we?' She switched the stare on to her husband for a second.

'Yes, of course, rather small, certainly,' he mumbled, carefully looking at nobody. 'Drawback of course, being small.'

'And then it's not really the type of house we're looking for, not the style, as my husband has probably told you already.'

'No, not the style.' Mournfully he fingered the long moustache. 'Not quite, certainly. Perhaps hardly at all.'

'Not at all,' Mrs Rathbury shouted, giving them everyone in turn a stare. 'However, we might as well see it.' Immediately she wheeled about and marched off, and her husband and the young estate agent hurried after her.

Miss Trant and Purton each drew a long breath, and looked at one another. 'You'll be wantin' them thar pars down at the Cottage, Miss,' said Purton very slowly. 'I'll go and get 'em.'

Miss Trant returned to the Cottage with her purchases, talked to Mrs Purton, dusted the drawing-room, then walked back, slowly, very slowly, to the Hall. As she sauntered up the drive, she thought she saw Hilary disappearing into the garden at the back of the house. A moment later the Rathburys emerged from the front door.

'Yes, we'll take it. But not a penny more than two hundred,' Mrs Rathbury was shouting to the agent. Then she saw Miss Trant. 'I'm just saying that we shall take it at two hundred. It's quite charming, quite charming, the sort of place that wants proper looking after. Several things to be done, of course.' She stared at Miss Trant, then through her, it seemed, at all the other Trants, as if to accuse them all of neglecting the place. 'We were fortunate in finding that young architect there to make suggestions.'

Mr Rathbury's moustache made some vague sound that implied it was in entire agreement with her. It was now Miss Trant's turn to stare. She caught the eye of Mr Medworth's assistant, who looked both triumphant and puzzled. Turning to Mrs Rathbury again, she saw with astonishment that that lady was actually smiling at her. True, the eyes had no part in the smile, but the rest of her face was amiably creasing.

'You never told us it was such a show place,' Mrs Rathbury shouted in great good-humour. 'I saw at once, of course, that it must be, and could be more of one, properly cared for. It was the young architect who told us all about it. Did he tell you he had come a hundred miles to see it?'

'I don't know,' Miss Trant stammered. 'I don't quite understand. Who is this?'

'What was the name?' Mrs Rathbury stared all about her as if the name must be written up somewhere. 'Oh yes, of course - Mr Static.'

There was no help for it. Miss Trant gave a little shriek of laughter. 'I'm sorry,' she gurgled. 'It's - it's such a silly name, isn't it?'

'Yes, rather; it is, certainly.' Mr Rathbury mumbled, evidently under the impression that he had been appealed to.

'Indeed!' Mrs Rathbury looked from one to the other in obvious disapproval. 'It's a name of some importance, I understand, in - in architectural circles. What was it Mr Static said he was an authority on?'

'Seventeenth-century panelled interiors,' replied the young estate agent, in what seemed to Miss Trant a rather queer tone of voice.

'Exactly! I ought to have remembered because I knew the name well. Seventeenth-century panelled interiors. This is a very good specimen, he said. But of course they want proper attention. A house of this kind is a responsibility, of course. Perhaps you're not interested in these things, Miss Trant. Tell Johnson we're ready to go back now.'

Miss Trant was fighting an impulse to tell her that she could not have the house after all. With this woman settled in the Hall, Hitherton would be impossible, even though it meant that Mrs Chillingford could begin a new saga. 'It's strange', she told herself, 'that I don't care more than I do. Perhaps it shows that I really am tired of living here.' And she answered Mrs Rathbury's questions meekly enough, said nothing about Hilary (which served her right), then referred her to Mr Medworth.

After lunch, during which Hilary was divided between the glee of the mischievous small boy and the natural shame of a solemn young intellect who has indulged his lower self, they drove to Cheltenham in Hilary's car. There she saw Mr Truby, who congratulated her on the result of the Sale, the gift of six hundred pounds, and the letting of the house, then told her that she ought to go away and enjoy herself. 'You're comfortably off now,' he added. 'Much better than we expected. I'll keep this sixteen hundred pounds in a deposit account for you until you decide what to do with it. Don't worry about money. What you want now is a change,' he concluded, with the air of a man who knew what a change was, even though he had never had one.

Miss Trant walked out of the dim office into the bright sunshine, feeling vaguely exhilarated. 'How queer and old-fashioned solicitors' offices are!' she cried to Hilary. 'Going to see Mr Truby is like walking into a Dickens novel.'

'How ghastly for you!' The Static shuddered. Then, as they found a tea shop, he observed mournfully: 'When you were in there, I took the car round to a garage to see what sort of price I should get for it. About seventy-five pounds, they said. That's about half of what it's worth. Isn't it a swindle? These garage people hate to pay cash for a car. They'll allow you anything nearly if they are selling you another.' And having thus descended to this ordinary low level of thought and feeling, he remained there throughout tea and his aunt smiled upon him. About half-way home, on a quiet stretch of road, she asked him to pull up. 'Do you think I might try to drive now?' she asked rather breathlessly. 'I have a licence because I've tried before, when Dorothy Chillingford had a car. Will you explain about this one?'

'Nothing in it. The thing practically drives itself. Why do you want to bother, though?' He jumped out and walked round the car.

'Because - if I can drive it, I'll buy it from you, Hilary; that is, if you really want to sell it.'

'You will!' cried the Static joyfully. 'Of course I want to sell it.'

'And I'll give you what you say it's worth, a hundred and fifty pounds.'

'Oh! I say! Will you really? But are you sure?'

'Yes, I am sure,' she said, firmly. 'That is, so long as I can drive it.'

'Of course you can drive it,' he cried, with mounting enthusiasm. 'Nothing easier! Let me show you where everything is. It really is a good little car, you know.'

And he did show her where everything was, and for the next hour she sat at the wheel under his tuition. So rapidly did she gain confidence that at last she drove them both home, passing two very large buses, a steam-wagon, and several jumpy rattling lorries, without slowing down to less than fifteen miles an hour, and finally sailing up the Hall drive, flushed and triumphant. Then followed ten minutes' further instruction on getting it in and out of the garage (which was not a proper garage at all but an old stable) and Miss Trant discovered once again the terrors and dangers of reversing, but was assured by Hilary that all was well with her.

'I'll give you a cheque in the morning,' she told him, as they sat at dinner.

'No hurry at all, you know,' he explained, though his face had brightened. 'Still, it would be rather useful. If we spent all tomorrow morning with the car - though you don't really need any more instruction from me, I can tell you - I could catch the afternoon train up to town. I hope you don't mind my running away at once, but the fact is, I must get hold of Carrera-Brown as soon as I can.'

'I don't mind,' she told him. 'I shall probably go away myself very soon, perhaps the day after tomorrow.' She was rather astonished when she heard herself announcing this departure. It was, so to speak, as much news to her as it was to him. Indeed, she was the more surprised of the two.

'Splendid!' he said, in an abstracted fashion, looking through her. She could see he was already busy meeting the other Statics.

That night she finished *Redgauntlet* yet once more, but this time she put it down without the smallest sigh. The dark mysterious hours found her guiding a little blue Mercia down roads that nobody knew, roads that wound through the shining hills of a dream.

IV

'Do you know - ' Hilary, began, looking down upon her from the carriage window.

'Well! Do I know what?' She smiled up at him. That pitless observer of the human race hesitated a moment. Then he continued: 'There's something different about you today. It must be the car.'

'Perhaps it is,' she assented. 'I'm beginning to feel reckless, Hilary. Do you know what number I shall be among the Statics?' The train began to move.

'Not less than the fifty-second millionth!' she called, and waved him good-bye.

On the way home she pulled up beside a black figure plodding up the dusty hill.

"What's this? What's this?' cried Mr Chillingford.

'Come in and see,' she told him, and before they had climbed the hill he had accepted an invitation to tea and learned all about the car.

'I feel like going away in it at once,' she confided, over the first cups.

Mr Chillingford lowered his spectacles and raised his eyebrows. 'By yourself?'

'Why not?'

'I don't know. No, of course. Why not?' He laughed and then they both laughed, and felt very friendly. Immediately afterwards, however, Mr Chillingford fell into such a profound reverie that he crumbled walnut cake all over his clothes.

'Well?' she asked, at length.

'I'm sorry. Dear me, what a mess I've made! I was thinking you ought to begin with Ely. Just think of it! You would go down from these hills into the Midland plain, getting lower and lower the further east you went, until at last you would find yourself - as it were - at the bottom of the basin. Then you would see that colossal tower shooting up - a sublime spectacle, my dear Elizabeth. You've not seen Ely, of course? No, I thought not. That miraculous octagon. There's a kind of barbaric splendour about the whole place! You must begin with Ely!' He was so excited now that he deposited his cup and saucer on the plate of sandwiches.

'Miss Trant, who had been staring at him in amazement, suddenly remembered, and cried: 'Of course! You're talking about a tour of the cathedrals.'

'Indeed I am. Wasn't that the idea? Of course it wasn't, though. How absurd of me! That was my idea, wasn't it? I said something about it the other day. I thought that was what you were going to do. What an old egoist I'm becoming! I was thinking you might call on my old friend Canon Fothergill at Lincoln. That is, if you began at Ely. And, mind you, that's the place to begin at. But then, of course, you are not beginning anywhere, so to speak. Just my foolishness!' And he laughed a little.

'Yes, I am,' said Miss Trant stoutly. 'I'm beginning at Ely, just as you suggest. And I *will* call on Canon Fothergill at Lincoln, if he'll let me. And you *shall* tell me where to go.'

Mr Chillingford scrambled to his feet, spreading walnut cake in all directions. 'I'll slip over to the rectory for my old map. It will be as good as a holiday to take a look at it again. I've done all this, every inch, in my time, on a pushbike, you know.'

But Miss Trant brought out a map and for the next quarter of an hour their two heads were bent over it. Mr Chillingford showered roads, towns, inns, naves, transepts, upon her, and in his excitement upset the milk jug. He brought out pencil and paper, covered two sheets with directions, crammed them into his pocket, then searched the room and declared they were lost. Miss Trant wanted to rush upstairs at once and hurl all her things into bags. 'I'll start tomorrow morning,' she announced.

'I shouldn't,' he warned her. 'It's Sunday tomorrow. Don't mistake me. I'm no Sabbatarian. Besides, there's more worship in going to look at Ely than in listening to me. But Sunday's a bad day to begin a journey. Wait a day. Start on Monday. There never was a Monday morning yet when I didn't want to be going somewhere.'

And it was on Monday morning that she did set out, after a tremendous Sunday of packing and instructions to the Purtons and letters to all manner of people. She had a last five minutes' talk with Mr Chillingford, turned perilously to wave to him nearly at the corner, and then went rolling down the hill, eastward out of Hitherton. The valley lay all golden in the deep sunshine; the morning was as crisp as a nut; the roads scrawled invitations, the very wires above hummed faint calls, to the misty blue beyond; and every turn of the wheel brought her a sense of mastery, and every milestone passed, bringing nearer the unknown and the gloriously irresponsible, gave her a new little thrill. Was she going across country to Ely? She was going anywhere, anywhere, wherever she pleased. This was the road to the first of the cathedrals, but it was also the road to - what? She didn't know, and delightedly she hugged her ignorance, vague and shining, a mist brightening with golden shapes, just like the morning itself.

In her bag were thirty pounds and a cheque book that would call at once on fifteen hundred more. And, snugly tucked away behind were all the nicest things she had, a dressing case she had only used once before, and four glorious historical novels, crowds of archers, Jacobites, conspirators, dragoons, crying to be let loose at the first hour of lamplight. They were all running away from Hitherton, into the adventurous blue, together. In a tangle of traffic at narrow Northleach she had to pull up beside a huge car that had come from the opposite direction. From this car a familiar long drooping moustache cautiously emerged.

'Miss Trant, isn't it? Thought it was,' it mumbled at her. 'Lovely morning. Not going far, eh?'

'Oh, good morning, Mr Rathbury,' she called out, loudly and clearly. 'Yes, it's absolutely wonderful, isn't it? And I *am* going far, hundreds and hundreds of miles until I am lost.' And she smiled, and did not stop smiling when she found herself confronted by a purple square of face and a grey stare.

'I beg your pardon,' shouted Mrs Rathbury, now purpler than ever from bending so far forward. 'Where did you say you where going? We were coming over to look at the Hall again. We may want to see you.'

'I'm going to be invisible.' Yes, she actually heard herself saying it. And then she turned her attention to the clutch and gears, for everybody was moving again.

'What address?' came the scream, now from behind.

'No address. No-o a-a-dre-esss.' She shouted it at the top of her voice. Not for years had she made such a noise. It was splendid.

Now the road emptied itself and broadened before her. A wind from the south-west caught up to her and coloured her cheeks. (It went on and on until at last it found the smoke from Higden's mill, where Mr Oakroyd was spending his very last day.) She shot forward and upward, then skimmed along one of England's little green roofs, this Miss Trant that nobody at Hitherton had ever seen and perhaps would never see.

CHAPTER THREE
Inigo Jollifant Quotes Shakespeare and Departs in the Night

I

WE have left all the hills behind; our faces are turned towards the long strands, salted and whistling, of the North Sea. Here, the land is a great saucer, patterned with dykes and arrowy roads. To the north and to the south are smudges of smoke, the bright webbing of railway lines, towers that are older than the distant fields they chime to, Peterborough, Ely, Cambridge. We are on the edge of the Fens. It is a place plucked from the water. Only here and there remains the old darkly gleaming chaos of marsh and reeds, alders and bulrushes, the sudden whirr and scream of wildfowl. All else is now deep pasturage and immense fields bright with stubble, feeding the windmills and the scattered red-brick farms. It is a country to make a farmer fat; these are fields to put beef and pudding and ale on a man's table. Yet it seems to be still haunted by its old desolation. Perhaps the sky, which can show a spread of cloud and blue by day, a glitter of stars by night, not to be matched elsewhere between Berwick and Penzance, is too big, too masterful, for a man's peace of mind, unless, like so many in the old days, he comes here simply to worship God. Perhaps too much is heard of its bitter neighbour, the North Sea, and of winds that come from the Steppes. Perhaps it is only because it is a hollow land, which every darkness turns again into a place of spectral marshes and monkish ghosts. Something desolating certainly remains, a whisper not to be drowned by the creaking of the heaviest harvest-wagons. The little farms seem lonelier than lighthouses. The roads go on and on, one ruled mile after another, but would never appear to arrive anywhere. The very trains, cautiously puffing along a raised single track, seem to be without either starting-places or destinations, and so wander undramatically across the landscape, only heightening, by their passing, the long silences. The vague sadness of a prairie has fallen upon this plain of dried marshes. Like a rich man who gives but never smiles, this land yields bountifully but is at heart still a wilderness.

Somewhere in the middle of this region, a narrow side-road finds its way to a hamlet, made up of about twenty houses, a tiny shop, and an ale-house, and then wanders on another mile or so in order to arrive at a house of some size, where it stops, despairingly. This is easily the largest house in the neighbourhood, a red-brick building in no recognizable style of architecture, and perhaps sixty or seventy years old. It was built by a strange gentleman from Australia, who had for years dreamed of a country mansion, and, once he was installed in it, proceeded very quietly to drink himself to death. Now, as certain sheds and newer out-houses, goal-posts and worn fields testify, it is no longer a country mansion. It is some years since James Tarvin, M.A. (Cantab.), married a woman ten years older than himself, bought with her money the desirable property known as Washbury Manor, and transformed it into Washbury Manor School, in which some fifty or sixty boys, preferably the sons of gentlemen, are prepared for the public schools and whatever else may befall them in this life. Letters from all over the world arrive now at Washbury Manor. Men and women in far-distant bungalows receive little scrawls from there and are very proud and boring about them. Quite a number of the small boys at Washbury have parents who are in India and Africa and such places, and not a few of the rest have no parents at all but merely guardians, persons who are conscientious enough but cannot be expected to discover the relative merits of all the preparatory schools in England. Not that Washbury Manor is a bad school; but, on the other hand, it is certainly not one of the best. One visiting uncle, a master in the merchant service, put it to himself and to anybody who might be listening: 'It don't smell right.' But he himself was not the kind of person that Mr Tarvin - it is his own phrase - wished to have associated with the school. Mr Tarvin could afford to be contemptuous of such criticism. He had references from public men, including a Colonial Bishop; some scholarships to the school's credit; pure air and water, a bracing atmosphere, perfect sanitation, good playing fields; and a teaching staff of three university graduates, Robert Fauntley, M.A. (Oxon.), Inigo Jollifant, B.A. (Cantab.), Harold Felton, B.A. (Bristol); a matron, Miss Callander, with a diploma in the domestic sciences; and an ex-regular non-commissioned officer, Sergeant Comrie, to take drill and carpentering. Moreover, the health and comfort of the boys are the care of no less a person than Mrs Tarvin herself, the daughter of the Rev. George Betterby. If you are a parent in India, is it not worth cutting things down a little, depriving yourself of a few holidays in the hills, we will say, merely to know that your boy is in such hands as these? Term by term, Mr Tarvin received tribute from the very frontiers of our Empire, and rarely had he to complain that one of his little iron bedsteads was without its weight of boy.

They are all in bed now, these boys, but they are not all asleep. Mr Felton has already looked in once at the older ones, who may be subject to the vaguely disturbing influences of Saturday night, and has told them to be quiet. All the other adult persons in the house are trying to forget the existence of boys. Mrs Tarvin has commanded the presence of Miss Callander in her drawing-room and is pleasantly occupied in bullying her. Mr Tarvin himself, having been told to keep out of the way for half an hour after dinner, has retired to what he calls his study, and there, pasty, damp, and breathing heavily, he has cast off both the schoolmaster and the anxious husband and has turned himself into a dozing middle-aged sedentary man, with a weak stomach lulled for a little while into a false peace. Mr Fauntley has disappeared on one of his mysterious Saturday night excursions. Sergeant Comrie is walking over the fields to the village inn, where he is regarded as a rich cosmopolitan character. Mr Jollifant is in his bed-sitting-room, a very small and stuffy apartment not far from the roof, which he prefers to the equally small and stuffy common-room because at this moment he is engaged in what he imagines to be literary composition.

He is sitting in a Windsor chair that he has tilted back to a very perilous angle, and his feet, enclosed in vivid green carpet slippers, are resting on the sill of the open window. There is about both his attitude and his apparel that elaborate carelessness of the undergraduate, though Inigo Jollifant, now in his twenty-sixth year, left Cambridge three years ago. He is a thin loose-limbed youth, a trifle above medium height. His face does not suggest the successful preparatory-school master. It seems rather too fantastic. A long lock of hair falls perpetually across his right eyebrow; his nose itself is long, wandering, and whimsical, and his grey eyes are set unusually wide apart and have in them a curious gleam. He wears a blue pullover, no coat, a generous bow-tie, and baggy and rather discoloured flannel trousers. He is smoking a ridiculously long cherry-wood pipe. There is about him the air of one who is ready to fail gloriously at almost anything. We realize at once that his History, French, English Literature, his cricket and football, are dashing but sketchy. At this moment he is ostensibly engaged in writing an elaborate essay - in a manner of the early Stevenson - entitled *The Last Knapsack*, an essay that he began many weeks ago, in the middle of the long vacation. His right hand grasps a fountain-pen and there is a writing-block on his knees, but never a word does he set down. He blows out clouds of smoke, keeps his feet on the window-sill, and balances his chair at a still more alarming angle.

There is a knock at the door, and then a face looks in, bringing with it a flash of eye-glasses.

'Hello! Who's that?' he cries, without turning round. 'Come in.'

'I'm sorry to trouble you, Jollifant.' And the visitor enters.

'Oh, it's you, Felton, is it?' Inigo twists his head round, and grins. 'Come in and sit down.'

Felton is about the same age, but after that there is no further likeness. He is a pleasant, earnest young man, whose rimless eye-glasses give him a rather misleading look of energy and alertness. Two years ago, he left the University of Bristol, at which he had spent four undistinguished years, with the determination to do his duty, speak the truth, and be friendly with everybody; and a certain sense of anxiety discovered in his face, voice, manner, suggests that he has not found it easy. Already he is beginning to approach life, or at least every succeeding new manifestation of it, with a slightly halting step and a little prefatory cough. He goes warily through the term, occasionally reading large dull biographies and smoking non-nicotine cigarettes and always agreeing with everybody, and then tries to forget his responsibilities in cautious foreign travel.

He sat down, then cleared his throat. 'Look here, Jollifant, I'm sorry to trouble you.'

'Felton, you do not trouble me,' said Inigo, regarding his companion as if he were a fairly intelligent fox terrier. 'It's true I was in the throes of composition. Throes! What damned silly words we use! Have you ever been in throes?'

'Yes, I see you were,' replied Felton, looking with something like reverence at the writing-block. He had a deep veneration for literature, so deep that he hardly ever made acquaintance with it. He did not know whether these things that Jollifant was always trying to write were literature or not, but as usual he was not taking any risks. 'It's about the washing lists.' he added apologetically.

'The washing lists!' the other cried, in an ecstasy of scorn. 'This is Saturday night, Felton. Think of that, Saturday night! Remember your orgies at Bristol. Now I'm prepared, as you see, to devote myself, in stern seclusion, to Art, searching for the exact Phrase. Don't forget that - the exact phrase. Takes a devil of a lot of finding. Again' - and he looked very severely at his visitor and took out the cherry-wood pipe - 'I'm prepared to come down from yonder height, as it were, to make merry with you, to exchange ideas, to hear you talk of the old wild days of Bristol. But no washing lists! Not on Saturday night!'

'I see what you mean,' said Felton. 'It's an awful nuisance, of course. But still, Mrs Tarvin said - '

Inigo held up his hand. 'Her words fall on deaf ears. That woman's a gorgon. Tonight, I refuse to believe she exists.'

'Well, we told you what she was like,' said the other. This was his fourth term at the school, and it was Inigo's third. Mrs Tarvin had been away, for a long rest-cure, during both the previous terms, so that Felton had known her for about eleven weeks, whereas Inigo had only known her for one. 'We told you what it would be like when she came back,' he added, with all the irritating complacency of the successful prophet.

'What you told me was a mere nothing,' Inigo cried. 'You said, for instance, that the food would be cut down a bit when she came back. It's not been cut down, it's been cut out, clean out. There's nothing left but the smell, which is worse than ever. Look at tonight's mess!'

'I know. Pretty bad, wasn't it?'

'Shepherds' pie - and no shepherd would ever touch it - for the second time this week, and prunes for the third or fourth! And she calls that a dinner - on Saturday night, too! And there she sits, the shapeless old guzzler, choking herself right under our noses with cutlets and cream and God knows what. That's the last refinement of torture. If she was in the trough with us, groping amongst the minced stuff and prunes and muck, it wouldn't be so bad. But to sit there, letting us see that real food still exists, letting us watch it being converted into that fat of hers, it's simply piling on the insult, it's devilish! If there's another dinner like that, I shall take sandwiches and chocolate down and eat them in front of her. It isn't that I care so much about food. My soul, Felton, is like a star and dwells apart, absolutely. But I ask you! Can you worthily instruct the young, can you wrestle with the problems of French and History, day after day, on prunes? It can't be done.'

'No. I see what you mean, of course. Though as a matter of fact,' he added hesitantly, 'I rather like prunes.'

'Under which king, Besonian? Speak or die!' Inigo shouted, pointing his pipe-stem at the startled Felton. 'He that is not with us is against us. Do you ask for Prunes, Felton? Do you creep down to that wretched female Tarvin, with your tongue lolling out, and say, "More prunes. Custard or no custard, more prunes"?'

'Don't be an ass, Jollifant,' Felton wriggled. 'Besides, I hate shepherds' pie as much as you do. It'll be like that all the term. I told you what it would be.'

'The whole subject', the other began loftily, 'is profoundly distasteful to me. Let me read you a sentence or two from *The Last Knapsack*, an essay celebrating - mournfully, you understand - the final extinction of the walking tour. Have you an ear for a phrase, Felton?'

'I don't know. Yes, I think so. But, look here - I'd like to slip up later and hear that - but what about those washing lists?'

Before Inigo could express his opinion again on the subject, there came a little knock at the door. It was Miss Callander, and she looked as if she had just retreated to her room in a shower of tears and had hastily quitted it in a cloud of powder. She was a distant connexion of Mr Tarvin's, a tall, rather plump girl of twenty-seven, who would not have been noticeable in the nearest town but who seemed in this wilderness almost a beauty, and was certainly too well-favoured to be successful as the school matron, especially since she had been appointed by Mr Tarvin during his wife's absence at the beginning of the year. She had only spent ten days so far trying to please Mrs Tarvin, but already she was beginning to realize the hopelessness of the task. For the past four years, she had been engaged off and on to a cousin who was out in Egypt. During the last three months, the engagement had been off, but even now she was meditating a letter that would put it on again.

Inigo beamed upon her snub nose, round and rapidly doubling chin, and large and rather foolish eyes. They were, he told himself again, the eyes of a stricken deer. 'This, Miss Callander,' he announced gravely, 'is an honour.'

'Oh, Mr Jollifant,' she fluttered, 'is Mr Felton here? Oh, I see he is. Mr Felton, it's about the washing lists - '

'Felton,' said Inigo sternly, turning round, 'what about those lists?'

'That's just what I was asking,' Felton began, hastily coming forward.

Inigo cut him short with a superb gesture, then smiled at Miss Callander with deep tenderness and looked for a moment as if he were about to pat her hand. 'You want them now, I take it?'

'I do, yes. As soon as possible. Mrs Tarvin's perfectly furious about *everything*.' And her eyes grew and grew and her mouth dropped.

'Say no more,' cried Inigo, with an air of immense benevolence. 'What man can do, we will do, at least if Felton will condescend to give me a little assistance.' He rummaged amongst a mass of papers on his table, found what he wanted, then added : 'Forward to the common-room. And the motto is, "One for all, and all for one" - absolutely. Lead on, Miss Callander. Master Felton, take these papers, and shake off that deep lethargy.' And off they went, with Miss Callander, giggling a little, in front.

By the time that Inigo had carefully filled and lighted his absurd pipe and had smiled dreamily for a few moments through the haze of smoke at his two colleagues, they had completed the lists. 'There now,' he said, as Miss Callander gathered up the papers. 'That's done with. What do we do now? I can't go back to that beastly little room of mine and try to write. The mood, Miss Callander, the precious mood, is shattered; the golden bowl, Felton, is broken. I shall try a little music.'

Miss Callander, at the door, turned wide eyes upon him. 'How can you, though? I mean, where will you go?'

'Aren't you forgetting', he replied with dignity, 'that there is an instrument - I won't say a piano, but anyhow something in the semblance of a piano - in our rotten schoolroom?'

'Oh, but Mr Jollifant!' she gave a tiny giggle that was a mixture of delight and apprehension. 'Don't you remember Mrs Tarvin said it wasn't to be used in the evening? She did, didn't she, Mr Felton?'

'She did, you know, Jollifant,' said Felton, with an earnest flash of his glasses. 'It's a shame, of course, but that's what she said.'

'My friends, my old companions in misfortune, I thank you for these words of warning, but I know nothing of such orders, tyrannical commands which - er - strike at the very roots of liberty. Is thy servant a dog that he shall not do this thing? The answer is, "No, decidedly not!" I go to play - as best I can, and by George, that's not saying much because half the keys stick all the time - I go to play, I repeat, upon the schoolroom piano. Open your ears - I mean yours, Miss Callander, because Felton's, as you can see, are open enough - and they shall drink in melody and harmony and what's its name - a spot or two of counter-point.' And Inigo marched downstairs to the dismal little schoolroom, once the drawing-room of Washbury Manor and now a cheerless huddle of desks and blackboards and yellowing maps. It was dusk now, and he switched on a naked and shivering electric light, then walked over to the far corner of the room and seated himself before one of those cottage pianos, with ochreous fronts and mournful blue-white keys, that are designed and glued and varnished for no other places but miserly institutions. The pedal creaked, the keys stuck together, the tone was sadly tinny, but it was a piano, and music could be wrung out of it.

It must be said at once that Inigo's playing, like his French and History and cricket, was dashing but sketchy. He was not of your cool and impeccable executants, delicately phrasing, to the last grace-note, their Bachs and Mozarts. His technique was faulty and his taste was worse. He himself thought little of his musical powers, and all his serious thought, his fine energies, were devoted to the composition of elaborate prose. In more expansive moments, he saw himself as another Pater or Stevenson. But he was not a writer, and never would be. Try as he might, he only succeeded in putting honest words on the rack, leaving them screaming, though of this he was happily unconscious. He was marked out to be one of those wistful adorers who never even catch a glance from the Muse. He would never create literature, though his life itself might be rich with its scents and flavours. He would always be one of its failures, though perhaps one of its happy failures, that company of humble aspirants - and at heart Inigo was humble enough - who discover more joy in the sight of a sadly botched manuscript than many a successful writer has found in a row of admired volumes. On the other hand, in his antics at the piano, which had made him so popular at school, at Cambridge, and at odd parties everywhere, those antics that he regarded with smiling contempt, there was really a glint of genius. His touch was light, crisp, and somehow deliciously comic; he could start the keys into elfin life; and not only could he read easily at sight, and improve as he read, the common sort of music, the songs and dance tunes that were so often demanded of him, not only could he play by ear and throw in a trick or two of his own as he played, but he was able to improvise the most amusing little tunes, cynical-sentimental things of the moment, not unlike all the other butterfly melodies that wing their way across the world and then perish obscurely, and yet all his own, with a twist in them, something half wistful, half comic, in their lilt, that belonged to nobody else. He would play these things until every foot was tap-tapping, and many a listener, vainly attempting to catch again the deft little phrases, would be maddened for weeks. But he would only try variations of key and manner until at last his ear was satisfied. He never tried to put them down on paper. It had not occurred to him that the world was being scoured for such tunes; and if it had occurred to him, he would probably have remained indifferent, having a *Last Knapsack* still to finish.

For several days an unusually impudent and delicious little tune had been capering at the back of his mind, and now, after some preliminary flourishes, he set out to capture it. He fumbled about for a few minutes in the key of D major, but then slid into his favourite E flat. The next moment the poor hulk of a piano leaped into life. The tune was his, and he began toying ecstatically with it. Now it ran whispering in the high treble; now it crooned and gurgled in the bass; and then, off it went scampering, with a flash of red heels and a tossing of brown curls. There was no holding it at all. It pirouetted round the room, mocking the desks and blackboards and maps: the air was full of its bright mischief. *Rumpty-dee-tidee-dee, Rumpty-dee-tidee.* But why try to describe that little tune or make any mystery of it? All the world knows it now, or did yesterday, as *Slippin' round the Corner*. What Inigo played that night was not quite the final melody that became so famous as a song and a dance tune afterwards: the butterfly was hardly out of the chrysalis yet; but, on the other hand, the lilt that came out then had not been blared and bleated and howled and vulgarized in every conceivable fashion, and still had all its enchanting mockery of things heavy and dull and lifeless. Inigo twisted it this way and that, sent little glittering showers of high notes over the melody, let it sink down in mock despair to the bass, then made it ring so triumphantly through the schoolroom that it shattered the place altogether and set up in its stead a room that was all long windows and gardens beyond and youth and happy folly. As he did this, Inigo laughed aloud.

'Mr Jollifant!' A voice at the door.

Rumpty-dee-tidee-dee. This was the best tune yet. It was what Saturday night ought to be. It danced clean over Washbury Manor School at the very first note, cleared the long sullen fields, and then went capering through bright towns that could not be found on any map.

'Mr Jollifant!' The voice was closer and louder, a screech.

Rumpty-dee-tidee. And friends you had never seen before joined hands with you, and away you went, past lines of laughing girls

'*Mr Jollifant!*'

And Inigo let his hands fall from the keys and awoke to make the discovery that Mrs Tarvin really existed and was standing before him, very angry indeed. There followed a moment during which he was able to examine distastefully and in silence her shapeless black figure, her grey hair with its odd ribbon in front, her steel spectacles, her long sallow face that always contrasted so dramatically and repellently with her bulk of body.

'Didn't you hear me calling?' she demanded furiously.

'I'm afraid I didn't.' Inigo smiled at her in a dazed fashion. The tune was still running through his head.

'Well, please stop playing at once, at once," cried Mrs Tarvin. She had a trick of repeating phrases, raising her voice the second time, that had been meat and drink to mimics at Washbury for years. 'I thought it was clearly understood that this piano was not to be played at all, not at all, in the evening.'

'But that's the only time I can play it, absolutely the only time,' Inigo replied, quite unwittingly falling into mimicry there and then. 'And after all, I give some of the boys music lessons. Music's an extra and - er - we share the profits. And I can't give music lessons unless I play myself sometimes, can I?' And he gave her a broad smile.

It was not returned. Mrs Tarvin had known Inigo only a week, but already she had begun to regard him as another of her husband's unfortunate appointments. 'The music lessons are not important, not important, at all,' she said coldly. 'And in any case, I don't see that it is at all necessary that in order to give them, you must play music-hall tunes as loudly as you can when all the boys are in bed, yes, long ago in bed.'

'The longer in bed, you know, the deeper the sleep,' he began.

'That will do, please, Mr Jollifant. The rule is that this piano shall not be played, not be played, in the evening.' And she swept round as if she were on a swivel, drew herself up, and marched out.

Inigo followed, whistling softly the night's tune, which now was not only deliriously lilting but also had a certain rebellious note in it. At the head of the stairs, on the way to his room, he met Miss Callander, who looked as if she had been standing there, listening.

'Oh, I heard her go down. Did she stop you?'

'She did, she did,' he replied. 'And just when I was beginning to enjoy myself. Did you hear the thing I was playing? A poor thing, but mine own.'

'Was it really? I thought it was lovely. You are clever.' Then she dropped her voice. 'I knew she'd stop you. She's been fearfully cross all evening and blamed me for all kinds of silly things just after dinner, and I really don't know what to do.' And she put a hand to her cheek and looked at him forlornly.

He took her hand and held it somewhat absent-mindedly. 'She thinks by keeping us on a low diet - I mean shepherds' pie and prunes - to crush our spirit. But she won't succeed, unless perhaps with Felton, who hasn't much spirit anyhow, and likes prunes, or says he does. But you and I, Miss Callander - ' and he completed the sentence by squeezing her hand.

She withdrew her hand, though not hastily. 'She's really awful, isn't she? And only a week of term gone! And weeks and weeks yet! What will she be like at the end? Better perhaps.'

'Worse, decidedly worse,' said Inigo impressively. 'Nine weeks more of her - it's unthinkable. Believe me' - and now his voice sank to a fearsome whisper - 'young as the term is, short as the acquaintance of this gorgon-like female and myself, the fates have already conspired together and woven a web and laid a train, and very soon - do you know what will happen here very soon, do you know what there will be?'

Her round eyes and parted lips were sufficient to frame the question. But Inigo's sense of the dramatic compelled him to wait a few moments. His stare was heavy with doom.

'A bust-up,' he said at length, 'and a bust-up of the most astounding and shattering proportions.' He gave her another fateful glance, then quite suddenly grinned at her, waved his hand, and went striding down the corridor, whistling his tune, that tune which is perhaps the *leitmotif* of the piece.

II

Sunday was surprisingly warm for a late September day. It was not, however, a pleasant and bright warmth, but sulky grey heat, as if the whole place had been shovelled into a huge dim oven. Not a breath stirred the surrounding fields, and all the air inside the school seemed to have been used over and over again. Midday dinner with the boys had been a misery, and Inigo, who had hacked off innumerable slices of boiled beef, had had some greasy traffic with carrots, and had then watched fifteen boys eat tapioca pudding, felt hot, sick, and cross.

'I was wrong about there being only two smells here,' he announced angrily to Felton, with whom he left the dining-room. 'There are two smells-in-chief, I admit. The smell of boy is the first, of course.

And the smell from the kitchen, which must be piled high with decaying bones and drenched in cabbage water, is the second. These are what's its name - dominant. But - are you listening, Felton?'

'Not more than I can help, I must say,' said Felton, without turning round. They were now going upstairs, and he was in front. 'But go on, Jollifant, if it amuses you.'

'Ah, Felton, even you feel the iron entering your soul. Where is that genial comradeship, that old West Country good nature? And let me tell you that it doesn't amuse me. But what I was going to say was that it's a mistake to imagine that there aren't other smells here, little old smells that live in corners, large vague smells that drift about the corridors, smells that - '

'Oh, do shut up!' Felton increased his pace. 'I've just had dinner.'

'And you want to wrestle with it in peace? You intend to turn it into an honest bit of Felton? These be mysteries, not to be tampered with or butted into by the profane.'

'I'm wondering what to do,' said Felton, standing at the door of his room.

'You're wondering what to do!' cried Inigo, patting him on the shoulder. 'Then I say you're lucky. I've got past that. I know that it's a warm Sunday afternoon in a smelly school miles from anywhere and there's nothing to do.'

'I think I shall go for a walk.'

'What! the same old round - through the fields, Washbury, over the old bridge, back down the road. Oh no, Felton, you don't mean it.'

'No, not that way. I thought of going along the dyke to Kinthorpe,' said Felton, with the air of a modest hero. 'You can get tea there, too.' And he nodded brightly and went into his room.

By the time Inigo had stretched himself across his two chairs and had lit his pipe, he had an inspiration. He knew that Daisy Callander was free until early evening. Why shouldn't he take her to Kinthorpe or somewhere to tea? She was not perhaps an enthusiastic walker but she could manage that distance. There were times when he half fancied he was in love with Daisy, though he never could shake off the knowledge that he had only to see half a dozen other girls to be quite sure he was not in love with her. He knew too that it was impossible to spend more than an hour alone with Daisy without flirting with her, because somehow there was nothing else left to do. But then he had no objection to flirting. He had no objection to anything, apart from work and from the baser and more violent crimes, that would pass the time. Languidly, he began to change some of his clothes, beginning with his collar.

There was a knock, and Felton looked in, all neat and shining.

The very sight of his trim brown felt hat, his dreary blue tie, his flashing eye-glasses, gave Inigo an awful sense of dullness. A walk with Felton would be like a stroll across the Gobi Desert.

'You're not coming, Jollifant?'

Inigo gave him a long head-shake. 'No, thanks. Some other time when I'm a stronger and saner man and the wild North-Easter does whatever what's his name - Mr Kingsley - says it does. But not today.'

'I thought not.' Felton grinned, rather surprisingly, and withdrew.

'And that', Inigo told himself, 'disposes of you, Master Felton. Now for the fair Daisy.' And he pulled what seemed to him a fine melodramatic face and even went over to the glass to see what it really looked like; and hurried on now with his toilet. The fair Daisy seemed fairer still, her company for two or three hours a rich prospect. The awful boredom vanished, dispersed by a tiny flame of excitement. He fell to whistling his tune.

A glance through the window showed him a few boys drifting out into the grounds. He cast upon them a look of pity. They would be soon assembling for their Sunday crawl, under the direction today of Tarvin himself. Then they would return to produce, under that same paternal eye, their laborious little weekly letters. Poor infants! What a Sunday afternoon they had! But then, just as he was turning away, two larger figures caught his eye. One was Daisy Callander. And her companion, stepping along so briskly, was the wretched and perfidious Felton. He had sneaked down and captured her, and was now taking her out to tea. He was coolly walking off with Inigo's whole afternoon. Inigo stared at their backs, then noticed the daft hat in his hand, threw the thing across the room, and then stared out again and this time saw nothing - apart from a few idiotic little boys - but a huge and faintly sizzling blackness.

There was just one moment when he might have wept out of sheer self-pity. But he gave his hat a kick, muttered words that he ought not to have known at all, sat down, and thought of Felton, of Miss Callander, of the whole burst afternoon, and suddenly he chuckled. Then he went to call on Fauntley, to borrow from that gentleman's ample store a detective tale.

Fauntley was lolling in his old basket-chair, sucking a pipe and finishing a whisky and soda. He was a large, sagging man, about fifty, with formidable eyebrows, a clipped moustache, a heavy jowl, and a face enpurpled by a host of tiny veins. He was also the only really able master in the school. Such scholarships as came its way were snatched by Fauntley, who now and then persuaded himself that a boy had ability and promise and so promptly crammed knowledge into him. Why he should ever have come to Washbury Manor or, having come, should have remained, was a mystery. He seemed to have drifted there out of some queer past. It would be an exaggeration to describe him as that familiar type (in fiction), the brilliant failure; nevertheless, he was a sound scholar - infinitely superior to Tarvin himself - and an old Rugger Blue, and he seemed like a man-of-war rotting in some dilapidated little harbour. He jeered at all modern literature (pointing out its mistakes in grammar), but read enormous numbers of detective stories. Once, and sometimes twice, a week, he disappeared for the whole evening, not returning until very late, and never offered any account of these expeditions. (Inigo periodically shocked Felton by suggesting that their older colleague had a mistress in one of the neighbouring villages.) He was very fond of whisky, and when he had taken a sufficient quantity of it he would either express at length his regret that he had never gone into the Church and then proceed to denounce all modern civilization, or relate with a certain scholarly distinction of phrase, which never appeared in his ordinary conversation, any number of dirty stories. Such was Fauntley. It was impossible to dislike him, but it was not difficult to feel that somehow one would be better off in some place where he was not. The sight of him frequently turned Inigo's attention to the thought of other careers.

'Well, Jollifant,' Fauntley growled amiably, putting down his glass, 'I'm sorry I can't offer you a whisky, but there isn't any more. I had to have that to take the taste of that damned lunch out of my mouth. Sit down.'

'I couldn't touch it even if you had any,' said Inigo, 'not at this hour. I can't drink whisky, somehow, until it's dark. And talking of whisky, it's my birthday tomorrow.'

'How old are you?'

'Twenty-six.'

'Good God!' And Fauntley regarded him closely. 'Twenty-six. I'd forgotten it existed. But where does the whisky come in?'

'I thought we might celebrate the great event, in the common-room after dinner - '

'If you're thinking of asking our worthy Mrs Tarvin,' said Fauntley - who hated her - with a grin, 'you'll be disappointed. The Tarvins are dining out tomorrow night, I happen to know. They usually do about this time every year.'

'All the better. Felton will be able to get tight in peace, the deep and treacherous dog. But I want two bottles of whisky for the occasion, and I thought you would know where I could get 'em.'

'Two bottles, eh? Stout feller!' Fauntley rumbled. 'The notice is too short for me to get 'em for you. I know, though. Comrie's the man. He'll get 'em for you by tomorrow night. You'll make sure if you let him know today.'

'Good. I'll see the dashing Sergeant, then,' said Inigo. 'But what becomes of him on Sundays?'

'You've noticed that fair-haired rather tall maid who occasionally waits at table? Her name's Alice.'

'And very suitable, too. I know the one you mean. The most buxom and least ill-favoured of our handmaids. But what about her?'

'Give a message to Alice,' remarked Fauntley blandly, 'and it will reach Comrie tonight.'

'Well, well, well!' Inigo cocked an eye at his companion. 'You'll pardon me for saying so, Mr Fauntley - '

'Fauntley, please,' that gentleman put in, 'even if you are about to insult me, as I see you are.' But he grinned amiably.

'But you seem to know a devil of a lot about what I might call the inner workings of this establishment. Now I thought I knew everything that's going on in the place - '

'Not you, Jollifant; you flatter yourself. But anyhow, you try it and see. Give Alice a note.'

'I will. And you'll join me tomorrow night?'

'Honoured!' grunted Fauntley. They smoked in silence for a minute or two. Then Inigo looked disconsolately out of the window.

'I suppose', he began, 'you wouldn't like to come out for a walk.'

'You're right, I shouldn't,' the other replied. 'And when you've been here as long as I have, you won't either. Besides, I never walk just for the sake of walking. I've no doubt Tarvin will let you take the boys out.'

'I've no doubt he would. And I've no doubt Mrs Tarvin would let me soak the prunes for tomorrow. It won't do. I don't want to live entirely for pleasure. Will you lend me one of your latest masterpieces of crime and detection, something very thin in clues and thick with suspicions?' He began looking about him.

Fauntley yawned. 'Take what you like. That one's not bad, *The Straw Hat Mystery*. It'll puzzle your tender brains. I'm going to sleep for an hour.'

Inigo crawled away with his book and, after a few minutes in his stuffy little room, he decided to go out and read under one of the five trees at the back of the school. On his way out, he came across one of the maids, who promised to give the note he handed her to the fair Alice, busy, it appeared 'a-tidying 'erself. Then he found his tree and proceeded to stun the gigantic and silly afternoon with *The Straw Hat Mystery* which he did not finish because he fell asleep. When he awoke he made a number of discoveries, the most important of them being that it was past tea-time and much cooler and that he was very stiff and had a slight headache. He limped round to the main entrance just in time to see Miss Callander and Felton arrive there, and to notice that they looked dusty and tired and out of spirits. They were in front, and he let them go without a word.

When Inigo came down, two hours later, to the usual Sunday night cold supper, he was feeling hungry. Everybody was there, but only Mr Tarvin was making an effort to talk. He was a spectacled pompous little man, with an unusual and quite misleading expanse of forehead and a large and shaggy moustache that had been trained to hide what would undoubtedly be discovered to be a weak little mouth. He had a habit of punctuating his speech with a curious explosive sound, which must be inadequately represented by 'chumha'. And this was the first thing Inigo heard as he reached the table.

'A - ha, Jollifant!' cried Mr Tarvin. 'Just in time, but only just as the - er - chumha - Scotsman said of his change.'

'What Scotsman?' Inigo inquired, with an innocent glance that immediately became less innocent when it moved round to Fauntley, who raised ponderous eyebrows.

'The exact Scotsman is not specified. Chumha.' And Mr Tarvin began rubbing his hands as he looked at the food before him.

There was the boiled beef, now cold, with beetroot and mashed potatoes. Mrs Tarvin, however, had a generous plate of cold chicken in front of her. Inigo examined it out of the corner of his eye, and then chanced to meet the wide gaze of Miss Callander, who suddenly lowered her eyes and was troubled by a delicate fit of coughing. They all champed their way through the first course, with Mrs Tarvin occasionally addressing a remark to Felton, Mr Tarvin and Fauntley throwing a word at one another, and Miss Callander and Inigo exchanging glances now and then across the table. Inigo was convinced that he was suffering from a fit of deep depression. 'My heart aches,' he told himself, poking away at a slippery piece of beetroot, 'and a drowsy numbness pains. Absolutely.' He seemed to have spent nearly all his glittering young manhood eating old meat with these people.

The plates were changed. Before Mrs Tarvin a dish of *crème caramel* and a jug of cream were placed. Then came, for the middle of the table and presumably the remainder of the company, the usual butter and the wooden slab of cheese - and stewed prunes. They were not even new prunes, Inigo declared angrily to himself; they were old and withered prunes, the very prunes some of them, he was ready to take oath, that he himself had rejected several days ago, prunes that by this time he knew shudderingly by sight.

'No, thank you,' he cried when the dish came his way. 'Not for me. I don't like prunes. Do you like prunes, Mrs Tarvin?' he added impudently. There was an instant hush.

'I don't think I've asked you, Mr Jollifant,' she replied coldly, 'to consult me about my taste in food. As a matter of fact, I used to be very fond of prunes, very fond of prunes - '

'I thought I was at one time,' Inigo put in recklessly, 'but now I find I can't stand them.'

'But I am not allowed now to eat everything I like,' she went on, 'not allowed at all. I have to be careful, to be very careful.'

'Certainly. Very careful. Chumha,' said her husband.

'When you are young, you can eat anything, anything at all,' she pursued, 'just as sometimes you imagine you can say anything or do anything. Though that is often a mistake, quite a mistake.' She looked at him steadily through her steel spectacles, then slowly turned to her neighbour. 'What were you saying, Mr Felton?'

'And of course, Fauntley, you can't - er - chumha - go on spending public money like - chumha.' Mr Tarvin was rushing in too.

'Did you have a good walk this afternoon, Miss Callander?' Inigo roared across the table. 'Have some cheese?'

Ten minutes later, the first to leave the table, they strolled out into the garden together. 'I must have a cigarette after that,' she whispered. 'Can I have a cigarette, please?'

'You can,' said Inigo. 'But tell me, did you enjoy your walk with Felton this afternoon? I must have the answer to that question before I pour out to you the secrets of my heart.'

'Oh, must you! Well, of course I did.'

'You did,' he said with a stern melancholy. 'Then the secrets of this heart are ever denied you.'

'Well, then - ' she hesitated. They were still in the light of the doorway, and she took the opportunity of showing him her large liquid orbs. 'If you feel like that, I'll confess. I didn't enjoy it much. He's - Mr Felton's - dullish, isn't he?'

'Felton is very dull. You set my mind at rest. I intended to ask you myself to go for a walk.' And he explained at length how he had missed her, then went on: 'We'll talk sympathetically under the stars, and tonight I shall call you Daisy.'

'Oh, will you? I don't know about that. But listen - you're absolutely in Mrs Tarvin's bad books. I heard about last night from her; she was furious. And then tonight - those prunes. I thought I should have screamed when you asked her if she didn't like them - the greedy old thing. But really, you'll have to be careful or there's sure to be trouble.'

'I am a man', announced Inigo, with a fine Byronic air. 'born for trouble. It is only when I'm with you, Miss Cal - I mean Daisy, that this restless heart is stilled. Not altogether stilled mind you, because Beauty itself - er - '

'Oh, do be quiet,' she cried, after waiting in vain for him to tell her what Beauty did. 'You're too absurd, and worse than ever tonight. I don't think it's safe being out here with you.' Then she lowered her voice, drew closer to him. 'But really she is an awful old cat. I'm sure I shall never stick it, I really shan't. She hates me like poison already.'

Inigo murmured sympathetically and drew her arm into his. They walked slowly, close together, over the lawn. The night was large and cool-breathing, deep purple with a faint gold glimmer of stars, full of owl-haunted distances. Inigo, squeezing her arm within his, was already embracing the night itself, with which he had fallen instantly in love. Miss Callander herself, however, was not only shedding certain defects of form and feature, but was even escaping from her own trite prettiness; the night lent her beauty. Could she have borrowed its silence too, she would have been throned even higher in Inigo's imagination.

'I can't do anything right for her,' she continued in a rapid whisper. 'She grumbles at everything. Oh, and do you know she won't let Mr Tarvin talk to me alone a single minute? She won't really. She comes flying up at once, saying "What's this, what's this?" The day before yesterday he came and said something to me just outside the door, and she was at the other end of the garden, miles away, and she saw us and came hurrying up - you wouldn't think she could move so fast, but she can - saying " What's this, what's this?" It's because he's about ten years younger than she is. She keeps her eye on him all the time. As if I wanted - I mean, a dingy little middle-aged man like James Tarvin - isn't it ridiculous? He's my mother's cousin, you know. She can't forgive me for his having engaged me when she was away.'

Inigo let her run on, content to give her arm an occasional squeeze and drift into an amorous reverie. They halted near the shrubbery and she grew silent as he glanced from the stars to the dim ivory round of her cheeks. But a noise in the shrubbery made her jump and she clutched at him. He slid an arm around her. 'All right,' he muttered, 'it's nothing.' And the arm tightened about her unresisting body.

'I thought - it might be Sturry,' she gasped. Sturry was the gardener, a long, shambling, melancholy creature who was subject to epileptic fits. These fits were perhaps the most exciting events at Washbury Manor, and at any time when you were taking a class, droning away at French or History, you might glance through the window and see Sturry falling into a fit outside. All the boys kept their eye on him whenever they could, hoping that it might arrive at their turn to throw up a hand and cry 'Please, sir, Sturry - !', sounding gloriously the alarm.

'What would Sturry be doing mooching about here now?' But while Inigo put the question - and tried to make it sound tender and protective - he could not help thinking that it was useless to ask what Sturry was doing anywhere and at any time.

'I don't know,' she went on, in a tiny troubled voice, 'but he's so horribly queer isn't he? He follows me up and down. He comes and stands and stares. I see him staring through the window at me sometimes. He frightens me. Yes, he does, really.'

'Poor girl,' he murmured, drawing her closer. 'Never mind the loathsome brute. He won't hurt you.'

She said nothing but let her hand rest idly against his coat. Her large eyes, deep and expressionless, were fixed upon his; her face itself, so close now, was a mysterious silent world; everything of her waited. Inigo knew that the moment had arrived. He kissed her.

'No, no,' she whispered when it was done. 'You really mustn't.' Her face went back about three inches, but was still tilted towards his. He kissed her again, then again, and held her close while she showered upon his face a host of little kisses. All this they did with a certain vague suggestion of absent-mindedness, as if it was really happening in their sleep so that they could not be held responsible for it. Inigo felt triumphant but at the same time a trifle foolish. The trouble was, he had nothing to say. What he was feeling was too strong for the usual idle pretences and yet it was not strong enough to put real words into his mouth. He was rather relieved when she gently disengaged herself and began to move forward.

Before they had moved ten paces, there was another rustling in the shrubbery. 'Who's that?' Inigo called sharply. A figure shot out and ran past them. Miss Callander gave a little scream, swung round, and tripped heavily over a stone. Inigo, prepared to give chase to the retreating figure, stopped and found her stretched at full length, whimpering a little.

'It's my ankle,' she moaned. 'I can't get up. I'm sure it's broken.'

It wasn't, but it was badly sprained, they discovered. Inigo got her gingerly to her feet again, and she put one arm round his neck and slowly hobbled back to the house.

Somebody came peering out of the doorway. 'Is that you, Daisy?' he called. 'And who - chumha - is that?' Mr Tarvin walked to meet them.

'Miss Callander tripped and fell and sprained her ankle,' Inigo explained. And the lady herself, turning a face pale with suffering upon the staring little headmaster, gave further details.

'We must get you indoors at once. Now lean on me. Chumha.

Allow me, Jollifant. That's right. Th-a-at's right.' And Inigo found himself dispossessed by his superior, who promptly put an arm round Miss Callander's waist, drew her own arm round his neck and retained the hand he held, and did it all with a certain gusto. The two of them so affectionately entwined, tottered towards the doorway, and at every step there seemed to be more of Miss Callander and less of Mr Tarvin. They were actually standing, swaying there in the light, and Mr Tarvin was consoling his burden with soft little chumhas, when footsteps came pattering up the hall. Mrs Tarvin burst round the corner.

'What's this, what's this?' she flung at them, almost before she could see anything. 'James! Miss Callander!'

All three began explaining at once, though Mr Tarvin, in spite of his deficiencies, was easily the loudest and most voluble.

'Indeed! Very unfortunate, most unfortunate, though why Miss Callander should choose to wander about in the dark, I can't imagine. Just take hold of my hand, please, Miss Callander, and see if you can't walk. No, James, stand away, stand away. Not at all necessary, quite unnecessary. Now Miss Callander, if you have no objections to leaning upon me. I will find you a cold water bandage. Yes, cold water, absolutely cold. We shall manage very well, quite well in fact, by ourselves, James.' And Mrs Tarvin moved off, jerking forward her victim and leaving the two men staring at a back that seemed to rustle with indignation.

'Well - er - Jollifant - er - thank you,' said Mr Tarvin; and with an embarrassed chumha he followed, though not too closely, the two women.

Inigo stared after him, and when they had all disappeared he still hung about, filling and lighting his pipe, and feeling vaguely as if he had just slipped out of a theatre in which an idiotic play was being performed. For ten minutes nothing happened at all; nobody came; there was not a sound. Then a noise behind made him turn round, and, with a shock of surprise, he found himself looking at a girl he had never seen before, quite a pretty girl in bright blue, with cheeks like an apple.

'Please, sir,' she began. And then he realized that this was Alice, the maid that Fauntley had mentioned, who was to take his message; but Alice without her uniform, in her best clothes, a free and perhaps saucy Alice.

'I took that message, an' Sergeant Comrie 'e says 'e can get them two bottles of whisky tomorrow an' 'e'll let you 'ave 'em in the afternoon an' please will you give 'im the money then. An' 'e says', she continued, breathlessly, 'will Old Rob Roy do?' ·

'Will Old Rob Roy do what?' Inigo inquired solemnly. 'I don't know because I've never met the old gentleman. But he sounds as if he could do almost anything.'

She giggled, and then opened her eyes wide at him. 'It's the name of the whisky, you know it is. An' will it do, 'e says?'

'Couldn't be better,' said Inigo heartily, though he had never heard of it before. 'It's for my little birthday party tomorrow night,' he added in a confidential whisper. 'Suppose I give you the money, could you pass it on and take the bottles in for me? Just, you know, as a special birthday favour.' Alice could, and he counted out the twenty-five shillings, gave it to her, then found another half-crown. 'You know, I think Comrie's a very lucky man. I didn't recognize you, you're such a tremendous swell in your Sunday clothes. I hope Comrie appreciates them.'

'Oh, I don't go with 'im every time 'e likes,' cried Alice, tossing her head. 'I likes to please myself about that. Sometimes I goes out by myself.'

'Yes,' said Inigo vaguely, for this was an invitation to which he did not feel he could respond. Nevertheless, he beamed upon her. 'I can see that you're a proud girl, Alice. But I hope you're not too proud to accept this for taking my message.' And he pressed the half-crown into her palm and folded her fingers round it. His glance fell upon her ripe and smiling mouth. The night was still working obscurely inside him. There was something very inviting about those generous lips.

'Ah, Jollifant,' said a voice behind him. Inigo jumped. Mr Tarvin had returned.

'Alice here', said Inigo blandly, 'has been taking a message for me, haven't you, Alice?'

'Yes, yes, of course, one of the maids. Alice. I didn't recognize who it was. Chumha.' And he looked at her with such interest that Inigo made a note of it, for the benefit of Fauntley.

'I was just saying the same thing myself,' Inigo pursued. 'I was saying that she was so smart in her Sunday clothes - they are your Sunday clothes, aren't they, Alice?'

'Let me see,' Mr Tarvin reflected, 'you've been here how long now?' He seemed to be in no greater hurry to get rid of her than Inigo was. And it was this last query, keeping him staring there another minute, that was his undoing.

'Oo!' cried Alice.

The two men turned round. Too late! Mrs Tarvin was upon them. 'What's this, what's this? Really now I can't understand, I really can't understand - '

'I've just been - er - chumha - '

'Good night, everybody.' Inigo left his unhappy headmaster to explain everything. When he reached the landing that led to his own room, he ran into Felton.

'What have you been doing all night, Jollifant?'

'There are times, Felton,' said Inigo, solemnly shaking his head, 'when the sight of your bright innocent face, those unstained eye-glasses, that cherubic mouth, the wild yet shy gambols and romps that have brought so many happy hours to Bristol and even Clifton - '

'Oh, do shut up about Bristol!'

'The very pink that now mantles your youthful cheek - all these things, Felton, at times, I say, go to my heart and there lay a what's its name - a heavy burden, and I tell myself that Washbury Manor has much to answer for. This is one of the times, Felton. I grieve for you. Good night.'

III

'Having drunk your health, Jollifant,' said Fauntley, his fingers closing round the bottle of Old Rob Roy, 'I will now proceed to give you a little good advice.' He spoke in that unusually careful and dignified manner often found in men who have just accounted for half a bottle of whisky and are busy pouring out the other half.

This was Monday night and the little birthday party. The revellers had the place to themselves, for the Tarvins were dining out and Miss Callander had retired early, to rest her ankle. Indeed the tiny common-room, which had sufficient haze of smoke and reek of Old Rob Roy to be a highland den, seemed to have removed itself altogether from Washbury Manor. Perhaps one of the trio, Felton, can hardly be described as a reveller. He did not like whisky and was secretly troubled all the time by the thought of what his companions might say or do under its influence, but being a good-natured and gregarious youth, he did his best, by drowning his tots of liquor in soda water and then taking blind gulps at the stuff, by smoking quite a number of his non-nicotine cigarettes, by laughing whenever the others laughed, to be one of the party. And perhaps Fauntley, who was there to deal justly with the Old Rob Roy, did not quite succeed in revelling. With Inigo himself, however, there can be no such reservations. He was there to do the honours, to drink with and beam upon his companions in misfortune, to forget, to expand. He was not really very fond of whisky but already he had had a great deal more of it than he was accustomed to, and now his lock of hair seemed longer and more troublesome than usual and his smile a trifle broader, his gestures had a certain amplitude and nobility, and his spirit, discovering again the enchanted richness of life, was taking wing.

'But before I give you this advice,' Fauntley continued, 'I should like to ask you a few questions, in what is - you must understand, Jollifant - a purely friendly spirit. No discourtesy is intended.' He brought out these remarks with the care of a pleading K.C. In a few more glasses' time, he would stand at the familiar cross-roads, being compelled to go one way and discuss his lost position in the Church and the decay of civilization or to go the other way and talk bawdy. At the moment, however, he was still free and so was enjoying his capacity to choose, develop, expand, any theme. 'My first question is this. Have you any money?'

'About two pound ten,' replied Inigo.

'No, not actual money, cash in hand, but means, income, capital.'

'Oh, that! I've a private income of about sixty pounds per annum, derived, gentlemen, from investments. One is the Western Gas Company, and the other the Shuttlebury Bag and Portmanteau Corporation. I may add that the Bags and Portmanteaus are a bit rocky.'

'Very well. You can't live on that, can you? Still, it's something,' said Fauntley, examining the stem of his pipe with great gravity. 'My next question is this. What about your people? Have you any expectations? Have you anybody dependent on you?'

'Neither.' Inigo took up his glass. 'I am, my friends, a man without family. You see before you a Norphan. As a matter of fact, I've an uncle - he's in the tea trade and lives at Dulwich - who sort of helped to bring me up until I left Cambridge. I was staying with him during the Long. He's a pleasant old stick and the only man I know what still wears a straw hat.'

'I know a man who wears one in winter,' Felton put in modestly.

'Have another drink, Felton,' said Inigo, pushing across the bottle. 'In winter, too, eh? There's more in you than meets the eye. An all-the-year-round-bounder, eh? I must tell my uncle that; he'll be furious. But where does this lead us, to what dark clue, Fauntley?'

'My advice to you, Jollifant, is this. Get out of this place. You're only wasting your time. You don't like it, and I don't think it likes you.' Fauntley emptied his glass and relit his pipe. 'I don't mean go to another school. There are plenty of prep, schools better than Washbury, much better, and there are some worse. I've known one or two a damned sight worse.'

'You stagger me,' cried Inigo.

'Well, I don't know,' said Felton, 'I've heard of schools - ' But what he had heard was never revealed because his troubled piping was completely drowned by Fauntley's heavy bass.

'When all's said and done, these prep, schools are not your damned Board or Council schools or whatever they call 'em now - reading and writing factories. A gentleman can still teach in 'em. Don't forget that, you youngsters. These are the only places left for a gentleman.'

'No doubt,' observed Inigo sadly. 'But it's pretty ghastly being a gentleman, isn't it?'

'It's nearly played out,' said Fauntley. 'And so, by the way, is this bottle. There's another somewhere, isn't there, Jollifant?'

'There is, and I'll open it. But what am I to do when I get out?"

'Well, of course, that's your affair,' said Fauntley, who seemed to think that up to this time the conversation had been on some public question, and had all the appearance of a man who had successfully settled it. 'I don't pretend to know about these things. But you write a little, don't you? Why don't you become a journalist?'

'Because I was born at least thirty years too late,' replied Inigo. 'Now if I'd been writing in Henley's time - '

'Good feller, Henley!' Fauntley ejaculated this with such an air that the wondering Felton, who only knew Henley as the man who was captain of his soul, thought the two must have been at Oxford together.

'I could have done something,' Inigo pursued wistfully. 'It's too late now, though. Why, I'm working at a thing now, an essay on *The Last Knapsack* - about walking tours, you know - that Henley would have jumped at. But I'm absolutely certain', he added, with prophetic truth, 'that there isn't a paper in the country would take it now. No, I've thought about that, and it's useless. Some day, perhaps, I may - ' And he finished the sentence with a graceful gesture; that, no doubt, of a man accepting or refusing several wreaths of laurel.

'That's no good then,' said Fauntley so heartily as to be almost brutal. 'What else is there? Of course you're devilish clever at the piano - I've heard you - always reminds me of a feller who was up at Merton in my time. He was the cleverest feller I ever heard at a piano, could play and sing you anything, though I can't say it ever did him any good in the long run. The last time I heard of him, he was seen opening oysters - professionally, I mean - in a bar in Sydney. Still,' he conceded, 'you might be able to make something out of it.'

'Some fun, that's all. But, by Jingo! I concocted a gorgeous little tune the other night - Saturday, it was. Did you hear it, Felton? It's about the best I've struck.' And he began whistling his little tune and it sounded better than ever.

'Let's have it, Jollifant,' said Fauntley.

'What do you mean? Go down to the schoolroom?'

'I do. A quick one all round - ' and he tipped some Old Rob Roy into the three glasses - 'then some music'

'Right you are !' Inigo drank his approval.

'But look here,' Felton began, signalling an alarm with his eye-glasses.

'No time to look there, Felton,' said Inigo sternly. 'Drink up. He's worried because the Tarvin stopped me on Saturday,' he explained to Fauntley.

'She's out,' said Fauntley, 'and I don't know if it would matter if she weren't.' And he drank confusion to the woman. 'Bring your glasses and a syphon. I've got the bottle.' And Felton, sorely troubled, followed them down.

'A little one before you begin,' Fauntley suggested, and so Inigo had another drink. He had never seen a keyboard that looked so inviting. He felt he could do anything with it, any mortal thing. He liked this phrase so much that he found himself repeating it: 'Any morr-tal thinggg.' It gave him a feeling of joyous confidence. *Terum, perum, perum - pum - pum, trrrum.* That was the fine opening flourish. Now he was sliding into his tune, gently, gently at first. *Rumpty-dee-tidee-dee -* it was undoubtedly better than ever - *rumpty-dee-tidee.* He played it through softly.

'Is that it?' asked Fauntley, out of a golden mist of Old Rob Roy.

'It is. D'you like it?'

'Well, I don't pretend to have any ear, but it seems to me absolutely first-rate, Jollifant, far better than most of the things you hear nowadays. You ought to get somebody to print that. *Rumpty-dee.* No, I haven't quite got it. We'll have it again in a minute. Here's luck!'

Inigo emptied his glass in reply, then began playing again. He went through half a dozen tunes of his own, and Fauntley tapped his feet and Felton nodded his head, though a trifle dubiously.

'Bravo!' cried Old Rob Roy, speaking through Fauntley. 'You've got a touch, you know, Jollifant, a wonder-ful touch. And a talent, distinctly a talent.'

'You heard those tunes of mine?' said Inigo, wheeling round excitedly. 'I have a phrase describing 'em, thought of it the other day. They're like a family of elves in dress suits. How's that?'

'Not bad,' said Fauntley, 'but I'd rather have the tunes. Let's have that first one again.'

And Inigo, deciding that as a phrase-maker he was above the heads of his present company, went back to his *Rumpty-dee-tidee-dee*, and this time he crashed it out fortissimo, so that instead of slyly hinting that you might slip round the corner, the tune now loudly defied anybody or anything that would keep you in your place and ended by fairly hurling you round the corner. Fauntley kept time with his glass on the little table near the piano, and even Felton tapped his feet. There was such a noise in the room that a car might have been driven up to the front door, the door might have been opened without anybody there being any the wiser.

Concluding with a final crash, Inigo sprang to his feet.

'And that's the tune', he cried, 'that the wretched Tarvin woman, that putter of prunes on other people's plates, stopped me playing the other night.'

'A damned shame!' growled Fauntley. 'She's an old spoil-sport.'

'Yes, I don't like her much, I must say,' added Felton, now throwing discretion to whatever winds Old Rob Roy may have known.

'Like her, Felton! I loathe her. What a pair they make! I've not told either of you yet what happened last night.' And he plunged excitedly into an account of the proceedings of the night before, beginning with Mr Tarvin's discovery of Miss Callander outside the door. As soon as he had brought Mrs Tarvin on to the scene for the first time, Inigo's narrative began to lose its grasp upon truth until at last it was an Arabian Night of embarrassed 'chumhas' and 'what's this, what's this?'

'Oh, damned good, damned good!' Fauntley was rolling in his chair. 'I don't believe a word of it, Jollifant,' he roared. 'But it's damned good.'

'Honest truth, I assure you!' Inigo roared in reply. He was sitting down now and the three of them had their heads together. 'So she came along, crying "what's this, what's this, what's this? I can't understand, I really can't understand. Now tell me, tell me, tell me." "Well, you see," said poor old Tarvin, "you see - chumha. " "No, I don't see chumha. I don't see chumha at all," she screamed back at them. "I see you talking to a girl, a girl, quite young, a young girl. I cannot have you talking to a girl, cannot have it all, not at all."' Inigo stopped for a moment, exhausted.

'She never said that, though,' Fauntley roared again. 'You can't tell me she said that.'

'No, I know she didn't.' Inigo sprang up, flung back his wandering lock, then slapped his knee. 'But don't you see I'm giving you the soul of the thing, absolutely? That's what she meant.'

'Is it, is it, indeed?' It came in a scream of rage from the door at the other end. There stood Mrs Tarvin.

The shock, the sight of her standing there, coming at the end of a long crescendo of excitement, cut the last binding thread of self-control in Inigo. Up jumped Old Rob Roy himself to answer. 'How now, you secret, black, and midnight hag!' he thundered down the room.

'What!' she shrieked, and swept forward, followed by her husband. 'What did you say? You're a drunken rowdy. I've never been so insulted in all my life. And by one of our own masters! I've never heard, never never heard, of such a thing. The schoolroom a tap-room, mimicry and insults and abuse! Why don't you say something, say something, James? Tell him to leave the place at once.'

'You ought to be ashamed of yourself, Jollifant,' said Mr Tarvin as sternly as he could. 'You're - er - drunk. Chumha.'

Fauntley was trying to rouse himself. 'He's a bit tight, Tarvin. Birthday. Get him to bed.'

'Pardon me, Fauntley, but I'm perfectly sober,' said Inigo. 'And I refuse to be got to bed.'

'Is this - this - this fellow to stay here?' demanded Mrs Tarvin of her husband, in a passion.

'Of course not. Expect resignation,' muttered Mr Tarvin.

'He must leave in the morning, in the morning. I won't have him here a moment longer, not a moment.' Her rage seemed to increase.

'Quite understand. Chumha. Disgraceful business,' her husband muttered again. 'Rather awkward, though, to leave in the morning.'

'And why, pray?'

'Well, to begin with, must have term's notice. Chumha.'

'In short,' said Inigo, making a sweeping gesture but speaking quite distinctly, 'if I leave in the morning you must pay me a term's salary. Fifty-two-pounds. A mere pittance, but mine own.'

'I don't care about that,' cried Mrs Tarvin, looking at Inigo as if he were a kind of reptile, then glaring at her husband. I won't have him here any longer, not a day, not a day. I knew what it would be from the first, from the very first. Another of your ridiculous appointments. I'll have him out tomorrow, whatever it costs.'

'Very well, my dear,' said Mr Tarvin, who knew only too well where all the money came from. 'We will have to manage somehow - chumha - for a week or so. You will - er - have your term's cheque in the morning, Jollifant, and leave us then.'

'I should think so indeed, I should think so,' cried Mrs Tarvin. At this moment, Inigo was trying to close the lid of the piano and not succeeding very well because he had failed to notice that a large matchbox had been left on the keys. 'Don't touch that piano, don't touch it,' she went on. 'Take yourself off to bed and get ready to leave in the morning.'

'I am not leaving in the morning.' Inigo announced loudly.

'Certainly you are.'

'Oh no, I'm not. I'm leaving tonight. Now.'

'Don't be an ass, Jollifant,' said Fauntley, putting a hand on his arm. 'You can't leave tonight. It's impossible.'

'Not at all impossible. An excellent idea,'

'There's no train,' Fauntley pursued. 'You couldn't go anywhere.'

'I can walk,' said Inigo triumphantly. 'I can put a knapsack on my back and walk. I leave tonight. It's not raining, is it? Is it raining,

Felton?'

'I - er - I don't know,' stammered poor Felton, who had been busy trying to efface himself for the last five minutes.

'I'm surprised, very surprised, at you, Mr Felton,' said Mrs Tarvin severely. 'I expected better things of you.'

'Felton was dragged into this', said Inigo, 'because I told him it was my birthday. Felton can't resist a birthday, can you, Felton? Mr Tarvin, I'm leaving tonight and so I will ask you to make my cheque out now.' He spoke very slowly and carefully.

'This is - er - chumha - ridiculous, Jollifant. You'll have to go, of course, but still - er - chumha.'

'Let him go, let him go,' cried Mrs Tarvin. 'We shall only be spared trouble in the morning. I don't see why we should have to make out cheques at this time of night, but the sooner he goes the better, and if he has to sleep in a ditch it's no concern of ours, no concern at all. Mr Felton, kindly remove these filthy glasses and open all the windows. This place is disgusting, disgusting.' She turned a still quivering back upon them and marched out.

Quarter of an hour later, Inigo had his cheque in his pocket and had packed his immediate necessaries in a knapsack. 'I'll tell you where to forward the trunk and the suit-case,' he said to Fauntley, who was looking on. 'Keep an eye on these things, will you, until I want them? It must be twelve, isn't it? And I don't feel a bit sleepy and it's a fine night and I've finished with this place and I needn't look for another for some time and I don't give a damn. I call it a glorious exit.'

'And I call it damned silly,' said Fauntley, grinning. 'And God knows how we shall manage those classes next week, or what sort of blighter the agencies will rake up for Tarvin. But good luck, Jollifant! Here, there's a spot of whisky left. We'll have a parting drink.'

They were having it when Felton looked in. 'You're really going then? I told Miss Callander you were. She looked out of her bedroom and asked me what was the matter. Can I do anything, Jollifant?'

Inigo shook him by the hand. 'Not a thing but say good-bye. I commend your soul to the Eternal Verities, Felton, though I haven't the least notion what they are. We shall meet again sometime, I feel it in my bones.' By this time, he had put on a raincoat and swung his knapsack over it, found his hat and a fierce ash stick, and was ready to go. Fauntley went out with him. As they passed her door, Miss Callander looked out. 'I'll be with you in a minute,' Inigo whispered to Fauntley, and stayed behind.

'You really are going?' Miss Callander, in her dressing-gown, looked rather like a pink rabbit. She opened her eyes as wide as possible and her mouth hardly at all.

'I'm sacked and I'm going.'

'You crazy boy!' she whispered. 'I'm awfully sorry. It will be my turn next, very soon, and really I shan't be sorry, I really shan't.'

Inigo looked at her steadily, with a small friendly smile. 'I should try Egypt if I were you.'

She nodded confusedly. 'I've just been - been writing there. Oh, but - I've got something for you.' She produced a little packet. 'It's only some biscuits and chocolate, but I don't suppose you've got anything to eat with you, have you? And you'll get awfully hungry.'

Inigo was really touched. It came to him in a flash that nobody had done anything like this for him for years. He had been living almost entirely in a world of services for money. 'Daisy Callander,' he cried softly, 'you're a brick. I'm tremendously grateful. I'd forgotten how hungry I should be in an hour or two.'

'Where are you going?'

He stared at her. 'Do you know, I'd entirely forgotten that. I've no idea where I'm going. I shall just walk and walk. Goodbye - and good luck!' He held out his hand.

She slipped her hand into his instead of shaking it. Then she raised her face a little. 'Good-bye,' she said, rather tearfully.

He realized that she wanted him to kiss her. Strangely enough, though he had never liked her more than he did at this moment, he did not want to kiss her. But he did kiss her, gently, then gave her hand a final squeeze, and hurried downstairs to find Fauntley waiting for him at the front door.

'Fine, but coldish and black as pitch,' said Fauntley. 'In an hour you'll wish you'd stayed here and gone to bed. You'd better change your mind now.'

'Not I,' said Inigo, peering out, 'I like the smell of it. I'll push on, Peterborough way.'

'You're a young ass, Jollifant.'

'And I'll let you know what happens to me, Fauntley, give you an outline of my adventures till we meet again.'

'I repeat, Jollifant, you're an ass. And if I were twenty years younger, I should come with you.'

Two minutes later, Fauntley had bolted the door and Inigo had turned out of the grounds into the lane, walking quickly westward.

CHAPTER FOUR
Mr Oakroyd on t'Road

I

WHEN Mr Oakroyd dashed out of the house and hurried down Ogden Street with his little basket trunk in one hand and his bag of tools in the other, he had no idea where he was going. He only knew he was going somewhere, that night, at once. The thought of taking a train at such a late hour somehow frightened him, for it seemed the act of a desperado. He had only once taken a train at night in all his life and that had been in the company of six hundred other citizens of Bruddersford. He saw himself being arrested at the ticket office.

'Na Jess!' somebody cried.

'Na lad!' he called back, hurrying on and wondering who it was. He walked so quickly now and was so busy with his thoughts that outside T'Mucky Duck, turning into Woolgate, he ran full tilt into somebody, a big man.

''Ere, weer the 'ell are yer coming to!' shouted the big man. Then he saw who it was. 'Eh, it's Jess Oakroyd. Weer yer going, Jess?'

'Off for me holidays, Sam,' replied Mr Oakroyd, slipping away and leaving the big man staring.

These little encounters seemed to make the situation more desperate. It was then that he thought of Ted Oglethorpe's nephew, who had said last night that he could have a trip whenever he wanted one. Loading at Merryweather's in Tapp Street, up to eleven o'clock or after, and then going somewhere down South - where was it? - Nuneaton. That was it. He felt immensely relieved at the thought that Ted would give him a lift down South. It would probably mean sitting on the bales at the back of the lorry all night, but this prospect did not daunt him. He rather liked the idea of jolting his way out of Bruddersford in this fashion.

Tapp Street, near the centre of the town, is a short street full of offices and warehouses, and any time after seven it looks dark and is almost deserted. There was only one sound now to be heard in the street, but no sooner had Mr Oakroyd, turning the corner, heard it, than he quickened his pace at once. It was the sound of a lorry engine, an urgent throb-throb. As Mr Oakroyd trotted up towards it, the engine burst into a roar. In another minute the lorry would be off. 'Hi!' cried Mr Oakroyd, and fairly ran now. It was quivering with impatience.

'Here, Ted,' shouted Mr Oakroyd, 'I'm coming wi' yer.'

A face he could not see distinctly looked from the driver's seat.

'Less noise, mate,' it said hoarsely. 'An' if yer coming, yer'll have to get on at the back. There's only room for two 'ere in front. 'Urry up. Take it or leave it.'

This was certainly not Ted's voice, but Mr Oakroyd did not trouble his head about that. 'All right,' he gasped, and hoisted his two bags on the back. Fortunately the lorry was not fully loaded and there was room at the sides, where the tarpaulin-covered bales or pieces did not come to the very edge. But he had still to hoist himself up, and he had not succeeded in doing this when the lorry started, so that he was carried several yards down Tapp Street with his legs swinging in mid-air. It was only by a tremendous effort that he pulled himself over the side, and even then he barked his shins and knees. After resting a minute or two, he contrived to remove himself and his two bags to where there was space enough between the backboard and the tarpaulin pile for him to sit down and make himself snug.

It was grand. They bumped and rattled on at a surprising pace, and Mr Oakroyd in triumph watched the Bruddersford warehouses and shops and trams start up, quiver, and then retreat. With great dexterity, he filled and lighted a pipe of Old Salt, which had itself somehow achieved a new and adventurous flavour, and smoked it with a real old saltish air, like a man on the lookout to make the landfall of Cape Cambodia. Through valedictory puffs of smoke, he saw Bruddersford itself slide away, the hills rise up, a vague blackness, the street-lamps of distant and ever-retreating suburbs take on the shape and glitter of constellations. Other towns, Dewsbury, Wakefield, closed round him and then shook themselves off again. It was colder now, and he shivered a little in his thin mackintosh. He was still warmed, however, by a feeling of triumphant escape. He didn't care where they landed in the morning. They were going on and on, and it was grand.

Then there came a great moment. He had been dozing a little but was roused by the lorry slowing down, sounding its horn, then swinging round into a road that was different from any they had been on so far. It was as smooth and straight as a chisel, and passing lights showed him huge double telegraph- posts and a surface that seemed to slip away from them like dark water. Other cars shot past, came with a blare and a hoot and were suddenly gone, but the lorry itself was now travelling faster than he thought any lorry had a right to travel. But at one place they had to slow down a little, and then Mr Oakroyd read the words painted in large black letters on a whitewashed wall. *The Great North Road.* They were actually going down the Great North Road. He could have shouted. He didn't care what happened after this. He could hear himself telling somebody - Lily it ought to be - all about it. 'Middle o' t'night,' he was saying, 'we got on t'Great North Road.' Here was another town, and the road was cutting through it like a knife through cheese. Doncaster, it was. No trams now; everybody gone to bed, except the lucky ones going down South on the Great North Road.

'By gow!' he cried, 'this is a bit o' life, this is. Good old Ted! Good old Oglethorpe! I owe him summat for this.' And he yearned with gratitude towards the thought of Ted and his companion at the wheel, settled himself as snugly as he could, and in spite of his excitement soon began to doze again.

He might have fallen fast asleep had he not been wakened by a very curious incident. There was somebody shouting. The lorry made a grinding noise, seemed to hesitate. 'Hey there!' came the shout. 'Wait a minute, wait a minute.' It was a policeman. The lorry had passed him now, but he came running after it. There was a roar, a fearful rattling, and the lorry rushed on, obviously being pressed to go as hard as it could. The policeman dropped behind, but he was near enough for Mr Oakroyd to see him. He stood still but moved his hand. Above the din of the lorry sounded the policeman's whistle, that horribly urgent shrilling. Again and again it sounded, but now they were rapidly gaining speed and soon left it far behind. Mr Oakroyd, looking and listening still, his face above the rattling backboard, was startled and amazed. The whistle rang in his ears yet, asking questions. What did it mean? What was Ted up to? Why had the policeman tried to stop them? Had they been going too quickly? This was the obvious explanation, but somehow it did not satisfy himself. There was something very queer about this. He was quite awake now.

Having decided to act queerly, the lorry did not return to normal behaviour. It raced along at a monstrous pace, jolting Mr Oakroyd until he was breathless, bruised, and terrified, and several times it seemed in danger of crashing into other cars, only swerving at the last moment and being followed by angry shouts. Mr Oakroyd had begun to wonder whether it would be possible to creep along to the front to yell at Ted, ask him if he had gone crazy, when suddenly the lorry swung round, throwing him against the backboard, and turned down a narrow sidestreet. It went several miles down this road at the same mad pace, and the jolting was now worse than ever. Then it turned again, this time into a road still narrower, a winding lane full of ruts and overhanging branches of trees that seemed to miss them by inches, and now it was compelled to slow down to what seemed in comparison a mere crawl. Mr Oakroyd was able to take breath, look about him into the mysterious night, and think a little. He had hardly collected his thoughts, however, before the lorry, arriving at a tiny open space where this road met another, came to a standstill, much to his relief. It was all right going down the Great North Road in the middle of the night, but this had been a bit too much. He rose, gingerly, to his feet.

'Where's that screwdriver?' he heard from the front. It was the voice of the man who had spoken to him in Tapp Street.

It went on: 'That's right. Better stay 'ere, Nobby, and gimme the office if yer see anybody.' The man was climbing out.

'D'yer think 'e took it?' asked the other.

Mr Oakroyd was astonished. That wasn't Ted's voice. Ted was not on the lorry at all, then.

'Whether 'e 'as or 'e 'asn't, I'm risking nothing,' said the first man. 'There's no going straight through now, and 'owever far we go round, this lorry's got to 'ave another bloody number before we see daylight. 'Ere, Nobby, yer might as well get down. Chuck us them number plates.'

At this point Mr Oakroyd thought that he might as well get down too. He fell rather than climbed out - for he was stiff and shivering with cold - and tottered round to the front, rubbing his hands.

''Ello, 'ello!' cried the first man, staring. 'I'd fergotten all about yer, mate. You've 'ad yer liver and lights shaken up all right, 'aven't yer?'

'I have an' all,' replied Mr Oakroyd grimly. 'But where's Ted?'

'Ted? Ted? Oo the 'ell's Ted?' demanded the other. And then he stepped forward and peered into Mr Oakroyd's face. 'And oo the 'ell are you, anyhow? 'Ere, Nobby, this isn't 'im.'

'Isn't it?' said Nobby, stepping forward too. He was a large man, well muffled up, with a very small hat crammed down on his head. It was his turn now to stare at Mr Oakroyd. 'No begod, it isn't at all. It's a stranger. He's a stranger to me, Fred.'

'And to me. 'Ere, wot's the idea?' he demanded fiercely.

'Ar d'yer mean wot's the idea?' asked Mr Oakroyd valiantly.

'I mean wot's the bloody idea, that's wot I mean,' he repeated with passion.

Mr Oakroyd felt very uncomfortable indeed. 'Well, this is Ted Oglethorpe's lorry, isn't it?'

'No, it isn't Ted anybody's lorry, this isn't. It's our lorry, this is, and I want ter know wot yer doing on it.' This Fred was a hoarse-voiced truculent sort of fellow, one of those who pushed their faces close to yours when they talked, and at every succeeding word he seemed to grow angrier.

Mr Oakroyd might feel uncomfortable, and indeed he could not help feeling a little lost and forlorn, miles from anywhere in the night as he was, in the company of two fellows whom he now suspected to be downright rogues; but he was anything but a coward and he had his own share of pugnacity. 'I come on it because I thought it belonged to a friend o' mine,' he said sturdily. 'And you said nowt to stop me neither when I said I were coming.'

'I took yer for somebody else,' said Fred sullenly.

'And I took you for somebody else,' said Mr Oakroyd. 'So that's that.'

'Well, yer came and yer 'ere and now yer'd better be moving on.' And Fred, turning his back on Mr Oakroyd, began whistling.

'Half a minute, though,' said Nobby, 'we'd better have a bit of a talk about this.' And he beckoned Fred, and the two of them walked away and began whispering. Mr Oakroyd overheard several phrases, of which one - 'knows too much' - was repeated more than once by Nobby.

'If you want to change these numbers,' Mr Oakroyd called out, 'get on wi' it. It's nowt to do wi' me.'

'Not so loud, not so loud,' said Fred, returning with his companion. 'All right, Nobby, I'll get on with it. You can do the patter. Only for God's sake keep it quiet.' He busied himself with the front number plate.

Nobby brought his large mysterious bulk close to Mr Oakroyd, and when he spoke his accents were bland and conciliatory. 'And where might you be making for, Mister?'

'Well, you see, I thowt I'd move down South for a bit,' explained Mr Oakroyd. 'Leicester way p'raps. I've been there afore an' I'm out of a job and so I thowt I'd try a move.'

'Going at a funny time, wasn't you?' pursued Nobby, still blandly but with a certain significant emphasis.

'Ay, I was moving late - like you. But this 'ere friend o' mine had told me he'd be there late, you see, at Merryweather's i' Tapp Street.'

'That's all right, Nobby,' grunted Fred, bending over his task. 'Saw it further down and it got off about ten minutes afore we did.'

'Quite so, quite so,' said Nobby smoothly. Then he lowered his voice. 'The fact of the matter is, Mister - I dare say you thought one or two things about this job was a bit queer like, didn't you? - but the fact of the matter is, me and Fred here hasn't got a licence - driving licence, you know - between us, and so we're having to do a bit of dodging.'

'It's no business o' mine,' replied Mr Oakroyd reflectively, 'but I don't see how changing t'numbers is going to help you if you haven't got a licence. You can be pulled up, just t'same. Still, you know your own business.'

Nobby made a smacking noise with his lips, perhaps to suggest that he was thinking deeply. 'It's no good, Mister,' he said at length, 'I can see it's no good trying to deceive you. You're too smart for that. Well, it's like this.' And now he whispered with a most engaging conspiratorial air. 'A genelman of my acquaintance is a partner in a firm.

Right. He has a bit of a barney with the other two partners, decides to have a split. Right. He takes so much stock, they take so much. But he can't get his, they won't part. It's his but they won't part till they're forced. He comes to me and asks me to get it away for him. Once it's gone, all right, no trouble. It'll save a law job. They can't get at him 'cos it's his stuff, but they could get at us for getting it out of the warehouse. We knew that, me and Fred, when we took it on, but we're sportsmen, we are, and we'll take a bit of a risk obliging a friend, we will.'

'Ay,' said Mr Oakroyd, who did not believe a word of all this. 'So you're keeping it quiet like. And who did you think I was?'

'Well, you see, Mister, there was a feller in the warehouse we'd got to know,' began Nobby hopefully.

'Ay,' said Mr Oakroyd, cutting him short. He had suspected some time that he had travelled with a lorry-load of stolen goods, probably pieces of expensive cloth. The trick had been worked before in Bruddersford, and he knew all about it. At the moment he did not feel any particular loyalty towards the manufacturers of his native town, whose warehouses could all be rifled for all he cared, so that his conscience did not trouble him overmuch, but at the same time it was not easy to feel comfortable in such company and he thought that the sooner he left it the better. Yet when he considered the chill darkness, the lonely place, his own position, any company seemed better than none for the time being.

Fred appeared now. 'If they're looking for WR 7684, they'll be looking a bloody long time,' he announced. 'Now what's on? Is this where 'e gets off or does 'e work 'is passage a bit farther?' And he glanced from Nobby to Mr Oakroyd.

The latter regarded him without enthusiasm. 'T'other's bigger rogue, I'll be bound,' he told himself, 'but he is a bit friendly wi' it. This chap 'ud knock you on t'head wi' a big spanner as soon as look at you.' He thought it wiser to let Nobby answer for him.

'He's all right,' said Nobby. 'We can take him a bit farther. He's a sportsman, he is. Best thing we can do is to lay up a bit. Can't get through to London, now,' he added, lowering his voice and addressing himself to Fred; 'that's finished. We'll have to wire him tomorrow and make the other way.'

'All right, mate,' said Fred. 'I could do with a bit of shut-eye and a drink and a bite of something.'

'So could I,' said Nobby, who seemed to be thinking deeply.

And Mr Oakroyd realized that he could, too. He felt cold and hungry, heavy for lack of sleep.

'Not a bleedin' chance round 'ere,' said Fred disgustedly. 'We're right off the rotten map.'

'Half a minute, half a minute,' cried Nobby. 'Where are we?'

'Somewhere between Rotherham and Nottingham. There's a signpost there. See wot it says. But 'urry up, for God's sake. Let's get moving.'

'Good enough!' cried Nobby, after he had inspected the signpost. 'I've been round here before all right. You can't lose me, chum.'

'Wot's the idea?'

'I'll show you,' said Nobby, with enthusiasm. 'You shut your eyes and open your mouth and see what God sends you. We can lay her up a bit and have our drink and shut-eye all right. Drive on, Fred. I'll show you. Get up at the back, Mister, if you're coming with us.'

'I'm coming all right,' said Mr Oakroyd, who had been shivering for the last ten minutes. He moved off, to climb up again.

'Big Annie. Keeps the Kirkworth Inn,' he heard Nobby say, in reply to some further question from Fred. 'You must have been there, or heard of her. She's all right, Annie is.'

For the next hour and a half they threaded their way slowly and drearily through narrow by-roads, sometimes having to go back for a missed turning. Mr Oakroyd was very sleepy now, but he felt chilled through and as empty as a drum, and so could do nothing but fall into an uneasy doze for a minute or two. All the earlier excitement of the night had left him, and more than once he could not help wishing, in spite of himself, that he was back in his own bed. As the lorry went rattling and jolting into the most cheerless hours of the night, he began to regret, in a numbed fashion, that he had ever set eyes on it.

When they pulled up at last outside the Kirkworth Inn, a lonely house at a cross-roads, with a wide entrance to a yard at one side, the situation did not seem to be much better. The inn stared at them through the gloom with blind eyes. Mr Oakroyd could not see them ever finding their way into it. But he climbed down with the others and stood looking up at its shuttered windows.

'Sure it'll be all right?' asked Fred uneasily. 'We've made a 'ell of a bad break if we tell 'er oo we are and then there's nothing doin'. Got us taped then.'

But Nobby was still confident. 'Leave it to me. She knows me and I know her. It'll be all right.' And he walked boldly up to the door and rapped upon it. Nothing happened, so after waiting a minute or two he rapped again. They heard a window being pushed up, and then a very angry female voice cried: 'Wot is it? Wot yer making that noise for? Wot d'yer want?'

Nobby called up: 'Is that you, Annie? It's me, Nobby Clarke. You remember me?'

'Who is it?' she screeched.

'Nobby Clarke. You remember me. Been here before, pal of Chuffy and Steve and that lot. Remember the Yarmouth do, Annie?'

'Oh, it's you, is it? Well, wot yer want coming at this time for, knocking me up?'

'You slip down and I'll tell you all about it, Annie. Me teeth's chattering here so much I can't talk.'

The head withdrew, grumbling, and after a minute or two the door was opened and Nobby went in.

'Nobby's pullin' it off,' the relieved Fred confided to Mr Oakroyd. 'Soon as I see 'er come down, I knew it was all right. They've only got to listen an' Nobby'll talk 'em into anything. Gor, 'e can talk.' And Fred spat out very noisily to show his appreciation, then lit about half an inch of cigarette.

Nobby came bustling out in triumph. 'All right, chums,' he cried. 'It's a go. We can camp here a bit. Shove the old bus round at the back, Fred, up in the yard. You go round with him, Mister. We'll let you both in there.'

Mr Oakroyd followed the lorry round the yard, took out his little basket trunk and bag of tools, and was then admitted with Fred into a kitchen at the back of the inn. A lamp had already been lit there, and Nobby, now revealed as a tall fattish fellow, with close-cropped hair, a purple expanse of cheek, and a huge loose mouth, was blowing at the hot ashes, now heaped up with fresh wood, with a gigantic pair of bellows. The kitchen was untidy and dirty, and its owner was untidier and dirtier still, an enormous figure of a middle-aged woman mysteriously wrapped about in yards and yards of filthy flannel.

'This is Annie, Mrs Croucher,' said Nobby, putting down the bellows to wave a hand. 'And this is Fred - Fred - '

'Smith,' put in that gentleman, whose appearance was even less reassuring than his talk. His face was long and thin and was all twisted to one side, and he might have been any age between twenty-five and forty-five.

'Fred Smith,' continued Nobby blandly. 'And he's on the job with me, he is. And this other's a chap who's been travelling with us owing to a bit of a mistake.' And he looked questioningly at Mr Oakroyd.

'Oakroyd's my name.'

'Oakroyd's his name, and he's a sportsman else he wouldn't be with us.' And Nobby fell to blowing the fire again and soon had it blazing.

'Well, lads, wot's it yer want?' demanded their hostess. ''Cos if it's steaks and chips and feather beds, you've got a bloody hope.'

'Anything, Annie, anything,' replied Nobby. 'A bit of bread and meat, if you've got it. And a drink. What's it to be, chum? Beer's too cold. I'll tell you what. I'd like a drop o' tea with some rum in it, good old sergeant-major's.'

'That's the stuff, mate,' said Fred.

'It'll do me a treat,' said Mr Oakroyd, who was just beginning to feel warm again but still suffered from a gnawing hollow inside him. He looked hopefully at the formidable Annie.

'Anything to oblige,' said Annie, 'and I'll take a drop wi' yer. 'Ere, Nobby, put this kettle on.' She produced the remains of a cold joint of beef, a loaf of bread and some butter, four half-pint mugs and a bottle of rum. She and Nobby made the tea, Fred hacked away at the joint, and Mr Oakroyd, not to be left out, cut half a dozen thick slices of bread. He was beginning to enjoy himself again. This was a queer lot, to be sure, but it would all make a grand tale to tell. He rubbed his hands as Nobby brought the steaming teapot on to the table, and the landlady, who was not disposed to be incautious even at this hour of the night, measured out a noggin of rum.

All three of them fell with fury upon their sandwiches and washed them down noisily and happily with the tea, which was very strong, very sweet, and well laced with rum. After the landlady had gulped down a hot mixture that was as much liquor as tea, she set her massive flannelled bulk, arms akimbo, before the crackling fire, and watched them with an indulgent, almost maternal eye. 'That's putting some 'eart into yer, I can see,' she observed complacently. 'And wot's the next move, lads?'

'Shut-eye,' announced Fred, from the depths of his enormous sandwich.

'That's right,' said Nobby. 'Just pass the little old brown jug, will you, Mister? This'll stand a bit more rum. Yes, we'll have to kip down for an hour or two, Annie.'

'It'll 'ave to be down 'ere,' said Annie. 'But put a bit o' wood on the fire an' you'll be all right.'

'Leave it to us, Annie. And here's the best.' Nobby raised his mug and emptied it in her honour. 'You've done us proud, you have. We're all right. Leave it to us.'

'Going to,' said Annie. 'Gettin' back to bed now. I'll 'ear 'ow the game's goin' and all the news in the morning. And for God's sake don't show a light in front. And 'ere, I'll take the damages now. It'll be six shillings the lot, which is cheap enough, seein' yer've 'ad a noggin o' rum between yer.'

'Good enough,' said Nobby, fumbling in his pockets.

Then Mr Oakroyd, full of tea and rum and beef and bread, feeling cosy, companionable, and sleepy, did a foolish thing. 'Here,' he cried, 'I'm a chap as likes to stand me corner. I'll pay for this. Six shillin', is it?'

He searched his pockets but could only discover a solitary sixpence. He must have put all the loose money he had with his week's wages on the table at home. But he had four five-pound notes enclosed in an old envelope and tucked away in his breast pocket. 'Half a minute,' he said, and in his anxiety to foot the bill promptly, he was clumsy and brought out all four bank-notes.

'Gor!' cried Fred, bending forward. 'Oo's this we 'ave with us? - Mr bloody Rockiefeller. Been touchin' up a bank, mate?'

Mr Oakroyd looked, to see three pairs of eyes fixed on his bank-notes and, feeling uncomfortable, he hastily put three of them back in the envelope and held out the fourth. 'Can you change this, Missis?'

'No, I can't,' she replied very emphatically. 'An' if I could, I wouldn't. Yer don't land me with one of 'em, oh no! Yer've been doin' well, 'aven't yer?' she added significantly.

'All right, Mister. All right, Annie,' Nobby put in smoothly. 'I'll settle this. Six shillings.'

'Be good then, an' turn that light out as soon as you get down to it.' And Big Annie removed the bottle of rum, locked the door of the bar, and retired. The three men yawned and, on the advice of Nobby, who insisted upon repeating: 'Boots off's half a bed,' they took off their boots. In the survey of the room and discussion that immediately followed, Mr Oakroyd, to his gratified surprise, was awarded the old sofa in the corner.

'You're best off there, Mister,' said Nobby earnestly, 'and you're entitled to it, as a sportsman. Isn't he, Fred?'

''E can 'ave it for me,' muttered Fred, spreading himself across two chairs.

Mr Oakroyd would have liked to have smoked a last and even more adventurous pipe of Old Salt, to have heard tales of Big Annie and Chuffy and the 'Yarmouth do', to have talked about the Great North Road, but he was tired out and now that he was warm and comfortably stretched out on the sofa, with a little glow of rum inside him, he could hardly keep his eyes open. He was aware vaguely that Nobby was bending over the lamp, blowing it out, that now there was only a flicker of firelight; dreamily he felt the lorry jolting him again, caught a ghastly glimpse of the Great North Road; and then fell fast asleep.

II

A strident voice filled the kitchen. Mr Oakroyd grunted, half-opened his eyes and then closed them again. For a few blessed moments there was a silence. Then the voice came again, screeching and cutting like a bad circular saw. This time Mr Oakroyd stirred, shook himself, and opened his eyes as widely as he could. What he saw astonished him. For years he had opened his eyes in the morning to see the front bedroom of 51 Ogden Street, Bruddersford, and now, for a minute or two, he could not make out where he was. It took him some time to recollect in order the events of the previous night, to realize that this was the first morning of his travels and, incidentally, the last Tuesday in September. The soul of him still slumbered and what was awake was yet only the mere creature of habit, so that the feeling of being uprooted and suddenly dropped in some strange place brought him no pleasure. And he was still heavy and bemused from lack of sleep; his head ached a little; his body was stiff and sore. It was not a pleasant waking. Last night he seemed to have fallen asleep in an atmosphere of friendliness, but now everything seemed to be different. He raised himself so that he could look over the neighbouring table, and caught sight of the enormous back of the landlady, who was padding out of the kitchen into the passage, and a dirty-looking girl in her teens was just coming in from the yard.

'Hello!' he said to the girl. He was standing up now, stretching himself.

She stared at him dully. "Ello!' she said. 'Time you woke too.'

'What time is it?' he asked. He did not possess a watch. Bruddersford has an elaborate system of factory buzzers - usually known as 'whews' - that keeps its humbler citizens informed of the time.

"Alf-pass-teight. Missus told me to wake yer.' Mr Oakroyd looked about him "Ere,' he cried, 'where's t'other two?'

'Gone.'

'Gone?' He looked at her, bewildered.

'Missus said so. I never seed 'em. They must ha' gone before I come in.'

He looked out into the yard. No lorry was there. He turned round to find Big Annie herself regarding him with marked disfavour. Grimy, swollen, purple-faced, with little greedy bloodshot eyes, she seemed even more unpleasant and formidable now in daylight than she had done last night.

'That's right,' she cried shrilly, 'they've gone an' long since. Time you went too. I can't do with yer 'ere.'

'All right, all right, Missis,' he replied, trying to smile at her and not succeeding. 'I don't want to be in t'way. But I've no but just now wakened up. Give us a chance. I suppose I can have a bit of a wash like an' summat to eat, a bit o' breakfast?'

'No, that yer can't.' She was quite passionate in her refusal.

'Why, what's up, Missis? I can pay for owt I have.'

'No, yer can't pay for it, not 'ere. I don't want your sort 'ere.'

'Ar d'you mean "my sort"?' he demanded, his pugnacity aroused. 'What's wrong wi' my sort? If you said them sort as brought me here last night, yer friend Nobby an' t'other chap, I'd know what you was talking about. I know that sort, let me tell you - '

''Ere,' she cried in a fury, 'I don't want any bloody argy-bargying. They've gone, and that's all about it. You go now, sharp as yer can. I've told yer I don't want yer 'ere.' She turned and went padding away. At the door, however, she wheeled round. 'An' don't try comin' 'ere again either, 'cos yer won't get in, let me tell yer. Huh. My sort!' She gave him another elephantine snort and then turned her back on him again.

Mr Oakroyd pulled his little brown cap firmly over his head, fastened his mackintosh to the basket trunk again, and took up his bag of tools. 'I'm off then,' he said to the girl. 'I suppose there's other places where I can get a wash and a bite. I don't seem to be what you might call in favour here. What's matter with her?'

'I dunno. Old bitch!' the girl said vindictively.

'Well, you know her better ner I do,' observed Mr Oakroyd. And I must say this going out mucky an' empty's nowt i' my line. Nar where do I get to from here? Where's t'nearest place where I can get a bit of a wash and suchlike, summat to eat?'

The girl came out into the yard with him. 'Yer best way's to yer right, straight on then,' she said. 'Capbridge is first, but that's no good, only a little place. Yer want to foller the road on to Everwell. Yer'll be all right there. There's tea-rooms and all sorts in Everwell.'

'I should think so with a name like that,' said Mr Oakroyd. 'And how far's this Everwell then?'

'Five or six miles. Turn to yer right and straight on then, through Capbridge, and straight on again. Yer can't miss it.'

'Any trams or buses or owt?'

'There's a bus comes past 'ere at two,' she replied.

'Two! I'll 'a' pined to death afore two,' he cried. 'I mun walk, that's all. And tell your missis from me not to kill hersen wi' doin' ower many good works an' kind actions, tell her she owt to look after hersen a bit more, she's wearing hersen away to t'bone.' And still chuckling over these ironical thrusts, he turned away and made for the road on the right, a bag in each hand.

There were signs that the day would be warm later on. Already the heavy autumn sunlight was dispersing the light mists, and though there was still a faint chill in the air and a glitter of dew on branch and stem, Mr Oakroyd stopped shivering after he had gone a dozen yards and very soon found himself quite warm. Not that he felt much better than he had done. His eyes were still weighted with sleeplessness; his unwashed face felt unpleasantly stiff; and he was so empty inside that he discovered that his first pipe of Old Salt would have to be postponed until after breakfast, whenever that would be. He walked for a mile down the narrow twisting road without meeting anybody, then, on hearing a light cart come rattling up behind him, he set down his two bags, which were beginning to make his arms ache, and waited at the side of the road.

'Hey!' he cried, when the cart was almost upon him. 'You going to Everwell, mate?'

'No, I'm not,' said the driver, and passed him without another word or glance.

'That's another o' Big Annie's tribe, I'm thinking, lad,' muttered Mr Oakroyd as he watched the cart disappear round the next corner. He picked up his bags and set off again, not quite so briskly this time.

Another twenty minutes brought him to Capbridge, which consisted of seven ruinous brick cottages, a few hens, two dirty children, a brown mongrel limping about uneasily, and an actual bridge not quite three yards long. It was at this bridge that Mr Oakroyd halted again, to rest his arms and to look about him in disgust. Somehow the sight of the place annoyed him. 'Daft little hole,' he told himself. 'I wouldn't ha' a bit o' food given here, I wouldn't.' There was an ancient signpost near the bridge that said: 'Everwell 4 mls.', and after casting a somewhat melancholy glance at this, he moved on again. 'They don't know a mile when they see one round here.' he concluded angrily. 'I've come three now if I've come a yard, and I'll bet this next fower mile's more like ten.'

He had not covered the first of those miles, however, when luck favoured him at last. He met a cart turning in his direction out of a field and this time he was able to beg a lift, though it took several minutes to explain to the driver, a little old whiskered fellow nearly as deaf as one of his own sacks, exactly what he wanted. And by the time he had made it plain to his companion that he was travelling about, that he wanted a wash and brush-up and some breakfast, Everwell itself was in sight. It was a straggling dingy little place that looked somehow as if it had been dropped there, as if a dozen streets or so from some dreary district in a city had been plucked out and suddenly planted there, and not at all as if it had ever grown.

'Y'oughter go to Poppleby's,' quavered the ancient driver. 'Poppleby's eatin' place. It's rare and good there, it is.'

'Right you are,' roared Mr Oakroyd. 'I'll go there. Where is it?'

'Yes, it's the best there is. I goes every Saturday night and has meat-and-'tater pie, every Saturday. I 'as a pint over at Old Crown, then goes for me meat-and-'tater pie.'

'I said "Where is it?"'

'Ay, cheap enough for them as can afford it,' said the old man. Then, when they turned the next corner, he pointed with his whip. 'Yon's Poppleby's. Yer can get down 'ere.' He pulled up.

Mr Oakroyd descended and collected his luggage. 'That'll do me nicely,' he cried loudly.' And thanks for the lift.'

'Eh?' The old man leaned forward.

'Thanks for the lift.' By this time Mr Oakroyd was hoarse. 'I say, thanks for the lift.'

'O' course you can, any time,' replied the old man mysteriously. He looked at Mr Oakroyd reproachfully. 'I call that a silly question,' he said at length, and he drove away, grumbling.

The notice, in large if faded letters, ran: *Good Pull Up. Poppleby's Dining-Rooms. Cyclists Catered For.* Mr Oakroyd regarded it with satisfaction. In the window were some yellow lace curtains, two bottles of lime juice and soda, four withered oranges on a plate, a slab of boldly checkered brawn, labelled *Poppleby's Best,* some little cakes covered with what had once been bright pink icing, and innumerable generations of flies. Mr Oakroyd did not stop long examining the window, but the sight of it did not lessen his satisfaction. He opened the door and was immediately assailed by the smell of food, which was strong enough to suggest that people had been eating day and night without cessation in that room for the last thirty years. It made Mr Oakroyd's mouth water. For the last hour and a half he had wanted food, and here, it was plainly evident, was food in plenty. So richly steeped was this dining-room of Poppleby's in the atmosphere of cooking and eating - the oilcloth on the tables was covered with crumbs and the stains of recent meals, the very walls and furnishings were greasy with fat, and the air itself was boiled and toasted and fried - that only to walk into it was to be nourished at once. A person who was not very hungry or not very robust might find a mere entrance sufficient to satisfy or blunt the appetite, but such a hungry and robust person as Mr Oakroyd could only walk in to discover that he was even hungrier than he imagined, to wait for Mr Poppleby with a watering mouth.

This is exactly what Mr Oakroyd did. The room was empty and only the flies were stirring. He sat himself down on one of the benches, coughed and tapped his feet, then finally tapped on his table with a pepper-pot.

'Morning.' The man shot up from behind the counter as if he were part of a conjuring trick. It could only be Mr Poppleby himself. All of him that was visible, his large round face, the top of his long apron, his shirt-sleeves and the arms that came out of them, was the same shade - whitish and faintly greasy. Even his eyes were a pale grey, had a jellied look.

'Morning,' said Mr Oakroyd, still staring. 'Er - lemme - see - er - '

'Tea-coffee-cocoa-bacon-and-egg-bacon-and-sausage-kipper-boiled-egg-plate-of-cold-meat-bread-and-butter,' said Mr Poppleby, keeping his prominent eyes fixed on Mr Oakroyd's with never a blink.

Mr Oakroyd gazed at him with admiration, then removed his little brown cap, possibly as a tribute. 'That sounds a bit of all right. I'll ha' a pot o' tea and you can do me two rashers and two eggs. And plenty o' bread, Mister,' he added.

'Pot - of - tea - two - rashers - two - eggs - four - slices - bread.' Mr Poppleby turned away.

''Ere, I say,' cried Mr Oakroyd. 'Can I have a bit of a wash afore I start? Been on t'road most o' t'night - wi' a lorry,' and he added this not without a certain touch of pride.

'Certainly you can 'ave a wash, my friend, certainly,' replied Mr Poppleby with impressive gravity. 'You just come this way and I'll find you a wash. I'm not saying it's usual - it isn't usual - but it's no worse for that, is it? You don't want to sit down to your food all dirty, an' I don't want to see you sitting down to it all dirty, and we're two feller men, aren't we? That's right, isn't it? Well, you come this way then.' And off he went, with Mr Oakroyd in attendance. They arrived at a tiny scullery, and Mr Poppleby waved a hand to indicate the presence of a little enamel bowl, a large bar of yellow soap, and a towel that had seen long and desperate service. ''Ere you are, my friend,' he continued. 'You can wash 'ere to your 'eart's content. And while you're 'aving your wash, we'll be dishing up your bacon and your eggs. That's fair dealing between man and man, isn't it? Give a man what he asks for - in reason, y'know, for there's reason in everything - but anyhow, *try* to give a man what 'e asks for - that's my motto.' And thus concluding a trifle unctuously, Mr Poppleby withdrew.

'Who does he think he is - Lloyd George?' muttered Mr Oakroyd as he took off his coat. He saw that the envelope was still safely stowed away in the breast pocket. 'To hear him talk, you'd think he was offering me a steam bath wi' shampoos an' finger-nail cutting to foiler.' Nevertheless, when he had spluttered over the enamel bowl and had rubbed himself hard with the only corner of the towel that was not slippery, he felt twice the man he had been, and when he returned to the dining-room, passing on his way through a zone newly enriched by the smell of frying bacon, he gazed benevolently at the impressive figure of Mr Poppleby, who was engaged in depositing a pot of tea beside a plate of bread, a cup and saucer, a long pointed knife, and a two-pronged fork.

'Your bacon and your eggs'll be ready in one minute,' said Mr Poppleby, returning to his counter.

'Good enough,' cried Mr Oakroyd, rubbing his hands. 'I'm fair pining, I can tell you.'

'We'll soon put that right.' And no consulting surgeon could have said this more impressively. 'So you've been on the road, eh?'

'I have an' all,' said Mr Oakroyd. 'Come down t'Great North Road last night.' But, somewhat to his surprise, this did not appear to impress his host.

'Well, what I say is this,' Mr Poppleby began even more weightily than before. 'It's all right if you take it all in the right way. What I mean is, if it makes you more yuman, it's all right. If it doesn't it's all wrong. If I've said it once to customers 'ere, I've said it a thousand times, just standing 'ere like I am now, talking to somebody like yourself. "Does it", I said, "make you more yuman? 'Cos if it doesn't, keep it." I take a broad view, and when I say yuman, I mean yuman. I believe - ' and here he fixed his prominent eyes unwinkingly upon Mr Oakroyd - 'in yumanity.'

'That's right, Mister,' replied Mr Oakroyd heartily but with a certain philosophical sternness. 'I see your point and I'm with yer.' He would have been better pleased, however, he admitted to himself, to have seen the bacon and eggs. A knocking from some place behind suggested that they were now ready.

'What I say is, ask yourself all the time "Is it yuman?" If it isn't, don't touch it. Let it alone. Pass it by. That's my motto - yumanity first - and that's the rule 'ere, as you saw right off when you asked for a wash. Take the yuman line, I say, and it'll pay you every time.' He now condescended to hear the knocking, and brought out the bacon and eggs. 'There you are, my friend,' he said, and he said it in such a manner that it was impossible to believe that he had merely carried the dish a few yards. He seemed not only to have done the cooking but to have gathered the eggs from distant roosts, to have cured the bacon himself, to have made the very crockery.

Mr Oakroyd, after telling himself that he wished the cooking had been done by someone a little less human (for the eggs were fried hard), ate away with the utmost heartiness and dispatch. Every mouthful seemed to be taken in under the auspices of Mr Poppleby, who leaned over the counter and never took his eyes off his solitary customer. By the time he had arrived at his third slice of bread, Mr Oakroyd was ready to open the conversation again. He felt friendly, expansive.

'What allus beats me', he announced, 'is this here "Cyclists Catered For". What's difference between cyclists and t'other folk as comes?'

"Am chiefly,' replied Mr Poppleby thoughtfully. 'Cyclists is great on 'am. I've seen the day when one of these cycling clubs would run me right out of 'am by six o'clock Saturday. Mind you, I'm not talking about last week, nor the week before, nor last year, nor the year before that, I'm talking about before the War. Properly speaking, there's no cyclists now, not to call cyclists. You might get one now and again, coming on a bike, but there's no real cycling, couples off together, and clubs, and suchlike. That's gone, that'll never come back. When I started 'ere, it was all traps and carts and whatnot on week-day, and then cyclists - with a few regular locals coming in, of course - at week-ends. Now, it's all cars and lorries. And what 'appens? They don't stop at a place like this but goes on to big towns and stops there. That's what's hit this business so 'ard, my friend. It isn't what it was, I can tell you.'

'Nowt's what it wor,' said Mr Oakroyd with a kind of cheerful melancholy. 'I've seen some changes i' my time. You take textile trade nar - '

But Mr Poppleby was not taking it. 'That is so. And what's it amount to, what's the real difference between them times and these? That's the question I always ask.'

'And you're quite right, mate, to ask it,' Mr Oakroyd put in warmly.

'And what's the answer? What's the answer?' And Mr Poppleby hurried on so that he could supply it himself. 'It's less yuman, that's the difference.' And he paused, triumphantly, gazing at Mr Oakroyd, who was busy lighting the pipe for which he had long been waiting. Secure on a foundation of bacon and eggs, Old Salt was again delicious. Mr Oakroyd slowly sent a few of its kindly blue clouds rolling through the air, and waited for Mr Poppleby to continue.

'I've no need to tell a man like you what I mean by "yuman",' Mr Poppleby went on. 'I mean there's less of the good old man-to-man spirit. It's take what you can get and run, nowadays. Money and grab and rush, that's what it is. When you're running a business like this, you see life, you know what's 'appening in the world, you talk to all sorts. Of course there's some men in the catering that's as ignorant as you like - and why? - 'cos they don't make use of the hopportunities of the business; they see a customer come in, gets 'is order, serves it, takes the money, and finish. I like to live and learn. I talk to my customers and they talk to me, and that's 'ow I go on. I'm learning from you.'

'Ay,' said Mr Oakroyd, who could not help wondering, however, what it was that the other was learning from him. 'He doesn't gi' me a chance to tell him nowt,' he told himself, and, feeling that he had had enough of Mr Poppleby's conversation, he said: 'Well, what's t'damage?'

'Lemme see,' replied Mr Poppleby. 'Pot-of-tea-two-rashers-two-eggs-four-slices-bread. That'll be one and eight. And a fair price if you ask me.'

'Ay, I dare say,' said Mr Oakroyd, who thought it stiffish. He felt in his pockets and once again produced the solitary sixpence. 'I shall ha' to ask you to do a bit o' changing for me,' he remarked, producing the envelope from his breast pocket.

'We'll try to manage that.' Mr Poppleby made a noise that faintly suggested he was laughing. 'You want the change and I want you to 'ave it, and we're both satisfied and nobody's the worse. That's the yuman line, isn't it?'

But Mr Oakroyd was staring in front of him open-mouthed. The envelope was not empty, but all that it contained was a dirty half-sheet of paper on which was scrawled 'Wishing you a Merry Xmas & a Happy New Year. XXX'. All four bank-notes had disappeared. He ran through all his pockets, hoping against hope that somebody had merely played a trick upon him. But no, they had gone. He had been robbed. And now he understood why he had been given the sofa to sleep on last night, why Nobby and Fred had departed so early, why the landlady had hustled him out of the place before he had time to think.

''Ere,' he cried, 'I've been robbed. Look at this. I'd twenty pound i' there last night, fower five-pound notes, and sitha, there's nowt there but a bit o' paper. I've been robbed and I know who did it.' But when he looked at Mr Poppleby, he saw that that gentleman was regarding him coldly, with raised eyebrows.

'It'll be one and eight,' repeated Mr Poppleby.

This made Mr Oakroyd very angry. 'I tell you I've been robbed o' twenty pound. I haven't one and eight. I've got sixpence, and there it is, and that's all I have got. And I know who did it and where it happened too. It were two fellers wi' a lorry at t'Kirkworth Inn last night.'

'Are you trying to tell me you lost twenty pound, four five-pound notes, at the Kirkworth Inn last night?' demanded Mr Poppleby. 'Because if you are, I'm going to ask you what you was doing with so many five-pound notes and at such a place. It sounds fishy to me. But that's no business of mine; you go your way and I'll go mine - though the sooner you get back to where you come from, the better, I think, my friend; but in the meantime you owe me one shilling and eightpence, whichever way you look at it. And that's what I want from you - one and eight.'

'And that's what you can't get from me, Mister,' cried Mr Oakroyd, exasperated. 'Aren't I telling you that I've nobbut sixpence in t'world? 'Ere, look 'ere.' And rising to his feet, he turned out his trousers pockets. 'Twenty pounds I've lost, all I'd got but this here sixpence. Eh, but I was a gert blunder-heead!'

'You're not the first that's tried it on.' said Mr Poppleby, steadily.

'Ar d'you mean?' cried Mr Oakroyd. 'I'm not trying anything on. When I come in here, I thought I'd twenty pound i' my pocket. I didn't know I'd been robbed.'

'And I didn't know, neither,' observed the other, eyeing him suspiciously. 'This has happened before 'ere, I'll tell you. And I go on trusting people. You come in 'ere and you 'ave my eggs and my bacon and my tea - '

'Ay, and your bread and your lump o' washing soap and your mucky towel and your drop o' water,' Mr Oakroyd added with great bitterness. 'Go on, go on. You've lost one and eight and I've lost twenty pound, and it's bad luck for both on us, but it's a dam' sight war for me. 'Ere, there's sixpence, and that knocks it down to one and two. Well, I'll settle wi' thee, lad.' And Mr Oakroyd, in a frenzy of irritation, rushed to his bag of tools and took out a chisel. 'You see that chisel? It's worth more ner any one and two, is that, and you can ha' that for your one and two. And when I can pay your fowerteen pence, I will, for I'd rather ha' that chisel than all t'shop you've got. Ay, even if you cleaned it up,' he added vindictively.

Mr Poppleby came forward, picked up the sixpence, and examined the chisel. 'A chisel's no good to me,' he said slowly, 'but I suppose I'd better let you go. I like to take a yuman line - '

'Yuman line! T-t-t-t. Yuman nothing!' Mr Oakroyd was very scornful as he gathered his things together.

'That'll do, that'll do,' Mr Poppleby's philosophical vanity was hurt now. 'But let me tell you, my friend, you can't do these sort o' things 'ere. Don't try it again. I tell you, you can't do it.'

'And let me tell you summat, Mister,' said Mr Oakroyd, moving to the door. 'There's summat you can't do, neither.'

'Ho, indeed! And what's that?'

'You can't fry eggs.' And Mr Oakroyd, chuckling, closed the door behind him.

Down the sunny length of Everwell he wandered, a man desperately situated. He had not a penny, was far from home and, indeed, not certain where he was, had no work at a time when work was scarce, and had not even an insurance card. Yet before he reached the southern end of the town he was chuckling again.

'I had him nicely about them eggs.' And he lifted to the sun a face still wrinkled and brightened by the pleasures of repartee.

III

It was late in the afternoon when Mr Oakroyd saw the curious motor-van. Since leaving Poppleby's Dining-Rooms, he had struggled down some eight or nine miles of dusty road, forever changing his basket trunk from the right hand to the left and his bag of tools from the left hand to the right, he had had a bite of bread and cheese and a mouthful of beer from a friendly lorry-driver, who had not, however, believed a word that Mr Oakroyd had told him, and he had slept for two hours under a hedge. Now he was moving on again, very slowly because, for one thing, he was tired and rather dazed after his nap, and, for another thing, he did not know where he was going and was wondering what to do. The motor-van caught his eye at once. It was drawn up under some trees just off the road, and was a most unusual vehicle, something between a rather long delivery van and a caravan proper. A little window had been let into the side, but it had no chimney nor any of the shining contrivances of the real caravan. Paint and polish it had none; the car itself seemed old and rusty; and the wagon or caravan part of it had a woefully weatherbeaten look. After noticing all these details with a craftsman's eye, Mr Oakroyd might have passed on had he not heard, from the back of the van, the sound of sawing, a sound that made him prick up his ears at once. And it took him not more than a minute to arrive at a certain conclusion.

'Yond chap can't handle a saw,' he announced to himself, and walked across to investigate, emboldened by his plight and the knowledge that he, Jess Oakroyd, could handle a saw. Once at the back of the van, he dropped his bags, lit his pipe, stuck his hands in his pockets, and thus fell easily into his role of spectator.

The man with the saw looked up as Mr Oakroyd approached and then dubiously set to work again. He was a thick-set fellow in his early forties, with black hair cropped close, eyes almost as black as his hair, and a broad clean-shaven face as red as the scarf he wore in place of collar and tie. Though he was in his shirt-sleeves and his brown check suit was shabby, he looked far more dashing and dressy than Mr Oakroyd or any of Mr Oakroyd's friends. Nevertheless, his appearance did not clash at all with that of the van. There was about him an air of vagabondage that Mr Oakroyd recognized at once, though he could not have put a name to it. Without obviously being anything definite himself, the man yet called to mind strolling actors and soldiers and sparring partners and racing touts and cheap auctioneers.

He looked up again after Mr Oakroyd had been standing there a minute or two. 'Nice day, George,' he remarked with a wink.

'Ay,' said Mr Oakroyd; and then, not to be outdone in this matter of handing out names, he added, dryly: 'Nice enough, Herbert.'

"Ere,' said the man, straightening himself, 'now I ask you. Do I look like Herbert?'

'Nay, I don't know.' Mr Oakroyd paused a moment. 'But I'll tell you what you *don't* look like, if you ask me.'

'Go on, George. I'll buy it.'

'You don't look like a chap as knows how to use a saw,' replied Mr Oakroyd, softening the severity of this criticism with a companionable grin.

'Oh! Now we're 'earing something, aren't we?' He dove into his waistcoat pocket, fished out a packet of Woodbines and a box of matches, and lit up. 'Do you know all about saws, George?' he inquired amiably.

Mr Oakroyd's reply to this was to fetch his bag of tools and dump it down at the other's feet. 'You tell me what you're trying to do, mate,' he said earnestly, 'and I'll soon show you what I know about saws.'

''Ello, 'ello!' the man cried in mock astonishment. 'What's the ruddy idea? You a tradesman, George?'

'I am an' all,' replied Mr Oakroyd, not without pride. 'I'm a joiner and carpenter by trade.'

'Well, I'll tell you something now. My turn, see. You don't come from round 'ere. You come from Leeds.'

'Nay, I don't. I come from Bruddersford.' And this seemed to Mr Oakroyd a different thing altogether from coming from Leeds, and so he was triumphant.

'Near enough,' said the other complacently. 'Knew you came from that way. Tell it in a minute. Bruddersford, eh? Know Lane End Fair?'

'Tide, you mean.'

'That's right. Lane End Tide. All "tides" round there, aren't they? Don't call 'em fairs.'

'Course I know it,' said Mr Oakroyd.

'So do I,' exclaimed the man in triumph. 'Been there many a time. I gave it a miss this year but was there last year. What are you doing round 'ere? Looking for a job?'

'Ay, I'm looking for a job, nar,' said Mr Oakroyd bitterly. 'I'll ha' to get one right sharp, too. I've been landed properly, I have.' And next minute he was telling the story of his lost twenty pounds. It was the third time he had told it that day, but it was the first time he had found a listener who believed him.

'Where did you get the fivers from?' asked the other, at the end of the story. 'Back a winner?'

'Nay, I never put owt on horses. But another chap had backed a lot o' winners seemingly.' And encouraged by the reception of his previous recital, he now told the story of the drunken sportsman and his bulging pocket-book, to all of which his companion, now sitting on the steps of his van, listened with a quick and humorous sympathy.

'Easy come, easy go, that,' he observed. Then he reflected. 'What did you say the name of that feller was, the one with the lorry? Nobby Clarke? I've known a few Nobby Clarkes in my time. One or two'ud have taken the milk out of your tea. Was he a little feller with a turned-up nose, Cockney twang, bit of a boxing man, lightweight?'

'Nay, this chap was a big fat feller wi' a big round bilberry face on him the size o' two,' said Mr Oakroyd. 'A smoothtalking chap, he wore, though I thought he were a bit of a rogue as soon as I clapped eyes on him.'

'I believe I know that feller. Nobby Clarke. Nobby Clarke? A feller like that used to go round with *Mason's Magic and Mysteries*, and 'e might have called 'imself Nobby Clarke. I shall remember 'im. If I saw 'im myself I should know in a minute. Never forget a dial. I meet a feller and say "'Ello, saw you at so-and-so five years ago, six years, seven years, ten years ago," whatever it is; and 'e says "That's right. I was there. Don't remember you"; and I says "No, but I remember you." I'm right every time. Marvellous, isn't it?'

'And so you're one o' these as goes wi' t'tides - fairs - like?'

'That's me! My name's Jackson. What's yours?'

'Oakroyd. Jess Oakroyd.'

'Oakroyd. Good enough! Well, mine's Jackson - Joby they call me - Joby Jackson. Everybody in this line o' business knows me. Been in it twenty years, and been in it longer only I started in the old militia and then joined up again in the War. Done everything - you ask anybody - Joby Jackson. Boxing shows, circus, try-your-luck games, everything. I've run shows of me own - Human Spider and Wild Man o' the Amazon. You can't name a place where they 'ave a fair or a race-meeting I 'aven't been to, you can't do it. I know 'em all. England, Scotland, Wales, Ireland, Isle o' Man, Isle o' Wight, you can't lose me. Marvellous!' He jerked a thumb over his shoulder at the van. 'On a steady line now. I'm selling 'em something. Got ter do it - isn't enough money about for the old games - you've got to sell 'em something now. Rubber toys is my line, rubber dolls, rubber animals - you blow 'em up' - and here he blew away, for he was a man who illustrated his talk with innumerable rapid and vivid gestures - 'and there y'are. Seen 'em? Good line - plenty o' profit - easy to carry - all flat, you see, light as a feather. Get a good day and they sell like beer in barracks. Some days you can't sell anything - you wouldn't get buyers if you were offering bottles o' Scotch at ninepence a time. But get a good day - ' and after a little overture of winking, he unloaded in rapid dumb show a host of invisible rubber dolls and animals upon an invisible multitude - 'marvellous. Only thing is, too much competition! They're all tumbling to it, all coming in now.

When a few more gets in, I shall get out, see? I'll try something else, sell 'em something new. That's the idear, isn't it, George?'

'And you go round i' this?' Mr Oakroyd looked at the van.

'That's it,' replied Joby, with enthusiasm. 'Take a dekko at 'er. Not exactly a ruddy Rolls-Royce, but she moves, George, she moves. You can't get more than twenty miles an hour out of 'er, 'cept down steep 'ills, but that's enough, what d'you say? Got 'er for fifteen quid - a gift; then 'ad a winder put in, then a bunk, then a couple o' bunks. If I don't want to sleep anywhere else, I sleep in there, see? I'm sleeping in there tonight. Got a little stove in there, carry all my stock in it, stall and all. 'Ere, I was trying to patch up the old stall when you come 'ere. It got a nasty knock yesterday. Like to see what you could do with it? I'm no good with my 'ands. Funny thing isn't it? I can sell anything, do the patter, but can't use my 'ands; must 'ave been born a ruddy gentleman. Like to 'ave a do at the old stall, George? I'll see you're all right.'

'Leave it to me, mate,' cried Mr Oakroyd, delighted. 'Let's have a look at t'rest of it. Got any nuts and bolts and three-inch nails?' Together they pulled out from the floor of the van the remaining pieces of woodwork, and Joby discovered that he had some spare nuts and bolts and plenty of long nails. 'Nar then,' said Mr Oakroyd, 'you tell me what you want and I'll set you up i' no time.' And in another minute he had his bag of tools open and his coat off and was happily at work.

''Ow about a drop o' Rosie Lee?' said Mr Joby Jackson. He was very fond of this queer rhyming slang, most of which must be omitted from any record of his talk because it is incomprehensible to ordinary people. Even Mr Oakroyd, who was acquainted with this kind of slang, though he rarely used it himself and, indeed, associated it with rather disreputable characters, was sometimes puzzled. But he was not bewildered, of course, by any mention of the famous Rosie, and he was more than ready for a drink of tea. So Joby strolled away to fill the kettle, returned with it to busy himself in the van, and then came out again to sit on the steps and watch Mr Oakroyd at work.

'Fond o' tarts, George?' he inquired.

'Nay, I've had all t'tarts I want,' Mr Oakroyd grunted in reply, still bending over his saw. He quite understood that the question did not refer to things to eat.

'Tarts or booze - or both,' said Joby reflectively, 'that's where the bother begins. You wouldn't be 'aving to mend that stall now if it 'adn't been for a tart. I've 'ad a pal with me lately - Tommy Muss they call 'im. Silly name, isn't it? Clever little feller, though, Tommy. I've known 'im years. 'E used to go round with Oxley's Circus, one time, then 'e ran a little ball-on-a-string game - one o' them where you gets a watch, that is if you're lucky and the, feller that's running the game don't 'appen to lean on the board when you're 'aving your go, see - but 'e wasn't good at it, wasn't Tommy. So 'e come round with me. You can manage by yourself at this, but it's better with two. Booze isn't Tommy's trouble, though he can shift it as well as the next. It's tarts. Can't keep away from the women, and they can't keep away from 'im. Good-lookin' little feller, Tommy, an' got a bit o' ruddy swank, yer know - and they like it, George, they like it. And 'e's the best mouth-organ player you ever 'eard in all your natural, easy the best - never 'eard anybody to touch Tommy with a mouth-organ - play anything - marvellous! There was a piece about 'im once in *The World's Fair*. 'E oughter 'ave gone on the stage as a mouth-organ turn. I've told 'im so many a time. 'E's a mug. ''E could 'ave been getting twenty quid a week. 'E wouldn't bother, though, too busy square-pushing, taking the girls out, see. Well, anyhow, there's a tart 'e's 'ad 'is eye on some time - black flashing sort o' bit she is - and 'er and another woman runs one of these palmistry Gipsy Queen stunts, see. We kept coming across 'em working the same fairs - and I saw Tommy was working 'is points. 'Alf a minute, we'll 'ave the Rosie now, George.'

Joby mashed the tea in a mess-tin, stirred some sweet condensed milk into it, then poured his companion's share of the rich brew into a large thick cup, across which was written Moseley's Coffee Taverns Ltd, and retained the mess-tin for his own use. He also brought out of the van a biscuit tin containing two-thirds of a loaf of bread and some butter.

''Ow's this, George?'

'Grand!' replied Mr Oakroyd, munching away. He looked about him and would have sighed with pleasure if he had not been so busy eating. Everything was still and the sky was a fine blaze of gold. The tea was exactly the strong and sweet mixture he preferred, and not for years had he enjoyed a slice or two of bread and butter as much as he was doing now. 'I'll make a right job o' this stall,' he told himself, turning a grateful glance upon his host. And after a few puffs of Old Salt, he announced: 'I'll get on wi' t'job nar,' and returned happily to work.

'You were saying summat about yer pal and this here Gipsy Queen lass,' he said, when Joby had cleared away the things and was sitting down again on the steps.

'Lemme see,' reflected Joby. 'Oh yes - about that bit o' bother we 'ad yesterday. Well, you see, yesterday we're at a little place called Brodley, thirty or forty mile away, where there's a bit of a fair. This tart's there and Tommy's squarepushing 'er as 'ard as 'e can go, see. 'E's the sheek of Araby there all right. But this tart 'ad been going round with a feller called Jim Summers. This feller's tried all sorts and just now 'e's running one o' these try-your-strength things - yer know what I mean

- down with the 'ammer and up she goes and rings the bell - no good now, played out. 'E's a big feller - fourteen stone easy - and used to be a bit of a fighting-man - a slogger, you know, trained on booze. Well, this tart 'ad been going round with this feller, Jim Summers, and then she'd given 'im the go-by, see. You know what they are, and I expect 'e'd taken too many loads on and knocked 'er about a bit. But if 'e couldn't 'ave 'er, nobody else would, neither - that was 'is line, and 'e's a big feller, gilled arf the time and with a nasty temper. Tommy gets away with it and with this tart yesterday properly, and Jim Summers is on the same ground and 'ears about it, comes lookin' for 'em. This tart and the other Gipsy Queen - a fattish woman, comes from Burnley - 'ad packed up 'cos there wasn't much doin' anyhow. Tommy comes round the back of the stall. "'Ere," 'e says, "I'm off with this tart for a day or two, and I'm off now. I don't want any bother with a mad-drunk 'eavyweight like Summers. Join yer later on, Joby" 'e say. "Right you are, Tommy," I says. I knew 'e knew what the programme was, see. Nottingham Goose Fair starts a week this Thursday. Ever been? Marvellous! It's one of my best pitches, and I'm getting a fresh lot of stock in for it, pickin' it up at Nottingham before the fair starts. So I'm just working a lot of little places, filling time in, like, not too far away. We 'ad it all worked out - me and Tommy, always do, yer know - so that 'e knew the programme, and I knew 'e'd join me soon as 'e could, might be tomorrow, might be next week. This tart might be working the same places, and if she wasn't, 'e'd see 'er at the Goose Fair. So off 'e went, and where they went to I don't know, so I can't tell you. It didn't bother me. I didn't want to foller 'em in their Abode of Love. But I knew what was coming to me - Jim Summers. Up he comes, just after Tommy'd gone. 'E'd been in the boozer at dinner-time and 'e was nasty, very nasty." 'Ere," 'e says, giving the old stall a bang or two, "where's that um-pum-pum-bloody-um-pum-pum little pal o' yours?" 'Strewth, you ought to 'ave 'eard 'im. Top of 'is voice, too. "Don't ask me," I says - and I don't mind telling you, George, I was wishing I was a long way off, though I can use 'em a bit. "You know," 'e says, "and you're going to bloody well tell me or this something-something stall o' yours goes up in the air." And 'e begins kicking about a bit, see. "'Ere," I says, "you leave that alone." But 'ow's the repairs going, George?' He stood up and began to inspect the other's handiwork.

'You tak' hold o' that end,' said Mr Oakroyd, now in command. 'We'd better fix her up and see how she stands. Steady, mate, steady! Nar then, drop it in.'

They spent the next half-hour rigging up the stall, Mr Oakroyd making certain improvements at the owner's suggestion. When no more could be done - Joby declaring that it was now better than ever - they took it down and packed it away in the van, well content.

'I passed a boozer about two miles down this road,' said Joby. 'What about 'aving a can or two?'

This brought Mr Oakroyd out of his pleasant dream of craftsmanship, and he was troubled. 'I could do wi' one,' he said dubiously, 'but I have nowt. I'd better be thinking what to do wi' mysen.'

'That's all right, George. You're with me, see. 'Ere, you're not doing anything, are yer? Well, you stay with me till Tommy comes rolling 'ome again - might be a day, might be two days, might be a week. You'll 'ave somewhere to sleep, your grub, and I'll see you've something to be going on with when 'e does come back. I'm going to a little place called Ribsden tomorrer - got a weekly market and there's a bit of a fair on - and you can give me a 'and, see? What say?'

'You're not doing this because I have nowt, are yer?' demanded Mr Oakroyd severely, his independence up in arms. 'I don't want - what's it? - charity, you know.'

'Charity nothing!' cried Joby. 'Oo d'yer think I am? Lord Lonsdale? I want yer to give me a 'and, see. Besides, you've done me one good turn already. Can't I do you one?'

'You can an' all,' said Mr Oakroyd. 'I'll be right glad to stop till your mate comes back.'

'Put it there if it weighs a ton,' cried Joby. And they shook hands. 'Is everything in? 'Ere, shove your tools in the van. And put that in as well. Is that yer luggage? Looks like four days at Sunny Southport, that does. 'Strewth, I 'aven't seen one o' them things for years. Get in. We'll run 'er down to the boozer - too far to walk. Now then, Liz, let's give a turn to the old 'andle. She's startin', she's startin'. No, she's not. Now then, Liz, what about it? There she goes. J'ever 'ear such an engine? Sounds like one o' them electric planners startin'. She 'asn't 'ad any oil in 'er since I left Doncaster. Now then, 'old tight, George, we're off.'

'What happened wi' this chap you were talking about, this chap Summers?' shouted Mr Oakroyd as they went rattling down the road.

'A bobby come round just when the bother began,' replied Joby. 'And Summers slung 'is 'ook. I packed up just after that and come down 'ere. Where 'e went to I don't know. I'm wondering what 'is programme is. Sure to see 'im at Nottingham, but 'e'll 'ave got over it by then.'

'Ay, let's hope so,' said Mr Oakroyd, who found that he too kept wondering what the movements of this Summers might be. He could only hope that this chap had never heard of the place they were going to tomorrow, Ribsden. He had never heard of it himself before. After a little while he remarked casually: 'I suppose you chaps is allus coming across each other, aren't you?'

'You bet yer life!' replied Joby heartily. 'Can't go anywhere without seeing some o' the boys. Same old crowd, same old round, year after year. Marvellous!'

'Ay, I suppose so,' said Mr Oakroyd thoughtfully, and began to think about other things.

They had two pints each at the little public-house, and Joby was the success of the evening there. In less than ten minutes the taproom was his kingdom. His talk became more and more staccato and yet more dramatic; he showered winks and nudges upon his companions; he showed them how Bermondsey Jack went down to a foul from the nigger, how Dixie Jones got in with his left, how his old friend, Joe Clapham - 'best welter-weight we ever 'ad - but a mug, see - fight anybody - do it for nothing' - had two years of glory, laying 'em all out, going through the lot 'like a dose o' salts'; he took them through fairs and boxing-booths and race-meetings and pubs from Penzance to Aberdeen, and told them about three-card men and quack doctors and bookies and 'tecs; and the later it grew the more often his 'Marvellous!' rang through the admiring tap-room. Even the landlord was impressed and insisted upon standing him a farewell pint. As for Mr Oakroyd, he wandered through an enchanted country. Being a respectable Bruddersford working-man, he had no desire to be one of these people or to pass his life in their world. But to hear about them and it, perhaps to meet some of these people, to dive into this fascinating world, this was enchantment. He drank his beer, pulled away at his Old Salt, and sat there, never missing a word or a gesture, dazed and happy. And when they drove back to the convenient harbourage at the side of the road, the talk still went on, and by the time they were settling down in the van, taking off their boots and coats and then stretching out on the bunks and rolling in a blanket each, they had arrived at football and a common enthusiasm, so that it was very late indeed before Mr Oakroyd said 't'United' for the last time and Joby Jackson had no more full-backs and centre-forwards to bring out for his inspection. A grand night.

They were silent. The queer little noises of the night crept into the dark van. Mr Oakroyd listened to the strange rustling and scratching for several minutes, and was then startled by a sudden melancholy screech. 'Eh, that's a funny noise, isn't it? It gives you the creeps.'

'Owl,' explained Joby. 'I don't mind it - used to it. Tell you what I can't stand. Trams. 'Orrible sound at night, trams. If I'm in a place where there's trams, I never go to bed till they've stopped. Can't get to sleep for 'em - gives me the 'eart-ache or the stomach-ache. Ah, well,' he added drowsily, 'not a bad life this, not while yer can stand up and chew your grub. Keep going and see a bit o' life, I say, we'll all be dead soon enough. What say, George?'

'There's summat i' that,' replied Mr Oakroyd, with true Bruddersfordian caution. But in truth he was really still a little dazed by the wonder of it all. 'I maun tell our Lily about this chap,' he reflected. 'She'll be right amused.' And there was a moment, in the shadows of sleep, when he caught her smiling at him across the wastes.

<h1 style="text-align:center">IV</h1>

The next morning they were up and away very early. 'Take us an hour to get there,' Joby explained. 'And I want a good pitch.' They made a quick breakfast, tea and bread and boiled ham, and were bumping down the road before the sun had struggled through the clouds.

'Bit colder than it wor,' said Mr Oakroyd.

Joby gave the morning an expert glance. 'Weather's breaking. Won't be so warm today, you'll see. Might rain. If it doesn't today, it will tomorrer. Rain's no good to us. A couple o' weeks of it and yer see me going to the nearest three brass balls, selling the little 'ome up. Talk about sailors! We're the blokes that 'ave to watch the weather.'

Ribsden, a squat little town not unlike Everwell, but rather larger, was already in a bustle when they arrived. The combined fair and market filled the square and was creeping up several streets leading to it. Joby secured a pitch that pleased him, however, for it was just at the junction of the main street and the square and - as he pointed out at once - 'dead opposite a boozer' - The Helping Hand. They were not able to keep the van with them, but had to take out everything they wanted, stall and stock, and then park it up a side-street in a line of other cars and carts and caravans. Together they set up the stall and began decorating it with rubber dolls and animals, most of which had to be inflated. From time to time, Joby would give a shout, recognizing some acquaintance, but everybody was too busy to talk, except the onlookers, the local crowd, which was made up of little boys who were so interested that they got in the way and had to be cursed out of it again, little girls who jumped up and down on the pavement in an ecstasy of anticipation, a policeman with a ginger moustache who apparently did not like markets and fairs, and a policeman without a moustache who apparently did like them. Mr Oakroyd enjoyed every minute of it. He enjoyed the bustle and hammering and shouting, the setting up and decoration of the stall, upon which he now turned a proud parental eye, the autumn snap in the air and the first gleams of sunlight, the now thoroughly adventurous flavour of Old Salt, and the companionship of the knowing and voluble Joby. He did not see himself as a salesman of rubber dolls, though he soon became expert in blowing them up and setting them out; but taking it all in all, it was - as he admitted to himself more than once - 'a champion do'.

Joby completed his preparations for the day by tacking a number of little placards to the posts of the stall: 'Don't forget the Little Ones,' they screamed at the passer-by. 'Shops Can't Compete'; 'We lead. Others follow'; 'British Workmanship Can't Be Beat' - which was probably true enough and worth saying, even though all Mr Jackson's stock seemed to come out of boxes bearing foreign labels. To crown all, in the centre of the cross-bar at the top was a larger placard, glorious in scarlet, announcing that 'Joby Jackson is Here Again. The Old Firm'. Having done this and surveyed his handiwork with great satisfaction, Joby had leisure to turn his attention to his neighbours.

One of them had just arrived to claim a little space on the left, dumping into it an easel and a box. He was a tall seedy man dressed in a frock coat that shone in the sun and looked greenish in the shade. He wore no hat, and had a grey mop of hair at the back of his head but none at all in front. His eyebrows were so large and so black that they did away with the necessity of closely shaving the face below them, a fact of which their owner had recently taken a generous advantage.

'Morning, Perfesser,' said Joby to this personage.

'Good morning,' said the Professor, who had a hollow booming voice. 'Ah, it's Mr Jackson. Good morning. Neighbours again, eh? I think I saw you at Doncaster.'

'You did. Got a good stand 'ere.' And Joby jerked a thumb at The Helping Hand.

'Ah yes. I'd never noticed that. Well, it might be useful, Mr Jackson. I've known the time when - ' And he completed the sentence by raising a large dirty hand towards his mouth, which brought from its cavernous depths a sound suggesting laughter. Then he looked very grave. 'Nothing much for me here to day, Mr Jackson. A mere stop-gap, nothing more.'

'Same 'ere,' said Joby. 'Where you been since Doncaster, Perfesser?'

'Places without a name, you might say,' the Professor boomed mournfully. 'Little markets, miserable affairs, pounds of cheese and yards of muslin and ducks and hens. Rural solitudes, Mr Jackson. And I was carrying the wrong line too. If I'd been running the rheumatic cure or the digestive tonic, all might have been well, but at the present time I'm doing the Character and Destiny business and it's a town business, absolutely a town business. I thought of changing over, but there wasn't time to get the bottles. And you must have bottles nowadays, must have bottles. They won't swallow the pills, Mr Jackson. That's not bad, eh?

Just keep an eye on that box will you? I'll be back in about ten minutes.' And the Professor strode away.

'Yon'd chap'ud make a good loud speaker,' said Mr Oakroyd, who had been listening with delight to this dialogue.

'That's what 'e is, if you ask me,' replied Joby. 'Clever feller, though, the Perfesser. Known 'im off and on years. All patter, y'know. Marvellous! 'E'd sell 'em anything. No expenses, all profit, in 'is line. Clever feller. Edjucated, y'know - that's what does it. They wouldn't believe you and me if we tried it on the same as 'e does. 'E'd make 'em believe anything, sell 'em the boots off their feet.'

'Ay, I dare say,' Mr Oakroyd observed thoughtfully. 'But he hasn't got fat on it.'

'Too much booze - lives on it - telegraphic address: Blotting Paper. 'Sides, the game's not what it was, and that's a fact. Too much edjucation about for fellers like 'im. They're beginning to rumble 'im.' Then he changed his tone, so suddenly that he startled Mr Oakroyd. 'Nar then, lady, take yer choice. Ninepence, one shilling, one-and-six, two shillings, all guaranteed not to burst, tear, burn, or drown, the best rubber on the market today. Pick where yer like, they're all the best.' It looked as if their first customer had arrived.

There was now a steady flow of folk round the stalls, from which issued startling brazen voices. So far the crowd was chiefly composed of women with baskets; the pleasure-seekers would come later; but for those who, like Joby, catered for the family, the day's trade had begun. Mr Oakroyd, hanging about at the back of the stall, discovered a new interest in life. He had never helped to sell anything before, and now it seemed to him an amusing gamble. Would the little boy with *H.M.S. Lion* on his hat succeed in dragging his mother over to see the rubber animals? Would the woman with the carpet bag, who talked incessantly to her companion and turned over dolls and animals without ever looking at them, end by buying anything or was she merely there to have her talk out in peace? Joby seemed to know, as a rule, and some people he left entirely alone, some he took gently into his confidence in the matter of rubber toys, and others he bullied outright into buying. Mr Oakroyd, trying to be helpful but not finding much to do, regarded his new friend with admiration.

'Got the idear, George?' said Joby, looking straight in front of him but twisting his mouth round and winking very rapidly, a method of address that suggested unfathomable confidences. 'Take note o' the patter and prices, see. Might want yer to take on a bit soon.'

A minute or two later it would have been almost impossible to hear this message because their neighbour on the right suddenly opened the day's campaign. Even when he began, this linoleum merchant, he was coatless, perspiring, in a fury of salesmanship, and every moment he became more tempestuous, banging his rolls of linoleum, his little table, his own hand, anything and everything, and worked himself into such a frenzy that it made you hot to see him, made your throat ache to listen to him, and turned the purchase of a roll of linoleum into an act of common kindness. 'Now I'll tell yer whattam going ter do, people,' he would yell. 'Just to make a start, I'm not going ter sell yer linoleum, I'm going ter give it ter yer. Here y'are.' And he would unroll a length and bang away at it in a passion. 'Now that's not oilcloth, it's the very best lino-carpet pattern, rubber-backed - and there's four yards if there's an inch an yer couldn't buy it under fifteen shillings in any shop in this town or any other town.' Here he would draw a deep agonized breath, then give the roll another bang. 'Five shillings. Four and six. Four shillings. Well, I'll tell yer what I'll do. Three and six. Three and six, and I'm giving it away. All right, then. Here! Pass me up that other piece, Charlie. Now then,' he would burst out afresh, beating the new piece unmercifully, 'there's three yards here - yer could cover a landing with it and it 'ud last yer a lifetime - and I'll put the two together. Six shillings the two.' He would glare at the crowd, mop his brow, and run a finger round his sopping rag of a collar. 'It's not oilcloth I'm trying to sell yer,' he would begin again, and his voice was the last despairing shriek of reasoned conviction in a world hollow with doubt and fear. If anyone there said that it was oilcloth it seemed as if the man would have vanished in flame and smoke.

On the other side, the Professor, who had returned to set up his easel, was standing in silence, frowning upon three small boys who were waiting there to see if he would do anything to entertain them. *Do You Know Your Fate?* asked the easel, and then went on: *Professor Miro Can Tell You. What Is the Message of the Stars? Destiny! Will Power! Personality! The Chance of a Lifetime!! Don't Miss It!!!* But so far the good people of Ribsden, bargaining and chattering in the light of the sun, seemed to care nothing for the dark secrets of this life. Perhaps the Professor's hour would strike when the night stole down upon them, beckoning its old troupe of ghosts. Meanwhile, he tried, quite vainly, to intimidate the three small boys with his immense eyebrows, and stood there, in a dignified silence, nursing a packet of coloured papers.

The Professor's other neighbour, a broad-faced, spectacled young man, very carefully dressed, was as noisy as the linoleum merchant, and looked like a bank clerk in a frenzy. Nobody seemed to know what he was selling or even if he was selling anything at all. He held up a number of plain envelopes, shook them in the faces of his audience, and talked continually of one Walters of Bristol. 'When Mis-ter Wal-ters of Bris-tol', he roared in the manner of one discussing his friend the Prime

Minister, 'gave me these envelopes, he assured me that in every one of them there was a bank-note, and he sent me down here to sell them to you purely and simply as an advertisement. Mr Walters knew and I knew that there was no money to be made out of this. It's a good advertisement. And when Mis-ter Wal-ters guaranteed that there was a bank-note in every one of these envelopes, that was good enough for me. I knew that Mis-ter Wal-ters of Bris-tol would not send me on a fool's errand, I can assure you, people.' And he went on assuring them and shaking his mysterious envelopes in their faces.

A little after noon, the Professor left his stand and approached Joby. 'I was wondering, Mr Jackson,' he began, in a confidential whisper, 'if you had a spare shilling about you. Just until tonight, you know.'

Joby nodded towards The Helping Hand. 'Going in?'

'Yes, I thought that perhaps a little - er - '

Joby cut him short. 'You come with me, Perfesser. 'Ere, George, you can take over a bit, eh? Shan't be long.'

So Mr Oakroyd was left in charge, and before Joby had returned, he had sold a vermilion stork with wooden feet, a policeman on traffic duty, and a shrimp-coloured and dropsical rubber infant, taking four shillings in all, of which, he knew, at least half-a-crown was sheer profit. This was good business.

When Joby came back, an hour later, he brought with him a bottle of beer and two meat pies. 'Yer can't stir in there now,' he explained, 'so I got yer these, see. Knock off and get outside these, then 'ave a walk round. Wotcher done?'

Mr Oakroyd, attacking the first of the meat pies, reported his sales. 'A bird, a bobby, an' a bairn, for fower bob.'

'Yer a ruddy poet, George, if yer ask me,' said Joby in great good-humour. 'The Perfesser's still in there. We shan't see 'im now till closing time. 'E's found the 'elping 'and all right. 'E'd lowered about five when I left, and all buckshee. 'E could talk a feller into givin' 'im a bucketful. Clever feller, the Perfesser, but I wouldn't like to see the coloured menagerie 'e sees some o' these nights.'

By the time Mr Oakroyd had finished his two pies and the bottle of beer, had walked round the fair and market and explored the town, and had returned to have a smoke with Joby, it was nearly tea-time. 'Not much doing now till about six,' Joby told him. 'Yer can take on a bit, see. 'I'll 'ave a dekko at the old van, a drop o' Rosie, and a word wi' some o' the boys. Don't forget them monkeys is two bob apiece - they're extra special, they are - they cost me ninepence.'

The linoleum merchant and the friend of Mr Walters of Bristol had each large audiences, but there appeared to be a temporary slump in rubber toys. Very few people even looked at the stall, partly, no doubt, because its two neighbours were so much more exciting and noisy. The only questions Mr Oakroyd found himself answering referred to Joby himself and not to his stock-in-trade.

''Ello! This is Joby Jackson, isn't it! Where's old Joby today?'

'Knocking about,' Mr Oakroyd would reply, and the inquirer would saunter off again.

This happened several times, and Mr Oakroyd began to assume a knowing air with these fellow professionalists of the road. But he was not able to do more than make a beginning. The tide that had carried him along so smoothly these past twenty-four hours suddenly turned against him. One of these fellow professionalists who had been moving aimlessly through the crowd caught sight of the stall, stopped, and stared. Mr Oakroyd, staring back at him, came to the conclusion that he was not a pleasant-looking chap. After standing there a minute or two, the man came closer and examined the stall, its placards, its rubber dolls, its uneasy salesman, with little bloodshot eyes. He was a big man, whose huge shoulders were encased in a dirty football jersey; there was three or four days' stubble on his great prow of a jaw; and he looked as if he had recently wakened from a drunken sleep to find himself in a very bad temper. As he stood there, signs of intelligence began to dawn in his face, but the sight was not a pleasing one.

It was Mr Oakroyd, however, who broke the silence at last. He could not stand this scrutiny any longer. 'Like a doll, mate?' he asked, with dubious good-fellowship in his tone and glance.

'Like a doll!' the large man spat out in contempt. 'Do I look as if I wanted a bloody doll, do I now, do I?' Then, suddenly appallingly, he became as angry as a goaded bull. 'Where's that - ' and he proceeded to apply a number of words to the absent Joby that shocked Mr Oakroyd, accustomed as he was to most of them. 'Where is 'e? d'y'ear?' And he brought his huge fist down on the stall so that every stork and monkey and policeman hanging there started dancing, and then he leaned forward and pushed his face nearer to Mr Oakroyd's.

'Well,' he roared, 'wot d'yer say, yer silly-looking - ?'

Mr Oakroyd kept perfectly still and quiet. This, he knew, was Jim Summers. It couldn't be anyone else but Jim Summers. He remembered everything he had heard about Jim Summers. And he tried to think, and it was difficult. 'Now I'll tell yer whattam going ter do, people,' came the voice on the right. 'And it isn't oilcloth I'm selling yer.' Joby might be back any minute. Meanwhile, he wasn't here, and Jim Summers undoubtedly was. 'When Mis-ter Wal-ters of Bris-tol,' the left boomed steadily, 'came to me and gave me these envelopes - ' Mr Oakroyd looked Jim Summers in the eye.

'He's not here,' he muttered.

'Can't I see 'e's not here! I'm asking where 'e is. Yer not a bloody stuck pig, are yer? Yer can talk, can't yer? This is 'is stall, isn't it?'

Still Mr Oakroyd made no reply.

'I'd like ter give yer something uttud make yer open yer mouth,' said the angry Summers, looking very ugly. 'Well, I can wait 'ere a bit.'

Mr Oakroyd found his voice now. 'It's not a bit o' good your doing that, mate. Joby Jackson's not here.'

'Ar d'yer mean 'e's not 'ere,' cried the other contemptuously. 'This is 'is stall, isn't it? Think I don't know it!'

'Ay, but' - Mr Oakroyd fumbled, then hurried on - 'you see, I've bowt it off on him.'

'Oh, since when?'

'Yesterda',' replied Mr Oakroyd. 'I took it on mesen, so you won't find him here, mate.'

Mr Summers looked puzzled. Not being a man of intellect, he took some time to arrange his ideas. Then suddenly he shook himself, banged the stall again, and shouted: ''E's been seen 'ere this morning. You bought this? You've 'ell as like, yer rotten little liar.'

'Here, here, here, here! Less of it, less of it. What's it all about, eh?' This was the policeman with the ginger moustache, the one who apparently did not like markets and fairs. Now he looked very severe indeed.

'I come 'ere asking for a feller,' growled Summers, 'and this feller 'ere says 'e don't know where the feller is and says that this stall 'ere is 'is and I was telling im it wasn't 'cos I knew it belonged to this other feller, d'yer see?'

'Well, I don't see what you've got to make such a lot of noise about,' said the policeman. 'Either it's his or it isn't, and one way or the other, it don't seem to me to be much o' your business.'

'I was only telling 'im I knew it wasn't, d'yer see?'

'All right, all right, I know what you was doing,' cried the policeman angrily. 'And I say it don't seem to me to be much o' your business.'

'That's right,' Mr Oakroyd put in, feeling it was about time he said something. It was, however, a very unfortunate move. The policeman, who up to now had been eyeing Summers very suspiciously, transferred his unpleasant stare to Mr Oakroyd himself, who did not find it easy to meet it.

'Well, it may be none of his business,' said the policeman, still staring, 'but it's my business all right. If you ask me, there's something a bit queer here. Now you say this here outfit belongs to you and not to this other feller he's talking so much about?'

'Ay,' replied Mr Oakroyd, hesitating. 'In a manner o' speaking, you might say - '

'What d'you mean "in a manner o' speaking"?' the policeman demanded. ''Ere, let's have a look at your licence.'

Mr Oakroyd stared back at the policeman, open-mouthed. He knew nothing about licences, had no idea what a licence would look like, how much it cost, where it would be obtained. All that he did know, with a sickening certainty, was that he ought to have a licence, if his story were to be believed, and that he could not think how to begin to explain why he hadn't one.

''E's got no licence,' said Summers triumphantly.

'Who's talking to you?' the policeman demanded angrily. Then he turned to Mr Oakroyd again and repeated, with maddening deliberation: 'Let's have a look at your licence.'

Fortunately for Mr Oakroyd, the policeman's high-handed methods were too much for Jim Summers, whose temper was always uncertain and who disliked the Force. At that moment he might have been compared to a smoking volcano. He pushed his face between the other two, and repeated, very slowly and ominously: 'I said "'E's got no licence."'

'And I say "Who's talking to you?"' cried the policeman, giving him a push. 'You get back a bit.'

'And 'oo the bloody 'ell d'you think you are?' shouted Summers, raising a huge fist. 'Touch me again, yer ginger pig, and I'll flatten yer.'

'Another word and you'll come along with me,' retorted the policeman, stepping back.

''Ello, 'ello! What's the row?' It was Joby, and with him was a short, thick-set, smiling man.

At the sight of Joby's companion, Summers gave a roar. 'Muss, yer - ' He rushed at him but both Joby and the policeman threw themselves in the way, and the next moment they were all so many whirling arms and legs. Instantly the crowd surged round and its pressure drove them against the stall which rocked with the fight. Mr Oakroyd, at the other side and cut off from the combatants, could do nothing but try to keep the stall in place. A shower of rubber birds and monkeys descended upon the battlefield. *Crack!* went the stall and another shower of dolls fell, so that Mr Oakroyd began sweeping those that were left into the boxes at the back, and then, crawling underneath, contrived to pick up a number of those that had fallen. He returned to hold on and sway with the stall. He had undertaken 'to mind t'stall' - as he told himself - and what he could do, he did. There was no room for him in the fight, even if he had wished to join it. The redoubtable Summers, having sent little Tommy Muss into the dust, given Joby a black eye, and battered the policeman, was now being overpowered. The policeman had had time to blow his whistle, which brought his colleague from the other end of the market-place, and the two of them secured the person of James Summers and finally marched him away, followed by the cheers and hoots of the crowd.

Mr Oakroyd immediately came round to the front of the stall and began picking up the remainder of the fallen toys, while Joby and his friend gasped and swore and wiped their faces and dusted their clothes.

"Ere, didn't take any names, did 'e?' asked Joby, still panting for breath.

'He didn't take mine,' said Mr Oakroyd.

'We're off then. What d'yer say, Tommy? If they wants us for the witness-box, they must find us, see. 'Ere, get this stuff away, sharp as yer can. Come on, Tommy. That's right, George. Sharp's the word, or we'll never do it. But they've got ter get 'im ter the station, see.' He turned to look at those members of the crowd that were still lingering about. 'Nar then,' he cried, 'it's all over this time. No more performances today, people. Out o' the way, you lads.' And the linoleum merchant and the friend of Mr Walters of Bristol, taking advantage of the fact that a crowd was already assembled at their elbows, roared out their patter again and drew all but the most obstinate of the spectators into their audiences.

'I'll get the van, see,' said Joby, 'and run it as near as I can, just round the Johnny Horner. Soon as yer 'ear me toot, run with as much o' the stuff as yer can carry. Get the stall down, George, and anything that's broken bad, leave it.' And he hurried off.

'A troublesome business, Mr Muss,' boomed a voice above them as they packed the things.

"Lo Professor!' said Tommy, looking up. "Ow goes it? We're sliding out.'

'Quite right, quite right, Mr Muss,' replied the Professor. 'I should do the same myself, have done before today. Very inconvenient these police-court affairs. Besides, if you go into the box, it creates a prejudice against you in the profession. Not that Summers doesn't deserve whatever he gets - a hooligan, a tough, Mr Muss - these low types are a disgrace to the road. They can't carry their beer, that's the trouble.'

'There goes the old van,' cried Tommy. 'Now then, Professor, you don't know us, do you?'

'I've never seen you in my life before,' the Professor replied gravely. 'And I'll drop a word to the boys. Summers won't give names, of course, because you'd be hostile witnesses, though I doubt if he's the sense to see that. I'll keep an eye on these things for you.'

Two hurried journeys each were enough. Mr Oakroyd was hustled into the back, the other two sitting in front; and they rattled out of Ribsden as fast as the van would take them. Mr Oakroyd had no idea where they were going and his backward vision of the town and the road that followed it told him nothing. The long day, the excitement of the fight, the hasty departure, had left him rather tired, and after the first few dramatic minutes of the escape from Ribsden he gradually sank into a doze, lying full length on one of the bunks. When, finally, they stopped and he struggled out, he had not the faintest notion of the distance they had come or the time they had been on the road. He found they were standing in a long village street, outside a small public-house. The landlord came to the door.

'The wife in, Joe?' cried Tommy.

'Yuss, she is. 'Ad 'er tea some time back though.' replied the landlord.

'Tell 'er I'm 'ere. 'Alf a minute, though, I'm coming in.' And Tommy, giving a wink to the other two, went inside.

Joby passed the wink on to Mr Oakroyd with the undamaged eye 'Tommy's got the tart in there,' he remarked. 'Been there two days, see. 'E came into Ribsden on chance of finding me there, but didn't think 'e'd find Jim Summers there. What 'appened, George?'

Mr Oakroyd related his adventures with Mr Summers and the officious policeman, and, when he had done, Tommy emerged from the public-house, followed by a gaudy youngish woman several inches taller than himself.

'What-how, Jowby!' she cried, waving a hand. 'All the best! I wish I'd bin there to see. 'E's got what 'e wanted, 'asn't 'e, the swine? Gor! - but you got an eye. You want a bit o' stike on thet eye, down't 'e, Tommy? Come in and 'ave one while I getcher a bit o' stike.'

'What about it, Joby?' added Tommy. 'Coming in now? The old box of tricks be all right there.'

'No, I'll pull 'er out, Tommy, and find a place for 'er. Going to kip in 'er tonight, see. 'Sides, me and George'll 'ave to see what the damage is and try to straighten up if we're working that place tomorrer. See yer later, Tommy.'

'I'll be 'ere,' said Tommy.

'Get in front, George,' said Joby, climbing in again. And off they went down the long street. 'Tommy's joining up again to-morrer, see, and the tart's follering on, doing the palm business. She's all right, but a 'ole night with the two of them together - with 'er sitting on 'is knee and slapping 'im and drinking 'is beer - 'ud get on my ruddy nerves.'

'I dare say. She looks nowt i' my line,' Mr Oakroyd remarked dispassionately.

Joby halted at the last shop in the village, where he bought some food, and then they found a camping place by the side of the road, about a mile outside the village. There they repeated the programme of the previous evening, examining and putting in order the stock and the stall and then having a meal. But this time Joby went to the public-house, the one in which Tommy and his temporary bride were staying, unaccompanied by Mr Oakroyd, who said that he was too tired to move. It was true he was tired, but he was also feeling rather out of it. Joby's pal had come back, and now, he knew, he was not really wanted. Tomorrow he would have to go on alone. 'Nay, I'll get to bed, Joby lad,' he said, and watched him walk down the road back to the village, but neither saw nor heard anything of Joby's return, two hours later, so deep was this, his second – and probably his last – night of sleep in a caravan, with only a three-ply breadth between him and the stars.

V

'Well, George,' said Joby, the next morning, 'yer done me a good turn or two, see. I'd like to keep yer on the job a bit longer, but yer see 'ow it is. And this oughter straighten us up a bit.' And he handed over an extremely dirty bit of paper that turned out, much to Mr Oakroyd's surprise, to be a pound note.

'Nay, I don't know as how I can tak' this,' he said doubtfully. 'You've given me summat to eat and sup and a bed like, and I've done nowt to earn this.'

'Yer the first West Riding feller I ever knew to look sideways at – what do you Tykes call it? – a bit o' brass. Nar then, George, put that in yer pocket.'

And Mr Oakroyd did put it in his pocket and even tried to mumble some words of thanks, an agonizing task to any true Bruddersfordian, who always tries to arrange his life so that he will be spared such appalling scenes. Mr Oakroyd himself had always regarded with suspicion any person – not counting affected southrons and the like – who showed a readiness to say 'Please' and 'Thank you', and was genuinely troubled afterwards by the thought that perhaps his travels were already sapping his manly independence and might lead him to indulge – as he said himself – 'in all sorts o' daft tricks'.

'And I'll tell yer what, George,' Joby continued, 'if yer've found nothing, get a lift to Nottingham next week – Thursday, Friday, Saturday – Goose Fair, and take a look round for me and Tommy, see. All the boys'll be there, and I might be able to find something for yer. Good tradesman, eh, George? 'Andle a saw, every time, eh? That's the stuff. Don't ferget, Nottingham.'

'Ay, if I've nowt on, I will.'

'Good enough! What's the ruddy move now then, George? We can give yer a lift on the way, can't we? What say?'

Mr Oakroyd shook his head decisively. 'Nay, you go one way and I'll go t'other. You've had enough bother wi' me. Where do this here road go to?'

''Alf a minute, 'alf a minute.' Joby scratched his head, looked at the road, frowned at it, then scratched his head again. 'Tommy fetched me 'ere - ter call at 'is boozer - but I been 'ere before. I've been everywhere, I 'ave. Yer can't lose me. I know, George, I know. 'Ere, go down this road, keep round to the left - 'bout six miles - and yer'll come to a place called Rawsley. Biggish place - twenty or thirty boozers there - good 'uns some of 'em. A feller called Thompson - Jimmy Thompson - used to keep one - knew 'im well, used to be a welterweight, and tidy with 'em, too. That's the place - Rawsley. They 'ave a fair third week in July - not so bad, neither - best round 'ere. Yer might easy pick something up there, see. 'Ave a look at Rawsley, George.'

Mr Oakroyd brought his basket trunk and his bag of tools out of the van and then stood waiting for Joby to come out too. It was quite late in the morning and there was every indication now that the fine autumn weather they had been having had at last come to an end. There had been rain earlier on, and though it was fine now, the sky was overclouded and it was much colder than it had been. It was the wrong kind of day on which to go off on your own again; the road looked cheerless, the whole prospect forlorn. 'A poor do,' thought Mr Oakroyd, waiting to say good-bye.

When Joby did come out he brought with him a little package loosely wrapped in brown paper. 'Yer'll want these, George,' he said. 'Yer don't pass nothing on the way to Rawsley, see.' He handed over the package. 'Sandwiches - our own ruddy make,' he explained, looking almost apologetic. 'If yer don't want 'em, give 'em to the poor, George, give 'em to the poor, but for God's sake don't start arguing the toss about 'em.'

'All right, Joby lad, I won't,' said Mr Oakroyd, putting on his old mackintosh and stuffing the sandwiches into the pocket. 'And I hope I see thee agen afore so long.' He held out his hand, feeling that he might go to any lengths now after such a desperately emotional speech.

Joby shook it enthusiastically. 'Well, George, I'll tell yer something. Yer the best Yorkshire lad I've met for a long time. I'm not fond of 'em as a rule, see. I don't get on with 'em.'

'Ay,' replied Mr Oakroyd gravely, 'we tak' a bit o' knowing.'

'But you're all right, George, you are,' Joby continued, persisting with this imaginary Christian name to the very end. 'And any time yer want to find me, just drop me a line to *The World's Fair* - that's our paper, see - Joby Jackson, care of *The World's Fair*. That'll find me all right every time. So long, George, and all the best!'

Half a mile down the road a spatter of rain overtook Mr Oakroyd, and at the end of the next half-mile it was raining in good earnest, so that he thought it wiser to shelter under some trees. He sat down on his two bags and pulled out his pipe and pouch. But there were only a few crumbs of Old Salt left, enough perhaps for one small pipe, and he wisely decided that this was not the time to smoke them. 'I must save 'em till I've had summat to eat,' he told himself. He sat there in his chilly and glistening mackintosh, forlornly watching the raindrops dance on the road and an occasional faded leaf flutter down to his feet. A postman on a bicycle went past, then a large closed car; and that was all the traffic there was. Try as he might, Mr Oakroyd could not drown a little voice that kept asking him if he had not been a fool to leave home and wander about like this. True, he was better off than he had been two mornings ago, for then he had had nothing at all and now he had a pound. But what was a pound? And what was he to do now? There weren't many Jobys about. This thought brought him closer to the heart of his melancholy. It was the joyous reunion of Joby and his pal Tommy that had really made him feel so desolate. Joby had been a good sort but he didn't want him, Jess Oakroyd, not after his own pal had come back. Nobody wanted him, except Lily, who was far away in Canada, and even she didn't seem to mind their not being together. There wasn't a chap in Bruddersford who would care twopence where Jess Oakroyd was and what had happened to him. Even Sam Oglethorpe wouldn't bother his head five minutes about him. And his own wife and son were glad to be rid of him. And yet he was a friendly chap really, only too willing to put in a good bit of hard work for somebody and then have his pipe and pint afterwards with a mate or two. At least, so it seemed to him, but as he thought it over and over, in a dragging and dreary fashion, his mind grew shadowy and fearful with doubt. Perhaps there was something wrong with him. But now his feet touched solid ground and he sprang up, erect. 'There's nowt wrong wi' me,' he declared sturdily. 'I'll ha' summat to eat.'

He pulled out the sandwiches and, remembering how Joby had given them to him, he felt a little more cheerful. As he munched away, the sun came struggling through again and the rain dwindled to a few glittering drops. The road looked more inviting now than the chill damp shade of the trees, and he hurried through his little meal, lit the last shreds of Old Salt, then walked out into the sunlight. He was wandering on again. The thought brought him a tiny thrill of pleasure now. As he trudged down the road, he mused upon that first fine clatter down the

Great North Road, the Kirkworth Inn, Mr Poppleby and Joby and the Professor and the rubber dolls. Their images were still popping in and out of his mind when he reached a cross-roads and saw that the signpost to the left pointed to Rawsley. As he turned down this new road, a sudden excitement took possession of him. He even stopped, put down his bags, took the pipe out of his mouth, and spoke aloud.

'Eh,' he cried, 'but I've seen summat this week. I've had a bit o' fun on me travels if I never see nowt no more.'

Perhaps that began it all. They were brave words, manfully spoken from the heart, and we do not know how far such words may travel nor what they may set in motion. A minute or two later, he turned a corner and saw that the length of road before him was empty except for a single stationary object some distance away. It was a small car. He walked towards it, leisurely, incuriously. He did not know that this was to be, for him, no ordinary car, that he was casually crossing the threshold of another world.

CHAPTER FIVE
Miss Trant is Almost a Second Columbus

I

THE car was the same two-seater Mercia that had carried Miss Trant so bravely out of Hitherton four days before. It was not perhaps the same Elizabeth Trant, certainly not the one Hitherton had known. She had been running about, discovering England, all by herself; marching into hotels and demanding beds and breakfasts and dinners and lunches; talking about roads and cars and cathedrals to strangers, mostly men. This was something. Indeed, after you had lived with the Colonel for twenty years at Hitherton, it was a great deal, a wild rush of independent life. But it was nothing - mere touristry - compared with her other adventures. The little car had taken her farther than the most distant cathedral, the loneliest hotel. It had plumped her into the middle of other people's lives, the most fantastic places in the world. She had not forsworn her allegiance to the historical romance - and had read two out of the four she carried with her - but now she regarded its figures with a different eye, meeting its conspirators and dragoons on something like terms of equality. Indeed, she could afford to pity them, for though they had to grapple with all the urgencies of life they appeared to have been denied all but a crumb or so from its vast stores of comic relief. She was beginning to feel now that she knew both. After the first splendid hour or two of escape, Monday had not been an exciting day. Ely, she found, was just fifteen miles too far, so she stayed that night in Cambridge a town she had visited before at The Lion in Petty Cury. Term had not yet begun and the little grey town, which she remembered as a riot of rowing enthusiasts, salmon mayonnaise, ices, and lawns lit with Chinese lanterns, was now pleasantly empty, only engaged in decking out its windows with a new stock of caps and gowns and college ties and tobacco jars. She had a little stroll before dinner, ate heartily, then sipped her coffee in the glass-covered lounge, which pleased her because it reminded her of being on board ship. By this time, she was eager to talk to somebody, and did her best with her neighbour, a large upholstered sort of woman who stared straight in front of her, above a magnificent Roman nose.

'I find it more tiring than I thought it would be, driving by oneself, I mean,' explained Miss Trant.

'Do you?' said the other in her deep contralto voice.

'Perhaps it's because there's nobody to share things with,' Miss Trant continued, eagerly, 'all the little difficulties and dangers and triumphs, you know.'

'Indeed!' The woman still stared straight in front of her.

'It may be because I'm inexperienced, of course,' Miss Trant faltered. It was not easy to talk to this nose.

'I dare say.' said the other, achieving her very lowest notes but not moving a muscle of her face.

Miss Trant looked at her and wondered sadly why people should be so unfriendly. The next moment, however, the woman's face lit up and she jumped to her feet with surprising agility. A boy about eighteen had just entered the lounge, obviously her son. The woman had not been unfriendly but simply absent-minded. Miss Trant felt relieved. She looked about her again, only to meet the gaze of the man opposite, a man with protruding grey eyes, admirably adapted for staring fixedly at strangers, and a heavy greying moustache that he fondled as if it were a privilege to have access to such a creation. She made the mistake of meeting his stare very frankly. It brought him over to the vacated chair at her side.

'Mind if I sit here?' he inquired, in a thick voice.

'Not at all,' said Miss Trant, looking hard at the chair he had just left.

'Thanks. Awfully quiet here, isn't it?' he continued, his eyes bulging at her.

'Is it?'

'Well, dontcher think so? I know this place pretty well, come here three or four times a year, you know. Not much to do here in the evening, specially if the boys aren't up. Usually drop into the pictures myself.'

She may have led a quiet life, but she was no fool. There was no mistaking his doggish inviting air. And a minute or two ago, she had been telling herself that people were too unfriendly. And now this. It was too absurd. She wanted to laugh, and some little sound must have made its way out.

'Pardon,' and the man leaned forward.

Her amusement somehow brought her into command of the situation. She fixed her eyes upon the heavy moustache, as if it were a curious museum exhibit, and remarked: 'I was wondering if all the men in my family had decided to go to the pictures. I'm waiting for them now, and they're late.'

'Oh, waiting for them, are you?' There was a change in his tone.

'Yes,' she continued hastily. 'My father, my two brothers, my husband, and our two boys. Quite a crowd of them. They're awfully late.'

He stared at her, but it was quite a different stare. 'Yes, time's getting on, isn't it?' he mumbled. He pretended to look at his watch. 'Time I was moving on.' And he moved.

He left Miss Trant wondering at herself, at her impudence, her courage, her staggering presence of mind. She felt as if she were a schoolgirl again and yet a woman of the world, though no woman of the world, she reflected, would have ever stooped to such a ridiculous fifth-form trick. Something - money or freedom or both - had changed her. She wanted to unbosom herself to somebody very badly now, so she wrote a long letter to Dorothy Chillingford. Then she went to bed.

Next morning, about eleven o'clock, she was at Ely, enraptured by the dramatic splendours of the cathedral. It was at the top of the tower that she made the acquaintance of the fierce little elderly man, apparently the only other visitor there. He had very bright eyes, pink cheeks, a bristling beard, and one of those old-fashioned turned-down collars that always suggest that their wearers are William Morris socialists or vegetarians or leaders of surprising little religious sects. She never learned which of these he was, never knew his name, business, or place of address; but nevertheless they were soon on very friendly terms. It was impossible that they should be silent when they were standing on the high tower together, looking down upon the sunlit plain of Cambridgeshire. He had a map with him and insisted upon pointing out to her every landmark on the horizon. Then they explored the rest of the cathedral together, and she found him a most learned and entertaining companion, in spite of his staccato dogmatic manner. 'Do you know anything about brasses? You don't, eh? Then I'll explain.' And he would explain, and he hurried from one part of the building to another, explaining. Miss Trant felt sometimes as if she were back at school, but it was impossible not to like him.

Both of them, it appeared, had left their cars outside The Lamb, so they walked back there together and shared a table for lunch. It was during this meal that Miss Trant let fall a remark that was of some consequence because it led to a change in her programme.

'Isn't it a pity, we can't build like that now, make really beautiful things?'

'No pity at all,' he cried, putting down his fork. 'We can; we do. My dear young lady, don't you believe that stuff. All rubbish! The world progresses. We can build when we want to. I don't say we build anything like Ely here - we don't want to - not our style - all wonder that, cultivated by barbarism, no knowledge of the universe in it - but I say we can build as well, can build better. Look at the new County Hall in London. Have you seen it? Look at the Bush Building. Have you seen that? Have you seen that enormous block of offices near London Bridge? You must get that idea out of your head at the earliest possible moment, you really must, if you'll forgive my saying so. You say you are going round looking at the cathedrals - that's the plan, isn't it? Well, have you seen Liverpool?'

No, she had not seen Liverpool.

'Go to Liverpool at once,' he commanded, and was so impressive that she felt she ought to hurry away at that very moment. He was as bad as Mr Chillingford. And what a pair they would make!

'Now you can't say I'm not interested in these medieval creations,' he continued earnestly. 'You can't say I don't appreciate them. This morning you probably thought I was a little too interested and appreciative, the way I dragged you round and talked your head off. But at Liverpool there's a brand-new cathedral, finished the other day - so to speak. Not a town-hall or a railway station or a block of offices, but a cathedral, the very thing you're talking about.'

He paused to take breath, and Miss Trant, who was reminded a little of her father, regarded him with friendly amusement.

'Now what's it like, this cathedral? Is it a little shuffling jerry-built hotch-potch thing? It is not. It's large, it's solid, it's enduring. It's beautiful, it's sublime. And who made it? The men of today. Don't be misled by this medieval nonsense. We're better men than they were, and we live in a better world. Building was their chief trick; it's not ours; but when we want to build, we can outbuild 'em. You never give a thought to most of our building,' he lectured away, for ever taking up his fork and then putting it down again. 'Take the big liners - there's building for you. Look at one of 'em.' He said this as if there were several just outside the window. 'There's adaptation to ends, there's beauty of design, there's solid craftsmanship and workmanship, everything there in a big liner. You go to Liverpool, look at the cathedral, then take a peep or two at some of the liners in dock, and you'll soon change your mind about our building. You were going there anyhow, I suppose?'

Miss Trant found herself compelled to say, untruthfully, that she was. It would have been terrible to have told him that she had never even thought about Liverpool; he would never have eaten any lunch.

'Then go there at once, my dear young lady,' he replied, eager as a boy. 'See it before this nonsense takes root in your mind. I insist upon your going there next. It's only a pleasant day's run from here. I'll show you on the map after lunch.' And he fell to gobbling his lunch, he was so anxious to have done with it and to show her the map.

Miss Trant sat there, eating daintily, and envying his complete absorption in the matter in hand. It might be babyish, but it must be great fun, she thought, to be swallowed up by things like that. She could as well go to Liverpool as to Lincoln or York, and she decided she would go there, if only to please him. It would, too, be a friendly gesture towards the eagerly-forgetting-all-about-yourself, which only needed what she determined now to call 'a swallower'. Buildings and anti-medievalism and progress were apparently all swallowers for this old gentleman, now galloping rather noisily through his blackberry tart. Perhaps she had served other people's swallowers too long; it was time she had one of her own. But then there might be one waiting for her at Liverpool.

'Here you are then,' cried the old gentleman enthusiastically, pointing to the map. 'Huntingdon, Kettering, Leicester, Derby, Macclesfield, Warrington, Liverpool. Almost a straight run across country.'

She examined the route carefully. It seemed to take her through a number of industrial towns, places with trams and lorries and narrow main streets. 'Will there be a lot of traffic?' she inquired dubiously.

'Traffic! What's wrong with traffic? Why, I can give you thirty years, but I like traffic. The more traffic the better. I like to see a place bustling alive. It does me good to drive through a town that's got some trade. It's - it's inspiring. You're not going to tell me that you're frightened of traffic.'

'Yes, I am,' she said firmly. 'I don't like it at all. If I'd more experience, I might not mind it so much, but, as it is, I'm terrified. I never know which side I ought to pass a tram on, and when the great lumbering things look as if they're going to pin me between them I can't possibly console myself by thinking the town is very busy.'

'Pass them on any side. I do.' He waved an arm carelessly. 'I like these little problems of driving. They keep me young. In and out, in and out, stop, go on, in and out again - nothing pleases me better. It will you soon, too, you mark my words. But you've nothing to be afraid of on this route.' And he went over the route again, and made such a fuss about it and was so friendly and absurd that she felt herself compelled to fall in with his plan.

'But I can't go all that way today, of course,' she told him.

'Perhaps not, perhaps not,' he cried, rather testily. Then he ran his finger over the map. 'You could get as far as Macclesfield,' he finally announced.

She looked for herself. 'Leicester would be quite far enough for me.'

'Leicester! A stone's-throw, a mere stone's-throw! You could have tea there, then run on to Macclesfield. That's the place, obviously.'

Miss Trant shook her head. She did not see why she should be dictated to in this fashion. 'I shall have done quite enough by the time I reach Leicester.'

'My dear young lady, I don't believe you can read a map, I really don't believe you can. You're talking nonsense, you know.' He seemed quite irritated. 'You couldn't have an easier run than to Macclesfield.'

She smiled at him. 'Yes, I could, and I'm going to. Just as far as Leicester.'

'It's ridiculous,' he exploded. He slapped the map angrily with his open hand. 'Really, you know, you're not *trying*. It's most annoying the way you're not trying.'

Her only reply to this absurd protest was a little peal of laughter. The whole idiocy of the situation burst upon her. 'I'm sorry,' she faltered at last.

'So am I,' he ejaculated. 'Very.' And he marched out of the dining-room and banged the door behind him. The door at the other end of the room then opened to admit the head of the waiter. 'Did the gentleman call?' he inquired.

'No, I don't think he did,' she replied. 'He went out.'

The waiter withdrew and had no sooner closed his door than the other opened and the old gentleman marched in again. He walked straight up to her, looking pinker and more bristling than ever. 'I beg your pardon, my dear young lady, I really beg your pardon,' he said earnestly. 'Most stupid of me. You must go as far as you like and stay where you like, of course. It's no business of mine at all, is it?' Then he smiled and turned himself into a very charming old gentleman indeed. 'But you will go to Liverpool sometime, won't you, and remember what I said?'

'This very day,' said Miss Trant, and they became more friendly than ever.

She never learned his name, and after a time remembered nothing of him but a voice and vague patch of pink cheek and bristling beard; but she always believed afterwards that it was he who really began it all by hurling her across country towards Liverpool. If he had not insisted upon her going there, she would say, nothing would ever have happened, thereby forgetting that she had been busy turning herself into one of those persons round whom things always happen, and also forgetting, as we all do, that the one road we have chosen out of a hundred is not the only road lined with adventure. Perhaps she was right, however, in saying that the particular adventures she did have were really set in motion by the nameless old gentleman who shot across the map. But she never arrived at Liverpool, and to this day has never even caught a glimpse of the town of Macclesfield.

II

She spent Tuesday night at Market Harborough. The next morning, she ran through Leicester, or rather lost herself in what seemed a nightmare of traffic and unlabelled streets and then miraculously found her way out of it, pushed on through Derby, and by lunchtime was out in the rising open country beyond. She came to a village clustered about an important junction of roads, and saw at the corner a pleasant little hotel that promised lunch. There were two cars already drawn up before the front door, but she was able to slip in between them. It was then she noticed that the car in front seemed exactly like her own, the same kind of two-seater and painted an identical light blue. She entered the hotel wondering idly what sort of people owned this twin car.

There were only two persons having lunch. Miss Trant was given a small table in the opposite corner, but as the dining-room was quite narrow she was not far away from her fellow-lunchers. They were a curious pair. The woman was about her own age, a large square blonde with a wandering nose and a mouth that was so big, so loose, and so vividly and inhumanly carmined, that it seemed to have no connexion with the rest of the face, to be a dreadful afterthought. She was cheaply but showily dressed, a jangling sort of woman, and she talked very quickly and loudly and was evidently in nervous high spirits. Her companion was nervous but not in high spirits. He was a neat compressed little man, with dark hair parted in the middle, pince-nez about a button of a nose, and tiny moustache. He looked vaguely uneasy. Miss Trant told herself that he reminded her of a rabbit.

Before Miss Trant had finished her soup, there were sounds of other arrivals outside, and in a few minutes four men, three stout and one thin, clomped in and seated themselves at the other end of the room.

The large blonde woman, who was half-way through her lunch, had been fussing some time with a heavy coat. Now she stood up, took it off, and exclaimed, in a curious mincing accent apparently assumed for everybody's benefit: 'This cowt's an orful nuisance. I'll have it pet in the caw.' She looked about for the waitress, but the waitress was ostentatiously busying herself with the men's table, so she walked out with the coat herself, obviously enjoying the little fuss she was making, and returned in a moment.

'All ri'?' inquired her companion, in a weak high voice that was exactly what you expected from him.

'I told the man to pet it in the caw, deear,' replied the woman, reseating herself and attacking the boiled mutton with an indescribable air of luxurious pleasure.

Miss Trant had just decided that she had watched and wondered at this odd pair long enough, when the telephone bell rang. The telephone was in the dining-room, and the waitress answered it. Everybody else looked at her and listened intently, finding it impossible, as usual, to be indifferent to a telephone. 'Yes, it is,' cried the waitress through the mouthpiece. 'That's right.' Then she listened. 'How should I know?' She listened again. 'Like what?' she asked, frowning. 'Oh, I see.' And then her glance went travelling round the room and finally rested on the odd pair. It was very exciting as nobody even pretended to eat. 'Well, I don't know,' said the waitress dubiously, still looking the same way. Miss Trant shot a glance there too, and noticed that the little man seemed very restive. 'I dare say it might be,' the waitress continued, 'but why don't you give the name. I'll ask if you give me the name. All right. Hold on a minute.' She put down the receiver and called out to the little man: 'Beg your pardon, but are you Mr Tipstead? Mr Eric Tipstead?'

Miss Trant saw him start up involuntarily, saw the woman give him a sharp warning glance, lay a hand on his arm, and give a lightning shake of her head. 'No, no,' the woman cried hastily, too hastily.

'It isn't, eh?' the waitress called out.

'No - er - certainly not,' the man quavered in anything but a tone of certainty. He seemed desirous of appearing as if he were not really very sure just then what his name might be.

The woman, however, had no such subtle reservations in her manner. 'Johnson's the name, Miss - Johnson,' she cried. She evidently shared with the waitress a conviction that it was more polite to talk about 'the name' than to say 'your name' or 'our name'.

'Perhaps she had worked in an hotel,' Miss Trant told herself. She had missed nothing of this.

'Not the name,' the waitress informed the telephone. Then after a pause: 'Well, I can't help that, can I?' The tone in which she said this suggested that it was no business of hers if her patrons chose to tell lies, though she had her own private opinion of them. Then she replaced the receiver and hurried out with her tray.

Miss Trant was now positive that the little man, the very uneasy little man, was Mr Eric Tipstead. To begin with, he looked exactly like a Mr Eric Tipstead. Then she was certain she had heard the woman addressing him as 'Eric deear'. And why should he have started up when he heard the name, why should the woman have restrained him? Johnson too! Nothing could be less convincing. Johnson was mere impudence.

She kept her eye on them. They were now eating away for dear life, wanting to get away as soon as they could but equally determined to have their three shillings' worth each if it choked them. In another five minutes they were hurrying out, and Miss Trant heard a car give a familiar gasp or two, then a rattle, then a roar immediately afterwards. Never had a car sounded so guilty; there was nervous apprehension in every diminishing hoot. Miss Trant was left to ponder the mystery of Mr Eric Tipstead and his partner, without whom the dining-room was very commonplace, just so much boiled mutton and treacle pudding, so many fat men and whisky advertisements She was aching to ask the waitress what had been said to her on the telephone, but even in her new character of independent woman, who dashed from Ely to Liverpool and stalked in and out of hotels, she could not do it. The waitress herself trotted about, looking as if she could tell a tale if she wanted to, and she had dropped some remark that had made the four men roar with laughter. It was most irritating. Miss Trant did not bolt her lunch Tipstead fashion, but on the other hand she did not linger over it as long as she might have done. And she gave the waitress only fourpence, instead of sixpence.

There were at least half a dozen cars and vans standing outside the front of the hotel now, but she was astonished to find that her own car was not there at all. She stood on the threshold, staring in bewilderment. Then she walked round the assembled cars. It was not there.

'I'm looking for my car,' she explained to a man who was hanging about the door. 'I left it here.'

'Ar,' said the man, looking wise. 'Blue two-seater was it?'

She replied, eagerly, that it was.

'Ar. It's round the corner 'ere. 'Ad to shift one of 'em about 'alf an hour ago.' And he led the way round the corner.

There it was, much to her relief. She climbed in, and was about to start the engine when she noticed there was something strange about the dashboard, something strange indeed about the whole interior.

'All right, miss?' the man asked.

'All wrong. This isn't my car.' She got out and looked at it.

'Then whose car is it?' the man, anxious to be helpful, walked round the car after her.

'I don't know whose car it is, I only know it isn't mine. It's like it but it isn't it. I'm afraid that sounds ridiculous. Well, I suppose my car must be about somewhere.

The man began to stare at her and as he stared his mouth slowly opened.

'I remember now,' she went on, not bothering about him, for he seemed very stupid. 'This car was in front of mine when I went in to lunch. I noticed that it seemed extraordinarily like mine. Yes, this is the one.' She broke off; it was impossible to talk to that fish-like stare. 'What's the matter?'

'They took it,' the man said slowly.

'Who took what? Do you mean my car? Did someone mistake it for this? I know. Was it - ' she hesitated.

'About 'alf an hour ago,' the man put in. 'Just after I'd 'ad to move this. A couple comes dashing out, gets in, goes off without a word. Smallish feller with eye-glasses, it was. His wife picks up a big coat that's lying over the side, puts it on, and then they're off without a word.'

'The Tipsteads!' cried Miss Trant.

'I beg yer pardon, Miss.'

'That's the name of the people who took it, or at least I think it is. Tipstead.'

'If 'e was that by name, 'e wasn't that by nature,' the man observed rather bitterly. 'As I say, 'e gives me nothing for my trouble but goes off without a word. And then 'e goes and takes the wrong car, seemingly. Now if 'e'd only said something. They were trying it on, if you ask me. I says to myself at the time, I says "You're in a bit of a 'urry, aren't you." Going off like that without a word! I might 'ave known!'

'But this is absurd!' cried Miss Trant. "They've taken my car and now they're miles away. What on earth am I to do?'

'I should take theirs if I was you,' said the man with an air of deep cunning.

'But I don't want theirs. They've got all my things. Which way did they go?'

'Took the north road.' And the man pointed.

'I wonder if I could overtake them,' she mused. 'I suppose I could drive this one. But how do I know this is theirs? It might belong to somebody else.'

'That's theirs all right,' he replied. 'I saw 'em come up in it. It's the spit image o' yours, too.'

She got into the car again, started it up, and ran it backwards and forwards once or twice. It was as easy to handle as her own, and was indeed a twin Mercia. Finally she reversed it round to the front of the hotel, with the vague idea of consulting the landlord. At that moment a motor-cycle came tearing up to the hotel. It stopped just as she stopped.

'Where is he, where is he?' cried a very angry feminine voice. 'Where is he? - you - you – ' here it choked a little - 'you big vamp, you!'

Miss Trant looked round and was astonished to find that the furious little woman who had just jumped out of the sidecar was screaming at her. 'What on earth are you talking about?' she cried.

The woman was even more astonished. As she stared, her face fell. 'Oo, I'm sorry.' She was now joined by the young man who had dismounted from the motor-cycle. 'This isn't her, Willy,' she wailed. Then she looked at the car, and her eyes grew round and her mouth opened. 'This is our car, isn't it, Willy? I'm sure it is.'

Willy, a very stolid young man, looked it over carefully and announced that it was certainly their car.

'I know what he's done,' she wailed again. 'You needn't tell me. He's gone and sold it. Three hours away and the first thing he does is to sell the car. She's made him sell it.'

'We'll see about that,' said Willy, unmoved. 'We can ask, can't we?' And he looked at Miss Trant.

'I don't know what you're talking about,' said Miss Trant, looking from one to the other, 'but I can assure you this car doesn't belong to me.'

'Then what are you doing in it?' Willy broke in, rudely.

Miss Trant, who was annoyed, gave him a sharp glance. 'Please be quiet a moment,' she commanded. 'Otherwise I can't explain. This car belongs to some people who have just gone off in my car.'

'That's right.' This was from the first man, who felt it was time he took charge of the situation. 'You see, a party comes out, gets in this lady's car, goes off without a word - '

'What sort of party?' asked Willy.

'A little-ish feller with eye-glasses - '

'Eric!' cried the woman. 'I knew it, I knew it. What did I tell you, Willy?'

'Sounds like him all right,' Willy agreed.

'A biggish woman, fair-'aired, 'is wife was,' the man continued.

'His wife!' The way in which the agitated little woman let loose these two syllables confirmed Miss Trant. This was Mrs Eric Tipstead. She was small and dark, like her husband, but looked altogether more energetic and purposeful. She was one of those little stringy women who never seem to tire.

'They left the hotel in rather a hurry,' Miss Trant began.

'Yes, I'll bet they did,' said Mrs Tipstead grimly, folding up her mouth.

'And they ran off in my car. That was about half an hour ago.'

'You hear that, Willy?' cried Mrs Tipstead. 'In for a penny, in for a pound. Taking cars now! She goes and makes him take this lady's car right under her nose.'

'Hold on, Sis, hold on,' Willy put in. 'He didn't mean to take it, you bet. Did he?' And he appealed to Miss Trant and the other man.

'No, of course he didn't,' said Miss Trant.

'It's as easy to explain as anything you could wish for, considering, that is, it's a bit of a mix-up,' said the man. And he began an immense narrative of what would obviously have developed into an enormous narrative if Miss Trant had not cut it short by giving a brief account of the affair as she saw it.

'There's no doubt this is his car, then?' asked Miss Trant at the end of her story.

'Not a bit. Look, there's his bag.' She pointed to the luggage in the dicky seat. 'And - and - look there, Willy - that's hers.' She plucked out the suitcase and flung it down on the road. 'The impudence of it, with a bag and all!' And then, quite suddenly, surprisingly, she burst into tears and had to lean against her brother, who did not support her very tenderly or even adequately. Miss Trant, who was still sitting in the car, looked on and felt very foolish.

'What are you going to do then, Sis?' asked Willy, a practical man clearly at a disadvantage.

Some choking sounds from Mrs Tipstead might have been interpreted to mean that she intended to follow her erring husband.

Miss Trant came to the conclusion it was time she intervened. The relations between Mr and Mrs Tipstead and the large blonde were no business of hers, and the thought of being in any way entangled in their affairs made her shudder; but the fact remained that her car and most of her best clothes were being rushed into the North somewhere by Mr Tipstead at that very moment. She was confident that, whatever he did, he would not return to the hotel with the car. He must have known that it was his wife who rang up when they were having lunch.

'The point is', she said clearly and calmly, 'do you happen to know where these - where Mr Tipstead is going? The very moment you came I was just setting out to try and overtake them. The man showed me which road they took. And we're only wasting time, you know.'

'Yes, I do know,' replied Mrs Tipstead, calmer now. 'At least I've a good idea. If I hadn't, I couldn't have come so far. I got her address and they're going there. I found a letter she'd sent him, found it this very morning. I'll bet he doesn't even know he's lost it yet, but he's going to know very soon, mark my words. She's got a house at Sheffield, and they're going there.'

'Can you drive this car?'

'No, I can't, and that's another thing. Never would let me touch it, artful monkey! Said I might hurt myself! A lot he cared!'

'Then you must come with me,' said Miss Trant. 'That's the only thing to do. If you really think they've gone to this address you have, we must go there, too. I don't want this car of yours and I certainly do want my own and all my things that are in it.'

'That's so,' said Willy, obviously much relieved. 'I'll have to get back anyhow, Sis. You'll get to Sheffield easy before dark, and this lady'll look after you.'

'Oh, I can look after myself all right,' exclaimed Mrs Tipstead. 'And it does seem best, doesn't it, Willy?' Then she turned to Miss Trant and suddenly became very stiff and genteel. 'I'm sure it's very kind of you, Miss - er. I'm Mrs Tipstead.'

'My name is Trant.'

It seemed as if 'Very pleased to meet you' was only prevented at the last moment from popping out. Perhaps the absurdity of it in that situation dawned on Mrs Tipstead just in time. All she said, after some hesitation, was: 'Very - kind indeed, of you, Miss Trant.' Then she turned aside with her brother.

Miss Trant hunted for a map in the car but could not find one. There was one hanging in the hall of the hotel, however, and she traced the route to Sheffield on it with her finger. When she returned to the car, she found Mrs Tipstead sitting in it and staring straight ahead, down the road to the North, like a small damp fury.

It was a fantastic journey. The road crossed the valleys of the Dove and the Derwent and wound about the lower spurs of the Peak. They ran along green troughs powdered with dust; they sailed up towards great castles of vapour, rosy Himalayas of cloud; they sank through hollows of blue air cupped round with grass; and all the hills, the dales and dingles, the farmhouses came curving to meet them, steadily shone or gloomed for a moment, then slipped noiselessly away like places in a dream. So it seemed to one part of Miss Trant, which saw nothing, knew nothing, but this pageantry which went, mazed with wonder, flashing a wing, through the golden afternoon. But she was triune; and the other two of her were very differently occupied. One was busy with the mechanism of the car, and a little dubious of the matter of gears. The other - it was a fair division - had to attend to fellow humanity which was present in the form of Mrs Tipstead. At first, Mrs Tipstead was very stiff, very quiet. Miss Trant did not know what to do with her. It is not easy to make conversation with a strange woman, a woman moreover, with a social background very different from your own, when you are helping her to overtake a runaway husband. It is all the more difficult when two-thirds of you are busy elsewhere, up on the hill, down among the gears. Miss Trant did what she could, however, and very soon Mrs Tipstead, who was not equal to the task of keeping up her stiff genteel manner, began pouring out her confidences.

Miss Trant had murmured something about tea.

'I reely couldn't, you know, Miss Trant,' Mrs Tipstead cried into her ear. 'I believe a mouthful would choke me. You don't know how I feel, I'm that worked up.' There was genuine distress in her tones, but there was also a certain melodramatic gusto. Obviously she rather liked the thought of being choked by a mouthful.

Miss Trant said nothing because there did not seem to be anything suitable to say. One of those vague little sympathetic noises would have done, but you cannot make them in a car, at least you cannot possibly make them loud enough to be heard. It is not easy, she reflected, saying anything to someone who confessed to being 'worked up'. You really ought to shout back: 'I hope you'll soon be worked down.'

'It's pretty country, isn't it?' Mrs Tipstead remarked quite unexpectedly. 'I've always been fond of this part. I like a bit of nice scenery, don't you? Eric now - my husband - never cared for it much. There, I'm beginning again. I won't say another word.' And she threw herself back against the seat.

'Do go on, unless you really don't want to,' said Miss Trant. She wanted to add to this, to say something tactful, sympathetic, but discovered she could not frame a sentence that would suggest the right attitude, something between brutal indifference and equally brutal curiosity.

The other was silent for a minute or two, but her thoughts demanded relief. 'I shouldn't have minded half so much,' she declared suddenly, 'if he'd been honest with me, if he'd had it out with me. But to go sneaking off like that! Just leaving a bit of a note! I shouldn't have known anything if it hadn't been for that letter she sent him I found this morning, the one with her address on, this address we're going to in Sheffield. Not that I didn't know something was going on. I knew that all right. There's no smoke without fire, is there? When me lord's out night after night, I knew there was something on. "Business," he says, leaving me to look after the shop. You see, we've got a shop - nice little business - sweets and tobacco and newspapers and fancies - and he does a bit in the insurance line, too, and of course that does take him out at night. But it never took him out as much as all that. Besides, I could tell the diff'rence - you always can, can't you? - because he'd try to sneak out and then if I faced him with it, he'd go off in a minute, fairly screaming at me, telling me I didn't understand what business was. You always know, don't you, when they get angry like that about nothing, they're hiding something. It's their consciences, if you ask me. They know they're doing wrong, silly babies. Well, I pretended not to see. You can't do anything else, can you?'

There was a large car coming towards them, travelling at a great speed almost in the middle of the road, and Miss Trant had to attend to this car. When they had passed it, she found it quite impossible to settle any problem in conjugal tactics. 'I don't know,' she replied.

'No, of course you don't. I was quite forgetting. Well, I've always said you've got to have it out right at the first, as soon as you notice anything, or you've got to leave it alone, keep your dignity, you see. And I left it alone, soft thing that I was. And this is what's happened. Catch me doing it again! But I thought I knew him all right.' She thought about this for a moment, then went on: 'And so I do. It's her I don't know. But I've heard a few things about her, and if I didn't know what I do know, you wouldn't see me here now. If she'd been a bit different, he could have had her and welcome. I've got my pride. But if you ask me, he's just been dragged into this, couldn't help himself. She's said "Come" and he's gone. I know him.'

She said no more but stared fiercely ahead, down the road that led to Sheffield, where her Eric was waiting to be rescued.

Remembering that odd pair in the dining-room, Miss Trant concluded that this view of the situation was probably the right one. She had now to transform those vague figures of fun into the real people of Mrs Tipstead's vehement declarations. It was strange; it was rather frightening. For the moment she was repelled by the thought of this sheer thrust of life beneath these grotesque surfaces. It would not do. She told herself she ought not to feel like that. It was mean, cowardly, snobbish perhaps; it was - horrible thought - what people call old-maidish. She had not the slightest desire to be married, and especially at this moment, but she shuddered at the idea of being old-maidish. She must not mind being jostled by things, by people, by life; she must be ready to take hold herself.

'Only eight miles to Sheffield now,' she announced.

'Do you know, Miss Trant - ' Mrs Tipstead hesitated. 'It wouldn't make any difference, would it? - I mean to getting there in time. But I'm beginning to feel I'd like a cup of tea, if we could find a nice place. I haven't had anything since breakfast, and I'm beginning to feel a bit faint, and I think just a little something would do me good. What do you think?'

'I'm sure it would,' replied Miss Trant heartily. 'We'll stop at the next decent place.'

They pulled up at a little tea-room and had the place to themselves. Tea meant confidences to Mrs Tipstead, and as soon as she had poured the first two cups she began the story of her dreadful morning, the discovery of the letter, the summoning of her brother Willy, who knew the road and so had suggested telephoning to one or two hotels where the runaways might have halted for lunch. 'We didn't do that till we'd started off ourselves, you know,' she explained. 'From

Lichfield, you know. That's were we live.'

'Lichfield! Then that's why she said Johnson.' Miss Trant felt like Sherlock Holmes, an old favourite of hers. And she had spent hours and hours - it seemed like years - reading Boswell's *Life of Johnson* to the Colonel, whose robust passion for Boswell and Gibbon had now closed the eighteenth century to his daughter for ever.

'Who said Johnson?' Mrs Tipstead stared over the piece of buttered tea-cake she held.

'Why, that woman, when the waitress asked if they were called Tipstead.' And she told the story of the telephone call.

'It just shows you, doesn't it?' Mrs Tipstead was bitterly triumphant. 'He'd have never had enough off to do that. But trust her! This isn't the first time, if you ask me. I've heard about her. What's she like?'

Miss Trant gave a brief and unflattering description.

'I thought so. I've never set eyes on her, that's the funny thing. As far as I can make out, she's only been in the place about three or four months, came as a barmaid. She'd been on the stage a bit before that, Willy says. You know the sort. But then I don't suppose you do, Miss Trant, a lady like you. I don't know much about that sort myself, I'm sure, never being one for theatres and going to hotels and all that. That's Eric's style, though, always was. He always thought he could have done well on the stage, and I dare say he would - comic, you know, when he gets going, good as a pantomime. I've laughed sometimes till I've had to tell him to stop. That's what attracted her, I'll be bound, that and his looks. Going there night after night, putting it on a bit and playing the comic, you know, that's what did it. And me waiting on in the shop, night after night!' She halted between anger and tears. 'Aren't you ready for another cup, Miss Trant? I'm sure you are.'

Miss Trant was not quite ready. She was indeed rather busy trying to reconcile this Mr Tipstead, so dashing, so droll, so fascinating to the other sex, with the little rabbit of a man she remembered at the hotel.

Mrs Tipstead poured out another cup for herself, and having tasted it, plunged into further confidences. 'I'll tell you what it was that turned him. I thought it was the best bit of luck we'd ever had when it happened, but you can never tell how things'll turn out, can you? This last March he won a first prize in a competition - five hundred pounds.'

'Five hundred pounds!' Miss Trant was genuinely astonished. She could not imagine Mr Tipstead winning a prize of any kind, let alone one of five hundred pounds.

'Five hundred pounds,' said the wife, with mournful pride. 'Sparklets they were - funny little bits of sayings, you know. He'd been trying and trying and better trying at it for months, filling in coupons and sending 'em up with a sixpenny postal order every time, till I said "Oh, for goodness' sake, Eric," I said, "you might think we're made of postal orders. You've wasted enough time and money on them things if you ask me," I told him. I knew he was clever at them, but it seemed to me they only took the first they came to and gave 'em prizes and his were never at the top of the bag. Well, not two weeks after - it was a Tuesday afternoon - two young fellows came, one with a camera, and told us he'd got the first prize. They took our photographs - "Mr and Mrs Tipstead receiving the cheque from our representative" they called it - and they put in a long piece about how pleased we were and what we were going to do with the money and all sorts. I wanted him to buy a bigger insurance book with it or move into a bigger shop, but no - he wouldn't have that, and of course I couldn't say anything. He'd won it, not me. So he must cut a dash with it, buys that car outside there, some new suits of clothes and one thing and another. And what with getting all this money and having his photograph in the paper and what he said and having a car, it just turned his head. "Lord Tipstead" they began calling him down in the town, Willy told me; taking him off, you see - though there was a lot of jealousy in it, if you ask me. And of course all these silly girls began making a fuss of him - they've nothing better to do now, girls haven't. Then this one comes along - regular home-wrecker, she is, from what I can see, the sort you'd think you'd never come across off the pictures. Don't you think this butter tastes funny, Miss Trant?'

'It's margarine. I can't eat it.'

'I don't blame you. You ought to have another of these cakes. What was I saying? Oh, I'd finished, hadn't I. You really must excuse me, Miss Trant, it's so strange meeting you like this and I'm that bewildered today I hardly know what I'm saying. If you met me ordinary times, you wouldn't know me.'

There was no reply to this, so Miss Trant put a question instead. 'Have you any children?'

'I haven't. Not that we haven't wanted them, me especially, and it's been a great trouble to us. Perhaps it's as well as things are turning out, though you wouldn't be so lonely, would you?' She choked a little, coughed into her handkerchief, drank some tea, and looked tearful.

'Won't you have another cake?' This was very inadequate, but it was the best Miss Trant could do at the moment.

'Well, do you think we might halve one between us, I really couldn't eat a whole one. No? Well, I won't bother. I'll finish this and then we'll go. Yes, when you're treated like this, you don't know whether to feel glad or sorry you haven't any children, you really don't.

And when I think what I've done for that man! There's nothing I haven't done for him. I've given him my whole life.'

These phrases came out too glibly, they were not from the heart, but from the newspapers and the penny novelettes. If Miss Trant had liked the little woman less, she would have let them pass, but now she felt she couldn't. 'You know, I'm awfully sorry, Mrs Tipstead, and I'd like to help if I can. And you mustn't think I'm unsympathetic if I say that I never understand what that phrase means - about giving your whole life, you know.'

'If you'd been a wife, Miss Trant, you'd know soon enough.'

'Well, I haven't, of course. I've only been a daughter. But do you mean that all the time you've been married you've been sacrificing yourself, never enjoying the life you had together or anything?'

'I've enjoyed nearly every bit of it,' cried Mrs Tipstead warmly. 'I know Eric's had his faults - a bit extravagant and silly - thoughtless, you know - but you couldn't want a better husband. I won't say we've always had the best of luck - we haven't - but we've enjoyed ourselves, I can tell you.'

'You wouldn't have preferred being single, then?'

'Single! Me!' she cried in horror. 'Living by myself, nobody to look after, nobody coming in and out, no bits of jokes and bits of comfort! I may have had a lot to do for him, but I've never begrudged it, never, except just lately perhaps, brushing his coats and ironing his trousers so that he could go out and meet that - that - fat painted barmaid. You needn't ask me that, Miss Trant.'

'Then you really haven't given your life, you know. You've been living it just as you wanted to live it all the time. I mean, I don't see what more you could have done with it. You don't mind my saying this, do you?'

Mrs Tipstead shook her head, then was silent for a minute or two, struggling through into honesty. When at last she spoke, her voice sounded different; it was quieter, more sure of itself. 'It's a funny business, isn't it? I've thought a bit about it lately. And I see what you mean. If you do give a lot, it's only because you want to. But it's terrible when it's all thrown back in your face. You must wonder why I'm running after him like this. Of course I'm still fond of him - but I've got my pride the same as anybody else, and perhaps a bit more than most. But I know Eric, and I've nearly had trouble with him before. He's weak, Eric is, for all he's so clever and all that, and this woman's simply got hold of him and made him do what she wanted. He never wanted another wife, not he. He only wanted somebody to show off in front of, somebody who didn't know him like I did; he never wanted to be landed into this; and I'm sure he's miserable even now and he'll be worse tomorrow. If he can tell me to my face, he doesn't want to come back, that'll be different; I'll go away and never say another word. But he won't, you'll see.'

'I'm sure you're right,' said Miss Trant, remembering the uneasy little figure in the hotel.

'A wife knows, Miss Trant,' Mrs Tipstead observed earnestly. Then she looked up and, with a startling change of tone, cried: 'Well, Miss, I hope you're not going to charge us for butter when we've had nothing but margarine.' And after wrangling with the waitress, she then proceeded to wrangle with Miss Trant, who wanted to pay the bill herself. Mrs Tipstead did not want to pay it, she wanted to divide it scrupulously into two, and she had her way.

A few miles brought them to pleasant hilly suburbs and very soon they were threading their way towards the vast haze that was Sheffield.

III

Miss Trant sighed with relief. This was the street they were looking for, and though it was not far from the centre of the town, it had been very difficult indeed to find, and she was weary of stopping to ask the way, turning in crowded streets, dodging trams and lorries, all of which she had been doing for the last hour. It was a grimy and melancholy street, one of those that have steadily fallen in the social scale these last forty years, that begin by housing prosperous merchants and bank managers and gradually decline to the humble level of theatrical lodgings, corset agencies, palmists' consulting-rooms, and other and more dubious enterprises. The other end of the street, not far away, was blocked by a high wall. They had stopped the car a few yards round the corner, and now looked down the street, wondering what to do.

'Look,' cried Mrs Tipstead, pointing. 'Isn't that it? It's just like this.'

The car stood outside a house about half-way down on the left; it was the only one in the street. Miss Trant was sure it was hers. What a pity she couldn't take it without a word! But some explanation was necessary, of course. Perhaps she could get it back without being involved in the affairs of the Tipsteads.

'Hadn't I better go first?' she asked. 'I shall have to see your husband, of course. What's the name of this woman?'

'If you mean her second name, I don't know. It was just Effie on the letter. So far as I can see and from what Willy said, everybody in the town just called her Effie. They would, wouldn't they?' Mrs Tipstead added vindictively.

'Well, I simply refuse to go up to that house and ask for Effie.' She thought for a moment. 'Perhaps you had better go first and inquire for your husband.'

'No, that wouldn't do. I'll tell you what. I'll get out here and wait a bit. You drive right up to the house and ask for Eric - Mr Tipstead - you see, and I'll - I'll - come in later on.' She was very excited now.

After some hesitation, Miss Trant agreed, though she did not understand what Mrs Tipstead intended to do and could not imagine her waiting outside in the street very long. She drove up to the house, discovered that the car really was her own, with all its luggage there just as she had packed it in that morning, then knocked at the door, not very loudly because she suddenly felt quite uncomfortable, almost guilty, as if she were a spy. This feeling did not last long, however, and as nobody came she gave the door, which did not look as if it had had any attention from anybody for years, a good sound rapping. Then she noticed there was one of those old-fashioned bells that have to be pulled out. She gave it a little tug, but it did not move. She gave it a hard tug and immediately fell back with about a yard of wire in her hand. At that moment, of course, before she could release the wire, the door was opened.

'Good evening,' said the man who had opened the door. He had a thick husky sort of voice.

'Good evening,' gasped Miss Trant, feeling very foolish. She let go of the bell handle and it hung down absurdly, at the end of its yard of wire.

'You've had a bit o' bother with that, have you? Out of date, you know, out of date. All electric now, isn't it. You can't stir for it,' he observed amiably. He was a stout elderly man with a prominent reddish nose, an expanse of grey-bristled jowl, and a pair of spectacles pushed up to his damp forehead. One hand clasped a newspaper, and the other, now that the door was open, replaced in his mouth a short clay pipe. He wore neither coat nor collar, was lax in the matter of buttons, and altogether was a figure of unlovely ease.

'Is Mr Tipstead here, please?'

He took out his pipe to think this over. 'Tipstead? Tipstead? Nothing to do with the Bird-in-Hand Friendly Society, is it? 'Cos that's two doors down. We're always getting 'em here.'

'No, it hasn't. I was told Mr Tipstead was staying here. He took my car by mistake, and I've got his.'

The man's eyes grew rounder, then one of them gave her a wink. He leaned forward. 'Our Effie's chap, you mean,' he whispered. 'I've heard about that car. Didn't know his name was Tipstead, though. "Eric" she calls him. "Eric or Little by Little," I said, right off. And he didn't like it, neither. Come in.'

No sooner had Miss Trant followed him into the dilapidated little hall than the large blonde herself, Effie, bounced out of a back room, crying: 'Who is it, Unkerlarthur?'

'Half a minute, half a minute! You'll soon know.' And Uncle Arthur ushered Miss Trant into this same back room, a rather small and dark apartment that contained a bewildering assortment of small tables and knick-knacks and fretwork brackets and photographs. Among these, not unlike a knick-knack or piece of fretwork, was seated Mr Tipstead, nervously pulling at a cigarette.

Miss Trant addressed herself to him at once. 'You probably remember me. I was lunching at the next table to you this morning. You went off in my car - '

She could say no more. Mr Tipstead sprang forward excitedly, and he and his Effie began explaining at the top of their voices. They continued for several minutes, first one of them taking the lead, then the other, correcting one another, as they went along. But it was Effie who concluded the explanation. 'And so we found your name and address on one of the bags and were going to write this very minute, weren't we, Eric, to tell you how it had happened, and Eric was going to offer to drive it back for you, weren't you, Eric, to make it all right, and we'd sent a telegram to the hotel to ask about his car, you see, because that was left behind and somebody might have got it, hadn't we, Eric?'

'Your car's outside.'

'Outside!'

'Yes,' Miss Trant went on, 'I came up here in it.'

'Thank God!' cried Effie, blowing hard. She had dropped the manner she had assumed at lunch, probably finding it too great a strain in such a crisis, and was clearly now her own natural self, dramatic, voluble, vulgar.

A weak smile lit up the face of Mr Tipstead, who still had that vague hunted look. 'Well, that's a bit of all right. And thank you very much, Miss - er - Trant. That's it, isn't it - Miss Trant? We got the name right, you see. And we can just change over now, can't we? Drive it all right? Yours was O.K. It's the same bus, you know, but a bit newer than mine.'

'Just fancy!' And Effie's eyes, which were her best feature and looked quite bright under her thickly pencilled lashes, travelled from Mr Tipstead to Miss Trant, from Miss Trant to Unkerlarthur who was leaning against the door, puffing at his little clay, and enjoying every moment of the scene. Gaiety itself, Effie invited them all to fancy with her. 'You've no idea what a load you've taken off our minds,' she told Miss Trant. 'It was just spoiling everything, wasn't it, Eric?' She smiled hugely at that gentleman and threw an arm about his shoulders. It was a fine solid arm coming out boldly, imperially, from the short sleeve of her lilac silk jumper, and it seemed to announce at that moment that it was ready to protect an Eric it contrived to diminish from all the trials and assaults of this world. Mr Tipstead wriggled a little in its embrace.

'Now then, Miss Trant,' Effie continued, 'do sit down and make yourself at home. And Unkerlarthur, if you're going to stop in this room, you'll have to go and put a collar and a coat on and make yourself look respectable; we're not just by ourselves now. Aren't you playing at the theatre this week?'

'I am that.' And Uncle Arthur blew out his cheeks, sent his hands sawing backwards and forwards and, in short, gave an excellent imitation of a trombone player. 'Pom-pom-poppa-pom. Pom-pom-poppa-pom. It's a musical comedy - *The Girl in the Garage* - this week - augmented orchestra - so I'm in. You'll soon be rid of me. I'll have to go and change soon.' And he gave Miss Trant, who had turned to look at him, a prodigious wink. We know, don't we? - the wink said to her.

Miss Trant did not know, but she smiled at him. She liked Uncle Arthur, somehow, and the thought that he was one of those mysterious creatures who creep from under the stage and sit so coolly, blowing or fiddling away, in their little deep trench, gave her a thrill. She had always been fond of the theatre - the whole enchanted absurdity of it - and had never been able to go often enough.

'I'm sure you must be tired, Miss Trant,' Erne continued. 'Now do sit yourself down and make yourself at home.'

'I won't, if you don't mind. Now that we've settled which car is which, I think I'd better go.' And it occurred to Miss Trant, when she had said this, that she had not the faintest idea where she was going.

Effie looked really disappointed, almost aggrieved. 'Oh, but after coming all that way and bringing Eric's car and us taking your car nearly all the day and you coming right out of your way like this! We can't let you run away like that, can we, Eric? Hello! What's the matter with you, Eric? No, don't interrupt him. He's thought of something, thought of it deep down in his little head, all by himself, and he'll tell us if we'll keep quiet a minute.'

This was badinage heavy enough to make an elephant wince, but it had no effect upon Mr Tipstead, who still stared at Miss Trant, with his round little mouth open. 'I've just been trying to work it out,' he said at last, giving his weak laugh. 'This is what I can't understand. How do you come to be here, Miss Trant? This address wasn't on any of the bags was it?'

'I've no idea,' replied Miss Trant easily. 'I never looked at the bags.'

'Well, I never did! I never thought of that.' Effie looked from one to the other. 'You just came here and we'd got your car and you'd got ours and I never thought any more about it. Well, how did you know we were coming to this house? Hello! What's that?' There was a repeated knocking at the front door. 'Unkerlarthur, go and see who that is.'

'It's somebody come to put the rent and rates up, 'cos he's seen two cars standing at the door.' remarked Uncle Arthur, with a waggish glance all round. They could hear him chuckling down the hall.

'Well, you don't mind us asking, do you,' Eflie pursued, 'but really it does seem funny, doesn't it, you coming here – '

Mr Tipstead held up his hand. 'Half a minute,' he said, listening. Then he rose to his feet, a very shaky little man. There was a sound of voices in the hall.

'What's the matter? Who is it?' cried Effie, now looking alarmed.

'It's her,' said Eric in a very small voice. It really seemed as if all his colour had ebbed away; he was obviously terrified.

Mrs Tipstead marched into the room, a little figure but compact, charged with energy, all bristling. She halted, gave a quick glance at the astonished Effie, then surveyed the shrinking figure of her husband. 'Well, Eric, I've followed you, you see.'

Effie made a last desperate attempt to carry off the situation with a high hand. 'Here,' she cried, 'who told you to come in here? What do you want?'

Mrs Tipstead was fully equal to the situation. The question presented her with a magnificent cue. 'What do I want?' she cried. She pointed to the wretched Tipstead. 'That's what I want. My husband.'

'O my God!' groaned Uncle Arthur at the door, and he promptly shut it and left himself on the other side.

'Now then, Eric,' his wife continued briskly, 'I'm not going to argue with you here. You can take your choice here and now. Just make up your mind whether you'll stay here with this woman or go back to the shop with me. One or the other. And it's the last time, mind.'

'Eric, no; you wouldn't, would you, Eric!' As she shrieked this out, Effie looked as if she were about to fling herself bodily at poor little Mr Tipstead, who would certainly have gone down like a nine-pin. He shrank back, moistened his lips with his tongue, and looked utterly abject.

'Not after all you've said, Eric,' moaned Effie, who was rapidly going to pieces.

'You be quiet and leave him alone,' commanded Mrs Tipstead. 'Let him make his own mind up.'

There was a silence.

'Well?' asked Mrs Tipstead. Eric looked up, looked down, cleared his throat, swung one foot, cleared his throat again, swung the other foot, then made a sound that bore no resemblance to any known word.

There was another silence.

It was Miss Trant who broke it, shattered it completely. Miss Trant, who had no business to be there at all. At the sight of Tipstead standing there, so dumb, so abject, a kind of angry shame had begun to take possession of her mind, had pricked and then at last gored her until she could bear it no longer.

'Oh, for goodness' sake, say something or do something!' she cried to him, stamping her foot and beating her hands together. 'Don't stand like that. Do have some courage, and either go or stay. Anything, anything but this! It's - it's - absolutely vile.' She was too excited to be surprised at herself, though this was perhaps the most astonishing speech she had ever made.

He said nothing but at last he did something. Slowly, with bent head, absurdly, pitiably like a small boy in deep disgrace, he walked to the door, opened it, and went out. He was going back home. Without saying a word, his wife immediately followed after him. The two left behind never moved. Effie stared at the open door, her lower lip hanging foolishly. A few moments later, Mrs Tipstead marched in again.

'He'd left his hat in here,' she announced. She picked it up from the sideboard, flashed a smiling glance at Miss Trant as she passed, and went out, this time closing the door behind her. There came the sound of a car being started outside in the street.

Before Miss Trant could do anything at all, Effie suddenly became alarmingly active. She ran to the door and then came running back again, crying 'Oh, he's gone, he's gone. I've lost him, I've lost him' - or something that sounded like that. With a final gesture of despair, she flung one arm along the mantelpiece and knocked over a large pink vase. Perhaps the hideous cheerfulness of this object enraged her, for now she picked it up and hurled it into the fender, instantly smashing it to pieces. Then she threw herself into the armchair and burst into a storm of tears, sobbed and sobbed, her whole body shaking and her feet drumming on the floor.

It was an alarming spectacle. Effie was no chit of a girl but a woman on a very generous scale. The room did not seem large enough for such convulsions. It was incredible that they could have been set in motion by Mr Tipstead. 'In another minute', Miss Trant thought, 'she'll be in hysterics,' and saw herself trying to hold Effie down as she had once had to hold down a maid at home. She was annoyed with herself for not having gone before this, but on the other hand she felt she could not go now, not at this moment. 'Don't, don't!' she cried, and moved a step or two forward, with the intention of doing something. But she did not know what to do. The usual consolatory little actions seemed absurd, like trying to give a pat or two to an earthquake.

'Now what's up here?' Uncle Arthur was puffing and blowing before them, looking from one to the other. 'Has that chap gone?' he asked Miss Trant. 'I thought I heard him. Nay, lass, bear up, bear up.' He gave his niece an affectionate slap or two on the shoulder. 'You're well rid of him. He was nowt but twopennorth o' copper. Nay, lass, take it easy, take it easy.'

Effie refused to take it easy. Violently she shook herself free from his hand, drummed her feet on the floor again, and cried louder than ever.

'Well, you must have it out, I suppose,' he observed philosophically. Then he glanced at the hearth. 'Gone and smashed an ornament and all,' he said to Miss Trant, lowering his voice and speaking confidentially. 'Can't help it, you know. Temperament, that's what it is. We've all got it; runs in the family. If we're up, we're up, but if we're down, we're down. It goes with talent, you know, and it's always been the same i' this family. Her mother - she was my sister - could sing *The Volunteer Organist* and such like and make a whole club-roomful cry - but if she were cross, she'd raise the roof, break anything. And her grandfather - my father, you see - was the best euphonium-player the Old Dyke Band ever had - I've known 'em come fifty miles to hear his *Death o' Nelson* - but if he didn't want to play, he wouldn't play, you couldn't make him. It wasn't beer, you know,' he added earnestly, as if to arrest the thought that surely must be uppermost in his listener's mind. 'He liked a drop, but it wasn't that. It was temperament. It runs in the family. I'm a bit that way myself. But I'll have to be off.' He was dressed for the theatre now, for he was wearing a very old dress coat and waistcoat, a queer turned-down collar and about an inch of black tie. He caught Miss Trant's surprised glance, and winked at her. 'Ar,' he remarked complacently, 'I know what you're thinking.'

'Do you? Well, what am I thinking?' Miss Trant was amused.

'You're thinking "He's gone and forgotten to change his trousers," that what's your thinking.'

Miss Trant laughed. 'Well, as a matter of fact, I was.' And with good reason, for he still wore the same trousers he was wearing before and they were blue.

Uncle Arthur winked again. 'What the eye doesn't see, the heart won't miss,' he observed. 'I'm only on duty, you might say, from the waist up, and I could wear a kilt or clogs and it 'ud make no difference you see. You notice next time you're at the theatre, and you'll see what I mean.'

Effie was being overlooked and so she stopped crying, to exclaim indignantly: 'That's right, Unkerlarthur, go on, don't bother about me! Standing there talking about trousers and kilts! And look at me!'

'Well, you feel a bit better now, Effie lass, don't you?'

'No, I don't.' And to prove it she began again.

'Well, I must be off,' he said hastily.

'And so must I.' said Miss Trant.

'No, no, Miss Grant,' cried Eme, 'don't leave me to myself. I won't be responsible if I'm left to myself, I won't really. Don't go'

Uncle Arthur stared at Miss Trant in pained surprise. 'Nay, Miss, have a heart. You're not busy, are you? Well, stop on a bit and keep her company.'

'Nobody wants me, nobody,' moaned Effie.

'Course they do, Effie lass,' said her uncle heartily. 'Miss Dent here will stop and look after you a bit. I'm off then! Be good!' He gave Miss Trant a last wink as he went out.

Effie sniffed a little, then began to dry her eyes. 'I'll bet I look a sight, don't I?' And undoubtedly she did. 'Do sit down and make yourself comfortable. I don't want to keep you here if you've anything to do, of course, but I wish you'd stay a bit. There's nobody here, and if I'm by myself tonight, I shall get the jimjams, what with all the excitement there's been today and the state I've been in this last week and the way he went off just now. If Unkerlarthur hadn't been working at the theatre this week, he'd have stayed with me - he's a good sort is Unkerlarthur - and this is really his house; well, really, me and my sister Elsie and him we all join in it, and we let rooms to theatricals, you know, as well, because my family has always been concerned with the profession, and I went on the stage for a time and then had to leave, it was too bad for my nerves, and Elsie - she's younger than me and very talented - she's still on, doing concert party work, you know.' All this came out in one unbroken torrent while she was still dabbing her eyes and patting her hair. How she contrived to say so much and say it so quickly, having apparently been in hysterics two minutes before, was a mystery.

'Now, Miss Grant -' Effie began again.

'Trant,' the lady put in, correcting her.

'Oh, you must excuse me. Of course it's Trant, isn't it. I had the name right at first, and then what with one thing and another - Did you catch my name? Longstaff, it is.' She stood up and examined herself in the mirror. 'First thing I must do is to tidy myself up a bit. I'll just slip upstairs, if you don't mind. Take your hat off, Miss Trant, and rest yourself properly. What about a cup of tea and something to eat?'

'It's awfully kind of you,' said Miss Trant, who was really touched by this show of hospitality. She was not merely an intruding stranger, she was the villain of the piece, for had she not brought Mrs Tipstead to this very door? It was clear, however, that Effie was anxious to keep her there, probably because she needed a listener more than usual this melancholy evening. 'But I had tea, you know, some time ago,' Miss Trant went on. 'And I really don't think I want any more, thank you.' She took a sensible interest in food, and had already begun to wonder about dinner.

'Ah, that's afternoon tea, you mean,' said Effie, 'but we go in for high tea in these parts, though as a matter of fact in this house supper's the big do, and I'll tell you why. You see what with Unkerlarthur being at the theatre and then us letting rooms to the profession, none of them really wants anything solid till the shows are over, about half past ten to eleven, that's the time they want a proper set-to, and so Mrs Moore - that's the woman that looks after the house - goes away in the afternoon and then doesn't come back till about nine or half past and then cooks something hot for everybody, you see.'

'That's a very queer way of living,' said Miss Trant. 'I don't understand how anybody sleeps after that.'

'They don't, you know, not early. But they can stay in bed in the morning. And they couldn't have a solid meal just before the show. Take these we've let to this week - I've not seen them but Unkerlarthur told me they were here again, and they've been here before - the Four Romanies - acrobats, you know - you'll probably have seen 'em - they're a good turn - well, if they'd their dinners at night and then went on to do their show, they'd have to be taken to hospital in ten minutes. And even Unkerlarthur has to wait. I've heard him say many a time "Give me a good plateful of steak and kidney pudding and you just might as well push a cake of soap up the old trombone." Can't play, you see, after that.'

'I see. But you needn't wait, eh?'

'Oh, no, not at all. They weren't expecting me, anyhow, tonight. That's why I say let's have a bit of something now. I could nip out for something in a minute. Just rough-and-ready, take-us-as-you-find-us, you know.'

Miss Trant was not anxious to take them as she found them. 'Look here,' she said, 'won't you come out to some hotel and have dinner with me? And by the way, I can't possibly leave Sheffield tonight. I must find an hotel to stay in tonight, and I must go and put my car away too.'

'With having these Romanies here - though one of 'em's only a dwarf - you never saw such a little man - we're rather full up, though I dare say I could squeeze you in here somewhere - '

'Don't trouble, thank you,' said Miss Trant earnestly. The thought of being squeezed in there was too much even for her new adventurousness. 'Probably you can take me to some hotel where I can stay and we can have dinner too.'

'I'd love that,' cried Effie enthusiastically. 'It's very nice of you, I'm sure, and if it's not saying too much, I don't mind telling you it's just what I need a night like this, I mean having a little friendly outing. Hello!' She broke off, and listened. 'Front door again. Hope it's somebody for the Bird-in-Hand this time. I'm getting nervous.' She giggled uneasily, departed, only to return the next moment with a telegram in her hand. 'It's for Unkerlarthur. What's he doing with telegrams? Here, I'm going to open this. It's all in the family.' She did open it and, characteristically, read it out at once. 'Here, listen to this. *Show bust all stranded send other basket passenger train also three pounds anything wheres Effie. Elsie.* Well, I don't know! What do you think of that?' She stared at Miss Trant.

'I don't think anything of it,' replied Miss Trant, 'because I don't understand it. What does she mean?'

'She doesn't know I'm here, you see,' cried Effie excitedly. 'And I'll bet anything she rang up Lichfield to tell me, and they told her I'd gone, they didn't know where. Rawsley this is from. I knew they were at Rawsley all last week. It's just like her, too, sending a long telegram like this - over a shilling, you see. It's a funny thing those girls have always got money for telegrams, doesn't matter how broke they are. They never write, nobody on the stage ever writes.'

'Yes, but what does it mean?' Miss Trant was now so curious that she was quite impatient. These little glimpses of that mysterious world behind the painted scenes excited her.

'Well, don't you see, the show's suddenly busted - she was with a concert party, pierrot troupe, you know - and they're all stranded. The old business. No salaries for a few weeks, then one morning the manager or the fellow that's running it isn't there, and they're all up a gum tree. That's what happened to them at what's its name - Rawsley.'

'Where's that?'

'It's somewhere in the Midlands, not above thirty or forty miles from Lichfield. That's all I know. I never heard of it before. It's one of these small towns, you know, that some concert parties try out when they've finished a season at the seaside. And now she wants her other basket sending on, by passenger train, you see, so she'll get it in good time, and a pound or two to get her out of the place. Some mangy old ma's probably claimed her basket till she gets paid for her rooms. I'll get that basket - it's got all her other props in - off in the morning, and if Unkerlarthur's got a spare quid or two - 'cos I haven't - I'll post that on too, first thing.'

'You've got her address, of course?' Miss Trant did not inquire out of mere politeness; she was really interested.

Erne looked blank. 'Well, if that isn't just like her! She sends a long splathering telegram and never puts her address in it.'

'Can't you send it to the theatre?'

'They've not been showing at a theatre because there isn't one at Rawsley. It's one of those holes where you do three nights at the Corn Exchange or all next week at the Assembly Rooms. Don't I know 'em! Nowhere to dress and all draughts and the curtain never works. It'll have to go to the post office, that's all, and take its chance - I mean the money. The basket'll have to go to the station. It's what I call a mess. Here, I'm going to tidy up, and then we'll go out and talk about this after. Won't you come up?'

'No, thanks. I might as well wait until I get to the hotel and then I shall have my things.'

'All right. I shan't be long. You have a look at our photos.'

The walls were covered with photographs, and Miss Trant spent the next quarter of an hour examining them. It was like catching a glimpse, in a peepshow, of another world. There were photographs of large ladies in tights, massive Dick Whittingtons and Prince Charmings, or small ladies in ballet skirts or pierrot costume. There were photographs of gentlemen in evening dress, in battered hats and monstrous-check trousers, in nothing at all but leopard skins and laced boots. Niggers and fairies and tramps and pierrettes stared out with the same wide impersonal smile. Nearly every photograph had not only a dashing signature, followed by a brief but imposing description of the writer - *Leading Comedian in 'Hot Times', Trincipal Girl 'Mother Goose', Starring in 'The Doodahs'*, and so forth - but also flung out, with a prodigality of exclamation marks, some such message as *Heaps of Love!* or *All the Best!!* It was impossible not to believe that the subjects of these photographs were living in a whirl of success; they seemed to smile out of a glittering triumph. Only by making an effort could Miss Trant realize that these radiant creatures might be stranded in little towns and be reduced to spending their last shillings on SOS telegrams. But she was aided by the sight of a post-card, crammed with broad grins and frills and pompoms, sent by Elsie herself, now so forlorn at Rawsley. It was all curiously fascinating. Here was a world that seemed as far away and fantastic as any of those she explored so eagerly in her favourite fiction, that of the embattled Huguenots or the Young Pretender, and yet it was only just round the corner. Indeed, she had one foot in it at that moment. That was an exciting thought, and though she laughed at herself a little, nevertheless the foolish little thrill of it remained, like a tune going on somewhere at the back of her mind.

Then Effie bounced in. Miss Trant had hoped that Effie would depress her evening's toilet to the level of this disastrous day. She looked forward to seeing Effie more cheerful in mind but far more subdued in appearance. Actually, however, Effie was now more flamboyant than ever; her hair was a wilder gamboge; her eyebrows and lashes were astonishingly blackened and her mouth was a fiercesome daub of vermilion; her dress was a vivid green; and she carried an imitation Spanish shawl that promised to be the final catastrophe.

'I don't know whether to wear it or not,' she mused. 'Pretty isn't it?'

'I shouldn't wear it if I were you,' Miss Trant counselled earnestly. She was relieved to find that her companion immediately and quite meekly put the shawl away. It was soon apparent, however, that Effie had made her final onslaught upon the day's melancholy upstairs in her room; she had called up her last reserves from her wardrobe and dressing-table and had gained a brief victory; but now she could do no more. Her appearance was hardily triumphant, but her manner became more and more subdued. When the car had been put away, the room secured at the hotel, and they sat down to dinner, Effie chattered no longer. Over the soup she looked as wistful as it is possible for a person so large, so bright of hue, to look when eating soup. After that she became sentimental, confidential. She would not talk of Elsie or Unkerlarthur; her thoughts were with Mr Tipstead.

'I didn't think anything of him at first, you know, Miss Trant,' she confided mournfully. 'Thought he was a little swanker. He kept coming in and there was a bit of talk about him because he'd won a prize in one of these competitions. But that got nowhere with me, I can tell you; and I'm used to admiration and men saying silly things, what with being on the stage and then hotel work; they all run after you, you know, or pretend to, just to pass the time. But he kept coming in and coming in, and we got to exchanging bits of jokes, you know; and he'd make me laugh sometimes. You wouldn't think he was droll, would you?'

'I shouldn't,' replied Miss Trant promptly and with decision.

'Well, he is. But that was nothing. I've met 'em far funnier than him - make a cat laugh, some of the fellows I've known would. Then, one day, I was walking round in the afternoon - off duty, you know, and nothing much to do - and he comes along, and we go for a bit of a walk and sit down, and he asks me about my life, where I've been and all that, and then he tells me all about himself, how he's married and it's all been a mistake and how his wife doesn't understand him and won't think about anything but making money - '

'I must say I think that's nonsense,' Miss Trant put in. 'I should think she understood him only too well. But men always say that, at least they always do in books and plays.'

'Well, in real life, they'll say anything for twopence, that's my experience. And we'll always believe 'em. At least,' she added, with a sudden gleam of sagacity, 'we'll believe 'em if they tell us what we want to believe. Anyhow, that started it. I felt sorry for him, and he said how sorry he was for me - and you can do with a bit of sympathy when you've had nothing but a row of great fat fellows all talking silly round the bar every night. And then all of a sudden quicker than catching 'flu - he got a real fascination for me; couldn't keep my mind off him. I'd have gone anywhere, any time, to see him. But you know what it is.'

'I'm not sure that I do,' Miss Trant replied, with some hesitation. There came, unbidden, to her mind the thought of a tall Scots ship's doctor, a deep voice, a glint of hair about prominent cheek-bones. Hugh McFarlane. How queer to think of him now! But then, hadn't she suddenly thought about him the other day, when Mrs Chillingford had told her that Dorothy was engaged? It was time she forgot about him. She knew less about him now than she did about - Mr Tipstead. Yet, really, that was queer, too. She hardly noticed what Effie was saying. Something about her being pretty. The word startled her into attention.

'Pretty!' she cried. 'Don't be absurd. I'm not pretty, and never was.'

'My words but you are!' exclaimed Effie in all seriousness. 'And don't think I'm flattering you, either, 'cos I never flatter anybody - that's not my way. Course you're pretty. I only wish I was half so pretty. You've got lovely hair and eyes and teeth - they're your own, aren't they? - and nice features and a nice slim figure. Mind you, Miss Trant - if you'll let me say so - I don't think you make the best of yourself. Your style's too quiet - of course, it's ladylike and all that, but you can have too much of the ladylike, if you see what I mean.'

Miss Trant did not see what she meant, or did not choose to see. Effie told her and produced, among other things, what she called 'some tips and wrinkles you won't find in any of the books of words', and this she did with great precision and fluency but still with a certain melancholy, as if life were all over for her and she was only shouting a few last messages to the fading shore. Most of this advice Miss Trant instantly decided to ignore, not having any desire to look like a human oleograph, but now and again she heard something that left her more determined than ever to take stock of herself. Indeed, she was all eager attention, having been started into it by the initial compliment. Elizabeth Trant of the Old Hall, Hitherton-on-the-Wole, was sitting in the dining-room of an hotel in Sheffield with a barmaid, a large, loud, and badly painted female who had failed that day to capture another woman's husband; and because she had just been told she was pretty,

Colonel Trant's daughter was pleased and excited at once, perhaps better pleased and more excited than she had been for years. Hitherton would never have believed it.

Was it this conversation, was it the sight of those photographs in the sitting-room, was it merely a sudden lack of interest in cathedrals, at Liverpool or elsewhere, or was it a combination of all these things that made Miss Trant offer her services? She will be seen arriving at other decisions but at none really of greater importance than this, which is of such moment indeed that everything related up to now has been a mere overture to it. It came easily enough, and as usual with nothing to indicate that here was a little lever that might move whole worlds. Effie had returned to the subject of Mr Tipstead, whose sun was still setting with her; then she had passed rather mournfully to talk of herself and her own prospects, and hinted at trying the next day for a place in a certain gentlemanly bar in Sheffield, where apparently she might be able to piece together a broken heart; and finally and momentously she arrived again at her sister Elsie, waiting in Rawsley for her basket and some money. It was then that Miss Trant made her offer.

'If you like, I'll take them down for you tomorrow,' she announced quite calmly. 'No, it won't take me out of my way because really I haven't got a way. I was going to Liverpool to see the cathedral but I'd much rather go to Rawsley and see your sister.'

Effie agreed with enthusiasm. It was arranged that Miss Trant should call at the house next morning for the basket and whatever sum Unkerlarthur might be able to raise at such short notice. There would be no difficulty, Effie pointed out, in finding Elsie in a town of that size, where everybody knew everybody else's business. She launched upon a description of Elsie that soon became a bewildering biography, and at last Miss Trant had to cut her short, pleading that she was tired and would like to go to bed early. That was quite enough. Instantly, Effie was for rushing her upstairs at once and putting her to bed with her own hands, and by the time Miss Trant had excused herself from any such treatment, she was tired indeed.

The day had been so long, so eventful, so cluttered with other people's lives, with Tipsteadery, that it seemed to press upon her now, a weight and huddle of experience not to be borne without some little respite of darkness and quiet. Thus it was a relief to see the last of Effie, now almost tearful again and threatening huge embraces, to meet the chill emptiness of the hotel bedroom, as impersonal as a packing case, to slip out of the day altogether, after having crowned it with a little gesture of one's own. In short, Miss Trant did not regret her change of programme and slept well.

IV

Thus it was that she found herself, on the Thursday afternoon, on the road a few miles from Rawsley. Behind, on top of her own bags, was a theatrical basket, the property of Miss Elsie Longstaff, and in her handbag was a letter from Effie and an envelope in which she had seen Unkerlarthur place a dirty pound note and an equally dirty ten shilling one; all he could muster. She had hinted that she could lend Elsie some money herself, but Unkerlarthur had insisted on sending this thirty shillings. It had never occurred to Miss Trant that she, a stranger, was being trusted with these things, and neither Unkerlarthur nor Effie had pointed out this fact or shown the least hesitation; all of which says something for the company we are keeping.

The rain that had driven Mr Oakroyd under the trees had compelled Miss Trant to put up the hood of her car. With the first appearance of the sun, she had stopped to take down the hood, and this time had stopped altogether. The car refused to start again. She cranked away until she was breathless and aching. She pressed the self-starter until at last it would not even make a noise. When she was not attending to one or the other, she was hopefully flooding the carburettor. It was useless; the engine would not start, never even gave a promising little cough or splutter. She looked wistfully at its mysterious pipes and wires and cylinders. 'How absurd these things are!' she told herself. 'It looks just the same, exactly the same as it does when it's going, and yet it won't go.' There was nothing for it but to wait until someone came along who knew more about the interior of a car than she did. As the roads now are crowded with people who know all about such things, her position did not make her feel uneasy. The road to Rawsley, however, was singularly deserted that afternoon. Ten minutes passed and brought not a soul. Then a little figure came into the struggling sunlight. And this, of course, was Mr Oakroyd walking into his adventure.

When he came closer, Miss Trant noticed that he was carrying a bag of tools and, of all things, one of those absurd little basket trunks, and the very smallest she had ever seen. When he came closer still, she noticed that this sturdy middle-aged workman had a broad pleasant face and eyes of bright blue. His brown cap was on the back of his head and looked too small for him, and this cap and the ridiculous little basket trunk made Miss Trant want to laugh. What she did do, however, was simply to smile at him and to ask if he knew anything about cars.

He did not raise his cap, he did not touch it in salute, but he pushed it further back on his head. In this way he contrived to give the lady some sort of salute and also keep his independence at the same time. 'Well,' he replied to her question about cars, 'I do and I don't, as you might say.' And he smiled back at her, his face wrinkling pleasantly in the sunshine.

'I wonder if the "do" part of it would apply to this car, because I can't make it start, you see. I wonder if you'd mind having a look at it. I'm sure you could do something with it.' Miss Trant had great confidence in all men who carried bags of tools about with them, and would have been surprised to learn that joiners usually know very little about internal-combustion engines.

'What I mean is this,' he went on, following his own thoughts stubbornly. 'I've nivver driven a car i' my life. Cars as cars has nowt to do wi' my job. But where I've been working, they've a lot o' lorries and I've spent many an hour watching t'lads set 'em to rights, so I've picked up a bit about 'em. Nar do you understand me, Missis - I mean, Miss?'

His caution, his broad North-country speech, and certain whimsical details of his appearance all delighted Miss Trant. 'I see. But I'm sure you could find out what's wrong with it.'

'I might and I might not. You can nivver tell wi' these things. I'll have a do at her, though. Nar what have you done so far?' And he listened to her tale of cranking and petrol flooding with the deep solemnity of a man about to take over a job. When she had finished, he remarked: 'I'll bet it's either t'plugs or magneto. She won't start if her plugs is mucky. We'll have a look at 'em.'

Cheerfully he set to work, first pulling out the car's tool box, then unscrewing one plug after another. 'They're none so bad,' he observed, 'but we'll give 'em a bit of a rub up while we're on t'job.'

It was while he was giving them his bit of rub up that the sky suddenly darkened. From the massed clouds in the West there came a vague roll or two of thunder, and the next minute there was something more than a mere shower, there was a downright pelter. Mr Oakroyd hastily covered up the engine and then helped Miss Trant to raise the hood. 'Come inside and shelter,' she cried, climbing in. After a moment's hesitation, he followed her, and there they sat together, looking through the windscreen at the downpour, a very queer pair indeed.

'Eh, I've left that basket o' mine out,' he exclaimed, and brought it in. 'I've all my clothes i' that, an' they wouldn't dry so quick once they'd gotten sopped through.'

This last remark was made, in his excitement, in a brogue so broad that Miss Trant could hardly understand it. 'I'm sure you must come from Sheffield,' she said, after a pause. 'I was there last night.' This nice little man reminded her of Unkerlarthur.

'Nay, I don't,' he replied, apparently in some surprise. 'I belong many a mile off Sheffield. I came from Bruddersford. Nar, I'll bet you've heard o' Bruddersford, haven't you, Miss?'

'Yes, that's where they make cloth, isn't it? But that's in Yorkshire too, surely?'

'Ay, I should think it wor. It's more i' Yorkshire ner Sheffield. You couldn't have owt more Yorkshire ner Bruddersford. An' I've lived there all my life, except for a bit when I was down South, till this week.'

'And where are you going to now?'

'Eh, I don't know. I was just going to have look round this Rawsley place today, but I don't rightly know where I'm going.'

'I'm rather like that, too, at the moment,' Miss Trant remarked. The parallel amused her.

'I nobbut set off o' Monday night,' he continued, a trifle dreamily. 'And what is it now? It's nobbut Thursday, isn't it? Well, it seems like months sin' I was i' Bruddersford, I've done that much and seen that much these three days. I'm fair capped wi' mesen. It's like being one o' these chaps on t'pictures. And nobbut three days!'

Miss Trant could have clapped her hands, just as she used to do when she was a little girl and as she had never thought of doing for years. 'But how queer!' she cried. 'I've been just like that too. I've been away since Monday and all kinds of things have happened and I feel as if I'd been away months and was quite a different person. Don't you feel that too?'

'I do an' all.' He was as delighted as she was.

'Do tell me all that's happened to you,' she commanded. 'But tell me your name first.'

'Oakroyd's my name. It's a right old Bruddersford name.'

'And mine's Trant, and that's an old name, too, in Gloucestershire. And now you must tell me all your adventures since Monday night. I'm sure you've had adventures, haven't you?'

'I have that. I've had so many, I don't fairly know where to start. It'll tak' a bit o' time.'

'Never mind about that, Mr Oakroyd. It's raining hard and we can't do anything until it stops, and I want to hear all about it.'

After some hesitation, he told the whole story, with Lily and his wife and Leonard, the twenty pounds and the dismissal, the lorry, the Great North Road and Nobby and the Kirkworth Inn, the caravan and Joby Jackson and the fair and Jim Summers, in short, with everything in it. Miss Trant, who occasionally asked questions and insisted upon all the details, enjoyed it all and decided that Mr Oakroyd himself was adorable. In return, she told him enough to prove that she was really a fellow-adventurer. Then the sun came out again to brighten the last spatter of rain.

'Nar we'll have a do at them plugs,' said Mr Oakroyd, who liked to push on with a job once he had put his hand to it. His 'do' was crowned with success, for the car started easily. Miss Trant waved him back to his seat, and they moved towards Rawsley. The town began, as so many small towns do, with a railway station, and on the opposite side of the road, about a hundred yards farther along, was a corrugated iron hut labelled 'Mounder's Station Refreshment Rooms'. Miss Trant's eyes were caught by a pink bill pasted on the wall of this hut, near the doorway. She pulled up, then got out to examine the bill. It told her what she wanted to know: *The Dinky Doos*, in their Musical Medley of Fun and Frolic, were to be seen, it proclaimed, in the Assembly Rooms, Rawsley; and among the promised attractions were 'the Dainty Numbers' of Miss Elsie Longstaff.

While she was reading this notice, a middle-aged woman appeared in the doorway. Perhaps she was Mounder herself, for she had the mournful resignation of one doomed to be encased in corrugated iron and to serve station refreshments.

Miss Trant turned to her. 'Can you tell me if these people' - she pointed to the notice - 'are still in the town?'

Mrs Mounder immediately folded herself up, her arms, her face, her whole body, being compressed at once, so that she seemed the very image of bitter stoicism. 'Yes indeed they are,' she replied grimly. 'They're in here.'

'What! Do you mean they're in there now?'

Mrs Mounder shut her eyes, put her lips away altogether, and nodded her head so violently that the whole of her seemed to rock slightly. 'Came an hour ago, six of 'em,' she said at last, 'and ordered one pot of tea and one plate of bread-and-butter, and they've asked for two lots of hot water already, and some of 'em's eating what they brought themselves. And sitting there jabbering away and ordering me about! They'll get no more hot water, I can tell you,' she added, looking sternly at Miss Trant, as if to anticipate that lady's request that they should be given still more hot water.

'Oh, what a shame!' cried Miss Trant, remembering their plight.

'You might well call it that, Miss. If everybody went on like that, I couldn't keep a door open.'

'No, I was thinking about them,' said Miss Trant, boldly correcting her.

'Them indeed!' Mrs Mounder sniffed. 'Don't you worry about them. They've impudence for anything, they have. We've heard about them.'

'Well, I'm coming to see one of them, and I'll have some tea too.'

She turned away to invite Mr Oakroyd, who was still sitting in the car, to have some tea with her. At this moment, however, two men, looking rather bedraggled, approached the hut, and in the narrow space between the road and the doorway there was hardly room for the three of them. The men stepped back to let her pass, but as they did so, the one in front, a fair youth with a wild lock of hair and no hat, called out to Mrs Mounder: 'Good afternoon, Madam. Have you Dinky Doos here?'

It sounded as if he were an officer of health inquiring about some infectious disease. Miss Trant smiled as she hurried past them. She heard the second man cry: 'Lead on, Jollifant,' noticed that he carried a large flat case that looked as if it contained some musical instrument, and wondered if they were theatrical people too. They disappeared into the Station Refreshment Rooms. Then Mr Oakroyd, a little diffident, followed them, and Miss Trant, who had returned to her car for her hand-bag, was last of all. In the doorway, she lingered a moment and heard an astonishing clatter of tongues coming from the inner room. 'I'm quite excited,' she told herself happily.

CHAPTER SIX
Inigo Meets a Member of the Profession and Turns Pianist

I

WE left Inigo Jollifant hurrying away from Washbury Manor in the darkness of Monday night. We have just seen him arrive at the Station Refreshment Rooms in Rawsley on Thursday afternoon. In order to understand how he came to be there at all, we must know what happened to him during those three days, or, to be more precise, those sixty-four hours that began at 12.30 a.m. on Tuesday.

Then it was that Inigo decided that Fauntley had been right. He ought to have gone to bed. The night was not warm enough and certainly not light enough to make walking very pleasant, especially after a long day of French and History and birthday celebrations. He ought to have drunk more Rob Roy or less. As it was, Rob had played him false, for after conjuring him out of the school, out of his bed, he had not stayed with him and kept him glowing inside but had gradually dropped behind, and now, at the end of half an hour's walk, had slunk away altogether. A little more Rob or a little less, and he would have been in bed now. So Inigo argued, and incidentally entertained himself, as he walked the last half mile or so of a familiar side-road that linked Washbury to the world. When he came at last to the main road, running north and south, he was back again in the world, but there was little of it to be seen as nothing was happening in it. He turned to the right, then spent the next minute wondering which of the faint points of light was the North Star, and the next ten minutes wondering about stars in general. It was, as usual, a cheerless meditation. If you are going to bother about these things, he decided, you have to turn astronomer, to weigh them and measure them, out of sheer self-defence.

A rumble that he had heard behind him for some time turned at last into a lorry. This was the first vehicle he had seen on the road. He turned round and gave a shout when it came near. It pulled up, but the driver seemed dubious when he was asked for a lift.

'It's all right,' said Inigo, 'I'm on a walking tour.'

That was sufficient. The driver realized at once that a man on a walking tour is an enemy to nobody but himself, and may safely be given a lift.

'But I can't take yer far,' the driver shouted as they rumbled on again. 'About ten mile and no more. That's where I finish. I live there, yer see.'

'Where?'

'Near Dullingham. And I'll tell yer what. Yer can get a train at Dullingham Junction. Yer wouldn't think it but yer can. It's the only place for miles and miles where yer can get a train at this time o' night is Dullingham Junction.'

'Splendid!' cried Inigo at the top of his voice. The lorry appeared to be full of suits of armour carelessly packed. 'I like to hear that. You wouldn't imagine anything ever happened at a place with a name like that, would you? Dullingham Junction! Where do they go to, these trains?'

'I dunno. Up Lincoln and Grimsby way or Doncaster way I dare say, but I don't rightly know. I've never been on 'em but there's a feller I know, feller called Harry Briggs, works at the station and I know he's on duty at night for this train. Always late too, he tells me. I'm not sure he isn't on this week.'

'I'd like to have a look at this station.'

'That's right,' roared the driver. 'I'll put yer down close to it.' And then he went on to shout of other matters, the chief of them being a very awkward journey he had just made to Northampton, and he so often demanded agreement that Inigo, who felt that he ought to be sympathetic, made himself hoarse before the ten miles were covered.

At last the driver pulled up and pointed. 'There y'are. See them lights. That's Dullingham Junction. Yer just go down that bit o' road and yer there. See if it's Harry Briggs.'

The road curved down sharply to the station. As he descended, Inigo could see the signal lights, the faint gleam of the metals, and a dim yellow glow from somewhere in the station itself. His spirits dropped at the sight. There was something very melancholy about Dullingham Junction. The wide night itself was somehow not so cheerless as this half-hearted attempt to drive it away, this sad glimmer of light. It was so quiet too. He could not imagine a train ever arriving there. The usual cheerful railway bustle seemed as remote from this little station as Paddington itself. He began to ask himself what he was going there for, whether it would not be better to return to the main road, and about twenty yards or so from the entrance he stopped and leaned against the wooden rail at the side of the road. Dullingham Junction only confirmed his opinion that he was indeed a young ass.

Perhaps he would have turned away (and walked out of this chronicle altogether) had he not heard a most astonishing sound. The sound itself was pleasing and its unexpectedness, its daft incongruity, were ravishing. He listened in delight, telling himself that he had judged Dullingham Junction too hastily. It was saying that he was not a young ass, that this is still a world in which midnight exits may be rewarded, that he has not everything who has bed and breakfast. Somebody in Dullingham Junction was playing the banjo.

If this was Harry Briggs, Inigo decided as he drew nearer, then Harry Briggs was wasting his time in the service of the London and North Eastern Railway, for this banjo was not being fumbled with but was being *played*. The night retreated hastily before its impudent twanka-pang, twanka-pang. Tired as he was, Inigo found that his feet itched to break into a double shuffle. If the station had been crammed with grinning coons, buried under melons and cotton blossoms, he would not have been surprised.

He walked through the booking office, where only one tiny light was burning, and on to the dim and empty platform. The banjoist, now in a happy fury of syncopation, was obviously in the waiting-room. Inigo peeped in through the half-opened door. At one side of the little fire was Harry Briggs or one of his colleagues, a young man with a round red face, and at the other side, sprawling on the seat, was the banjoist himself. One was so busy playing and the other staring and listening, with his mouth wide open, that Inigo stood there, several minutes without being observed.

With a final and triumphant wag of his head, the banjoist concluded his performance. 'How about that, my boy?' he cried, holding up the banjo as if inviting it to share in the applause. 'You've heard that? Now where are you going to hear the next like it? Can I rattle the old banjo or can I not?'

'You can that, Mister,' replied his audience earnestly. 'My word, you've got a touch, you 'ave!'

'You've said it. I have got a touch,' the banjoist remarked with dignity. His utterance was rather thick and there were other indications that he had been refreshing himself very generously earlier in the night. Apart from this thickness, however, his voice was peculiar. It was a curious, harsh drawl, and though he could not be said to have a definite American accent, nevertheless his accent was not quite an English one. It was so unusual that it excited Inigo's curiosity.

'You 'ave got a touch, and I don't care where the next one comes from,' his listener went on, enthusiastically if a trifle vaguely. 'What about giving us just another, Mister? 'Ere, do you know *'Er 'Air was Golden?'* And, fixing his gaze sternly on his companion, who looked rather startled, the railwayman sang very slowly and solemnly, with the most lugubrious portamentos, the following ballad:

> Errair was go-olden on the day
> She gave 'er love to mee-yer,
> And though it's long since turned to gray,

> We're still in sympathee-yer,
> And 'and in 'and -

But here he was interrupted.

'No, no,' cried the banjoist. 'No, don't know it. And between you and me, stationmaster, it's not quite my style. A little too heavy on the sentimental side, too much heart message, for me, a matter of taste, you know, a matter of taste.'

'Ar, ar, I like a good ballad.'

'You like 'em tender and trew, I can see that,' said the banjoist, with a droll glance. 'That's because you stay up so late by yourself, waiting for the midnight express. Did you ever see *The Midnight Express* - the drama? I played in it once for three nights in Montreal!'

Inigo chose this moment for his entrance.

'Hallow, hallow!' cried the performer. 'What's this?'

The railwayman jumped to his feet, looking startled, and was then annoyed because he had felt frightened for a moment or so. "Ere, what's the idea?' he demanded angrily. 'Coming creeping in like that!' Then, having taken a good look at Inigo, he moderated his tone. 'Beg your pardon, but you made me jump. What is it you want?'

'I want a train,' replied Inigo, though up to that moment he had not really thought about trains.

'Oh, you want the 1.20, eh? Where do you want to go to?'

'Where do I want to go to? Now that's rather a puzzler. Let me see,' Inigo meditated. 'Well, what about Stockport?'

'Stockport! You can't get to Stockport on this line.'

The banjoist now took charge of them. 'Stockport,' he repeated, rather condescendingly. 'Ever been to Stockport?'

'Never set eyes on it,' Inigo told him.

'Then my advice is - don't bother. There's nothing there, not at all. I know it well, my boy. I've been there; I've been everywhere. If you do go, you ask 'em. Ask 'em at the Red Lion if they don't know me. They'll remember me all right. Morton Mitcham, that's my name. They'll remember Morton Mitcham.' And he stood up, perhaps to show exactly what it was they would not be able to forget. He was certainly not a person who would be easily forgotten. He was tall but very thin, and his clothes, a light check, merely hung upon him. There was a Shakespearian cast about the upper part of his head, for he was bald on the crown but had very thick dark hair at each side, bushed about his ears. His eyebrows were immense and dramatic; his nose boasted a fine curve and a rather richer colouring than the rest of his face; his long upper lip and his long pointed chin were blue; his slightly hollow cheeks were blue below and brown above; and indeed his whole face had that curious parchmenty look that comes from exposure, at some time or other, to hotter suns than this country ever sees. His collar and tie reminded Inigo vaguely of Tenniel's Mad Hatter. Altogether, Mr Morton Mitcham was an unusual person; his appearance was as puzzling as his accent, oddly combining the tropical planter, the tragic actor of the old school, and a rather down-at-heels senator from one of the remoter states of those that are united.

'I was listening to you playing the banjo,' Inigo told him. 'And by jingo, it was good too. It's a rattling good instrument played like that.'

'It is. But it's a difficult instrument, let me tell you. Yes, sir. It's good, as you say, when it's played like that, but how often is it played like that?'

'Ar,' said the railwayman fervently. 'That's right.'

Mr Mitcham fumbled in a waistcoat pocket and finally brought out about an inch and a half of dusty cheroot. 'Indian cheroot,' he explained. 'There's nothing to beat 'em once you acquire the taste. I had twenty boxes of the very best given to me once when I was up at Bangalore. I never knew who sent 'em, didn't know a thing. "To Morton Mitcham Esquire from an admirer" - that's all it said, on a plain card. Woman's handwriting, though. I've one or two of the boxes still, in there.' He pointed to a very large and disreputable bag on the seat. 'I've carried 'em round ever since. But no cheroots in 'em. Ha, ha!' Nor did it seem likely that he had any stock of cheroots with him, for the one he was lighting now had evidently been smoked before. He began putting away his banjo in its case. 'You a musician?' he inquired of Inigo.

'I play the piano from time to time.'

'A professional?' And he raised his immense eyebrows.

'No, a very ordinary amateur.'

'Ah, pity!' Mr Mitcham lowered his eyebrows, but did not condescend to explain why it was a pity.

Inigo suddenly remembered the chocolate and biscuits that Daisy Callander had given him, and now he brought them out, inviting the others to eat with him.

'You're a traveller, a campaigner, a trouper, my boy, I can see that,' cried Mr Mitcham approvingly, helping himself and carefully extinguishing the cheroot. 'Give me a few biscuits and some chocolate and a few bottles of whisky, rye for choice, and I'll face anything. Blizzard, shipwreck, anything. I once lived for a fortnight on nothing else, up on the Black Hills between Wyoming and South Dakota – '

'South Dakota!' Inigo's cry was ecstatic. The man must really have been there because you couldn't *think* of South Dakota, couldn't just lift it out of some mental map.

'Yes, South Dakota. There were two of us. Let me see, what was that fellow's name? Ah, yes - Sheerman. He was an ex-Wesleyan minister who'd been running a quick-lunch bar down in Denver. Hardest winter they'd known for forty years, and the two of us walked right into it.'

'Have another biscuit,' said Inigo enthusiastically.

'Thanks, my boy, I will. Of course we'd whisky there too, any amount of it. Perhaps you're thinking whisky wouldn't shake down with biscuits and chocolate, but let me tell you, they're fine together. If you've got a flask with you, just try it.'

'Sorry, but I haven't.'

'Always carry a flask,' said Mr Mitcham severely. Then he turned to the railwayman, who was demolishing a gigantic sandwich. 'What about that tea you were talking about, station-master?'

The other mumbled something in his sandwich. Evidently he was dubious now that there were three of them.

'You're not Harry Briggs by any chance, are you?' Inigo asked him.

He was Harry Briggs; admitted the fact with delight, and insisted upon Inigo explaining exactly how he came to hear of him. When the identity of the lorry-driver had been fully established, Harry Briggs at once changed his attitude towards Inigo, who felt he was now regarded almost as an old Dullinghamian. His round red face beaming at the thought of what coincidence could do, Harry Briggs set to work now to make some tea.

Mr Mitcham fastened the straps of his banjo-case. 'Just a little hobby of mine, you know,' he remarked airily, tapping the case. 'But it's most useful; made the evening go all over the place. "Ask Morton Mitcham to come in and play his banjo," they'd say. Guest nights at Residencies, you know, and that sort of thing. I've played to at least half a dozen colonial governors in my time, and they simply ate it, simply ate it - all except one and that was old Lord Stennenfield.'

'What was the matter with him?' asked Inigo. 'No soul?'

'Deaf as a post, couldn't hear his own brass cannon going off. And the best bridge-player east of Alexandria, they used to tell me. That's what he wanted, you see. "Get the card tables out," he shouts, right in the middle of my performance, I walked straight out. You can't do that to Morton Mitcham.'

'Quite right,' murmured Inigo. 'You're an artist, sir, I can see that.' And he saluted him with a stick of chocolate.

'Well, I've been told so. I've been asked to give lessons by a colonial governor. I'll give you his name - though this is in confidence, gentlemen.' And he looked sternly at Harry Briggs, who was standing open-mouthed, with a kettle in his hand. 'It was Sir Elkin Pondberry.

"Damn it all, Mitcham," he said to me, "you'll have to teach me how to play that thing." "Very proud, Sir Elkin," I told him, "but it can't be done." "Damn it all," he said, "it must be done." "It would take years," I told him. "Then you'll have to stay here years," he said. "I'll have you kept here, Mitcham, damned if I won't." "Can't be done," I told him, "I'm catching the next boat up to Bangkok." And he had to give in. But I told him about Stennenfield - they were meeting at Singapore very soon - and showed him how to deal himself four aces and four kings. "Damn me if you're not a genius, Mitcham," he said when he'd got the hang of it. "I'll try that on old Stennenfield." And he did, and it was the great joke that year in all the clubs out there. I heard about it up at Hong Kong.'

'Hong Kong!' cried Inigo, who was feeling rather dazed. 'You've held the gorgeous East in fee, absolutely. But what about those aces and kings? You're not a conjuror, are you?'

'Not exactly a conjuror. I've never bothered about illusions and the mechanical trick acts, you know. But sleight of hand's a hobby of mine. I think I can do most things with a pack of cards.'

'You've got a heap o' talent, if you ask me, Mister,' said Harry Briggs, who had now made the tea. 'I wish I'd only got a bit of it. You wouldn't catch me 'ere. You've got a touch on that there banjoey, my word! 'Ere, 'ave a drop o' tea. One'll 'ave to 'ave the cup and other the saucer.'

'It passes the time, it passes the time,' said Mr Mitcham, and with an apparent absence of mind, he took possession of the cup. 'I've found these little accomplishments useful now and again on my travels, and polished 'em up a bit as I went along. I learned a trick or two in the sleight-of-hand business from an old Chink I met one time in Shanghai, and then another time one of the Frenchified niggers you get in New Orleans showed me one or two things I didn't know about playing the banjo when I was down there. Though one of the best players I ever heard - in a class right above all these New York jazz-band men, and, mind you, I've heard them all - was an old Irishman I struck down in Sydney.'

'There's a cousin o' mine there,' Harry Briggs put in eagerly, 'same name as me, except he's Jim, and he drives a van for a laundry. You might 'ave come across 'im.'

'What, Jim Briggs of the laundry!' cried Mr Mitcham, with a wink at Inigo. 'I knew him well. He told me he'd a cousin down here. "Look him up," he said, "if you're ever at Dullingham Junction."'

'That was clever of 'im, seeing that I've only worked 'ere six months and it's two or three years since we 'eard from 'im. You can't pull my leg, Mister.'

'Well, it's fifteen years or more since I was there,' remarked Mr Mitcham imperturbably. 'I've been all over since then. I'm a wanderer over the face of the earth, I am, my boys. I've only been back in the Old Country two years, just looking round, you know, visiting a few old friends.'

'Ar, a gentleman o' leisure like, now,' Mr Briggs observed with respectful envy.

'You've hit it,' said Ulysses, in his queer harsh drawl, now American, now English. Once more he brought out the stub of cheroot, this time a very small and dusty stub, lit it, and blew out clouds of smoke in a manner that contrived to suggest leisure, a rich indolence, a return at last from innumerable and astonishing journeys round and round the globe.

'*Heureux qui, comme Ulysse, a fait un beau voyage,*' said Inigo, who was wondering how this incredible personage had ever been able to land himself at Dullingham Junction in the middle of the night. It was really surprising that he had been able to find this small island of ours at all.

'That's right, my boy,' he replied condescendingly. Then he yawned. 'What about that train of yours?'

'Should be 'ere this next half-hour,' said Harry Briggs, slowly turning himself into a railway official again. 'She's an hour late tonight. I'll just 'ave a walk round.' And he lumbered out.

'I don't know whether I shall bother catching it,' said Mr Mitcham, settling himself down on the seat. 'I'm going on to Nottingham, just to see a few old friends, you know. But I might as well wait until the morning now. I missed a connexion down the line.'

'Did you?' yawned Inigo. 'Where was the place?'

'Um - I don't remember.' For once, it seemed, that unusual memory of his had failed him.

Inigo had a suspicion that Mr Morton Mitcham had not missed any connexion. Mr Morton Mitcham was a very unusual person, either a great traveller or a great liar. Inigo decided that he wanted to see more of him.

What he did see, however, was Mr Tarvin. He and Mr Tarvin were struggling through deep snow up a hill, and when they were half-way up, Mr Tarvin stopped and looked round, saying: 'All this is South Dakota then. Chumha. Just call the boys, Jollifant,' and he called the boys, though there were none to be seen. But the next moment they were there, a whole crowd of them, making the most extraordinary humming noise. It made Inigo so angry that he shouted at them, but they made more noise than ever. Then he stared so fiercely at the nearest boy, young Withington, that he stared himself out of South

Dakota altogether, back again into the waiting-room, where Mr Morton Mitcham was sleeping with his mouth wide open and snoring prodigiously.

Inigo stretched himself out at full length on the seat and used his knapsack as a pillow. He listened to the snores for a minute or two, then slipped away again, not into South Dakota this time, but into oblivion. There he stayed, though once or twice it seemed as if the darkness and quiet were being mysteriously invaded, as if there were alarms and skirmishes on some distant frontier.

II

Somebody was shaking him. He opened his eyes, to see a black moustache, large and badly trimmed, and it annoyed him so much that he closed his eyes again. 'Now then, sir, now then!' it said.

Inigo did not feel called upon to reply.

Time you was moving if you want the 6.45,' it went on.

This remark was so extraordinary that it opened his eyes again. The waiting-room looked quite different in the morning light. He stared at the porter. 'Where's Morton Mitcham?' he asked.

The porter shook his head. "Tain't on this line. I never 'eard of it.'

'It's not a station but a man. He was sitting there last night, talking about banjos in Bangkok and conjuring in Singapore. Unless I dreamt him.'

'I shouldn't be surprised. I'm that way myself,' said the porter earnestly. 'Let me 'ave a few or a bit of tinned salmon last thing, and I'm off, all night. The stuff I've seen! Banjos and Singapore's nothing to it.'

'I don't know that I care for Old Rob Roy,' Inigo mused. 'He's split my head open and left a sort of dark brown taste in my mouth, as if I'd been chewing some of his Highland peat. But look here, where's what's-his-name - wait a minute - Harry Briggs?'

'Ar, now you're talking! You didn't dream 'im, I can tell you. Went off duty a bit back, he did. You missed the 1.20, didn't you? Going North, aren't you, sir?'

'Am I?' Inigo thought it over. 'I suppose so, but before I go anywhere I want a bath and a shave and some health salts in a tumbler of tepid water and then some tea and toast. And perhaps an egg - you never know - one of those young and tender eggs, the little brown ones. Now,' and he produced a shilling, 'what do you think about that programme?'

'Thank you, sir. Well, what I think is you'd best get on to Grantham on this next train. Dullingham's no good to you, I give you *my* word. Get anything you like at Grantham, anything you like.' And the porter smacked his lips at the thought of this roaring metropolis.

So Inigo went to Grantham. He sneaked through the early morning sunshine to the Angel and Royal, where he slipped into a bathroom before most of its guests had looked at their early cups of tea, and had to keep several of them at bay because he stayed so long luxuriating in nakedness and warm water. By the time he was fit to appear at the breakfast table, he was ready for anything it had to offer. After breakfast he smoked his pipe and stared, in a rather dreamy fashion, at several newspapers, and it was half past ten when he finally took the road.

It was only because he was the prospective author of *The Last Knapsack*, that prose elegy of pedestrianism, that Inigo chose to walk out of the town, which offered him innumerable trains and buses. Walking did not seem very pleasant that morning; the day was warm already; the westward road was dusty and never free from motor traffic; and he did not feel inclined to exert himself. It was better when at last he was able to turn down a side-road, which brought him, after many a corner that seemed alarmingly like a blank end, to a small red-brick inn and bread and cheese and beer. There was nobody to talk to at the inn, for the landlord evidently had other work to do during the day, his wife had so little time to spare that she appeared even to serve the beer under protest, and there was no company; but Inigo lingered there until two o'clock, in a dreamy reverie. When he sauntered on again, skirting fields of stubble and bright but decaying woods, the beer within and the sun without conspired to make that reverie dreamier still.

He did not know where he was or where he was going, and he did not care. He drifted like a leaf down the vacant lane. The whole burnished afternoon was only an idle fantasy. 'I move among shadows a shadow,' he told himself over and over again, for his mind was a shining jumble of quotations from the more melancholy anthologies. Here everything was golden, and nothing real perhaps except the dust. 'Golden lads and girls ... come to dust.' That was how it went, and that too he repeated with swelling vowels that sent little shivers of pleasure down his spine. He came at last to a place of exquisite shade and peace, where the lane turned into a narrow road and great branches hung over a grassy space at the corner. It was a place where a man could meditate or perhaps sleep for an hour. But someone had left a little car there. There was plenty of shaded space on either side of the car, but the sight of it, suggesting noise and fuss, kept Inigo standing where he was. The car spoilt the place. He looked at it in disgust. Then he looked at it in astonishment. He went nearer.

Yes, there it was. Along the bottom of the windscreen was a notice printed in bold crimson letters: *Take heed for the end draweth nigh*. In the rear compartment were a number of placards, two or three feet square and printed in even bolder crimson letters. Inigo did not scruple - for clearly this was no time for scruples - to take out two of them. *And the stars of heaven fell upon the earth, even as a fig tree casteth her untimely figs, when she is shaken by a mighty wind. And the heaven departeth as a scroll when it is rolled together; and every mountain and island were moved out of their places.* Then he turned to the other, which said: *And I beheld, and heard an angel flying though the midst of heaven, saying with a loud voice, Woe, woe, woe, to the inhabiters of the earth by reason of the other voices of the trumpet of the three angels, which are yet to sound!* He carefully replaced the placards and stretched himself on the grass by the side of this strange apocalyptic little car.

It was very quiet. The few sounds there were, a distant creaking, a vague twittering, were so remote that they might be coming from another world, another life. He stared out of the shade about him into the shimmer of green and gold beyond. The whole afternoon had been insubstantial. Now it all seemed little more than so much painted silk, quivering at a breath. Its fragility hurt him; he closed his eyes. But the ground he was resting on was solid enough, and the blades he pulled were the old sweet blades of grass. He opened his eyes again. The car itself, though a little battered, had very definite substance. He noticed it had been fitted quite recently with a new set of tyres. Inigo juggled idly with the thought of these tyres. Perhaps the prophet who owned the car bought them because he expected to be still running about in his car when the cities were sheets of flame and the mountains were fading like smoke. He might run right through Armageddon in it. That would be a record indeed; a non-stop run into the new heaven and earth. And all the journalists and advertising men, poor ghosts, biting their spectral lips because the very last edition had been printed, sold, withered away, long before! These fancies made Inigo feel more comfortable, though there was still a little hollow place, as hollow as the world without, inside him. He yawned, shut his eyes, wondered who owned the car, then fell asleep.

He awoke about an hour later, sat up, and discovered that the owner of the car was there, fussing with it. For a minute or two, Inigo could only blink at him, but he decided that the man looked disappointingly unprophetical. Their eyes met.

'Hello!' cried the man. 'Do you think I disturbed you? I must have done, mustn't I? But you weren't here, were you, when I first came? It's very warm this afternoon, isn't it?' He spoke in rather high chanting tones, and as he spoke his whole face beamed. He was a man of about forty, and he had curly auburn hair damply clustered about a somewhat lumpy forehead, gold spectacles, prominent cheekbones, a small curling moustache and too many teeth. He was very neatly dressed in a dark blue suit and a black tie, and there was something vaguely evangelical about his appearance.

'I don't think you disturbed me,' Inigo replied, 'and it doesn't matter if you did. It's stupid to fall asleep like this, gives you a headache - but I was awfully tired.' And he yawned.

The other flashed his spectacles at the knapsack. 'You've been walking, haven't you? I should think you're taking a holiday, aren't you? What splendid weather we're having, aren't we? Perhaps you're going about alone, are you?'

'I wander lonely as a cloud, absolutely.' Inigo struggled to his feet.

'Ah, I recognize that, you know,' cried the other enthusiastically. 'That's Wordsworth, isn't it? About the daffodils, isn't it? A beautiful piece too, don't you think? Now you're probably not feeling like walking, are you? I wonder if I could give you a lift. I'm going on to Oxwell. Do you know it? Are you going that way at all?'

'To tell you the truth,' said Inigo, 'I don't know where I'm going. I'm just wandering about for a day or two, on a kind of holiday.'

'That's splendid, isn't it? Though, mind you, I don't envy you because the work I am doing - and it takes me all over the country - is better than any holiday, much better. Do you know what I'm doing? Of course you don't. I'm organizing secretary to the Second Resurrectionists. Perhaps you're a Second Resurrectionist, are you?'

'No. I'm not even a First Resurrectionist. I'm afraid I never heard of them before.'

'Is that so?' The man's face clouded for a moment, then brightened again. 'But there, you have now, haven't you? I thought you might be one because we're holding one of our special gatherings tonight at Oxwell, and I thought you might be on your way there. I'm going there myself, but I told you that, didn't I? Yes, the special meeting for all the East Midland district - including both Ephraim and Gad - '

'Ephraim and Gad!' cried Inigo. 'What have they got to do with it?'

'Ah, that puzzles you, does it? You recognize them of course? Well, I must explain, mustn't I? One moment, though. I must tell you my name.' He looked quite grave when he said this: 'I'm E. G. Timpany.' Then he smiled again.

'And my name's Jollifant, Inigo Jollifant - rather absurd, isn't it?'

E. G. Timpany held up his hand. 'No, no, no. Not at all. You mustn't say that. I know the name. Yes, I do. A Mrs Jollifant is one of our prominent workers in the South-Western district - that's Simeon, you know. Exeter is the headquarters of Simeon, and Mrs Jollifant is, I believe, an Exeter lady. Yes, she keeps a teashop there. A relation perhaps?'

'I don't think so,' replied Inigo. 'But tell me about Gad and Ephraim, and why Exeter is in Simeon.'

'We divide up our country as Jehovah divided up Canaan among the twelve tribes. I was the humble instrument of the command. At the Annual Convention, someone complained about the confusion between the various districts. Our President turned to me. "Perhaps Mr E. G. Timpany can suggest something," he said. At that very moment, I heard a Voice. And the Voice said "Look in your Bible." In a flash, I saw what we were to do. "Are we not the Children of Israel?" I said, for we believe that the great Anglo-Saxon race is descended from the ten lost tribes, just as the British Israelites do, only we have looked further into things than they have. "We will divide up our territory as Canaan itself was divided," I said.' He stopped and took out his watch. 'Time is getting on, isn't it?' ' I suppose it is,' said Inigo, disappointed. He did not want to lose Mr E. G. Timpany.

'Now I want you to do me a favour, Mr Jollifant. I'm sure you're an educated man, aren't you? Have you any profession?'

'I'm a schoolmaster of sorts.'

'A university man perhaps?'

'Cambridge. A Third in French, and a History Special.'

'A Special, eh? That's splendid, isn't it?' cried Mr Timpany, whose notion of a Special was evidently quite different from that of the university authorities. 'I knew, though, I knew. I could tell in a moment. You always can, can't you? Not that I'm a university man myself. I'm not. I'm self-educated. I left school when I was fifteen - a day school in Wolverhampton, it was - and all I've had since has been a Correspondence Course - in Accountancy, and very poor, I thought, not at all thorough - and some evening classes in Commercial Spanish. That was before I discovered the great teacher, Mr Jollifant - the Bible, the common, everyday, beautiful old Bible.' And he suddenly produced one from nowhere, like a conjurer. 'I'm sure you're not one of these so-called higher critics, are you?'

Inigo truthfully replied that he wasn't, but tried to convey the impression that he might have been a higher critic if he had cared about that sort of reputation.

'But there I go, talking and talking away,' said Mr Timpany. 'What I wanted to ask you, as a favour to *me*, was to come with me to Oxwell. You'll be very welcome, Mr Jollifant. There's a high tea at half past six - people coming from all parts, you see - and then a gathering afterwards. I want you to come simply as my guest, *my* friend, if you don't mind my calling you that, and I'm sure you don't, do you? Now what do you say? I'd like nothing better than to stay here and talk to you about some of our Second Resurrection truths, but - as you can see, can't you? - I haven't the time.' And he smiled his wide innocent smile, with its flashing confusion of ivories, and passed a hand over his damp forehead and auburn curls.

There was no resisting this invitation. Inigo packed himself and his raincoat and knapsack (both of which found a place among the texts from *Revelations* at the back) in the little car, and off they went. They slowly chut-chutted down the winding lanes, crawled through half a dozen villages, for Mr E. G. Timpany was an excessively cautious driver, so that there was plenty of time for people to read the notice on the windscreen: *Take heed for the end draweth nigh*. If such people grinned, as they frequently did, Inigo gave them a solemn and prophetic stare, but if they looked puzzled or startled - and one little girl and a man in a milk-cart really did look startled - he beamed upon them with the air of a man bringing glad tidings. His companion did not talk much because there were so many corners and cross-roads and the like to be carefully negotiated, but from time to time he let fall some information about either the Second Resurrection movement or himself. So far as Inigo could gather, then and later, the Second Resurrectionists took their stand on some fantastic interpretation of the twentieth chapter of *Revelations*, believing that Satan was let loose, given almost unlimited powers, about 1914, when he instantly set to work deceiving the nations and gathering them together for battle, that worse was soon to follow, more and bigger battles, floods and earthquakes, fire out of heaven, all within the space of the next two or three years, after which the sea would give up its dead, the sun, the moon, stars, and the round earth would vanish like clouds, and there would be an end of all material things. In addition to this apocalyptic dream, there were astonishing theories about the ten lost tribes and the Great Pyramid. It was all very confusing, not unlike hearing somebody describe a nightmare. Mr Timpany's own history, or such scraps of it as Inigo caught, seemed simplicity itself. The central fact in it was that he had sold what he called 'one of the best insurance books in Wolverhampton' to devote the remainder of his life, three years at the most, to the Second Resurrectionists. When Inigo applauded such courage and faith, Mr Timpany was very modest indeed, and pointed out that once he had come to believe in the Second Resurrection view of the future, it was impossible for him to remain in the insurance business.

'I want to talk to people about our S. R. truths,' said Mr Timpany, 'and I felt it wrong to take their money, just as you would, wouldn't you? What was the use of my trying to persuade a man to take out a twenty-years endowment policy, a thousand pounds, we will say, with benefits at a premium of fifty-one pounds ten, when I knew so well in my own heart that everything was coming to an end long before then? The very last day, I remember, a man came to me because he wanted to take out an education policy for his two boys, and I had to tell him outright that his boys never would be educated, not as we know education, you see. It was the least I could do, wasn't it? It wouldn't have been honest to have gone on, would it? Not that I wanted to, but in any case it wouldn't, would it?'

Inigo thought this over. 'I think it would,' he announced at length, as gravely as he could. 'After all, I suppose people only insure themselves to set their minds at rest, because they feel assured about the future. Well, they'd have had that, you see. And their future is settled anyhow, you believe. They'd really have had their money's worth, you see.'

Mr Timpany did not see, and they were at Oxwell before the question was settled. Oxwell proved to be a miserable little town, and Mr Timpany explained that it had only been chosen as the scene of the gathering because one of the chief Second Resurrectionists in the district happened to live there and it was he who was providing them with the hall for the meeting and the tea. 'Mr Grudy is one of our old stalwarts, a strong character and very deep-thinking man,' Mr Timpany went on to explain, 'entirely self-made and quite well-to-do. He's a farmer and corn-chandler and horse-dealer and several other things besides. Quite a patriarchal character, and one of our most substantial S.Rs. I'd been taking a message to one of his married sons when I met you,' he added, as if that somehow clinched the matter.

There were several cars, a trap or two, and a little bus standing outside the hall, a red-brick building of small size and less dignity that evidently served the town as a recreation-room. People, mostly women, were already buzzing in and out of the place, and Mr Timpany, with a hasty excuse to Inigo, immediately dived among them and finally disappeared for some time, leaving Inigo outside, staring at the people and at the large notices that surrounded the door. These were even more fiercely apocalyptic than those in Mr Timpany's car. In crimson lettering, bright as arterial blood, they announced a speedy end to all familiar things. *And in those days, they screamed, shall men seek death, and shall not find it; and shall desire to die, and death shall flee from them.* The Second Resurrectionists, all washed and brushed, stiffly erect in their best clothes, passed in and out and shook hands, asked one another how they were and said they were quite strangers. Inigo moved nearer the door and was pleasantly assailed by the smell of freshly cooked ham. He remembered that he had had nothing since breakfast but a little bread and cheese. Yes, he was hungry. Then his eye was caught by the furious crimson of another placard: *Therefore I will shake the heavens, and the earth shall remove out of her place, in the wrath of the Lord of hosts, and in the day of his fierce anger.* He was also feeling very dirty and untidy.

'This is Mr Jollifant.' Mr Timpany was beaming upon him once more. 'Mr Grudy.'

'We are very pleased to see you here today,' said Mr Grudy in a very deep voice. There was certainly something patriarchal about him. He was a gaunt elderly man carefully dressed in black. His eyebrows were bushy, intimidating; his nose had a masterful Semitic curve; his long white moustache was not altogether of this world. It was a face you could see framed in the smoke of a desert sacrifice.

Inigo said he was very pleased too, and then took Mr Timpany on one side and asked him about washing and brushing. Mr Timpany remembered that Inigo would have to spend the night somewhere. He consulted Mr Grudy, who advanced upon Inigo again. 'There is room in my house for you tonight,' he said. 'You will stay with us.'

Inigo, wishing he could reply in the same grand manner, could only stammer something about thanking him awfully, better not, lot of trouble, very decent, easily manage somewhere though, to all of which Mr Grudy paid no attention.

'There is a place for you,' he announced. 'My wife is superintending the preparations for tea, but my niece shall take you to the house.' And he stalked away, followed by Mr Timpany.

Inigo waited for the tall bony female with the large nose, the daughter of Ephraim or Gad. To his astonishment, however, Mr Timpany returned with a girl about twenty, all rosy and smiling, quite a pretty girl. And this was Mr Grudy's niece, Miss Larch, the maiden of the tribe, who would wait upon him. Inigo, an almost painfully susceptible youth, shook her hand enthusiastically and accompanied her to the house, which was only about quarter of a mile away, in the highest spirits. There, it is true, he was handed over to an elderly woman, who showed him into a neat little bedroom; but when he had washed and brushed himself and returned to the hall, Miss Larch, still rosy and smiling, was waiting for him. He wanted to shake hands with her all over again. She wore a charming blue dress that gave place, at the knee, to silk stockings of a most admirable contour; the five freckles dotted about her small nose were delicious in themselves; she had large blue eyes, thickly fringed, and they seemed to twinkle when they turned upon him. It was incredible that she should be a daughter of either Ephraim or Gad.

'You don't look a bit like a Second Resurrectionist,' he boldly confided on the way back. And then, of course, he had to tell her what a Second Resurrectionist did look like, and drew a strong picture of a bony female that made her laugh. Didn't she look like that, then? She didn't, he replied with fervour, and left her more rosy and smiling than ever. But he too didn't look like one, she told him. He wasn't one. Then what was he doing there? He explained shortly, then drew from her an explanation of her own presence on the scene. She had lived there for the last eighteen months, Mrs Grudy being her mother's sister, and she helped in the house and it was all very, very dull, though her uncle and aunt were very, very kind, but there was nothing really to do and everybody who came was either old or stuffy or both, and nobody talked about anything but the Bible and the lost tribes and the Pyramids, and sometimes she thought it was silly and then at other times she had to believe in it, they were all so sure about it, and then she felt she was awfully wicked and was a bit frightened, yes, awfully frightened sometimes. It all came out in one breathless rush, and it was evident that Miss Larch - Freda - had not exchanged confidences with anyone for a long time. By the time they reached the hall, they were not so much friends as fellow-conspirators, for Youth, when it is exiled into the kingdoms of the old, at once turns itself into the strongest of secret societies. At the door, Inigo glanced meaningly at the crimson letters, and Freda glanced at them too. Then their eyes met.

The door was closed but they opened it softly and peeped in. Some sixty or seventy people were sitting at the long tea-tables. They were not eating but listening to Mr Grudy, who was apparently concluding an address from the platform at the far end of the room. He boomed on for some little time before Inigo could make out what he was saying, but his final quotation from the Bible he carried in his hand came clearly enough, and Inigo, peeping over Freda's shoulder, heard it with a sense of incredulity, as if all Oxwell were some fantastic dream.

'And it shall come to pass,' roared Mr Grudy, 'in that day, that his burden shall be taken away from off thy shoulder, and his yoke from off thy neck, and the yoke shall be destroyed because of the anointing. He is come to Aiath, he is passed to Migron; at Michmash he hath laid up his carriages.' Then, after a suitable pause, Mr Grudy stepped down from the platform. 'Let us have tea,' he said in a milder voice, and instantly there was a babel.

'It looks as if we've come to Michmash, absolutely,' muttered Inigo. Mr Timpany had reserved a space for them next to him, but the table was so crowded and the others had been sitting there so long that not much of the space was left, for they were using long wooden forms and not chairs. Freda sat down, then Inigo jammed himself between her and Timpany, who was almost steaming. 'Warm in here, isn't it?' he said to Inigo. 'But a splendid gathering, really splendid!'

It may have been a splendid gathering but it was certainly a very odd meal. Inigo remembered other high teas but none higher than this. The forms were a solid mass of eaters and drinkers, and the tables were a solid mass of food. There were hams and tongues and rounds of cold beef and raised pies and egg salads; plates heaped high with white bread, brown bread, currant teacakes, scones; dishes of jelly and custard and blancmange and fruit salad; piles of jam tarts and maids of honour and cream puffs and almond tarts; then walnut cake, plum cake, chocolate cake, coconut cake; mounds of sugar, quarts of cream, and a steady flood of tea. Inigo never remembered seeing so much food before. It was like being asked to eat one's way through the Provision and Cooked Food departments of one of the big stores. The appetite was not tickled, not even met fairly; it was overwhelmed. The sight of these tables drove hunger out of the world, made it impossible to imagine it had ever been there. Inigo ate this and that, but he hardly knew what he was eating, he was so warm, so tightly wedged in, so amazed at the spectacle. The Second Resurrectionists were worthy of the colossal meal spread before them. This highest of high teas had met its match. If they had all been forty years in the wilderness, they could not have dealt with it more manfully. They were not your gabbling, laughing eaters; they did not make a first rush and then suddenly lose heart; they did not try this and taste that. No, they were quiet, systematic, devastating; they advanced steadily in good order from the first slice of ham to the last slice of chocolate cake; and in fifty minutes the tables were a mere ruin of broken meats, the flood of tea a pale and tepid trickle. Inigo, who retired early from the conflict, though he had to stay where he was, with Mr Timpany steaming on one side and Freda delicately grilling on the other, looked on with wonder and admiration. Across the table were two middle-aged women with long yellow faces, almost exactly alike, and a little round man who had no teeth and whose nose and chin came within an inch of one another as he worked away. It did not look as if three such persons would be able to do more than skirt the fringes of a high tea, but actually they walked right through and emerged unruffled at the other end. Above their heads, high on the opposite wall, was yet another of Mr Grudy's crimson placards, which began: *And the light of a candle shall shine no more at all in thee.* Inigo stared, now at the people, now at the placard. It was all very odd, absolutely.

Tea was over. Freda disappeared; Mr Timpany was borne away by the daughters of Ephraim and Gad; and Inigo strolled outside to taste the air, which had a novel and delicious flavour. After that he smoked a pipe and sauntered up and down the road, keeping an eye on the door so that he should not miss the fair Freda. A few belated Resurrectionists, whose work had kept them from the last Grudy high tea but two that this world would know, hurried into the hall. Then a large car arrived and carefully deposited on the road several persons who evidently could not be expected to grapple with a high tea. There was a tremendous middle-aged woman, purple and commanding, who was attended, as such women so often are attended, by a thin depressed-looking girl in a frock she had never liked. There was also a tall man with an excessively long and lean and brown face and a military bearing. Inigo watched these three new arrivals sail, drift, and march into the hall. Then he caught a glimpse of Freda's blue frock in the doorway.

'Well,' he asked her, 'when does the meeting begin?'

'In a minute,' she replied. 'The nobs have arrived. Did you see them? They won't come to the tea, they're too grand. That woman with the red face and the big nose is Mrs Bevison-Burr, and that's her daughter with her - she never says a single word and wears the most awful clothes. And the man with them is Major Dunker. He's rather nice, but he's a bit cracked.'

'Never mind. We're all a bit cracked.'

'You may be,' retorted Freda, 'but I'm not - '

'I know what you're going to say next,' he told her.

'You don't.'

'I do. You were going to say "So there?"'

'No, I wasn't,' cried Freda. Then she made a little face at him, plainly asking for more. This was Freda's idea of conversation. After sitting in corners so long and listening to stuffy old people who said things that were either silly or downright frightening, to contradict a young man who smiled at her and had nice eyes - it was lovely. So Inigo exchanged a little more of this stuff - 'sandbag badinage', he called it - and had time to reflect that if she had worn steel spectacles or scaled three stone more, he could not have done it, would have been elsewhere. As it was, he too was happy, delighted with Freda herself, with the phrase he had just made, and with his own ironical reflections.

It was time, however, for the meeting, the gathering, the convention - whatever it was - to begin. The tea things had been cleared away, the tables moved back, and all the forms ranged in front of the little platform. Now Mr Grudy, Mrs Bevison-Burr, Major Dunker, and Mr Timpany marched on to the platform and looked as if they were about to sing a quartette. Everybody else made a rush at the forms. Freda and Inigo were among the last, with the result that they had to squeeze in at the end of one of the back forms. Freda was jammed against a very stout woman, who smiled at her and patted her hand. Inigo was jammed against Freda and in order to sit there at all he had to hold on to the form itself, just at the back of Freda. There was really only half of him on the form.

Mr Grudy stepped to the front of the platform and surveyed them with a benevolent patriarchal stare, as if he saw before him his shepherds and bowmen and handmaidens and flocks and herds. Then he lifted a hand. Immediately everybody leaned forward and covered their faces. Inigo was not sure what was about to happen, but he leaned forward too, with a sharp jerk, so that the arm behind Freda slipped up and landed somewhere in the neighbourhood of her waist. She shook herself and whispered something. 'Sorry, couldn't help it,' he began whispering, and at the same time, by a gigantic effort, contrived to remove the innocently offending arm. She gave him a fierce little Sh-sh-sh. Mr Grudy was opening with a prayer. It was rather a long prayer, and Inigo was so uncomfortable, his body twisted at a fiendish angle, that he found it impossible to listen to it. Nevertheless he was in sympathy with it, for Mr Grudy continually referred to captivities and migrations across great deserts and Inigo felt them in every limb. When everybody sat up again at the end of the prayer, Mr Grudy stood there, very erect, and did nothing but look at them for at least two minutes. Inigo wondered what would happen next.

'Jee-ee - ' sang Mr Grudy.

Everybody jumped up at once - except Inigo. He sat there a second too long; his end of the form went down and he fell with a crash; the other end shooting up and slightly forward, hurled a little round man - it was the toothless one - into the seat in front; and there was a confusion and uproar. The hymn could not begin until the little man had been restored to his own row, the seat had been put back in its place, and Inigo, crimson, dusty, and furious, had scrambled to his feet.

'Jee-ee - ' sang Mr Grudy again, and this time they were off. Inigo did not sing, for the hymn was one he had never heard before. He felt foolish. When they came to sit down again, he felt still more foolish because the few inches allotted to him had now been swallowed up. He was about to abandon the seat altogether, to go and lean against the wall, when Freda captured about six inches from the large lady on her right and offered it to him so prettily that he could not refuse. And there he sat, very close, for the rest of the evening.

Mr E. G. Timpany was called upon to address them. Moist and triumphant, he stepped forward, clutching at a large bundle of notes, and looked all gold spectacles and teeth and preposterous auburn curls. He beamed upon them. For such moments as these he would gladly have sold all Wolverhampton. He produced figures, compared the numbers in Ephraim with those in Dan, was convinced that Gad would soon outstrip Issachar and even gave them percentages. Indeed, he made such good use of his correspondence course in accountancy that Inigo expected him at any moment to remember his other course and drop into Commercial Spanish. It was impossible not to like Mr Timpany, he was so innocently happy, so naively proud of his position as organizing secretary. Inigo found it quite painful to think that just when Mr Timpany was beginning to enjoy this life, he would either have to quit it or be compelled to admit he was a fool - unless it was possible for the Second Resurrectionists continually to postpone Doomsday.

Mrs Bevison-Burr, the commanding woman, came next. Her subject was Unbelief. She referred to Unbelief as if it were a very obnoxious person who was in the habit of insulting her every morning and evening. Mrs Bevison-Burr commanded them to do all manner of things to Unbelief. She did not hold out any great hopes for them when they had done all these things. Only a few of them were wanted by Jehovah, but the least they could all do was to settle Unbelief. They were asked to remember that Unbelief and Bolshevism were one and the same. There was a little more about Jehovah, to whom she referred as if he were a prominent politician staying at her country house. Mrs Bevison-Burr was not a success, though her presence there was evidently gratifying to most of her audience.

Major Dunker followed. His themes were the Pyramids, international relations, and earthquakes. Holding a little note-book very close to his face, he talked at some length of pyramid inches, which determined all the chief dates in the world's history, but it was difficult to follow this part of his speech because of the note-book. He passed on to international relations, which were rapidly approaching a supreme crisis. We were on the eve of the greatest and the last of all wars, the real Armageddon. But worse was to come. Earthquakes. Everybody had noticed that in recent years there had been more and more storms and floods and earthquakes, and scientists had all been baffled by these phenomena. All over the world they were investigating to discover the causes of these disturbances. They could find nothing. The causes were not in the mere rise and fall of the barometer nor even in spots in the sun. Forces were being let loose upon this planet that had formerly been restrained. These were the first activities of the newly released Prince of *Darkness. And when the thousand years are expired, Satan shall be loosed out of his prison.* And having delivered this quotation in the same dry tones he had used throughout, the Major abruptly concluded. He was, Inigo decided, quietly and decently mad.

Mr Grudy called for the testimony of other friends. Nobody spoke for a minute or two. Then a man with a black beard jumped up, said something about King George the Fifth being the ninety-ninth in succession from King David, and then sat down again. He was followed by a shrill little woman, who declared that she had dreamt four times that year of an angel waving something that looked like a golden coal-scuttle over the dome of St Paul's. Mr Grudy nodded approvingly at her, but there seemed to be a general impression that she had not done well in putting herself forward in this way. After that there was another wait. Then Mr Grudy stepped forward again and was about to address them when there was a stir at the back of the hall.

'I see that our friend, the Reverend Higginworth Wenderby, has arrived,' cried Mr Grudy. 'I am sure he will be pleased to give us his testimony. It is a privilege to have him here with us.'

A tall stout man in black climbed on to the platform, and stood there, panting and mopping his brow, while they applauded furiously. He was a curious figure. He had a mane of dark hair and an unusually large, white, wet face, which retreated at the forehead and the chin. 'My dear friends,' he boomed, 'please allow me a moment. I cannot talk to you without breath, and I have come here in such haste that I have no breath.' Everybody applauded again, including Inigo, who looked round and saw that a change had come over the whole meeting. Everybody seemed expectant. They were leaning forward now, all eager attention.

Mr Wenderby held up a large white hand. 'My friends,' he began, softly this time, 'it is a joy to address you once more, and there are not many joys in this vale of suffering and sorrow. We live here in sin, and Death is busy among the people. The husband must go from the wife, and the mother must weep over the departed child.' He continued in this strain for some time, his voice as artful and moving as a passage for muted strings. The matter was nothing, the manner everything; and even Inigo, who had disliked the man at sight, found himself vaguely moved. As for the rest of his audience, they frankly abandoned themselves to the luxury of easy emotion. Some of the women sobbed. Freda stirred uneasily and bit her underlip. Inigo sat there in both physical and mental discomfort.

Mr Wenderby paused and let his huge head droop. Then he raised it, higher and higher, until at last his white wet face seemed to shine in the light. 'But have I come here, my friends, to bear testimony to these things?' he asked, without raising his voice. 'Are they strange tidings, these of sin and misery and death, that I should come and relate them to you? Have I nothing more to say? Is this the end of our message?' He stepped forward another pace, so that he stood on the very edge of the platform. 'No,' he thundered. 'No, and a thousand times, no!'

'Ephraim!' yelled a voice in Inigo's ear.

'I beg your pardon,' he cried, startled. But the man, who had drawn up a chair just behind Inigo, took no notice whatever of him but stared fixedly at the preacher.

'I look for the Word, and the Word is here.' Mr Wenderby, now in full diapason, held up his Bible. 'And after these things,' he chanted, 'I heard a great voice of much people in heaven, saying, Alleluia; Salvation, and glory, and honour, and power unto the Lord our God. For true and righteous are his judgements; for he hath judged the great whore, which did corrupt the earth with her fornication, and hath avenged the blood of his servants at her hand. And again they said, Alleluia. And her smoke rose up for ever and ever.' Mr Wenderby then crumbled the world to dust and blew it away in one mighty shout. He led the faithful to their eternal home. He arrayed them in fine linen and took them through the gates of pearl and along the streets of pure gold to where the river of the water of life flowed from the throne of the Lamb.

The arms he raised seemed to lift most of his audience out of their seats. If they had groaned before, now they shouted. Only Mrs Bevison-Burr and Major Dunker remained unmoved. Mr Timpany had taken off his spectacles and was wiping them feverishly. Mr Grudy towered in his chair and his face grew bright in the glow of unseen desert suns. Inigo looked round in astonishment. The place was a pandemonium. Face after face, almost transfigured, caught and held his glance. This then was the secret, these moments, crashing in Dionysiac rout through months of boredom, glittering and trumpeting for a space in lives as quiet and faded as an old photograph. Something pitiful tugged at his heart, then was gone.

Mr Wenderby, dripping and paler than ever, blessed them fervently. All was over. There was a rush to the platform. 'What do we do now?' asked Inigo.

'Let's go, shall we?' said Freda. 'It wasn't quite so frightening this time, but it was bad enough. You feel better about it all outside, I've noticed.'

They walked up the road, cheerfully libelling all the Second Resurrectionists, but when they arrived at the house, Freda hesitated. 'I suppose I ought to go in, really. My aunt may want me to help her with supper.'

'Supper!' Inigo was horrified. 'There can't be supper, not after that tea. Surely none of 'em want supper - unless they're going to stay up all night.'

'Yes, they will. They're awful greedies, I can tell you. And Uncle will be bringing some of them in. That's why I don't want to go in. They'll talk and talk and talk, and I've had enough of it, haven't you?'

He admitted that he had had a good deal of it. They strolled about a mile farther up the road, stood on a bridge and talked nonsense, and then returned to the house. Freda did not go in, however, but crept up to a lighted window and peeped through a space between the drawn curtains.

'They are there,' she announced, 'and they're eating sandwiches. Didn't I say they would?'

'It's incredible,' Inigo cried softly. 'They can't go on putting it away like this. They simply will bring the world to an end. I can see Timpany's teeth just fastening on a wretched sandwich. Horrible, horrible! Come away.'

Freda had another peep, then joined him. 'Mr Wenderby's there. I don't like him, do you? He's the queerest of them all, I think. Do you know, he always calls me "Little Sister" - '

'Like his infernal cheek!'

'And - and - he always looks as if he wants to kiss me. He doesn't, you know - '

'I should think not.'

'But I always feel he would if I didn't dodge. He frightens me.'

'Then he's a vile brute,' cried Inigo. He was quite indignant. The arm he slipped round her, as she stood there looking so defenceless, so prettily forlorn, quivered with righteous indignation.

'Do you think so?' she murmured, not stirring except to lift her face a little.

'Beyond the pale, absolutely,' said Inigo firmly. He saw her fair face tilting until it caught the light. He saw the dark curve of her mouth. It was irresistible. He bent forward, and at that very moment the front door opened. Before anybody could come out, Freda had flown round the corner. Inigo went after her but by the time he had caught up to her they had been all round the house and were back again at the front door.

In the hall they met Mr Timpany. 'A splendid gathering, wasn't it?' he called to them.

They replied, breathlessly, that it was, absolutely splendid.

'Now don't tell me you're sorry you came, Mr Jollifant,' Mr Timpany continued. 'Don't tell me you weren't interested.'

'I won't,' said Inigo, shaking him by the hand.

III

On the following night, Wednesday, Inigo was sauntering through the streets of Nottingham. He had not gone there to look for Mr Morton Mitcham, though he had reminded himself with a certain quickening of interest, that this was Mr Mitcham's destination, where, like the gentleman of leisure he was, he had decided to look up a few old friends. At any moment, Inigo told himself, he might be passing an old friend of Mr Mitcham's. Inigo was there, however, because at the breakfast table that morning Freda had declared that she must go to Nottingham to visit a dentist. It then appeared at once that Inigo, who had been rather vague about his movements, was really on his way to Nottingham too. This astonishing coincidence had landed the pair of them on the same motor-bus from Oxwell, given them the same table for lunch, and finally, at Freda's request, had condemned them to spend the afternoon together, and some of it unnecessarily close together, in a huge sensuous cavern that called itself a picture palace.

Inigo did not care very much for films, especially in the middle of the afternoon, when their bludgeoning sentimentality, their glycerine tears, seemed downright blasphemy. This picture palace had an organ that was nothing but one gigantic, relentless, quavering *vox humana* stop, and listening to it was like being forcibly fed with treacle. However, Freda, having escaped from the wilderness of Oxwell, the captivity of the Second Resurrectionists, enjoyed it all. She munched chocolates, drank tea, ate little cakes, and coughed her way through two cigarettes; she laughed when the screen told her to laugh, stared mournfully when all was lost save love and the *vox humana* stop, shuddered and gasped and clutched at Inigo at all appropriate crises; and filled in the duller intervals in the programme by flirting with him. They were in there so long that Inigo was surprised to emerge, blinking, into broad daylight, and for a moment or so the sane and three-dimensional world about him looked quite unreal. It also made him feel rather foolish, and somehow he said good-bye to Freda, still rosy and smiling as she mounted the 6.15 motor-bus, with a feeling that was more like relief than regret. He returned to the mournful little commercial hotel where he had left his knapsack and there had a very bad dinner.

After wandering about the streets for quarter of an hour or so, Inigo turned into the nearest tavern for a glass of bitter. The place was almost empty, fortunately, for he wanted to be quiet and to think. What was he going to do? Should he wander on like this for a few days more, then return to his uncle's place at Dulwich and, once there, go the rounds of the scholastic agents? Did he want to go on teaching? No, he did not. But what did he want to do? He didn't know. He could afford to give himself a little holiday, but sooner or later he would have to decide about a job. This was an opportunity to experiment, certainly, but what was he going to experiment in? Journalism? His soul revolted, absolutely. It was while he was still telling himself how much his soul revolted or was prepared to revolt that the landlord came in and nodded to him.

'Breakin' up now,' said the landlord. 'But we can't grumble, can we? 'Ad a good month.'

Inigo never knew what to reply to remarks of this kind about the weather. People who made them always seemed to belong to a society of weather observers or even weather owners, and he always felt that he himself was too much of an outsider to do more than merely mumble something in response. He mumbled now, then hesitated, and finally remarked: 'I've just been wondering what to do. Now what would you do if you were a young man like me, with a little, just a very little, money of your own?'

'I wouldn't go into this business again,' replied the landlord promptly.

'You wouldn't, eh?'

'Wouldn't touch it, wouldn't have it given. Nothing in it now. All to pieces. What with dogs, football, pitchers, one thing and another - you can't sell beer, can't get 'em regular, yer know. Oh I wouldn't look at it.' He straddled in front of the fireplace and jingled some coppers in his pocket.

'Well, what would you do?' asked Inigo.

'If I'd my time over again, I wouldn't 'esitate,' replied the landlord, lowering his voice. 'I'd make a book, go in the ring. It's money for dust. They can't give it to you fast enough. Why, there's fellers come in 'ere - tut-t-t - ' And he tut-tutted away and wagged his head to show that mere words were failing him.

'Be a bookie, eh? That's no good to me, I'm afraid. Nothing in my line. I don't understand racing and I couldn't shout loud enough.'

'Don't need to shout, don't need to know anything,' cried the other. 'Some o' these fellers 'ardly know where they live. Doesn't matter. They get it all the same. Rolling in it, rolling! And where do they get it from, where do they get it from?' He walked right across the room to ask this momentous question and stood over Inigo, who told him he didn't know where they got it from. 'All right, I'll tell you,' said the landlord. 'They get it from mugs, like you and me. Mugs! Don't they, Charlie?' This was to a man who had just entered the room.

'That's right, Jack,' said Charlie, winking at Inigo. 'I don't know what you're talking about, but that's right.' And he sat down, pushed his cap to the back of his head, and began whistling very loudly.

"Ere, Charlie,' said the landlord, 'what's this about old Fred telling Jimmy you said I'd picked up a tenner on Cherry Lass?'

Inigo made his escape. The streets were lighted now and livelier, but the only entertainment they offered him was that of watching innumerable youths ogle innumerable pairs of over-powdered and under-nourished young girls, who took care to parade within easy reach of the various picture theatres. He soon came to the conclusion that these streets were not lively at all. They began to depress him. He thought once of going in, to add a few sentences to *The Last Knapsack*, but the image of that melancholy commercial hotel daunted him. No good literature could be composed in that hotel. 'It would all come out wrong,' he told himself. 'I should be putting down "as per yours" and things like that.'

He stopped outside a large and glittering tavern. It announced that it had a Singing Room, and Inigo did not remember ever having been inside a Singing Room. He walked in, to find himself facing a long curved bar that had far too many mirrors and electric lights. Business was brisk, so brisk that the bar counter was flooded, the change he received was all wet, and the beer itself had a nasty rinsed look. There were several swing doors, gorgeous with leaded lights, opening out of this bar, but there was nothing to indicate the one that would admit him to the Singing Room. He took a sip of beer, put the glass down, and determined to forget about it, and began dodging through the throng, to find the Singing Room. It was then that he heard, behind the back of a man who held one of the swinging doors open, the voice. 'In the absence of the pianist, ladies and gentlemen,' said the voice, 'I will not give you one of my famous banjo solos, but I will, with the kind permission of one and all, endeavour to entertain you with a few feats of sleight of hand.'

There was no mistaking it. This was the voice of that returned traveller, that gentleman of leisure, that looker-up of old friends in Nottingham, Mr Morton Mitcham.

Inigo pushed his way in. This was the Singing Room, and there, at the far end of it, near the piano, addressing an audience of about twenty men, youths, and girls, who did not seem particularly interested in him, was Mr Morton Mitcham. He wore the same light check suit, the same Mad Hatter collar and tie; and his eyebrows seemed larger, his nose richer, and his chin longer and bluer than they did before. 'I will open', he was saying, 'with a little trick I've performed in all parts of the world, America, Australia, India, and every important place in the U-nited King-dom - except Nottingham. Notice that, ladies and gentlemen - except Nottingham.' He held out a pack of cards. 'Now I want a lady or gentleman to take a card - '

'Any orders,' cried a waiter suddenly springing up from nowhere.

'Wairer, I wanternother double.' This was from a very ripe gentleman, who was sprawling at a little table by himself.

Inigo told the waiter to bring him a bottle of Bass and sat down not far from the ripe gentleman and near a middle-aged man and a little woman with eye-glasses who were sitting over two glasses of stout and placidly holding hands. Mr Mitcham stared at the new-comer, brought his immense eyebrows down and pursed up his lips. Inigo grinned at him and at last got a nod and a grin in return. Mr Mitcham, who clearly did not want to begin his trick until the waiter had returned, crossed over and calmly remarked to Inigo: 'I know you, my boy, and I see you know me. I'm just trying to place you.'

'We met the other midnight at Dullingham Junction.' said Inigo.

'Of course we did. And you had the chocolate and biscuits. And a merry little session we had, didn't we?' He lowered his voice. 'I'm just filling in the evening here, you know, just amusing myself. This isn't my kind of thing at all.'

'No, I should think not. Have a drink?'

'Thank you, my boy, I will. I'll have a whisky, just a - well, you might as well make it a double Scotch.' He lowered his voice again. 'If you told most people you'd seen Morton Mitcham here, they wouldn't believe, simply wouldn't believe you. But it amuses me, you know. And I like to show these boys and girls a thing or two. They've seen nothing, absolutely nothing.'

The waiter having returned and departed again for the double whisky, Mr Mitcham began his performance. A man in a brown hat far too small for him was persuaded to take a card. 'Look at that card, sir,' said Mr Mitcham impressively, 'examine it carefully. You may show it to any other members of the audience but don't let me see it, ha-ha! Now take this envelope, an ordinary plain white envelope, you observe, and place the card in the envelope and put the flap inside. Don't lick the envelope, sir, I may want it again. Now I take the envelope. It is impossible for me to see what the card is. Now follow me closely. I shall place the envelope - '

But here the ripe gentleman created a diversion. 'Never mind about cards,' he cried thickly. 'I wanner a bit o' music'

'I say, I shall place the envelope underneath this handker-chief - '

'I wanner a bit o' music'

Mr Mitcham frowned at him. 'All in good time, sir, all in good time. Just now I'm trying to entertain the company with this trick. I shall be much obliged, sir,' he said severely, 'if you will not interrupt.'

'Thaz all ri', thaz all ri'!' He waved a hand, and a large and idiotic smile slowly spread over his rubicund face.

'It is, you will observe, an ordinary handkerchief. I slip the envelope underneath - '

'Ber I like a bit o' music'

Mr Mitcham stopped and glared. Two or three members of his audience laughed, but a young man in a green cloth cap was very annoyed. 'Oh, put a sock in it,' he said to the ripe gentleman, who immediately and very loudly asked him what he meant by it.

'Now then, gentlemen, give order *if* you please,' cried the waiter, who had returned with Mr Mitcham's double whisky. They gave order, and Mr Mitcham was able to finish the trick, which he did by producing the card that was placed in the envelope from the middle of the pack, to the astonishment and admiration of everybody except the ripe gentleman and the two people who were holding hands. Inigo himself thought it a very good trick indeed. The young man in the green cap was loud in his admiration. 'Clever!' he cried aggressively. 'And new to me. Clever!'

'I seen it done once before,' said the man who had first taken the card. 'Fellow at the Hippodrome 'ere done it.'

'May I ask his name, sir?' said Mr Mitcham, frowning. 'Because that's my trick. I think you must be mistaken.'

'No, I'm not,' replied the other, mildly though firmly. 'I seen it all right. And I'll tell you his name. The Great Julius, that was him. The Great Julius. He was a Yank.'

'You're right, you're right.' cried Mr Mitcham, with hearty condescension. 'If it was the Great Julius, you're right. I taught him that trick in Philadelphia in 1910. There was no Great Julius about him then, I can tell you. He was just plain Julius Isenbaum, and nobody could be plainer. Yes, I taught him that trick.'

Inigo gazed at him in admiration, caught his eye, and indicated the presence of the whisky. The great man strode across, gave him a wink and 'the best, my boy!' and halved the liquor in one gulp. Then he produced a number of cards from his elbow, his knee, and the empty air, and finally asked the young man in the green cap, who still said 'Clever!' at intervals, to put the four queens wherever he liked in the pack. Mr Mitcham then shuffled the pack, held it up in one hand, held it up in the other hand, and put it down on the nearest table. The four queens, however, he produced from the pocket of the ripe gentleman, who had fallen into a doze. This delighted everybody except the ripe gentleman himself, who hit the table and cried: 'All a lorrer bunkum! Lessav a birrer music.'

'That's right. Where's Joe?' asked someone.

'Joe's the pianist,' Mr Mitcham explained to Inigo. 'Regular job here, you know, but hasn't turned up tonight. Here's the vocalist,' and he waved a hand at a rather short and flat-faced man who had just entered the room. 'He can't do anything, either. But I shall try 'em with the banjo soon, pianist or no pianist. I've kept a whole room going with that banjo in places where there wasn't a piano within two or three hundred miles. Believe me, my boy, I've travelled a hundred and fifty miles just to play it at a wedding party. That was up in Saskatchewan one time, Ninety-five or Ninety-six, I think it was.' He finished the whisky, then added: 'No, it wasn't. I'm not telling you the truth.' Inigo gasped. 'It was in Ninety-four,' Mr Mitcham concluded triumphantly.

Inigo glanced across at the piano, which was an ancient grand. 'Look here,' he said finally, 'I think I could knock something out of that, if you really want a pianist.'

'Of course you could,' cried Mr Mitcham enthusiastically. 'Didn't you tell me the other night you played? You're the very man we're looking for. Let me see - your name's just slipped - oh, Jollifant, is it? Of course it is.' He beckoned the vocalist and rose impressively at his approach. 'Meet Mr Jollifant, an old friend of mine, who's just turned up and who's one of the finest pianists that's ever stepped into this town. He's just promised to help us out.'

Five minutes later Inigo found himself sitting at the piano with some tattered sheets of music in front of him. It had been arranged that the vocalist should take his turn first. Inigo ran his fingers over the keys, which were very yellow, burned in places, and far too loose. The piano itself, however, was better than he had imagined it to be, and was certainly capable of making a terrific din. He dashed into the opening bars of the first tattered song, and the vocalist, in a voice so hard and so high that it hurt, proclaimed to the Singing Room that he lived in a la-and of rer-hoses but he drer-heamed of a la-and of sner- how. At the conclusion of this astonishing ballad there was a certain amount of applause, led by the ripe gentleman who had been beating time and humming in a vague sort of way. The vocalist treated his ravaged throat to a draught of stout, waited until six newcomers had sat down and given orders, then nodded to Inigo and declared, in his highest and hardest notes, that the woman for him in all the world was just his dear old mother. This was a sentiment that aroused the enthusiasm of the company, and one after another of them joined in until at last they were all asserting that the one woman for them was just their dear old mothers. By the time it was ended, the room was nearly full, and there was so much applause that the vocalist, now purple in the face, had 'to thank them one and all' and burst into an encore. Here again it appeared they had all a common enthusiasm, this time for dear old Ireland, especially the colleen in the cabin back in Connemara. Only Inigo, Mr Morton Mitcham, and the waiter appeared to have no tender memories of this colleen.

The vocalist departed; Mr Mitcham began tuning his banjo; the waiter collected orders and told Inigo to give it a name; more people came crowding in and filled the room with smoke and babble; Mr Mitcham whispered instructions and hummed tunes in Inigo's ear; the waiter dumped glasses of beer and whisky on the piano; the ripe gentleman vainly demanded more double Scotches; and Inigo emptied the glass in front of him and began to feel excited.

Off they went, softly at first, Mr Mitcham wagging his head to his lilting twanka-pang, twanka-pang, Inigo vamping away and putting in artful variations. More and more people came crowding in, to tapper-tap-tap with their feet. Mr Mitcham wagged furiously, quickening the pace. Inigo never lagged behind for a second and the louder and faster they went, the crazier were his elaborations. He would bring down both hands to crash and rumble in the bass and then would send them tinkling like hey-go-mad in the treble. 'Quiet!' cried Mr Mitcham, and then played as softly and solemnly as it is possible to play a banjo; indeed, you would not have thought it possible. Then after a minute of this - 'let her go!' he cried. And they let her go, in a triumph of twanging and panging and tinkling and crashing. And when it was done, the Singing Room let itself go too. There was such a din that the landlord himself looked in and was delighted to see how enthusiastic and hot and thirsty everybody appeared to be.

'With your permission, ladies and gentlemen,' said Mr Mitcham, after he acknowledged the applause, mopped his face, and drained his glass, 'a little impression of a military patrol. I may say that I first thought of this number when listening to some of our own brave boys up at - er - Allahabad.'

There was a great stamping of feet and banging of glasses, and a red-faced man roared out that the banjoist was a good old something-or-other 'wallah'. Mr Mitcham bowed his acknowledgements, then produced his impression of a military patrol, which he did simply playing a quickstep very softly at first and gradually increasing the tone. As no accompaniment was necessary, Inigo took another drink from those that were still steadily finding their way to the top of the piano, looked about him, and tried, not very successfully, to simmer down and give the appearance of being an old hand. The military patrol was a tremendous success, and Mr Mitcham had to give the latter half of it all over again. He then waved a hand to show that he was completely exhausted. 'You give 'em something,' he told Inigo, and emptied several glasses.

Inigo promptly played some of his own little tunes, finally arriving at the one we all know too well now, his *Slipping round the Corner*. While he was still strumming it quietly, he heard a queer clinking sound and saw the long lean figure of Mr Morton Mitcham moving about the crowded room. That gentleman of leisure was undoubtedly going round with the hat. Inigo had a shock, but it did not last long. 'In for a penny, in for a pound,' he told himself, and then added: 'If it is a pound.' He could hear the feet tapping to his tune. Perhaps he did not play it as well as he had done at Washbury Manor - now a little dark place thousands of miles away - but he ended by playing it even faster and louder. Nor did he end alone, for Mr Mitcham, presumably with the hat, returned to join in with admirable gusto, having picked up the tune. The whole Singing Room was slipping round the corner.

'Time, gentlemen, please!' the waiter shouted, but nobody appeared to take any notice of him, except the two performers, who came to a triumphant conclusion. There was no doubt about their reception. The Singing Room had not heard so enthusiastic applause for years. Three glasses were broken. There were cries of 'Encore' and 'Keep on, boys'. But Mr Mitcham, still the dignified performer in spite of his dripping face and the innumerable drinks he had consumed, shook his head at Inigo.

'Time, gentlemen, if you please!' cried the waiter again now in an agony of supplication. Several moist enthusiasts insisted upon shaking the musicians by the hand, and there was trouble with the ripe gentleman, who was crawling about the floor looking for his hat; but gradually the room was cleared. Inigo felt rather dazed. He saw Mr Mitcham very carefully counting a heap of small change. Then he discovered the landlord at his elbow.

'You can tickle 'em all right,' said the landlord, pointing to the keyboard.' 'Ere, 'alf a minute.' And he dragged Inigo to one side. 'If thirty bob a week's any good to you,' he said, lowering his voice, 'and all the drinks you want, the job's yours and Joe can go to 'ell.'

'Thanks,' Inigo found himself muttering, 'but I don't want the job, if that's what you mean.'

'What's the matter with it?' the landlord demanded. 'You won't get better money in this town, let me tell you.'

'But I'm not staying on in this town.'

'Ah, that's different, that is. Well, you can tickle 'em all right. Give us a call and a tune any time you're round this way. 'Ere.' And he dragged Inigo back again, to where Mr Mitcham was counting his coppers. 'This is my little contribution, gentlemen.' He threw a ten shilling note on the heap, drew Mr Mitcham on one side to whisper to him, then shouted to the waiter and walked away.

Mr Mitcham wrapped up the money in a handkerchief. 'I know a place where they'll give us a decent little feed, that is, decent for these parts. There's no food really here, of course; you mustn't expect it. Now what about giving ourselves a little supper? I've hardly had a bite all day, didn't want it, you know. I'm so used to feeding late. Come on then; it's not far, just near the station.'

They sat in the window of the upstairs room of the unpretentious little restaurant, which was almost empty. Inigo ordered a mere snack, but Mr Mitcham, who gave Inigo the impression of having been on short commons for a day or two, asked for large steaks and bushels of onions and potatoes. As soon as the waitress had gone, he brought out the handkerchief containing the money. 'Now, then,' he began, 'the landlord made it ten, didn't he? And the takings in the room were twenty-three shillings and ninepence ha'penny. That's exactly thirty-three shillings and ninepence ha'penny. Now what's half of that?'

'Sixteen and something,' replied Inigo. 'But why do you want to know? Are you thinking of dividing it between us?'

'Naturally, my boy, naturally! Like an honest trouper! No quibbling about shares, either. I don't say', he added thoughtfully, 'that some of this might not have been a little appreciation of my sleight of hand, and of course you'd nothing to do with that. That card in the envelope trick went devilishly well, you know. But - share and share alike, I say, and no quibbling.'

'I can't take any of it. It's jolly good of you, but I can't.'

'You can't?'

'No. You see - '

Mr Mitcham patted him on the arm and at the same time, with great dexterity, swept all the money away with the other hand. 'My dear boy, of course I see. You've no need to tell me.'

'I did it for a lark, you see - '

'Just for the fun of the thing and to oblige a friend,' cried Mr Mitcham enthusiastically. 'And naturally you wouldn't touch a penny of it. I know, because that's just how I feel myself. Done it myself many a time. Ask them in Toronto what Morton Mitcham did at old Reilly's benefit, or for that fire concert in 'Frisco, or the time when the stage hands went out at Melbourne. I know your feelings, know them to a hair, my dear boy. They're the feelings of a gentleman, a musician, a true artist. You remind me - everything you've done has reminded me of Captain Dunstan-Carew - played for me, played with me, scores of times out in India, and "Proud to do it, Mitcham," he'd say, and he was the best amateur pianist out there - *and* a Dunstan-Carew. You've both got the same touch - recognized it in a minute - a gentlemanly touch, but full of fun, plenty of devil in it.'

Inigo said he was proud to have the same touch as Captain Dunstan-Carew.

'But I'll tell you one thing, my boy,' continued Mr Mitcham. 'You may not let me give you a share of the takings, but you're going to let me pay for this supper. I insist. I don't care what you're having tonight, I insist. The supper is mine.' He looked first at Inigo and then round the room with such an air of noble generosity that Inigo found it difficult to remember that his own share of the supper would only amount to about tenpence.

'For that matter, of course,' said Mr Mitcham, after he had

wolfed in silence the greater part of his steak, 'the business tonight's been a mere piece of foolery with me. As I told you before, I think, it's not at all my line of country. But, the fact is, I've been unlucky just lately. You know what it is. Twenty years ago I was landed in the same damned hole. No, it was worse. I was down there in Memphis - '

'Not Memphis!' cried Inigo in delight.

'Memphis,' replied Mr Mitcham firmly. 'And I hadn't a nickel to my name. And you can imagine what a hole Memphis is when you haven't a cent.'

'Rather!' cried Inigo. 'You couldn't be in a worse place, could you?' He said this with conviction, though actually all that he knew about Memphis was that it is a city somewhere in the United States.

'You couldn't. Well, three months afterwards, exactly three months - where was I? I'll tell you. I was in a suite on the first floor of the best hotel in all New Orleans, and telegrams pouring in, just pouring in. Go here, go there, go everywhere! Three syndicates all eating out of my hand! I don't say it will be the same all over again *exactly*. Times have changed, my boy, you can take it from me. There's not enough money in this country. But as I was saying, I've been unlucky just lately. Vaudeville's gone to pieces here, absolutely to pieces. And what with one thing and another, these last few weeks I've just been living from hand to mouth; on little engagements picked up here and there, some of it damned near to busking. If it was summer, I wouldn't mind, but winter - you know what it is. You want a cast-iron contract in winter. I tell you, things have been so bad, I've even considered band work, but I couldn't get near, couldn't get near. The Union, you know - they've a union and it won't let an outsider come within a mile. Then I thought of concert-party work, pierrot stuff. It's a hell of a drop, of course. Mind you, I won't say I've never done it before. I've even done the black-face business, though that was in the days when it still had style.'

'But these concert parties or pierrots or whatever they call themselves, don't they just go round, hopping from pier to pier, so to speak, in summer? Won't they all have just finished?' And it struck Inigo that he had not seen any of these troupes for years. Did the men still bend their knees in an idiotic way when they sang choruses? What a life!

'Most of them have finished now, but some keep on through the winter, doing small inland towns, you know, where people are glad to see anybody.'

'They must be,' said Inigo, who was still turning over his memories.

'Well, I'll tell you what I'm going to do, and I want you to listen very carefully, my boy. I'm going to see a concert party tomorrw. And

I'll tell you why. I ran across two people I know - decent nice folks, man and wife, vocalists, but not, I think, absolutely bursting with talent - and they told me they were in a troupe that was running on through the winter and there might be a vacancy or two in the autumn. I saw a notice in *The Stage* saying they were at Rawsley for two weeks, that's not too far from here, and so tomorrow I'm running over to have a look at 'em. Now if you're doing nothing - but look here, what *are* you doing?'

Inigo gave a brief but spirited sketch of his own position.

'If you do anything but play the piano,' said Mr Mitcham earnestly, 'you're just throwing yourself away. I was watching your work tonight, and I said to myself, "That boy was born with it. A bit of experience, a few tips from an old hand, and he can go anywhere." And believe me, I *know*. I've seen and heard thousands.' Inigo laughed. 'Did you like my tunes?'

'Catchy stuff, very catchy stuff, and new to me. Where did you pick 'em up?'

'Out of the ether.'

'Ah, I never bother with this wireless myself,' said Mr Mitcham judiciously, 'but I've no doubt you can pick up a good tune or two occasionally if you listen long enough.'

'No, no, I don't mean that. I mean, they're my own tunes. I make 'em up myself.'

Mr Mitcham stared at him. Then he extended a long yellow hand. 'Shake that,' he commanded, 'and as hard as you like. Now you listen to me. There's a pot of money in those tunes if they're properly handled. You've got the gift, though, mind you, I don't say you don't need experience or a little advice from people who've had experience. After this, I can't let you go, I just can't. It would be a crime. You've just got to stick to the old man, my boy. Come with me tomorrow. If there's an opening for me, there'll have to be one for you too. If there isn't, we can move on. We'll try that stuff out somewhere.'

Inigo had come to the conclusion that it really would be rather a lark. 'But what do they call this pierrot troupe?' he asked.

'I'll tell you in a minute,' replied the other. He fumbled in his waistcoat pocket and finally produced a little newspaper cutting. 'Here it is. They call themselves "The Dinky Doos".'

Inigo gave a yell. 'But I couldn't be a Dinky Doo,' he gasped. 'Don't ask me to be a Dinky Doo.'

Mr Mitcham lowered his great eyebrows. 'What's the matter? Do you know the show?'

'No, but the name, the name! It would hurt, absolutely.'

'No, a mere nothing, that!' Mr Mitcham's face cleared, and it was as if the sun had risen upon those black hills of South Dakota he had once mentioned. He stood up, then patted Inigo on the shoulder. 'If I don't mind the name, you shouldn't. At your age, my dear boy, it doesn't matter what they call you or make you wear; you can get away with it. But look at me, at my age! I ask you, do I look like a Dinky Doo?'

He looked fantastic enough for anything, Inigo thought. All that he said, however, was that they might put it to the waitress, who was approaching with the bill. Now would you say', Inigo solemnly inquired of her, 'that either of us looked like a Dinky Doo?'

'Get on with you!' said the waitress, who understood this to be some sort of chaff but was too sleepy to bother her head about it.

'And that's the answer all right,' said Mr Mitcham as they walked down the stairs. 'Get on with it. I'll look you up in the morning. Where are you staying?'

And in the morning, quite early, Mr Mitcham arrived at Inigo's hotel, accompanied by his banjo-case and his large and disreputable bag. He did not say where he had been sleeping, and had the appearance of not having slept anywhere except in his check suit. Two little cross-country trains finally landed them in Rawsley, and in the early afternoon they walked past those Station Refreshment Rooms to which, later, they had to return. Mr Mitcham did not know where his acquaintances, whose name was Brundit, were staying, in the town, and it took some time to find their lodgings. Inigo did not see how it was to be done at all, but Mr Mitcham, pointing out once more that he was an old hand, declared that everybody in these small towns knew everybody else's business and succeeded in uncovering a trail that brought them at last to the temporary home of the Brundits. There, a little woman with five curling-pins stuck round her furrowed forehead gave them cheerless news. The 'Dinky Doos' were no more.

'And I'm sure I'm right sorry for them. Mr and Mrs Brundit, too. Very nice people, and them with a little boy of their own,' said the bepinned landlady breathlessly. 'Off he goes on Sunday, this chap that's running it all, and the young woman that plays the piano for them going with him, and not a penny they've had for weeks. And people in the town's saying all sorts of things about them - and of course you do want your money, don't you, especially these days, when everything's top price - but as I say, and I'm as much out as anybody, I feel right sorry for them, and didn't know where to look when they came and told me, and Mrs Brundit, such a dignified and lady-like person, not like some of them, crying the eyes out of her. And now they've gone down to the station to see about something, and they told me they'd be all having a cup of tea and a bit of a meeting down at Mrs Mounder's - that's the Station Refreshment Rooms, a tin place, just opposite - and that's where you're likely to find them, if you ask me.'

That is how they came to be at the Station Refreshment Rooms, entering them - or rather it - for there was only one large public room in the hut - at the same time as a slender fair woman and her surprising companion, a short but sturdy man who looked like a workman of some kind or other. The four of them seemed to Inigo to make a very odd quartette indeed.

There were only six people in the tea-room, and they were all sitting together at the far end. Obviously these were the forlorn entertainers, though they did not sound very forlorn, for they all seemed to be talking at the top of their voices and laughing a great deal. Mr Mitcham marched up the room to them, and he was followed by the fair woman who had just come out of the car. Inigo, for once unaccountably shy, hesitated, took off his knapsack, then stopped where he was. He turned to find that the little man who looked like a workman had also stopped. Their eyes met. Inigo raised his eyebrows and gave a little grin. The other replied with a wink.

'Are these here', he began, in a kind of hearty whisper, 'the thingumjybobs - *pier-rots*?'

'They are,' replied Inigo. 'They call themselves the Dinky Doos.'

'Eh, they get some daft names!' Then he added ruminatively: 'I know nowt about a Dinky Doo, but it seems to be a queer do all right. But it's been nowt but a queer do all t'week wi' me.'

Inigo was amused by his impressive tones and broad accent and earnest open face. 'Oh, how's that?' he asked.

'It began o' Monday night, when you were i' bed and fast asleep, lad - '

'Half a minute, my dear sir, half a minute! Let me tell you,' said Inigo, with mock solemnity, 'I was not in bed and fast asleep on Monday night. I never saw a bed that night - '

'Ner more did I. Nobbut a sofa.'

'I was in the waiting-room of a God-forsaken place called Dullingham Junction, listening to my friend over there playing his banjo. What do you think about that?'

'I nivver knew there were so many folk wandering about. Once you've fairly set off, you come on 'em all over t'place. Do you know where I was o' Monday night?'

'I give it up.'

'On a lorry wi' two o' t'biggest rogues you ivver clapped eyes on, coming down t'Great North Road.' And Mr Oakroyd's blue eyes fairly shone with pride. This time he had a listener worthy of him.

'That's the stuff, absolutely the stuff!' cried Inigo, beaming upon this droll little Yorkshireman, who was evidently a Romantic like himself. Then he looked down the room, to see Mr Morton Mitcham beckoning him with waves of his gigantic arm.

At that moment a voice came ringing from the centre of the group. 'Come on, you two,' it cried. 'Don't be shy. Hurry up and join in.' It was a girl's voice, casual but a trifle mocking. Inigo heard it with a curious little thrill of excitement that afterwards he was at great pains to explain. He has not forgotten it yet, and perhaps he never will. It came ringing - and up went a curtain.

'Nowt shy about yon lass,' said Mr Oakroyd. 'Well, we've come a fair way, we mun join in.'

And that will do very well for the last word now. It is the tag of the first higgledy-piggledy piece, with its glimpses of too familiar backgrounds, scenes that are undoubtedly set scenes, and of roads jogging invitingly out of them, with its scattered hints of discontent and rebellion and escape. Here they all are, our people, and for a little space we darken the stage that holds them, leaving them staring at one another.

BOOK TWO

CHAPTER ONE
In Which They All Become 'Good Companions'

I

'SHAME isn't the word for it, it isn't really, Miss Trant,' cried Miss Elsie Longstaff indignantly. 'I've been in work now since last April, five months and more, consecutive, and look at the position I'm in now - having to get a sub from home! In work since last April, Miss Trant, and haven't been able to have my hair waved for three weeks! And this last week, my dear! The suspicion, the looks, the tone of voice, the things we've had to put up with all through that dirty rotter! It's wicked.'

'It's the wickedest thing I ever heard of,' replied Miss Trant warmly. She really had begun to feel angry with this defaulting manager. 'Have another cup of tea?'

'Yes, thanks, I will.' Then, with a dramatic change of tone, Miss Longstaff went on: 'He got us to sign on right through till next summer. It looked a good contract. What was the result? I'd a nice pantomime offer, came in early - Dandini for seven weeks, opening at Middlesbrough - and of course I went and turned it down - flat. And now look at me!'

Miss Trant did, very sympathetically. Elsie was younger and prettier than her sister Effie, though neither so young nor so pretty as she appeared to be at a first glance. She was probably about thirty, a too determinedly golden blonde, with large blue eyes set wide apart, a face that narrowed sharply to a small pointed chin, and a discontented mouth. She looked like a knowing and slightly dishevelled doll.

'And apart from that,' Miss Longstaff added, rather tearfully, 'he's gone and broken up one of the best little shows on the road.'

'It really was a good pierrot troupe, was it?'

'Please don't say "pierrot troupe", Miss Trant. It makes me think of being on the sands and rattling a box round the crowd. Call it a "concert party".'

'I'm sorry. Concert party, then.'

'Well, honestly, Miss Trant, it was a *good show*. Don't go and think I say that because I was in it. That's nothing. I've been in shows, my dear, that I'd tell you frankly were dead rotten. I wouldn't want anybody who knew me, or anybody who appreciated my work, to see some of the shows I've been in. But this was good. With any luck, we could have coined money with it.

'What a shame!' cried Miss Trant, and then looked thoughtful. Perhaps it was at this moment that a certain crazy notion began bobbing in and out of her head.

'Yes, but what's so aggravating, so fearfully maddening, my dear,' cried Miss Longstaff excitedly, 'is that it's a better show still, now those two are out of it, or anyhow it's got the makings of a better show.'

'Weren't they good?'

'Duds, complete and unutterable duds. He did monologues and child impersonations. You never heard anything like it. He never got a hand. Mr Charles Mildenhall in his celebrated monologues and child impersonations! My dear, it was a scream. They used to think it was a skit, until he went on and on. As for that precious pianist he took away with him - Marjorie Maidstone, she called herself, after the jail, I suppose - she was easily the world's worst as a pianist. She daren't have looked Little Nelly's Instruction Book in the face. Thumping away with those big fat fingers of hers, playing slow when you wanted it fast, and fast when you wanted it slow, missing the repeats - oh, ghastly! If she ruined my act once, she ruined it fifty times. With a decent pianist, we shouldn't know ourselves. And now, because they've gone and done the dirty on us, the show's finished. Isn't it sickening. It makes you lose heart.'

'But can't you run it yourselves?' asked Miss Trant, who, in this new mood of hers, was dying to see somebody run something.

'Oh, we've talked and talked and talked, but it's no good. We've no money not a bean. We're four weeks owing as it is, and can't settle for our digs here, most of us, let alone pay off for the show. They've taken all our props at the hall here, to pay the rent. It's wicked. Just let *me* see Mr Dirty Charles Mildenhall. Just let me set eyes on him again, and will there be trouble? Oh won't there just! Child Impersonator! Can you beat it!' And Miss Longstaff gave three dabs at her right eye before drinking her tea.

Miss Trant, after glancing round the curious assembled company, began to question her companion about these debts, and Miss Longstaff replied languidly and with a despairing sniff. Oh yes, if all that was paid off and there was some money left to pay immediate expenses, the show could go on. And if there was enough money behind to rent His Majesty's Theatre, it could go on better still. It amounted to *that*. 'What a hope!' she concluded bitterly, and evidently felt that all this talk was merely turning a knife in the wound.

'Well, I don't know - ' Miss Trant hesitated. That crazy little notion was bobbing furiously now. She made an effort to pretend it was not there.

Miss Longstaff stared at her with widening eyes. Then she leaned forward, all eagerness now. 'Look here, Miss Trant, you don't happen to know anybody who could put the money up, do you? I can tell you this, honestly, there isn't a more promising little show anywhere. With any luck at all, it could have been an absolute riot. I'm sure you do know of somebody, don't you?'

Instead of making a direct reply to this, Miss Trant hesitated again, then finally murmured: 'I wonder how much money it would take - I mean paying all there is to pay already, and then carrying on.' Her voice trailed away into a speculative silence, broken at last by the voice of common sense, pointing out that she was a fool. But then, wasn't it high time she was a fool? You can't go on being cool and sensible all the time, for ever.

Miss Longstaff leaned forward again and whispered: 'Jimmy Nunn could tell you - he's been working it out, I know, because he's tried hard to get somebody to back us. He's our comedian - that's him, over there - and he's one of the best comedians going in Concert Party work - clever, and keeps it clean - and he's stiff with experience, knows it all from A to Z. You have a talk to Jimmy about it, Miss Trant. I'll bring him over.' And she slipped away to whisper to a queer-looking man in a brown tweed suit.

Miss Trant had never met a comedian before, and it seemed incredible that she should be meeting one now. If Mr Jimmy Nunn had walked across to sing a song or crack a joke or two to her, she would not have been surprised; but that Mr Jimmy Nunn should merely announce, in a rather husky voice, that he was very pleased to meet her and then quietly sit down, was astonishing. Nevertheless, there was something distinctly droll about Mr Nunn. His manner was grave and dignified, almost pompous, but he had obviously spent so much of his time being a funny man that this other manner sat uneasily upon him, so that by merely refraining from singing songs and cracking jokes, by talking quite seriously, he seemed to be playing a part, thus remaining a droll fellow in spite of himself. Miss Trant found his appearance quite fascinating. He was really of medium height but had the body of a large stout man and the legs of a short man; he had a bald patch in front and grey stubble of hair surrounding it, little eyes set too close together, a shining bulbous nose, and an extraordinary expanse of upper lip enclosed between two deep wrinkles; and his whole face had a curious air of being a mask that had been painted and rubbed and painted again times without number.

'Not in the profession yourself, Miss Trant?' he inquired, closing one eye and staring hard with the other. 'No? I thought not, though I used to know a Mrs Trant on the Macnaghten Circuit. No, I'm wrong; I'm lying. It was Brant. Brant's Merry Chicks - juveniles, you know - none of 'em over thirty. You're not in management by any chance?'

'I've never managed anything except a house,' said Miss Trant.

'If you can do that as it ought to be done,' Mr Nunn observed, with some solemnity, 'and take it easy, keep smilin', have a good word for one and all, then - I say - you couldn't do better. Isn't that so? Right.' He waved the whole matter aside. Then, lowering his voice a little, he went on: 'You were asking something about the show, what we're down the river for, what it would take to run it. Am I right?'

Miss Trant wanted to laugh, for though Mr Nunn's manner was quite pompous, it kept breaking down, and all the time he gave her the drollest looks out of the particular eye that happened to be open. 'Well,' she faltered, 'I was just - wondering - '

'Quite right!' said Mr Nunn, and produced from his inside pocket a cheap and very soiled notebook. 'I've got figures in this,' he announced proudly. 'It's here - most of it anyhow - in black-*and*-white.'

'That's the stuff, Jimmy,' said Miss Longstaff brightly.

'Just you run away and play, Elsie,' Mr Nunn commanded; and after making a little face at him and flashing a professional smile at Miss Trant, Elsie did go, joining the others, who had now formed one group at a neighbouring table.

'A good girl,' remarked Mr Nunn; 'looks well and not as afraid of work as some of 'em; but' - and here he lowered his voice and leaned forward - 'can't quite put it all over yet, hasn't just got - y'know – '

Miss Trant nodded and really felt she did know. 'I wish', she said softly, 'you would tell me about the people in this trou - party - show.' She almost felt herself blushing as she brought out this last word. It sounded so knowing and professional. 'You've had a lot of experience, haven't you, Mr Nunn?'

'That's right. A lot of experience. C. P. work, halls, panto, low comedy in legit., know it all. And, mind you, whatever I may say about these boys and girls, I'll say this, as a show - or what might be a show if it was pulled together now - it's good.' He found a cutting in the notebook and handed it over. 'Here's one of our adverts. They're usually all lies, but this one's the solid truth.'

The advertisement, which was from *The Stage*, ran as follows:

Wanted Known
Offers from 3 Sept, onward
THE DINKY DOOS
In a Non-Stop Programme of Clever Comedy and
Exquisite Vocalism. Played to enormous business at
Little Sandmouth, last. Many thanks T. Browning,
Esq., for hearty welcome, and Mrs James, G. Hudson,
Esq., and R. A. Mercer, Esq., for inquiries. Refer
Refer. Refer. Next, Pav. Shingleton.

Miss Trant read it through once, wrinkled her forehead, then read it again.

'Wrote that myself,' Mr Nunn remarked, not without pride. 'Always wrote the adverts for Mildenhall. Neat and effective, don't you think?'

'Yes, I should think so. But tell me, what does "Wanted Known" mean?' she inquired. 'Why "Known"?'

'Oh, I always put that in. And, of course, "Known" - well, you see - it's "Known" - isn't it, you see?'

This was not very clear to Miss Trant, but she said she supposed it was. And after that, she thought, it would not do to ask what 'Refer' meant, nor even to hint that it must be difficult to play to 'enormous business' in a place called Little Sandmouth, of which she had never heard before. 'But you were going to tell me something about the people here.' She dropped her voice. 'Who is that very tall, thin man in the loud, check suit?'

Mr Nunn glanced across, then shook his head. 'Not one of us,' he whispered. 'I've just been introduced to him. Name of Mitcham. A pro. Banjo-player.'

'I remember. He came in when I did, with that rather pleasant-looking, untidy youth with the lock of hair.'

'That is so,' said Mr Nunn. 'Not our lot at all, just visiting. But you see that other boy who's talking to 'em, that nice-looking one?' Miss Trant did see him, and had indeed been thinking for some time that he was an astonishingly handsome youth. He had a small head, carefully waved dark hair, and fine regular features, and was beautifully dressed. It was a pleasure to look at him, though Miss Trant decided she had no particular desire to know him. He was not the type of young man she admired. 'That's Jerry Jerningham, our light comedian and dancer,' Mr Nunn continued. 'And I don't mind telling you, he's a *find*. Works hard, got personality, puts it over all the time. You couldn't want a better dancer. If he plays his cards properly, he'll be up in the West End before long. They've only got to see him. The only thing is, he won't feed. I never struck a worse feed.' And Mr Nunn paused impressively.

Miss Trant stared. This seemed a curious complaint to make. 'Do you mean that he won't eat?'

Mr Nunn leaned back, banged his thigh, and gave a sudden guffaw. Then he looked grave again. 'Not at all. It doesn't mean eating. Far as that goes, there's only one member of this show that can't eat, and that's me. Got a wicked stomach - oh, downright wicked! - won't look at a thing. Bacon, eggs, ham, chops, steak and chips, bit o' pie - anything you really fancy, y'know - you wouldn't believe what they are to me. Poison, that's what they are. Give me a good supper,' he pursued earnestly, 'and you might as well fill me up with red-hot pins and needles. I haven't had a square meal for three years, just toast and charcoal-biscuits and beef-tea and bits of fish and chicken and jellies and shapes. And I've got to be funny on that, got to make a lot o' people laugh who are filled up with roast beef and Yorkshire and baked potatoes and greens and apple pie. Dear, dear, dear!'

He wagged his head so comically that Miss Trant had to laugh even while she was crying 'What a shame!'

'But this feeding I'm talking about', Mr Nunn went on, 'is a name in the profession for working up to gags. The chap that feeds has to ask the comedian questions and get angry with him and all that. You know the business.'

Yes, Miss Trant did know it.

'And I give you my word, Miss Trant, it's not so easy as it looks, and a comedian's got to have a good feeder. Now young Jerningham there hates it and so can't feed for nuts. That's good, isn't it? - can't feed for nuts. And properly speaking, it's his job to feed, but as luck will have it, Joe over there - he's our bariton, Courtney Brundit, but everybody calls him Joe - is as good a feed as you could wish for.' He indicated a powerfully built man, with a broad and pleasantly stupid face, who was smoking a short pipe and staring at nothing. 'I won't say I've not heard better baritone singers than Joe. I've heard a lot better, and so have you. But if you or anybody else told me you wanted to run this show and leave Joe out, I'd say, "Well, you can leave me out too." That's how I feel about Joe. He's not one of the brainy ones, Joe isn't, and you'll never hear him at Covent Garden, but he's got a heart of gold. You can't rile him, and he'll do anything for a pal, Joe will. Easiest-tempered man I ever knew, and a good job too because he's as strong as a horse. He was in the Navy one time and a heavy-weight champion. If you ask me, that's what started him off as a singer. If he wanted to sing, he sang, and nobody could tell him to shut up.' Mr Nunn chuckled a little over this, then drew a long breath and became serious again.

'That's his wife there, our contralto,' he began.

'What, the woman in the purple hat?' It was a peculiarly revolting purple hat and Miss Trant had been shuddering at it for some time. It completely dominated its wearer, a vague plumpish sort of woman who was knitting in a rather detached and stately manner.

'That's the one. Stella Cavendish she calls herself, but she's Mrs Joe Brundit. Big voice, a good classy rep, plenty of experience, and a real nice woman, though a bit inclined to put it on, y'know, now and again. Keeps Joe well in hand. But they're a nice couple to work with. They've got a little boy named George - lives with his aunt in Denmark

Hill - and you'd think there'd never been another kid in the world. But it's hard on them, this bust-up, I can tell you.'

'And who is that young dark girl who's got such a merry face? I like the look of her.' The girl in question was listening to Mr Oakroyd, who appeared to be telling her all about his adventures.

'Ah, I was coming to her.' Mr Nunn's face brightened at once. 'That's Susie - Miss Susie Dean - our comeedeeyen and the baby of the show. I knew her father and mother - both pros - dead now. That little girl's got it in her blood, absolutely born for it.'

'Do you mean that she's very good?' asked Miss Trant, who was interested.

'Good! She's a wonder. Mind you, she's young, and I don't say she's nothing to learn, but she's picking it up like greased lightnin' - better every week. There'll be no stopping Susie once she's got a toe on the ladder. If we don't see her name in electric lights in Shaftesbury Avenue before we're ten years older, I'll eat - I'll never touch another bottle of magnesia!'

'I'd like to see her on the stage,' said Miss Trant, glancing across at the piquant little dark face. 'She looks interesting - comical and clever. How old is she?'

'Twenty. And you can take it from me, my - Miss Trant, I mean - she is comical and clever. She's all over this show. The way she can get laughs! You've only got to let her sniff an audience - if it's only six free passes in four rows of chairs - and she's bubbling over. A lot of comedians wouldn't have stood for the way she gets laughs, I can tell you - lot of jealousy in the profession, Miss Trant; it's the curse of it - but I don't mind, bless her! Susie and me's the best of pals.' He looked across at the girl as he spoke, his queer lined face alight with affection; and Miss Trant, following his glance, saw the girl look up and blow a kiss to him. Miss Trant smiled, rather wistfully.

'If this show had gone as it ought,' Mr Nunn continued dejectedly, 'she'd have had a big chance. Somebody'd have seen her and snapped her up. Now she'll have to take what comes, and ten to one be jumped on because she's too good for the bit of business they'll tell her to do. She's taken it well, best of the lot, Susie has, kept her spirits up all the time, but it's rotten hard lines. And I'll tell you this, Miss Trant,' he was very impressive now, 'I blame myself for this.'

'Why surely not!' cried Miss Trant. 'I don't see how it could be your fault.'

'I don't suppose you do, but nevertheless you can take it from me it is my fault,' he replied, gloomily triumphant. 'Who's had most experience here? I have. I ought to have known. Who'd heard one or two queer things about Charlie Mildenhall? I had. I ought to have known. Who looked at the bookings and saw he'd gone and fixed up rentals right and left? I did. I ought to have known.' He looked at her with the air of one who has made everything plain.

'I'm afraid I don't understand.' Miss Trant looked apologetic. 'What are rentals?'

'Ah, you see, it's like this. As a rule a Concert Party works on a percentage basis. It gets - we'll say - sixty per cent of the gross takings, and the people who own the pavilion or hall or theatre or whatever it is take the other forty. Sometimes there's a guarantee - for thirty or forty pounds maybe - which means - '

'That your share will amount to at least the thirty or forty pounds,' put in Miss Trant, who was no fonder of being a pupil than the next person.

'Right! Well, that's fair enough, gives everybody a chance. But we don't like renting places in the C. P. world, I can tell you, and that's what I mean by rentals. You just pay out your money, and the people who's running the hall or pavilion don't care tuppence about your show so long as they get their money. This was a rental here in Rawsley - and half of 'em was rentals, like this. I did point it out at the time, five-and-twenty pounds! And you oughter see the place! Not worth five-and-twenty shillings! And he hadn't just taken it for one week, he'd taken it for two. Two at five-and-twenty a week, here, in this place! I ought to have known. He never meant to stay, not him. Didn't matter to him if it was twenty-five hundred pounds a week here - he wasn't going to pay it, and he knew it - oh yes, he knew all right!' Mr Nunn raised his voice. 'They've got every prop we have, and there they stop till we can pay the fifty pounds, so we've said good-bye to 'em. We've not had a treasury for four weeks.'

'Yes, Miss Longstaff told me.'

'Mr Jimmy Mug, that's me! I could kick myself from here to the dirty Assembly Rooms and back every time I think of it.' He was very excited now. 'A man of my experience! And seeing those dates too! I tell you, Miss What's-it, I can't look these boys and girls in the face. I give you my word I can't.' He gave a groan.

'There's Jimmy going on again,' said a voice.

'Now then, Jimmy, now then!' This was from Mr Courtney Brundit, otherwise Joe, who now came lumbering across to them. 'Don't you take any notice of him, ma'am,' he said to Miss Trant, and he gave Mr Nunn a tremendous slap on the back.

'Hoi!' cried Mr Nunn 'Steady, Joe, steady! You've got a hand like a sledge-hammer. Miss - er - Trant, this is Mr Brundit, Courtney on the stage, and Joe off.'

'Very pleased to meet you, Miss Trant,' said Mr Brundit, taking her hand in his huge fist and shaking it heartily. 'Now don't you let Jimmy start blaming himself,' he added in his slow good-humoured growl, 'because it's no more his fault than it's my fault or anybody else's fault.'

'That's all right, Joe, but - '

'But nothing, Jimmy! We can't have a chap with a stomach like yours - he's got an awful bad stomach, Miss - worst in the profession - going and upsetting himself for nothing. Here, you people,' he roared, 'we're not blaming Jimmy, are we?'

'No,' they chorused, to Miss Trant's astonishment.

'Who's been keeping our hearts up?' roared Joe again.

'Jimmy!' they cried.

'Good old Jimmy!' Joe prompted them.

'Good old Jimmy!' they all cried. Even Mr Oakroyd who was not the man to be left out of anything so hearty and friendly, came in at the end with 'Ay, good owd Jimmy!'

Then before Jimmy or Joe or anyone else could make another sound, they found themselves confronted by the proprietor of these Station Refreshment Rooms, Mrs Mounder, who stood there, terribly compressed now in face and arms and body, all erect and folded up, but with a head trembling with indignation.

'I can't do with yer,' Mrs Mounder was crying. 'Not another minute! Outside, everyone.'

'Now then, ma,' began Joe.

Mrs Mounder glared at him. 'One-and-fourpence and one-and-eightpence and two shillings, that's what one or other of yer owes me, and yer can pay me now, at once, and take yerselves somewhere else, sitting about and making yer commotion!' And from the torrent of speech that followed, they were at liberty to gather that she never, never did, couldn't keep a door open, couldn't do with them, and would show them trouble if it was trouble they were asking for. By this time she had lashed herself into such a rage that she made a mistake in her tactics. She singled out Miss Trant, crying: 'You too, Miss! I thought you was different, a lady, but seemingly you're another of 'em.'

'What!' cried Miss Trant.

'You 'eard what I said.'

Miss Trant rose from her chair, drew herself up to her full height, and marched towards Mrs Mounder as steadily as the old Colonel and the other fighting Trants had marched upon earth-works and counterscarps. She was pale and there was a kind of glitter in her fine clear eyes, but there was not the ghost of a tremble or a waver or a wobble.

'What did you say we owed you?' she demanded icily.

At this there was some expostulation from the company behind, but she turned round quickly and even held up a hand: 'One moment, please. I'll explain later.' Then there was not a whisper among them.

She faced Mrs Mounder again, looking her straight in the eyes. Mrs Mounder tried to compress herself into a yet smaller, tighter, harder mass of disapproval, and when she discovered it could not be done, she began to weaken. After a sniff or two, she replied: 'There's one and fourpence and one-and-eight-pence and two shillings altogether owing, though, upon my word, what with the hot water that's been called for - '

Miss Trant cut her short. She took out a ten-shilling note and lightly tossed it towards the woman. 'There you are,' she said, raising her chin another inch, 'and please bring me the change at once.'

The note had fallen on to the floor, and Mrs Mounder looked at it now, with her head trembling away. Miss Trant neither spoke nor moved, and the others at the back never made a sound. Then Mrs Mounder suddenly dipped, took the note, muttered something that nobody could catch, and hurried out.

Miss Trant turned round, quite slowly this time, quite calmly, smiled vaguely at everybody, and said 'Let's go now, shall we?' And off she went to the door, to receive her change and to give Mrs Mounder a last annihilating lift of eyebrow, while the others, bursting into talk again, came trooping after her. Between the doorway and the road, where they had met before, the untidy youth with the lock of hair caught up to her and introduced himself as Inigo Jollifant. 'That was magnificent, absolutely,' he remarked. 'But you paid for my tea, you know.'

'I was going to explain to everybody why I did that,' said Miss Trant. Then she hesitated.

'The gesture, of course, the gesture asked for it,' said Inigo sympathetically. 'One-and-fourpence here, one-and-eightpence there - no gesture! Pay for the lot - take that and get out - the only way to do it! As a matter of fact, I was thinking of that myself. But I haven't the style, you know.'

Miss Trant - who suddenly felt light-hearted, free, gay - laughed. 'This is my car. We'll stop here and wait for the others. The point is, though,' she went on hastily, 'I've suddenly decided to - to run this troupe - I mean concert party. That horrid woman decided me.'

'Splendid, absolutely!' cried Inigo enthusiastically. 'I was only wishing I could do it. But I've only got forty pounds to spare. I've told them, though, I was ready to join up - just for a lark, you know. I've been teaching in a prep, school, but I can play the piano, and from what I can gather, my sort of piano stuff is just what they want.'

'I wish you would,' said Miss Trant. 'I'd been wondering about it for the last half-hour and trying to find out things, and then when that woman talked like that, I suddenly thought, "All right then, I *will*." I don't know anything about it, so nothing could be more crazy.'

'Oh, hatter-mad, I agree,' said Inigo cheerfully. 'But a lark of colossal dimensions. And here we all are, rogues and vagabonds together.'

'I'm wondering now what we ought to do,' said Miss Trant, quickly, as the others came up.

'I know. Leave it to me.' Inigo turned to face the entertainers, and called out: 'I say, is there a place here where we might all have some supper and a sort of meeting?'

'Why, what's the idea, Jollifant?' This was from Mr Morton Mitcham.

'The idea is, I want everybody to have supper or dinner or whatever they decide to call it, with me tonight,' Inigo explained. 'You see - ' And he glanced at Miss Trant.

'The fact is,' said Miss Trant, rather shy again now, 'I'm rather thinking of - of running - the - the show. That is, if you'll let me,' she added hastily.

There was an excited cry from everybody, but Miss Susie Dean was first. 'You darling!' she flashed out, and then added, when the others had done: 'I don't know you, but I'm sure you are.' And everybody laughed at this, and Miss Trant blushed and shook her head.

'Now, about this supper then?' said Inigo, after the excitement had died down.

'What about that hotel in the market-place, Jimmy?' asked Mr Brundit. They'd do it. Might be a bit dearish, though.'

'Never mind about that,' cried Inigo, who guessed that his own ideas of expense might be different from the homely Mr Brundit's. 'What is the place? Would it do?' He turned to Mr Nunn.

'You mean The Royal Standard, don't you, Joe?' said Mr Nunn. 'Yes, they'd do it all right. Good room upstairs too, they tell me. Though if there's a man on this earth who'd make a worse show at a supper or dinner or anything where there's real eating than me, I'd like to meet him. You know, it's all poison to me, Mr What's-it,' he said to Inigo earnestly.

'Shame! Well, then,' cried Inigo, 'let's say half past seven at The Royal Standard, everybody! I'll go and fix it up. That's all right, isn't it, Miss Trant?'

Then the newcomers remembered they had rooms to find, and there was some excited talk about this. Finally, Inigo and Mr Morton Mitcham departed with the Brundits, who thought there would be room for one of them in their own lodgings and a place for the other next door. They were accompanied by Messrs Nunn and Jerningham. Miss Trant, having Elsie's hamper in the car, suggested that Elsie herself should come in too, and as Miss Susie Dean shared lodgings with Elsie, it was agreed that she should join them, whereupon Miss Susie scrambled in at the back, which was rather full of things, with the remark that it would do Rawsley good to see her there. So that was settled.

'Well, Miss,' said a voice, gruff but diffident, perhaps a trifle wistful, 'I'd better have them traps o' mine out o' t'car and be getting on like.'

'Oh, Mr Oakroyd!' cried Miss Trant, who had forgotten all about him. 'Where are you going?'

'Na, I don't know fairly.'

'He doesn't know where he's going,' cried Miss Susie Dean excitedly. 'He told me in there. Oh, he mustn't go, must he, Miss Trant?'

'Of course you mustn't go, Mr Oakroyd. You don't want to go, do you?'

'Well' - Mr Oakroyd rubbed his chin reflectively - 'I don't say I've owt on, as you might say. But I'm nobbut i' t'road here. You can't do wi' me.'

'I'm sure we can,' said Miss Trant. 'I'm sure there's something for you to do. Isn't there, Miss Longstaff? Isn't there, Miss Dean?'

'I'm sure I don't know really,' began Miss Longstaff, who was not interested in Mr Oakroyd and was surprised that a lady like Miss Trant should be.

'Of course there is,' put in Miss Dean, who had heard already about the Great North Road and Lily and all manner of things. 'And he must come to supper, mustn't he? If he doesn't, I shan't. We'll stand outside making noises. We'll throw things at the window.'

'Hurry up and get in, Mr Oakroyd, if you can find room,' Miss Trant commanded, and without another word Mr Oakroyd did get in, and after a struggle with the hamper and various bags, in which he was assisted energetically by Miss Dean, he did find room.

'Well,' he said, his honest broad face alight as they moved down the road, 'this is a do, this is.' He ruminated for a minute or two, then, catching some droll glances that his companion shot at him out of her lively dark eyes, he grinned afresh and banged his right fist into his left palm several times. 'This caps t'lot, this does.'

'Tha's reight, lad,' said Miss Dean coolly.

'Yond's a caution,' Mr Oakroyd told himself. Then he looked at Rawsley with the air of a man who has seen many other and better places.

II

At half past seven that night, all our friends were assembled in the upstairs dining-room of The Royal Standard - with one exception. Miss Trant was not there. The Misses Dean and Longstaff, on being questioned, said they did not know why she was late. They had found very nice rooms for her next door but one to their own, and had left her there. She had, however, said something about a bath - 'and you know what that means in these digs, my dear.' Their various dears did know what it meant, and were relieved. 'Though it wouldn't surprise me if something had happened to her, taken ill or lost her memory or all her money or something, right at the very crucial moment. That's the sort of thing that *would* happen, my dear.' This was the dark verdict of Miss Stella Cavendish, otherwise Mrs Joe Brundit, who was looking very festive and important and uncomfortable in her cerise, a dress that was rather too small for her now but had done good service some years ago during a season in 'stock', when she had played the Duchess of Dorking and other great-lady parts, all with a song in the third act. But if Mrs Joe, who had no illusions about the profession and was a great authority upon its ups-and-downs, especially the downs, was ready to be pessimistic about the non-appearance of their possible saviour, Miss Trant, this does not mean that she was out of tune with the festive evening. The Duchess of Dorking herself could not have surveyed and approved of the arrangements in better style. She hastened to congratulate her host, Mr Jollifant: 'Everything very nice, very tasteful, I'm sure,' was her verdict.

'Mrs Tidby - she's the proprietor - said the notice was too short,' replied Inigo, 'but that she'd do her best. And, she said, although she was not the one to say it, nobody in this town could do better. And she insisted upon telling me all about the annual dinner of the Rawsley and West Something-or-other Horticultural Society, which has been held here since 1898. So there!'

'All very nice, very tasteful,' repeated Mrs Joe, with bland complacency, casting her eye over the table, laid for ten. 'Though nobody knows better than I do', she continued archly, 'that so much depends on the orderer in these affairs. Get a good orderer and what happens? Everything tasteful, nothing tawdry. How many can you trust to order? Now there's Mr Brundit - Joe - he couldn't order, not to be satisfactory. He hasn't the manner. Joe's as gentle as a lamb and as strong as a lion; but he hasn't the manner. They'd say in a minute. "Anything'll do for *him*." They *know*, these people, Mr Jollifant. Now you're a gentleman. What does that mean? It means that it comes to you naturally, you're a born orderer.'

'Oh, I don't know about that,' Inigo protested, being the last person in the world to have any aristocratic pretensions. 'I don't know that you can say that - '

'I do,' said Mrs Joe firmly, holding up her hand. 'And when you've been as many years in the profession as I have, you'll know. I can tell it in a minute. I said to myself as soon as I met you: "He's untidy; he may not have much money; he's ready for his little joke with everybody; but - he's a gentleman." Oxford or Cambridge or Harrow, Mr Jollifant?'

'Cambridge,' said Inigo, staring.

'I knew. "One of them," I said to myself.' She was very triumphant. 'There's a *Stamp*. I've thought about it for George - that's our boy, you know. I said from the first, if that boy's bright - and you couldn't want a brighter - and if things will allow, he goes to one of those places. I don't care, I've told Joe more than once, whether it's Cambridge College or Oxford College - I'm not one of your silly boat-race people - but to one of them, things allowing, he goes.'

'Jolly good!' said Inigo heartily if a trifle absent-mindedly, for he was wondering when Miss Trant would come.

'*And* no stage. I've made up my mind about *that*. Joe says it would be nice to have him with us, and nobody knows that better than a mother, but what I say every time is that George must have his chance at something gentlemanly - a bank or estate agency. Concert singing I would not object to, but that depends on the Voice. So far, George has given no signs of having a Voice. If it comes, well and good. But no stage.'

'You're frightening me, Mrs Brundit,' said Inigo, smiling. 'Don't forget I'm apparently just about to join the profession myself.'

'Ah, that's your fun, Mr Jollifant, I know,' replied Mrs Joe, turning her head a little to one side and raising her eyebrows. 'Just a little experience for you, that's all. I believe you're a real musician.'

'I'm not,' said Inigo, laughing. 'Anything but that. I'm just a piano-pounder. Writing's the only thing I'm really interested in.'

'Writing? You have the look of an author too. Now if only I'd had the time, the things I could have written! The experience I have had, but never the time. What is it, Joe?' she inquired, for that gentleman was now standing at her elbow.

'It's quarter to eight, that's what it is,' said Joe rather gloomily. 'And Miss Trant's not here yet. I suppose she wasn't having a game with us, was she?'

'Oh, she wouldn't do a thing like that, Joe,' cried his wife. 'You could see at a glance she wasn't that sort. What I'm wondering is whether anything's happened to her. What if she lost her memory or was run over! Just when it seemed all right!'

'It'd be just our luck, Mag,' said Joe, his face falling They exchanged hollow stares, and for a moment or so Miss Stella Cavendish lost all resemblance to the Duchess of Dorking; she seemed to droop, to sag; she looked a tired woman who remembered she had a boy to support and that he was far away on Denmark Hill, that they had no money and some debts, that jobs were few and getting scarcer; a woman who had said good-bye to the easy elasticity of youth. Joe coughed. 'It'll turn out all right, you'll see,' he began gently.

Inigo turned away, for this was no place for him. He wandered round the room, keeping one eye on the door through which Miss Trant should enter at any moment. And all his other guests were keeping an eye on that door and were beginning to look anxious, though they kept up a little buzz of talk and pretended they did not care. Mr Jimmy Nunn had cornered the old waiter in order to tell him that the whole dinner would be regarded by Mr Nunn's digestive apparatus as poison and nothing less, and now he had Mrs Tidby (who had a sister who was just the same) in his audience, and appeared to be presenting the two of them with a little act in which he took the part of a too sensitive and suspicious stomach. But even he watched the door all the time. Mr Jerry Jerningham and Mr Oakroyd, who had discovered that they could not talk to one another, looked about them and grinned rather vaguely, but kept most of their glances for the door. Mr Morton Mitcham, who had unearthed a larger tie and an almost clean collar for the occasion, was playing Othello to the combined Desdemona of Miss Longstaff and Miss Dean, but when Inigo approached he broke off to ask the time. 'Eight o'clock, is it?' he cried. 'Well, well! I just wondered, you know.' His eye went round to that door, and then hastily retreated. 'Well, as I was saying, Miss Longstaff, Miss Dean, I only once played Jo'burg in a thunderstorm, a real thunderstorm - '

Inigo began to feel anxious himself now. Suppose Miss Trant really didn't turn up! What a horrible fiasco this supper - as all the players called it - would be with the show still in ruins, all their hopes scattered again! He went down the stairs, looked in several of the rooms there, then stood at the entrance for a minute or two, glancing up and down the square. When he returned he found the old waiter at the bottom of the stairs. 'We're still one short,' he explained. 'Look here, couldn't you take some cocktails - gin and Italian or sherry and bitters or something - upstairs to those people, and ask them to help themselves.' He had a cocktail himself at the bar, and no sooner had he swallowed it than he noticed a figure, an irresolute, hesitating figure, at the entrance. He rushed forward. It was Miss Trant.

'Come along, Miss Trant,' he roared. 'We're all waiting for you.'

'I'm sorry,' she stammered, still hesitating.

He stared curiously at her. What was the matter? 'You know,' he went on, in a lower voice, 'those people upstairs - the poor old Dinky Doos - had begun to think you weren't turning up, and they were feeling sick about it. They didn't say anything, which I thought jolly decent of them, but they were beginning to look a bit greenish, absolutely. You can't blame 'em, can you?'

'No, of course not,' said Miss Trant. 'And I'm sorry I've been so long. I - er - had to wait ages for a bath.'

'Oh, I knew you'd come all right,' said Inigo. His tone was cheerfully offhand, but he shot another curious glance at her as she came forward. 'Baths, of course - well, that's asking for difficulties, isn't it?' he babbled, leading her to the stairs. 'The old Rawsleyans have not yet quite grasped the idea of a bath yet. A panful - yes! Two panfuls - possible! But a bath, involving the contents of more than two pans or five kettles and the subsequent immersion of the human body – '

She stopped him at the foot of the stairs. 'Listen, Mr Jollifant. I feel I must tell somebody, and I think you'd understand. It's all very silly, of course - ' she hesitated.

'Go on, Miss Trant,' he said. 'You must tell me now. As for it's being silly - well, we're all a bit silly, aren't we? I know I'm ridiculous, absolutely.'

'I could have got here earlier,' she began hastily, 'only I suddenly discovered I wanted to - to run away. When I found myself alone again, I wondered why I had said I would go into this business. I don't know anything about it. I have some money, but not much really. And then it's all so different from the kind of life I have known. And when I thought about all this, I began to feel a bit sick about it and wanted to run away, to go back to my own kind of life, you know, to ordinary comfortable things - '

'Know! I should say I do,' cried Inigo softly. 'You get a crawly feeling somewhere at the bottom of your stomach, don't you? - you feel all cold and hollow inside - and then you curse yourself for having let yourself in for the thing - '

'That's it, exactly,' she replied, eagerly. 'But surely you haven't felt like that?'

'Of course I have. This very night, for that matter! I feel like that whenever I try anything new, but I say - Down with it! You'd never do anything if you took any notice of that, would you? I mean, all this is as strange and absurd and unreal to me as it is to you, really, but I don't care.'

'It's much worse, I think, for a woman. A young man can do anything for a time, it doesn't much matter - '

'And so can a woman, within reasonable limits. And this is well within 'em, isn't it?'

'I suppose so,' she replied. 'And if it *is* silly, I don't really mind. It's time I did something really silly. It's terrible being quiet and sensible all your life, isn't it?'

'Rather!' said Inigo, who had never tried it. 'And I'm awfully glad you didn't run away, you know.'

'And so am I. It was only a bit of me that wanted to, and it would have been mean and cowardly, you know, and I can't help thinking if I *had* gone, if I had sneaked back home - and I nearly did - I should have hated myself afterwards.' They were climbing the stairs now. 'I'm glad you understand, Mr Jollifant.' She drew a long breath, shook herself a little, then laughed. 'I feel better now. Thank you.'

'So do I, so don't thank me. And I'll do anything I can to help. I know nothing about this business, and I'm practically half-witted, except at times on paper - but there!'

They exchanged smiles at the top of the stairs, the smiles of two compatriots in a far and fantastic country. They were friends.

Inigo threw open the dining-room door. 'Ladies and gentlemen,' he roared. 'Miss Trant.'

A stir, a quick sigh, a buzz of welcome, and a clapping of hands; and she stood for a moment or two in the doorway, looking at them all, half-embarrassed, half delighted, no longer that familiar and only-to-be-expected figure, Miss Elizabeth Trant, who had stayed at the Old Hall so long that her youth had slipped by and all her bright looks been dimmed, but a mysterious Miss Trant who had popped up, come from nowhere, to save the show, and whose entrance lit up the room just as it lit up her face. As she stood there, she felt for a moment that she was a vivid and rather delightful person, one that even a busy Scots doctor might remember with pleasure. It was a moment well worth the whole six hundred pounds that had fallen to her last week out of the blue.

'And if you'll allow me to say so, Miss Trant,' said Mrs Joe, otherwise Miss Stella Cavendish, sweeping forward impressively, 'as pretty an entrance as one could wish for. It takes me back in a flash', she told the company, 'to the big scene in *The Rose of Belgravia*.'

'Take your seats, ladies and gentlemen.' Inigo called out.

'Now where are we going to sit, Jollifant?' asked Mr Morton Mitcham in his most dignified manner. 'Quite like old times, Mrs Brundit.'

'I should say so,' cried Miss Susie Dean. 'The good old times when we all played the baby in *East Lynne* - perhaps. Well, I'm going to sit next to Mr Oakroyd, because he's shy. Aren't ta, lad?'

'Noan too shy to gi' thee a bit of a slap, lass, if tha doesn't behave thysen,' replied the delighted Mr Oakroyd in his broadest accent. 'Yond's a coughdrop,' he announced to the room at large, and took his place beside her.

We have never heard that The Royal Standard in Rawsley is famous for its dinners, and as Mrs Tidby herself pointed out more than once during the evening, the notice was short, so that it would be absurd to pretend that the dinner Inigo gave that night was an exquisite and memorable repast. Nevertheless, it seemed so to the whole ten of them. There were special reasons why it should. Miss Trant enjoyed it without noticing what she was eating, not because she was not interested in food but simply because she was still excited about herself and everybody else. Inigo enjoyed it both as a meal (for his interior still remembered Washbury Manor School) and as a lark that would inevitably beget other and wilder larks. Mr Oakroyd was rather over-awed and dubious at first; there were too many knives and forks for his peace of mind; but the company of lively Miss Susie and the sight of a large glass of beer helped to reassure him, and soon he happily stared and grinned and ate like one who had suddenly found an appetite in fairyland. As for Mr Morton Mitcham and the other players, they enjoyed it because it was a splendid novelty, eating at that hour, and something of a novelty, perhaps, eating at all, certainly eating steadily through four generous courses. Miss Susie Dean, who confessed that she had been living entirely on tea and bread-and-butter and brawn and apples for the past week, declared she had forgotten there was so much food in the world, and was promptly asked not to be vulgar by her colleague, Miss Longstaff, who was so determined to be ladylike that she carefully left little of each course at the side of her plate, which was otherwise clean enough. Mr Jerningham contrived to wear an expression of faint boredom throughout the dinner, but dispatched it like an elegant wolf. Mr Joe Brundit, who joined Mr Oakroyd in his preference for a large glass of beer, demanded so many pieces of bread that he became an important figure in the waiter's reminiscences. But it was Mrs Joe and Mr Morton Mitcham who succeeded best in giving the dinner the air of being a prodigal feast. With them there seemed to be not four courses but fifty. The tomato soup, the mysterious little pieces of white fish, the boiled mutton, the blackberry and apple tart, were transformed by their histrionic gusto into a banquet of Lucullus, and they seemed to nod and smile at one another over the ruins of garnished peacocks' and nightingales' tongues. To see Mr Mitcham fill Mrs Joe's glass and then his own from the solitary bottle of Beaune was to catch a glimpse of the old mad bad days of the fine ladies and gentlemen who lived careless of the morrow, though the very tumbrils were rattling down the street. When they raised their glasses, the least you saw was a Viceroy or Governor-General of the old school and the Duchess of Dorking. It was a fine performance.

Even Mr Jimmy Nunn contrived to enjoy the dinner in his own way. It was not the soup and fish and toast, to which he restricted himself, that he enjoyed, but his abstinence. As he groaned 'Can't look at 'em - poison to me!', he did not seem to be refusing a little mutton and tart, but a gigantic host of dishes; waving away the very fat of the land. He referred to his stomach as if it were a haughty and eccentric guest he had brought with him. He crumbled his toast and sipped his whisky and soda ('Can't touch wine or beer') with a melancholy pride. He found time, however, to talk business with Miss Trant, who explained briefly and rather nervously her complete ignorance and comparative poverty.

'If you've two or three hundred you're ready to play with,' said Mr Nunn, 'that'll be more than enough. With any luck, you'll have it back in no time, and after that the profit begins, and you just lean back and count the boodle. I don't mind telling you, Miss Trant, if I'd half that, I'd be running the show myself. I wouldn't be sticking to the show if I didn't believe in it. I'm not like most of these boys and girls here. I could get another engagement - as good as this, if not better - tomorrow, 'cos I'm an old hand and well known in the profession. Matter of fact, I was getting twice their money, and might have got more if I'd stuck out for it. What are you people eating now? Blackberry pie? My word, you don't know your luck. I've nearly forgotten the taste of it.' He sighed hugely.

'You're not missing so much, Mr Nunn,' Miss Trant whispered. 'It's not very nice. The crust's too thick and stodgy.'

'It looks like Heaven to me,' he lamented. 'But as I was saying, I believe in the show. We all do, and if we'd had the money, we'd have wanted nothing better than to have gone on ourselves, running it on a profit-sharing basis. You see what I mean?'

'Yes, of course I do,' she exclaimed. 'I'm not quite so ignorant as that, you know.'

'Sorry, sorry! No offence meant, Miss Trant.'

'And none taken! Isn't that the phrase?' She laughed, then added, lowering her voice: 'As it is, I have to pay the company's debts - '

'You're not forced to,' he put in. 'You're not responsible for 'em. But it 'ud be better if you did. And then we could get all the props back, too.'

'Certainly. Well, I pay them, and the salaries, of course, and I suppose the expenses.' She was very business-like now, and was enjoying it.

'Yes, any expenses that crop up connected with the show,' he replied, 'such as railway fares, baggage fees, and all that, and anything that's wanted for production numbers, special costumes and effects, you know. But not costumes for individual numbers. We get them ourselves.'

'And if there's any profit, it belongs to me?'

He groaned. 'That is so, but don't put it like that, Miss Trant. Spare a poor man who's had nothing but toast and mush and a bit of a fish he's never heard of. Don't think we're going to lose money for the rest of our lives. You make me feel like a Jonah. Put it this way. You take all the profits.'

'That does sound better, doesn't it? And of course I should like a lot of profit, heaps and heaps of money, but somehow I can't believe there will be much.'

He looked very solemn and thoughtful, screwing up his face until it seemed all shining nose and upper lip. It was absurd that he should look like that and yet talk business so sensibly. 'I'll tell you what I'll do,' he announced at last. 'I was getting ten a week - I'll show you my agreement with Mildenhall tomorrow morning - '

'No, no,' cried Miss Trant. 'I don't want to see it. Go on, please.'

'Now, if you want me to, I'll produce for you. I'm sure none of the boys and girls would object to that. I know the business all through.'

'You mean that you would rehearse everything and be responsible for the programmes? That would be splendid, Mr Nunn. Just what I wanted! Thank you.'

'It's a pleasure, Miss Trant,' he said solemnly. 'And not only will I produce for you - and it means a lot of extra work - but I'll drop two pounds a week, making it eight. No, listen. Instead of that two pounds, I'll take 15 per cent of your net profits. Now I've worked that out somewhere' - he brought out his note-book - 'and you'll see it means - yes, here you are - it means that I'm not making up that two pounds unless you're making over thirteen a week net profit. Mind you, I'll tell you this - you won't make it at first. Don't expect it. We've got to pull the show together, and then again this is between seasons. Summer's over and it isn't winter. And another thing, we haven't got our dates right yet. We can't take Mildenhall's dates, at least not all of 'em, 'cos they're terrible. But that'll tell you whether I believe in the show or not.'

'I'm sure you do,' said Miss Trant warmly. 'And I'm only too glad to accept that arrangement of yours. One thing I want to change, by the way, and that's the name. I don't like it, and besides I think we ought to start all over again.'

'Not a bad name, you know,' he replied thoughtfully. 'And it's known. But that's up to you. We can easily find another, and, as you say, make a fresh start. That might put more heart into the boys and girls. Very superstitious, us pros, Miss Trant, and all sorts of little things bother us. Oh, and there's another thing. What about taking on these two new fellows? I've had a talk to 'em, and I advise it myself, but it's your business now, you know; you're the boss and you have 'em to pay.'

'Mr Jollifant we want, certainly,' said the boss, flushing a little, 'that is, if he's a good pianist. And I should think he is,' she added, hopefully.

'Heard him before we came on here,' said Mr Nunn, 'and he's first-class. He makes the last one we had seem like a piano-tuner in a fit. He's an amateur, but he's got real style. That other chap, Mitcham, swears by him, and he's got a lot of experience. I've heard of him before.'

'He's a very queer-looking man,' she said, dropping her voice. 'He looks like somebody very grand and important who's all gone to seed.'

Mr Nunn shut one eye and curved a hand round his mouth. 'One of the best banjoists in the profession, and a good conjurer,' he whispered. 'And one of the biggest liars. Wonderful! You have a talk to him. I don't say he hasn't seen a lot in his time, but to hear him talk you'd think he was the Wandering Jew's older brother. He's worth taking on just as a liar. Apart from that, though, he'll be worth his money all right. The conjuring'll come in as an extra, and he's just what we want for the band. We run a sort of little jazz band, you know, in the show, and a banjoist'll just make it up. I play the drums, and for a man who's forgotten what a square meal's like, I can rattle 'em a bit, I don't mind telling you.' And he picked up a knife and fork and gave a little ratta-tat-tat on a plate. 'Must use a knife and fork sometime, eh?' he observed, at the end of the performance.

Perhaps the company thought it a signal for silence, or perhaps it was merely because the dinner was finished, but everybody stopped talking and looked rather expectantly towards Miss Trant and Mr Nunn.

'Shall I talk to 'em?' asked Mr Nunn.

'Yes, do,' she replied. 'But you ought to ask Mr Jollifant. After all, he's the host. Do you mind, Mr Jollifant,' she said, turning to him, 'if Mr Nunn explains now what we're going to do?'

'That's the idea of the thing,' cried Inigo. 'To have a feed and then a grand pow-wow of the great chiefs. The idea, absolutely! Say on, Master Nunn.'

That gentleman rose to his feet. 'Ladies and gentlemen,' he began.

'Give him a hand,' cried Miss Dean, who was in high spirits. And they gave him a hand, and so enthusiastically that the waiter who was trying, though not trying very hard, to remove the crumbs from the table, was so startled that he retired precipitately. 'And not so much of the "Ladies and gentlemen", Jimmy!' his friend Joe called out, to the disgust of Mrs Joe, who was sitting erect, with her head a little to one side, her eyebrows well raised and her lips pursed up, as if all Dorking was looking at its Duchess.

'Boys and girls,' said Mr Nunn, 'I'm not going to say much. You've had a good dinner; I haven't; and you ought to do the talking. I only want to say that Miss Trant here, as you know, is going to run the show - '

Applause for Miss Trant, in which the speaker himself joins heartily. The lady smiles confusedly, blushes, and for a moment or two wishes herself back at Hitherton.

'And we're going to turn it into the best little Concert Party on the road today,' Jimmy continued. 'We're lucky to have Miss Trant behind us. I think you'll think with me that Miss Trant'll think - half a minute, I'm getting too many "thinks" in here, can't move for 'em. What I mean is, I hope Miss Trant will think soon she's been lucky too, to come across such a show.' Cries of 'Hear, hear!' and more applause. 'You'll all be glad to know that we're completing the party at once. Mr Morton Mitcham is joining us, and Mr Mitcham, both on the banjo and with the cards, is an artiste of great talent and long and wide and - er - thick experience - '

'Four times round the world,' that gentleman puts in, taking care to say it so that everybody will hear and yet contriving to appear as if he has merely spoken his thought aloud.

'Four times round the world,' Mr Nunn repeats with a certain droll emphasis, 'having played in Europe, Asia, Africa, America, Australia, and the Isle o' Man. Am I right, sir?' Laughter and more applause. 'Also the place of the late pianist - '

'A nasty fumbler if there ever was one,' remarks Mrs Joe with great bitterness.

'Will be taken by Mr Inigo Jollifant, who is new to the profession but is a first-class pianist as those of you who have heard him will testify. I ask you to remember too, boys and girls, that this is Mr Jollifant's supper, though, as far as I'm concerned, there hasn't been a supper. But you've all had one, and a good one.'

More laughter and still more applause. Mr Jollifant bows his acknowledgements, and seeing a welcoming smile on the face of Miss Susie Dean, he directs at her a specially companionable grin, only to discover that it is received with a haughty and disdainful stare. When he looks again he finds Miss Dean is pointedly drooping an eyelid at Miss Elsie Longstaff, and he comes to the conclusion that he has just been guyed by this dark and lively young lady.

Mr Nunn has stopped, to confer in whispers with Miss Trant, who nods her head rapidly. The table is all attention.

'Look here, what about - ' begins Mr Jerry Jerningham, but he gets no further, being fiercely requested by several of his colleagues to 'shush'.

'Now then,' remarks Mr Nunn, 'there's just one or two points. As you boys and girls know, there's no reason why Miss Trant should pay any salaries at all until we start working again. But' - here Mr Nunn takes a deep breath, and everybody looks relieved - 'but she says she is willing to pay two weeks' money to all the old members of the party, that is, everybody but the two who've just joined. That means we're being paid for this week and last. And there'll be no cutting. Salaries the same as before.' Here Mr Nunn, who is too old a hand not to know when applause is coming, stops speaking. He is not disappointed.

There is, however, a dissentient. It is Mr Jerry Jerningham, who now raises his beautiful head to voice a protest 'Look hare, Jaymy, thet's all raight about the two weeks' meney. Quaite generous, and all thet.' (Here we must break in to say that though there is no more graceful and exquisite young man in the Midlands than Mr Jerningham, his accent, a comparatively recent acquisition, unfortunately demands this kind of spelling. It is one thing to look at Mr Jerningham, and quite another thing to listen to him. The thousands who have crowded in from Shaftesbury Avenue since then to see Jerry Jerningham will not recognize this accent, for the simple reason that he afterwards dropped it and then picked up another during his successful season on Broadway. Even the one we are trying to capture now was the third accent he had had since he quitted, at the age of seventeen, the outfitter's shop in Birmingham.) 'But Ai cawn't agree to the same selery. Ai told Mildenhall Ai wasn't getting enough, considering the way mai ect was going, and he agreed - '

'Yes, you idiot,' Miss Susie cries heatedly. 'He'd agree to anything, considering-thet-he-wasn't-going-to-pay-you-anything-et-all. Fancy bringing that up! You're acting like a measly little Sheeny, Jerry Jerningham.'

'Just maind your own business, Susie,' he replies. 'Nobody esked you to bett in. Ai'm talking to Miss Trarnt and Jaymy.'

And neither Miss Trant nor Jimmy is looking with any great favour upon him. Both of them, indeed, are annoyed, and Miss Trant is quite ready to tell the beautiful youth that if he is not satisfied he can go. She glances with approval at the outspoken Susie. Jimmy is purpler than usual and might have been heard, a moment ago, muttering 'Little blighter', but after a swift whispered aside to Miss Trant - 'He's good, you know. Must try and keep him' - he now adopts a conciliatory attitude. Jerry has said that he is worth more than he is getting. All the boys and girls know that. They know that Jerry has been putting it across in great style, and will put it across in even greater style very soon. But the boys and girls will agree with him, Jimmy Nunn, that in times like these an artiste cannot get what he is worth and is sometimes lucky to get anything at all. Things being what they were, Jerry must keep on at the old rate, like the rest of them. If Jerry's big chance came he could take it. Miss Trant was not going to bind any of them down. She was playing fair with them, and they would play fair with her. To all this the boys and girls gave a hearty assent, and Mr Jerningham, whose chief desire had been to call attention to his own importance, gracefully signified that he would condescend to join them at the same salary as before.

'What's the programme then now, Jimmy?' Mr Brundit calls out, in a voice that reminds everybody once again that many-brave-hearts-are-asleep-in-the-deep-so-beware. 'Got to start again, haven't we?'

'I'm coming to that now, Joseph,' Mr Nunn informs him. 'First thing, then - rehearsals. We've got to rehearse as if we'd never seen one another. Isn't that so? Well, what I propose is this - and, by the way, I ought to have said that Miss Trant wants me to produce for her and be the general big noise until she's got her hand in - we stop here and rehearse.'

There are groans from the boys and girls, who have had quite enough of Rawsley. 'A place', Mrs Joe observes, 'that would take the blood out of a stone.'

'That's all right. I know how you feel about it,' Jimmy continues, 'and I'm all for the first train out myself. But one thing you've got to remember. We can't have a Treasury tomorrow - a little sub might be managed, that's all - because Miss Trant's got to have time to get her money through. It'll be Saturday or Monday before the ghost walks. And we'll have to settle up before we go. The other thing is, we've got the use of the hall this week and can rehearse there, and might get the use of it in the mornings and afternoons for a pound or two or for nothing if we stick out for it when we pay up, for part of next week. The date for next week's already cancelled. We could get a two- or three-night stand between here and Sandy bay, where we're going the week after, and try out the new show then. How's that? Oh, and another thing! We're going to change the name. Miss Trant doesn't like the one we've got and anyhow we ought to start afresh with another one - change the luck, y'know. Now, any ideas for a new name?'

Several of them suggest names, all of which, it is triumphantly proved, have been used before 'for ages, my dear, simply ages'. Mr Joe Brundit (it is impossible to call him Courtney at such a moment) quite solemnly proposes they should call themselves 'The Mugs' - he calls this 'catchy' - but is at once howled down. His wife brings out 'The Duennas', admits that she has forgotten what a Duenna is, but points out that it has a fine operatic flavour. Summarily rejected. Mr Morton Mitcham is heard remarking that 'The Wallahs', the name of a troupe he coached at either Simla or Bangalore in Nought Five, might be revived. His suggestion not meeting with approval, he rises - looking, as Miss Dean observes, as if he is never going to stop - and after clearing his throat in a very impressive manner and lowering his gigantic eyebrows at those persons who are still talking, he says: 'Miss Trant, ladies and gentlemen. While we are cudgelling our brains to find a suitable name for the show, I propose - as I have proposed on many occasians in many different parts of the world before today - that we should - er - exhibit our appreciation, that is, display our grateful thanks, to our host, my friend, and your new colleague, Mr Inigo Jollifant. Mr Jollifant and I have already had some - er interesting experiences together, have gone through bad times and good times. We met - er - in extraordinary circumstances - as Mr Jollifant will remember.' He paused, and everybody stared at Inigo, who began to feel that he and Mitcham must really have wandered across whole continents together. There was something compelling about Mitcham's epical imagination. 'And on that occasion, after a very short acquaintance, I told him he was a trouper, a good trouper. Those of you who are not - er - familiar with the Transatlantic Stage may not know the term. It is one, I may say, of the highest praise. I knew then that our friend, Mr Jollifant, was a good trouper. He has proved to all of you, ladies and gentlemen, tonight that he is a good trouper. And I propose that we all show our appreciation. Mr Jollifant!'

And they all do show their appreciation. Mr Jollifant is called upon to reply. He grins, thrusts back his lock of hair, grins again, and puts back the lock in its usual place. It is, he stammers, awfully good of everybody. He is overwhelmed, absolutely. He is not sure what a trouper is. His knowledge of America is very small and is chiefly derived from a study of *Huckleberry Finn*.

Here he is interrupted by no less a person than Miss Trant, with whom *Huckleberry Finn* is a very old favourite indeed, and who now boldly claps her hands and cries 'Isn't it glorious?'

'Isn't it!' Inigo replies, and looks for a moment as if he is about to sit down and spend the next half-hour talking to Miss Trant about that masterpiece. Then he remembers he is making a speech. 'As I said before, I'm not very sure what a trouper is, except that he or she is one who - er - troupes. Therefore, I don't exactly know what constitutes a good trouper. But if it means being a good companion, or trying to be a good companion, then I'm proud to be called one, absolutely. Somehow' - he was in earnest now, saying for once something that was very real and important, felt in the heart, and not being, in spite of all his easy chatter, one of that rapidly increasing horde of glib self-confessors, he could only stammer it out - 'somehow - there isn't too much - er - good companionship left - is there? I mean - people don't sort off - pull together now much, do they? Everybody's - well, not everybody, but a lot of people - are out for a good time - and that's all right, of course; I'm all for it; the more the merrier, so to speak - but it's nearly always their own good time and nobody else's they're out after, isn't it? An awful lot of hard nuts about now, somehow - and only soft in the wrong places. Well, of course, I'm not any better than anybody else, bit worse, I dare say, but I'd like one or two people to say I was a good companion. That's one of the things that's attracted me about this what's it - concert party; a good crowd sticking together. That's where the fun really comes in, isn't it? Look here. I'm making an awful mess of this, y'know. I can gas but I can't really talk - but' - he ends with a sudden burst - 'I could write it, and I will do before long. Thanks very much.'

'Listen, everybody,' Miss Trant calls out at once. 'Mr Jollifant has given me the name. I'm sure it's never been used before. We'll call ourselves 'The Good Companions'. What do you think of that?' She is very excited now.

'The Good Companions'. They are all turning it over and over tasting it.

Inigo approves of it at once and with enthusiasm.

'I like it too,' cries Miss Susie Dean. 'It's original, and it does mean something, not like the ridiculous Dinky Doos. That always made me feel as if I was something between a scented cigarette and one of those sixpenny packets of dye that Elsie here's always using. I like the sound of this new name. I don't know how it will look on the bills, though,' she concludes doubtfully.

'I do,' Mrs Joe announces in a very deep and gloomy voice. 'It will look rotten on the bills.'

'I agree. Not enough *dash* about it, if you ask me,' says Miss Elsie Longstaff, who is all for dash.

'Too haybrow, Miss Trant,' is Mr Jerningham's comment.

Mr Nunn closes one eye over it, then the other, and finally declares it is a bit on the stiff side and won't space well on the bills - but - it is out of the common and will do. Mr Mitcham comes down on the same side with all the weight of his experience. The combined enthusiasm of Miss Trant and Inigo is more than a match for the vague doubts and fears of the others.

'There it is then,' Miss Trant calls out in her clear voice. 'We'll call ourselves "The Good Companions".'

Here Mr Mitcham has an inspiration. After saying to Inigo: 'Now this is *mine*,' he rises to his full height and thunders: 'Waiter. Where are you, waiter? Ah, there you are. Waiter, I want a bottle of port.'

'Now what kind would you like, sir?' the waiter inquires, quite anxiously, as if the cellar is stocked with all manner of ports and he is gravely concerned lest the gentleman should not have exactly the right one.

'Oh, something drinkable. What have you got?'

'Well, we've the Tawny at three-and-nine the bottle, and we've the Old and Crusted at four-and-six.'

Then bring a bottle of the Old and Crusted,' and Mr Mitcham gives such richness to his vowel sounds that already the wine seems twice as old and crusted as it was before. 'And glasses round,' he continues, 'as quick as you can.' After almost chasing the waiter out of the room with his eyebrows, Mr Mitcham sits down with the air of a man who not only knows a good wine but also knows how to order a good wine.

'Now he'd make a wonderful feed if I can get him going. Got just the style,' Mr Nunn whispers to his neightbour, Miss Trant. 'And I've got a sketch or two that he can walk away with, right from the word "go".'

The Old and Crusted has arrived and so have the glasses. 'I'm going to give you a toast in a minute,' says Mr Mitcham, 'so fill up, everybody.' When they are ready, he lifts his glass and cries in a voice of such majesty that it brings Mrs Tidby upstairs from the bar: 'My friends, I give you "The Good Companions". Long Life and good luck to 'em.'

'I'll drink this', Mr Nunn declares, 'if it kills me.' And down goes his Old and Crusted with the rest.

'The Good Companions!'

Mrs Tidby, nodding and smiling at the door, is invited to drink the health of the new show, which she does with great gusto, smacking her lips over the Old and Crusted to indicate perhaps that there is nothing wrong with it.

It is now Mr Oakroyd's turn. Up to now he has been quiet because he is a diffident man and rather out of his element. All the others are members of the party, but he is only a guest. There had been some talk outside that tea-place about him doing something, but nothing has been said since and he is not one to push himself in where he isn't wanted. Tomorrow he will be wandering on his way again, but he has enjoyed tonight, and must say something to them all before they separate. So now he raises the large glass, which still has an inch of beer in it, and cries to them all: 'Well, I'm nobbut one o' t'audience, as you might say. But this is my bit. May you mak' good companions o' t'fowk as comes to see and hear you, and nivver look back.' And down went the inch of beer.

'Thank you, Mr Oakroyd,' Miss Trant calls out before anybody else could reply. And then she begins speaking in a low voice to Mr Nunn.

Miss Dean, who seems to regard Mr Oakroyd as her protégé, is delighted. 'Isn't he sweet?' she cries across the table, and turns to look at him, with her head tilted to one side 'You are sweet, you know, Mr Oakroyd, aren't you?' And her glance suggests that he is about six inches high and covered with pink icing.

But Mr Oakroyd is now summoned to the end of the table, where Miss Trant and Mr Nunn are in conference. He exchanges places with Inigo, who seems rather pleased to find himself next to Miss Dean, still smiling and altogether very attractive.

'Now listen, Mr Oakroyd,' Miss Trant is saying. 'Mr Nunn says that a handyman like you would be very useful to us - '

'Stage carpenter, props and baggage man, lights, doorman where needed, bill-poster where needed,' Mr Nunn rattles off this list with an easy air. 'And of course any odd jobs.'

'Ay.' Mr Oakroyd rubs his chin. You would not suppose for a moment that he is delighted. 'Well, I know nowt about theaters, nowt at all but what you can see from t'gallery. I could pick a deal up, I dare say. I can do owt I want to do wi' my hands as a rule. Is it summat you want doing or a reg'lar job?'

'We want you to travel round with us, Mr Oakroyd, as our handyman,' Miss Trant explained. 'And I'm sure you'd soon learn anything you didn't know that had to be known. About lights, for instance.'

A grin slowly broadens over Mr Oakroyd's face. 'One o' t' Good Companions, eh? By gow, I'll have a do at it, I will an' all.'

'And Mr Nunn suggests three pounds a week - '

'Plus train fares and any extra expenses,' Mr Nunn adds. 'And good money too. Coming in regularly - very good money'

'Would that be all right Mr Oakroyd?'

'Eh, I should think so, Miss. Three punds i' t' week and nobbut mysen to keep! Nivver thowt I'd end up as a the-ater chap! This beats t'band, this does.' And he chuckles away.

'That's all right, then, is it? Will you come down to the Assembly Rooms in the morning, Mr Oakroyd?'

'Nobbut say t'word,' says Mr Oakroyd earnestly, 'and I'll be down at half past six wi' my tools.'

'Half past six!' Mr Nunn gives a capital imitation of a gentleman who has just received a severe blow at the back of the head. 'There isn't such a time, not in the morning - never heard of it - don't believe it exists. Nay, lad. Half past ten's our time.'

'Day's half over i' Bruddersford by then. Happen to know Bruddersford, Mr Nunn?'

'I do know Bruddersford,' Mr Nunn replies in tragic accents. 'Everybody knows it, except the lucky ones. Ask Susie there about it. She calls it "Shuddersford". It's generally known to the profession though as "The Comedian's Grave"!'

'Eh, whatever for?' inquires Mr Oakroyd, his face quite wooden. 'I've heard tell of 'em calling it t'place where they hammer screws. You hear all sorts, don't you, Mr Nunn?' And he leans back in his chair and calmly stares at the ceiling.

Miss Trant, after looking at the pair of them, laughs a little, and Mr Nunn laughs too, and then Mr Oakroyd begins to chuckle again. 'They're a bit o' good company, this lot,' he tells himself, and when he remembers that he is not leaving them tomorrow but is going to travel all over the place and do odd jobs and have three pounds a week, he feels ready to burst.

Now they are calling 'Miss Trant. Spee-eech, Miss Trant. Spee-eech.' At first she shakes her head, but the boys and girls will take no refusal, as Mr Nunn is careful to point out to her.

'I haven't anything to say at all, you know,' she tells them, 'except that I'm sure we shall all get on very well together. You must forgive me if I make mistakes or say anything silly, because, as you know, I don't really understand this business. I haven't even seen you on the stage, which is rather absurd, isn't it? But I'm sure you're all very clever and work very hard and - and - tomorrow and afterwards when you're Good Companions you'll be cleverer still and work harder.' Laughter and applause. 'And now I'm going to bed. Yes, I am. I've had an awfully long and exciting day - it seems to have lasted about a week - and now I'm tired.'

'Oh, don't go, Miss Trant,' Susie implores.

'Why not?'

'Well, if you go, I shall feel I ought to go too, and though I'm tiredish too, I hate to think I'm missing anything.'

'I'm ready to go, Susie,' Miss Longstaff tells her.

'Oh, all right then,' cries Susie. 'I suppose all us feemiles had better trot off together, and leave the men to stay here until they're kicked out. Can't you just see them here when we've gone - going yaw-yaw-yaw and haw-haw-haw and all of 'em nearly dying of conceit? I do think men are ridiculous,' she concludes, putting her nose in the air.

'You stick fast to that opinion of the men, my dear,' Mrs Joe tells her, 'and you might have a chance of getting to the top of the tree.' And with that, the good lady rises, informs her husband that he can have another glass and no more, and stay just half an hour, then departs with the other three members of her sex.

And the men, sitting down again with that fine careless ease that comes when the women go, do have another and do yaw-yaw-yaw and haw-haw-haw, and while they are doing that, Inigo discovers that Jerry Jerningham, with his good looks and grace and weird accent, his determination to top the bill and have his name in electric lights before long or perish, his grave and almost ascetic devotion to his flimsy little art, is altogether an astonishing person; and Mr Oakroyd discovers that Joe, whom he recognizes at once as a man after his own heart, is not only partial to a pipe of Old Salt (to say nothing of a glass of beer) but is also a fellow enthusiast in the matter of football, at which little George will very soon distinguish himself - and surprise some of 'em, it appears - at Denmark Hill; and Jimmy Nunn and Morton Mitcham discover that they remember any number of 'pros' who have got there or dropped out or lifted an elbow too often or gone into management or taken a nice little pub somewhere. Mrs Tidby reappears, to hope everything was to their liking and to point out once again that the notice was short, and then to glance significantly at the clock. The old waiter yawns, pushes a few glasses about in an aimless fashion, returns with change on a little wet tray, smiles vaguely when told to keep it, then yawns again. They troop out into the deserted streets and stop a minute, with a faint shrinking sense of irony, to look up at the thinning clouds and the mild stars beyond. 'You going my way? Right you are. Good night, boys. Good night, ol' man. Goo' night.'

CHAPTER TWO
Very Short, and Devoted to Rehearsals

INIGO seemed to spend all his waking hours, the next few days, on the improvised stage at the Rawsley Assembly Rooms, pounding away on the ancient Broadwood Grand. Two of the notes, the first G in the treble and the lower D in the bass, were in the habit of sticking and even by the end of the first day he had come to know those two notes so well that they had taken on a personal life of their own, so that he appeared to have spent hours quarrelling with two obstinate little yellow men: Tweedlegee and Twoodledee, he called them. His wrists and forearms began aching by about twelve on Friday morning, and after that - though Sunday was a holiday - they went on aching until at last he forgot to notice them. It did not matter whether the Good Companions sang choruses, quartets, trios, duets, or individual numbers, he had to be at work. And if they stopped singing and took to dancing instead, then he had to work all the harder. For him there was no rest. Each member of the troupe prided himself or herself on having a large repertoire, known always as a 'rep', and insisted on going through it at some time or other with the new pianist, who soon began to dislike the very mention of 'reps'.

'I never knew there were so many dirty tattered old sheets of music left in the world,' Inigo confided to Miss Trant. This was after he had struggled through Jimmy Nunn's rep, which was the dirtiest, oldest, and most tattered of all. Many of Jimmy's songs, which did little more than announce that their singer was a policeman ('When you're going down the street. You will see me on my beat, For I'm a Policeman - *pom* - Yes, I'm a Policeman') or a postman or a waiter or some other droll public character, were in manuscript, and were further complicated by instructions scrawled in in pencil - 'Stop for patter', and so forth. Fortunately it did not matter very much what he played for Jimmy, who had no ear and no singing voice, and only demanded that the accompaniment should stop in various odd places in order that he should be able to point out that his father was a very mean man, or describe, with a wealth of unlikely detail, his wedding day. Indeed, the relation between Jimmy's singing and the piano was so vague that he had sung a whole verse of a policeman song to the accompaniment intended for a postman before either he or Inigo had noticed the mistake. 'Have to use the old uns, my boy,' said Jimmy, carefully removing from the piano a sheet that was dropping to pieces. 'They don't write real comic songs now, you can take it from me.' And Inigo was quite ready to agree that these masterpieces had obviously been written a great many years ago. His only hope was that he would be able to vamp the accompaniments by heart before most of the scores crumbled away altogether.

The respective reps of the two Brundits were in rather better condition than Jimmy's, being mostly composed of well-printed ballads, but they were far larger, especially Mrs Joe's, a very stout portfolio with 'Miss Stella Cavendish' printed on it in scarlet letters. 'I don't think there's a bigger and classier rep on the C. P. stage today,' she told him proudly. But it was not necessary to go through it all. Inigo was a quick reader and found this easy ballad stuff mere child's play. After Mrs Joe, with flashing eye and heaving bosom, had tunefully cautioned a son o' hers against doing something or other, had suggested that the roses in her heart would never bloom again like the roses in her garden, had commanded the red sun to sink in-toe the We'est, had waited for one Angus MacDonald to return from some mysterious campaign, had said good-bye to leaves and trees and kisses on the brow and practically everything, and had finally announced that she must go down to the sea again; in short, after Mrs Joe had tried over about half a dozen of her most popular numbers, she expressed herself as being not only satisfied but delighted, mopped her face with one hand and patted Inigo on the shoulder with the other, and told him he was a pianist with a touch, a talent, a soul, and in short was a downright find. 'You've got just the style for me, Mr Jollifant,' she cried warmly, and asked everybody present to agree with her. Inigo, who had been quietly enjoying himself by indulging in an ironical over-emphasis, looked round to see that Miss Susie Dean, who was standing near, was regarding him with a cool and speculative eye. At once the praise of the simple songstress made him feel uncomfortable. He glanced apologetically towards Susie - he thought of her now as Susie - but that young lady immediately tilted her nose a little higher than usual and looked away. Inigo then came to the conclusion that he was not such a clever young man as he had imagined himself to be.

Joe gave Inigo more trouble than Mrs Joe had done, though his rep was neither so big nor so classy. 'Joe's got the Voice but not the Training,' his wife explained. 'And if he's not going to get off the note again, he'll have to have some of his numbers transposed. I told that to the creature that ran off with Mildenhall, but, of course, it was no use talking to *her*. She couldn't play a straight accompaniment, let alone transpose. As I told Joe this morning, you're a real musician, so you won't mind putting some of his numbers down a semi-tone or a tone.' And Inigo did put some of them down a semi-tone or a tone, but nobody except Mrs Joe, who was quite triumphant, even imagined it made any difference. Joe's rough, powerful voice still refused to keep on the note; towards the end of a song it wavered between several different notes; and usually at the very end it wandered into another key altogether. Moreover, it cannot be denied that Joe was a very wooden vocalist. He stiffened his massive body, clenched his fists, and roared until he was purple in the face. It was not so bad when his themes were nautical and it was his duty to point out the various perils of the de-ee-eep, but when he tried to turn himself into a melodious victim of the tender passion, when he declared that he heard you whisper his name among the roses or admitted that he had been standing 'neath your window in the moonlight or confessed that he thought of nothing night and day but two bright eyes and two white arms, and stood there bellowing, fifteen stone of taut muscle and stiff bone, with his big chin jutting out, his forehead gemmed with beads of perspiration, and his two fists apparently ready at any moment to deliver a knock-out, then it was very hard indeed not to smile at honest Joe. Miss Trant, who chanced to enter the hall when one of his love lyrics was in full blast, had to retire to the back so that he would not catch sight of her face. 'What on earth makes Mr Brundit sing love songs?' she asked Susie afterwards. 'I don't mind what he sings, of course, but anybody less love-sick I can't imagine.' Susie laughed. 'I know. Poor Joe! - he sounds as if he's shouting for steak and onions, doesn't he? Mrs Joe - our Stella - makes him sing them. They don't go down badly, either. People must think it hurts him more than it hurts them, so they give him a hand. I adore Joe, though. He's a lot nicer than the men who *can* sing love songs, I can tell you. I've known some of them. Ugh!' When the two girls of the party came to rehearse their individual numbers with him, Inigo had an unpleasant surprise. He found that he enjoyed playing to Elsie more than he did to Susie. Elsie came first and ran through about half a dozen songs, mostly of American origin, songs at once plaintive and impudent, in which somebody had either never had a 'sweetie' or had just lost one. Elsie sang these in a little tinny nasal voice that seemed itself an importation from the United States, and after the last two she danced in quite an engaging and graceful fashion, making the most of her shapely self. To Inigo looking over the piano at her as soon as he could dispense with the few repeated bars of music that accompanied the dance-steps, she seemed very attractive, in spite of the fact that he had always thought her too fair and fluffy, too saucer-eyed, too scented, at once too demure and too flaunting, too much the ageing kitten, and had never had five minutes' amusing talk with her. Until then, indeed, he had seen her as a rather silly and empty woman - and, after all, she was a woman, several years his senior - and had set her down as 'affected and cosmeticated, and a bit hard and mean inside'. But now, when she twirled away, smiled at him, cried 'Quicker, please', smiled again as they increased the pace together, she seemed to have distinct charm, and he saw an audience warming to her act, thin and conventional though it might be. And when, at the end, pink and rather breathless, she clapped her hands and came over to him, crying 'Oh, thanks ever so much! That was topping. You do play beautifully, don't you?', and he replied 'That was fun, wasn't it, Miss Longstaff?', and she said that she couldn't be Miss Longstaff any longer but must be Elsie and he must be Inigo - then he began to feel they were really friends.

This was a surprise but not unpleasant. It was Susie who surprised him unpleasantly. To begin with, she was so disappointing. Jimmy Nunn, the Brundits, and even Jerningham, had all told him how wonderful Susie was; easily the best little comedienne on the Concert Party stage, they said, and a coming star on any stage; not simply hard-working and clever with a touch or two of originality but - you know. And he knew. He had watched her closely ever since they first met, which was only last Thursday but already seemed months ago, and was only too willing to believe anything they said of her. He could see her on the stage - the nimble but sturdy figure of her, the piquant dark face, flashing with fun, and the performance itself, a rush of high spirits, a mixture of charm and drollery with just a glint, the tiniest glint of pathos. And then when she came to rehearse with him, it was not like that at all. She sang a few songs in a husky little voice; they were poor things, flimsier than Elsie's, even, and she went through them listlessly, half-heartedly. She did a little step-dancing, but that was half-hearted too. Now and again she stopped him; he was too slow, too fast, or he must halt in such a place. That was all. It was woefully disappointing.

'I say,' he began, when she had done and was putting her music together.

'Well, what is it, Professor?'

'Those songs of yours - they're not much good, are they?' He saw her opening her eyes to stare at him. 'I mean - pretty feeble - eh?'

'Oh, do you think so?' There was rising and dangerous inflexion in her voice.

'Rather! Thin stuff, tissue paper, absolutely! You must get fed up singing 'em, don't you? Quite apart from the words, think of the tunes. What are they? Lord, I could invent half a dozen better ones in a morning.'

'Could you really?'

'With ease,' the rash young man continued. 'I don't say mine wouldn't be tripe, but there's tripe and tripe, isn't there?'

'I suppose so,' she said, softly now. 'I never touch it myself. But go on, please, go on.'

'Well, I mean to say,' he went on, a little less sure of himself, 'if those things are the best that are going, we'll pension 'em off and concoct some of our own. What do you think?'

'I'll tell you what I think,' she said fiercely. 'I think you've got a damned cheek. Now then! Sitting there coolly telling me my songs are all rot! And you haven't been in the show five minutes. Never seen an audience in your life! D'you think I'm in your - your - infant class! Oh yerse,' she went on, holding up her head and speaking in a throaty voice that was a vindictive imitation of Inigo's, 'ther's trape and trape, isn't ther? Oh, absolutely!' Then, with a furious sweep, she turned and caught sight of Jimmy Nunn, who was in conference in the body of the hall. 'Jimmy,' she called, 'just a minute, Jimmy. You'll perhaps be sorry to hear that I shan't be able to appear in the show. No, impossible! Mr Jollifant, who's so kindly condescended to play for us, says my songs aren't worth playing.'

'I didn't,' Inigo protested.

'Yes, of course you did,' she retorted. 'And what I'd like to know is - who do you think you are? The last pianist we had was pretty foul, but at least she didn't tell us what we had to sing.'

'Now then, you kids,' Jimmy called to them. 'Remember you're going to have something tasty for your tea, and I'm not. Pity poor James! Ease up, Susie. And you apologize, Jollifant. I don't care if you haven't done anything, say you're sorry. It's the only way with 'em. Take it easy, the pair of you.'

'I'm awfully sorry, Susie - '

'Miss Dean, thank you.'

'All right. Miss Dean then,' replied Inigo with dignity. 'I repeat: I'm awfully sorry if I've offended you. I didn't mean to.'

'Yes, that's the only way with 'em, isn't it? Well, it isn't with me.' Susie picked up her music. 'I'm sorry you don't like these numbers because you're going to hear them quite a lot. Anyhow, I'm going to sing them. And if you wrote the best soubrette songs in the world, here and now, I wouldn't sing them, not if you paid me to sing them. And that's that.' And off she marched, her head in the air.

Jimmy came up a few minutes afterwards, and Inigo told him what had happened. Jimmy whistled for a minute, then puckered up his face and looked drolly at his companion. 'There's one thing they didn't teach you at Cambridge, my boy,' he said finally, 'and it's something you'll have to learn at this job. That's tact. Don't say these things. Think 'em but don't put 'em in the book of words. In this profession, the men are bad enough. But the women! Touchy! Dynamite, my boy. One word and up they go! Besides, Susie's numbers are good enough. I don't say they couldn't be better. But you see what she does with 'em on the night. They all eat out of her hand.'

'But that's the point,' said Inigo. 'I should never have said anything - this is between ourselves - if I hadn't been so disappointed. I expected something wonderful from her, and I thought she was awfully dull.'

On hearing this, Jimmy gave an excellent imitation of a distinguished astronomer who has just been told that the world is flat. He groaned; he looked heavenwards; he beat his brow. 'What d'you think this is?' he cried, waving a hand at the empty hall. 'A command performance? D'you think them chairs with the bit of plush left on are the Royal Family? D'you think that pillar there's Sir Oswald Stoll, with his pockets full of new contracts?'

'Let me take a turn at this,' cried Inigo, good humouredly enough, though in truth he was still rather nettled. 'And do I think this piano is the box office of Drury Lane? The, answer is - I don't. And what then?'

Jimmy laughed. 'Only this. Susie wasn't bothering, that's all. Wait till you see her in front of an audience. I tell you, she can make a hit with the duddest number you ever shut your ears to. Leave it to her, my boy. Susie's all right.'

'I see.' Inigo played a little phrase, softly, reflectively, then ended with a sudden crash. 'You can expect some songs from me now, Jimmy, that is, if we can get some words. The tunes come easily enough, but I can't write the sort of stuff they want as words for them.'

'If my inside lets me alone for a day or two,' said Jimmy, 'I can do a bit that way myself. We'll get together and fit 'em in. This is how it works. If you've got a good melody, then I'll try to find words for it. If I've a likely lyric, you try to find a tune. And don't forget to try your hand on that opening chorus I've got ready.'

'Right you are. I'm going to show Miss Susie that I wasn't exactly talking through my hat just now. She said she wouldn't dream of singing anything I ever wrote. We'll see about that. I'll write something that'll make her eat her words, or I'll bust.' And, so fired by the scorn of Susie, who must be *shown*, he set to work in earnest, and the two of them spent all the next day, Sunday, with a wreck of a cottage piano, the pride of Jimmy's lodgings, and some music manuscript paper that Jimmy had unearthed.

On Monday morning, Inigo rehearsed with Jerry Jerningham, who carefully divested himself of his coat and waistcoat and then, for the next hour, worked like the nigger of legend. His voice was no better than it is now, was indeed the same plaintive and rather nasal croon, hardly worth calling a voice at all, yet most artfully adapted for the work it had to do. Jazz, which had begun as an explosion of barbaric high spirits, a splash of crimson and black on a drab globe, had become civilized; it was quieter, more subtle, and flirted with sentiment and cynicism; its first bold colours faded to autumnal tints; its butterfly gaieties were for ever fluttering down into melancholy; its insistent rhythms were like the soft plug-plugging of those great machines that now keep whole populations waiting upon them, devouring so much of people's time and yet leaving their minds partly free to wander - and to wonder; and in its own crude, jigging, glancing fashion, as it sang with a grin and shrug of home and love to the crowds of the homeless and unloved, it contrived to express all the sense of baffled desire and the sad nostalgia of the age. History, which attends to folk songs as well as the migrations of peoples, had produced this Jazz, and Nature, working obscurely in a long dark street in a Midland city, had produced a Jerry Jerningham, this Antinous in evening dress and dancing slippers, to match the event. Jerry's voice was nothing, yet it would have been impossible to find a better for these songs. And his feet, those two astonishing energetic and versatile commentators, said all the rest. As soon as he began pit-patting with those feet, Jerry suddenly became a real person, confessing things, making original remarks about life. His feet pondered, sank into despair, began to hope, took courage, laughed and carolled, became crazed with happiness, were touched with doubt, wondered uneasily, shrugged and turned cynical, all with a seemingly careless grace.

Inigo had found it difficult to like this beautiful and vacant young man, but now he found it easy enough to respect him. Jerningham might have a mind as blank as a new slate, and the most atrociously affected accent in the country; he might be all narrow ambition and conceit; but he was an artist - not merely an artiste, but an artist. And how he worked! It was his ambition to be the most graceful lounger, the best of all the idle fops of revue and musical comedy, and to achieve these butterfly perfections he trained like an athlete and toiled like a slave. Off the stage, Inigo had discovered that Jerningham could be easily ignored; but now at rehearsal he saw another young man, who knew exactly what he wanted, not merely from himself but from everybody else, and had made up his mind not to be balked; he was in his own atmosphere, and at once flashed into life, like a fish put back into water. Inigo played with unusual zest to the very end. Jerningham leaned against the piano, smiled across it, and then carefully wiped his forehead with a lilac silk handkerchief.

'By George! - but you can dance, though,' cried Inigo, enthusiastically. 'Hope my playing was all right? This syncopated stuff's rotten to read at sight.'

'Jally faine,' said Jerningham. 'Ai laike your playing. Jest what Ai warnted. You've got the Jaizz tech. You'll make a lat of difference to our baind too.' He mopped himself delicately again. 'Gled you laike my darncing. Ai'm pretty good at those steps, but Ai warnt some new ones very bardly.'

Inigo flourished a manuscript. 'You listen to this,' he cried. 'It's a song Jimmy and I wrote yesterday. The tune's one I've had in my head for some time, and now Jimmy's put some words to it.'

'What's the taitle?'

'*Slippin' round the Corner*,' Inigo told him. 'I'll play it to you while you're resting.' And once again the mischievous little tune came dancing out of the keys. Long before Inigo had finished, Jerningham was looking over his shoulder at the manuscript and humming and tapping his feet.

'Oh, but it's a wonderful little namber!' cried Jerningham, with unexpected enthusiasm. 'There's nathing going to tech it, nathing, Jallifarnt. And it's mai number, isn't it? Must be mai namber, Ai insist.'

'Yes, you can sing it,' Inigo replied, with grim satisfaction. He was thinking of Susie.

Jerningham was going through the words now. 'Ai must tray this now, Ai ralely must. You know you look like being a gold-maine, Jallifarnt. Now do pramise you'll let me sing this for at least two or three months before you send it anywhere?'

'Oh, that's all right. I wasn't thinking of sending it anywhere.'

'But mai dear boy, of course you must. There's pats of meney in things like this, pats. Shahly you knew thart!' And Jerningham opened wide his velvety brown eyes to stare at this strange fellow. 'But let's tray it now. Here's Jaymy and Mitcham. We're just going to tray this namber of yours, Jaymy.'

Jerningham took the manuscript - Inigo knowing the music by heart - and went through one verse and chorus rather slowly. Then he tried the second verse and took the chorus at quicker pace, his feet making little movements to the lilt of it. 'Now we'll tray it all over again, please, Jallifarnt, and we'll put the snep into it. Raight you are.' And when he came to repeat the chorus, he was accompanied by Mr Mitcham's banjo and Jimmy on the drums. The four of them sent everything slipping gloriously round the corner, and Inigo danced on the piano stool, improvised the most astounding variations and flourishes, and laughed in his excitement. 'Repeat, repeat,' cried Jerningham, and immediately stopped singing and began dancing properly, while the other three, their heads wagging away, slipped and slipped and slipped round the corner.

'But where, where, where did you get that duck, that perfect little fat duck of a number?' It was Susie who came rushing on the stage. They had not noticed she was about. They had not noticed anything.

'Never mind,' she cried. 'Tell me afterwards. Let's have it again, do let's have it again. I want to try it with Jerry.'

So off they went again, repeating the chorus, with Susie, very excitedly humming and putting in all manner of strange words, dancing away with Jerningham. After a minute or two, the men stopped.

'Go on, go on, boys,' she cried. 'You're not going to stop, are you? Can't I have it again?'

No, she couldn't, they told her. They were all blown.

'Well, now you can tell me,' said Susie. 'Whose is it and where did it come from? Tell me all about it.'

'It's mai new namber, Susie,' Jerningham panted.

'And there's the boy who wrote it,' said Mr Mitcham, pointing to Inigo. 'And as soon as he let me hear it, I said "That's a winner, my boy." I can tell 'em. Went back to my hotel once in Chicago and there was a waiter there - little Jew boy - heard him picking out a tune on the piano, very quietly - nobody about, you see. I went straight up to him - '

But he had to finish his anecdote in the wings, where Jimmy and Jerningham were taking deep breaths. Susie had not stayed to listen to it. She had rushed over to Inigo at the piano.

'Do you mean to say you wrote that?' she demanded.

He smiled at her. 'Well, Jimmy wrote the words, but I wrote the tune. It's - er - one of those little things of mine I believe I mentioned to you the other day. A poor thing but mine own: absolutely.'

Susie stared at him, breathing hard. 'And you've let Jerry Jerningham have it?'

'Yes, why not?'

'Well, you are a mean pig to give it to him like that, and not even let me hear it first. I didn't think you could be so - so - unfriendly, so spiteful.'

' But you said - '

'I know what I said. But of course I didn't mean it. You ought to have known I didn't mean it. Besides, I thought if you did write anything, it would be dreadful - they usually are - and not something really good like that. And just because - ' She paused.

'Because what?' He had stopped smiling now. He was busy trying to make head or tail of these remonstrances that came flashing out without any kind of logical sequence that he could discover, and at the same time he was telling himself how pretty she was. No, it wasn't just prettiness. Nor could vou call it beauty. But there it was, infinitely delightful and disturbing.

Now she suddenly dropped her indignation. 'It doesn't matter of course. It's nothing. But I thought we were going to be friends, and it's obvious we're not. That's all. I suppose you're writing another now for

Elsie Longstaff. No, I'm really cross now. I wasn't before, and you ought to have seen I wasn't. And I'm not cross now. Yes, I know. I thought I was but I wasn't. I'm just - well, I'm disappointed. That's all.' She lowered her eyes as she tried to look brisk and cheerful. (And Inigo, bewildered but not yet entirely unobservant, did not know which it was.) 'It really is a good little number,' she said, with all the brittle brightness of a conscientious hostess. 'And I must say, you're clever. You'll make quite a lot of money if you keep on turning out things like that.' And she strolled away, her head in the air.

This was Inigo's triumph, but he did not enjoy it. He sat there feeling rather ashamed of himself, though somewhere at the back of his mind was a cool little fellow who whispered that he had no reason to be ashamed of himself, that he had just been humbugged out of his triumph. Then she came back, ran across the stage, her face alight.

'I don't want you to think I'm bad-tempered, because I'm not, really I'm not,' she cried, putting her elbows on the piano and resting her chin in her hands. In this position she could look at him steadily, and she did look at him steadily. 'Now, aren't you sorry you gave that number to Jerry Jerningham instead of me? I know I haven't shown you yet what I can do, and I know that Jerry's very clever in his own way. I believe you were very disappointed in me the other day, weren't you?' she inquired, rather plaintively.

'Well, I don't know - ' Inigo stammered, feeling it impossible to look away and equally impossible to say what he had thought with his eyes still fixed on hers.

'Are you really a spiteful person? You don't look like one. I thought at first you were rather nice.'

'I am,' he replied, trying to be the good-humoured, rather whimsical middle-aged gentleman, and not succeeding at all. 'I'm usually considered specially nice. "Here comes that nice Mr Jollifant," they say.' He put on the indulgent smile of forty-five, but felt it wobble.

'Are you? I wonder.' She stared at him with a kind of innocent speculation for a moment. 'But you mustn't try to patronize me just because you're about three years older than I am, you know. We're just the same age really.'

This was his chance. 'Yes, yes,' he murmured. 'And now you're going to tell me that a girl is always years older than a man. I know. You've been reading magazine stories and light fiction from Boots'.'

'I wasn't going to say anything of the kind,' she protested, almost too swiftly. 'I was going to say I'd seen a lot more of life than you have. Then I thought I wouldn't. "It might hurt his nice little conceit of himself," I said to myself. So I didn't. If you want to be friends with a man, you mustn't ever say anything to hurt his precious vanity, and as that's always as big as a row of houses and tender all over, you have to be awfully careful.'

'Oh, do you want to be friends, then?'

'Perhaps.' She stood up now, gave a twirl or two. 'I haven't made up my mind - quite.'

'Do make up your mind. I'm all for it, absolutely,' he said, turning into an eager youth again. 'What's the good of being a Good Companion, if you're not friends.'

'Mr Oakroyd's my new friend,' she remarked, still twirling. 'Ahr Jess. Did you know his name's Jess? It's Jesiah, really. Isn't that too sweet? He comes to me and asks all about curtains and footlights and spot-lights and props, and he goes about looking so important when he's anything to do. He's already mended my basket for me. He says "It'll do champion nar, Soos." He calls me "Soos", and tells me all about Shuddersford and the Gurt North Roo-ad. We're very thick, I can tell you. I heard him saying to Miss Trant, "Her and ahr Lily's as like as two peeas." What d'you think of that?' She hummed a bar or two of *Slippin' round the Corner*, and tried a few steps. Then she smiled at Inigo.

'Do you know what you're going to do now, Mr Inigo Jollifant?' she cried softly. 'You're going to write another song, just as good as that, if not a wee bit better, and that number will be all for me. I can see it coming. And - listen - I'll promise to put all I know into it, and then one day a big manager from the West End will hear me singing it, and he'll send for you and he'll send for me, and we'll both make our fortunes. You'll have Francis, Day, and Hunter sitting on your doorstep, and I'll have fifteen agents fighting on the stairs. Now don't say you can't do it, because I know you can, you're so clever. Do you know, I said at once when I saw you, "That boy with the lock of hair and the ridiculous knapsack doesn't look like a pro, but he looks a clever boy." That's exactly what I said. And now, isn't that what you're going to do?'

And, strangely enough, Inigo admitted that it was. He even went so far as to add that already he had a tune in his head that might do, if Jimmy could dig up some words. 'And are we friends again now?' he inquired.

'But of course we are,' she replied. 'Though we don't know each other very well, do we? But we're going to work very hard together.' Then she looked him over rather severely 'But, you know, you mustn't take these little things so seriously. Mind that.'

Before he could reply, she was giving a lightning imitation of a pompous gentleman fingering a large, pointed, and very important moustache. 'Little things, you know, Mistah - ar - Jollifant,' she croaked. 'Me-ah difference of o-pin-yon, what! The kaind of thing that may happen at any mo-oh-ment - what!' Then she instantly became herself again, blew him a kiss, and tripped away.

Inigo stared after her and drew a very deep breath. Having had such innocents as Felton and Daisy Callander of Washbury Manor to deal with, he had come to see himself inevitably taking the lead, leaping from position to position and beckoning to the duller-witted who lumbered after him; but he could not help feeling that he had now more than met his match. Susie left him gasping. Being friends with her was going to be very exciting. It appeared that his imagination had probably not deceived him when, hearing her voice in the tea-room, it had seen a curtain go shooting up. That curtain was still going up, higher and higher.

CHAPTER THREE
In Which Colonel Trant's Daughter Goes Into Action, Sticks to Her Guns, and May be Considered Victorious

I

HAVING taken the plunge, Miss Trant found herself at once in another world. It was, so far, chiefly a world of tea and chops and telegrams. The tea and chops came from her Rawsley landlady, who was very interested, very sympathetic, but unpunctual with meals. It was her habit to offer Miss Trant odd cups of tea the moment she saw her coming in, whatever the hour; and the meals, when they did arrive, seemed to be always a chop - a 'nice chop', which apparently meant one that was burnt on the outside and quite raw in the interior. 'Sit you down and 'ave a cup o' tea, Miss Trant, and I'll do you a nice chop,' this was the good lady's formula. Fortunately, Miss Trant was hardly ever hungry that first week. Perhaps it was the telegrams that took away her appetite. Although the Trants had for generations made a trade, as it were, out of alarms and excursions, a telegram had still been something of an event at Hitherton, and even at the Old Hall the sight of a little brown envelope called up visions of catastrophe. But now the little brown envelopes fell in showers. The telegram was apparently the common method of communication in this extraordinary world, where everybody seemed to be 'wiring' everybody else. Prompted by Jimmy Nunn, armed with the current number of *The Stage*, she 'wired' the proprietors of Winter Gardens, Alfresco Pavilions, Kursaals, Chalets, and Playhouses, mostly in places she had never heard of before, and even such people as printers and costumiers had to be 'wired' too; and all these wires promptly produced other wires, some of them so compressed that they might as well have been in cipher, and others of a staggering length and fluency, like strange heads coming round the door and screaming at the top of their voices at her. Of all the others, only Mr Oakroyd, who frequently trotted round to the Post Office for her, shared her amazement at all this wiring. 'Eh! - we're keeping all t'telegraph lads i' t' country on t'run,' he would cry. 'It's war ner workin' for a bookie.' The waste of money appalled him, but he could not help being delighted by the dash and importance of it all. At the Post Office he soon became a familiar figure. 'If I bring yer onny more,' he would tell them, 'happen you'll be declaring a divvy this year'; and the three young women behind the counter would nod and say, brightly, if vaguely: 'That's right'; and they were all very friendly.

Living in such a world of telegraphy, Miss Trant felt she had no right to sit down and enjoy a meal at her leisure. She did sit down - though she always felt she ought to be standing up - but she ate her chops as hastily and perfunctorily as her landlady had cooked them. The latter, we may say, proffered a brief sketch of a dinner, and Miss Trant, in her turn, replied with a brief sketch of a diner. It was only late in the evening, when there were no more 'dates' to be considered and no more problems to be instantly solved, that she achieved any real sustenance. This she did by drinking a large cup of cocoa (a weakness of hers) and munching her way through innumerable buttered Digestive biscuits while staring at a book. The book was *Barlasch of the Guard*, borrowed on the payment of two-pence and a deposit of half a crown from the little stationer's in the market-place, and very slow the story seemed too, after all the telegrams. She was beginning to read these things with the air of an old soldier listening to a fellow veteran only a year or two older than herself.

The problems she had to solve were numerous and for the most part fantastic. One of the most reasonable was that of costumes. Like many other concert parties, the late Dinky Doos had made a practice of giving the first part of their entertainment in fancy pierrot costume and the second half in evening dress. The Good Companions had decided to continue this practice, though two members of the party had protested against it. Mr Jerningham had objected because he delighted himself in evening dress, which he would have worn in the morning if he could have done so. Mr Joe Brundit objected because he always had trouble with his dress collars - They fairly saw my head off some nights,' he grumbled - and was very gloomy about laundries. These gentlemen were allowed to argue with one another, but otherwise no notice was taken of them. Miss Trant discovered, however, that she disliked the pierrot costumes worn by the three women. They were cheap, faded, cottony things, and must be replaced at once. There popped up in Miss Trant, who had always dressed herself very quietly, partly because she had been timid and partly because she really thought a quiet style suited her, a long-hidden lover of the gaudy and fantastic in clothes, and this dashing creature hurried off in the car to the nearest large town and showed her shimmering cascades of silk, plunged her into orgies of apple-green and scarlet and lilac and jade, called down a rain of multi-coloured frills and tassels and pompoms. And she found two allies. Mrs Joe was useless, simply a born knitter and nothing more. Nor was Susie much better, for though her taste was reasonably good (Mrs Joe's was vile), she was much too impatient and not at all clever with her fingers, as she readily admitted herself. This was a disappointment to Miss Trant, with whom Susie was already a favourite. It was the fluffy Elsie, the one she liked least so far, who proved herself to be a treasure in this matter of costumes. Elsie had a passion for clothes; she had good taste; she could design, cut out, and sew like a professional tailor and needlewoman. She also had - as Susie said - a nose for clever, cheap dressmakers, and it was she who brought in the second ally, Miss Thong. There can be no doubt that Miss Thong really was a clever, cheap dressmaker and that she worked miracles for them those few days, but that is not the reason why she deserves a little space to herself. We must glance at Miss Thong because the image of her haunted Miss Trant at odd moments throughout that winter. Miss Thong has a part in the homely epic; it is a very tiny part - no more than that of a whispering ghost - but we cannot say it has no significance. Miss Trant remembers her to this very day.

She went with Elsie, who knew the way. They walked the length of an unusually monotonous street of little brick houses, which ended in some waste ground, a melancholy muddle of worn turf, clayey holes, wire-netting, and ramshackle fowl- houses made out of orange boxes, and a few dirty and listless hens. The last house on the left was detached from the row, but was yet so close to it, so obviously still a part of it, that Miss Trant felt that this house had just been sawn off, as if it were the crust of a long loaf. It looked like a slice too, for it was severely rectangular and only one room in breadth, being indeed the very narrowest house she had ever seen. It was not old; it was not dingy; it was newish, had a bright glazed look, and was immediately depressing. There were two little brass plates on the door; one said *Midland Guardian and Widows Fire and Life Assurance* and the other whispered *Miss Thong - Dress-maker*. The door was opened to them by the Midland Guardian, who had watery eyes, a drooping grey moustache, carpet slippers, and a coat and waistcoat that had seen far too much gravy and egg. Yes, yes, his daughter was in, and they could see her; but she was busy; she was always busy these days, always in great demand; and she wasn't too strong, not really strong enough for all the work that came. One of these days, he told them as they went into the tiny sitting-room, he would have to put his foot down, the girl was doing too much. And he shuffled out, to tell her they were there. 'I know the sort of foot he'll put down,' Elsie whispered. 'I'll bet she keeps him going all right. If he makes enough out of his insurance to keep him in whisky, I'd be surprised. Silly old blighter! But she isn't strong, either. She's a queer little thing.'

She was a queer little thing; no older than Miss Trant herself, perhaps, but very small and crooked, with thin hair pathetically bobbed, hollow cheeks, and a long nose that seemed to flush in a most unhappy manner. Her eyes were bright enough but she had hardly any eyelashes and the lids were slightly reddened. Perhaps she was consumptive. She looked as if she might have anything and everything wrong with that frail body of hers. It seemed as if one winter's night would extinguish her for ever. Nevertheless, as soon as she saw Elsie, her face lit up and she plunged at once into a gasping prattle that never stopped all the way up to the front room upstairs that was her workroom. When she learned that the troupe was to be re-formed under the direction of Miss Trant, she was genuinely delighted, almost in an ecstasy. She insisted upon telling Miss Trant all about the two performances of *the Dinky Doos* she had seen when they had been giving the show the first week.

'It was such a treat to me, you can't imagine,' she gasped. 'And then when Miss Longstaff came here - and I'd seen her only two nights before, singing and dancing there and looking prettier than a picture - well, well, it was a surprise! I stared at her, couldn't believe my own eyes! I must have looked a sketch.' Here Miss Thong laughed heartily at herself. 'Didn't you think I did, Miss Longstaff? Never mind, so did you, when you came on as that little girl in the choir. That was a skit, that was. Laugh! - you ought to have heard me. And that Mr Nunn - he's a comic, if you like. The way he went on telling everybody they was late! And then betting five pounds with that other one who was it? - that fine sing-ger - yes, that's him - Mr Brundit - oh, that was good! And that Miss Susie Dean! Isn't she a card? The way she took people off! Really enjoying herself, she was, you could tell just by looking at her. So pretty too! And what high spirits! Now don't you go and be jealous, Miss Longstaff, because I'll say the same for you. I'm not going to quarrel with the prettiest customer I've got, and a real famous actress too - no, no, no!' And Miss Thong cocked her head on one side, looked very arch and very cunning at one and the same time, and then laughed at herself so heartily that she burst into a fit of coughing and hastily put a handkerchief to her mouth.

Miss Trant stared out of the window a minute, then said: 'I'm glad you enjoyed the show so much, Miss Thong. At least, I imagine you did,' she added, with a smile.

'I haven't enjoyed anything so much, I don't know when,' cried Miss Thong. I went twice - did I tell you? It's not usual for me to go even once, but twice - then it's got to be extra special. I said to Pa - he doesn't like me going out much, you know - but I said to him "I know I'm very busy," I said, "and I know it costs money. But I must go again," I said, "because they're so good they've taken me right out of myself, what with their sing-ging and lovely dancing and their comics and all," I said. And when I heard they'd gone and broken up - oh, the news soon gets round in Rawsley! - well, I could have sat down and cried. And then

Miss Longstaff told me how they'd been treated, Miss What's it - Miss Trant, I beg your pardon. "What a shame!" I said. There I'd been sitting here, thinking how lovely they looked and trying to hum some of the songs and telling myself they hadn't a care in the world, and there they were all feeling as miserable as anything, not knowing where to look, you might say, and me here with my nice little business. And that only made me feel more miserable. You know how you can get sometimes?' And Miss Thong laughed again. 'But to think that you're beginning all over again!'

'And going to be better,' said Elsie. 'We've got two good new men.'

'Just fancy!' cried Miss Thong delightedly. 'It just shows you, doesn't it? You never know what's waiting round the corner, as I tell Pa. He'll never believe in anything. Oh, these business men, I say! He never would believe we'd get this house. But here we are. And isn't it nice here, Miss Trant?' She almost pushed them both over to the window with her. They looked out at the bald turf, the half-bricks and tin cans, the huddle of box lids and wire netting and hens.

'Very nice,' said Miss Trant. Then, with an effort: 'Very nice indeed.'

'Isn't it?' cried Miss Thong. 'It's so open. You're in the town and yet *not* in it, I say. Especially up here, looking right out. That's where all the boys down the street play - cricket and football - and though they're a bit noisy, I don't mind it - quite cheers you up to see them running about and hear them shouting. It's a bit of life, isn't it? I'm glad you think it's nice here. It's made such a difference to me having such a lookout. What with this house and the dressmaking doing so well, they'll be telling me soon I'm getting above myself. Perhaps I am, what with actresses coming too, eh, Miss Longstaff? Somebody said to me, the other day, when I told them, they said "You'll be going on the stage yourself next, Miss Thong." "And a fine sketch I'd look!" I said.' Here Miss Thong laughed and coughed again, and Elsie laughed a little too, and Miss Trant tried to laugh, but found it easier to turn away and undo the parcels they had brought with them.

They told her what they wanted, and she frowned and gasped out questions and nodded excitedly and busied herself clearing the work-table. 'There, you can go away,' she cried to the vanishing pieces of material, 'and so can you, and you, and you. Coat and skirt - blue serge and braid - for Mrs Moxon - that's the last of you for a bit and I don't care if you *are* promised. Semi-evening for Miss Abbey - wants it for whist-drives - and *you'll* have to wait. Yes, I'll do it for you, Miss Trant, Miss Longstaff, but don't - oh, don't - breathe a word to anyone in Rawsley I'm doing it, or my custom's gone! You see, I've promised and promised and better promised - and they come round and ask and ask - just as if a girl had twelve pairs of hands. But I'll do it for you. I don't care. They can all wait, that's what I say.' The little crooked creature grasped the edge of her table, stood as erect as she could, and, with cheeks paler than ever but with her great nose flushing triumphantly, she seemed to defy a host of clamouring Moxons and Abbeys, coats and skirts and semi-evenings. 'So there you are,' she cried. 'If I've to lock myself in this room, give out I'm ill again, I'll do it. Let's have a bit of life, I say. Now tell me what you want and show me what you've got.'

'We want a harlequin effect in some of the dresses,' said Elsie. 'We've got all sorts of remnants and lovely odd bits.' Look here. Sateens and light silks and *crêpe de Chine* and velvet.' And the next minute, the work-table had disappeared, and in its place was a crazy garden of fabrics, a rainbow carnival.

'Oh, I say! O-o-oh!' After this first rapturous cry, Miss Thong breathed hard, quivered with delight, pressed her hands together, and stared and stared, as if her eyes had long been thirsty and could at last drink their fill. Then she fell upon the glowing heap. 'Oh, look at this - and this - and these two together,' she babbled ecstatically. 'Here's some apricot velvet - lovely cap it would make, wouldn't it? And that old rose - let me smooth it out - look! - put that with it - wait till I get some pins - hundreds of pins - oh, aren't I silly?'

'I was like that the other day,' said Miss Trant, laughing.

'I'm always like that,' said Elsie, who was indeed nearly as excited as Miss Thong. 'They go to my head, I can tell you, Look at that, Miss Thong. Isn't it lovely?'

'Isn't it! Oh, deary dear! It's all lovely, and I don't know where to start or whether I'm on my head or my heels or laughing or crying, I don't really. Now aren't I silly?' And it certainly looked as if something dreadful would happen to Miss Thong, who was trying to laugh and cough and blow her nose and pick up some of the silks and fill her mouth with pins all at the same time. At last, however, she quietened down, the professional dressmaker taking the place of the enraptured woman, and they discussed the dresses they wanted. It was arranged that Elsie should help her when she was not wanted for rehearsal, during the remaining two days at Rawsley.

It was Wednesday evening when Miss Trant called there again. The thin little house, now besieged by the curiously melancholy dusk of autumn, that smoky blue into which the green and gold of summer has vanished, it seems, for ever, looked forlorn enough, but its glazed brightness had gone and there was something cheerful and brave, a hint of the indomitable, about that lighted upstairs window. Elsie was there, looking very pink and rounded and robust by the side of Miss Thong, who in the searching gaslight seemed frailer and uglier than before, like a worn-out witch, with that great nose and her dimmed eyes peering between their reddened lids. She was obviously tired out, yet greeted Miss Trant triumphantly. Two dresses were completed.

'And Miss Longstaff's is one of them,' she began.

'Elsie, I told you,' said that young lady.

'There now!' she cried to Miss Trant, nodding her head. 'She wants me to call her Elsie. Aren't I getting on? And it seems only a minute since I saw her on the stage. Well, then, Elsie's is finished and it's the loveliest thing you ever saw, Miss Trant, it really is. Do put it on, Elsie. Slip into my bedroom and put it on. Just to please me.'

After an interrogative glance at Miss Trant, Elsie nodded, went out, and returned in an incredibly short space of time an entirely different person. In that soft shimmer of blues and greens she looked almost beautiful.

'But what a lovely dress you've made!' cried Miss Trant with genuine enthusiasm. 'It's like a wood full of bluebells.' She turned to Miss Thong to congratulate her.

But Miss Thong's gaze was still fastened mistily upon Elsie. Her lips were quivering a little, and her long clever hands were clutching and twisting. 'Oh - Miss - Miss - Elsie,' she faltered, moving a step or so towards her. 'You do look beautiful in it. And I made it, didn't I? And to think of you - wearing it - sing-ging and dancing in it - going all over - thousands of people. Oh, I am silly - but - just to think - '

Elsie put an arm about her, held her for a moment, then stooped and lightly kissed her on the cheek. 'You're not silly, you're very clever,' she said softly. 'There. Isn't she clever, Miss Trant? We shall have to put her name on the programmes, won't we? Dresses by Madame Thong of Rawsley.'

'Oh, go on with you,' gasped Miss Thong, dabbing at her eyes and laughing and crying. 'I really must be tired. I don't know when I've taken on so. You must be thinking "She's a ridiculous little thing." Now aren't you? Never mind, we're all a bit silly sometimes. Best thing I can do is to put in a bit at Mrs Moxon's coat and skirt, that'll bring me to my senses. Two yards of braid to put on, plenty of machining, that what I want. There now, let's talk about the other things.'

So they settled down to talk about the other dresses and were very business-like. It was when Miss Thong began to discuss sending them on and to ask about addresses that Miss Trant, who was moved by the thought of their leaving this little woman and never seeing her again, had an inspiration.

'Tomorrow morning, you know,' she began, 'we leave for a place called Dotworth - '

'That's the three-night stand I told you about,' Elsie put in, nodding at Miss Thong.

'And then next week we go to a seaside place on the East Coast called Sandybay,' Miss Trant continued. 'Now if all the dresses will be finished by about next Monday or Tuesday, why don't you bring them yourself - you needn't carry them, you know; we can arrange about that - and then you can try them on.'

'And I could see you all on the stage too, couldn't I?' cried Miss Thong eagerly, her face lighting up.

'Of course you could. And it would be a nice little holiday for you too, after all your hard work. You could stay a day or two.'

'Oh, wouldn't that be lovely! Going to the seaside and trying on the dresses and seeing them on the stage perhaps and hearing it all again and better than last time and - oh - everything!' For a moment she saw it all, fastened on it in pure rapture. Then the light died out of her face. 'But I couldn't do it, Miss Trant. Oh, I wish I could, but I really couldn't.'

'Why not?'

'Oh! - so many things. There's - I don't know - I couldn't begin to think of it.'

'Of course we should pay your expenses,' said Miss Trant casually. 'Naturally, when you're working for us. It's the usual thing, isn't it, Elsie?'

'Done every time,' replied Elsie promptly and with a grateful glance at Miss Trant. Then she looked severely at Miss Thong. 'Now you're being really silly. I don't believe you want to see me in my dress. You come along. I'll get you in my digs.'

'Yes, of course, Elsie, Miss Trant, I know - but - oh, don't ask me! There's Pa. He'd never let me go, I know he wouldn't.'

'Where is he? Is he in now? Downstairs? All right, you leave him to me,' said Elsie grimly. 'If it's only Pa that's bothering you, I'll soon settle Pa.'

And off she went, there and then, leaving Miss Thong - as she admitted - 'downright flabbergasted'. It took Elsie exactly five minutes to settle Pa, and there could be no doubt - as a glance at her face promptly informed them - that on this question the Midland Guardian was settled once and for all.

'And didn't he mind then?' cried Miss Thong in wonder and delight.

'Not a bit,' said Elsie, still grimly. 'He liked it. And he'll keep on liking it.'

'Well, I'll come then. Yes, I will. I'll work and work and get them all finished and I'll bring them. I know there's an excursion from here to

Sandybay - four days or something - and that'll make it cheaper. I don't know how I'll get all the dresses to the station.'

'I do,' said Elsie. 'Pa will take them.'

'And I shall be able to come in and see you all for nothing, won't I?' cried Miss Thong. 'And perhaps go behind the scenes.'

'Of course! Madame Thong, dressmaker to The Good Companions,' said Elsie. 'Can't we put it in the programmes, Miss Trant?'

'We can and we will,' she replied, rising. 'We must finish making the arrangements now. I've still got heaps and heaps of things to do. I wondered at first how I should find anything to do, but now I seem to be busy from the crack of dawn.'

'I'm sure you like it, don't you, Miss Trant?' said Miss Thong. 'It's a bit of life, isn't it? That's what I feel about doing these dresses. Give me a bit of life, I say.'

And that was one of the things Miss Trant did not forget.

II

It was very exciting being at last on the move. She took with her in the car Jimmy Nunn and Mr Oakroyd, setting off early so that these two would have an opportunity of putting the stage in order, for the hall they were using at Dotworth, known as the Olympic, was a picture theatre. The others came on later, by train. On the way, she tried to be very cool about it all, told herself that it was, of course, a most absurd frolic, but nevertheless she was very excited. And that night she would see the party - her party - how ridiculous that sounded! - on the stage, acting before an audience, for the first time. Just before they arrived there she had to make a confession.

'You know, I feel thrilled already,' she told Jimmy.

He was rather troubled about this. 'Not that I don't understand; I do,' he said. 'I don't care if a man's been fifty years in the business, there's the same old thrill comes back. Opening night - all of a doodah! I know. I've had some opening nights in my time. It's that as much as anything that ruins a man's digestion.'

'Isn't yours any better?'

'Better! Worse and worse! Believe me, I've nearly forgotten the motions of eating. A knife and fork worries me. I ate so little at Rawsley that even the landlady complained, said it was putting her off her own feed, and her husband came to see me one night and got quite nasty about it, said their food was as good as anybody else's, and he was tired of eating my meals cold or warmed-up and being called a glutton by his missis into the bargain. But what I wanted to say is this. Don't expect anything here, Miss Trant.'

'What haven't I to expect?'

'Anything at all,' he replied promptly. 'The show's not in shape yet. This Dotworth isn't a real date. I know the place; played it once before, years ago. It's a dud. All we're doing, Miss Trant, is trying it on the dog.'

And Dotworth looked rather like a dog. 'One of these forlorn yellow little mongrels,' Miss Trant told herself. In the faint sunlight the little town looked yellowish, and there was something forlorn about the streets through which they were passing.

The Olympic was a very small place, sandwiched between an ironmonger's and a draper's. On a board in front was pasted one of their new bills. There it was - *The Good Companions* - in bold lettering. The sight of it gave Miss Trant a sense of achievement that was very pleasant.

'But look at that,' groaned Jimmy, pointing, 'just look at it, I ask you.'

Undoubtedly the bill was not very impressive. It suffered because underneath it was a highly coloured poster of a film. This poster showed several pairs of legs, apparently supporting The Good Companions' bill, and underneath these legs were letters of flame that said: *A Drama from the very Depths of the Soul.*

'That's what they do to you in these one-eyed holes,' said Jimmy. 'You'll have to cover that poster up, Oakroyd.'

Miss Trant had never heard of a 'one-eyed hole' before, but the term kept popping up in her mind during the afternoon and early evening, when she was busy running round Dotworth, going from the station to the Olympic, from the Olympic to her hotel. Dotworth certainly was a one-eyed hole, and by the time the doors of the Olympic were opened, she was convinced that the solitary eye would not be fixed upon The Good Companions. It was not the first time she had been anxious about the size of an audience, for she had helped at charity concerts and the like at Hitherton, but she had never felt so anxious before. When she saw the doors open and people walking past them, she positively winced. But if the people went in, she was not happy about them but busy wondering if they would enjoy it. Before the curtain went up, she was able to count the audience. There were ninety-three altogether; twelve in the one-and-tenpenny seats; thirty-seven in the one-and-twopenny seats (but these included ten free passes for people exhibiting bills): and the remaining forty-four were ninepennies at the back. She tried to do a little mental arithmetic but was not successful, so she called it three pounds and reminded herself that their next three performances could only be considered dress rehearsals.

'I'm not gone on these 'ere pierrots,' she heard somebody say.

'Give me pitchers.' Then, a minute later, the same voice went on: 'That is so. Just what I've said many a time, many and many a time.' The woman cleared her throat mournfully. 'Give me pitchers.'

Miss Trant felt like giving her a box on the ears. Pictures indeed! Still tingling, she sat down at the very end of one of the one-and-tenpenny rows, having agreed that for this first night she must keep in front. The great moment arrived. No footlights suddenly and beautifully illuminated the curtain, for there were no footlights. The stage was lighted from above, and now these lights were switched on and those in the body of the hall turned off. There came the thrilling sound of a gong, then the crash of a chord or two, followed by a run, on the piano. The curtain rose about a foot, hesitated, wobbled, then rose another six inches - then stopped - to reveal several agitated pairs of legs. There was some agonized whispering. Then a voice spoke out from the wings in desperation. 'Nay,' it said, 'shoo won't budge an inch.'

There was some clapping and jeering at the back.

'Sh-sh,' cried Miss Trant fiercely, turning round.

The curtain began wobbling again: jerked up another few inches; stopped again; then suddenly ran up at full speed, presenting the audience with a splendid view of Jimmy Nunn's back. But that gentleman was equal to the occasion. He did not run off but cooly turned round, made a face at the audience, and said: 'Oh, you're here, are you? Couldn't make out where you'd got to. I'll call the others. They'd like to see you.' And he put two fingers to his mouth and whistled, gave Inigo at the piano a nod, sat himself down behind the drums, and they crashed into the opening chorus. It was superbly done. Miss Trant felt as if she had just tobogganed over a chasm. She had not been so excited about anything for years.

It was very odd and amusing seeing her new friends on the stage. She had never known any professionals before, and it was quite different from watching amateurs. When you saw people you knew acting with amateur dramatic societies, they were merely themselves with parts stuck on to them: Mrs Corvison pretended to be a maid, and Major Thompson wore a wig and butler's clothes - and that was all. But with these professionals, you lost all sight of the private personalities; they simply came to life on the stage in another sort of way; and as you watched them, you could hardly believe that you really knew them as people. Jimmy Nunn, for example, was all drollery; he had an entirely new voice, very queer and squeaky; and the man she knew who had been so worried about percentages and his digestion completely disappeared. Mr Jerningham, whose dancing was so astonishing, became a vivid personality. Mr Mitcham was immensely dignified and impressive, and when he was repeatedly contradicted and fooled by

Jimmy and pretended to lose his temper, he seemed like an outraged ambassador. Elsie appeared to be ten years younger, and frivolity itself; though her stage personality appealed to Miss Trant rather less than her real one. Even the Brundits, whose singing interested Miss Trant less than any other part of the performance, simply because she had heard much better singing of this kind all her life, at least contrived to be imposing figures. Mrs Joe swam down the stage like a Queen of Song, and acknowledged any applause that came her way with the air of a duchess opening a charity bazaar. And Joe, when he was busy 'feeding' Jimmy, could say 'Well, I'll bet you a fiver, old man,' and produce a crumpled bit of newspaper, quite in the manner of a gentleman whose pockets are stuffed with fivers. As for Susie, who was best of all, she did not change; she was still her delightful self: but she seemed enlarged and intensified in this new atmosphere; she treated the stage as if it were her own hearth-rug and the audience as if it were composed of old friends attending her birthday party. Everything she did was deliciously absurd. She sang ordinary sentimental little music-hall songs, and by letting her voice slide down and down, by catching her breath at awkward moments, by a droll flick of a glance, she turned them inside out and then tossed them away with an easy scorn. Her dancing itself was a delicate parody, a sly comment on Elsie and Jerry Jerningham. And then she contrived to give lightning sketches of all manner of people; just a phrase or two, a walk, a gesture, a grimace, and you were reminded at once of somebody solemn and ridiculous you had known; if she only had to cross the stage, she would do it in character or caricature, and you had to laugh; she was always being somebody and yet she was always Susie too, for you were always conscious of the girl herself, with her dark eyes and tilted nose, her rather square shoulders, her sturdy figure. Unlike Jimmy Nunn, she did not seem to give you a set performance; her acting was a kind of witty romping, an overflow of high spirits; and it was all essentially feminine - 'Aren't they absurd, my dear?' it seemed to say; and Miss Trant, who remembered so well the times she had felt like that, but could do nothing but bottle it up, adored her. The fact that Dotworth evidently thought the girl an amateurish trifler, who ought to learn to sing a luscious ballad or redden her nose and be really funny, only stiffened Miss Trant's allegiance and fed the flame of her enthusiasm. Oh, it had been worth it just for Susie! This girl *had* to go on and on, that was certain.

When the final curtain came, the applause was only half-hearted. Miss Trant stood up and clapped fiercely. There was the company, *her* company and her friends, who had worked so hard all the evening and the whole week before this evening; there they were, smiling - for the curtain had risen again just to let them smile - and these poor Dotworth creatures could only stare or go poking about for their hats. It was not fair. Miss Trant clapped harder than ever, and then, when the lights came on, there was some staring in her direction, but she did not care. At least, one Miss Trant did not care, even if the other did - for now there seemed to be two of her.

There was the Miss Trant who had been growing up so quickly ever since she left Hitherton. It was this Miss Trant who had so suddenly, so recklessly, so absurdly decided to run the Concert Party, who had plunged into this shabby and adventurous world of minor theatres and had so far enjoyed every moment it had offered her, who had become passionately concerned with dates and rentals and seating and production numbers and costumes, who had already plucked out of this dingy wilderness of lodgings, makeshift theatres, and dull little towns, the fine flowers of work and comradeship and loyalty. But there still remained the Miss Trant who had lived so long at the Old Hall, Hitherton, the woman who had arrived in her middle thirties in a very different world, into which none of her new companions, except perhaps Inigo Jollifant, could ever have found their way; a world full of people who would see very little difference between travelling round with a concert party and singing in the streets. It would be idle to pretend that this Miss Trant had been banished for ever almost at a moment's notice. She was there in the background, wondering and sometimes wincing. She was ready to point out that this was all very well perhaps for a week or two's frolic, while they were moving obscurely in little towns, but that sooner or later the two worlds must clash and then there would probably be a catastrophe in one of them. She had her hour when there came a reply from Mr Truby of Cheltenham, the solicitor, who had had to be told something of what was happening so that he could make arrangements with the bank about forwarding money. Mr Truby had replied that he would do his best to carry out her instructions and did not anticipate any difficulty; he was as solemnly courteous as ever and showed no trace of surprise; yet there was that in his letter which announced in effect that Mr Truby was ready to carry out the wishes of any clients no matter how monstrous they might be, until such time as he received a medical certificate proving their insanity. And that was only a beginning. Very soon there must come a real test - and what would happen then? Could this tiny fantastic army of pierrots withstand the massed forces of Hitherton? Those forces could act through the glance of amazement, the lifted eyebrows, the horrified remonstrances, of a single person; and Miss Trant was aware of the fact, though she had not the least idea who the person might be.

She had not to wait for either the test or the person. They arrived together, on the Wednesday afternoon of the following week, at Sandybay.

III

Dotworth had been a failure: they had made neither friends nor money there, and they had all been glad to leave the place. They would really make a start, they told one another, at Sandybay, which some of them knew and proclaimed to be 'not a bad date'. Miss Trant had never heard of it before, but then she knew very little about the East Coast. It was certainly very pleasant after Rawsley and Dotworth, for it was a clean friendly little town, open to salt winds that as yet only had a healthy chill in them. In the mornings, when the October sun struggled through, there was a fine sparkle on the sea, the air was as crisp and sweet as an apple, and it was delightful to swing along the promenade. In the centre, the old part, Sandybay was still a fishing village, a fascinating higgledy-piggledy of boats, nets, capstans, blue jerseys, mahogany faces, and queer inns. On the outskirts, it was a residential town; it had a ring of little villas and two golf courses; and retired army officers and district commissioners abounded there, battling with weeds in the morning, trying a niblick in the afternoon, and bidding a quite unjustified Three No Trumps in the evening. In the spaces between these outskirts and the old fishing village, Sandybay was a growing but still 'select' resort; and here you found the Beach Hotel, the Sandringham Boarding-House, the Old Oak Cafe, the Elite Picture Theatre, Eastman's Circulating Library, the Municipal Bandstand and Floral Gardens, and the Pier. This Pier went forward about twenty-five yards, then swelled out in a rather dropsical fashion to support a Pavilion, which looked like an overgrown and neglected greenhouse. However, it boasted a stage equipped with floodlights, a spot-light, and an excellent curtain, a grand piano and several dressing-rooms for artistes, and seating accommodation for six hundred people. After achieving this Pavilion, the Pier went on again for about a hundred yards and ended in a subdued riot of little kiosks and automatic machines, the whole dominated by the Refreshment Room, where the very red-faced men who took out monthly angling tickets could obtain a little Scotch or Draught Bass. It is perhaps worth remarking, in passing, that our friend Mr Morton Mitcham had made the Refreshment Room his headquarters and had become a great favourite with both the staff (one blonde and one brunette) and the patrons, who included in their number two gentlemen who were nearly sure - after some prompting - that they had seen Mr Mitcham before, one in Singapore in Nought Three, the other in Sydney in Nought Eight. Mr Mitcham himself declared more than once that he remembered them both very well, and they were all very happy together.

It was the manager of the Pier who had engaged The Good Companions (on a 60 per cent basis, with a thirty-pound guarantee), for Sandybay was trying to extend its season until the end of October and had promised its visitors a 'First-class Concert Party every week in the Pier Pavilion' throughout the month. The fact that The Good Companions had found it ridiculously easy to find lodgings (with sitting-rooms wildly thrown in) suggested there had not been any rush of belated holiday-makers during this second week of October. And so far, this is, on Monday and Tuesday evenings, the attendances had been poor. Jimmy Nunn said there were plenty of people in the town, enough to give them a full house every night, but that they had no inclination to walk out to the Pier Pavilion. Miss Trant agreed with him. The town was bright enough in the morning, lit by the huge flickering gem of the sea, but by tea-time this brightness had faded, the waters were ghostly, the waves came lapping in melancholy, and the evening, twice accompanied by a drizzle of rain, was forlorn indeed, and there was nothing more forlorn in it than the echoing length of the Pier. A cosy theatre of the old-fashioned kind, all gilt and crimson plush, stuffy and glittering, would have been proof against such evenings, but this Pavilion, like nothing but a huge decayed conservatory, was helpless before the mourning mystery of the autumnal darkness and the moan of the sea. But there was time yet, they told one another; the end of the week was always better than the beginning.

Miss Trant had had an early lunch on this Wednesday so that she could see what was happening in the Pavilion, where Mr Oakroyd, assisted by Joe (who was not a bad hand with a paint brush), was making a little set for a new production-number-cum-sketch devised by Jimmy Nunn. This set showed the exterior of a cottage and consisted of a practicable door and window and a few square feet of painted canvas at each side. Mr Oakroyd and Joe had nearly finished and were now sitting in their shirt-sleeves triumphantly refreshing themselves with a bottle of beer and large sandwiches. Inigo and Jimmy Nunn were at the piano, trying over a new song. Miss Trant walked through the auditorium and then stopped in the centre gangway near the end of the third row of front seats, to examine the set, which was propped up, drying, at one side of the stage. She had just congratulated the two craftsmen, who were very proud of themselves, and was thinking what fun it was to be able to have things like that made, merely to have an excuse to return happily to the play of the nursery, when the Pavilion attendant, a man with one eye and a long melancholy face, came up to her and said: 'There's a lady askin' for yer, Miss Trant.'

'Who is it?' She was puzzled.

'I dunno, Miss,' he replied, looking at her sadly with his single

BOOK TWO / CHAPTER THREE

eye. 'She wouldn't give no name.'

'Well, ask her to come in here then, please,' she said, and exchanged a few more remarks with the craftsmen on the stage. Then she looked round. Somebody had just entered the Pavilion, was approaching her. It was her sister Hilda, and the very last person she wished to see at that moment.

So far Hilda has only entered this chronicle in the conversation of her nephew Hilary, who reported that she was 'frightfully down on' the idea that he should spend his time with *The Static*. For the last fifteen years she has been the wife of Lawrence Newent, of Porchison, Newent, and Porchison, solicitors; the excellent mother of his two children and the equally excellent ruler of his household in Cadogan Place. She is not unlike our Miss Trant in appearance, but shorter and stouter and glossier; is actually six years older but looks ten. As a wife, a mother, a mistress of the house, she is a sensible and capable woman; it is only as a social being, a member of society, or rather two societies, for she is always leaving one and struggling into another, that she is somewhat ridiculous. In her time she has been the victim of many passing enthusiasms and cults, but it is obvious that though they might necessitate a revaluation of the whole universe (there was Theosophy, for example) they never at their maddest urge came within a thousand miles of managing a pierrot troupe. But for the last twenty years, she has alternately condemned her sister Elizabeth for holding herself in too much and for wanting to break out. During the last years of their father's life she did not hesitate to say that Elizabeth had been foolish enough to allow herself to be submerged. At this moment - and it is written in her eyes as she approaches - she thinks the girl has emerged, broken out, with a vengeance.

They kissed. 'But, Hilda' - and Miss Trant gave a short nervous laugh - 'what a surprise!'

'Isn't it?' said Hilda, rather vaguely. She was busy looking about her. 'They told me I should find you here.' Her glance rested on Inigo's lock of hair, on Jimmy's puckered shining face above the piano, on Joe's shirt-sleeves, on Mr Oakroyd's sandwich and bottle of beer. And when her eyes returned to meet her sister's, all these things had been quietly extinguished or at least removed a great distance.

'How did you find me?' Miss Trant asked quickly.

Truby told me,' Hilda replied. 'He wrote. He seemed to think it was his duty to write, that we ought to know. And I agree.'

'Well, I think it was rather impertinent of him,' cried Miss Trant. 'It was no duty of his at all. I'm sure that's not the way Lawrence treats his clients. Not that I really mind, of course.'

'Naturally. Unless, of course, you didn't want us to know.'

300   THE GOOD COMPANIONS

Miss Trant coloured. 'That's absurd. I should have told you myself. I've had no opportunity yet, really. I've been so busy. Honestly, Hilda, I've never been so busy before. You've no idea what a lot there is to do.'

Hilda closed her eyes, an old trick of hers, effective for once because it seemed to remove still further the shirt-sleeves and bottles of beer.

'But tell me', Miss Trant went on, 'how you came to find me here.'

'I wired to Truby and he told me where you were. Then I came down the moment I could. It was fearfully inconvenient putting everything off today - you know what it's like in town now, the awful rush - but I simply had to come. Lawrence wanted to come himself. At first, when he heard about it, he laughed - exercising his precious sense of humour, as usual - but he soon saw it wasn't particularly funny, and he wanted to come because he thought you'd probably been encouraged to sign some perfectly iniquitous contract or other and would lose all your money. He says this business is full of the most awful swindlers, and he knows all about these things. So he wanted to come himself and get you out of it, he said. But I told him I must see you myself first. There was quite a good train from Liverpool Street, and then of course it didn't take me long to guess they would know something about you here. So there you have it, Elizabeth.'

'I see,' said Miss Trant slowly. Then she suddenly smiled and lightly touched her sister on the arm. 'Well, Hilda, I'm very pleased to see you.'

There was a silence between them. From the piano there came a soft tum-tum-tumming. From the other side of the stage came the voice of Mr Oakroyd, rather muffled with sandwich, saying very confidentially: 'I'll tell tha what it is, Joe. Ale you get from t'wood's bad enuff naradays, but this 'ere bottled stuff's nowt but fizz, blaws you up like a balloon.'

Hilda sent a glance of despair towards the stage, then moved away, down the gangway. Miss Trant followed her, and together they walked to the entrance, where they stopped.

'Now, my dear,' cried Miss Trant, 'I can see you're nearly bursting. Do begin.'

'And I can see you're ready to fly into a temper and talk all kinds of nonsense,' replied Hilda good-humouredly. 'And I refuse to have a quarrel in this absurd place, it would be too ridiculous.' Then she looked grave. 'But I must say something.'

'Well, say it, Hilda, say it at once.'

'But my dear, you must admit I have a right to know. You might at least have told me. What I can't understand is how on earth you came to be mixed up with these people at all. The last time I heard from you, you were down at Hitherton furnishing the Cottage and arranging to let the Hall. Then the next thing I hear - and from Truby of all people - is that you're wandering round the country with a lot of wretched pierrots. It's too absurd. Just as if you were a little stage-struck girl! How did it happen?'

Miss Trant told her, as best she could, how it happened, giving a very brief sketch of her adventures since she left Hitherton.

'And I suppose it is rather absurd,' she admitted, in conclusion. 'But one can't always be sensible, can one? After all, you've always done the sort of things you wanted to do, you know, Hilda. And this is something to do, and it's fun, and it isn't doing anybody any harm, in fact it's doing all kinds, of people some good, me included.'

'I'm not at all sure about that.' said Hilda.

'I am,' said her sister decisively.

Hilda stared at her and was silent for a moment. She gave the impression that she was deciding to change her course of action, discarding a whole set of remonstrances and appeals. 'Well, Elizabeth,' she said at last, quietly, 'I'm not going to be the tremendous elder sister and all the rest of it. I'm not going to pretend to be an old-fashioned snob. I won't remind you what Father would have thought of this - ' She saw her sister smile, and went on hastily: 'Yes, I know. He didn't approve of some of the things I used to do. I'll admit we shall have to leave him out because he hardly approved of anything that wasn't absolutely Victoria and Albert. But nobody has ever called me stodgy, have they? I'm not stuffy about the theatre and theatrical people. I've met them at parties - the successful ones, I mean - and I've invited them myself, and I'll admit I've been glad to see them and meet them. Everybody is, nowadays, except a few old freaks. But this sort of thing is simply shabby and fourth-rate. It's nothing but a crowd of beery men and common little girls trailing round from one dirty set of lodgings to another, living in the most awful kind of way on about twopence a week - '

'Splendid, Hilda!' cried Miss Trant. 'I never knew you were such an orator. I don't agree with you, but go on.'

'Well, you must admit, my dear, there isn't one of these people you'd dream of asking in even for a cup of tea at Hitherton.'

'I don't admit it. And even if I did, it doesn't prove anything. I refuse to regulate everything by what I might do at Hitherton. I've had rather a lot of Hitherton, you know,' she added, and in a tone of voice that helped Hilda to remember that she herself had taken care to have very little of Hitherton.

'Oh, I know you had a dull and rather awful time there,' cried

Hilda, rather plaintively. 'And you know that I didn't mind at all about all the money and everything coming to you.'

'Of course, my dear. You needn't tell me that.'

'Both Lawrence and I were glad, and we were hoping you would come and stay with us for some time and meet people and perhaps settle in town if you wanted to. I'd made all sorts of plans, Elizabeth - '

'I'm very sorry to have upset your plans, Hilda.'

'No, don't be absurd. But you must see that you can't possibly go on with this crazy scheme. If it were something decent, I wouldn't mind - though you must admit you don't know anything about business - but this is too ridiculous. To begin with, it's too dingy and futile for words. Then you don't know anything about this sort of thing.'

'Well, I didn't certainly. But I'm learning. And it's great fun. I like it.'

'And as Lawrence says, these pierrot people are probably robbing you right and left, just living on you and laughing at you behind your back.'

'No, they're not,' replied Miss Trant warmly. 'That's certainly not true. They're very grateful - and - and loyal - and awfully hard-working. They're just as honest and decent as any of the people I've known. The only difference is - they're more amusing.'

'For a time perhaps, that's all.'

'That may be. Perhaps one can only settle down with the kind of people one's always known, and been brought up with, but then I'm not settling down, I'm having a change. You see, I wanted something to do, and now I'm doing it. I'm quite willing to admit that I may get tired of this life pretty soon, but until I do I intend to go on with it, to finish my little adventure. So there you are, Hilda!'

'Oh, but don't you see - !' She was exasperated now. 'It's just like talking to one of the children, it really is. Don't you see that anything might happen while you're going on like this? We can't have you wandering round all winter staying in the most dreadful places by yourself, without a single person near you could trust to be sensible. And not only that, but what's going to happen to your money? You might easily lose every penny. It's monstrous, Elizabeth. Now honestly, have you made any money so far?'

'Not a ha'penny,' Miss Trant replied cheerfully.

'There you are!' Hilda was triumphant. 'You haven't, and you never will. I expect they're all hopeless, these people, or they wouldn't have been stranded like that.'

'No, they're not. Some of them are really clever, far too good for the audiences they're having. They really are, Hilda. Stay and see the' - she hesitated, then brought it out bravely - 'the show tonight.' She laughed. 'I'll give you a free pass, just as if you had exhibited one of our bills in your shop window.'

'No, that's not funny, Elizabeth,' Hilda snapped. 'And I can't stay tonight, and even if I could, I wouldn't. The whole thing's perfectly monstrous. Look at those people in there! You know very well you felt uncomfortable the moment I set eyes on them. Good Companions indeed! And all the time you're spending your money to keep these feeble creatures in - in - beer. And they're laughing at you, knowing quite well they don't even need audiences when they've got you to fatten on. And you could be doing so much now, staying with us and meeting the right kind of people, interesting men, and - oh - everything. I'd like to know how much money you've thrown away already'.

'Well, I don't propose to tell you, Hilda.'

'If you'd made some money out of it, that would be the tiniest excuse for going on,' cried Hilda, who plainly held, however, that it would really be no excuse at all, and was only using the first argument that came to hand. 'As it is, there's no excuse.'

'That's where you are wrong,' said Miss Trant eagerly. 'It seems to me all the more reason for my sticking to them. I'm far keener about it now than I was a week ago. We went to a place called Dotworth - a most deadly little town - and lost money there. Yes, it was a complete fiasco, I admit it. And after that, I told myself I wouldn't give up for anything, not until we were really successful. Can't you imagine what I feel about it, Hilda? I really like these pierrots - you'd like some of them too - and I think they like me and hate the thought of my losing money, and I should hate myself for ever if I ran away now and let them down. Besides, I should despise myself just for running away, throwing all the adventure away just to feel safe and comfortable, just because a few people might be shocked.'

'You're getting angry and excited now, my dear,' cried Hilda, raising her voice. 'I knew you would. And I knew you'd be absurd and stubborn about it. You stuck down there at Hitherton, wouldn't move, and now of course the minute you feel yourself free, you must go and do something absolutely senseless. Yes, wickedly senseless!' There were tears of vexation in her eyes. 'If you want to do something, have adventures, as you call it, there are plenty of things you could do that would be worth doing and wouldn't make you and the rest of us simply laughing-stocks. It's all so silly and useless. There couldn't be anything sillier. Singing old music-hall songs and joggling at the knees and repeating stale jokes! Going round making shopgirls giggle! Cadging sixpences from butchers' boys! And you of all people, Elizabeth! It's perfectly incredible. And you might be meeting men you could marry, instead of hobnobbing with broken-down actors in awful places like this.'

'I don't want to marry. And please stop, Hilda.' Miss Trant was not flushed now but pale. For the moment she could not stand up against this vehemence, in which there was real cutting scorn. She was at a grave disadvantage because she was still open to all the attack and could not produce a defence that she knew existed. It was not merely that Hilda would not understand her motives, but that she did not really understand them herself. They came from obscure but vital needs, from desires that had vanished underground, like the limestone country rivers, in girlhood. She did not know herself why there was something strangely satisfying about this life of dancing and singing and tinsel and limelight and odd journeys. She knew it was good to be full of plans, to be responsible, to be the comrade, perhaps the leader of these lovable creatures of the stage, but the rest she could not explain. So, for the moment, she was dumb, helpless.

Hilda saw her advantage but halted for a breathing-space before she pressed it home. And she was too late.

'Oh, Miss Trant!' cried a voice.

'Why, Miss Thong!' cried Miss Trant delightedly. 'I'm so glad.'

'Yes, isn't it nice? And what a journey! But here I am, with the dresses all ready. We've brought them too, you see. Elsie carried most, of course. Oh, but I'm interrupting, aren't I? I'm sorry, I'm sure. You know what I am, I get carried away.'

'It's all right,' said Miss Trant, smiling at her. 'This is my sister, Mrs Newent. And this is Miss Thong, who has been making some absolutely wonderful dresses for us.'

'Very pleased to meet you, I'm sure,' cried Miss Thong, who was bobbing about in an ecstasy. 'Though if I'm fit to meet anybody or even to be seen, I shall be surprised, I shall indeed. What with working at the dresses and putting people off and smoothing Pa down and packing up and the long railway ride and meeting Elsie at the station and seeing the sea - well, well - ' She began coughing, wrestled desperately, and gasped out her apologies to Hilda, who could not help staring at the queer rickety little mortal. 'There, if that doesn't just serve me right,' she concluded cheerfully. 'That's me all over. Talk, talk, get excited, won't let others get a word in edgeways, then I land myself! Miss Trant'll tell you how silly I am, Mrs Newark.'

'We must go into the Pavilion and look at the dresses,' said Miss Trant. 'Unless you're too tired, Miss Thong, and would rather wait.'

'I couldn't wait a single minute. I said to Elsie, "Just take me to Miss Trant and let her see the dresses or I shan't rest," I said, "or it's like being here under false pretences," I said, didn't I, Elsie? Where is she? She must have taken them in, all but these. Yes, do let's go in. Are you interested in these stage dresses, Mrs Newark? I'm sure you are, being Miss Trant's sister, and then having such nice taste yourself. You don't mind me saying that, do you? I know it's rather personal, coming from a stranger, but us dressmakers we can't help noticing, you know. I see in a minute. "She knows what's nice," I say to myself. "London style and good," I said to myself the very moment I saw you, Mrs Newark. You're sure you don't mind? I don't know what I shan't say before the day's out, and that's the state I'm in. Doesn't the air seem good? Can't you feel it going inside you?'

'I've only just arrived myself,' said Hilda. 'But the air does seem good here, I must say.'

'Doesn't it?' cried Miss Thong, with so much enthusiasm that the two of them might have been arguing for hours and have only just reached a triumphant concordance. 'That's exactly what I say. I felt the benefit of it as soon as I set foot outside the station. Elsie laughed at me the way I breathed in and out, but get it while you can, I say. Is this where we go?'

'Come along, Hilda,' said Miss Trant. 'You must see these dresses.' And then, a bolder stroke: 'I'd like your advice too.'

And Hilda followed them in, only making a few faint noises that perhaps suggested it was no concern of hers. She had been offering her sister advice about clothes for the last fifteen years and she was not going to stop now, even if the girl had suddenly turned herself into a manager of pierrots. Once inside, however, she was compelled to listen to the enthusiastic babble of Miss Thong, who seemed to think it was her duty to attach herself to this other visitor.

'So this is where you are then,' cried Miss Thong. 'Oh, isn't it nicely fitted-up? Proper stage too! And I shall see them all on it tonight and my dresses as well. Where will I be sitting, I wonder. I'd like to sit on my seat now, just to try it. Where will you be sitting, Mrs Newark?'

'I shan't be here. I'm going back to London.'

'Are you really? Isn't that a shame! But I expect you can see them any time, can't you, being Miss Trant's sister and able to come and go, I dare say. It's a treat for little me, I can tell you. The way I've looked forward to it, and coming on top of the journey as well! They *are* good, aren't they? And better still now than when I saw them! And fancy seeing the dresses you've made yourself coming out on to the stage, part of it all, as you might say, just fancy that!'

Miss Trant was examining a dress that Elsie was holding out.

'Oh, but this is perfectly lovely,' she cried. She looked up, caught her sister's eye, and saw a gleam of interest in it. 'Do look at this, Hilda,' she said.

'Yes, it is rather charming,' Hilda admitted. 'But too good for this sort of work, I should think.'

'Oh, no, Mrs Newark,' cried Miss Thong. 'You can't say that. It'll wear like anything and wash too. Just you take hold of it and have a good look.'

And Hilda did have a good look, at that and the others, and though she still maintained a rather stately and condescending attitude, as if she were looking down upon the dresses, their creator, and their prospective wearers, from a great height, she even went to the length of congratulating Miss Thong.

'I had thought of having a sort of mid-Victorian scene,' Miss Trant told her. 'Do you remember that pile of old songs we had at home? Some of them could be used. Do you remember how we used to laugh at them, though some were quite charming? And what became of the crinoline? Didn't you take it to town for a fancy dress?'

'Yes, but you couldn't use it for the stage,' said Hilda, forgetting herself. 'It's not bright enough. Besides, it's far too skimpy. Don't you remember how small it was? I meant to have it altered but I never did.'

'Yes, I know, Hilda, but I thought if you wouldn't mind lending it to me - a mid-victorian scene would be delightful, wouldn't it - Miss Thong could copy it more or less. You see how clever she is. I quite agree that it's not bright enough. Now what colours would you suggest, my dear?' she inquired demurely.

It was absurd, but Hilda found herself not only promising to lend the crinoline but also suggesting colours and materials and actually discussing the whole question with this fantastic little dressmaker that Elizabeth had picked up on her ridiculous travels. And by the time they had finished, she was ready for a cup of tea. But she did not stay for the performance in the evening. To have done that would have been to suggest that she had no will of her own at all, to say nothing of missing the Dexters' party. She insisted upon returning, as she had planned, by the 5.35, and said so a good many times, for somehow it sounded like a train that a strong-minded woman would catch.

'And mind you, Elizabeth,' she said at the station, 'I haven't changed my mind in the least. I think you're behaving dreadfully. The whole thing's too absurd for anything. And you really ought to see Lawrence as soon as you can, because you're probably being hopelessly swindled every minute. And do look after yourself, and the very instant you feel less mulish and realize how futile and wearing the whole thing is, let us know, just drop it, and run, and we'll see - at least Lawrence will - that these people don't try to take advantage.'

'Very well, Hilda. I will,' said Miss Trant, very quietly, almost submissively, and with only the tiniest flicker of amusement in her face. But she could hear the voice of another Hilda, busy explaining away the antics of her younger sister, Elizabeth, and even making social capital out of them 'Yes, my dear,' this voice was saying brightly, 'it's perfectly true. The crazy creature is actually running round the country, managing a concert party. Of course they're not the ordinary kind of awful fourth-rate people, but really good - one or two quite young and simply geniuses - and Elizabeth discovered them in some obscure place and said she would make them famous. And there she is, hiring theatres and designing costumes and all the rest of it. Oh, quite crazy, of course! But very amusing and original, don't you think? Exactly! Why not? That's what I say. As a matter of fact, I've given her some pretty good advice about one or two things she didn't understand.' And so that other voice ran on, while Miss Trant lifted her eyes demurely to meet her sister's reproachful glance.

After Hilda had given a final caution and a final wave from the 5.35 Miss Trant returned briskly to her little hotel, with a wind from the sea whipping the blood in her cheeks for her flying colours. She did not care now. There were no longer two Miss Trants, wrestling and jabbing in the dark of her mind, but only one, looking boldly upon the world out of two fine grey eyes. The test had come - and gone. If only these people would crowd in and enjoy her Good Companions, instead of staying miserably at home or going to the pictures or sitting in bar-parlours all night, she would be happy.

IV

Wednesday night was better than Monday or Tuesday: there were more people, especially in the cheaper seats, and, perhaps influenced by Miss Thong, who clapped everything, they were a trifle more enthusiastic. Thursday night was better still, but then Thursday was closing-day for the shops. Friday, however, was just as good as Thursday, and rather more appreciative. But none of these - as Mrs Joe said - were what you could really call Nights. There were still rows and rows of empty chairs (the Wood Family, Jimmy Nunn called them); the applause was feeble, scattered, and there was hardly an excuse for an encore; and it was difficult not to feel that the mournful night was drifting in and smothering such enthusiasm as there was in the half-empty pavilion. And now the great question was, Would Saturday be a Night?

'If Saturday's a fizzle,' Mrs Joe announced on Friday night, in the ladies' dressing-room, 'I shan't dare to look Miss Trant in the face, my dears. Dotworth didn't matter - '

'There wasn't tuppence in the whole rotten little town,' Elsie put in, rubbing her face far too vigorously. 'If they had a whist-drive there, they'd want to knock off and stay at home for six months.'

'But this place is different. It's supposed to be a good date, and after all it's only the middle of October. And look what we've done,' Mrs Joe added, dejectedly. 'Miss Trant will think we're a lot of Jonahs, that is, if she understands the expression, which I doubt.'

'Lucky for her!' cried Susie, that child of the theatre. She pulled her dress over her head, and then remarked on emerging: 'I must say I'd like to show her a real Night. She's cheerful enough - bless her! - but I fancy, a full house, money turned away, encores all round, five curtains, speeches, thanks from the manager - the usual "riot" that everybody talks about in the adverts, and hardly anybody ever sees - would buck her up no end. I know it would. And that new number of mine that Jimmy and Inigo have written is only waiting for an audience that isn't sitting there just to hear *God Save the King*. It's just crying out, ladies, for a few live ones in front.'

'Exactly,' said Mrs Joe. 'Experienced as I am - and very few artistes who *are* artistes have struck more dead frosts than I have in my time - I cannot, no, I can not, sing to chairs. I can feel the empty spaces, my dear, I assure you I can, and you've no idea how it wrecks my interpretation. I told Miss Trant this morning when I met her on the front: I said "Properly speaking, you've not heard me really interpret a song yet." But I didn't tell her why. I felt it would have been adding insult to injury - not that I've done her any injury, but you know what I mean?'

They did know what she meant, and they all sighed in chorus for a Night.

Jimmy Nunn and Mr Morton Mitcham, having what they called 'a quick one' with the manager of the Pier, Mr Porson, in the Refreshment Room on Saturday morning, could not keep away from the subject.

'Yes,' said Mr Porson, 'we're round about forty-three pounds so far. That means you'll just about make up to your guarantee tonight, unless of course there's a rush. A wet night might bring 'em in, though they're not fond of walking out to the Pier on a wet night. If it's fine, then they don't want to come inside, and if it's wet they don't fancy the Pier.' And Mr Porson added the short and rather cheerless laugh that he always tacked on to this observation, which he had made already at least fifty times this season, to say nothing of other seasons.

'If you ask me,' said Mr Mitcham impressively, 'I think we're getting going in the town. Some of the fellows who come in here, fellows who never go in to see a show, are beginning to talk about it. They've heard something, you see. If we were here another week, we'd be playing to capacity. I know. I've seen it before. But there you are, we're not.'

'Just what I think,' Jimmy Nunn admitted sadly. 'We've got going, but too late. And damned hard cheese, I call it. As I told you, Mr Porson, this lady who's the boss, Miss Trant, she's put up a lot of money for us - '

'A lot of money,' Mr Mitcham repeated emphatically, with the air of a man who knows money when he sees it.

'She's new to it, you see, Mr Porson,' Jimmy continued, 'and she's one of the best, a real lady too - general's daughter, they say. It's time she began seeing something for her money.'

'She'll think we've sold her the gold brick,' Mr Mitcham put in mournfully.

'And the show ought to go,' said Jimmy.

'It oughter go big,' said Mr Mitcham, who, in this despondent mood, seemed to become more Transatlantic.

Mr Porson had heard something like this, usually in this very bar, every week since April, but he immediately agreed that it was a good show. 'I don't say it's everybody's show,' he said judicially. 'It's not one of your bustling knock-'em-about, come-on-let's-have-the-applause shows. But I'll tell you frankly - I like it. You can put me down for that. It's a fine little show, and we're as disappointed as you are.' He finished his drink 'Well, I must be trotting.' Mr Porson was always trotting, as Miss Trant and Jimmy and other people who had business with him knew to their cost. He trotted so much that he could never be found. The other two watched him go, and then looked at one another with slightly raised brows, which announced that they had no great opinion of Mr Porson, that Mr Porson might be pleasant enough over a drink but nevertheless was a thoroughly incompetent person, the kind of manager who would ruin the chances of any show.

'What about finishing these and then walking down to see if there are any bookings?' Jimmy asked. The box office was at the entrance to the Pier. It took them ten minutes to reach it, but by the time they did they had quietly dismissed nine men out of every ten who had found their way, obviously by influence, my boy, into management, as creatures who merely cumbered the ground.

'Good morning, my dear, you're looking very bright this morning,' said Mr Mitcham to the young lady in the box office, who looked anything but bright. 'And how are things?'

But the young lady, who suffered a good deal from bronchial trouble, really did brighten now. 'Quite picking up today,' she replied. 'I've booked out about two and a half rows of the two-and-fourpennies already, and I've had several inquiries on the telephone. I shouldn't be surprised if a lot of the better-class people aren't coming, for once. I believe you're going to get a good house tonight.'

'Bless you, my child, for those kind words,' said Jimmy. Then he exchanged a glance with Mr Mitcham. 'It looks better, ol' man.'

'It's just as I said,' replied Mr Mitcham. 'We've got going in the town, though only at the last minute. Another week and it 'ud be capacity every night.'

'Well, a good send-off will be something. It'll cheer us all up and look well in the adverts. "Thanks for wonderful send-off at Sandybay. Last night a riot!" And I'll tell you what I think, Mitcham,' Jimmy added earnestly. 'Mr Porson ought to get more chairs in. He told me himself he'd lent about fifty to the corporation. Let him put 'em back, I say. There's time this afternoon. I'll leave a message.' Miss Trant herself saw the extra chairs being taken in, late in the afternoon. Mr Oakroyd was there, lending a hand.

'I suppose they're expecting something rather wonderful next week,' she said to him with a touch of bitterness. 'They don't want any more seats for us.'

'Nay, Miss Trant, they do,' he told her, pushing back his little brown cap as usual, for he always wore his cap and always saluted her in this manner. 'It's going to be a right big do, they tell me, and even wi' these extras ther'll nobbut be standing room for them as comes at last minute, I dare say. All t'fowk where I'm lodging and ther friends and relations is coming. I do knaw, and all t'better seats is booked up, two and fower a time.'

'Oh, but that's splendid, isn't it, Mr Oakroyd?' she cried.

'It'll be a bit of a change,' he admitted dryly.

She looked at him reproachfully. 'Is that all you can say?'

Mr Oakroyd did not blush because he was not in the habit of blushing, but he looked a trifle confused. 'Nay,' he protested, 'I'm right glad. It's champion.'

Miss Trant, rather excited now, returned to the Pavilion earlier than usual in the evening, and though there was the usual mournful drizzle, making the Pier look as forlorn as ever, already people were streaming along towards the Pavilion. Sandybay had discovered, at the eleventh hour, that The Good Companions were offering it an unusually good show. Ten minutes before the performance began, all the unreserved seats were filled and there were numbers of people standing at each side and at the back. In another five minutes, after a few more had been squeezed in, the 'House Full' notice was put up and they were actually turning money away. Miss Trant, who was sitting in a corner in the wings, near the ladies' dressing-room, had the news from Mr Porson himself, and immediately both dressing-rooms and wings buzzed with it: 'Turning money away, my dear'; 'Capacity to the roof, ol' man'; and they took turns at peeping through the curtain. 'Going to be a Night, my dear,' they cried to one another. 'What did I say? Something told me.'

'Now, Miss Trant,' said Mrs Joe, 'can't you feel a difference?'

Miss Trant could. The whole atmosphere of the place was changed. You knew at once that on the other side of the curtain there were no longer any cold spaces and empty chairs and yawns and languid stares; that everybody there was expecting to be delightfully entertained, had already met the players more than half-way, was only waiting to hum and laugh and break into gigantic hail-storms of applause. Miss Trant tried hard to be coolly amused at the excitement of the others, but she did not succeed. She was as excited as they were, and was only thankful that she herself had nothing to do. Oh, this might be absurd, but it was thrilling, it was fun!

Jimmy had a last-minute inspiration. 'Let's open with the band behind the curtain. Our two numbers. *Slippin' round the Corner*, then Susie's number.' Inigo had been able to score these two songs of his for the little jazz band, with some assistance from Morton Mitcham, and they had both been well rehearsed. They got their instruments and took up their places; Inigo at the piano; Jimmy at the drums; Mitcham with his banjo; and Joe, Susie, and Elsie respectively with cornet, violin, and tenor saxophone, instruments they all played in a slapdash but sufficiently adequate manner. In less than a minute they were waiting for the signal to begin.

House lights out and footlights up. Applause already. Then - one, two, three, and off they went. *Rumpty-dee-tidee-dee. Rumpty-dee-tidee.* Quietly at first, then louder, louder, then letting it rip. You could feel the whole house moving to its rhythm through the curtain. They were tapping; they were humming; they were eating and drinking it. A final flourish, crowned by Jimmy, who crashed his drum-stick against the hanging cymbal. A moment's silence. Then the Pavilion seemed all clapping hands.

'Instruments away,' shouted Jimmy through the tumult; 'All on and the opening chorus as usual! Come, on, come on. Now then, Inigo! Ready with that curtain, Oakroyd! Gosh! it's going with a bang tonight!'

And with a bang it went. They clapped when Joe warned them against the mighty deep, and clapped again when Mrs Joe discovered Angus Macdonald coming home from the war. They rose as one man when Elsie tunefully announced she was looking for a boy like them. They reduced Morton Mitcham to mere sweat and grinning bone, and he did so many tricks and played so many tunes that both cards and strings must have been red-hot by the time he had done with them. They roared with laughter every time Jimmy opened his mouth or crossed the stage. And when Jerry Jerningham did his slipping round the corner and Susie brought out her new song about going home, then they had no mercy but clapped and stamped and whistled and drummed their feet time after time to bring the two back again. When the final curtain came, it was nearly eleven, three-quarters of an hour past the usual time, and even then the enraptured audience would not stop applauding. 'Spee-ee-eech!' some of them were calling.

Jimmy beckoned to Miss Trant, who was standing in the wings, at once excited and exhausted, dithering, because instead of being a mere spectator she had seen both actors and audience. 'Come on and say something,' Jimmy's mouth shaped at her.

Instantly she waved a frantic negative. She could no more have tottered into that lighted space and spoken to the loud if friendly monster there than have flown to the moon.

'Ladies and gentlemen,' Jimmy began.

But that was the signal for another outburst, and in the middle of it the attendant could be seen pushing his way up to the stage, carrying a magnificent bouquet of roses. The lights were up now and everybody on the stage could see that approaching bouquet. The three women never took their eyes away from it. Mrs Joe was not without her hopes, for might there not be a Music Lover in the house? It flashed through Elsie's mind that probably some gentleman friend - Elsie was rich in gentlemen friends - was in front. Susie was already preparing a special smile and curtsy, for it was hardly possible that the bouquet could be for anyone else. If ever a girl had earned a bouquet, she had tonight. The attendant held it up, and Jimmy came forward with a skip and a jump to receive it. He read the label, and the three women held their breath. He turned and, with a droll gesture and smirk, handed it - to Jerry Jerningham.

Mr Jerningham, very warm, very tired, a little shiny perhaps, but still exquisite, bowed his acknowledgement very gracefully, then, after a quick glance at the label, which said *To Mr Jerry Jerningham from an Unknown Admirer* and said it in a flowing and feminine handwriting, smiled again at the audience and smiled at his fellow-players, three of whom were attempting to disguise looks of mingled amazement and disgust. And it may be admitted, here and now, that there was talk of that monstrous bouquet for weeks afterwards in the ladies' dressing-room, that we ourselves have perhaps not heard the last of it, that the Unknown Admirer may turn up again.

It was over at last. Inigo, hotter and even more weary than Mr Jerningham and not at all exquisite, hammered out something that approximated to *God Save the King*, and then, safe behind the lowered curtain, nearly fell off his chair. This is the boy that ought to have a bouquet,' said Mrs Joe, who had a great opinion of Inigo. 'Look how he's worked. And never even got so much as a hand!'

'Yes, it's a rotten shame,' said Susie, smiling at him. 'Look - his lock of hair's nearly coming out. Never mind, you were wonderful, Inigo, and the song's a darling, darling, da-ar-ling.' And off she ran.

Miss Trant found Mr Porson at her elbow, saying something about returns and a future date, but at the moment it was impossible for her to be quietly sensible. They were all still shouting congratulations to one another and clearing away their props. It was like the end of a crazy party. After a minute or two, she decided to wait outside until some of the others had finished changing. And very strange it was to go outside and find the night there, the glitter of the promenade, the mysterious and murmuring dark of the sea, the lonely lights far out, the chill salt breath that now seemed so sweet.

Out they came, dim shapes with jubilant voices. A cigarette went curving over the side like a tiny meteor, and a voice said: 'Ah, I'd rather taste the air than that.' They gathered round her. 'Well, this was a Night, wasn't it?' they chorused: and 'What a send-off!' and 'A riot at Sandybay, my dear!' Jerry Jerningham held out his roses to Elsie, who condescended to smell them. Mrs Joe found Mr Joe, who tucked her arm in his and gave the scene a pleasantly domestic flavour, so that you could almost see little George himself there with them. Inigo went dodging round so that he could place himself by the side of Susie, a bafflingly elusive girl. Mr Mitcham was still in the middle of an anecdote to which nobody was paying any attention. Jimmy Nunn came up, giving instructions to Mr Oakroyd. Then suddenly, all at once, they were telling one another how tired they were.

'And so am I,' cried Miss Trant, 'although I haven't done anything. I feel as if I could go to bed for three days. Thank goodness it's Sunday tomorrow.

'Yes,' said Jimmy, 'and by the way, I've looked up the trains for Winstead. I've got it down in my note-book and I'll look it up when we get to the entrance. No Through, of course. The usual cross-country business - an hour's wait at Mudby-on-the-Wash and then another hour at Washby-on-the-Mud, and so on. Who are you taking in the car, Miss Trant? You'd better let us know now.'

'Oh, good heavens. I'd forgotten!' she cried, in such droll dismay that they laughed. 'I was thinking I was going to have a nice quiet day here, breakfast in bed with a book and then a little sewing. I'd forgotten all about Winstead. Isn't it terrible? We've got to begin all over again.' And then they laughed at her again, for there was something in her tone that told them she was now much happier about it all and seemed to establish her companionship with them. They moved slowly towards the Pier entrance, planning the next day's journey.

CHAPTER FOUR
Mr Oakroyd Plays 'The Hunted Man'
for a Short Season

I

AT the beginning of that week at Sandybay, Mr Oakroyd was a happy man. Never in all his dreams of being an independent craftsman had he been so independent or so much the craftsman as he was now. He put in as many hours working as he had done at Higden's mill, and sometimes he put in a great deal more, achieving a day's labour that would have horrified every Trade Union secretary in the country. But you could hardly call it work; it was like a kind of hobby; it was nothing but a pleasant dream of work; and it made old Sam Oglethorpe, with his 'Joinery and Jobbing Work Promptly Attended to', his hen-run, and his cottage, look like 'two-pennorth o' copper'. When Mr Oakroyd remembered that only a week or two before, he had envied old Sam, he was amazed at his good fortune, which indeed had still something unreal about it. True, he had a lot to learn about this business; all this messing about with curtains and bits of scenery and electric lights was new to him; but then he was learning fast and liking it. So long as they did not want him to appear on the stage - he drew the line at that, even if it was only choosing a card out of a pack for Mr Mitcham - he was ready to do anything they asked him to do. And if he made any bit of a thing for these people, they were pleased and thankful and went on about it until he hardly knew where to look. This attitude towards work seemed to him astonishingly novel. At Higden's, if you didn't put all your back into a job, they asked you what you thought you were there for; but when you did put your back into it, finishing the job in fine style, then they said 'Ay, that'll do.' And he could not help thinking that these strange theatrical people - indeed, all these Southerners he was meeting now - did overdo this patting you on the back and making a fuss when you did some little bit of a thing: it made you feel soft. But he was also compelled to admit that it did oil the wheels and put heart into you when you had to tackle something new. Oh, the job was a gift! Then there was the travelling. Talk about being on t'road! Talk about being down South! Why, at this rate, there would hardly be anywhere in England where they hadn't been, after six months. The places these theatre folk had seen! Even Susie, only a bit of a lass, could talk by the hour, like Joby Jackson himself, about the towns she had been to, dozens and dozens of them. As for Mr Mitcham, if you only believed half he said, he must have played that banjo of his and done his conjuring in nearly every place under the sun, in places too where you would not think they would want to hear a banjo or see any conjuring. Such folk, who could afford to be particular, might well think nothing of Rawsley and Dotworth, but Mr Oakroyd had enjoyed himself in both these towns. They seemed to him delightfully foreign. At Rawsley the woman at his lodgings had given him for supper one night some little dry dumplings with bits of bacon in them, something that Bruddersford had never set eyes on; and in a pub there he had met a man who thought Bruddersford United was a rugby team. Dotworth was equally outlandish. There they had put nothing but Swiss milk in tea, called buns 'cakes', did not know that wool had to be washed and combed before it was spun, and got terribly mixed up between Yorkshire and Lancashire all the time. It was in a pub at Dotworth that he had been able to set a chap right very nicely. This was a scene he had often wistfully amused himself by imagining back at Bruddersford, when he dreamed of being a travelled man. He had imagined himself taking his pipe out of his mouth and saying quietly, 'Half a minute, mate! You're wrong there. I've been and I knaw.' And it had actually happened like that. This chap, who drove a cart and seemed to fancy himself, was laying down the law a bit and got on to talking about the Great North Road. He said it went through Lincoln and York, and all the Dotworth innocents, gaping at him over their half-pints, said that he was quite right. Then it happened. Mr Oakroyd took his pipe out of his mouth and said quietly: 'Half a minute, mate! You're wrong there.' Ho. 'e was, was 'e? Yes, he was, and had he ever been down the Great North Road? No, he hadn't, but he had pals who had and knew it well. 'Well, yer pals is wrong too, mate,' Mr Oakroyd had told him and the company. 'Great North Road nivver sees Lincoln and York. I've been and I knaw. Only come down it t'other night, on a lorry.' And for the next quarter of an hour he had told them a thing or two, and the landlord himself had stayed in the tap-room to listen.

Neither of these places, however, could compare with Sandybay. He was ready to put Sandybay in front of the other seaside towns he had visited, Morecambe, Blackpool, and Scarborough, not because there was more 'going off' there (most people say 'going on' but in Bruddersford they say 'going off' - a subtle and significant difference), for in that respect it was inferior to the other three, especially Blackpool, where there were more amusements than in any other town in the world. No, he preferred Sandybay because it had more of the sea about it. There were the boats drawn up on the beach, the nets and all the other paraphernalia, the lifeboat, and the fishermen themselves, with their blue jerseys, brown faces, and white whiskers, just like the fishermen in pictures. One old man down there was the very image of the man he had seen so often on the packets and advertisements of his favourite tobacco, Old Salt. Mr Oakroyd had actually spoken to him. He had a word or two with a good many of these fishermen, down at the beach or over a glass at one of the funny little pubs near the harbour. He found it hard to understand what they said, and they seemed to find it hard to understand him, but that only made it all the more interesting, like being among foreigners, except that they seemed to like a drop of beer and a pipe of tobacco and were not above cadging one or the other. Joe liked to talk to these chaps too, and sometimes went round with them. All the pierrots were friendly enough - 'they got on champion', as Mr Oakroyd admitted - but Joe was really the only one he could go about with a bit. Joe might be a singer - and a rare old noise he could make too - but he was a solid and sensible chap, with arms on him like two, who liked his pipe and glass of bitter and was a good talker when you once got him going. By the time they had reached Sandybay, the two of them were quite confidential. Joe talked to Mr Oakroyd about their George, and Mr Oakroyd talked to Joe about their Lily.

Then again, Mr Oakroyd was happy because so far he liked being in lodgings. He discussed this subject with Joe when the two of them were working at that little set in the Pavilion. Joe had been grumbling, saying he was sick of being in lodgings. He wanted a home of his own.

'Well, I can fancy that, Joe,' replied Mr Oakroyd, "cos you've been at it a long while. But being i' lodgings is a change for me, and I'm not pining for any home of me awn or wanting to go back to t'one I've got. It's a bit of a treeat to me being a lodger, Joe.'

'How d'you make that out?' asked Joe. 'It's not your own place. You can't do what you like. You've got to put up with anything they give you.'

'Nay, I find you're a deal better off. When I were at home, place didn't belong to me but to t'wife. She may ha' done what she liked but I knaw I didn't. And if I didn't put up wi' owt she gave me, I nivver heard last on it for days. If you tell t'woman at your lodgings you don't want rice pudding all t'week, she might bang t'door a bit as she goes out, but she won't stand there calling you ivvery name she can lay tongue to and then start afresh next morning or look at you as if you'd been trying to set fire to t'place.'

'Now, Oakroyd,' Joe protested, 'you're not going to tell me you were henpecked like that.'

'No more ner t'next man,' said Mr Oakroyd grimly. 'But I nivver even heard tell of a henpecked lodger.'

'Maybe. But you've heard tell of many a one that's been swindled and diddled and robbed. And if you haven't, there's one here, talking to you. Some of 'em would take the milk out of your tea and the laces out of your boots. They'd charge you for the stairs going up to bed if they could. I could tell you some tales.'

'No doubt you could, Joe,' said Mr Oakroyd earnestly, 'and I'm not denying that gurt fat woman I lodged wi' i' Dotworth were a bit on t'skinny side when it come to laying table. For all that, I'm doing better ner I've done for some time. Nah, as you knaw yersen, three pound i' t'week isn't a big wage. I've had more ner that afore today and thowt I were badly off. But when you've nobbut yersen to keep and you're i' lodgings it seems to me you get more out on it than you do at home. You pay your two pound or whativver it is to t'landlady and she treats you like a good customer, as if you wor somebody. At home you pay all you can but you're nobody. "Oh, it's you, is it?" they say when you come home. "Well, you'll have to wait for your tea 'cos I haven't finished what I'm doing. And how many times have I to tell you to tak' them big boots off when you come in! Look at mess you're making!" That's what you get at home, Joe. But when I walk into my lodgings, it's a bit different. "You're just in time, Mr Oakroyd," they say. "Your tea'll be ready in one minute. I shan't keep you waiting. Nice afternoon it's been, Mr Oakroyd." D'you see, Joe?'

Joe did see but was not convinced. 'And when you've lived a year or two on landlady's cooking, old man,' he said, 'you'll change your mind. There's Jimmy Nunn there always grumbling because he can't eat anything, but I sometimes think he's lucky. He knows he can't get it, but I think I'm going to get something and I don't.'

'Pass me up them inch nails, Joe,' said Mr Oakroyd. Then he reflected a minute or two. "Well, I must say I've seen better cooking i' my time than you get round these parts. That's because you're out o' Yorkshire. Down South here t'women doesn't bake and you can't get a curran' teacake or a flat cake or a fatty cake or owt like that. Eh, I'd a right good laugh yesterda'. Woman where I am - Mrs Cullin her name is - she's a widow woman - her husband were at gas-works here and had a good job too, she tells me - she's a decent clean little body, and friendly like - she tells me all sorts - well, Mrs Cullin, she says to me yesterda', she says, "Now, Mr Oakroyd, I'm going to give you a treat," she says. "I've a joint o' beef for your dinner and you're a Yorkshireman, so I'm going to give you some Yorkshire pudding with it," she says. In comes my dinner - bit o' beef, cabbage, potaters. I looks at it and says, "Here, Mrs Cullin, what about that Yorkshire pudding?" I says. "Let's have that first." She stares. "It's here," she says, pointing to t'plate. 'What!" I says. "You don't mean this bit o' custard, soft batter stuff, under t'cabbage?" "Yes, I do," she says. "If that isn't Yorkshire pudding, what is it?" "Nay," I says, "you mun't ask me, Missis, what it is. All I knaw is, it's no more Yorkshire pudding ner I am. It's a bit o' custard or pancake, likely enough." And then I tells her about Yorkshire pudding. And tak' notice o' this Joe, 'cos it'll happen come in handy some time.' Mr Oakroyd paused to relight his pipe, blew out a cloud or two of Old Salt, then continued.

' "To begin wi'," I says, "a Yorkshire pudding is eaten by itsen and not mixed up wi' meat and potaters, all in a mush. And it comes straight out o' tooven," I says, "straight on to t'plate. No waiting," I says, "or you'll spoil it. If you don't put it straight on to t'plate you might as well go and sole your boots with it. And another thing," I says, "you've got to have your oven hot, I do knaw that. Then if you've mixed right and your oven's hot, pudding'll come out as light as a feather, crisp and brarn, just a top and a bottom, you might say, wi' none o' this custardy stuff in t'middle. Nan d'you see, Missis?" I says. "Nay," she says, "I can't learn all that at my time o' life, and you're letting your dinner get cold wi' talking about your hot ovens," she says. And then we'd a right good laugh together, and I heard her telling her daughter - she's in a draper's - all about it last night. She has this lass at home and a lad, and another lad away i' t'Navy, and they're all courting - even t'sailor's young woman is allus coming in - so we see a bit o' company. And they're all coming o' Saturday night to see us.'

'That's the idea,' said Joe. 'You go on working the town a bit. That's what I do. Some of the boys and girls laugh at me, but I say it all helps.'

'It does an' all,' cried Mr Oakroyd. 'They tak' a right interest in t'pierrots at Mrs Cullin's. "Is it a good show?" they asks me. "Good show!" I says. "It's t'best show as ivver you've seen i' Sandybay," I says. "We're nobbut here just to pass an odd week, then we're off to t'big theaters - coining brass," I says. "Coining what?" they says. "Brass," I says, "and that's Yorkshire for money. You come and see Good Companions. You'll nivver get another chance, and when you read about 'em i' t'papers - and you'll be doing that afore so long - you'll be fair mad if you've nivver seen 'em. Best show on t'road," I says.'

And indeed this was Mr Oakroyd's opinion. He was fully convinced that there was no better concert party than The Good Companions in existence. It is true he did not know much about the others, had never even seen them; but then he could not imagine any one of them being better, could not imagine any other being as good, so that he was quite honest in his opinion. Nor was his enthusiasm merely part and parcel of his loyalty to his new friends and to his employer, Miss Trant. He had never been a constant theatre-goer or music-hall patron, though he still liked seven-pennorth of pit at the second house of the Bruddersford Imperial, but nevertheless he considered himself to be a man who knew a good turn when he saw it. Your Bruddersfordian is a hanging judge of anything that costs money. And Mr Oakroyd, after having seen the show from almost every possible angle, was convinced that The Good Companions were good turns. He thought least of Elsie, whose rather mechanical little frivolities he dismissed as 'summat and nowt'. On the other hand, the dancing of Mr Jerry Jerningham had no more staunch admirer in this island, and Mr Oakroyd did not hesitate to give out that he was something of an authority and no ordinary onlooker, for in his youth he had been considered one of the best clog-dancers in the Woolgate and Lane End districts of Bruddersford and had once taken third prize at the Pit Park Gala. For Mr Jerningham himself he had a contempt. 'Yond', he would say, 'is war ner a big lass. Starves his belly to clothe his back, I'll be bound'; and, becoming more mysteriously West Riding in his turn of phrase with every added insult, would conclude by muttering that Mr Jerningham 'wer war ner a pike sheep head', which final and awful judgement was not the less devastating because nobody understood what it meant. But Mr Oakroyd made a clear distinction between Jerningham the man and Jerningham the dancer, and for the latter he had a genuine admiration. And Susie was a favourite with him, on and off the stage. She was obviously a good turn, though he could not always make out what she was getting at, and she was a lively, bonny, and friendly lass, reminding him so much of their Lily that he found her company nearly as delightful and yet disturbing as did Inigo himself. Inigo too he admired as a piano-player and liked as a friendly young chap with not a bit of swelled head about him. (In Bruddersford you are always on the lookout for swelled heads, and if a man does anything at all out of the ordinary there, his head has to be measured at once.) There was too a special bond between him and Inigo, because, as he explained to Joe: 'We're both i' t'same boat, both amachoors, as you say, who comes at t'same time and is trying to show you what we can do.' And it was clear from Mr Oakroyd's tone, as he said this, that he thought the two of them were not only trying but succeeding.

For Miss Trant he had a tremendous respect, though he took pains not to show it. There was something about her - he knew it was there but did not care to discover exactly what it was - that commanded this respect, and it was something he had never found in Sir Joseph Higden, Bart, and other men of wealth and standing for whom he had worked in Bruddersford. None of The Good Companions (who had talked it over more than once) knew how much money Miss Trant had, whether she was really rich or merely in possession of a decent income with a few hundreds to spare for this whim of hers; but it was Mr Oakroyd's opinion that she had plenty of money and had it so long that she never thought about it. 'Brass might graw on trees so far as she knaws, or cares,' he said of her; and this opinion, which would have enraged a democrat of an earlier generation, only tended to increase his wondering respect for her. Bruddersford had its rich and its poor, but he never remembered meeting anyone there like Miss Trant. The two of them were like beings from two different planets who had yet discovered points of contact and sympathy. If Miss Trant had been a man, perhaps his attitude would have been different, but not only was she a woman but, in his eyes, a very personable young woman. He had talked about her to Susie, one afternoon, when the two of them walked the length of the pier. Susie was very fond of Miss Trant and thought her - as she said - 'really swish and a dear', but of course practically middle-aged, with nothing but a deadly spinsterish sort of life in front of her once she had left The Good Companions. Mr Oakroyd had immediately protested against this view of his employer.

'Nay, Soos,' he said, 'you're off your horse there, lass. I wouldn't be so capped if Miss Trant didn't marry afore so long. She may have a chap, nah, nobbut waiting for her to say t'word. She's young eniff for onnybody; you've nobbut to look at her to see she's one o' the classy sort that happens to ha' got plenty o' gumption; and she's right nice-looking into t'bargain. And if I were a chap, coming courting here, Miss Trant 'ud be t'first I should go for, so nah you knaw.'

'So that's it, is it?' Susie pretended to be very disgusted indeed. 'Well, you are a fraud, Mr Jess Oakroyd. And after I've been so nice to you! What about me, yer gurt nowt?'

'I wouldn't be paid to wed thee, Soos,' he declared, delightedly. 'A chap 'ud nivver have five minutes' peace and quiet to hissen wi' thee, for tha'd be kissin' him one minute and tormenting him t'next minute and then thrawing pots and pans at him minute after. If tha wasn't telling him he mun nivver leave thee for half an hour, then tha'd be telling him tha were leaving him ivver, till t'poor lad wouldn't know whether he wor on his head or his heels.'

'And very nice for him too,' she replied. 'He'd like it. Though you're simply talking rot, of course. You don't know anything about me really, not the least thing, and it's simply cheek to say I should go on like that. But do you really think I would?'

'I'm saying nowt,' he began.

'And about time, too!'

'But I do knaw this. There's a lad i' this company I've got my eye on, and I'm feeling right sorry for him already.'

'Now what - just exactly what - do you mean by that, Mr Oakroyd?'

'He may be a good pianner-player. I don't say he isn't. They tell me he might easy mak' a lot o' money out o' t'songs he's doing. I don't doubt it. But I've had my eye on him, and I say I'm right sorry for him. If he goes on t'way he's shaping, he'll land hissen in a mess, choose how it works out. If this lass he's getting so sweet on won't have him, then he'll nivver knaw no peace. But if she does have him he'll nivver knaw no peace neither.'

'I never heard such stuff in all my life,' cried Susie. 'As if I - he - anybody - oh, don't be silly! And if he was getting like that - and of course he isn't; he hasn't known me five minutes, not that that makes much difference, I admit - well, it wouldn't be my fault, would it?'

'Not so much your fault as his misfortin,' said Mr Oakroyd, with a grin.

'Nah, lad, nah, lad!' Susie snapped her fingers at him. 'And if somebody had told me that a carpenter from Shuddersford could be beastly nosey, just like an old woman, I wouldn't have believed them. Now just run away and do some work instead of talking scandal that you've made up yourself and' - here her voice sank and took on a blood-curdling vibration - 'poisoning the mind and betraying the heart of A Young Girl, hardly more than a Chee-ild and a Norphan. Go, Sir Jess.'

And that wicked baronet, pulling his little brown cap further down, did go, giving her a wink as he went. He entered the Pavilion through the stage door. If anybody had told him a fortnight ago he would be marching in through stage doors! Inside there was a nice little job waiting for him. When he had done that, had a chat with Joe and one or two of the others perhaps, smoked a pipe or two of Old Salt, there was the grand walk back to his lodgings and tea at the end of it. 'Good afternoon, Mr Oakroyd; your tea's just ready and I've done one of our special fat kippers you like so much.'

'Nah that's a bit of all right, Mrs Cullin,' he would reply; and then have his tea and a look at the paper, then a walk round and perhaps half a pint somewhere, then back to the Pier, taking his time; his own man, a chap that was knocking about a bit, and one of The Good Companions. Eh, but it was grand!

'Nay, lad,' he warned himself, 'steady on, steady on a bit. Tha's not asleep and dreaming. There's bahnd to be a catch in it somewhere.'

And the second half of that week at Sandybay brought the catch.

II

It was a letter that destroyed his peace of mind. He had soon seen that he could not cut himself off entirely from the folk at home. They must know where to find him, for though they might think they were better off without him, be glad to see the last of him, still there they were, his wife and his son, and if anything happened to them, they would want to let him know and he would want to know. There was also the question of Lily's letters. It took over a fortnight for a letter to find its way to her out there in Canada, and more than another fortnight for a reply to come back; in fact, you could reckon it six weeks, there and back, even if she replied almost at once. He had - as he said - 'studied this' when first he joined the troupe. He could write to her as usual, and indeed he intended to write more often now that he had so much to tell her. But how was she going to reply? He could not give her his address six or seven or eight weeks ahead, for he would not always know where they would be then. He saw that she would have to write to him at 51 Ogden Street, Bruddersford, as before, and the letters would have to be sent on to him by his wife or (and that was more likely) by Leonard. All he had to do was to let them know at home where he would be the next week, and he could always find that out. He asked Joe about this, and discovered from him that all that was necessary was to give the name of the troupe, the hall, and the town: Mr J. Oakroyd, The Good Companions, Pier Pavilion, Sandybay - that is how you did it, and that is what he sent home, the week before at Dotworth, together with a short letter saying that he had got a job with some pierrots and telling them to send on Lily's letters. And he had written again, giving them his Winstead address, before a reply came.

It was on Thursday afternoon that he found a letter waiting for him at the Pavilion. He hurried away with it to a quiet corner and was delighted to discover that it contained a letter from Lily. But she did not say much. It was still very hot out there; she was all right but taking it easy because of the baby that was coming, which she was sure was a boy; and her husband, Jack Clough, was working very hard and looked like getting a rise very soon; and they sent their love to all. When he had read this letter through a second time, Mr Oakroyd began to feel miserable. It brought Lily back so sharply to his mind, which could not hold a clear image of her face nor hear her voice distinctly yet was most vividly, poignantly conscious of her. The letter did this, yet at the same time it made painfully plain the distance between them. There she was, but this was all she could say. Tomorrow he would sit down, sucking away at his moustache, pressing so hard on his pen that it spluttered ink on the paper, in an agony of endeavour to tell her something of what he felt and thought, and he would say little more. If only she was here, listening to him, or he was there, looking at her! Not a word yet about him going out there. He folded the letter with mournful care and put it in his inside pocket.

Something had been sent with it. He glanced down at the name at the bottom of the scrawl. It was a short letter from Leonard. He cast a rather negligent eye over it. He was not very interested in what Leonard had to say. But when he had gone through it once, he drew in his breath sharply, pushed his cap to the very back of his head, and began all over again, this time attending carefully to every single word. And this is what he read:

> Dear Father,
>
> We got your letter and I am sending you a letter which came from our Lily. I am having to write because Ma says she will not write because she is too ashamed for you and will not trust herself she says to say a word to you. What have you done, you must have done something because after you had gone a few days a bobby called one night and asked about you and where you were. We could not say we said. And that is not the end of it, Mrs Sugden told Ma the police had been watching the house and Joe Flather told me they had been to Higdens and asking at the club. So you had best keep away from here and keep out of the way or try a disguise or they will get you. Albert Tuggridge says it is too risky writing, they can open all letters and track you down that way but I am risking it though we are not telling anybody where you are. Ma is disgusted but I must say it is a bit of excitement and agree with Albert that if you have done anything you must have been the tool of others and been used by a gang of crooks. We were surprised you had got a job with some pierots and think you ought to watch out there. United lost again, what a team. I have been moved up to fourth chair at Gregsons allready.
>
> Your aff. son,
> Leonard

After he had read it a third time, he tore it up and, still clutching the fragments, crept quietly out of his corner, a hunted man.

For the rest of that day, he thought about that letter - a policeman calling at 51 Ogden Street; police watching the house; police inquiring at Higden's; police going along to the Club - and the more he thought about it, the more uneasy he became. 'Nay, but I've done nowt,' he kept telling himself; but that had no effect. He had been so busy and happy in his new job that he had almost forgotten the astonishing series of events that had taken him to Rawsley, or at least he only remembered them as episodes in a tale he had to tell. But now they returned to arrange themselves in a sinister sequence. There was the money that drunken sportsman, George, had said he had had stolen from him. The police had announced that they had a clue, a valuable clue. That very day he had quarrelled with his firm and quarrelled with his union, had torn up his insurance card (the act of a desperate man), and had run away. And that was not all. There was that lorry, loaded with stolen pieces, that he had travelled down on: the police had been after that. And those two fellows, Nobby and Fred, and that horrible fat woman, Big Annie, all of them ready, no doubt, to swear his life away. Even then he had not finished. There was that row at Ribsden Fair, the policeman who had wanted to see his licence, the flight and all the rest of it; he had been in that, and the policeman had had a good look at him. Why, everywhere he had been, he had been mixed up in something that was against the law, at every single step on the road! That fellow who kept the dining-room where he had had to leave a chisel. Poppleby his name was, that fellow would remember him and would give information as fast as it was wanted - taking the 'yuman line' as usual, the big, pasty-faced mess! Looking back, Mr Oakroyd saw these hostile witnesses springing up all along the line of his travels. 'I've done nowt,' he concluded mournfully, 'but I haven't a leg to stand on.'

Mr Oakroyd was a respectable working-man, not a member of the criminal classes, and therefore he did not regard the police as his natural enemies. On the other hand, his social level was not that of those comfortable and well-dressed persons who think of the police purely and simply as their protectors, who see them as so many stalwart, kindly, humorous, obliging fellows, all with big hearts of gold beneath their blue tunics. He and his friends in Bruddersford had no quarrel with the police but neither had they any tenderness for them. Their attitude was one of wary neutrality. A bobby was all right in his place, though he had a nasty trick of not keeping in his place. Mr Oakroyd in his time had known several policemen, had exchanged half-pints of ale and remarks about football with them, and had found them good, bad, and indifferent, like other people. Of their superiors - sergeants and inspectors and that lot - he was rather suspicious, believing that they were rather too fond of having 'cases' to be entirely just men or desirable companions. And of the Law itself, with all its mysterious routine and artful tricks, he had a real horror. 'You keep out, mate.' he had heard many a time, had repeated himself more than once. Neither he nor any of his friends was one of your born lawyers, a type known to every ship, every regiment, every factory, and not popular, the kind of men who always have their 'rights' off by heart, know exactly what you can't be made to do, and positively welcome the chance of standing up in a court of law. Mr Oakroyd knew very well that he was innocent, except in that matter of the insurance card, but he was ready to go to considerable lengths in order not to be compelled to prove his innocence. The idea of establishing his innocence and putting himself right with the authorities never once occurred to him; if the police were looking for him, then it was his business to keep out of their way; and if there are any persons to whom this attitude seems incomprehensible, then they simply do not understand Mr Oakroyd or anybody else in Ogden Street, Bruddersford.

The only satisfaction Mr Oakroyd had was the gloomy one of knowing now exactly where the catch was. By the next day, after much troubled reflection, he felt a hunted and haunted man. He had never noticed any policeman before in Sandybay, but now they seemed to spring up round every corner. He walked past them with his heart pounding away, and their suspicious eyes seemed to be digging in his back. And something was always turning up to remind him of his horrible position. Thus, in the afternoon, the Pavilion attendant, Curtis, the man with one eye and the long melancholy face, had to begin chattering.

'I see in the paper', said Curtis, 'where they've got that feller that did the big jewel robbery in the West End.'

Mr Oakroyd grunted.

'Made no mistake, got him fair and square,' he continued with enthusiasm. 'They only wanted a bit of time, that's all. Now, *he'll* get a bit of time.' And Curtis, who seemed to have found a subject that released him from his usual melancholy, laughed at his own pleasant wit. 'Fellers say to me, "Oh, they'll never get him," but I've said all along, "You wait and see, chum. Give 'em time." What d'you say, Mr Oakroyd?'

Mr Oakroyd only grunted again. He looked at his companion with shrinking distaste. One eye was lighted up and seemed to rove all over him maliciously, while the other, the glass one, was fixed on his face in a cold dead stare. The effect was most sinister.

'People can say what they like about the police,' Curtis went on, 'but I know a bit about 'em and I like to foiler these cases, and the conkerlusion I've come to is just this, Mr Oakroyd: Give the police time and they never miss their man.'

Mr Oakroyd merely made a clicking sound with his tongue and stared about him.

'Never miss their man,' the other repeated emphatically, at the same time tapping his listener on the arm.

Mr Oakroyd drew back sharply. 'Ar d'yer mean "Never miss their man"?' he said irritably.

'The feller they want they find,' said Curtis. 'It may not be this week. It may not be next week. But sooner or later' - and here he held out a large and dirty hand, then suddenly closed it - 'got him!' After this dramatic conclusion, he looked at Mr Oakroyd triumphantly out of his one eye.

'Nowt o' t'sort!' cried Mr Oakroyd angrily. 'If you ask me, they miss as monny as they catch.'

Curtis shook his head and smiled pityingly. 'That's what a lot o' people think, but they don't know. It's organization that does it. Organization, that's it.'

'It's all me eye,' said Mr Oakroyd.

'No, chum, it's all *their* eye.' And Curtis laughed again, and was so irritating that Mr Oakroyd told himself he would like to give him 'a bat on t'lug'.

'Friend of mine's got a brother-in-law in the Metrotropilitan - you know, up in London, proper Scotland Yard man. You ought to hear the tales he tells. Not a dog's chance, they haven't got, these fellers that's wanted.'

'All me eye and Betty Martin!' muttered Mr Oakroyd.

'What with photographs and fingerprints and telegraphs and wireless and flying squads!' cried Curtis ecstatically. 'Not a dog's chance! They give 'em a bit of rope and then - got him!'

'Ay, you did that afore!' Mr Oakroyd sneered. He was now thoroughly exasperated. 'What do you want to keep doing that for? It looks so daft. Got him, got him! You look as if you're trying to catch bluebottles.'

'I was just illustrating, so to speak, the way they can do it,' said Curtis meekly.

'Well, what's it got to do wi' you?' demanded Mr Oakroyd. 'Onnybody 'ud think to hear you talk they were makking you t'chief constable o' town - '

'All right, all right, chum. What's the matter with you?'

'Nowt's matter wi' me,' replied Mr Oakroyd, 'only don't keep on about it like that. You've told me. Well, let it drop, mate. I don't like to hear a man going on i' that fashion. Like a dam' bloodhound! They've done nowt to you.'

'Ar, you're too soft-hearted, that's it, Mr Oakroyd,' said Curtis, looking rather relieved. 'It does you credit in a way, but believe me, you can't afford it, not in these times. These fellers is best out of the way. I like to see 'em getting under lock and key.'

'I think yond's Mr Porson,' said Mr Oakroyd and so put an end to this unpleasant conversation. He took care to have no more little chats with Curtis after that. But now, any out-of-the-way incident began to look sinister. Things that would normally have excited his curiosity and given him the chance of indulging in the most delightful speculations, now made him all the more uneasy and secretive. There was, for example, that little talk he had with the chauffeur outside the Pavilion on Saturday afternoon, when he was helping with the extra chairs. Between two loads, when there was nothing to do, this chauffeur strolled up to him. He was a soldierly-looking chap in a fine blue uniform.

'Hope you don't mind me asking,' he said, 'but haven't you something to do with this troupe, The Good Companions?'

'That's right,' said Mr Oakroyd, with a touch of pride. 'If you want to knaw, I'm t'stage carpenter and property man for 'em.' He looked at the man. 'And I've seen you about t'place somewhere, I'm thinking.'

'Big blue Daimler,' said the chauffeur. 'You'll have seen it in the town. We're staying at the Great Eastern Hotel, on the front there. We've seen this show twice, and when I say "we", I mean the missis - not the wife, you know; she's at home - the Daimler's missis. I've seen it once too. We're coming again tonight. It's a good show.'

'You won't find a better, mate.'

'That is so. And it's not being patronized as it oughter be. Have a fag?'

'Nay, I nivver touch fags. I'm a pipe man missen.'

The chauffeur lit his cigarette and gave Mr Oakroyd a companionable nod or two. 'Well, you're like me, I expect. One place today and another tomorrow.'

'That's it,' said Mr Oakroyd, who liked this sort of talk. 'We're allus on t'road. Packing up again tomorn.'

'And where is it this time?' asked the chauffeur, with a casual air that seemed a bit overdone.

'Place called Winstead next week,' Mr Oakroyd replied, with all the nonchalance of a man who is ready to go anywhere at a moment's notice.

'Winstead, eh? Lemme see, that's a smallish town, sort of market town, in Northampton or Bedfordshire, isn't it?'

'Nay, I don't fairly knaw,' Mr Oakroyd admitted, still quite at ease. 'To tell truth, I've nivver set eyes on t'place.'

'And where after that?' the other pursued.

'Nah then, I'll ha' to think a bit. Is there a place called Haxby?'

'There is. It's Coventry way. Is that it?'

'It might be. I've heard 'em say summat about Haxby.'

The chauffeur examined his cigarette. 'And then where?' he asked.

'Well, there wor some talk about Middleford,' Mr Oakroyd admitted, 'but that might be t'week after or it might be monny a week after for all I knaw.'

'You couldn't get to know, I suppose, and give me a sort of a list?'

Mr Oakroyd stared. Then his easy friendly manner suddenly disappeared. 'Here, what's the idear?' he demanded. 'What's it matter to you where we're going?'

'I just wondered, that's all,' said the chauffeur, looking rather surprised. 'No harm in asking, is there?'

'There might not be and then again there might,' said Mr Oakroyd, eyeing him suspiciously. 'But I can't see what it's got to do wi' you, Mister. It's not all plain sailing i' this business. Yer nivver knaw who you're talking to,' he observed severely.

'That is so,' said the chauffeur.

'A chap i' my position has to be careful. I can't say what I like to onnybody as comes up and asks. There's wheels within wheels,' he added mysteriously.

'Well, if you want to know why I'm asking,' said the chauffeur, suddenly confidential, 'I'll tell you, though I'm not supposed to. It's the missis that wants to know.'

'The missis!' cried Mr Oakroyd, staring.

'Lady I'm working for,' explained the other, with a grin. 'If you ask me, she's taken a fancy to this troupe of yours. She's always taking a fancy to something. Too much money and not enough to do, that's her trouble. Widow, y'know, and rolling in money. And this morning she asked me to come and find out where you people was going to. Wants to come and have another look at you, though she didn't say so. So there you have it.'

'Ay,' said Mr Oakroyd reflectively.

'And you can't tell me any more?'

'That I can't.'

'All right. No harm done, is there?' The chauffeur gave him a nod, rather a contemptuous nod. 'So long!' And off he went.

Mr Oakroyd rubbed his chin and watched the retreating figure. 'Nay, lad,' he told it, 'tha's coming it a bit too thick. Missis wants to knaw! Missis nowt!' He did not believe this fantastic story, and still felt uneasy and suspicious, and therefore took care not to mention this encounter to any of the party. Perhaps if he had mentioned it, some of them might not have been so puzzled by the arrival of that bouquet for Mr Jerry Jerningham and by several other incidents that occurred later.

That last performance at Sandybay, as we know already, was a Night, and Mr Oakroyd enjoyed it as much as any of the others. Their triumph was his triumph. His broad face beamed in the wings throughout the show, and was so ruddy and shining that it looked - as somebody said - like an extra spot-light. But when it was over, when the last applauder had gone and all the props were put away, he saw the shadow creeping over him again. And was there ever such luck! There he was, as snugly suited as any man in England - and yet, Wanted. At any minute they might say 'Got him!' - and then where was he? Worse off than he was before. It made him sweat to think of it 'Done nowt,' he said again, very bitterly this time, 'but not a leg to stand on!'

'Now, Mr Oakroyd,' cried Miss Trant gaily when they were all standing at the Pier entrance, 'you must decide. Will you go in the car again, or would you rather go by train this time? Which do you think is the more romantic? I know you're a romantic person - like me.'

And then he had to think quickly, desperately. Which was the safer? That was the point. He saw himself being collared in a station. He saw himself being hauled out of the car. 'Nay, I don't fairly knaw,' he stammered. 'I mun think a minute, Miss Trant.'

'He's spoilt, that's what he is,' said Susie. 'But that's because he's our little mascot, aren't ta, lad?'

'Owd thi tongue, lass,' cried Mr Oakroyd. 'I'll go i' t'car, thank yer, Miss Trant.' Yes, the car would be safer. And he was not going to leave it at that. He would show them.

When he met Miss Trant the next morning he was very self-conscious, but she was too busy to notice that or anything else about him. 'Good morning, Mr Oakroyd,' she said. 'You're in good time.'

His face fell. A casual glance, and she had recognized him. But then, of course, she was expecting him. Then Susie joined them. There was usually a second person taken in the car, but never more than two because they carried as much luggage as possible. He greeted Susie with a sheepish grin.

'Hello, hello!' she cried. 'What's this? Look, Miss Trant. Do you see what he's done?'

Miss Trant smilingly examined him. 'You do look a little different,' she said.

'He's shaved his moustache off,' cried Susie.

'So he has,' said Miss Trant.

'He's tired of being behind the scenes. Is that it, Jess? Or did you leave it with your landlady as a little souvenir?'

'Don't be disgusting, Susie,' cried Miss Trant.

'I'll bet it makes me look different,' said Mr Oakroyd fingering his upper lip. 'Allus does, shaving off a moustache.'

'It doesn't much, you know,' Miss Trant told him.

'It's just the same sweet face from Shuddersford,' Susie assured him.

His heart sank. It looked as if he had given himself a stiff and raw upper lip for nothing. 'But don't you see owt else different?' he inquired, rather wistfully.

They both looked again. This time Miss Trant was first. 'I know,' she cried. 'You've got a new cap, Mr Oakroyd.'

'It looks the same to me, about two sizes too small,' said Susie.

'No, the other one was brown,' said Miss Trant.

'I believe it was,' cried Susie. 'And this is grey. I remember now. The old one was what they'd call in Yorkshire a mucky brown, in fact it was a mucky old cap. You can see he wants to be an actor now - what with being clean-shaven and going in for being dressy like that.'

Mr Oakroyd grinned nervously, and pushed the cap back a little, for being the same size as the other, that is, too small, it went sliding back equally well. But though he grinned, he was at heart very disappointed indeed. For one wild moment, after he had shaved that morning, he had had a vision of Miss Trant and Susie looking at him as he came up and wondering who it was. 'And half a crown gone on a cap an' all,' he told himself, 'and I liked t'owd un. Seems to me I'll ha' to grow a beard and wear a big trilby if I'm to disguise mysen. This is a hopeless case.' And he had already written to Ogden Street to say he would be in Winstead this coming week. If the police had got hold of that letter, it might be all up with him. He did not look forward at all to Winstead.

III

There is no pleasanter market town in all the East Midlands than Winstead, with its cobbled square and broad High Street, its fine fifteenth-century Parish Church, Elizabethan Market Hall, and old gabled houses. It is not a market town and nothing else, for it manufactures gloves, hosiery, and lace in a discreet gentlemanly fashion; there is plenty of money in the town; the shops in the High Street have quite a metropolitan air; Munsey's Cafe has an orchestra (piano, violin, and 'cello) and gives a *thé dansant* twice a week; and every ten minutes or so a bus comes into the market square from one or other of the numerous villages that regard Winstead as the centre of all things. It has one picture palace, and one small theatre, the Playhouse, which occasionally sandwiches a concert party in between two seasons of stock companies.

The Good Companions were at the Playhouse, and were doing better business there than they had done at Sandybay. The audiences were not wildly enthusiastic but they were fairly large and responsive every night, especially in the more expensive seats. Winstead - as they all told one another - was proving a good 'date'. All the players liked the town, with the exception of Jerry Jerningham, who hated the thought of playing in any place smaller than his native Birmingham and said that he was 'eating his hawt out in these little tawns'. Their lodgings were better than usual, they agreed; cleaner, more comfortable. They were fortunate in the weather, which was the best golden October brew, its sunshine as mellow as the old red-brick walls. Miss Trant, at home in such a place, enjoyed every hour there. Elsie discovered in the younger Mr Long, of Long and Passbury, estate agents and auctioneers in the High Street, a gentleman friend of her residential season at Cromer, two years before, and a friend ready to combine business with pleasure by taking her out in his two-seater. Susie pottered about, contentedly enough, though in secret she too sighed for cities and crowded streets; and if she was ever alone in her excursions, that was not the fault of her colleague, Inigo Jollifant. Mrs Joe, who was beginning to feel prosperous again, planned and began executing some vast knitting work, told her landlady all about George, and occasionally made a stately entrance into Munsey's Café. Joe himself strolled about in the sunshine with his pipe, listened to Mr Morton Mitcham's reminiscences, and played snooker with Jimmy Nunn. Jimmy, in his search for a digestion, had discovered a little chemist, just at the back of the High Street, who was a very droll card and might be worked up into a new number and act.

These people, however, were not wanted by the police. Mr Oakroyd, who was convinced that he was, did not enjoy himself at Winstead. Everything conspired to rob him of his peace of mind. The very sunlight only lit up his face before the eyes of every passing policeman. On the very second day there he had had an alarming experience. He had decided that it was no use skulking in his lodgings, though he was very comfortable and quite at home there, and so went boldly out, in the full light of the afternoon, to explore the town.

At the corner, turning into the square, he ran into a police sergeant, a large, unpleasant-looking chap, went right into him, with a bump. "'Ello, 'ello!' the sergeant growled. Mr Oakroyd gave him one startled glance, muttered something, and hurried away as fast as he could go without actually breaking into a run. He walked across the square, dodging between the buses, and then, slackening his pace, went down the High Street. There he met Jimmy Nunn, who was carrying a tiny parcel that only a chemist could have wrapped so neatly. Jimmy stopped him. 'Did you ever hear of this stuff, Oakroyd?' he said, holding up his packet. 'Pepsinate, they call it.' And he kept Mr Oakroyd there for five minutes listening to a description of Pepsinate, which had, it appeared, arrived at its final test, namely, a fight to a finish with Jimmy's stomach. At the end of these five minutes, Mr Oakroyd chanced to glance across the road. There, standing on the pavement and looking directly at him, was the large sergeant.

He hurriedly said good-bye to Jimmy, but this time took care not to appear as if he was running away, and merely sauntered along, stopping now and again to examine a shop window. The first time he ventured another glance across the road, the sergeant was still there and apparently still keeping an eye on him. The second time he glanced across, however, the sergeant was not to be seen. Mr Oakroyd pushed back his cap in sheer relief and admitted that he was a fool to frighten himself in this fashion. He stood staring idly at the side window of a boot shop. After a moment or two, he was still staring but no longer idly. There was something blue moving above that pair of gent's box calf. It was a reflection in the mirror at the back, and it was a reflection of a policeman's uniform. The sergeant was just behind him. He stooped down, pretending to tie a lace, and cocked an eye at the pavement, waiting to see a pair of regulation blue trousers move past. They did not come. Suddenly, he lunged forward and hurried off, without a glance behind him. As he went, he thought he heard a deep voice saying "'Ere, half a minute!' A few yards farther on, he slipped across the road, between two cars, and was just about to break into a run when he caught sight of another policeman eyeing him severely. The place was full of policemen.

'A nice little place like this an' all! What do they want so monny for?' He asked himself angrily. 'Gurt idle nowts! Waste o' fowk's brass, I calls it.' By this time, however, he had taken the first turning out of the High Street down a narrow sidestreet, and had come to another road full of shops. Here there were no policemen to be seen. Immensely relieved, he lit a pipe of Old Salt, and walked slowly along. A picture of a large steamer pulled him up. There was also a picture of a man standing in a cornfield, holding out his hands, and saying 'Come to Canada'. He spent several minutes looking at these and other pictures and thinking about Lily and Canada. The shop was a Tourist and Shipping Agency, and Mr Oakroyd, peeping in, could see a number of booklets spread out on the counter. He had examined some of those little books before, and they had a kindly trick of bringing Lily a bit nearer. Some of them might have a map that would show him just where she was. He went in and began turning over the booklets. Nobody bothered about him, and when he had looked them all over, he slipped two of the largest into his pocket and walked out. And there, looking straight at him, blocking up the whole pavement, was the sergeant.

'Well?' said the sergeant.

'What's up?' Mr Oakroyd stammered, his heart thumping away.

'What do you want to run away for?' The sergeant sounded very fierce indeed.

'Nay, I weren't running away,' replied Mr Oakroyd.

'And what's the idear 'aving this brogue?' the sergeant went on. There was a suggestion of good humour now beneath his fierceness. 'What d'you think you are now - Lancashire comedian?'

'What do you mean?' asked Mr Oakroyd desperately. 'Sorry,

Sergeant, but I don't foiler yer,' he added, more politely.

The sergeant stepped forward and looked at him so intently that his heart turned to water. It must, he thought be all up now. But the sergeant was beginning to look puzzled. 'You're either Jimmy Pearson,' he said finally, 'or his twin brother.'

'Nay, I'm not. I knaw nowt about onny Parsons. I'm a - I'm a - stranger here, Sergeant.'

'What's your name?'

'Oa - ' he began, then recollected himself. 'Oglethorpe,' he announced boldly. 'Sam Oglethorpe. And I come from Wabley i' Yorkshire.'

'And you sound as if you do, Mister,' said the sergeant. 'Well, you're the very spit of a feller called Pearson that used to live here. When you give me that bump in the square, I said to myself. "That's Jimmy Pearson come back. I'll 'ave a word with him." Not too fond of us, Jimmy wasn't - used to make a book now and again - but we didn't mind him. And the way you was dodging round was Jimmy all over.'

Mr Oakroyd saw that it would not do to pretend he had never seen the sergeant before. 'After I'd gi'en you such a bump at t'corner there, I thowt I'd better keep out o' t'road,' he said, with an appearance of great candour.

That was all right then. They were friendly enough when they parted, but the encounter had given Mr Oakroyd such a shock that its surprisingly happy ending did nothing to quieten his fears. If anything, he was more uneasy than before. He had given the sergeant a wrong name, and trouble might come of that. He had another shock the following night during the performance, when he was at the top of the little ladder working the light. Jerry Jerningham had just kicked both legs in the air when Mr Oakroyd noticed a policeman's helmet bobbing about in the wings. He nearly fell off the ladder. They had found him. He was free to descend now but he stopped where he was, in the hope that the policeman might overlook him. The next moment, however, he was looking down on the policeman's upturned face.

'Finished up there?'

'Ay.' said Mr Oakroyd reluctantly.

'Just come down a minute then.' said the policeman. At every step he expected to find the policeman grasping his collar. It was horrible.

'They said you'd be the feller to tell me,' said the policeman amiably, indeed quite apologetically. "Ave to 'ave a look around yer know. Council here's very particular. Fire and all that. Won't take a minute, but I've to ask a question or two.' And he pulled out a note-book and immediately looked grave and important.

Mr Oakroyd breathed again. 'Owt I can tell you, I will, mate.' he said earnestly, with the air of a man who was ready to put out a fire with his own hands.

The worst of it was that you never knew when you were safe even for an hour. The most innocent things suddenly became sinister, menacing. Thus, on Saturday morning, his landlady, Mrs Mason, whose husband was a porter at Long and Passbury's, the auctioneers, told Mr Oakroyd at breakfast-time that he must make sure of being in to tea. 'It's Milly's birthday today,' she announced, 'and we're having a bit of a spread and we want you to join us, if it's not asking too much. And Milly's young chap's coming too. You'll like 'im, a bit of good company he is. Six o'clock we're 'aving it becos that's as soon as he can get here.'

Mr Oakroyd liked nothing better than such festive occasions. Not only did he promise to be there but he arranged to get two tickets for the show that night for Milly and her young man, of whom he had heard vaguely but had never seen, as a birthday present. At half past five he was in the parlour, listening, with a show of interest for once, to the ponderous talk of Mr Mason, a very slow and solemn man, not too fond of work. Mr Mason seemed to think this was a suitable moment to discuss his attitude towards religion. 'Give me a bit of ritchool,' he was saying, 'I likes a bit of ritchool, Mr Oakroyd,' when his daughter Milly, a big bouncing girl, who earned good money at the glove factory and had no respect for her father, blew in like a coloured and scented gale and told him to 'dry up about his old ritchool'. Mr Oakroyd wished her many happy returns and handed over the tickets. For this he was soundly kissed, for he was in favour with Milly, who liked to think she was in touch with theatrical life and had retailed Mr Oakroyd's gossip to some profit during the week to the other girls at the glove factory. Then Mrs Mason, crimson, shining, and unfamiliar in her best, bustled in and said that tea was ready when they were.

'Tom's not 'ere yet,' said Milly. 'We'll wait. If he keeps us much longer, he'll 'ear from me when 'e does come.'

'Don't let 'im 'ear too much from you, Miss,' said her mother, delighted at such a spirit but not above giving a warning.

'She'll get 'er master yet in Tom,' Mr Mason observed ponderously. 'Or if she don't, then I'm surprised. 'E's big enough'

Tom was big enough. He was nearly six foot, very straight, very broad in the shoulders. He had a red face, a small clipped moustache, a twinkling eye, and any amount of jaw. In his new grey suit, he looked both stalwart and trim, and he was the kind of young fellow that Mr Oakroyd at any other time would have taken to at once, but now somehow he did not like the look of him. There was something unpleasant about the way in which he marched in, heavy on his feet.

'Comes in as if he's going to lock us all up,' cried Milly, asking them all with her eyes to admire him.

'Well, you be careful then, my girl,' said Tom with mock gruffness. And then he and Milly laughed, and Mr Mason and Mrs Mason laughed. Mr Oakroyd did not laugh; he only smiled vaguely; he was feeling rather uneasy. Tom had heard about him and the troupe, and was very pleased to meet him. Mr Oakroyd said he was very pleased too, and tried to look pleased, especially after he had had his hand almost pulped. They went in to tea.

Mr Oakroyd brightened up at the sight of the tea. There was boiled ham; there was tinned salmon, with vinegar; there was even jam pasty; it was a proper knife-and-fork, company tea that Bruddersford itself would not have despised. It reminded him of old times at home. And then no sooner had they got sat down than Mr Mason spoilt it all.

'Well, Tom,' said Mr Mason, 'arrested anybody lately? 'E's in the Force, Tom is,' he added, turning to Mr Oakroyd.

Mr Oakroyd nodded, and felt himself turning all colours. This was a nice mess he had landed himself into, having to eat all this tea right under a bobby's nose. 'Best thing tha can do, lad,' he told himself desperately, 'is to car quiet, say nowt.' And this was easy enough for a time, while Milly and her Tom were busy chaffing one another, but after that there was no escape for him. Grateful for the tickets and anxious to be polite, Tom insisted upon talking to him, asking him questions.

'Where did you say you came from?' said Tom.

'Leeds,' said Mr Oakroyd.

'I thought you said it was Bruddersford the other day, Mr Oakroyd,' cried Mrs Mason.

'It's all t'same,' replied Mr Oakroyd. 'You can't tell where one ends and t'other begins.' Nothing could be further from the truth, he knew, than this, but it might pass among these strangers. Indeed, strangers who actually visited the West Riding were inclined to take such views, seeing one endless town where natives could see half a dozen entirely different and warring communities.

'We don't often get 'em from your part down here,' said Tom reflectively. 'Funny thing, though, there's another chap just come here who's from your part, judging by your talk. Our sergeant was telling us about him. He was the very spit image of a little bookie that used to be here called Jimmy Pearson - '

'I've 'eard of him,' said Mr Mason with great solemnity.

'So the sarge follered him round to have a word with him, and then it turns out it wasn't the same feller.'

'Case o' mistaken identity you'd call that in the Force, wouldn't you?' said Mr Mason with even greater solemnity. 'Ar, I thought so.

Mistaken identity, that's what they'd call it, Ma.'

'Fancy!' cried Mrs Mason. 'Let me give you another cup of tea, Tom. Pass the stewed pears to Mr Oakroyd, Pa.'

'And this little feller came from Yorkshire the same as yourself,' said Tom, who was not the man to leave a tale half finished. 'Same sort of name too. The sarge did say what it was. Og - something or other.'

'It 'ud be Ogden,' announced Mr Mason complacently. 'Know the name well. I've sold at least two up in my time.'

'No, it wasn't Ogden,' said Tom. Then he looked at Mr Oakroyd. 'It was longer than Ogden. A real Yorkshire sort of name, it was. I thought you might know the name. You might know the man. Our sergeant said it was a bit fishy the way this feller kept getting out of his way at first, but he thinks everything's fishy, he does. That's the way they get to be sergeants.'

'I don't like a suspicious nature,' cried Milly. 'Don't you ever 'ave a suspicious nature, Tom, whatever you do.'

This seemed to Mr Oakroyd a very sensible remark. He himself tried to convey the impression that he could not be bothered with anything at that moment but stewed pears and custard and brown bread and butter. But he was not to be left alone.

'I was wondering if you might know this Og - something chap,' Tom said to him.

He shook his head. 'I've not heard tell of another Yorkshire chap here, but there may be onny number of 'em for all I knaw.'

Mr Mason had been ruminating and now he pronounced judgement. 'Tom won't 'ave a suspicious nature. Tom'll be too easy-going, that'll be his trouble.'

'No, it won't,' cried Milly. 'Will it, Tom?'

'He'll be there when he's wanted,' said Mrs Mason. 'Pass your cups up while it's nice and hot.'

'I've got eyes in my head,' said Tom, and as he said this his gaze wandered round the table and seemed to come to rest significantly on Mr Oakroyd, who was so disturbed by it that the pear he was cutting with his spoon suddenly shot off his plate and landed among the lemon-cheese tarts.

'Eh, dear!' cried Mr Oakroyd. 'Look what I'm doing.'

'You'll 'ave to be given in charge, Mr Oakroyd,' said Mr Mason waggishly. 'Here's a case for you, Tom. Damaging tarts with a pear.'

They laughed at this, and Mr Mason, thus encouraged, immediately took charge of the conversation. 'And joking apart, quite apart,' he began, just as if there were all manner of humorous diversions going forward elsewhere in the house, 'mentioning no names and intending no offence, I say it's time there were a few more cases in this town. Yes, and in other towns, a lot of other towns. And I know what I'm talking about - '

'No you don't, Pa,' said his daughter. 'Shut up.'

'And mind your elbow,' said his wife. 'Here, move that custard or he'll have it over in a minute.'

'There's people walking about the streets today', Mr Mason continued, 'that ought to be serving their time in gaol. Hundreds of 'em. We don't know when we're rubbing up against 'em. Isn't that so, Mr Oakroyd? You know that.'

'Ar d'you mean?' cried Mr Oakroyd, startled.

'Take no notice of 'im, Mr Oakroyd,' said his hostess. 'And make a good tea. You're not eating anything.'

'No offence and only in a manner of speaking,' said Mr Mason grandiosely. 'My meaning is that you're a man who sees the world, you're knocking about like meself, and you know it as well as I do. Wanted men, that's wot they are, and walking about the streets today as free as me and you, Mr Oakroyd. If I'd my way - '

'If you'd your way,' cried Milly, 'we'd all be in a mess next minute. Running down the police like that! Now you tell him something, Tom.'

'That's right,' said her mother. 'Give Tom a chance. And give Mr Oakroyd a piece of sandwich cake. He's eating nothing.'

'Well, I don't say we can work miracles,' said Tom, though he said it with an air of a man who might manage one or two if he tried. 'We can't and it isn't to be expected. But we know more than you people think we know. We can't pick a needle out of a haystack. And we can't afford to make mistakes.'

'Course you can't, Tom,' said Mrs Mason, who apparently had given this matter a great deal of thought. 'Pass your father's cup, Milly.'

'I've done nicely,' said Mr Mason. 'I want to listen.'

'Put it this way, then,' Tom continued. 'Supposing you're wanted for something, Mr Mason - '

'Don't take me, Tom. I'm too easy. Anybody knows where to find me in this town. I'm there at Long and Passbury's, have been for twenty years. It's money for nothing if it's me you're after. Take Mr Oakroyd 'ere. He's on the move. Nobody knows anything about ' im.'

'There's plenty knaws all about me,' Mr Oakroyd protested indignantly. What did this fool of a chap want to drag him in for! And why couldn't they change the subject! Surely they had been at it long enough!

'All right,' said Tom, 'we'll take Mr Oakroyd here. He's wanted. D'you see?' He looked very fierce and suddenly pointed a finger at the unhappy Mr Oakroyd. 'You're wanted. We're after you.' The Mason family laughed heartily at this by-play.

Mr Oakroyd had had enough of this. It might have been to his advantage to learn what happened when men were wanted, but he simply could not sit there any longer. 'Half a minute,' he cried, getting to his feet. 'What's time?'

'Only ten to,' Mrs Mason told him. 'You've ample time, Mr Oakroyd. You said this morning you wouldn't have to set off until quarter past seven.'

'Ay, I didn't knaw then,' he muttered. 'I've a right lot to do early on i' the-ater. I mun be off, Mrs Mason.' He departed to wash himself, leaving the others to rise from the table at their leisure.

Just as he was opening the front door, a heavy hand fell on the shoulder. He jumped. 'Eh!' he gasped, and turned round. It was Tom, looking a policeman every inch of him.

'Look out for us tonight, Mr Oakroyd,' said Tom heartily. 'You'll hear us clapping. And thanks for the tickets.'

'By gow! you made me jump,' cried Mr Oakroyd, and hurried away. He was determined that this Tom should not clap eyes on him again that night or any other night. He felt miserable. What with the salmon and the pears and the sandwich cake and all the shocks he had had, he felt queer inside.

'Good house tonight,' said Jimmy Nunn. 'Winstead's been a good date. I'm sorry to leave it.'

'Well, you can have it for me,' Mr Oakroyd told him. 'I reckon nowt o' t'place.'

'Why, what's wrong with it?'

'Iv'rything,' he replied bitterly, and went about his business.

IV

Mr Oakroyd felt that he could not go on much longer: his secret was weighing him down. 'I mun tell somebody,' he admitted to himself, 'or I'll be going right clean off me dot.' Some of the others were beginning to ask what was the matter with him. Jimmy Nunn thought he had the look of a man on the fringe - just on the mere fringe - of stomach trouble: one who 'would know about it later on'. Susie said he was homesick, pining for a sight of Bruddersford. Joe simply shook his head. It was a bad business. Mr Oakroyd felt ashamed of himself. He would have to tell somebody but he could not bring himself to do it, and felt worse every day.

They were now at Haxby, playing at The Kursaal, a horribly draughty building that had once been a small roller-skating rink. The audiences were not bad, though apt to be restive and noisy at the back.

The town itself, they all agreed, was hateful; a dark and dirty place, full of empty butchers' shops and men without collars who stood about waiting for the racing specials; and they complained of their lodgings, which were all smelly and uncomfortable, haunted by long-lost cabbages and prickly with old horsehair furniture. It was one of those places in which there is nothing to do during the day. They all hung about or went for listless walks or did some mending or tried to find cheerful company over a bottle of Guinness, and were glad when it was time to walk round to the stage door.

Haxby did not give Mr Oakroyd any of the shocks that Winstead had provided, but it seemed to depress him even more. There was something so dark and slinking about it. And his landlady, an elderly woman with a long yellow face, was not at all friendly but appeared to watch his every movement with suspicion. Nobody was better pleased than he was when Haxby was shut out, the lights turned up on the stage, and Inigo was rattling away on the piano, but even at the theatre they noticed he was out of spirits.

On Thursday night, however, he was a changed man. It was Inigo who remarked it first. 'Only another three nights in this hole, thank God!' he said, as they were standing together in the wings before the show began. 'Every time I come here I pass fifteen little butchers' shops and every one has nothing but an old, old leg of mutton in the window. I can't see them again, I really can't. They turn me up, absolutely, especially as I'm still finishing their elder brother at my digs. Gosh! what a town!'

'Nay,' Mr Oakroyd protested, 'it's noan so bad as all that. It's not t'place I'd like to come to for my holidays, but I've seen waar places ner this i' me time.' His voice had quite a new ring in it.

'Hello, hello!' cried Inigo, staring at him. 'What's happened to you, Master Oakroyd? Why are you now our little ray of sunshine? There's mystery here.'

Mr Oakroyd seemed rather confused. 'Nay, nowt's happened - much.'

'Come, come, this won't do,' said Inigo. 'You have a hidden life. There must be fairies at the bottom of your garden, as Mrs Joe points out sometimes in the key of E flat. What's happened?'

'Nowt - only I met a chap from Bruddersford today.'

'Ah - so that's it,' said Inigo. 'Do you hear that, Joe? Master Oakroyd's himself again because he's met a fellow-Bruddersfordian on this desert trail. Let the word go round, and song and cheer be all our what's its name.' And the word did go round, with the result that Mr Oakroyd was thoroughly chaffed all the rest of the night. Undoubtedly, they said, the little man had been homesick.

Mr Oakroyd did not care what they said. He had a welcoming grin for them all. He was happy again, haunted and hunted no longer. A chance meeting that afternoon had wakened him out of his bad dream.

After dinner (a bad one), he had gone for a stroll round the main streets of the town, smoking his Old Salt and wondering whether it would be worth while having a glass of ale before the pubs closed for the afternoon. Outside the White Hart, the largest pub in the place, he had noticed a little car and there had seemed something familiar about it even at a distance. As soon as he was close enough to see that the back seat of this car had been converted into a kind of large box, Mr Oakroyd recognized it at once. He knew that car well for he had spent a whole day working on it. That box arrangement (to hold samples) was nothing less than his own handiwork. And there were the Bruddersford registration letters. That car was the one used by Mr Ashworth, one of Higden's travellers. Mr Ashworth was probably inside the White Hart, where he would be giving a good account of himself, at that very moment.

(And let it be said here and now that this encounter with Mr Ashworth does not involve any undue stretching of the arm of coincidence. Those who imagine it does are simply living in ignorance, not being acquainted with the West Riding trade. Every week, travellers, local men with broad shoulders and broader vowels, leave Bruddersford to visit all the towns in this island, to cross the seas to Gothenburg, Amsterdam, Antwerp, Lille, and Milan, to sail round the globe itself and pop up in Sydney or Buenos Aires. Higden's is one of the largest firms in Bruddersford, and you might meet a man from Higden's anywhere and at any moment.)

Then Mr Oakroyd had an inspiration. He would tell his tale to Mr Ashworth, who had always had a word for him and was undoubtedly a chap with a head on his shoulders. He entered the White Hart. Mr Ashworth was not in the bar and not in the Smoke Room, which meant that he was not downstairs at all, for he was not one of your tap-room men. While Mr Oakroyd was hesitating, he was asked what he wanted, and was then told that one gent was still having his lunch in the coffee-room upstairs. That was Mr Ashworth. Mr Oakroyd found him in a corner of the deserted room, eating cheese and biscuits and looking idly at a newspaper.

Mr Ashworth, a big man with a vast expanse of red cheeks, several chins, and prominent light blue eyes, glanced towards the approaching figure of Mr Oakroyd, then stared at him. 'Here,' he called out, 'I know you, don't I.'

'That's right, Mr Ashworth,' said the other, walking up. 'How are you getting on?'

'Why, it's Oakroyd! What are you doing here? I heard you got stopped at Higden's. Dam' shame too, the time you'd been there! Here, sit you down.'

But Mr Oakroyd first explained how he came to be in Haxby at all, and then said, in conclusion: 'And I'd like to tell you about summat that's been right bothering me, Mr Ashworth, if you wouldn't mind.'

Mr Ashworth, who had probably been rather bored, did not mind at all. 'But we're not stopping here, lad,' he said. 'We'll find a corner downstairs and have one. Then we can talk in comfort.' And they went downstairs, had a double whisky and a pint put before them, and then Mr Oakroyd plunged into his tale, beginning with his adventures with George, the night before he left Bruddersford, and ending with Leonard's letter. 'And, as you see for yersen, Mr Ashworth,' he concluded, 'I've done nowt - nobbut tearing up me card, that is - but what wi' one thing and t'other it looked to me as if I hadn't got a leg to stand on.'

'But how did they come to be looking for you in Bruddersford?' the other inquired.

'All through that big daft George business,' replied Mr Oakroyd. 'That's t'only thing that could ha' started 'em. This bobby, you see, Mr Ashworth, tells me not to foiler this George, and he sees me face and he knaws where I live, Ogden Street, 'cos I told him. Nah then, when this chap, George, says after that he's been robbed, this bobby remembers me and begins making a few inquiries like, and they find out I've taken me hook all of a sudden and that starts 'em off.'

Mr Ashworth looked at his downcast face for a minute then burst into a sudden and startling roar of laughter. 'Well, I'll be damned! Nay, Oakroyd, lad! That was George Jobley, wasn't it?'

'Ay, that's t'name. Do yer knaw him?'

'Know him! T-t-t - ' Mr Ashworth went on making this t-t-t noise for about two minutes. 'I'd be a sight better off if I didn't know him. He's had many a quid of mine for something that didn't run or couldn't run. But I remember that business. It was all nowt. He was in the rats. He's never lost any hundred and twenty pound, not he, and he admitted it after. That's the bit they never put in the paper, of course.'

'D'you mean to say', demanded Mr Oakroyd, 't'police hasn't tak'n t'case up?'

'I should think I do mean to say it. Case! There isn't enough case to make a pigeon egg. If you've been fancying yourself as one of these chaps they're all looking for and can't catch, you can stop this minute. I don't care what your lad wrote, it's all nowt. He's been reading penny bloods.'

'Are you sure, Mr Ashworth?'

'Certain. You can go and walk up and down Woolgate all day tomorrow, and I'll give you five bob for every time the police look twice at you. Nay,' he concluded in his broadest accent, 'they've summat better to do than bother wi' thee, lad.'

'Well, by gow! you've tak'n a load off my mind, Mr Ashworth,' cried Mr Oakroyd fervently, 'you have an' all! It's been spoiling t'best job I ivver had. Eh, I don't knaw I'm born nar.' He rubbed his hands, finished his pint, then relit his pipe. When he saw that his companion had also finished his drink, he said earnestly: 'Nah you'll ha' one wi' me, Mr Ashworth. You've right set me up.'

Five minutes later, deep in his second pint, he observed happily: 'You knaw, Mr Ashworth, when I tinkered up that car o' yours, I nivver thowt I'd soon be a bit i' t'same line mesen. But we're both on t'road, aren't we?' He smoked luxuriously for a minute, and then added: 'And nah there's summat I've been meaning to ask you all along and I mun do it afore I forget.' He took a pull at his beer and looked speculatively at his companion over the top of his glass.

'How's that new centre forrard doing for t'United?'

Mr Oakroyd was himself again.

CHAPTER FIVE
Inigo Jumps Out of a Train and Finds Himself in Love

I

'NOW this', said Mrs Joe impressively, taking up the last little heap of cards, 'is what's sure to come true.'

'What was all the rest then?' Inigo asked.

'Look here, Inigo,' cried Susie, 'whose fortune is this, mine or yours? You're not a bit funny. Go on, my dear. Don't take any notice of him.'

Mrs Joe was examining the cards with sibylline gravity.' I see here great success for you, my dear. Money, admiration, power, everything - a really great success. And it'll come quite unexpectedly in a Five.'

'Five what? Can't you tell?'

'No, it's just a Five. And it'll all come through a dark man, a very dark man.'

'Perhaps it's a nigger,' suggested Jimmy Nunn.

'Oh, shut up, Jimmy!' cried Susie. 'You're old enough to know better. How am I going to meet this man? That's what I want to know.'

'Talking of niggers,' said Mr Morton Mitcham to nobody in particular, 'I was in New Orleans one time and there was an old nigger mammy there who could tell fortunes. She did it with melon seeds. She told me I was going to break my arm within a week. "Don't you go to de North or de West, sah," she said to me. But I did, though. And just a week after that, in Nashville -' He paused and looked from one to another of them.

Joe took his pipe out of his mouth. 'You broke your arm, like she said,' he prompted.

'No, I didn't do just that,' said Mr Mitcham solemnly, 'and I won't pretend I did. But just one week after that I was with a fellow - and I'll tell you who he was; he was old Horace Carson who used to go round with the *Woman in a Barrel* illusion - and he broke his leg. Queer, wasn't it? And another time, out East, there was an old Chink - '

'Well, Susie, you can't want a better fortune than that, my dear,' said Mrs Joe. 'You'll have a lot of worries and trouble in a Two, as I said, but after that everything's going to be bright for you, and I'm sure I wish I could say the same for us all.'

'Don't you think you could if you tried hard enough?' asked Inigo, looking innocent.

'There he goes again!' cried Susie. 'Pretending he thinks it's all nonsense, and all the time he's dying to have a good fortune himself and is furious because he can't have one.'

'Don't be a scoffer, Mr Jollifant,' said Mrs Joe earnestly. 'I've known people to scoff at these things once too often, like that young fellow who came to the Rawston Repertory when we were there. What was his name, Joe?' she called across to him.

'What was whose name?' asked Joe.

'That young fellow who came to the Rawston and who'd once been in a lawyer's office or somewhere and didn't believe in bad luck and good luck and all that.'

'Oh, that chap,' said Joe. 'I remember him well. Best solo whist player I ever struck, he was. Knew every card in your hand. I remember him all right.'

'What was his name?' screamed his wife. 'Don't keep telling me you remember him. All I want is his name.'

Joe thought for a moment. 'I've forgotten his name,' he confessed.

'Just like you, Joe,' and she dismissed him with affectionate scorn. 'That's Joe all over,' she explained to the others at her end of the compartment. 'He'd keep on for an hour telling me he remembered him, if I'd let him, and then he doesn't even remember the man's name. Well, as I was saying, this young fellow came to the company and told us all there was too much of this superstition on the stage and he didn't believe in it, and to show us he didn't believe in it, he went out of his way to do all the things that bring bad luck, and put things in the dressing-room, spoke the tag at rehearsals, and everything. He'd show us it was all rubbish, he said. Well, what came of it?' She asked this in a low thrilling voice and fixed her gaze upon Inigo.

'Well, did anything come of it?' asked Inigo, who felt that he was capable of following this young man's example himself.

'I should think it did,' cried Mrs Joe triumphantly. 'He had his notice in less than a month.'

'Served him right, too,' said Susie very severely. 'But how did it happen?'

'Oh, we all complained to the management about him,' replied Mrs Joe. 'Either he goes or we do, we said, and so he had to go.' She stared at Inigo, who had suddenly burst out laughing. 'Funny to you it may be, Mr Jollifant, but it wasn't funny to us and it went to our hearts to have to do it but we couldn't have him deliberately ruining the luck for everybody. And he brought on his own bad luck, didn't he?'

'But don't you see - ' Inigo began, but then stopped because it was obvious that she did not see. Moreover, Susie was telling him to be quiet and not to talk about things he did not understand.

'Ai don't believe mech in these things,' Mr Jerry Jerningham announced, fluttering his long eyelashes at the company.

'You don't believe in anything,' said Miss Longstaff, who appeared to have wakened up specially to make this remark. 'All you believe in is yourself and White's dancing shoes and that stuff that says handsome men are slightly sunburnt.' It was clear that Mr Jerningham could not be numbered among Elsie's gentlemen friends.

'Dewn't you be so personal,' said Mr Jerningham, permitting his exquisite features to register indignation. 'You're always passing remawks. And Ai know whai. Oh yes, Ai know whai.' There was - as the ladies told one another afterwards - bouquet written all over him.

Susie began chanting a little composition of her own:

'Pretty Mister Jerningham
Came from Birmingham,
Where he'd been learning 'em,
And some say turning 'em
Up up up.'

'Now then, you girls,' said Jimmy, 'leave the boy alone. You're only jealous. If there's no more fortune-telling going on at that end, we'll have the cards back, please. What about another game of solo, Joe?'

'It's getting quite warm in here,' Mr Mitcham observed, and began taking off his overcoat.

'Exit the Silver King,' murmured Susie. This was the name they had given Mr Mitcham's overcoat, which was no ordinary garment. It had first made its appearance at Haxby (where Mr Mitcham had bought it in a second-hand clothier's for twenty-eight shillings), and immediately it had seemed as if another person had joined the party. Mr Mitcham was now described as 'travelling an overcoat', just as some players are said to 'travel' a mother or other relative. It was a gigantic plaid ulster and its collar was decorated with a few inches of fur from some mysterious and long extinct species. It had the air of having been round the world far more times than Mr Mitcham himself, and of having seen places that its owner would never be permitted to see. At any moment (as Inigo had remarked), you felt that this astounding overcoat might begin to supplement Mr Mitcham's travel reminiscences or set him right in a loud voice. And Jimmy Nunn swore that he had to take out an extra railway ticket for it and that every time it was taken into a third-class carriage its fur stood on end. Such was the Silver King, which Mr Mitcham now folded and, after some difficulty, found a place for on the rack.

After Haxby The Good Companions had had several three-night and two-night stands in the same neighbourhood, and it was now the middle of November. This Sunday journey to Middleford was the longest they had undertaken so far, for Middleford, as everybody ought to know, is one of those grim coal-and-iron towns of the North-East. Miss Trant had taken Mr Oakroyd with her in the car, on which he now kept a knowing eye, but all the other eight of them, as we have seen, were travelling in this train and they filled the compartment. They had been there for the last three hours, exchanging stories, playing cards, telling fortunes, eating sandwiches and chocolate, reading, smoking, yawning, dozing, staring out of the windows at the vague grey places that went wobbling past. It was a raw day - and, as usual, seemed all the more raw because it was Sunday - and at first the railway carriage had been miserably cold, but now it was not merely snug but downright stuffy. Jimmy Nunn, Joe, Mitcham, and Jerningham played a few more languid hands of solo whist; Mrs Joe knitted; Elsie closed her eyes again; Susie read a few more pages of *The Pianola Mystery*; and Inigo wrestled with several large Sunday newspapers.

'Hello!' said Jimmy, wiping the window and peering out. 'This looks like Hicklefield. We're running to time today.'

'Don't we change here?' said Inigo.

'We do,' Jimmy replied. 'And we've just twenty minutes. Time to get a drink.'

'Everybody changes here,' said Mrs Joe, putting away her knitting. 'I seem to have spent half my life in this station. Every time I've ever gone North, they've run me into Hicklefield, to change trains.'

The others agreed that Hicklefield was inevitable, and told one another how often they had met people they knew in the refreshment-room. They were now running slowly into the gloomy cavern of the station itself. Then a curious thing happened. Jimmy Nunn, who had let down the window and was looking out, gave a little cry and then suddenly sat down in his corner.

'Well, I'll be damned!' he gasped, staring before him. All the colour had drained out of his queer puckered face. He looked ill.

'Jimmy! Jimmy! What's the matter?' they were all crying.

He was pressing his hand now on his heart. His lips were blue. 'All right. It's nothing,' he groaned. 'Just a bit of - of - an attack, that's all. Get me - that bag down - ol' man - you'll find a flask in it. That's it. Ah - that's better!' The colour returned to his face, beginning with his nose, so that for a moment or two he looked as if he had his comic make-up on and there seemed a horrible touch of drollery in his still chattering teeth.

'Jimmy, my dear!' said Susie, her hand on his shoulder. 'What's happened? You did give me a fright. Don't do it again, will you?'

There was no time for more. The train had stopped now. Inigo and Morton Mitcham said they would see the baggage into the next train, which was already waiting at a neighbouring platform. The others were going off at once to the refreshment-room, but Jimmy, who was still shaky, refused to accompany them, so Susie insisted upon taking him over to the Middleford train. But when Inigo had finished with the baggage, he found Jimmy sitting there alone.

'Where's Susie?' he asked.

'I packed her off to get a cup o' tea for herself,' Jimmy replied. 'Is Mitcham trying for a quick one?'

'He is,' said Inigo, helping the porter with the smaller things, which they were spreading on the seats. 'There's still ten minutes, but I'm not going to bother. I don't like these lightning drinks.'

After a few minutes, Joe and his wife came along, announcing they had seen and spoken with Tommy Verney and Mabel Ross, late of The Merry Mascots. 'They're resting now,' panted Mrs Joe, 'then opening at Warrington in *Cinderella* - Baron Hardup and Dandini.' Then Elsie and Jerry Jerningham dis-engaged themselves from a group of people (the *Money for Dust!* Company on the Broadhead Tour) at the end of the platform, and came hurrying along, chanting the names of all the acquaintances they had seen. Then Mr Morton Mitcham, magnificent in the Silver King, stalked up, to point out that he had had two while some fellows, there before he was, had not been able to secure a single drink. 'It's an art as much as anything else,' he concluded triumphantly, and Jimmy and Joe acknowledged that he was undoubtedly a fast worker.

'Where's Susie?' asked Inigo.

Mr Mitcham thought he had seen her in the refreshment-room, talking to some people. 'There's three minutes yet,' he added. 'She can make it - easy. Did I ever tell you how I once caught the Twentieth-Century Limited?'

At this moment, however, a porter slammed the door. Jimmy and Mrs Joe both tried to look out of the window at the same time. 'By jingo!' cried Jimmy anxiously, 'but she'll have to hurry up. I can't see her, and they're getting their flags and whistles ready.'

'Just a minute!' said Inigo. 'Do let me have a look.'

'Can't see her anywhere.' said Jimmy.

A whistle sounded.

'There she is!' cried Jimmy. 'Eh, what's your name, guard? - half a minute! Oh, the silly devils! Gosh, we're off! She's missed it!'

'Then so have I,' roared Inigo. 'Get back, Jimmy. I'm getting out.' The train was actually moving now, though very slowly. He opened the door, dropped out, and fell flat on his back on the platform.

Jimmy fumbled desperately in his pocket while the others were shouting. 'Here!' he cried. 'Tickets!' He threw out two tickets which fell on the platform and were picked up by a porter, whose attention was then directed to Inigo by the frantic gesticulations of Jimmy. The next moment they were out of the station.

'Well I'll be - ' Joe did not say what he would be, but simply blew out his breath. The others, however, appeared to agree with him. 'For the minute', said Mrs Joe, 'I didn't know I'd a heart in my body.'

'Well, I've thought for some time he was sweet on Susie,' said Elsie, 'but I didn't know it was as bad as that.'

'I've seen it all along,' said Mrs Joe, with a huge sentimental sigh. 'That's what I call love, that is.'

'Oh, he's gone on her, is he?' said Joe, staring innocently at his wife.' Is that why he went and jumped out?'

'Of course it is, Joe. Don't be silly,' said his wife sharply. 'And you needn't look so surprised about it. He hasn't gone wrong in his head. If I was stranded like that, you'd jump out of a train, wouldn't you?'

Joe rubbed his chin and looked bewildered. 'I suppose so,' he said finally.

'You don't seem very sure about it.'

'All right then, I would,' said Joe. 'You try me and see.'

'And then go and break your neck, I suppose,' said his wife, still sharply. 'And then we'd be in a fine mess, wouldn't we? I've never heard a man talk in such a silly way as you do sometimes, Joe,' she concluded severely.

Joe looked at her in despair. Then he looked at Mr Morton Mitcham, who in his turn was looking at Jimmy. All three gentlemen exchanged glances, and they were glances of a deep philosophical significance, such as may be exchanged among members of a sex not entirely devoid of reason, not wholly given over to whims and fancies and irrational outbursts.

II

'And did you really jump out just to keep me company?' said Susie.' I think it's sweet of you, Inigo.'

Inigo himself, though he did not say so, thought it was rather sweet of him too. He had just been admonished by the North-Eastern Railway, had still a good deal of that railway's dust on his clothes, and had not quite recovered from his encounter with that railway's platform. The porter had handed over the two tickets that Jimmy had thrown out, but Inigo had neither overcoat nor hat, and felt chilly, shaken up and somewhat ridiculous.

'The very first thing we must do now', said Susie rather sternly, just as if he had proposed a few games of chess, 'is to find out when the next train goes to Middleford.'

'Yes, I'd thought of that myself,' said Inigo meekly.

Together, they examined the indicator, which informed them that the next train to Middleford would leave No 2 Platform at 7.45 p.m.

'Over four hours to wait here,' said Inigo.

'And when will it arrive at Middleford?' asked Susie. 'That's what it doesn't say. About the crack of dawn, I suppose.'

'The time-table over there will tell us that,' said Inigo, and led her towards it. After much pointing and running up and down of fingers, they discovered that the 7.45 arrived in Middleford at 11 o'clock.

'That'll be all right,' said Susie. 'Jimmy or one of the others will be sure to meet us. They'll look up the train too, and they'll have got us some digs. This isn't the first time this has happened to me, as Jimmy will tell you.'

Here she was stopped by a cough. It came from a middle-aged woman dressed in black who had been glancing at the time-table next to theirs. She had a long angular face, and her lips were tightly compressed. Inigo had noticed her when they first came up, for she was looking at the time-table as if there might be something wildly indecent in it. And now she coughed, not apologetically but peremptorily; it was like a tap on the shoulder. They looked at her, and she looked steadily from one to the other of them.

'Maybe you're theatricals?' she asked at last.

Yes, they were.

'Changing trains here?' she asked.

Changing and losing trains, they told her, and then exchanged quick, glances. 'Busybody?' Inigo's glance asked. 'Probably looking for lodgers,' Susie's replied.

'And when did you come in?' she inquired. After they had told her that too, and had even indicated the direction of the train, she looked at them more fixedly than ever, arid finally said: 'You don't happen to have been travelling with a Mr Nunn?'

'What, Jimmy Nunn!' cried Susie.

'James Nunn,' she replied firmly.

'I should think we were,' said Susie. 'We're all in the same show, The Good Companions. And Jimmy's an old friend of mine. D'you know him?'

The angular woman paid no attention to this question. 'Pierrot troupe, is it?' she said. 'And where are you going to now?'

Middleford, they told her.

'And where to next week?' she asked.

This was very puzzling. Susie looked at Inigo and hesitated. 'Well, if you want to know,' said Inigo, in that special no-concern-of-yours voice we always employ with that opening phrase, 'we're going to a place called Tewborough.'

'Not far from here,' said the woman.

'We're playing at the Theatre Royal there.' said Susie, not without pride.

'Humph. Not much good'll come o' that,' she said grimly, looking still more angular. 'What is it you call yourselves? *Good Companions*? And you're sure Mr Nunn's with you, are you?'

'Of course we are,' replied Susie, rather indignantly. 'We shall see him tonight or tomorrow morning. D'you know him? Can we give him a message?'

'James Nunn'll want no message from me. I saw him on that train, and if I'm not mistaken he saw me.' She looked hard at them both, then gave herself a little shake. 'I'm his wife,' she said quietly, and began walking away.

Inigo stared. Susie gasped, then ran forward. 'I say though,' she cried, stopping the woman, 'how extraordinary! I've known Jimmy for ages and never knew - '

'He'd a wife. No, I'll be bound you didn't.'

'But listen! I'm Susie Dean, and Jimmy used to know my father very well.'

'And I knew him too,' said this astonishing Mrs Nunn quite calmly. 'I might have known you were Charlie Dean's girl, for you've the look of him.'

'But how wonderful!' cried Susie. She was almost dancing with excitement.

'Is it?'

'Of course it is.'

'Why?' said Mrs Nunn, without the least flicker of interest. 'I don't call it wonderful. It takes more than that to surprise me. Good afternoon.'

'But surely you're not going away just like that,' said Susie. 'I mean, not *saying* anything at all. You simply can't go like that.'

Mrs Nunn gave her a long level stare. 'What is it you want to know?' she demanded.

'Well, it isn't exactly that I want to *know* anything,' Susie explained,' but you see - meeting you like this - '

'Without any intention of being rude and while thanking you for answering any questions I might have asked,' said Mrs Nunn, in a very angular voice, 'I must tell you that you're a good deal too excitable. You get out of the habit of working yourself up about nothing or it'll grow on you, Miss. And that's all there is to it. Good afternoon.' And she marched off without another word.

'Well, of all the dried-up, bony, beastly women!' cried Susie, rejoining Inigo, who had hung back. 'Did you hear her?'

'Jimmy saw her,' Inigo announced. 'He saw her on the platform when he was looking out of the window. Don't you remember how queer he went?'

'And no wonder!' said Susie. 'But isn't it strange? I never knew he had a wife.' And for several minutes she exclaimed at this discovery and then sketched in various accounts of Jimmy's past, in all of which no blame was attached to him.

'We've heard of the skeleton in the cupboard.' said Inigo meditatively.

'And she's it,' Susie put in quickly. 'And now we won't talk any more about her. The point is, where are we going?' They were now out of the station and had wandered into what was presumably one of the main streets of the town.

'So this is Hicklefield,' said Inigo, looking about him with distaste and shivering a little. 'Methinks the air doth not smell wooingly here, my Sue. In fact the place gives me the hump, absolutely.'

There was a light fog over the town. The shuttered shops and banks and warehouses were vague shapes and like the scenery of some dismal dream. Cars came sliding from nowhere, twisted this way and that, hooted like wounded monsters, then slipped away into nothingness. Ponderous trams loomed up, creaking and groaning, stopped to swallow a few morsels of humanity, and lumbered off to unimaginable places. A policeman, an antique taxi-cab, a man with newspapers, a woman in an imitation sealskin coat, and a few other persons and things, were standing there, apparently waiting for Doomsday to break. Nothing broke the grey monotony but the pavement itself, which was startlingly black in its grime. There was no colour, no sparkle of life, anywhere.

'My God!' cried Inigo. 'Let's get out of this, Susie. Another minute of this and I give up hope.'

'We'll jump on that tram', she said, pointing, 'and see what happens. Come on.' They raced down the street and boarded the tram just as it was moving off, to the delight of the conductor, who plainly had not expected anything at all to happen that afternoon. The top of the tram was covered, and they climbed up there and sat in a curved little place in front.

'Now this is much better,' said Susie, peeping out at a moving Hicklefield.

'Isn't it?' he replied. 'Like being on a galleon.'

But he was not looking at Hicklefield but at Susie herself who seemed more vivid and radiant than ever, and as he looked at her he found himself possessed by a most curious feeling, a kind of ache, made up of wild happiness and sickly excitement. He realized at once that this place, the front of this tram in Hicklefield, was the only place in the world for him, and when he thought of other places, where there was no Susie, from the Savoy Grill to the sunlit beaches of Hawaii, they appeared to be nothing but desolations. He realized in a flash that it would be better even to be miserable with her than to be anywhere else, for so long as she was there the world would still be enchanted, whereas if she were not there it would be a mere dark huddle of things. He knew now he was in love with her, and would go on being in love with her for ever and ever. This was it, there could be no mistake. He had jumped out of the train simply because he could not bear being without her; he had jumped and had fallen, head over heels over head over heels, in love.

'Susie,' he said, 'I say, Susie.' And then he stopped. His voice sounded ridiculous, like the bleating of a sheep.

'Well, Inigo?' Her dark eyes were fixed upon his for a moment, then suddenly their expression changed. She was looking at the conductor, who was now standing at Inigo's elbow. They asked him where they could go, if there was any chance of getting tea at the journey's end, and he told them that about half a mile or so beyond the terminus there was a fine big hotel, standing on a main road and largely patronized by 'motterists'. It was, they gathered, a most sumptuous establishment, and Inigo decided at once that they must go there and have tea. As it was nearly an hour's ride to the terminus, they would neatly dispose of the time before the evening train.

After the conductor had gone, Inigo had no further opportunity of telling Susie what had happened. It was she who began talking now. He smoked his pipe, watched the delightful play of her features, and listened half-dreamily to what she had to say. Now and again her voice was completely drowned by the groaning of the tram as it mounted a hill. It was all as odd and queerly moving as a dream: the mysterious stretches of Hicklefield darkening below them; the little place, so cosily their own, on the tram; Susie, with her eyes deepening into reverie, lost in remembrance; the tale of her past that progressed as they progressed, a dream within a dream: it was all so strange. He has never forgotten it.

'You're in for an awful time, Inigo,' she began, smiling vaguely at him. 'I'm going to tell you the story of my life. No, I'm not really, but I can't help thinking about everything in the past. It's all going jumbling away in my head. Meeting that woman, I suppose. I keep thinking about my father. Did you hear her mention him? He was on the stage, and so was mother. They were both in musical comedy. He was a baritone lead in touring companies, and she used to do soubrette parts. French maids as a rule. She was half-French and she'd an awfully good accent. They used to play in those funny old jiggety-joggety things, *The Country Girl* and *The Geisha* and *The Circus Girl*. They were both playing in *Florodora* when they got married, in Manchester. I can remember a dressing-case thing Dad always had with him and it was a wedding present and had something on it, you know: "With the Best Wishes of the Florodora Company, Manchester", and all the rest of it. It's silly but I just want to cry when I think of that. I don't know why, exactly, but I can sort of see them there in Manchester and their *Florodora* and "Tell me, Pretty Maiden" and everything - little, little figures, all very excited and happy, and when I think of them, these little figures are all in a bright light, but they're ever so tiny and all round them is a huge blackness, and it's back there in nineteen hundred and two and not one of them knows what's going to happen. Do you see, Inigo? I'm sure you don't, and I simply can't begin to make you understand how I see it. But it's just - sort of - life, the real thing, and either you've got to laugh at it, or cry, a bit when you see it like that, really you have. Now say I'm silly.'

He shook his head, and the look he fastened upon her offered her everything he had. But she was not thinking about him. She was still groping among her memories. When she began again, it was in a very subdued voice, and he could only catch an occasional word here and there. It was something about her mother, who had died only a year or two after Susie was born. He gathered that she had been looked after then by an aunt for several years. Then he heard more, for the tram was quiet and she was raising her voice a little.

'That's the queerest part and the one I remember best,' she was saying, 'when Father decided to take me round with him on tour. I was about five or six when that began, and it went on for several years. It's all such a funny muddle, though bits of it are frightfully clear. Going round dozens of towns, but they all seemed alike. Only sometimes the landladies called me "poor little dearie" and sometimes "puir wee lassie" and sometimes "doy" and sometimes "hinny" - I remember that awfully well. And often when there was a matinée, Dad would take me with him, and when he was on I'd be held up in the wings and sit in the dressing-rooms, sitting on comedians' knees or in chorus girls' laps, and I'd be given chocolates, and everything was always so queer and smelly - grease paint and powder and gas, you know - but I'd hear the band playing and people laughing and clapping, and I loved all that. It was horrible sometimes at night, though, when I had to go to bed before Dad went down to the theatre, and sometimes the landladies were horrible, with huge red faces and smelling of whisky. And the rooms too. I can see one now - it seemed enormous, with giant pieces of furniture and awful dark cupboards with Things in them waiting to spring but on you - and the blinds weren't down properly and the horrible greeny light of the lamp outside in the street shone in, and I'd shiver and shiver there every night, creeping down under the clothes and just waiting for something to come - bump! But then sometimes when Father came back, I'd wake up and go downstairs and he would be having his supper and perhaps he'd give me some. He adored cow-heels, done in milk and with onions - and so do I. We had scores and scores of little jokes we used to repeat over and over again. Dad said that bringing out these jokes was the only way he had of furnishing the home. He didn't drink much, not then anyhow, but I always knew when he'd had one too many because he always came and cried over me and said I must promise never to go near the stage, and always ended by giving me what he called elocution and ear-tests and telling me I had only to work hard to get to the top one day because it was born in me. But he was a darling, very handsome and with a jolly good voice, and all the landladies adored him and so did most of the women in the companies he was with; even I could see that. But then he decided it wasn't good for me any more, and I had to live with another aunt near Clapham Common and go to school - oh, hateful!'

By the time he had learned how she fought against the dull horrors of life near Clapham Common, how she returned to her father when she was fifteen, went into concert-party work with him when she was sixteen, saw him taken to hospital, to die there, when she was seventeen, how she had struggled on her own ever since, they were at the terminus. The town had long been left behind. There was nothing to be seen but a tiny shelter and the road that wandered into the gathering darkness. But half a mile down that road, the conductor told them once again, was the grand hotel on the main road going north, the hotel patronized by 'motterists'. Off they went, at a brisk pace. 'Hope you don't mind stepping out, Susie,' said Inigo, 'but the fact is, I'm finding it rather cold now without a coat.'

'I'll run all the way if you like,' said Susie. Then she put a hand on his sleeve. 'Poor Inigo! I never thanked you properly, did I, for leaving the train just to keep me company?'

Inigo stopped and seized the hand that had just touched his sleeve. He was trembling a little. 'Susie,' he began, 'I must tell you now. I've made a tremendous discovery. I - I - adore you.'

'But, Inigo,' she cried, 'how nice! I thought you did, though. Do keep on, won't you?' She made a little movement that suggested she was ready now to walk on again.

He had hold of both her hands now. 'Yes, but it's much more

serious than that. It's not just friendliness. It's everything, every mortal blessed thing and for ever and ever.'

Her hands slipped away. 'You sound as if you were about to propose,' she said lightly. 'It's not as bad as that, is it?'

'Of course it is,' he cried. 'And I am proposing and anything else you like. I'm in love with you, absolutely, frantically. It's marvellous. It's terrible.' The next minute he would have taken her in his arms but she was not there to take. And then they were walking briskly down the road again.

'I'm sorry,' she said at last, and said it quite gravely.

'I don't see what you're sorry about.'

'Well, you're rather a darling, aren't you?'

'I don't suppose I am,' he replied rather gloomily. Then he brightened up, and said eagerly: 'But if you think that now, it will probably be all right, won't it? I mean, I'm ready to give you a little time, though it's frightfully hard - or will be frightfully hard - just sort of aching about you.'

'Don't be absurd, Inigo.'

'I'm not. That's how I feel. All the time you were talking in that tram, I was just dying to kiss you. I am now. I don't know why I don't, except that - well, this is the kind of love - '

'Well, what kind is it? Do go on, Inigo.'

'I won't go on,' he said gruffly. 'I'll tell you some other time. You're simply laughing at me.'

'My dear, I'm not,' she protested. 'And to show you how serious I am, I'll tell you a secret. I've rehearsed this conversation heaps of times.'

'What! With me?'

'No, not with you, stupid, with nobody in particular, just a rather vague but frightfully attractive young man who was in love with me. And he would say a lot of the things you've just said - though he usually went into detail far more - you know, said what it was about me that made him fall in love - and then I'd reply and say how sorry I was - '

'Just as you told me how sorry you were.' Inigo put in, a trifle grimly.

'And then I'd tell him we'd always be the dearest friends but that I'd made up my mind I'd never, never marry. I would tell him that I'm wedded - as they say in the books of words - to my Art. And then very, very gently I would tell him to go away and fall in love with someone else, someone who could love him back, but usually he said he would do nothing of the kind, all other girls having lost their charm for him for ever. I liked that part,' she confessed, 'and usually left it at that!'

'There's only one thing you've forgotten, Susie,' said Inigo reproachfully. 'I'm a real person, not a vague, but attractive young man you've just imagined. Doesn't that make any difference? It ought to, you know.'

'It does. Now I'm really glad, really excited.'

'Well, there you are then,' he cried triumphantly.

'And I'm really, really sorry. That's the difference, but that's the only difference. And now let's talk about something else. Shall we?'

'There's nothing else in the world to talk about, absolutely,' said Inigo gloomily.

'There is. There's the hotel to talk about, and I can see it. It looks like a big one, doesn't it, really "motteristy"? Let's have an enormous tea. It must be my tea because this is all my fault.'

So these two infants arrived at the hotel, which was evidently used as a halt by motorists going north and south on this main road. A number of cars were standing before the entrance. Big as it was, the place looked cosy and inviting.

Inigo looked at his watch in the lighted doorway. 'We can just manage an hour here.' he said, trying to sound as if the conversation along the road had never taken place.

'Then that's just right,' said Susie, 'and I think you're very clever to have planned it so nicely. But then you are clever, aren't you, Inigo? And I like you.'

'I'm cold, hungry, and an ass,' that young gentleman replied, and made a desperate attempt to smooth his hair before a waiter caught sight of him.

III

Tea would be served, they were told, in the lounge. There was a large bright fire in the lounge, and there was also a large bright woman. She stood out from the other guests, the assorted 'motterists', like a cockatoo among thrushes. Indeed, she was not unlike a cockatoo. A tiny curved beak of a nose jutted out of her purply-red face; she had big staring eyes and a little round mouth, daubed a fearsome vermilion; her clothes were gaudy and expensive; every time she moved there was a glitter of jewellery; and she seemed to have enough flashing odds and ends of handbags and little boxes to stock a small shop. She sat alone, not far from their table, and was easily the most conspicuous person or object in the room. Susie and Inigo, however, had a further reason for remarking her gorgeous presence, for from the moment they entered she stared at them. At first she gave them a puzzled stare, but that soon changed into a plain stare, which went on and on and did not appear to mean anything.

'Why does she do it?' Inigo whispered. 'There isn't anything wrong with us, is there?'

'That's what I've been wondering,' Susie replied softly. 'I've been trying to go over myself and I seem all right. You looked a bit blue at first, but now you're thawing out nicely,' She handed him his cup. 'She must be wondering if she knows us.'

'She doesn't know me - thank God!' he muttered.

'No, but she may have seen *me* somewhere,' Susie went on with a flash of pride. 'When you think of it, I've played to thousands and thousands of people all over the country, and I must see somebody who had seen me sometimes, mustn't I?' And then she became very gay, very sparkling, and was so prettily attentive to Inigo that he began to think she must be in love with him a little, after all.

'Unless', he told himself, as he gloomily devoured a piece of shortbread, 'she is doing it out of kindness, just to make up for not caring about me.' By this time he could no long bother his head about the woman who stared. He did not even know if she was still there, for he had gradually moved round his chair until at last he had his back to her. When he had finished his shortbread, however, he noticed that Susie was looking up, with a rather puzzled expression on her face.

'What's the matter?' he inquired. 'Is the starey bird going?'

'Now I know I'm intruding,' said a voice just above his head.

Inigo jumped with surprise, and as he jumped he sent his fat armchair rolling back. It bumped heavily against something, and Inigo, turning round, discovered to his horror that the something was the flashing bosom of the staring woman. She gave the chair a push. He gave it a frantic tug. The result was that the chair shot forward and hurled Inigo against the tea-table. One of his hands knocked over the hot-water jug, and the other flattened itself against a plate.

'I'm sure I must be intruding,' cried the staring woman.

'Not at all,' said Susie, trying to smile sweetly at her and at the same time keep an eye on the hot water, which was now creeping about the table.' Won't you sit down?'

'Not at all! Rather! Absolutely!' roared Irigo, who did not know what he was saying. He waved a hand towards a chair - it was the hand that had just been flattened against the plate and there was a piece of bread-and-butter sticking to it. 'Sit here - there - won't you?' he went on. He waved his hand again, and most of the bread-and-butter went on the chair.

'I ought to introduce myself, oughtn't I?' the woman was saying.

'Do be careful of the hot water,' Susie cried to her.

'No, don't sit there,' Inigo roared again. 'It's all bread-and-butter.'

Having said this, Inigo could say no more. He suddenly lost control of himself. The woman herself, with her staring eyes and little beak of a nose and her magnificent finery, her unexpected arrival, his jump and subsequent antics with the chairs and bread-and-butter, the watery ruin of the tea-table - all these things made a combined assault upon him. The next moment, everything in the lounge, everything in the whole world, seemed wildly absurd. He flung himself down in his chair and gave a yell of laughter.

'I'm Lady Partlit,' their visitor announced, sitting down.

This was quite enough for Inigo, who went off into another fit of laughter. It would have been the same if she had been Mrs Jones, if she had merely remarked that the weather was cold. He was helpless now. Whatever happened, whatever was said, would be screamingly funny.

Susie gave Lady Partlit their names, but she only just managed to get them out in time. Her eyes were very bright and she was biting her lips. The next minute she too had fallen helplessly into the giggles.

Lady Partlit smiled at them both a trifle vaguely. Her voice, however, was triumphant. 'I thought I knew you,' she said. 'You're in a concert party called 'The Good Companions', aren't you? Of course you are. I saw you at Sandybay a few weeks ago.'

'Yes, we were there,' Inigo spluttered. He looked hard at the teapot in the hope that he would somehow be able to control himself, but it was hopeless. He pulled out his handkerchief, tried to wipe his eyes, and exploded again into silly laughter.

'I saw you three times,' said Lady Partlit. 'So good, I thought you were. Such a change!'

'I'm glad!' Susie faltered, trying not to look at Inigo. 'It's nice to think ' But then she went off again. 'Oh, do stop it, Inigo. You *are* a fool.' With an effort, she got her face straight, turned to Lady Partlit and said apologetically: 'You must think we're awfully rude, but it's just his silliness, and now - now - he's started me off.' And she giggled again.

'Not in the least,' said Lady Partlit, still smiling. 'And - er - where are you people going to now, if you don't mind my asking?'

'Middleford,' replied Susie, and brought out the name as if it were the greatest joke in the world.

'That's it. Ha-ha,' roared Inigo. 'Middleford. Ha-ha-ha-ha. Sorry, but I really have to laugh when I think of Middleford.' And he buried his head in his hands and yelled with laughter. This torrent swept away any tiny reserve remaining with Susie, who promptly joined him. Lady Partlit looked from one to the other of them; her eyes opened wider and wider; her little round mouth gradually widened; her rather heavy cheeks began quivering; then finally she burst into laughter too, a queer soprano sobbing that made the other two want to go on and on for ever.

And there were the three of them, shaking, watery-eyed, helpless.

'Oh dear, oh dear, oh dear!' cried Lady Partlit, dabbing at her eyes. 'I don't know what it's all about, but I haven't laughed so much this long time. I like a good laugh too.' Her speech was far homelier now than it had been before, and any suggestion of the great lady had completely vanished. They saw before them a kindly, rather silly, rich woman in her early forties, who waved away their apologies for their astonishing behaviour.

'I'm sure it's done me good,' she told them. 'I wasn't expecting to have such a good laugh in this place. My word! Now won't you let me order you some more tea? Are you sure? Well, what about some cocktails if the bar is open? Or some chocolates? Have a cigarette?' She produced a gold case, and the three of them lit cigarettes and settled down to talk.

'Don't forget our train, Inigo,' said Susie. 'You know how long it took us to get here, over an hour and a half.'

'What's this?' asked Lady Partlit, and when they told her, said eagerly: 'Now you mustn't think of going to the station that way. I've my car here, and Lawley will take you down there in no time, and all nice and comfortable, and you'll be able to stay here all the longer. And that'll be nicer for me too. I was going through to Yorkshire tonight, and just stopped here for tea, and then I thought I wouldn't go any farther tonight because Lawley says there'll be fog farther up later on, and so I said I'd stay here and go to bed early after dinner with a nice book. Now what do you say to that? Let Lawley take you to the station.'

Susie accepted at once, and though Inigo would rather have returned as they came because he could then have had Susie to himself, he could not offer any objection.

'You mustn't think it strange, my coming up like this and talking to you,' Lady Partlit continued, 'because for one thing you must count me among your admirers. I've never seen such a good show at the seaside before, and I've told all sorts of people about you. Such an original name too! And then, another thing is, I'm almost in the business myself in a way of speaking. My late husband - he was Sir Joseph Partlit - you may have heard of him - was very interested in the theatre business himself just as a sideline, you know, and he left me a controlling interest in two West End theatres and some productions.'

Susie's eyes lit up at once and flashed a message to Inigo. 'Here', they said, 'is the Fairy Queen.'

'What's the matter?' asked Lady Partlit.

'Nothing at all,' said Susie, 'except that you're the person we dream about every night. Two West End theatres! Productions! Not musical comedy or revue, by any chance?'

'As a rule, yes. I'm glad too, because I like them best, though I like a good romantic play too.'

'I can hardly believe you're real,' cried Susie smiling at her.

'But you mustn't think I've really anything to do with this business,' Lady Partlit explained amiably. 'I'm just a little nobody in the background. All I do is sign things now and again, though I like to keep popping up and seeing what they're doing. Helps to keep me busy, you know, and a widow without children like me hasn't much to do. But don't run away with the idea that I've much say in it.'

'You've enough say in it to take my breath away. Lady Partlit,' said Susie sturdily. 'Mr Jollifant there - you can call him Inigo; he likes it - may not care, because he's only an amateur slightly disguised, but as for me - ! And if Jerry Jerningham were here, I wouldn't be answerable for him. He'd probably want to kidnap you.'

The effect of these last two remarks was astonishing. Lady Partlit's ruddy cheeks were now like two mounds of pickled beetroot; her eyes were soft and bright; her bosom heaved and flashed.

'You remember him, don't you?' asked Susie, who had observed these significant symptoms. 'Our light comedian and dancer.'

'Oh, yes, I do. I thought he was - wonderful,' Lady Partlit faltered.

'He is,'said Susie. 'Isn't he, Inigo?'

'Absolutely. Jerningham himself may be a terrible - ' But here he stopped because he received a kick on the shin from Susie.

'A terribly good dancer,' that young lady prompted.

'Exactly!' cried Inigo. 'I must say he's the best step dancer I've ever seen.'

'And so marvellously good-looking of course,' said Susie.

'Yes,' said Lady Partlit faintly.

Susie gave a little laugh that struck Inigo as being the most unreal he had ever heard. 'It's funny', she said, 'the way Jerry attracts all the women in the audience. They'd run after him if they could, but they can't. He's never to be found.'

'Is - is he married?' Lady Partlit brought out this question in a tiny stifled voice.

'Who on earth - ' Inigo began, but was immediately kicked into silence again.

'Oh no, he's not married,' replied Susie brightly. 'He's not even thinking of it. He thinks about nothing but his work. He's very hard-working and frightfully ambitious - like me.'

After this, the talk that followed seemed merely casual, but it had a trick of working round to Mr Jerry Jerningham. Susie gave Lady Partlit a list of all their future dates she could remember. When at last the car came round for them, Lady Partlit slipped away and returned with a large box of chocolates for Susie and a box of cigarettes for Inigo, and was almost tearfully affectionate in her farewell, though her regret at their departure did not compel her, they noticed, to accompany them to the station.

'Well,' said Inigo, when they had seated themselves in the big limousine, 'I must say I don't understand that old girl. I think she's a bit mad.'

'Idiot! Don't you see,' Susie hissed, 'she's the person who sent Jerry that bouquet at Sandybay. She adores him.'

'Gosh!' was Inigo's comment. But he listened patiently while Susie discussed various aspects of this strange affair. They sat there in comfort, while the limousine rolled through the murk of Hicklefield. When it came to a stop at the station, Susie sighed luxuriously. 'People can say what they like,' she said wistfully, 'but it must be marvellous to have a lot of money.'

And anybody who saw her getting out of that limousine must have thought she had a lot of money. Her sketch of a very rich and bored young creature, the spoilt darling of fortune, was only offered to an audience of two porters, a taxi-driver, and a nondescript, but nevertheless it was superbly done. Her hatless and overcoatless companion who came out shivering slightly, was left somewhere in the air; he was there, but not in the picture; it was not until he opened the door of an empty third-class carriage for her that he returned to the picture and she was Susie Dean again.

IV

'Figure or no figure,' said Susie, 'I must have some.' She was examining the box of chocolates that Lady Partlit had given her. They were very large aristocratic chocolates, and by the time they had eaten two or three, the last glimmer of Hicklefield had left their flying windows. Once again Susie pointed out that it would be marvellous to have a lot of money. She dwelt rather wistfully on the subject of riches.

England is pre-eminently the country in which it is difficult for two to agree: if one turns realist, the other turns idealist; a cynic instantly creates a sentimentalist. Inigo stoutly denied that money, beyond a necessary competence, was important; he denounced the life of luxury, even going to the length of refusing a third chocolate; and he declared that Susie's attitude pained him. In a very short time, however, the lover overcame the philosopher in him.

'If that's what you think,' he said, rather gloomily, 'I'll make a lot of money. I don't want it, but I'll do it just for your sake. Didn't you say

I could probably make something out of songs?'

'Heaps and heaps,' she told him. 'If the right people hear them, I'm sure your fortune's made, Inigo. I really mean that. You've got a gift that could easily be a gold-mine.'

'Well, there you are then. I'll make a lot of money for you.'

'But I don't want your money, you absurd creature. I want to be rich myself, all by myself.'

'I don't believe you know what you want,' he declared, seeing that it was obvious she did not want him.

'That only shows you don't know anything about me,' she said. Then she thought a moment. 'I want to be a star. I want to be Susie Dean - bang! - like that. Enter Susie Dean - bang! "Here she is!" I want them to say. Not just for myself, either, but for my mother's sake and my father's sake - to make up for all their dreary journeys and digs and hard work and rotten pay and no chances. I know it won't make up for all that, yet I feel it will in a way if I go right to the top. Not that I don't want it myself, of course,' she added.

'Of course,' he said.

'I believe you're being sarcastic'

'No, I'm not. Go on.'

'Well,' she said, looking at him but not seeing him, 'I don't care about having my photographs in papers and little paragraphs about me and my name up in electric lights - not that it wouldn't be rather nice, you know - but that's not what I think about. I'd like to have a nice little flat - where managers rang me up and asked me to look at parts - and a dresser who adored me and perhaps a very cosy car, small but frightfully posh; and enough money to spare to give all sorts of people delightful surprises, holidays, and presents; and now and then I'd like to run away from it all; go on a voyage perhaps under some other name, and not let anybody know who I was, and then somebody would come up and say, "You do remind me of Susie Dean," and then I might admit I *was* Susie Dean, and everybody on the boat would say, "That's Susie Dean," and they'd probably get up an entertainment specially so that I could appear in it, and - oh - all kinds of things.' She ended breathlessly.

'It sounds a lonely sort of life to me,' said Inigo cheerlessly.

'Oh, but I'd have heaps and heaps of friends,' she cried. 'I couldn't exist without 'em. You'd be one, wouldn't you, Inigo?'

'I suppose so.' He saw himself somewhere dodging in the background, holding her cloak, while all manner of important and handsome males held her attention.

'You do sound miserable about it. I don't believe you want me to be successful. I believe you're one of those men who can only be friendly if they're allowed to patronize.' She looked haughtily out of a window through which there was nothing to be seen. He tried to look out of the window on his side too, but found it impossible to avoid glancing at her. After a minute or two, however, he noticed she was peeping at him. He smiled, and instantly she jumped round and faced him.

'Aren't we absurd?' she smiled. 'We're nearly as bad as Joe and Mrs Joe. Last summer they bought a ticket for the Calcutta Sweep, and one day, just before the draw was announced, they began to talk about their chances. Then when they'd awarded themselves a favourite, they began to wonder what they would do with the money. Joe said he would buy an hotel at one of the big seaside places. Mrs Joe said she would invest all the money and live on the income from it. No hotel for her, she told him. He insisted on his hotel. They argued for hours and got crosser and crosser and crosser until it ended in a quarrel and they never spoke to one another for two days, the poor darlings. Now come and sit on this side and then you won't have to stare at me and make me think I've done something dreadful to you.'

Inigo rose and stood for a moment looking down on her and listening to the rhythmical rattle of the train. 'It's melancholy, you know,' he said slowly. 'I ought to be happy here alone with you, Susie. I believe it's been my idea of happiness for some time.'

'Why, Inigo?'

'I'm not going to tell you again. What I was going to say is that it's rather melancholy. But then there's always been something melancholy to me about Sunday night, something a bit heart-breaking, absolutely.'

'I know,' she replied softly. Then she looked fierce. 'No, I don't.' she said in a loud voice. 'Sit down here, Master Jollifant, Master Inigo Absolutely, and if you don't cheer up, I'll shake you. Unless, of course,' she added, peeping at him, 'you're sad about me.'

So they sat side by side and talked idly as the train went clanking through mysterious regions of night towards the still distant Middleford. As time went on, Susie said less and less, began to yawn, and drooped away from him, into her corner. She had just nodded off to sleep when a ticket collector came in and wakened her. Then she yawned and drooped again, and this time her head sank in his direction until finally it rested against his shoulder, where it remained, to his delight. There was perhaps a certain bitter flavour of irony in this delight, for she had made it plain that he had little to hope from her and this was only the surrender of sleep. But it had something trusting in it, and his hopes revived under the slight pressure of that head against his upper arm. The very cramp that soon invaded his limbs took on a romantic beauty.

Where it was the train stopped, shortly after ten, Inigo never knew. It seemed a fairly large station. Susie opened her eyes, sighed then went to sleep again, leaving Inigo praying that nobody would disturb them. At the very last moment, however, when the whistle sounded, the door was flung open to admit some raw November night and a large man. Inigo looked at the man in despair. The man looked at Inigo with cheerful interest. He sat in the middle of the opposite seat, removed his hat, mopped his brow, re-lit the stump of a cigar, put a fat hairy hand on each knee, and blew little benevolent clouds of smoke at Inigo and the sleeping Susie. He was a well-developed specimen of a type of large man seen at all race meetings, boxing matches, football matches, in all sporting clubs and music-hall bars. His head was pear-shaped, beginning with an immense spread of jaw and ending at a narrow and retreating forehead, decorated by two little loops of hair, parted in the middle. His eyes protruded; his nose shone; his little moustache was ferociously waxed. There was a suggestion that innumerable double whiskies were hard at work illuminating his vast interior. All these details Inigo noted with distaste.

The man removed the stump of cigar and winked slowly, ponderously, at Inigo. 'Just caught it,' he said companionably. 'In the bar of the White Horse at ten, and here I am. That's moving, y'know, that is.'

Inigo merely nodded, but that seemed quite enough to establish a firm friendship with this genial intruder.

'Here,' he said, producing a flask as unexpectedly as a conjurer, 'have a drink of this. Go on, there's plenty for all. No? Well, will your wife have one? No, she's not your wife, is she? She's your sweetheart. Our wives and sweethearts,' he proclaimed, holding up the flask, 'and may they never meet.' He drank this toast with enthusiasm.

'Mind you,' he said sternly, 'that's just my fun, that about wives and sweethearts never meeting. If I say that to the missis, she just laughs. She knows me well enough to know that that's my fun. My wife is my sweetheart, and we've been married twelve years at that. Twelve years and always the best of pals – the best,' he added fiercely, as if Inigo had just contradicted him. 'The very best,' he went on, 'the very, very best. Here's to her.' And he took another pull at the flask.

'Anything she wants,' he observed, 'she can have - in reason. There's reason in ev'rything, isn't there? All right then. She's only gotta ask, that's all. She knows it. Her mother knows it. "You're lucky," she says to my wife. "You're lucky." She wasn't lucky - that's my missis's mother I'm talking about now - and I say she wasn't lucky. She got nothing. The old man wouldn't part. But that's not me. Get on the right side of me, and there's nothing I've got you can't have. My missis knows that. She's on the right side of me. We're the best of pals, the very best. And the same with the wife's mother - just the same - the very best. Here's luck to the old lady.' This toast apparently emptied the flask, which was now laid down on the seat, while its owner, after breathing hard, looked at Inigo, looked at the unconscious Susie, and slowly and sentimentally wagged his head.

At any other time, Inigo might have enjoyed this gentleman's society, but now he found it difficult even to tolerate him. Somehow that railway carriage was not the place it had been an hour before.

'Pretty!' said the stranger, still wagging his head at them. 'Very pretty! As good as a picksher to me.' He sighed hugely as he stared at Susie. The last draught from the flask appeared to have washed away any lingering reserve, and now he was very tender and mellow indeed. 'I know what it is. I've done my courting, holding her up half the day and half the night, the same as you now. Happy times - you can't beat 'em. Look at her now, just dreamin' there, happy and trustin'. And a nice little girl you've got hold of too, young feller, I can see that. Look after her, and then you'll be one of the lucky ones, like me.'

'It's been a rotten cold day,' said Inigo desperately.

'What's a cold day to a warm heart?' cried the other reproachfully. 'Don't tell me you've noticed it's a cold day. I'll bet your little sweetheart there doesn't know it's a cold day. Ah, I wish I was your age, young feller. Put your arm round her properly. Cuddle up to her. Don't mind me. I've been young. I'm young yet. I know what makes the world go round. It isn't money. It's love. It's two hearts beating as one, as the song says.' He leaned back, tried to fix a goggling stare on Inigo, and sang softly, beating time with one hand: 'My swee-eet-heart when a boy-yer - in days of long ago-er.'

Inigo closed his eyes and pretended to go to sleep. It was all he could do. The wretched song went droning on for some time then gradually died away, to be succeeded finally by a snore. Inigo moved his cramped limbs cautiously, and let his thoughts go jog-jogging with the train through the night.

'Mid-ford! Mid-ford!'

Immediately the stranger opened his eyes, sprang up, grabbed flask, hat, bag, and vanished.

'Are we there?' cried Susie. 'I must have been asleep. Who was that?'

'That', said Inigo with deliberation, 'was our fellow-passenger, a large and rather tight gentleman with a mind like a cheap Christmas card. And most of the way he's been calling you my little sweetheart.'

'Poor Inigo, how disgusting!' she said coolly. 'Do look out and see if you can see Jimmy or anybody there.'

He crept out, very stiff and feeling rather cold. 'I can see Jimmy farther up the platform,' he announced at the door. Then he stood there looking up at her. Their day was all over now. 'Well, that's that,' he said, a trifle mournfully. 'Come along, Susie.'

She looked at him curiously. 'Help me down,' she said. 'I'm rather stiff.' Then when she had got down and her hand still rested in his, she cried softly: 'Cheer up. And thank you for looking after me, Inigo. There!' And it came and went so swiftly, that kiss, that he hardly knew if it had really existed.

'Susie!' he cried.

'There's Jimmy.' And she hurried away, waving a hand.

We catch a last glimpse of him following her down the platform.

CHAPTER SIX
The Black Week

I

IT began, that awful week, before they reached Tewborough. It began -
at least for eight of them - on the Sunday night at Middleford. The week
at Middleford was a steady plodding affair, but it could boast one
exciting event. This was the visit of a rich and eccentric old lady, Mrs
Hodney. She had driven in by car to the town to see her solicitors on
Wednesday, had stayed to see the show, and after it was over had
insisted upon being introduced by the local manager, who knew her as
a 'character', to Miss Trant, to Jimmy, to everybody. She was so
delighted with them all, she said, that she wanted them to do a queer
old woman a favour. Would they all go out to her house, Custon Hall,
twenty miles away, on the edge of the moors, and give a performance
on Sunday there for her, her maids, and any of the villagers who were
not too stupid to enjoy themselves for once on a Sunday night in
November? They must not think of it as a matter of business - though
she was rich enough to pay for her whims, and if twenty pounds would
compensate them for their trouble, there it was - but they must think of
it as a matter of cheering up a lonely old woman who found it difficult
to be pleased with anything and who would not be staying long in this
world. Thus Mrs Hodney, a very staccato but vehement old lady, who
patted all the younger players on the back as she talked.

So it was arranged that all the actual performers should stay in
Middleford on Sunday night, catching a cross-country train on Monday
morning to Tewborough, and give a special show (in evening dress) at
Custon Hall, which would have waiting for them, they were assured, a
very large drawing-room; a grand piano, and a good supper. 'And mind
you,' said the local manager, 'the old lady'll do you well. She's a queer
old stick - I've heard all sorts of tales about her - but she's taken a fancy
to you and she'll see that you're all right, I give you my word.' This visit
was the great topic during the latter part of the week. Miss Trant had
waived any claim to part of the fee, so that it meant they would receive
two pounds ten shillings each, and there were many exciting
discussions, between Joe and Mrs Joe, Elsie and Susie, as to what might
be done with this windfall. Then again the command performance - as
it came to be called - was both a compliment and an adventure. Miss
Trant and Mr Oakroyd were pitied because they would not be there.
Had they been going anywhere else, these two might have stayed on
too, but Tewborough was no ordinary date and there was much to be

done on the Monday. At Tewborough they were playing at the Theatre Royal, a real theatre, not a mere Pavilion or Assembly Room or anything of that kind. Miss Trant knew nothing about Tewborough and, curiously enough, neither did any of the others, but she had seen an advertisement in *The Stage*, offering this theatre at a fairly moderate rent, and for once she had acted on her own responsibility and had taken it for a week, in spite of Jimmy's advice. 'It's buying a pig in a poke,' he said darkly, but Miss Trant, who could be both venturesome and obstinate on occasion, refused to be warned, and was encouraged by most of the others, who were anxious to see themselves on the stage of a real theatre again. Having thus committed herself to Tewborough, Miss Trant considered it the great date of the year, their grand opportunity, and it was necessary that she and Mr Oakroyd should travel by car as usual on Sunday so that they could get to work at once on Monday. And they refused to be pitied because they were missing the command performance, for to them would fall the pleasure of first seeing Tewborough and its Theatre Royal.

There had been some difficulty at first in finding anybody or anything to take them out to Custon Hall, which could not be reached by train. The garage proprietors of Middleford seemed curiously reluctant to send one of their larger vehicles to Mrs Hodney's remote village. At last, however, a man was found. His name was Dickenson; he owned a bus, he said, that could seat twelve and had taken eighteen in its time; and he would drive them there and back for two pounds. Under that, he told them, he would not budge; and they found they could not make him budge. Nevertheless, they were all relieved when they heard about Mr Dickenson and his bus.

The rendezvous was Jimmy's lodgings, and by half past six, the appointed time, all eight were there, in evening clothes and carrying instruments and portfolios of music and an astonishing assortment of cloaks, overcoats, shawls, and scarves. They were all in high spirits. This was a break in the routine, an adventure. Mr Morton Mitcham, looking gigantic and very impressive in the Silver King and a long green scarf, said once again that it was quite like old times, and Mrs Joe, struggling with her two woolly coats, an imitation Spanish shawl, and a very worn opera cloak, once more agreed with him. All they wanted now was Mr Dickenson and his bus. After another five minutes, these two arrived and brought with them a flat-faced youth, one Arthur, who blew on his hands a good deal and appeared to have no roof to his mouth.

'You're a bit late,'said Jimmy, pleasantly.

'Late!' cried Mr Dickenson bitterly. 'I'm early to what I thowt I was going to be. Bother I've 'ad with 'er, haven't I, Arthur?'

'Ee oo ah,' replied Arthur, and then blew on his hands. Having done that, he went on: 'Ee oh oo ee oo ah.'

'That is so,' said Mr Dickenson. 'And now if we're going to start, let's start. Though I'd as lief go back hoam and call it off, I would that.'

'Now what sort of night is it going to be, driver?" Mrs Joe inquired graciously, in her best Duchess of Dorking style.

'It's going to be a mucky cold neet, Missis,' said Mr Dickenson. 'Tickle 'er up, Arthur. And get in, all on yer, and let's get off.'

'These rugged North-country characters,' Mrs Joe was heard to murmur. 'Rough perhaps but staunch as oak.'

'I wish his bus was a bit less rugged,' said Susie, looking inside.

It was certainly not a very luxurious vehicle. To begin with, it was obviously very old, and when the engine started everything else started too, jumping and rattling in sympathy with it. The seats were very narrow and hard, and it had not a proper enclosed body but was merely roofed in with some sort of canvas. And though it may have held twelve persons, the fact remains that when the eight of them, with their instruments and music and wraps, were all inside, there was not an inch of room to spare. Once they were on the road, the jolting was very unpleasant, but nobody grumbled much. It was all part of the adventure of the command performance.

'This to me', gasped Mrs Joe in the darkness, 'is Romance and a great change. A drive out into remote places, the show in a different setting, against the background of one of our stately old mansions, an appreciative audience, a pleasant repast to follow.'

'Not so much of the "follow",' said Elsie. 'I vote we have the supper as soon as we get there. I thought that was the idea, and I've had nothing but a cup of tea and a bun since half past twelve, and I'm peckish now.'

'Now you settle that between you,' said Jimmy Nunn. 'You can't expect that to interest me. A drink of something a piece o' dry toast, and perhaps a bit o' chicken - breast - that's quite enough for me. I dare say there'll be chicken.'

'Sure to be.' This was the deep grave voice of Mr Morton Mitcham. 'They always do you well on these occasions - that's my experience, ladies and gentlemen. Everything of the best - champagne too, with luck, though being a woman she may be a bit slack about the drinks. You ought to have seen some of the spreads the old colonial governors - Sir Elkin Pondberry and one or two more - used to give us, after command performances. Sumptuous is the only word - sumptuous!'

'Well, I'm for splitting it like,' said Joe, rather apologetically. 'A bit o' supper before we start, and a good bite after we finish. One'll put heart into us before we begin.'

'And completely ruin your upper register,' said his wife coldly. 'I know what happens to you. You'll fill your stomach, and then you'll stand in front of Mrs Hodney, trying to sing, with your upper register in rags.'

'I can't sing at all empty,' he pleaded, 'and you know you said yourself at tea-time. "Save your appetite for tonight." So I say a bit before and then a good bite to come home on.'

'If Mrs Hodney, obviously a lady, refined if a trifle eccentric, heard you at this moment, she'd ask for your name to be crossed off the programme,' cried Mrs Joe. 'And I shouldn't blame her, Joe. I should say at once, husband or no husband and as good a baritone as you'll find in concert-party work, it serves him right and teaches him a lesson.'

This mention of the programme immediately set them all talking at once. They wondered if they had really chosen the best numbers. Would Mrs Hodney like this item and that? They were still talking about the programme when the bus suddenly came to a stop. As it was impossible to see anything inside, Inigo looked out of the flap at the back.

'Are we there?' somebody called out to him.

'We don't seem to be anywhere,' he replied, and got out, to find himself in a cold and drizzling blackness.

'We're eight mile off,' said Mr Dickenson, who was now examining the engine. 'Give 'er another turn, Arthur. It'll be teeming down in a minute. That'll do, Arthur. Let 'er alone.'

'Eh oh oo ah oh ee,' said Arthur mournfully.

'Well, I'll 'ave to get ruddy mag out, that's all,' said Mr Dickenson, who did not seem to be in a very good temper. 'I thowt she was bitching 'erself up all along. 'Ere, 'old this. Now then, we'll try that. Give 'er another turn, lad.' The engine began spluttering noisily. 'That'll do. It'll be pouring down in five minutes and 'ere to Custon's one o' the foulest roads you ever set eyes on. I ought to 'ad more sense than to come on this daft trip.'

'Never mind, you chaps,' said Jimmy, who had joined Inigo outside. 'We'll soon be there, and then you can put some beef and beer away and make yourselves cosy by a big fire.'

'Ee oh oo ah oo,' said Arthur, and blew on his hands very despondently.

'This expedition would be gayer, I think, without Arthur,' said Inigo, as he and Jimmy climbed in again. 'There is something about Arthur that depresses me - a sort of "Quoth the Raven" sound about him.'

The bus went very slowly now but rattled more fiercely than ever. Apparently the roads were narrow, winding, and steep, and it was clear that Mr Dickenson was not enjoying himself. The drizzle was steadily turning itself into a downpour, and very soon the passengers too found it difficult to enjoy themselves. Not only were they bumped about most unpleasantly but they also began to feel odd drops and trickles of rain. Evidently the canvas top was by no means watertight. They pulled their wraps and scarves about them, held on grimly to the backs of seats or whatever else there was to hold on to, and assured one another that it would not be long before they were there. But never had any of them known eight longer miles.

At last, however, they stopped, and Inigo, looking out again, reported that they had arrived at a large gateway leading to a drive.

'This is it,' yelled Mr Dickenson. 'Custon 'All, this is. Shall I take it right in if I can get in?'

'Oh, yes!' they cried happily, in chorus, he must take it up to the very door if he could. Already they saw the triumphant arrival, the great front door of the Hall wide open, the lights shining out, the stir of excitement among the crowd of retainers and villagers. As they went curving round the drive and everybody was trying to collect instruments and music and wraps, it was instantly decided that they should have something to eat and drink before beginning the show, for it was eight o'clock now, half an hour later than the very last moment they had expected to arrive at, and they all admitted they were hungry - all, that is, except Jimmy Nunn, who said he was dying of thirst. Out they tumbled, cold and rather damp and a little battered, hollow inside perhaps, but still in good spirits, delighted to be there, and ready to give old Mrs Hodney the show of her life. They emerged into a downpour of that slashing cold rain of the moorland, but that did not matter when they were at the very door of the Hall.

That door, however, was closed, and there were no lights at all in the lower rooms, and nothing anywhere but a faint glimmer in one or two of the bedrooms. The house looked an inhospitable black mass.

'I thought you said they were expecting you.' said Mr Dickenson, giving a most unpleasant short laugh.

'So they are,' said Jimmy uneasily, as he pulled at the bell handle.

'This part of the mansion', Mrs Joe observed hopefully, 'is little used, no doubt. Everybody is busy with various preparations at the back. Come under the porch, my dears, until the door is opened.'

Jimmy tugged away at the bell and at last a flicker of light was seen below. The door was opened a few inches, then another few inches. 'What d'you want?' asked a voice.

'Come along, please,' cried Jimmy impatiently. 'We're the concert party, "The Good Companions", come to give the show.'

The door was opened wide now but only in order that an elderly and weary-looking manservant could stare at them in amazement. 'What is it you want?'

Jimmy explained again.

'Well, you've come to the wrong place,' the man told him.

'Nay, they've not,' cried Mr Dickenson, 'this is Mrs Hodney's, I do know.'

'Of course it is,' said the man.

But when Jimmy explained at greater length, the man still stared in amazement. 'Well, it's no use your coming here tonight, or any other night as far as I can see. Mrs Hodney's poorly, right bad. She had a stroke o' Thursday and she's in a bad way. Doctor's here now and he's sent for a nurse. That's how it is.'

'Well, I'll be - ' Jimmy gasped.

'Just hold on a minute,' said the man. He let the door swing to, and they heard him walking away.

Then the voice of Arthur prophesying woe was heard above all others. 'Ee ee ah oo oo oh, oo ee eh, oo.'

'By gow! Arthur,' cried Mr Dickenson bitterly, 'you're right an' all.'

'If Arthur makes another sound,' said Susie in a low tense whisper, 'I shall scream and scream. I can't bear it.'

Now the door was flung wide open and they found a pocket electric torch shining on them. 'I don't understand this,' said a very testy voice from behind the torch, 'and I don't want to understand it. I haven't the time to spare. Mrs Hodney's very ill indeed, very ill. I doubt if she'll recover but we're doing our best. Now kindly go away and make as little noise as you can. Good night to you.' The torch vanished; the door was swiftly but quietly closed, locked, bolted.

'Good night to *you*,' cried Jimmy softly. 'With love and many happy returns of the day. Creep away, boys and girls. It's all off.'

'My God!' This was from Elsie, and for once she spoke for them all.

'Do yer meantersay - ' Mr Dickenson began, but was cut short by Jimmy.

'I meantersay,' said Jimmy, 'that we're going back to Middleford as sharp as we can, and the sooner you get that bus started the better.'

'Beef and beer!' cried Mr Dickenson, in a very ecstasy of savage irony. 'Cosy by a big fire! Gorrr! You're mugs yerselves and you've made me into one.'

'Ee oh oo oo ur oo oo,' said Arthur indignantly.

This last remark enraged Mr Jerningham, of all people. 'Oh, you shet erp,' he screamed.

'Ho, ho! And what's Arthur want to shut up for, eh?' Mr

Dickenson sounded very menacing. 'Nar, for two blurry pins - '

'Kindly start your car, driver,' said a forlorn and dripping object, with astonishing dignity. 'And don't talk about pins in that way when ladies are present.' And having delivered this reproof, Mrs Joe climbed into the bus, removed her sodden opera cloak, sneezed twice, and burst into tears.

'Ladies!' Mr Dickenson sneered. 'Gorrr!' He was then tapped upon the shoulder. After that he was taken to one side.

'Now you see me, don't you,' said Joe, speaking very softly. 'I'm a quiet sort of chap, I am. But I'm feeling sorry for that old lady in there. And I'm very disappointed because there's no show. I'm also very hungry and I'm wet. And that's my wife who's just spoken to you. Now, another word, just one more word, from you, and I shall have the great pleasure of relieving my feelings by knocking your silly ugly head right off.' And as he spoke, Joe came nearer and nearer, a most formidable figure even in the darkness. 'Just say some more, that's all,' he added, almost persuasively.

'Be ready to give 'er a turn, Arthur,' said Mr Dickenson despondently, and he sought his seat in front.

The return journey was horrible. It seemed to go on and on for hours and hours. Three times the bus had to stop, twice for engine trouble, and once because Mr Dickenson had missed the way. On the other hand, the rain never stopped at all, and the canvas cover merely acted as a distributor. There had not appeared to be any room to spare on the way up, but now everybody was in everybody else's way, and everybody was very wet and cold and hungry and so snapped at everybody else, and everybody else, being also very wet and cold and hungry, promptly snapped back again. Mr Morton Mitcham, attempting a reminiscence of a similar experience, was told at once that nobody was interested. When Mr Jerningham complained that he was wet through, he was informed that a drop of water would do *him* good. Elsie announced that this time she really was through with the rotten Stage. Mrs Joe pointed out, between sobs, that she had always been one to take the Bad with the Good, but that having ordered a complete outfit for little George, boots and all, on the strength of this extra engagement, she was now at the End of her Tether. Susie told Inigo how depressed she was at the thought of Mrs Hodney, the queer little old woman who had been so lively the other night and was now dying perhaps in that lonely dismal house; but when, in sympathy, he put his hand on hers, she pushed it away, said it was like a fish, so cold and wet, and asked him not to be a fool. Jimmy Nunn groaned from time to time, but only uttered three words during all the journey. 'The Good Companions!' he cried, with a ghastly chuckle, and after that nobody spoke for quite a long time.

Middleford was going to bed when they finally arrived there. They considered desperately, miserably, their chances of obtaining food and drink and hot baths at that late hour on Sunday. They heard already the outraged tones of landladies preparing to retire. Shivering, their best clothes so much sodden pulp, they crawled out of the bus, and it seemed the last straw when Jimmy plaintively announced that he would have to collect five shillings each from them to pay for it. While they were fumbling for their money, however, Inigo, who had disappeared for a moment, came back and said quietly: 'It's all right. I've paid him. You can settle up some other time. Let's get away.'

It was a miserable party that met next morning to catch the eleven o'clock train to Tewborough. They stared at one another's pale faces and reddened noses; they listened to one another sniffling and sneezing; they talked gloomily of aspirin and quinine; they yawned and shivered and groaned. Mrs Joe and Elsie had colds in the head; Susie said she felt feverish; Jerry Jemingham was watery about the eyes; Inigo's voice was rather hoarse; Joe moved stiffly and talked of 'rheumatics'; and as for Morton Mitcham and Jimmy, both of whom looked queer enough at any time, they were now a sad spectacle indeed, Mitcham being nothing but a gaunt yellow ruin, and Jimmy, who really looked ill, a stricken gargoyle. It was just their luck, they told one another, that they should be in such a state when Tewborough and its Theatre Royal were awaiting them. They admitted, however, that a packed and enthusiastic house on the first night might pull them through. 'Ill as I ab,' said Mrs Joe, between sniffs, 'I cad respod to the publig. That's my tebremend. Tewborough's a big dade and we'll blay ub to id.' This was the only topic that could rouse them out of their staring and shivering apathy.

It was tea-time when they arrived there, and too dark to see anything of the town as the train crawled into it. Miss Trant and Mr Oakroyd were there on the platform. Inigo seized hold of Mr Oakroyd at once. 'You've got to save our lives,' he said. 'We had a hell of a time last night.' Briefly he described the great fiasco. 'You were lucky to be out of it, I can tell you,' he concluded. 'Now then, what about Tewborough? How are you getting on? What's it like?'

Mr Oakroyd drew him to one side.' I've nobbut been i' t'place a day, as you knaw,' he said cautiously. 'But you've got to talk of a place as you find it.'

'Well,' said Inigo impatiently, 'and how do you find it?'

'Here,' said Mr Oakroyd, bending forward and curving a hand round his mouth. 'It's bloody awful.'

Having delivered this verdict, he looked solemnly at Inigo, shook his head, then stumped away to find the baggage, with the air of a man who would continue to do his duty whatever it cost.

II

Cathedral cities, market towns, ports forgotten by the sea, spas long out of fashion, all these can decay beautifully, and often their charm increases as the life ebbs out of them. Industrial towns, like steam engines, are only even tolerable if they are in working order and puffing away. Tewborough was like an engine with a burst boiler lying on the side of a road; it was a money-making machine that had almost stopped working, for only a wheel here and there shakily revolved or a pulley gave a groan or two; it was a factory that could now show you nothing but broken windows and litter and mouldering ledgers and a mumbling caretaker, it was nothing but an old cash-box containing only dust and cobwebs and a few forgotten pence. Trade in Tewborough had nearly disappeared altogether, and it was quite obvious that it would never come back again, would always prefer other and pleasanter places. It was a town of dwindling incomes, terrifying overdrafts, of shopkeepers who lived by stretching one another's credit, of working men who were rapidly becoming nothing but waiting men, their chief occupation being to hang about the doors of buildings that were known - with a fine irony - as Labour Exchanges. Tewborough had always been one of the ugliest towns in the Midlands, and now it was easily the most depressed and depressing. Its wealth had long ceased to accumulate but its men still decayed. The days when Tewborough's coal and lace-curtains and tin-tacks were in brisk demand everywhere, when many a local man who still liked his tea in a pint pot could 'buy up' the county's Lord Lieutenant and was known to have shaken Gladstone himself by the hand, these days had gone and had left nothing behind them but a few public buildings in a bad Gothic style, two be-whiskered and blackened statues, some slag heaps, disused factories and sidings, a rotting canal, a large slum area, a generous supply of dirt, rickets, bow legs, and bad teeth - and the Theatre Royal.

When Mr Oakroyd brought out his verdict on the place, he and Miss Trant had not spent a whole day there, but their roseate visions had long faded and vanished. It was impossible to like the town, though they had both tried hard and had perhaps succeeded in concealing a little of their dislike for it from one another. Miss Trant told herself she had never imagined that any town could be so hideous and depressing: she wanted to run away at once and never even think of it again. Sitting in the dingy coffee-room of the hotel, with a plate of congealing mutton fat in front of her, she had felt she was ready to cry at any moment. She knew already that Tewborough could not be amused by their show or any other show. When the man at the hotel had heard she had taken the Theatre Royal, he had stared at her and then given a short and disconcerting laugh. 'Having a pop at it, are you?' he had said. 'Well, I suppose there's nothing like trying. You're not the first, and I dare say you won't be the last, even yet. I thought old Droke was looking pleased with himself, last time I saw him. Met him yet? He's a queer old stick, if you like, as rum as they make 'em round here - and rummer. Well, well, well!' And Miss Trant did not like the sound of this at all.

Early on Monday morning she made the acquaintance of Mr Droke, and though she did not spend much time in his company, it left her in no doubt that Mr Droke certainly was as rum as they made them. He was a very little old man, with an immense head and quite tiny legs and feet, so that he looked like a dirty and dingy gnome. His senile voice came whistling through his browny-white moustache and beard, and he had a horrible trick of coming quite close and punctuating his jerky statements with vigorous upward nudges of his elbow. 'It's a good theatre,' he would say. 'Isn't better round here, go where you like.' Nudge. 'Been some famous actors there, they tell me. I don't know 'cos I wasn't here then, I wasn't.' Nudge. 'Had a shop in Liverpool then. Sold it and came back here. Got a shop here now.' Another nudge. Miss Trant in retreat and Mr Droke in close pursuit, ready for the next nudge. 'Belonged to my brother, this theatre did, and he left it to me. I don't bother with it much, too busy, and don't care about theatres. They used to be always wanting me to be doing this and doing that to it, but I couldn't be bothered, d'you see, and having my shop too and trade being so bad. Nothing wrong with it, though, nothing at all.' Nudge. 'A good theatre still. All fads, that's all. Nothing wrong with it. You're not faddy, are you?' More nudges. 'Well then, it'll suit you all right, very cheap at the price, very cheap. Too many faddy people now, aren't there? Don't know what they want.'

Miss Trant was not sure that she knew what she wanted but as soon as she saw the outside of the building, she knew at once that she certainly did not want the Tewborough Theatre Royal. Her heart sank. Its position was bad, for it was down a dark side-street; and its appearance was worse. Missing panes of glass, unpainted and rotting wood-work, dirt and litter, everywhere. The only things that were bright and new there were their own playbills, and they looked pathetic, so young and hopeful, so utterly out of place. The inside was worse than the outside. It was smaller than most old-fashioned theatres, but it was built on the usual plan, with stalls, pit, dress circle, and separate gallery. The seats in the gallery were narrow wooden benches, and those in the pit were similar benches with backs to them, and both pit and gallery stank abominably. The stalls and dress circle had the usual plush chairs, but they were all old and worn and stained. At one time the place may have made a pretty show of gilt, but now the dust and grime were so thick on the gilding that it returned no answering gleam to the lights. On the ceiling and the proscenium were some cracked nymphs and peeling cupids. Such carpets as there were on the corridors were threadbare. Old playbills lined the greasy walls: *Are You a Mason? The Girl from Kay's*; the Tewborough and District Amateur Operatic Company in *Dorothy*; *The Face at the Window*; *Dr Faustein in his Great Mesmeric, Thought-Reading, and Mystical Oriental Entertainment*; and here and there were yellowing photographs of heroic actors in togas or bag wigs, bewhiskered old 'heavies', and simpering leading ladies of the Nineties, all of them catching her eye as she passed and whispering: 'We're dead and gone.' She peered through a dirty glass door labelled *Saloon Bar* and saw a counter and a few bottles all thick with dust.

'That's shut up now,' said Mr Finnegan. 'We 'ad the licence taken away. 'Ard on a management, very 'ard!' This Mr Finnegan, to whom she had been handed over by Mr Droke, was called the manager, but he was obviously a general factotum in receipt of a mere pittance. He was old, shabby, and gently steeped in liquor, and such a pitiful figure that at any other time Miss Trant would have felt sorry for him, but now, as he shuffled down these grimy corridors with her, she could only regard him with distaste. When they returned to the auditorium, its atmosphere seemed more unpleasant and oppressive than ever: it was like walking into a drawer full of old rubbish that had not been turned out for twenty years. Miss Trant shuddered.

'Oh, but it - it's awful!' she cried. 'All so dirty and depressing.'

'Well,' Mr Finnegan mumbled, 'I don't say it wouldn't do with a clean-up, but - bless yer - it's a prince to some. You're new to it, aren't yer? Thought so; tell it in a minute. Wants tidying a bit, I dare say, but wouldn't be worth it just now. And theatres is all alike when you come in during the day and they're all empty, all alike they are: put you off if you don't know 'em. I've seen this place packed to the roof - everybody here - mayor and corporation, everybody! When Wilson Barrett opened 'ere with his Sign o' the Cross, there was over a nundred pounds in the youse, over a nundred pounds, Monday night, and that was when a quid was a quid, when you could buy something with it. Can't do that now, of course. There isn't the money in the town.' He shook his head mournfully.

The faded crimson curtain began shaking too. It gave a creak, then finally parted and rose. Two figures in shirt-sleeves walked on to the stage, and Miss Trant, approaching, discovered that one of them was Mr Oakroyd. When she drew near, she saw that he was very gloomy and disgusted.

'Eh, Miss Trant,' he cried, 'it is a mucky noil at t'back here. You nivver saw such a muddle. We'll have some trade on getting this right, we shall an' all. Come and have a look at it.'

Miss Trant went round, looked at the stage, peeped in a dressing-room or two, sent for Mr Finnegan (who could not be found), telephoned to Mr Droke (who did not reply), and went in search of two charwomen to assist Mr Oakroyd and his shirt-sleeved colleague, who had a glassy stare and a perpetually open mouth.

'He's not all there, isn't Charlie,' whispered Mr Oakroyd. 'That's his name - Charlie. He's a bit soft but he'll ha' to do. If he were right, he wouldn't be working here. If this is a the-ater, give me them pavilions and kursals ivvery time. This is nowt but a rag-bag. It'll cap me, Miss Trant; if we do much here. Town's got a bit of a miserable look about it.'

'It has,' replied Miss Trant emphatically. 'And I never saw a miserabler.'

'No more did I,' said Mr Oakroyd. 'We've nobbut been here a two-three hours, you might say, and it might improve a bit on acquaintance, but so far it's a right poor do.'

Mr Oakroyd, as we know, was not difficult to please. No man can live in Bruddersford for over forty years and be hypercritical; your Bruddersfordian is never one of those sensitive creatures who are entirely at the mercy of their surroundings. But already Tewborough had been too much even for Mr Oakroyd. Before meeting the others at the station, he returned to his lodgings, thus making further acquaintance with the town and disliking it more. His terse comment to Inigo summed up his view of the whole situation, the theatre, the town, the lodgings, everything. After making that comment, he walked away, partly because he had to see to the baggage but also because he had a good sense of the dramatic. After a few minutes he returned to Inigo's side.

'You and me has to share rooms,' he announced.

'Oh, how's that?' Inigo asked. 'Is the town full?'

'Nay, there's nowt on here at all. But they won't let. We'd a right job getting lodgings and they've all got to share. It's allus alike. Less brass fowk's makking, less they want to mak. If you go to a place where they're as throng as they can be, they're allus ready to mak' a bit more. You come to a place like this here, where all town's on t'dole and they're all pining, and you can't get 'em to let you have a room or two and sell you a bite and a sup o' summat. Fowk's so badly off, they won't be bothered.'

'Reluctant as I am, Master Oakroyd, to break in upon this deep philosophical strain,' said Inigo, 'I must put a question. What are the digs like?'

'Well, you'll see for yersen in a minute,' replied Mr Oakroyd. 'There's plenty o' room, I will say that. We've getten a big bedroom, with a gurt double bed in and one o' these little uns, campbeds. It's number nine, Billing Street, and it's right handy for t'the-ater. But by gow! - I don't know whether I'm not feeling up to t'mark or what - but there's summat about this place that seems to tak' t'heart right out o' me. I hope you don't mind being wi' me, lad,' he added shyly.

'Of course I don't,' said Inigo, who didn't.

"'Cos I'll be right glad of a bit o' company i' yond place,' he concluded.

There was certainly something very cheerless about Billing Street. It was narrow and dark, and had far more than its share of listless ailing women and children with grey faces and reddened eyes. It had two or three little warehouses with broken windows; a greengrocer's that seemed to have nothing but potatoes and paper bananas for sale; a chip-and-fish shop that smelt of tallow; a tiny grocer's that apparently specialized in black lead and sardines; a furtive little newsagent's, full of announcements about special wires and tips from the course; an undertaker's, with a specimen brass plate and a blackening wreath in the window; a herbalist's establishment, adorned with a large placard that said *Your Stomach Wants Watching*, a number of mysterious green packets, and a highly coloured drawing that had some reference to skin diseases; a second-hand shop filled with bamboo tables, flat-irons, and rolls of oilcloth; and two of the dingiest and dreariest-looking little public-houses that Mr Oakroyd, a man of experience, ever remembered encountering. Just behind the street was a building with a fantastic tower, a sinister conglomeration of pipes and ladders and tanks, and this, it appeared, was a sulphuric-acid works. Nobody seemed to knew whether it was still making acid or not, but if its pipes and vats were idle, their smell was not, for it descended into the street in sudden and sickening gusts.

Number 9 was the largest house in the street, and it looked the gloomiest. You could only imagine it existing in a perpetual series of dark Novembers. No sooner had Inigo set foot in it than he thanked God that he was not there alone. No wonder Mr Oakroyd had talked about 'a bit o' company'. The bedroom was quite large enough for two of them and it seemed reasonably clean, but there was something strangely chill and depressing about it.

Inigo sniffed. 'What is this queer smell? I've met it before. Wait a minute. I know. It's just like the smell of old magazines. When I was a kid, I used to dig out ancient copies of the *English Illustrated Magazine* from the lumber-room, and they had a smell just like this. Odd, very odd!' He looked about him. 'Not very jovial, is it? I feel as if there were a body in the next room.'

'There is,' replied Mr Oakroyd grimly.

'What!' Inigo jumped.

'Well, it's as good as one,' Mr Oakroyd went on. 'T'land-lady's owd mother's i' there, ower eighty and bedridden. You'll hear her coughing. I only hope she'll last t'week out. They've all gotten summat wrong with 'em here. It's war ner an infirmary. Mrs Mord - that's t'landlady - her you've just seen - she's not ower-strong - '

'A bit blue about the face, certainly,' said Inigo gloomily. 'I don't know that I want to hear any more.'

'You might as well nar we've started. Her husband's been off his work a long time - he wor a clurk in one o' them ware-houses - and I don't know fairly what's he's got, but I've nivver seen a feller so swelled up, all purple he is and puffed up; it taks him five minutes to do owt for his-sen and he can hardly talk. Eh, he's in a bad way. You'll be seeing him soon.'

'I won't.'

'And you haven't to excite him - that's what t'landlady says - he hasn't to be excited - '

'I don't want to excite him. I don't want to set eyes on him. I'm sorry for him, very sorry for him - he sounds like a human fungus - Hello! - what's that?'

'That's only t'owd lady coughing.'

Inigo breathed hard and looked thoughtfully at the things he was unpacking.

'Ay, they're a rum lot here,' Mr Oakroyd continued 'There's a sort o' young woman. I haven't had a proper look at her, and Mrs Mord says nowt about her, and I don't know who she is.'

'For the love of Mike,' cried Inigo, 'don't tell me there's something wrong with her too! It'll finish me, absolutely.'

'Well, all I knaw is she doesn't seem to do owt and there's summat funny about her. When you're going up and down t'steps or along t'passage, you suddenly see her face peeping out from nowhere and then she lets out a sort o' laugh and next minute you hear her scampering away as if somebody wor after her. I've seen her three times nar and I'm getting a bit used to it - '

Inigo had stopped unpacking. He was now sitting down and staring at his companion. 'She sounds as mad as a hatter,' he said despairingly.

'Ay, I fancy she must be a bit soft. They seem to run to it here. There's a feller at the the-ater called Charlie and he's not quite all there. No harm in him, yer know; just hasn't got twenty shilling to t'pound.'

Inigo stood up. 'I'm going,' he announced.

'Nay, lad, stick it, stick it! It's best we can get. And I only got in here 'cos I said there'd be two of us.'

'There must be an hotel. I shall go to an hotel. You can come too.'

'Nay, I'm going to no hotel. I've takken these lodgings and I'm staying here. They've gone to a lot o' bother to get it right for us. It's all nowt. Stick it, nar you're here.'

'All right,' Inigo replied gloomily. 'I shall spend most of my time at the theatre. That's the only thing to do. No wonder you said it was bloody awful. The adjective was justified, absolutely.'

'Eh, I wasn't talking about this place,' said Mr Oakroyd.

Inigo looked at him with horror. 'What were you talking about then?'

'Well, t'general carry on. Town itself, to begin wi', and t'the-ater.'

'Theatre?' Inigo's voice almost rose to a scream. 'Don't tell me there's anything wrong with that!'

But Mr Oakroyd insisted upon telling him what was wrong with the theatre, and they were half-way through tea before he had done. 'This Tewborough do's a washaht,' he concluded, 'and you can mak' up your mind about that. We shall do nowt here.'

'This is where we look sick,' Inigo groaned. 'I told you about last night, didn't I? And everybody's half dead today. All the way we've been saying that only a good week here will pull us together. Tewborough or death has been our motto, absolutely. Lord help us!'

It certainly looked, Mr Oakroyd admitted, as he took out his pipe and packet of Old Salt, as if they were in for it.

III

'Talk about a frost!' cried Mrs Joe, immediately after the performance on Monday night.

'You could skate on it for weeks,' said Susie gloomily. 'And I'll swear I've a temperature of 102.'

'And I'm sure you look it, my dear,' Mrs Joe told her. Then she went on, passionately: 'Was there an audience at all tonight? Was there *anybody* in the house? I thought I heard a sound once from somewhere, but was I mistaken? Does Tewborough know we're here?' she asked wildly.

'It knows but it doesn't care,' said Susie.

'I said to Joe last night: "Mark my words, Joe, this is going to be a bad week. I feel it in my bones," I said. Tomorrow, I shall spend most of the day in bed - and what a bed, my dear! - I'm sure it's one of those beds that rise in the middle, like a camel. And the room has no outlook and no cosiness. Not over-clean and the walls all covered with photographs of Oddfellows. But I shall spend most of tomorrow in it, nursing myself, and, then I shall come down again tomorrow night, but if I'm no better the next day I shall *not* be here, I shall go sick. The last thing that can be said of me is that I disappoint my public, but what I have to ask myself now, my dear, is this: Have I got a public in Tewborough? - and - Is it worth it?' Mrs Joe produced these questions with an air of triumph.

'No, it isn't worth it,' said Elsie crossly, 'and I wish you'd shut up. What's the good of talking?'

'Jimmy looked really bad tonight, I thought,' Susie said reflectively.

'I expect we all looked bad.' Elsie sniffed hard. 'I know I feel rotten enough, and feeling rotten isn't a hobby of mine like it is of Jimmy's. Me for some aspirin tonight. Come on, Susie, you *are* slow. Let's get out of this thing they call a theatre. Theatre Royal - my God! Theatre Dustbin - if you ask me. Oh, ca-ar-m on!'

On Tuesday night there were exactly fifty-three people in the audience. It was miserable when they kept silent, and it was worse when they applauded, for then you seemed to hear the empty spaces mocking the thin faint clap-clap-clap. Not that they applauded often. All the heart had gone out of The Good Companions. They trailed through the performance, and the only time they showed any signs of liveliness was when their growing irritation got the upper hand. Elsie complained bitterly of Jerry Jerningham; Susie openly accused Inigo of murdering her accompaniments; and even the good-humoured Joe began grumbling. Several of them declared it was high time Mr Oakroyd had learned his business, and were instantly told by that indignant little man to go and mind their own, which was, he asserted, 'in poor fettle'. Jimmy Nunn was strangely listless, and it was queer and disconcerting to see him so quiet, so yellow, and shaky. Miss Trant, who felt very apologetic about her disastrous venture, though it was she and not the others who would suffer most from the certain dead loss on the week, tried to smooth out these prickly relations and to cheer everybody up, but the heart had gone out of her too. The dismal town and the miserable waif of a theatre kept her spirits for ever sinking, for to leave one was only to encounter the other.

Wednesday brought a fog, not one of the choking yellow London horrors, but still a good thick blanketing fog, which settled on the town early in the morning and stayed there all day. The Good Companions sat huddled in their several rooms, trying to make the most of tiny fires and horsehair armchairs or sofas, reading papers that seemed to describe another planet, under greeny-white tattered gas-mantles, dozing and shivering and occasionally getting up to peer out of the steaming windows at the grey woolly nothingness outside. Of all of them, perhaps Inigo was the most cheerful, simply because the aspiring author in him now rose to the occasion. That author, who worked more fitfully than ever in these days, had not yet finished *The Last Knapsack*, having set it aside on the plea that wintry weather brought about an unpropitious atmosphere, but nevertheless he now made his appearance again.

'Off with the motley and on with the inkstand - that's what I say,' Inigo told Mr Oakroyd, in their common sitting-room. 'I was in the middle of a song, but I can't think about songs now. The mood, the mood - Master Oakroyd - is dead against any pierrotry. I was intended to be a man of letters and not a mountebank, and today I begin an essay - very bitter - that I shall call *England's Pleasant Land*. It will deal with the town of Tewborough, with a few such other resorts thrown in, and will be devilish ironical, bitter, absolutely. It will relieve my feelings, and it'll also make some of 'em sit up.'

'That's the idear,' said Mr Oakroyd; puffing comfortably at his pipe and beaming across the hearth at his companion. 'If you can't do it wi' Tewborough, you'll nivver do it with owt. But who's these that's going to be made to sit up?'

'Well - er - the - er - people responsible for such a state of things,' replied Inigo, vaguely but severely.

'I nivver knaw who they are,' Mr Oakroyd confessed. 'Other fowk allus knaws, though. It's allus either capitalists or t'workingmen, or it's this Parlyment or t'last, or it's landowners and employers or it's Bolshies. I can nivver mak' nowt out on it mysen, can't tell whose fault it is, but then I'm not one o' t'clever sort. It's allus all a right muddle to me. But you'll mak' summat owt on it, I dare say. And while you're at it, just slip in a nasty piece about yon' Droke who owns t'the-ater. Put us i' t'cart and right, he has. I call him a mucky mean old man, who owt to be going round wi' a little rag-and-bone barrer, he owt. But get thysen going, lad. Get it aht o' thy system.'

Inigo nodded gravely, lit a pipe, then without hesitation and with a fine flourish wrote at top of his first sheet: *England's Pleasant Land: by I. Jollifant*. Nor did he stop there. He actually began the essay itself. 'It is eleven o'clock,' he wrote. Having stared at this for a minute or two, he crossed it out and put in its place: 'I have just looked through the window, which is gemmed with moisture.' This did not please him, so out it came, and he began a new sheet, at which he frowned for nearly ten minutes. Then he wrote: 'Outside, this morning, the spoil of many clanking years - '; crossed out 'clanking'; crossed everything out; then drew six faces and absentmindedly decorated them with curly moustaches; then sighed, filled and lit his pipe again, and leaned back in his chair.

From the hall outside came the sound of a very slow dragging footstep. Mr Oakroyd looked up from his newspaper.

'That'll be Mr Mord,' he announced, 'and he's coming in here - if he can nobbut manage it.' Mr Oakroyd said this with a certain relish, as if he rather liked breaking bad news.

Inigo groaned. We have already heard Mr Oakroyd describe their landlady's husband, and since then Inigo has had two encounters with the purple and swollen invalid. 'I'm sorry for him, my heart bleeds, absolutely,' Inigo muttered quickly, 'but I can't stand having him about. It's like watching a ghastly slow-motion film. Have I time to get out?'

He had not time to get out. There was a vague knock at the door. Then the door opened slowly, very slowly, a maddening inch or two at a time, and finally admitted the stricken Mr Mord, who looked purpler and puffier than ever. He stood just inside the room for at least a minute, and then, having partly recovered from the journey, he produced, with all the care of a man saying something for the first time in a foreign language, the words: 'Good morning, gen-cl-men.' Then he nodded, very slowly. Then he smiled, and his smile was so leisurely that there was time to remark the appearance and disappearance of every crease in his dark swollen face. Then he made a step forward, then another step forward, then another. He saw a chair, seemed to examine it very thoroughly, and finally moved towards it. 'I'll take - a seat - if - it's all - the same - to you - gen-el-men,' he said; and when he spoke it seemed as if every syllable was an achievement. Then he lowered himself into the chair, carefully placed a puffy hand on each knee, turned his head round slowly to look first at one and then at the other, and ended by attempting speech once more. 'Seems - to me - a foggy - morning,' was his verdict. 'Used - to get - lot o' fog - here - one time.'

'Rather, yes! Awful lot of fog! Nasty thing, fog! Never liked it myself.' Inigo found himself jerking out these idiotic phrases at what seemed an incredible speed. 'Must excuse me now, Mr Mord. Awfully busy. Have to rush off.' And off he rushed, at least until he found himself outside the room, when he stopped and wondered where to go and what to do. The bedroom was miserably cold and cheerless, and he would have to sit in his overcoat there and probably have to listen to the old woman coughing in the next bedroom. If he wandered about the house, at any moment he might meet that mysterious and terrifying female who peeped round corners, gave a sudden screech, and then went scampering away. On the other hand, he could not possibly stay in the sitting-room and watch Mr Mord's horrible slow-motion performance. He went to the front door and looked outside. It was chill and ghostly. He crept upstairs to his bedroom, snuggled under his overcoat on the bed, and read a stained old copy of *Tom Bourke of Ours*.

It was chill and ghostly too in the theatre that night. They played and danced and sang like people in a miserable dream. Nobody was completely laid up yet, but nobody was any better. There were more grumblings and complaints, and it looked as if there would soon be downright feuds between the various bickering and snarling members of the troupe.

On Thursday the fog turned into black rain. This was the day on which most of the shops closed in Tewborough and the surrounding districts, and there were hopes of a better audience for that night. Mr Oakroyd, who had been round to the theatre for half an hour, returned in the middle of the afternoon to smoke a pipe with Inigo by the fire, and told him there were a few scattered bookings.

'Shop fowk here's got a bit more to spend than t'other fowk, so happen we'll ha' summat like a nordience tonight,' he remarked. 'But if it isn't one thing, it'll be t'other.'

'And what do you mean by that, my sage Bruddersfordian?' asked Inigo lazily.

'Bother wi' t'troupe.' replied Mr Oakroyd with great promptness. 'Bound to be a bit of bust-up soon, mark my word. All at it. And some on 'em'll get rough edge o' *my* tongue afore so long an' all, way they're going on. And there's owd Jimmy there, looking fit to drop, right poorly. And another thing. When I were going on, I saw yon Morton Mitcham coming out of a pub and I could see he'd had a few. Well, just afore I leaves the-ater in he comes wi' that chap, Finnegan - both on 'em a bit goggly - and they've getten a bottle o' whisky wi' 'em, a full un. They'll be at it nar, pair on 'em. Just you keep yer eye on yon Mitcham tonight. If he isn't three sheets i' t'wind by tonight, call me a liar, lad.'

Inigo could not keep an eye on Mr Mitcham before the performance began because Mr Mitcham was nowhere to be seen. When the curtain went up, he was still missing. There were more people in the theatre that night than there had been on all the other three nights put together; the place was about half-full, a good many people having come in from neighbouring small towns and villages, and it had a livelier air; with the result that the players themselves felt more cheerful. The only exception was Jimmy Nunn, who was more listless and shaky than ever. At the end of the third item, a song by Joe, and while the audience was still clapping, Mr Mitcham made his entrance. His make-up was very sketchy and he appeared to have a rather glassy stare. He was fairly steady but nevertheless contrived to knock a chair over before he sat down himself. For quite ten minutes, during which his assistance was not required, he sat, a huge huddled figure, staring at his banjo. At the end of that time, when Jimmy Nunn was about to announce the next item, Mr Mitcham suddenly sat up and began playing. Jimmy, who had no idea what was wrong, stared at him, but there was no help for it. So Mr Mitcham went on playing, very loudly and at top speed, and the rest of them had to pretend that it was part of the programme. Ten minutes, quarter of an hour, twenty minutes passed, and still Mr Mitcham went twanging away, until at last the audience, half-admiring and half-bored, burst into applause. Then he stopped, staggered forward, bowed, and suddenly roared out: 'La'ies Shenelmen! - one thing wanner say - one thing - thas all - jus' one.' And then, taking a deep breath, he bellowed: 'Four times roun' the worl''; and bowed again. At this the audience applauded again, while the other performers, now stiff with horror, tried to look as if nothing out of the ordinary was happening.

Smiling idiotically, Mr Mitcham now held up a long shaky hand, and said: 'Prosheeding ennertainmen' - permission, la'ies an' shenelmen - few fea's leshermain. Will any la'y - any shenelman - *Any* la'y - *Any* shenelman - any-any-anybody' - he stopped for a moment - 'take-a-card?' And he held out his banjo.

Inigo, catching an agonized glance from Jimmy, immediately started playing as loud as he could, and Joe was able to hustle Mr Mitcham off the stage in such a way that the incident appeared to be a well-rehearsed gag. Once in the wings, Joe took care that it should not be repeated, hurrying the protesting Mitcham down to the dressing-room, while the others went on with the performance.

Miss Trant always confessed that she went in terror of drunken men, but there was no sign of it that night. She was so angry that she insisted upon seeing Mr Mitcham as soon as she could. Even when he rose or wobbled to his feet, towered above her, and brought out again that large idiotic smile, she found she was not at all frightened but only wanted to shake some sense and decency into the great silly old disgusting baby.

'Goo' eening, Miss Tran',' he said genially. 'Goo' housh to-ni' and I gorrem goin', didden I now?'

'Please go home at once, Mr Mitcham,' she cried. 'You ought to be ashamed of yourself.'

He looked pained, and for a moment or two regarded her in silence with reproachful goggly eyes. 'Mish Tran', these not wordsh of a frien',' and he wagged his head mournfully. 'No, no, no. Who gorrem goin'? Didden I? Four time roun' the worl' -four times, mindjew - *Four* - an' still gerring 'em goin' - Morton Mitcham.'

She turned away in disgust and looked appealingly at Joe, who had not returned to the stage. 'Come on, ol' man,' said Joe. 'Just you get yourself going.'

Mr Mitcham seemed to regard this as a brilliant though bitter repartee. 'Clever, clever,' he said, shaking his head, 'bur nor wordsh of a frien'. Bur if I'm nor wanned, I'll - go.' And he suddenly went reeling away. Joe took charge of him, telling Miss Trant that he would be back at the theatre before the second half of the show began. For a moment now, Miss Trant felt inclined to go too, to turn her back on the wretched theatre and let herself cool down in her room at the hotel. She made up her mind that Mitcham should leave the troupe as soon as possible. She was still furious. To behave like that, just when things were so bad for her, was downright disloyalty, and the thought of it angered and then saddened her.

This was not the worst the evening had to offer, however, for in the middle of the second half of the show, Jimmy Nunn suddenly collapsed. He had sung one of his two songs - or at least had struggled through it somehow - and had made his first bow and then retired to the wings to make some slight change in his costume: Inigo was already playing the opening bars of the second song; when Jimmy, instead of changing, stared vacantly for a minute, gave a curious little moan, and would have fallen full length if Mr Oakroyd, who was standing by, had not caught him in time. Under his comic make-up (as a postman) his face was deathly pale; his lips were blue; and there were horrible little convulsive movements in all his limbs. Mr Oakroyd knew that poor Jimmy always carried a small flask of brandy about with him, and this was discovered in the dressing-room. Miss Trant, trembling, managed to force some of the brandy between the blue lips, while Mr Oakroyd supported the head and shoulders. There was some confusion on the stage, but all the time Inigo was still playing the same idiotic *pom-pom-poppa-pom, pom-pom poppa-pom* for that second song which now might never be sung again. The audience was growing restive; there was some stamping of feet at the back.

Jimmy stirred; some colour returned to his cheeks; and he opened his eyes. He was able to sip a little more brandy.

'We must get a doctor,' said Miss Trant.

Jimmy shook his head. 'No. No doctor,' he muttered. 'All right in a minute. Carry on show.'

It was Mr Jerry Jerningham, of all people, who took command of the situation now. He darted into the wings, exchanged a word with Miss Trant, then, pale but fairly composed, returned to the stage, stopped Inigo, and said: 'Ladies and gentlemen, Ai regret to announce thet Mr Jaymy Nen will nat - are - be able to continue his pawt of the - er programme - awing to ar - sudden indisposition.' Here he stopped for a moment, and there was a noise somewhere in the auditorium. It seemed as if somebody was trying to get out in a hurry. 'The next item - ar - will be a bahlad by Miss Stella Cavendish.' At which the audience clapped, as audiences always do; Mrs Joe walked over to the piano, looking very dignified but in such a flutter that she spilled half her music; Mr Jerningham, that intrepid exquisite, gravely took a seat; and the performance continued.

They got Jimmy to his dressing-room and he was still muttering that he did not want to see a doctor when there came the sound of voices from the corridor outside. 'Well, I don't knaw, Missis,' Miss Trant heard Mr Oakroyd saying. The next moment a thin middle-aged woman in black had stalked into the dressing-room and, ignoring Miss Trant and Joe, was bending over Jimmy, who was staring at her with his mouth wide open.

'And how are you now, James?' she said, still examining him closely.

Recovering now from his first shock of surprise, he gave the ghost of a grin. 'Not so bad, Carrie. What - you doing here?'

'You look badly, James. I thought you did earlier on. It won't do, James. You're a sick man. You're not fit to be sitting here, with that silly paint on your face. You want looking after.'

Miss Trant, who had been too astonished to speak at first and then had not known what to say, now made a slight movement.

'I dare say you're wondering what I'm doing here,' said the determined woman, looking at Miss Trant with an unfriendly eye. 'Well, I'm Mrs Nunn. And as soon as they gave out he wasn't well, I came round to see him. And it's lucky I happened to be here. I knew you were coming here because two of your troupe I saw the other Sunday at Hicklefield Station told me you were coming. You saw me out of the window that day, James,' she added grimly.

'Yes, I did,' said Jimmy, and left it at that.

'Yes, yes, of course, I see,' said Miss Trant hastily. She felt very embarrassed. 'We've been trying to persuade Mr Nunn to see a doctor. I know he hasn't been well all the week.'

'And never likely to be,' cried Mrs Nunn scornfully. 'Nothing proper to eat, wet clothes, and dirty lodgings, I know! He ought to be in bed now. Tewborough Theatre Royal! Well, he's going to hear what I've got to say now. He's heard it before but this time perhaps he'll believe me.'

This left Miss Trant no alternative but to go and leave this strangely united pair alone. Joe had already stolen out, so now Miss Trant followed his example. About a quarter of an hour later, in the wings, she found herself confronted by Mrs Nunn again, and it was quite obvious that that determined woman had decided what was to be done. The very look of her reminded Miss Trant of a coiled steel spring. 'James Nunn is coming with me,' she announced at once. 'He's in a poor way and I'm going to look after him. You must manage as best you can without him - '

'Well, but naturally, I don't want him to go on playing here when he's so ill,' Miss Trant protested. This extraordinary woman seemed to imagine they were ready to drag poor Jimmy on to the stage if necessary. 'But where - I'm sorry, but I don't quite understand - where is he going?'

'With me,' replied Mrs Nunn promptly and firmly. 'I live about twelve miles away, between here and Hicklefield. I've got a shop. That's why I came today, half-day closing. James Nunn's gone his way and I've gone mine, but we're husband and wife, nothing alters that, and I'm not going to stand by and do nothing when he's in such a state. I told him where it would land him before he'd done but he wouldn't have it. Now he's beginning to learn.' She looked as if she were about to turn away, but brought out another remark as if it were a postscript. 'Your troupe's not got enough go in it, not half enough go; you want to keep them up to the mark better, Miss.' And with that she stalked away.

Miss Trant, gasping a little, stared after her, and wondered what she ought to do. Finally, she stayed where she was for another ten minutes or so, then went down to Jimmy's dressing-room again. Jimmy would want to see her before he went, and after all she had a right to know what was going to happen to him. But the dressing-room was empty. It was incredible that they could have gone like that, without another word, but there it was; they could not be found. Jimmy's astonishing wife had spirited him away, just as if she were a witch. 'I shall believe in a minute she *was* a witch.' she told herself miserably, as she drifted back down the dingy smelly corridor. Her head ached and she felt ready to cry at any moment. Oh, this wretched, wretched Tewborough! She stayed to see the end of the performance, which had dwindled into a mere dismal sketch of their usual show, and to tell the others what had happened. Too tired and dispirited to join in their wild surmising and speculating, she crawled to her hotel, lay awake and listened to the black rain still falling on Tewborough, and felt alone in an ugly and incomprehensible world.

The next morning, as she sat scribbling letters over the coffee-room fire, a visitor was announced. It was Mr Morton Mitcham. He looked ancient and bilious; longer than ever but more ruinous; and he seemed to come creaking into the room, an unmelodious jangle of bones. He came forward, one hand clutching his sad sombrero and the other nervously fingering the immense buttons of his overcoat, the Silver King. Miss Trant remembered this name for his overcoat - she had forgotten all about it, and it returned unbidden - and then she told herself that she could not possibly send him away. And in any case, with Jimmy absent, it would not be wise, she reflected.

'Miss Trant,' Mr Mitcham began very solemnly, in his deep harsh drawl, 'I am here to make what apology I can - for last night. I understand that I nearly let down the show - at a difficult time, too - and I believe I also offended you personally.' His eyes stared hollowly at her above his sunken and yellow cheeks. 'I'm sorry. I'm very sorry indeed. I throw myself upon your mercy, believe me.'

'All right, Mr Mitcham,' she said hastily. 'I'm sure it won't happen again - '

'It will *not* happen again.'

'Very well, then' - and she felt like this gigantic creature's school-mistress; it was absurd - 'we won't say anything more about it.'

'Miss Trant, this is generous of you. It's - it's wonderful.' Then, rather surprisingly, he stopped, lowered his massive, eyebrows, and looked at her with something like disapproval. 'But it won't do,' he went on, with an air of mournful reproach. 'Something *must* be said about it. I ought to be ashamed of myself and I *am* ashamed of myself; but I doubt if I'm sufficiently ashamed of myself. Tell me here and now, Miss Trant, how disappointed and disgusted you are. For me, Morton Mitcham, the oldest and most experienced member of the party, the man who ought to see you through, the one trouper you ought to be able to depend on - to behave like that! Gah! - it makes me sick to think of it. And Jimmy ill too! The show right up against it! And what am I doing? Rub it in, Miss Trant, rub it in. Ask me how I'd like you to tell people that Morton Mitcham let you down. You can't say too much or put it too strong,' he went on, just as if she really had said all these things. 'I deserve it, every word of it.'

She could not help smiling. 'If you insist, of course, I will say that I think you behaved very badly - or at least very stupidly, and that I was really angry about it last night. In fact, I had made up my mind - '

He held up a hand. 'Pardon me for interrupting,' he said earnestly, 'but there's just one thing I've got to tell you. It couldn't have happened anywhere but in this place. Tewborough, Miss Trant, has been my what's-its-name - my Waterloo. Yes, it's downed me. I don't know whether I'm getting too old for the road or what - but here, in Tewborough this week, I've touched rock bottom.'

'So have I,' said Miss Trant, not without bitterness.

'I'm an old traveller, a bit of a vagabond, if you like,' he went on, with a certain mournful gusto, 'but I'm an artist too. The temperament's there, all the time, a lion waiting to pounce. I must have *something* - a bit of adventure, a bit of good cheer, a hand from the audience, a new show going well, anything will do, I don't ask for a lot. But in Tewborough - so far as I'm concerned - there's been *nothing*. The place, the people, the rooms, the theatre, the show frozen out every night - believe me, Miss Trant, I'm an old trouper, four times round the world, but I've nerves and all this has just got on 'em. I'll put it to you frankly - I'd just got to light the place up somehow, and yesterday I overdid the illuminations. And that's how it is.'

'I understand,' she assured him. And she did. She could almost find it in her heart to envy him his toping. 'It's all been a mistake, I know,' she said wearily, 'and I think we're all having a bad time and suffering from nerves. It's not like the same concert party. But you must help me out now, especially since poor Jimmy's been rushed off somewhere - I don't know where - by his wife. We're in an awful muddle now.'

'Miss Trant,' he said very impressively, 'you have here a man who's going to see you through, whatever happens. Whatever you're doing, making up a new programme, anything, you can count on Morton Mitcham. I'll give half a show, if you like; it won't be the first time I've done it. Only say the word, whatever it is, and I'm there.'

'Thank you,' she cried, still amused but also rather touched.

'Thank you.' And then he added gravely: 'I should like to shake hands on that, Miss Trant, if you don't mind.'

So they shook hands, and then Mr Mitcham immediately became his cheerful and reminiscent self again and insisted upon telling her all about various places he had visited that were not unlike Tewborough, though it was hard for anybody but Mr Mitcham to see any resemblance. Then he departed, after assuring her again that she had in him, Morton Mitcham, the man who would see her through, the man who was prepared, if necessary, to keep the show going by himself.

And that very night he was compelled to keep his promise in part, for a dreadful thing happened. Jimmy was absent; but then they had expected that. But Jerry Jerningham was missing too. At first they imagined he was merely late, and after waiting a few minutes they began without him, a sadly depleted troupe playing to a sadly depleted audience. No message had been received from him at the theatre, and finally Miss Trant sent Mr Oakroyd round to his rooms to see what had happened. Meanwhile, the others carried on as best they could. The absence of both Jimmy and Jerningham made a terrible hole in the programme. Susie and Mr Mitcham, however, contrived to fill up and supply some comic relief, gagging desperately. When Mr Oakroyd returned, he had a story to tell that only heightened the mystery. 'Woman at his lodgings doesn't knaw where he is,' said Mr Oakroyd. 'He said nowt to her. But a car come this morning, she says, and he went off in it. He didn't tak' onny luggage - she took notice o' that, you can bet yer' life, 'cos she'd want paying afore she'd let him tak' owt away - and he didn't let on where he was off to or say owt at all to her. But it wouldn't cap me,' he concluded, 'if he hadn't ta'en his hook bart luggage, just gi'n us the go-by.'

'I don't know what that means,' said Miss Trant rather peevishly, 'so I can't say whether I agree with you or not.'

Mr Oakroyd shot a curious glance at her. This was not like Miss Trant. 'I mean', he said shortly, 'he's gone off, luggage or no luggage. I can't say it plainer ner that.' It must be confessed that all their tempers were a trifle frayed by this time.

Miss Trant walked away without another word. It did not matter where Jerningham had gone, the fact remained that he was not where he ought to have been, that he had let them down. She was hurt, angry. When the interval came, she found that Elsie and Susie were no longer on speaking terms and that Mrs Joe had a complaint to make about the conduct of Mr Morton Mitcham, who seemed to imagine, Mrs Joe observed, that the programme belonged to him. Miss Trant refused to listen to any of them. 'Don't be babyish,' she snapped, to their astonishment, and turned her back on them. She had had as much as she could possibly stand, she told herself; the whole week a grim fiasco, money thrown away; Jimmy ill, missing; Jerningham missing; the rest of them getting drunk or wrangling, not making the slightest attempt to help her out; no loyalty, no comradeship; the whole thing in ruins. She felt she was sick of it all. Here she was, stuck in this awful place, trudging through black streets, her time spent in either a dingy hotel or a dirty broken-down theatre, and this misery was costing her more than the most expensive holiday she could devise for herself. She could not hang about and watch the performance trailing to an end; she wanted to go to bed, to read something distant, gay, and adventurous, to forget Tewborough and its horrible Theatre Royal and The Good Companions - the very name made her wince; but first, there was something to be done.

That was why, when the show was over, Mr Oakroyd said to them all: 'Miss Trant's gone home, but you've to look at notice-board by t'door.' On the notice-board was a sheet of paper that summoned them all, in the name of E. Trant, to attend a meeting on the stage the following day, Saturday, at noon: *Urgent.*

IV

At noon on Saturday they were all there, not excluding Mr Oakoyd, whose pipe was still in his mouth but quite cold and empty and whose little cap was as far back on his head as it could possibly go, two facts that proved beyond doubt that he was uneasy in his mind. They were all uneasy, subdued; and when they spoke their voices were quieter than usual. It was a morning as cold and grey as slate. Every few seconds one of them either coughed or yawned, and they all looked tired. Inigo, glancing every now and then at Susie, wondered if she too was ill, or all her sparkle was gone and she was pale and heavy-eyed. Nothing had been heard of either Jimmy or Jerry Jerningham, and they all had the air of being survivors after a shipwreck.

'I think you'll agree', Miss Trant began, with a curious return to her earlier half-nervous, half-detached manner and clipped speech, 'that we've got to decide what's to be done. To begin with - about tonight. Is it worth while giving a performance at all?'

'No, it isn't,' said Elsie. 'Last night was ghastly. They'll be throwing things tonight.'

'Preposterous!' This was from Mr Morton Mitcham, who drew himself up to his full height and menaced Elsie with his eyebrows. 'Why shouldn't we give a show? There are six of us, aren't there? I call it turning good money away not to give a show. Why, one of us - just one of us - is too good for Tewborough, let alone six of us. I've known the time when a whole drama and vaudeville show thrown in were done with less than six. I myself - allow me to say - '

'Oh yes, we know!' Elsie put in rudely. 'Out there in Timbuctoo, way back in Eighty-three, you worked miracles. We know all about that.'

'You know nothing,' said Mr Mitcham with great scorn. 'You haven't had a chance to learn. You've been nowhere. You've seen nothing. Ignorance, that's your trouble, young lady, sheer ignorance.'

'Oh, you go and - ' Elsie exploded.

'Now that won't do, my dear,' Mrs Joe cried hastily. 'Do not let us forget ourselves, please. We're having our Trials and Troubles I know - or if I don't, then who does, my word! But don't let's descend to Name-calling and - and - Baydinarge and Rudenesses.' And Mrs Joe sat up erect, looked very dignified indeed for about two seconds, but then unfortunately was compelled to sneeze.

'Well, I say - give tonight a miss,' said Elsie sullenly.

'And I say you're rotten mean,' Susie blazed out, 'to think of it. Here's Miss Trant dropped an awful lot on the week and you don't even want to give a chance to get something back. After all, it's Saturday and there's sure to be some sort of a house tonight. What's the sense of turning the money away, as Mr Mitcham says. We can give them a jolly sight better show even now than they can appreciate, if I know Tewborough.'

'Half a minute, though, Susie,' said Joe in his slow honest fashion. 'It's Miss Trant who's asking us if it's worth it, so I don't see you can fairly blame Elsie for saying it isn't. It seems to me it's for Miss Trant herself to decide. I'm sure we'll all do our best, but if she thinks this is going to give us a bad name, and it might, then she'd better call it off.'

'What do you think?' asked Miss Trant, turning to Inigo, to whom she felt closer, in this present mood, than she did to any of the others, for, like her, he was a newcomer to this world.

Inigo shrugged his shoulders. 'It's all the same to me. If it was a matter of leaving this graveyard of a town, I'd say, let's go at once, for I believe it's simply this place that's done us in, absolutely. But if we've got to stay here, we might as well give the show tonight. It's practice for us; it might brighten somebody's evening here; and though I'll bet all the money we take tonight won't go very far, it'll help you, Miss Trant, to bring down the loss a bit. On the other hand, if you say, Let's pack up and go, on to the next place, over the hills and far away, I'm your man, absolutely.'

There was a murmur of assent, but Miss Trant sprang to her feet, walked a yard or two, then faced them all. 'But now I come to the next thing,' she cried. 'Are we going to other places? Is it worth while going on at all? That's what I'm asking myself.'

She stopped and there was a little chorus of exclamations, through which the voice of Mrs Joe could be heard repeating, in tragic tones: 'I knew it. I knew it.'

'Please don't misunderstand me,' Miss Trant went on. 'It's not money I'm thinking about, though I've lost a good deal, as you must realize, especially this week. And you mustn't imagine for a moment I'm rich, because I'm not. It was only because some money came unexpectedly that I was able to do this at all. But it isn't that, though naturally it's rather dreadful continually losing money. It's something else –' She hesitated.

'May I say something, Miss Trant?' said Elsie, rather sulkily. 'If it's this week that's bowled you over, I hope you'll remember you brought us here, that it was your idea taking this stinking brute of a theatre.'

'You *are* the limit,' cried Susie, looking as if she was ready to silence her for ever. 'Won't you be quiet!'

'Why should I be?' demanded Elsie.

'Grrr!' There was exasperation, indignation, disgust, and we know not what beside in this fierce noise that Susie made.

But now she turned to Miss Trant: 'You're not really going to chuck it, are you, Miss Trant? I know we've done badly so far, but really we haven't had a chance yet.'

'Not a dog's.' said Joe gloomily.

'I realize that just as well as you do,' Miss Trant told them. 'It's not that at all. It's - it's - what has happened this week that makes me feel I've had enough of it. Oh, I know this place has been awful and I brought you here. I never ought to have rented this dreadful, abominable theatre - I know that - I made a mistake, and I'm paying dearly for it. But you might have stood by me - '

'Stood by you, Miss Trant!' cried Mrs Joe, throwing up her hands and glancing round with a look of deep despair. 'Never was any manager of mine so stood by as you've been by me this week. If it had been Drury Lane I couldn't have done more, and wouldn't have done so much. Night after night, I've come here rising from a Sick-bed. "No," I said to Joe, when he begged me to stay in and look after myself, "my Duty's there. If it was anybody but Miss Trant, I wouldn't do it," I told him. Weren't those my very words, Joe?'

'That's right,' said Joe, staring very hard at nothing in particular.

'I've no doubt whatever you did your best, Mrs Brundit,' Miss Trant went on, a trifle wearily. 'But I can't get away from the feeling that the party as a whole has let me down this week. This was my special venture - I admit it's turned out to be a very silly one - and you ought to have backed me up. Instead of that, the party has gone to pieces - '

'You can't blame us because Jimmy had a heart attack or whatever it was,' Elsie interrupted. 'And as for some people - ' She stopped and looked significantly at Mr Mitcham, who for his part tried not very successfully to pretend she wasn't there.

'Yes, yes, that was our bad luck,' cried Miss Trant impatiently. 'That couldn't be helped, but other things could - quarrelling, not bothering about the show, not trying to make the best of it, leaving the rest of us in the lurch - oh, you must know what I mean! If you don't, it doesn't matter; I'm only trying to explain myself. I feel the whole thing's gone to pieces.'

'I'll never, never forgive Jerry Jerningham as long as I live for going off like that,' Susie exclaimed.

'That boy's yellow,' said Mr Mitcham, and he said it in such a way as to hint that he had known this all along and was rather surprised that the others had not noticed it too.

'I suppose he *has* gone,' Susie said doubtfully.

'Yes, he must have gone,' Miss Trant replied, with a kind of weary contempt in her voice. 'He's left his things behind, but probably he preferred to go without them rather than stay here. You called again this morning, didn't you?' she asked Mr Oakroyd, who was dismally sucking his empty pipe in the background.

'Ay, I went and left t'message to say we was having a bit of a meeting here, if he came back. T'landlady said she'd heard nowt, and I fancy by t'look on her she'd just been takking stock o' his booits and shirts and collars to see how much they'd fetch in case she heard no more on him.'

'We've seen the last of that bright boy,' said Elsie. 'He'd a lot to say about Mildenhall, when he went and did the dirty on us, but he's no better himself, as he'll hear from me if ever I set eyes on him again.'

'Well there you are,' Miss Trant told them. 'The first real test - and - look what's happened. Can you blame me if I feel we can't go on? It's not been easy for me to do what I have done - I don't mean about money, but simply that I knew nothing about the Stage and didn't understand this life - I had to take what seemed to me an awful sort of plunge. And what attracted me, I think, more than anything at first was the way you were all so loyal and kept so cheerful and friendly under the most horrible conditions. And now - well - I'm afraid I don't see it like that any more.'

After her voice had trailed away into silence, nobody spoke, nobody stirred, for what seemed quite a long time. It was so quiet that they could hear, coming from the forgotten world into that strange shrouded place, the sound of the factory buzzers in the town.

Then Susie stood up. 'No, I suppose I can't blame you, Miss Trant,' she said tonelessly. 'But - oh, I'm sorry. You don't know how sorry I am.' There were tears in her voice now, and she swung round and walked to the side of the stage, where Mr Oakroyd was standing.

'Nay, lass,' he said, 'tak' it easy, tak' it easy.' Then he rubbed his chin hard, tried to push his cap further back still, finally pushed it off his head altogether, picked it up and jammed it on again, then stepped forward and manfully spoke up. 'Nar then,' he began, 'I don't suppose onny on yer want to hear what I've got to say, but as nobody seems to be saying owt just nar, happen you'll listen a minute. And I say, Stick it. Don't give up, Miss Trant. Have another do at it. Nar don't get into your head I'm saying this 'cos I don't want to lose mi' job - I don't want to lose it, I'll tell you straight, specially nar as I knaw t'ropes - but it isn't that. I fair hate thought o' a thing coming to nowt afore it's got started. Nivver let it be said that this here Tewborough took all t'heart out on us. Tewborough be damned, I say. We can show it.'

'That's the stuff, Master Oakroyd,' cried Inigo enthusiastically. 'I'm with you there, absolutely.'

'It's nobbut a matter o' turning a corner,' said Mr Oakroyd earnestly addressing himself to Miss Trant. 'It's allus same wi' iverything. Stick it, get round t'corner, and you're there. Gi' this up nar and it's all flummoxed, might as well nivver ha' started. Nobbut go on a bit, and you nivver knaw, happen in a fort-nit or fower week you're coining brass and they can't mak' enough on you. Nay,' he cried reproachfully, 'we're on t'road, aren't we? There's down's as well as ups. This here's down all right. What of it? We'll get on t'road agen, chance it, and - mark my words - if we're not up, right at top o't'tree, a'most afore you can say Jack Robi'son, nay, I'll eat this cap.' And Mr Oakroyd, carried away by his own eloquence, plucked off his cap, held it out, jammed it on his head once more, and turned away.

'Darling!' cried Susie tearfully as he passed her.

He replied by giving her a wink, not a jolly impudent wink but a stammering embarrassed wink, which announced that he knew quite well that he had been making a fool of himself. It would take a man years to live down such an emotional outburst in Bruddersford.

There was hardly time for the others to say anything before the voice of Mr Oakroyd, this time raised in expostulation, was heard again, coming from that part of the theatre to which he had retired. Everybody looked up and waited expectantly. Something was about to happen, their attitudes said, and they were glad of it.

A large, glittering, jangling woman charged into the centre of the group on the stage, and looked about her wildly.

'Lady Partlit!' cried Susie and Inigo together, at once recognizing their acquaintance of the hotel outside Hicklefield.

'Yes, yes. How d'you do? Of course!' Lady Partlit babbled, trying to see everyone at once, so that she seemed to be spinning like a top. 'I'm sorry to come like this. Must be intruding. But they told me - here. Is he here? Oh, where is he?' And she beat her little fat hands together.

Miss Trant was staring, amazed. 'I don't understand,' she began blankly. 'Who - what - is it -?'

Susie darted forward. 'Is it,' she gasped, 'Jerry Jerningham?'

Lady Partlit was at once so excited, anxious, confused, that she looked exactly like an agitated parrot. 'Yes, of course, Mr Jerningham. It's been all *all* a mistake, I assure you, and of course I can explain everything to him when I see him. Are you sure, are you really sure, he's not here? Because,' she concluded wildly, 'he's gone.'

They assured her that Mr Jerningham was not there, and would have asked her all manner of questions - for they were all bursting with curiosity - but she did not give them time. 'Miss Trant, are you?' she went on, rushing across to jangle in front of that astonished woman. 'So disturbing for you, of course, and so nice of you not to mind about my coming like this.' Then she rushed back to Susie, whom she apparently regarded as the one member of the party likely to be sympathetic. 'A complete misunderstanding from beginning to end, I do assure you, Miss Bean, Miss Dean, and all meant in the friendliest way. But he simply went off, went off without a single word, and I was sure I should find him here. And of course you're all thinking it's so strange of me, coming and behaving like this, intruding too, but I had to come if there was *any* chance at all of explaining to him, you see. And of course it's worse than ever, with no one here knowing anything about him.'

'He's been missing for two days,' said Susie.

'Yes, I know that. *That* I can explain,' Lady Partlit began, when a sound made her look across and she gave a little scream. 'There you are,' she gasped.

And there Mr Jerningham was, looking anything but his usual exquisite self. He jumped and turned crimson at the sight of Lady Partlit, who now hurried across the stage towards him.

'Go away,' he screamed, backing a step or two.

'But it's *all* been a mistake - '

'Ai don't waarnt to hear anything,' he shrieked. Then, with mounting fury, he added: 'Thet man took away mai trousers. He deliberately took them away. You told him to.'

'Only to brush them,' Lady Partlit wailed.

'Nat to brush at all,' Mr Jerningham cried, wagging a finger at her. 'He just took them away. Then he laughed at me. Look, look, what Ai had to put on.' And everybody looked at once and discovered with joy that Mr Jerningham was wearing a pair of very dirty khaki trousers of a kind that might possibly be used by an under-gardener faced with a morning's rough work. When Mr Jerningham saw all their eyes fixed upon his awful trousers, he was angrier than ever with poor Lady Partlit, and told her to go away at once and that he never wanted to set eyes on her again. Distressed and still babbling, she was led away by Susie, who accompanied her to the stage door.

'Very sweet of you, my dear, I'm sure,' said Lady Partlit, brokenly, tearfully. 'I felt so unhappy about it, and you will say as little as you can, won't you? I've an old friend lives near here, not twenty miles away, and I came specially to see - to see you all. That was on Thursday, and then I sent a note, just a friendly note, to Mr Jerningham, and sent the car round for him, to bring him out. I thought - he's so clever, isn't he? - and I thought I might be able to help him, though I didn't tell him that, my dear, didn't tell him how I might be able to - you know - assist him in his career, because I thought - well, we ought to be friendly first, because you can help a *friend*, can't you? And then of course I never knew my friend would be called away like that, and never dreamt for a moment there would be that difficulty with the car on Friday afternoon, and I do assure you, my dear, that it was all a mistake and a misunderstanding about the - the trousers. He's so *bitter* about them, isn't he? I'm sure he'll never forgive me, but perhaps some time soon, you'll perhaps just - er - say something to him, will you? But of course don't *talk* about it, will you? I know I can rely on you not to do that. And if there's anything, anything, I can do for you, at any time, my dear - you're so clever too, aren't you? And it's been so nice of me - I mean, of you - that is, so nice seeing you again, hasn't it? Do I - Oh, here - yes, of course. Dear, dear, I must stop one minute before I go out - so upsetting rushing in like this, and then - everything such a mistake - hasn't it? Good-bye.'

Susie stood looking after her a moment, drew a deep breath, then returned to the stage, humming a little tune that seemed to amuse her. Mr Jerningham was still apologizing and protesting to a bewildered Miss Trant, but he gave no sign of being willing to gratify everybody's curiosity. Susie took him aside as soon as she could. 'Do you know who that was?' she inquired, not without malice.

'Mai dear Susie,' he protested, 'down't talk about that harrible woman. She's a fet middle-aged vemp, thet's what she is.'

'You know she's Lady Partlit and very rich, don't you?' Susie went on.

'As a metter of feet, Ai do,' he replied loftily, 'and Ai don't care.'

'But what you don't know, my dear Jerry,' she continued softly, 'is that she practically controls two West End theatres, mostly running musical comedies and revues.'

'Mai God!' Mr Jerningham turned pale and looked at her with horror. 'And to think -!' The thought was too much for him, but as he looked away it chanced that he caught sight of the trousers he was wearing. 'Ai don't care,' he said stoutly, 'she shouldn't have told the man to take mai trousers.' Nevertheless, he was thoughtful for some time, and it was many weeks before he completely lost a certain brooding air.

'Of course, this does make *some* difference,' Miss Trant was saying, when they returned to her side. She let the others chatter a little while she considered their position. She did not understand yet exactly what had happened to Jerningham, but it was quite clear that he had not deliberately absented himself. He had vehemently insisted on the fact that it was no fault of his he had missed last night's show, and was genuinely indignant at the suggestion that he had failed them.

'Nar then,' cried the voice of Mr Oakroyd triumphantly, 'what about this?' Somebody was with him.

'Well, boys and girls!'

'Jimmy!' cried Susie, rushing at him. The next moment they were all round him, nearly shaking his hand off.

'There's a doctor in Mirley - that's where I've been - who's a marvel, a wonder, a miracle,' Jimmy announced solemnly. He still looked rather pale and shaky, but he was obviously much better. 'He's only young and he's got a bit of a squint and his teeth stick out - but, let me tell you, he could raise the dead, that chap. I went to see him, and he talked and tapped, and tapped and talked, until I got fed up. "All right, doc," I says, "don't mind me. Give me six months and get ready to sign in the space provided for that purpose on the form." He laughed. "Nonsense," he says, "I can make a new man of you. When did you see a doctor last?" So I told him. Four years ago. "Thought so," he says. "And what have you been doing to yourself since?" So I told him. Trying this and that. "Thought so," he says again. "Now you listen to me." And he gives me some medicine to take and tells me what to do with myself. Then it was my turn, and by this time the wife wasn't in the room. "Have I to stop here and do no work?" I asked him. "Because if so, I shall be dead anyhow. If you tell me right out", I told him, "to get back to the boards, where I belong, you'll complete the cure. And don't just tell me," I says, "but tell my wife as well." So he told me to see him again and then he'd let me know. I tipped him the wink all right. He knew what was what. "Do him no harm to get back to work," he said this morning. "May do him good." Collapse of the opposition! So here I am, Miss Trant, boys and girls, and so long as I take one dose before meals and one after, I'm fit and ready to crack the old wheezes.'

'We were only talking just now, Jimmy,' said Joe, 'about whether we could give a show at all tonight.'

'Give a show tonight!' cried Jimmy. 'I should think we do give a show tonight, if I've to give it all by myself. Tonight, one hundred and twenty-five members of the Mirley and District Cooperative Society - prevented, owing to un-fore-seen cir-cum-stances, from having their monthly whist-drive and dance are coming to Tewborough, and for what? - to see The Good Companions at the Theatre Royal, where they will occupy the dress circle on special terms given 'em by Mr Nunn. Now let's get busy and see if we can't pack the house.'

'Let joy and what's-its-name be unconfined,' roared Inigo, doing a little step-dance. 'Now what do you say, Miss Trant?' he asked, lowering his voice. 'Do The Good Companions go on?'

'They do,' she replied, smiling and flushing a little.

'We'll learn 'em yet,' said Mr Oakroyd, perspiring with enthusiasm. 'We will an' all. Tewborough 'ull noan do us down. Tewborough's nowt. It's getten a right slap in the eye this morning.'

They played well that night, and a circle packed with members of the Mirley and District Cooperative Society was not slow to appreciate their efforts. (Even the Treasurer, a deacon at the Baptist Chapel who had misgivings about any form of entertainment that ventured further than a cantata, was heard to laugh several times.) 'I don't say it's been a riot,' Susie observed, when the show was over, 'but I'll swear it's the nearest Tewborough's got to a riot since the Number Two Touring

Company of *A Royal Divorce* first came here in the year Dot. And we pulled together, didn't we, children?'

The children admitted that they had and returned to their various lodgings, which were all either so dismal or sinister that already a place had been found for them in the archives, with the cue - 'My dear, did you ever play a hole called Tewborough?' well content, happy in the knowledge that the party was itself again and that tomorrow it would seek fresh streets and lodgings new. Thus ended the Black Week.

CHAPTER SEVEN
All Stolen From the Mail Bag

I

From Miss Elsie Longstaff to Miss Effie Longstaff

c/o Mrs Bottomley,
23 Jagger Street,
Luddenstall,
Yorks.
19 December

Dear Effie,

I got the things alright and ought to have written before this but we did some Three Nights and you know what it is don't you, all packing and etc. Now we are here for what you can call a run! - till into the New Year at a sort of concert hall and picture place combined, not so big but comfy and clean, good stage and lighting etc. - all marvellous compared with what we have been playing lately I can tell you! Comfy rooms here too and on my own at last, Thank goodness, I got sick to death of having Susie Dean poking about all the time, not that we are not friends we are but you know what it is, my dear! Show looks like going well here, Good old Yorks. I say, if you can get them going up here they will stick to you alright every time. I had one encore last night and could have had another but of course I was told programme would not stand it. Too much Susie Dean and J. Jerningham in the programme if you ask me these days, what with the piano player writing songs for them as well and all that! His name is Inigo Jollifant says its real too! - and he is quite a nice boy but the way he goes mooning round S. Dean and the way she keeps him dangling would make you sick if it didn't make you laugh. Kids game, I call it, but then thats all they are!

Well we look like having a nice Xmas for once. Playing Xmas Eve and then just one show on Boxing Day. Can you get off to come up, I don't suppose you can, and I am wondering if I could manage it just for Xmas Day as it's not so far. Are you still at the George or have you gone to the Vic as you said you might, and does Charlie come in and Jimmy and that tall fellow with the specs and all that lot, if they do just give them my love and tell them to be good boys till I come back! And guess who I saw here the very second day. I went into Leeds in the morning looking round shops - I nearly bought a new coat in a little shop just off Briggate that was having a sale, large wrap in front and straight inlets carried down back and collar and cuffs and flounces lovely fur, just like real, and only £4 19 6 reduced from seven gns, but I couldn't run to it though if I wear my old black much longer they will be throwing things at me in the street. Well I got in the train to come back in the afternoon and guess who got into the very same carriage, you should have seen him jump, that boy we met at Scarborough year before last when I was with The Bluebells, you remember! It was the taller one with the light moustache who acted he was tight that time, Sunday night at the Crown, and he told me he would come to Luddenstall whenever I liked and gave me his office address and tel. no. so I shan't exactly be lonely. He asked to be remembered to you and I had to tell you that his friend was married now. I am sorry for his wife, what do you say, my dear!

I am getting you some hankies, will let you have them tomorrow or day after. If you have not got anything for me yet make it a pair of silk stockings bit darker than usual shade I like to go with my red, if it will run to it. Give Uncle Arthur my love and tell him I am getting him a pipe once again, and let me know soon as you can if you can come but if you can, no bringing Ethel Golliver this time, you know what it was last time she came along! I like a bit of fun, my dear, but Ethel would get me run out of this show and out of the town as well! Is it true she is living with - you know, the fellow we used to call Pink Percy - doesn't surprise me! Chin-chin, Effie, my dear and all the best for Xmas!

Elsie

II

From Mrs Joe Brundit to her sister, Mrs Sorly, of Denmark Hill

c/o Mrs Andrews,
5 Clough Street,
Luddenstall,
Yorks.
21 December

Dearest Clara,

You will be glad to hear the Luck is in for once - we are here right over the Holidays and the rooms are very nice, the landlady most obliging person - so that there will be no difficulty about George coming - isn't that splendid! If Jim can see him on the train at King's Cross or get someone to see him in, someone *dependable* of course, then either Jim or who ever it is seek out a carriage for Leeds with some nice person who is coming to Leeds - and ask them if they would mind keeping an eye on George on the way - specially not letting him go into the corridor by himself or play with the window. Perhaps if you could spare the time, my dear, it would be best - and any nice person would be glad of the company of such a bright boy as George, don't you think? Of course this is further on than Leeds but then we can meet the train there and that means no changing for him, and Joe has found out the *exact* train, which is 8.45 *in the morning* from King's Cross, please don't forget - 8.45 in the morning, and the day after tomorrow, that is the 23rd. You could send us a wire saying he is safely off. Here is the P.O. for the fare, *half* of course. And I know you will see he has his proper things with him and is well wrapped up for the journey - it is *much colder* here of course than it is with you - and has a bun or two and perhaps a bit of chocolate and some of those comic picture papers to look at. You can imagine, my dear, what a relief it is to have someone like you that a Mother can trust!

So this is going to be a proper Christmas for us for once and I am sure I don't know which is the most excited about it, Joe or me, for we have been buying toys and things for George's stocking - not that he believes in S. Claus still of course, I know that, but surely he will like to hang his stocking up - and we have made arrangements for a real Christmas Dinner - and Miss Trant has got George an invitation to a big Children's Party there is to be in the town on Boxing Day afternoon. Now that money is coming in regularly again, not missing a week here and a week there, with rooms and meals to pay for all the time, it makes such a difference, gives you *Confidence* again - so that - touch wood - things look altogether brighter and when we have our own dear child with us and have a happy Christmas altogether, I shall be a new woman! Would you believe it - a month ago I was in the *Depths* of Despair - we were all in them, even Joe, who may have his faults but hardly ever gives up hoping and taking a cheerful View, as you know - and then everything suddenly turned round. The Show is going magnificently - good houses every night and you could not want a better audience, a real taste for Good music into the bargain. I have been asked to give two items at a Sacred Concert here, in connexion with the. Wesleyans or Congregationals, I forget which - and Joe has been offered 15/- for two items any Sunday evening at the Labour Club here, Mrs Andrews' husband being a member and though a little rough and ready perhaps a gentleman at heart. So we have *Everything* to be thankful for as things have turned out.

It seems to be the same with everybody here - though Goodness knows it can't last. Jimmy Nunn, our com., says he is better than he has been for the last two years and looks it - and our pianist keeps up well and is as I said he was from the first as nice a young fellow as you could wish to find - and Miss Trant is a perfect lady to us all, does everything she can for us - and everybody is not only on speaking terms, and you know how rare that is, but is really friendly and nice - so that we might almost be a Happy Family. I am sure I have never wanted George to know anything about the Stage or to see me at work, and I have told you so many a time - haven't I - but I am sure if there ever was a Time or Place where it was right for him to do so, this is it!

The enclosed bag is offered with love, Clara, and gratitude for what you have done for George - and best wishes for a Happy Christmas, though it may not seem as if I meant it when I am taking George away from you just at this festive season, but you can imagine what it means to a Mother! As soon as I saw it in the shop I said to Joe - That will just do for Clara, she'll love it. And he said, No she won't, what put that idea into your head. And we argued about it quite a time before I found he was looking at the wrong thing and thought I was pointing to a fretwork outfit - just like a Man! He sends his love and best wishes to you and Jim and says if you can put it into George's head that he wants a clock-work train and a signal box etc. - so much the better.

Your loving sister,
Mag

III

From Jimmy Nunn to Mrs Nunn

c/o Mrs Shaw,
17 Clough Street,
Luddenstall,
Yorks.
23 December

Dear Carrie,

Just a line to let you know where I am and to say I am feeling better than I have done for the last year or two, and to wish you the Compliments of the Season. And I mean it too - a Merry Christmas and a Happy New Year - so don't you go sniffing about it. We can be friends in our own way even if we can't settle down together any more. I think kindly of you, Carrie, honestly I do, and I wish you to do the same for me. I know you don't want to come round the country with me and don't want to have anything to do with the Boards any more, and you know very well I can't spend the rest of my life sitting in the back of that shop of yours, doing up a parcel now and again. If we are both happy in our own way there's nothing to grumble at, I say. If Alice had lived, it might have been different. Never you mind what people say - tell them to mind their own business. Or say it's by doctor's orders I am still on the move.

I am glad to say you're wrong about this Show. Seeing it that night at Tewborough, when everybody and everything was all of a doodah, gave you a wrong idea of it, I can tell you. It's got going properly now and they are eating it here, and before long we shall be making money out of it and good money too. And what you say about the boss, Miss Trant, is all wrong too. She's one of the very best. And who do you think I ran into the other day in Leeds - old Tuppy Tanner - he's opening at the Royal panto there tomorrow as Baron Hard-up. Just the same only fatter than ever - and he was telling me his daughter Mona is playing principal girl at Birmingham this year - makes you think a bit, doesn't it - time flies. It doesn't seem more than a year or two since we all had that season together in Douglas - do you remember - when Tuppy fell into the sea and you nursed his little girl through the measles or something - and now she's getting her twenty a week at Birmingham and engaged to be married, Tupp tells me. Wasn't that the time poor Jack Dean kept getting so tight and got into trouble with that little Italian woman who was at the Palace and we had to keep hiding him? Little Susie here is always asking me about him - and, my word, I could tell her some tales if I wanted to - make her hair curl even though she has knocked about a bit herself - but of course I draw it mild. I don't suppose you want to know about her because you never liked poor Jack and he never liked you, but Susie is coming on fast and the first time a big man who knows a winner when he sees one happens to look at her act - it's good-bye to the Concert Party for little Susie. And I shan't try to stop her - let her have a chance, I say. I wouldn't know what to do with it, if I had a big chance now - I'm getting on and lazy - and the old round is good enough for me. If you ever wanted to see my name up in electric lights, you shouldn't have kept me back that time when old Wurlstein came round at Glasgow with the contract in his pocket. You didn't want to risk it but I did - but there - that's all done with - I'm up here and you're there with your shop, and we're both comfortable.

What about this for a letter! I'll be writing the Story of My Life next, after this. Now Carrie, no harm done between you and me, what do you say, and all the best for the New Year. If you see that young doctor, tell him I'm still taking that stuff and he's a marvel.

Yrs,
Jimmy

IV

From Jerry Jerningham to Lady Partlit

c/o Mrs Long,
6 Bury Road,
Luddenstall,
Yorks.
24 December

Dear Lady Partlit,

Thank you very much for the cig. case which arrived at The Ionic yesterday. How did you know we were playing here - did you see it in *The Stage* - it was a bit risky sending such a lovely case like that. Yes I was very surprised to get it and hear from you after what went on between us at Tewborough that week, but I must say I have been thinking some time I was too hasty and that after all it was not your fault so I will say now I am sorry - and not just because you have given me such a *beautiful* present and said such nice things in yr letter about my work. I am also sorry you are going out of England for a month or two because I should like you to see the Show again now it is going better and I have more chance, having got four new nos. - three of them written by our pianist who I must say is clever and a coming man in the song-world if only he takes his work seriously like I do. I must say the Show is going better than ever I thought it would now - though as you know it has got at least four dud people in it, and you are right when you say that I am wasted in this C. P. work, though I cannot grumble about the way my act is going here - two or three encores every night, and more wanted. But you have guessed right when you say it does not satisfy me and I am working hard all the time at new steps etc. so that when my chance does come the people who give it me will not regret it.

No I do not spend my time walking out pretty Yorkshire girls as you suggest - though if I wanted to I have no doubt I could do so alright - but even if they were a lot prettier than they are I should not let them take up my time just now. And if I was rude I am very sorry and thank you once again for the lovely present. I have just had a new photo taken and thought you might like a signed copy.

Sincerely yours,
Jerry Jerningham

P.S. - A letter sent to my perm. ad - 175 Fiscal Street, Birmingham, will always be sent on to me.

V

Mr Morton Mitcham to Gus Jeffson, Esq., Eccentric Club

The Ionic,
Luddenstall,
Yorks.
26 December

Dear Sir,

Re. your article 'Touring Out East' in last week's *Stage*, you say your Co. was the first to play Penang, but I was there with the old *Prince of Pimlico Co*, a good three years befor that, running down from Singapore. Refer 'Thirty Years in the Straits Settlements' by J. G. Thompson Esq. for account of Show and a photo of party, self inclined. *And* I'm still going strong - now playing at Ionic here, successful winter season with well-known Good Companions Co. (E. Trant & J. Nunn). Forgive correction and accept good wishes of another old pro who has done his share of Touring Out East - those were great days.

Believe me, Yrs. truly,
Morton Mitcham

VI

From Susie Dean to Miss Kitty Mackay, 'The Multi-Million Girl'
Co. Empire, Cardiff.

c/o Mrs Wright,
11 Jagger Street,
Luddenstall,
Yorks.
27 December

Darling Kitty,

Your letter only arrived this morning - after wandering round all over the place - but I see you are in Cardiff so this will get you at once. It was sweet of you to think of me like that - I shan't forget, my dear! - and three months ago I would have jumped at it, jumped at anything nearly - to say nothing of South Africa! I've always *longed* to travel - to go *everywhere* - wearing white and helmets and anything - and some day I will - with a private carriage or whatever it is the stars do have. But now I have just got to turn it down - don't ask me for exact reasons, my dear, you know how one feels about a thing! - it isn't the money - there's absolutely *nothing* wrong with your man's offer, I assure you, and I know I am lucky to get it - and here it is only Five a week, though marvellously regular, I can tell you, like clockwork - which of course makes a difference. But I have simply got to go on with this Good Companions show just now - it's been made out of the ruins of Mildenhall's rotten old Dinky Doos - an angel of a woman, very erect, y'know, and tweedy, and straight out of the Old Moated Grange from Little Widdleton-on-the-Wortleberry yes, the real thing - popped up from nowhere in a car - blushed a bit and looked very brave - paid everything and started us off again, all on her own, not knowing the first thing about it! If you could only see her - you would see at once it was the maddest and loveliest thing that ever happened, her doing this. And she lost money hand-over-fist for weeks and weeks - and not a murmur - and now she is beginning to get a little back again - and before she *makes* some. I don't stir an inch from this show - not if they offer me Daly's though I must say they haven't given any signs of doing so yet.

Has ta ivver played Luddenstall, lass? - its nobbut a little pla-a-ace i' Yorkshire - and as usual looks like a Gas Works all spread out - but I will say this, they know a good show when they see it here - packed house every night, *really*, and giving the little girl a hand every night - you should just hear them! And they ask us to parties - I was the regular Belle of the Ball at a dance here on Boxing Night after the show - presented the prizes and was given a box of chocolates as big as a suitcase - nay, lass, shut oop! Really though, as far as Luddenstall and district is concerned, we have the Leeds pantos knocked flat. And I have a feeling the luck's going on - and that sooner or later *Something* will happen. So no S. Africa just now, you see.

The two Brundits are still with us - and I'm glad, though they're not exactly Covent Garden, are they? - but darlings all the same. Good old Jimmy is still here - better too - and though I know all his jokes off by heart, about as well as he does - he seems to be as good a little comedian as there is in C. P. work - and better than some up aloft among the electric lights. Jerry Jerningham's here too - and going strong, I must say, and better to work with than he used to be - and the girls here follow him round with their tongues hanging out, as usual - but always from the tabs he's the same as ever, 1 gent's outfit, 1 dose of brilliantine, 5 cigarettes, 1 good opinion of himself, 3 bleats - and then nothing - that's our little friend Jerry. Then there's our new pianist, who let himself be called Inigo Jollifant - he's an amateur really, was a schoolmaster, Cambridge Varsity and baggy flannel trousers and the same weird tie every day and 'Give me my pipe' and all that, wants to write books and is very Lofty and Highbrow when he remembers to be - but quite clean and *really* very very clever and he's writing the most marvellous numbers for me, miles and miles beyond anything that comes from Shaftesbury Avenue these days. One of these nights, somebody from the West End or thereabouts will hear these numbers and then, my dear, I assure you his fortune is made - absolutely, as he always says. He is really rather sweet and we have lots of fun together - No, my dear, I'm *not*, quite decidedly not - we are just good friends, that's all, at least on my side. You don't say a word about Eric - I do hope it's all right.

If it was Canada instead of South Africa, there's a little man here who would be just dying to come with you. He is our property man and stage carpenter - a little Yorkshireman, not little really but you think of him being little because he is such a darling - and he too popped up from nowhere and is now one of the family - you should have seen him and heard him this Christmas here, telling all these other Yorkshire people where he had been and what he had seen - eh, it wor right champion, lass! He wants to go to Canada because he has a daughter there - ahr Lily he calls her - and because I'm supposed to be like her (Lord help me!), he simply adores me. Oh, I forgot there's also an old boy called Morton Mitcham, banjoist and conjurer, we picked up on the road - very weird, Laddie, very weird - not a bad turn, but easily the champion liar of the Profession! He certainly has knocked about in his time, but if he was a hundred and fifty years old and had never stopped touring, he would still be lying, the yarns he spins!

Yes, I know it all sounds very queer - and I'll bet we are easily the oddest C. P. on the road - but honestly we're the nicest too, and I only wish you were nearer and could come and have a look at us. Well, that's all, my dear - but don't forget I really am most affectionately grateful for the offer, and you do understand, don't you, why I can't accept. But don't go and imagine I'm glued to the piffling C. P. business! Not a bit of it! Very shortly, you'll see, I shall be Blossoming Out - and then I shall expect a cable from S. Africa when the news gets through. Best of luck to you all, Kitty darling.

Ever Yours,
Susie

VII

From Inigo Jollifant to Robert Fauntley, Washbury Manor School

c/o Mrs Jugg,
3 Clough Street,
Luddenstall,
Yorks.
29 December

Dear Fauntley,

Many thanks for sending on those odds and ends so promptly. I ought to have written before, I know. Now I have to send this to the school and risk its being forwarded on to you. If the envelope looks messy at the back, you will know that Ma Tarvin has steamed it open - using a hot prune for the purpose: and if you don't get it at all, you know she has destroyed your letter - ha ha! Your Washbury news was welcome but all very strange - like a message from Mars. Glad I am that the fair Daisy has departed - may she marry the outpost-of-Empire lad in the Sudan and may he be bronzed and lean and carry her photograph, in a silver frame, with him into Wildest Africa. The new man - vice Jollifant - certainly sounds a shrimp - a lesser Felton - and who would have thought that possible? I sent Ma Tarvin *a Christmas Card!!* It was the sweetest I could find, with little birdies in the snow and it said:

A heart-felt wish through rain or shine
In memory dear of Auld Lang Syne

or something like that. (Ask her about Christmas Cards when you get back.) Then, passing a dirty little shop here the other day, a most highly coloured and vulgar postcard caught my eye - the caption was 'You can see a lot at Blackpool' and you can imagine the picture above - and this I dispatched, naked and outrageous, to friend Felton in his beautiful refined home at Clifton. Felton is the only human being who still collects picture postcards - the British Museum and South Kensington kind, of course - but I have the feeling that mine has not been added to the collection. Dear, dear!

Can you imagine being a Pierrot in Luddenstall, Yorks! Can you imagine Luddenstall! It is a smallish town, black as your best hat, and it is joined on to other and bigger towns, equally black, by tram lines. I never saw so many trams. They turn them into mountain railways here; you see them going up vertically. All the streets here are at an angle of at least 45 degrees, everything built of stone, and they run down from a bleak hillside that is really the end of a huge dark moor. Last Sunday, I walked miles and miles on this moor - it has black stone walls like snakes twisting across it - until at last it began to frighten me. It's ridiculous to say this place is in England - quite another country really. Both Miss Trant (she runs this troupe - God knows why! - and comes from the Cotswolds) and I, after much discussion, have agreed upon that. The people here work - the women never stop - and go to football matches, drink old beer (very good stuff), listen to Handel's Messiah about twice a week, and make you eat cheese with cake.

I am, as you see, *chez* Jugg. It's a capital name for the gentleman because nearly every time I see him he has a jug in his hand, being among the most stalwart devotees of the aforesaid old beer, which has to be 'fetched i' jug'. He can give old Omar himself points in not believing in anything, for he has cut out the book of verse, most of the loaf, and the Houri stuff, and just sticks to the jug, though he has added a clay pipe and is one up on Omar there. He is very dry and cynical. Mrs Jugg reminds me vaguely of Henry the Eighth (she must be roughly the same shape, I think); she works harder than anybody I have ever heard of; and always looks so terribly exasperated that you would think her cooking would be atrocious, because everything she does is slammed in at the last minute, but it all turns out to be beautiful in the end - it's like a conjuring trick. The only amusement she has is going 'to t' chapel o' Sunday neet', but after a lot of argument I persuaded her to accept a ticket to our show the other night. What was the result? 'Eh!' she said. But it's a long sound she makes, rather like a sheep. 'Eh!' she said, 'it wer right good but I missed most on it because I fell asleep. Seat were so comfortable and I wer so tired.' Which seemed to me rather pathetic. I've been a fortnight here now and so am very pally with both Juggs. They are the best people I've lodged with so far, and this is our best town, in spite of its being so queer. We've had some horrors, I assure you. You don't know what Merrie England is like until you tour it with a pierrot troupe.

Do you remember telling me I ought to do something with those little tunes I used to improvise? Well, I am making them into songs now - and everybody seems to like them - and the people in the show, especially the chief girl here (her name is Susie Dean and besides being a most delightful girl, she really is a genius - you wait!), seem to think I ought to make some money out of them. I think I shall try soon. I've written two essays - quite good too - and sent them to several papers, but they've come back - 'Editor regrets', etc. - every time. It staggers me when I consider the bosh they do print, but I suppose it's difficult for an outsider - a pierrot at that! - to get in; and I feel like trying to make as much money as I can out of this silly song-writing stunt and then write at leisure. Meanwhile I pound the keys every night and take it easy during the day. We're an amusing crowd - we had a really jolly Christmas, best I ever had, I think - and though I don't see myself going on with this for ever, so far it's more fun than ramming French and

History into the offspring of our Empire builders and then trying to eat the Tarvin rissoles and stewed prunes. Luddenstall is as ugly as an old road engine, but it has one advantage over Washbury Manor, my dear Fauntley - it's alive! And so am I - never more so. And I hope you are too, and will have a good New Year.

Yours sincerely,
Inigo Jollifant

VIII

From Miss Trant to Mrs Gerald Atkinson (nee Dorothy Chillingford), Kenya Colony

Luddenstall, Yorks.
31 December

My dear Dorothy,

Your last letter only arrived here two days ago. I am so glad you are finding things so much better and that Gerald has got the extra land he wanted. You sound so happy. Isn't it fantastic - you out there, and me here? No, I have not been back to Hitherton at all. If we had been nearer these holidays I should have gone, just to see your dear father and mother, the Purtons, and everybody, but it could not be done - so I sent letters and little presents instead. It's been the *most* absurd Christmas I ever had - here in this dark and bleak little Yorkshire manufacturing town, where everybody talks like our delicious little Yorkshire property man, Oakroyd, whom I described to you before. Of course everybody seems dreadfully rude at first. You go into a shop and they say: 'Well, what do you want, young woman?' - though the 'young' is rather comforting. But I am used to it now, and really nobody could have been kinder and nicer than these people and we were lucky - for once! - coming here during the holidays because they are Christmassy sort of people. As you insist on having what you call 'theatrical intelligence', I may say that I am actually at last making a *Profit!* - that is, on each week, though of course I have not yet made up what I have lost so far. But it's so exciting to have really crowded and enthusiastic audiences, enjoying everything, and it's made the most wonderful difference to the members of the party, who are working splendidly now.

It's ridiculous, of course, but I am becoming the complete theatrical manager. The other day I actually had an offer for the whole troupe - and refused it! After the show one night last week, a card was handed in with a request for an interview, and in came a large fat shabby man, rather beery and pimply but very amiable (too amiable!),

and he was Mr Ernie Codd, from Leeds. He insisted on shaking my hand
and breathing on me for about five minutes, and in a very wheezy voice
kept saying 'Pretty little show! Taking little show! Congrats on the show,
Miss Bant! I'm Ernie Codd! They all know Ernie! Now listen here, just
listen!' When at last I succeeded in getting back my hand and assuring
him I was listening, he said something about having the scenery and
props and script of a revue (I think it's name was 'And You're Another!'
- I know he said it was 'a Winner and a sure-fire Screamer!') and one of
the neatest little troupes of dancing girls I had ever set eyes on outside
the West End radius, and he would take over my Good Companions,
lock, stock, and barrel at Fifty Per, or sign them on separately with
myself, Miss Bant, as assistant manager on a profit-sharing basis. I am
trying, my dear, to give you an impression of the way he rattled all this
off, with any amount of gesticulation and heavy breathing. It took me
twenty minutes - and even then I had to bring in Mr Nunn - to make
him believe that I had no intention of accepting his offer. I never saw a
man so surprised - or at least appear to be so surprised - as he was when
he finally understood that we did not want to be taken over by Mr Codd
and his friends. I was very amused (and would have been more amused
if Mr Codd had been rather cleaner and not so much given to shaking
hands) but I was also rather thrilled. Mr Nunn, who knows all about
these things and is my chief adviser, was delighted, and said that though
he would not trust Ernie Codd as far as he could see him, the offer was
a feather in our caps. It must all sound very silly to you, miles and miles
away, but you must allow me my little triumphs. Things really are
looking up.

Some local Commercial Travellers' Association gave a children's
party here the other afternoon and somehow the secretary got hold of
my name and insisted on Susie - the very charming and clever girl I told
you about - and I giving the prizes. We loved it. And talking of children,
I must tell you about Mr and Mrs Joe Brundit, my baritone and soprano.
I hope you remember my description of them because the story rather
hangs on that. But, as I told you before, they have a little boy called
George, whom they both worship. He lives with an aunt at Denmark
Hill, but they were able to have him with them this Christmas here. For
days they thought and talked about nothing else. Every penny they had
went on toys for his stocking and for treats for him. When the time
came, they were nearly delirious with excitement. I remember hoping
then that he was a nice little boy who would appreciate what they were
doing for him. And of course - that sounds pessimistic, but you know
how wretchedly things so often turn out - he wasn't a nice little boy, but
a horrid sulky stupid little wretch. He didn't like any of the toys they
gave him, and told them so very plainly. He didn't like Luddenstall, and

kept saying he wanted to go back to Denmark Hill. He broke some things at their lodgings and was very rude to the land-lady, who promptly slapped him (a thing I have been tempted to do myself), with the result that Mrs Joe quarrelled with her at once and finally had to find new lodgings for them all. They brought him to the theatre and he was such a nuisance that everybody said he must not be allowed to come again. He went to the children's party, got into mischief at once, then was sulky and cross, and ended by being sick. Never was there such a disastrous visit! And all the time the poor things have been pretending they were not disappointed or anything, until we did not know whether to laugh or cry. On the whole, I felt more like weeping. Poor simple Joe! - and poor simple Mrs Joe! - she is tremendously dignified and superior, as I told you, but really, if anything, she's the simpler of the two. They have decided now that George isn't strong - put it all down to ill health - though the little wretch is really as strong as an ox and only wants a good slapping from time to time to keep him in order. My dear, if you are going to be so absurd, I shall begin to wish I had never told you about that episode - for that's all it was. Of course I haven't seen 'Dr Hugh McFarlane on my travels'. Why should I have? I don't even know if he lives in this country, though I must confess I feel confident he does live somewhere, still exists. I don't suppose he would even recognize me now. Yes, I know 'there is such a thing as a Medical Register', as you put it - I'm sure you're becoming quite Colonial and brusque these days - but I have never had a peep at it, no, not the tiniest peep. If you could see me these days, you would understand why I am not worrying about any episode from ancient history. In less than a week, we move on again. Did I tell you I had made Hilda cooperate with me? - she helped me with some dresses for a sort of mid-Victorian song-scena we are giving now - and one that I planned myself!

For the last few days, the hill-tops to the West have been white, and I had a glimpse the other morning of the moors there, all silent and almost covered with snow, quite lonely and terrifying, and now it is beginning to snow properly down here and all the black roofs and hard lines are disappearing so that even Luddenstall looks rather like a place in an old fairy-tale! And very soon the bells will ring in the New Year. I hope it will be a happy one for you, my dear. I'm sure it will, though. And somehow I like the sound of it too. Love to you both.

Yours,
Elizabeth

IX

And as the snow drifted high on the moorland above and came whirling down in soft flakes to the valley below, until at last every roof in Luddenstall was thick and whitened and all the streets were touched with Northern magic; as they raised their glasses and joined hands and sang in chorus, the bells that seemed as old and mysterious as the flying and feathered night itself rang out the Old, rang in the New - the last letter of all was being carried through in a black and dripping railway cutting in the hills, to be slung with a thousand others on board a liner that would soon go hooting through the dark to Canada:

My dear Daughter,
    I am writing these lines to say I am still in the pink and hoping you are the same. We are now in Good Old Yorks, and so had a good and merry Xmas. I had my Xmas dinner with landlady and Family and had goose and pudding and etc. I wish you had been there Lily, to keep your old Father company. I went on tram to Bruddersford and called at 51. Your Mother was looking poorly but when I asked her said she was alright and as she was a bit short with me could get nothing out of her. Albert is still there but did not see him and was glad not to but I saw our Leonard who is doing well. Your Mother told me you had not written to her only to me so I think Lily you had better write to her as well sometime for she is your Mother when all is said and done and as I say is looking poorly. The Good Comps. are going well here and will do so, if I know any thing, at other places on the road. Wishing you and Jack a Happy New Year and all the best. Keep on writing to me at 51 and they will send on. And keep your heart up Lily we will have a good laugh the two of us yet together. With love and kisses,

from yr Father,
J. Oakroyd

BOOK THREE

CHAPTER ONE
A Wind in the Triangle

I

THE March wind went shrieking over the Midland Plain. Under a sky as rapid, ragged, and tumultuous as a revolution, all the standing water, the gathered thaws and rains of February, filling the dykes and spreading over innumerable fields, was ruffled and whitened, so that the day glittered coldly. There was ice even yet in this wind, but already there were other things too, shreds and tatters of sunlight, sudden spicy gusts, distant trumpetings of green armies on the march. Unless you were one of the patient men of the fields, following the great shining flanks of your horses across the ten-acre and already hearing the sap stirring, you did not know what to do in the face of such a wind. It was up to all manner of tricks, 'Grrrr! Get indoors and stay there!' it would go screaming. 'Poke the fire! Whe-ew!' And it might send a lash of hail after you. But then not quarter of an hour later, it might be crying 'Come out, come out! The year's begun', promising primroses, and spilling a little pale sunlight down the road. The moment you did go out, however, it would give a sharp twitch, darkening the sky again, and with a long *Whe-ew Grrrr!* would sting your cheeks and set your eyes watering. A most mischievous wind.

Away it went, across the central plain of England, until at last it pounced upon those three little industrial towns, Gatford, Mundley, and Stort, that are known as the Triangle, and more recently, since the towns gave themselves up to the mass production of cheap cars, the Tin Triangle. There are very few towns in this island so close together as Gatford, Mundley, and Stort, and a stranger might easily imagine they were all one town. On the other hand, there are hardly any other towns that seem farther away from anywhere else: Gatford jostles Mundley and Stort, and Mundley and Stort creep closer to one another; but the three of them appear to be almost as remote as a constellation from any other place of importance. Those short non-stop runs on the railway from Gatford to either Manchester or Birmingham always seem miraculous; and when that daily procession of brand-new cars, shiny saloons or chassis with drivers perched on boxes, slides away down the London Road, it strikes the visitor as a most hazardous enterprise, an adventure. The Trianglers themselves, too, regard this daily departure of new Imperial Sixes and Lumbdens and Baby Sceptres as part of a great adventure. Nowadays cars pour out and money pours into the Triangle. It is said that J. J. Lumbden, the son of old Lumbden who kept the bicycle shop in Cobden Street, Gatford, is worth nearly half a million and steadfastly refuses the most gigantic offers from America. The Sceptre people are building yet another factory between Mundley and Stort. And nobody can say there is anything tinny about the Imperial Six, the pride of North Gatford and Stort, where every other man is a mechanic. There is hardly a schoolboy in the Triangle, even in South Gatford, where there are detached villas and tennis clubs and boulevards, who does not groan with impatience, to think he is wasting his time with stuff about Magna Carta and Rivers of South America and Adverbs when he might be working in one of the car factories, swaggering out at half past five, very black and knowing. Useless to talk to the Triangle about bad trade and what might be done with the unemployed; it never knew such days before; Gatford is nearly twice the size it was twenty years ago, and Mundley and Stort, invaded by mechanics from every part of the Midlands, are growing visibly, at the rate of so many new little red bricks per fine working day. These are adventurous times for the three towns. The March wind, itself supremely adventurous, pounced upon them with glee. Here, it seemed to shout, was something better to play with than naked fields and branches and thin tremulous sheets of water.

It swooped down and charged the steady swarm of cars, the trams that lumber from Gatford to Mundley, Stort to Mundley, Gatford to Stort, the buses that dodge and hoot at and overtake these trams. It whipped off a loose tile and even a chimney-pot here and there. After seeking out any tattered posters on the hoardings and turning them into drums, it rounded up all the odd pieces of paper in the streets and compelled them to join in a witches' Sabbath. This most mischievous wind then found an open window on the second floor of a building in Victoria Street, Gatford, sent some papers skimming from the table to the floor, and compelled a certain gentleman, who had been staring at some figures and now found himself shivering, to look up and speak crossly to his companion and employee. This is Mr Ridvers, but when he is in this tiny office he calls himself the Triangle New Era Cinema Co., and it is from here he controls the destinies of The Tivoli Picture Palace, Gatford, The Coliseum Picture House, Mundley, and The Royal Cinema, Stort, the only three cinemas of any importance in the district.

'For God's sake, Ethel,' he said, 'shut that window. Look at those letters - all over the damn floor. Besides, it's cold.'

From behind her typewriter, Ethel gave him a curious side-ways look. She was a girl in her twenties, with a rather flat Mongolian face, hard staring eyes, and a thick daubed mouth. 'It was you who wanted it open,' she remarked. 'Told you it was cold.'

'Well, I want it shut now,' he grunted, without looking up again from the papers in his hand.

'All right, all right,' and she closed the window. There was nothing respectful in her tones, and there was something downright disrespectful in the way she moved. The exaggerated thrust and lift of her shoulders gave the impression that her body was making really impudent remarks about her employer. There was a suggestion that it had the right to make such remarks and that he knew very well it had.

Mr Ridvers examined the figures before him a minute or two longer, then stood up and threw the papers on the table. He found a half-smoked cigar in the ash-tray, relit it, and pulled furiously at it, frowning all the time. Ethel watched him out of the corner of her eye with amusement. He had been in a bad mood all morning and now he was obviously very angry indeed. As a matter of fact, he was a middle-aged man who ate too much, drank far too much whisky, took too little exercise, and was plagued by an outraged liver. He had his grievances, but it was really the sudden cold lash of the wind that had now put a sharp edge on his temper.

'Well?' And there was a certain malice in Ethel's query.

'Well nothing!' he exploded. 'These returns are worse than I thought. It was Stort last week. I suppose it'll be Mundley this week. I'd never have believed it. These flaming little pierrots are knocking hell out of the returns.'

'I told you what it would be.'

'Oh, for God's sake, don't start that! Never knew a woman yet who didn't think she'd gone and told me everything. People here must have gone balmy. Pierrots!'

'They're crowded out every night,' said Ethel.

'Yes, I know they are. I'm not silly. Even so, they oughtn't to have knocked us like this. Damn it all, there ought to be enough money in these three towns to keep us going as usual even if they are crowded out. I've given 'em good programmes.'

'I don't know about that,' Ethel replied coolly. 'You know very well you cut it a bit on the renting.'

'What if I did? Matter of fact I had to cut it to show Farrow and his Syndicate a good margin. And what diff'rence does it make, what I paid for the renting. They've never seen the bloody pictures before, have they? Well then! No, it's this pierrot show that's done it. Who ever would have thought it! Talk about luck!'

'I hear they're putting the prices up too,' said Ethel, who seemed to delight in flicking him on the raw.

'They would!' cried Mr Ridvers bitterly. 'That means all the less money for us. Seems to me if these people spend two and four they've finished for the week. Luck! They won't even let me smell it.' And Mr

Ridvers made a number of sounds to express his disgust and then savagely jammed his cigar against the ash-tray.

'I don't know what you're going on like this for,' said Ethel, who probably knew very well. 'A few bad weeks won't kill you.'

Mr Ridvers made a large gesture of despair. 'Oh, have a bit of sense, Ethel. Won't kill me! I don't know what you sit there for, I honestly don't.'

'Oh, don't you?' cried Ethel, staring at him hard. 'Well, I'm not always sitting here, am I, *Mister* Ridvers? Trying to turn me into a dummy or what?'

'All right, Ethel, easy, easy,' he replied, giving her shoulder a perfunctory pat, under which it squirmed. 'But I've told you before. Farrow and his P.P.H. Syndicate,' he went on, with ferocious deliberation, 'are making me an offer for my three halls. You know that? All right then. That-offer-is-to-be-based-on-two-months'-returns-of-these-three-halls. The price is according. Or, if they don't like the look of them, they won't deal. They'll buy elsewhere. Or - what's a damn sight worse - they'll come here and build their own. And you know as well as I do what's happened to our returns. And I ask you, who'd have thought a piebald, blink-eyed, bread-and-dripping little pierrot show, filling in time till it can get a pitch on the sands again, would have knocked 'em all silly here like that!'

'I went out to Mundley last night to see them,' said Ethel. 'Fellow took me. Packed out they were too. It's a clever show - bit slow in parts, 'specially the women, but it's clever. They've a boy there who dances - name's Jerningham - who got me all right. Talk about dancing! And looks! He's got the film fellows well beaten, that boy has. Tricky songs too.'

'You're sillier than I thought you were,' Mr Ridvers growled. 'With your dancing boys! They've another week at Mundley Rink, haven't they, after this? And then back to Gatford here again. I see they've got the Hippodrome plastered with bills already. And I went to Billy Roberts and told him I didn't want 'em back if possible and he owed me a good turn or two and he said he'd stiffen the terms - they hadn't taken it again then, you see - and make this woman who's running the show rent it and shove all sorts of responsibility on to her. But that's not frightened her, seemingly.'

'Why should it?' said Ethel. 'I know it wouldn't frighten me. She's safe as houses here now - can't lose.'

Mr Ridvers thought for a few moments. 'Here,' he cried finally, 'where is this woman or whoever it is that's running these 'Companions' or whatever they call themselves? Over at Mundley, I suppose?'

'No, she's not. They're all here, in Gatford, been staying here all the time and just running out to Stort and Mundley at night for the show. Her name's Trant, and she's staying at The Crown.'

'You seem to know a devil of a lot about them,' said Mr Ridvers, facing her across the table. 'Quite one of the pierrot fanciers, aren't you! Must be the dancing boy. Well, don't start any tricks, that's all.'

'I don't start tricks,' she replied shrilly. 'And if I did, I wouldn't ask your permission, Mr Charlie Ridvers. You get your money's worth out of me, don't you? Start tricks! You're a nice one to talk.'

'Oh, dry up,' said Mr Ridvers. 'Can't you see I've enough damn bother on my hands without you making trouble? I'm worried, that's what I am, and I don't mind admitting it.' He took down his hat and overcoat.' I'm going across to The Crown to have a little bit of a talk to this pierrot woman - what's her name? - Trant. That's what I'm going to do.'

'And a fat lot of good it'll do you,' cried Ethel. 'What can you say to her? Silly, I call it.'

'Never mind what you call it. And never mind what I can say to her,' he replied, with an air of a man who had produced a crushing retort. He had no idea himself what he could say to this Miss Trant that would be of the slightest use, but he looked both knowing and truculent. 'What's it now? Half past two? Back just after three, I dare say.' With his hand on the knob, he stopped, turned round and looked darkly at Ethel. 'She's going to hear something from me, good or no good.'

'Go on then, get it off your chest,' she replied. 'Perhaps you'll feel better after that.' She gave the typewriter carriage a push so that it shot across and rang its little bell, a contemptuous, dismissing little bell.

All the way down the stairs, Mr Ridvers told himself that Ethel was getting altogether too uppish and was not much use in the office any longer and not very much use anywhere else the way she was these days, and that it was always the same if you allowed yourself to have a bit of fun with them because the little bitches took advantage in a minute and it was time he stopped having these little games. The wind was very lively as he walked up Victoria Street, and he damned it heartily. It whistled round his legs, tried to snatch his hat, flung scraps of waste paper at him, and made him feel liverish again. At The Crown he found he had to stop at the bar and add two more whiskies, very quick ones, to the supply he had taken in during his early lunch; but they did not make his grievances seem any less or restore his lost temper.

II

The Crown is the oldest and most comfortable hotel in The Triangle, and Miss Trant had stayed on there because she liked the place and had been able to claim the small sitting-room upstairs for her own use. She was in there now, talking to Inigo Jollifant, who had just had lunch with her. These two were now very good friends indeed, and Inigo had been giving her all the news of the troupe, for she had only just returned from a visit - the first since autumn - to Hitherton. On the little table were a number of papers, rough accounts, and letters, that she had been looking over during the morning.

'I don't know what to do,' she was saying, raising her voice as the wind rattled the old window-frames. 'To tell you the truth, I haven't been able to think properly since I came back. I feel - do you know? - restless.'

'My own feelings, absolutely,' said Inigo. 'It's the wind, I think - the wind on the heath, brother. Spring's on the way, that must be it.'

'On the way!' she cried. 'It's here.'

'Not here,' he corrected her gravely. 'Not in Gatford. There may be a spot of it somewhere on the edge of Mundley or Stort. But tell it not in Gatford.'

'Well, it may not be here, but it's everywhere else. You should see the flowers at Hitherton - already.'

Inigo looked at her curiously. 'Shall I tell you what I think? I think you're tired of it - not of us - '

'Certainly not of you,' she interrupted. 'None of you.'

'No, not of us, as people, but of the business itself. I suspect you've had enough now.'

Miss Trant laughed, quickly, nervously. 'And I was thinking just the same about you all through lunch - the very same thing - that you were tired of it but would not admit it.'

'The two ama-chewers, eh! Had enough!' He thought for a moment. 'No, I can't say I've definitely felt that, not quite that.' He hesitated.

'Suppose' - and she held him with a level glance - 'Susie left us?' The instant look of horror on his expressive face brought a smile to her own. 'There you are, you see,' she cried in friendly triumph.

'As a matter of fact,' he remarked, serious now, 'Susie herself is rather restless. And she doesn't seem to be particularly keen on this Bournemouth offer. None of the younger ones are, you know. Jerningham seems uneasy about it, and Elsie - who you would think would jump at it - doesn't seem very interested. As I told you, it's the old hands, Jimmy and the Joes and Mitcham, who are all for it and so worried because you won't decide at once. They think it's a marvellous offer, absolutely, and so it is from their point of view - resident season, guaranteed and all the rest of it. All their dreams come true.'

'I know, poor dears. It's just what they've been wanting. There's no reason why we shouldn't accept it. After all, I needn't be there, not all the time, need I?'

'Not at all. You can take the whole summer off, if you like.'

'But really I don't like. That's the trouble. Please don't tell the others this, will you? But somehow the idea of going there, just settling down in Bournemouth for nearly six months doesn't appeal to me, and on the other hand, I don't just want to march off, though of course if they thought they could get on without me, I could leave altogether.'

'Oh, don't do that,' cried Inigo, alarmed. 'Besides, although we must be making money now - quite a lot, I imagine - you can't have got back all you've spent yet.'

'No, I haven't,' she admitted, with an involuntary glance at the papers on the table. 'We're doing so wonderfully well here that there really is good profit, so good that I feel like a bloated profiteer and capitalist, but actually I'm still about two hundred pounds to the bad. And the people who have taken my house at Hitherton now say that all kinds of things must be done to it - it's very old, you know, and has been rather neglected, and apparently I must do them and I shudder to think what it will cost.'

'Well, there you are then. You must carry on and rake in the dibs, shekels, or boodle. We can't allow you to retire still losing on the show.'

'I don't want to retire,' she told him emphatically. 'I should hate to. It's just that - well, like you - I feel restless and don't know .what to do.'

'I rather think that Jimmy and Mitcham and possibly Joe, the anxious lads, are downstairs in the bar, in the hope of getting the latest bulletin or ultimatum. I rather think so.' Inigo concluded lightly.

'Oh dear!' Miss Trant stared at him. 'I know they're dreadfully anxious about the Bournemouth business. Inigo, will you please slip down and tell them to wait a little longer because I may want to see them? I can't see them this minute though because I must make up my mind first. I hope waiting down there doesn't mean having a lot of drinks.'

'It does,' replied Inigo gravely. 'Always. And more especially at a crisis, when the beverages come to hand almost mechanically. However, I'll slip down and tell them.' He went out but almost immediately afterwards popped his head in the door. 'A gent to see you,' he announced. 'Name of Ridvers and smell of whisky. Will you have a look at him?'

Miss Trant, surprised, said she would, and the next moment Inigo had gone and a heavy man, of a somewhat swollen and purplish cast of countenance, was standing in the doorway. His bowler hat was tilted towards the back of his head and he had a cigar in his mouth. He came in without removing either hat or cigar.

'I am Miss Trant,' rising and regarding him with no great favour. 'Do you want to see me?'

'That's it. My name's Ridvers, and I don't mind telling you I'm the Triangle New Era Cinema Company, *Un*limited. Well known here, *very* well known, *not* a stranger to the district.' He paused, looked at her, then took out a cigar and looked at that, shooting a little cloud of smoke at his companion.

'I'm afraid I don't understand,' said Miss Trant, stepping back from the smoke.

'You're Miss Trant who's running these what's it Companions pierrot show, aren't you?' said Mr Ridvers heavily.

'Yes. What do you want?' And she looked pointedly first at the hat, then at the cigar, then at the whole man.

But Mr Ridvers was not to be hurried. His manner said very plainly that he had his own methods of approach to a topic. He pursed up his thick lips, stuck the cigar between them again, half-closed his eyes and wagged his head, and then growled through the cigar: 'Doing damn well here, aren't you?'

'I beg your pardon?' Miss Trant looked at him in amazement.

'Not-at-all, not-at-all.' He rested himself against the back of a high chair, took out his cigar, stared at her, and said again: 'Doing damn well here, aren't you?'

Miss Trant still stared.

'And do you know' - and here Mr Ridvers used his cigar as a pointer and contrived to spill some ash over the chair - 'at whose expense you're doing so damn well? At mine. And I'm here to have a little talk about it.'

'I don't want to have a talk about it,' she cried.

'P'raps not. But I do.' He made movements that suggested he was about to sit down.

This was too much for Miss Trant. 'Will you please go away at once?' she suddenly blazed at him, much to his astonishment. 'How dare you come in here behaving like this! I don't want to talk to you about anything.' She turned her back on him and opened the window, instantly admitting a cold and disturbing rush of our old acquaintance, the March wind, which at once determined to try and choke Mr Ridvers, with his own cigar smoke.

He coughed, spluttered, and cursed. But he was really shocked, for he had his own code of manners and now they had been outraged.

'I hope you don't call yourself a lady,' he exclaimed, in genuine indignation. 'What's the idea? Going on like that!'

Miss Trant swept round, marched past him to the door and threw it open. 'Now will you please go?' she said, white with annoyance. 'If you don't go, I will, and I shall ask the proprietor to turn you out of my room.'

Mr Ridvers advanced and looked closely at her for a moment. Then he gave his hat a tap to bring it forward, made a clicking noise, exclaimed 'Well, my God!' and went click-clicking down the corridor. When he reached the bar again, he was in a very bad temper. Tom Ellis himself, the landlord, was there, talking to two strangers, a long thin oldish fellow in a ridiculous overcoat and a short man with a peering monkey face.

'Let's have another, Tom,' said Mr Ridvers gruffly. 'I need it.' Then, after swallowing half his whisky, he burst out with: 'That's a bitch of a woman you've got upstairs, Tom.'

'Who's this you're talking about, Charlie?'

'Trant or whatever her name is,' said Mr Ridvers heartily. 'Running a pierrot show here, till the sands are ready again, I suppose. Hello, what's the matter with you?' Tom was nodding and winking at him.

'These two gentlemen here', said Tom, whose business it was to keep in with everybody, 'are members of that troupe. Very good show, they tell me.'

'And let me tell you, sir,' said the taller stranger, who is no stranger to us, being no other than Mr Morton Mitcham, 'that's no way to talk about a lady in public' And his eyebrows completed the rebuke.

'That is so,' said his companion, Mr Jimmy Nunn, sternly, and shutting one eye as he looked at Mr Ridvers. 'Just keep your bitches to yourself.'

Mr Ridvers gave a short laugh and cast a contemptuous eye over the rickety pair. 'So this is what they're all paying their money to see, is it, Tom? Tut-t-t-t. Broken-down old pros. Buskers. I wish I'd known what they looked like when I saw that woman upstairs. She's not all there, Tom.' He tapped his forehead. 'You want to keep an eye on her. Pierrots! Tut-t-t-t.'

'Who is this - er - gentleman?' And the irony Mr Mitcham, raising his eyebrows to a monstrous height, threw into that last word was stunning.

'Now then, gentlemen,' said Tom. 'Let's be friendly. This is Mr Ridvers who runs the cinemas round here.'

'Ah!' said Mr Mitcham significantly, looking at Mr Nunn.

'Ah!' replied Mr Nunn.

'What are you ah-ing about?' demanded Mr Ridvers truculently.

'Do you remember that ninepence we threw away the other afternoon in that dirty little place, Nunn?' Mr Mitcham inquired.

'And we wondered how people could pay money to go in,' replied Jimmy. 'Is that the place? And you thought it was raining in all the pictures, they were so old.'

'And you were asking me how the management had the face to have that cracked old piano and a girl to play it who'd never had any lessons. That's the place, isn't it, Nunn? Yes, I thought so.' He sighed deeply.

'You're very funny, aren't you?' said Mr Ridvers, looking from one to the other very fiercely. 'But don't think I'm going to take it from *you* because I'm not.' He did not say from whom he would take it, but there was a suggestion that he had taken it from somebody quite recently. 'Couple of buskers! Going round with the hat! Dirty pierrots! Let me tell you this, the pair of you, and you can tell that - '

'Easy, Charlie, easy,' said the landlord, who looked anything but easy himself.

'You want a good mouth-wash,' cried Jimmy angrily to Mr Ridvers. 'It's asking for a good clean-out, that big mouth of yours.'

'I've been in places where you'd have had a bullet through you - like that – zip! - for saying less than you've said about a lady.' And Mr Mitcham, drawing the Silver King round him with a noble gesture of scorn, attempted to wither the furious cinema proprietor with one magnificent glance.

'Go and have a look at yourselves,' roared Mr Ridvers, at the same time attempting to have a closer look at them himself, a movement that made them back a little, for Mr Ridvers, with his heavy shoulders and great thrusting jowl, was at that moment a very formidable figure. 'I'll say what I like, and you won't stop me and you know you won't. Do you see? I'll say what I like.'

'That's the way, Mister,' said a cheerful voice from behind them. 'That's the way to talk. Let a man say what he likes, that's my motto - s'long as he doesn't hurt anybody. Morning, boys. Any news? Hello, what's up?'

'I'll tell you what's up, Joe,' said Jimmy in tones that did not conceal his relief. And he plucked Joe by the elbow and in two whispered sentences told him what had happened.

The massive Joe then stepped forward and examined Mr Ridvers curiously, as if there stood before him some new kind of creature.

'Well,' said Mr Ridvers, standing his ground but not looking as if he was certain of it, 'what's wrong with you?'

'I'll tell you what's wrong with me,' said Joe softly. 'I'm a pierrot, same as these two. A dirty little pierrot. A broken-down pro. Just the same. Miss Trant, the lady upstairs, pays me my money. Just the same. Now I'll tell you what's the matter with you. You've two names. One's Mud and the other's Walker.' He jerked an enormous thumb towards the door. 'Off! Outside! You've just time. Oh!' - and here Joe wagged his head wistfully and a certain rapturous note crept into his voice - 'I could give you such a slugging. You're just the right shape and size, you are.'

Mr Ridvers had reached this conclusion even before Joe announced it. He departed. He ought to have stopped when he reached the door, turned round, scowled at them all, and produced the sinister laugh, the old hollow 'Ha! Ha! Ha-ha-ha-ha- *ha!*'; and indeed it is a pity he cannot be brought in every other page or so now to give us a warning 'Ha! Ha!'; but the fact remains that he went without a backward glance and in complete silence. He was, however, at boiling point, and a theatrical scowl, a little fist-shaking, and thirty seconds' sinister mirth, would have done him good. In Victoria Street the wind welcomed him boisterously as an old playmate, but his only response was to demand that it should first be damned and afterwards blasted. And when Ethel asked him if any good had come of his little talk, his reply was of such a nature that her typewriter was heard no more that day in the office of the Triangle New Era Cinema Company.

III

Mrs Joe put down her cup, then cocked her head in order, it seemed, to give her full attention to the wind. 'Just listen to that, my dear,' she remarked complacently, rather as if she had shares in some company that manufactured March weather. 'Wild, I call it. March came in like a lion and it seems to be going on like one. That makes it all the nicer to be in here, doesn't it?'

Susie, who was sitting in an enormous chair, specially introduced into that room for the benefit of Joe, curled her legs underneath her and snuggled down. 'Couldn't be nicer,' she said lazily. 'I love it when it's rotten outside and I'm not there and haven't to be there for an hour or two. It makes railway carriages cosier, even.' And she rubbed her cheek against the side of the chair.

'When Joe went out to see if there was any news,' Mrs Joe continued, 'I was saying to myself I could just do with a nice little chat. I must get my work.' Having found a complicated and very untidy piece of knitting, bright pink in hue, she beamed across the hearth at her visitor, then settled herself in her chair, and looked cosy and confidential yet still majestic, like a queen off duty.

'Now this is really nice,' she exclaimed. 'You know, if only George was here and in rather better health than he was at Christmas - you remember he was not at all well then, though Clara says he is all right now - do you know what I should call myself?'

Susie from the depths of her chair replied that she didn't.

'Stop!' cried Mrs Joe in a startling and dramatic fashion, at the same time sitting bolt upright. 'Stop! I've no right to ask for Everything. I don't say - I *won't* say - if only George was here. I'll say this. Do you know what I call myself now? I call myself - for once - a Happy Woman.' She looked triumphantly at Susie and then looked severely at her knitting and shook it a little, just as if it was about to interrupt with some impudent remark.

'You like it here, don't you?' said Susie.

'To be quite honest with you, my dear, I do. It suits me', replied Mrs Joe with decision, 'down to the ground. I dare say I can do my share of grumbling. If Things aren't going well, I face the fact and ask others to do the same. When they do go well, I say so. Just now it would be a sin to grumble, it really would.'

'But I'm not grumbling,' Susie protested.

'Quite so. Here we are, nice and cosy together, having our little chat in front of a fire, a good fire, a most liberal fire I call it- '

'They're jolly good about fires round here, aren't they?'

'I can say that for mine, Mrs Pennyfeather,' cried Mrs Joe with judicial enthusiasm. 'She'd never stoop so low as to send in about four pieces and a shovelful of dust and call that a shilling scuttle. Most liberal in the matter of coal. Well, here we are, listening to the wind blowing outside and not caring about it at all, and knowing that tonight we'll have a good audience, an appreciative audience, out at Stundley or Gort or wherever it is we're playing this week. Yes, Mundley, of course. That's the one, isn't it - the one where the trams go all round the funny dirty statue in the middle - Mundley? I find these three towns terribly confusing, don't you? Though of course as Dates they couldn't be better. And then such unusually good rooms these are too, aren't they? Look at this one. Have you noticed the oil paintings?'

As nearly every bit of wall space was covered with brownish canvases, framed lavishly in gilt but mysterious and curiously cotton-woolly in their subjects, Susie could reply with truth that she had noticed the oil paintings. 'I've been wondering for some time', she said, peeping out of her chair to have another glance round at them, 'what they're about. They don't seem to be *about* anything much, do they?'

'The work of Mrs Pennyfeather's uncle, I understand,' said Mrs Joe, whose tones now took on a certain new dignity, befitting the tenant of such a room and art gallery. 'An amateur - he was a seedsman or ironmonger, I forget which - but very gifted and quite up to professional standard. Above it in some ways, I think.'

'I must say, Mrs Joe, they all look alike to me,' said Susie. 'Yet they don't seem to have any sort of subject - unless it's the inside of a mattress - you know, one of those brown woolly ones - he's been trying to paint.'

'Moors and Glens, I believe, were his favourite subjects,' said Mrs Joe. 'He seems to have been fond of Highland scenery, though Mrs Pennyfeather tells me he was never up there. We once played Aberdeen and Inverness and saw just the same kind of scenery through the carriage window, in the train, you know, not quite so brown perhaps and not so many deers and stags about, but very like. You must admit, my dear, they give the room a Tone. It's a relief to me after so many calendars and photographs of Oddfellows and that class of thing. A woman who's gone to so much expense and trouble with a Home so rarely lets. Now where would you find a nicer room to sit in than this? As a matter of fact' - she dropped her voice – 'I know they're still paying off on that chair you're sitting in and the oak table there and the bookcase behind you, she practically told me so, the other day. And you know how Joe is set on having a Home of Our Own - well, put him in that chair, let him take a look round this room, and you can't drag him away from the subject. "Oh, for a Home of Our Own!" You should hear him go on about it. Though I must say, things being as they are and our work what it is, how we should get a Home of Our Own and what we should do with it when we have got it, I don't know, and if he does, then he doesn't tell me. Men never *really* think at all, as you'll find out for yourself one of these days, my dear.'

'I've done all the finding out about them I'm going to do,' Susie announced very promptly.

'That I cannot believe,' Mrs Joe retorted, 'or I should be sorry for you. But you must agree with me that if you're lucky with rooms, the next best thing to having a Home is playing a resident season. Now we've been lucky with the rooms here, and this is practically a resident season, isn't it?'

'Resident - with tram rides,' replied Susie. 'Though I usually go out to Mundley by bus.'

'With Tram Rides or Bus, certainly,' said Mrs Joe quite solemnly. 'But staying on in the same rooms makes it resident, I think, dear. Though of course compared with a whole summer season at Bournemouth, this is nothing. When I heard of that offer,' she continued, more animated now, 'the moment I heard of it, Susie, I said to Joe "The Luck has completely changed. We're made." And he agreed, though he says Bournemouth's not quite his style. Which is ridiculous of course but you know how Joe will pretend to be so rough and ready. "A big town," I told him. "A town with Tone and Taste - and Money of course. Five months at least guaranteed. It's a Miracle." If you'd gone round the coast and told me you were trying to find a place for a resident season, I should have told you without the slightest hesitation - "Bournemouth, by all means," I should have said at once. And Bournemouth now it is. But nothing so far seems to have been done about it, nothing. I hope there's no haggling about terms. Now that we are getting on, we mustn't be greedy. Surely the Bournemouth people wouldn't haggle?'

'The terms are quite good.' said Susie indifferently.

'Then they should be wired - at once.'

'Yes, I suppose so,' Susie continued, staring into the fire. 'I suppose we ought to think ourselves lucky.'

'Undoubtedly. Remember Rawsley, where Miss Trant found us,' said Mrs Joe earnestly. 'Bear that horrible place in mind, my dear.'

'I know. Only six months ago too. Oh, I've thought about all that.' Susie shook herself out of the chair, leaned her elbows on the mantelpiece, and tapped the fender with one foot. 'Yes, it's a marvellous offer - a plum - the sort that C. P. people are always telling you they're getting and somehow weren't able to accept - the liars? But - I feel a bit of a pig about this - but' - she wheeled round swiftly, facing her companion - 'Oh, Mrs Joe, I don't - I really, honestly don't - want to spend the whole summer in C. P. work at Bournemouth - '

'Just what I said to Joe about you,' the other cried in mournful triumph. ' "Susie doesn't want to," I told him. I saw it at once. He didn't of course, but then he never notices anything, never. Now why don't you? Tell me.'

Susie moved her shoulders impatiently and pouted down at the fire. 'Everybody's beginning to tell me I'm restless, and it's true, I am. The weather, I suppose - bit of nerves - swelled head, if you like. I've had too many good audiences this year, all of a sudden - not good for the little girl. Now she doesn't know when she's well off.' She laughed, rather bitterly.

Mrs Joe was maternal. 'Now don't be foolish, Susie. Nobody is saying anything about you.'

'I wouldn't care if they were,' cried Susie wildly. 'It isn't that. I suppose I'm always thinking something absolutely marvellous is going to turn up, and then when you all come along and say "Hooray! Six months in Bournemouth! Susie will continue to sing Number Twenty-seven on the programme! Twice daily! Outside in the afternoon, but if wet in the shelter! Bring the children!" then I see the same old stick-in-the-mud business going on and on, and I think - oh hell!'

'Not hell!' cried Mrs Joe reproachfully.

'Yes - *Hell!*' Susie repeated, ready now either to laugh or to cry. 'I just see myself stuck there. With those three numbers of Inigo's, I could go anywhere, anywhere. They're too good for concert-party audiences.'

'Not too good,' said Mrs Joe, 'but in a different style perhaps.'

'I'm sorry. I didn't mean too good really, but not what they want. Anyhow - ' She stopped suddenly. 'Oh, I am a fool. I'd forgotten what I slipped in to tell you. About Coral Crawford. Now this is what gets my goat, and you can't blame me. I brought the paper and put it down somewhere. Here we are. Now,' she went on sternly, 'you remember Coral Crawford, don't you? She was with the *Larks and Owls* Company with you, and left just after I joined, didn't she?'

'I should think I do remember her. Coral Crawford. One of the most outrageous Borrowers I ever shared a dressing-room with.'

'Well, then,' cried Susie, 'what did you think of her, honestly?'

Mrs Joe replied as if she were giving a reference: ' As a turn, hopeless. As a companion, a fellow-performer, a lady, no better, being deceitful, untrustworthy, given to lying, to say nothing of borrowing everything that could possibly be borrowed and some things that a self-respecting girl would never dream of wanting from anybody else, and never returning anything without being asked times without number.' She leaned back and added: 'What about her?'

'You remember she said she was fed up with C. P. work and left us to try and get into the chorus?' said Susie breathlessly. 'She got in. I've never heard of her since - until this morning. Now read this.' And she stuck the folded newspaper under her companion's nose. 'Starring - *starring*, mind you - in a new show at the Pall Mall! Doesn't it make you want to scream? Coral Crawford! Read it. Playing with Tommy Mawson and Leslie Wate and Virginia Washington! Great success! Should run for ever! Look what they say about the show! Coral Crawford! Bang at the top! I'm not jealous, honestly I'm not - it's nice seeing people you know getting there - but that girl - a star at the Pall Mall already! Help! When I read that this morning in bed I could feel myself going hot and cold and pink and yellow all at once. I wanted to gnaw the sheets and blankets, I really did.'

'Well, well!' Mrs Joe still stared at the paper. 'Of course the girl may have improved a lot since we knew her. I've known it happen in the most surprising way,' she said dubiously.

'Och - tripe! Not possible. Improved! She'd nothing to improve. There wasn't anything there. Anyhow, there she is - Coral Crawford - Crawly - at the Pall Mall, and here I am, taking the tram out to Mundley every night to sing Number Thirty-three on the programme! Isn't it enough to make you sick? And then you talk to me about six months in

Bournemouth, jogging on through the same old show! I know - I know - I oughtn't to grumble - I'm not grumbling. Miss Trant's an angel - you're all angels - and I suppose I ought to shut up. But there you are. And *now* do you understand?'

'You think this isn't good enough for you?' said Mrs Joe softly, staring at the fire.

'I don't mean exactly that,' Susie was penitent. 'I don't, really.'

'Yes, you do,' the other replied, quite gently. Her hands were still now, resting idly on her knitting, that knitting which might go on and on, from town to town, and be taken into dressing-rooms and railway carriages and all manner of strange lodgings, and grow more and more complicated and shapeless and useless until at last it would disappear and never be heard of again. 'And you're right,' she added, in quite a different tone of voice. 'You are too good, Susie. I used to think I was.' This was slipped in wistfully.

'And so you are,' said Susie stoutly. 'Miles and miles.'

'Do you think so, really?' cried Mrs Joe, brightening at once. 'Well of course when I'm in voice, there's no doubt I am. It's the delicacy of my voice that kept me out of big work. And after all good training and long experience, Taste and Interpretation - they must count for something, mustn't they?'

'Course they must, you absurd thing!'

'What you want, what you're pining for, Susie, is a big Chance. That's why you're restless. I know, my dear. Well keep on quietly, doing your best, and it'll come, that's what I say. I don't say *how* or *where* it'll come because I don't know, but come it will. I feel it. And you're still very young, aren't you?'

'I suppose so,' said Susie gloomily, 'though at times I feel a thousand, I can tell you. And telling yourself how young you are doesn't seem to make much difference if you're not satisfied. Every time I hear about anybody in the profession suddenly doing so marvellously, like Crawly, I always try and find out their ages. So does Jerry, I discovered the other day. He's pretty poisonous, of course, but he does understand about things like that. Jerry'll get there soon, if it kills him.'

'Your Chance might arrive', said Mrs Joe, 'at Bournemouth. That wouldn't surprise *me*.'

'It would me. Unless you mean six nights at the local Picture Palace. Bournemouth! Pooh!'

'Again, it might arrive here,' Mrs Joe went on impressively, 'in Gatford - or even Gort - I mean Stort, or Mundley. Yes, you can laugh, my dear, but I say it *might*. I've known it happen before and in far worse places, far, far worse - in Sheer Holes.'

'All right then, it might,' said Susie in tones that suggested the maximum of possible unbelief. 'Let's talk about something a bit more cheerful or I shall weep. Would you like the latest about Elsie and her Pink Egg?'

'Her what?' Mrs Joe was startled.

'Well, he looks exactly like one. You've seen him, haven't you? - the great gentleman friend. She thinks about nothing else now. Sees him every day, nearly. D'you know what she's gone and done? - bought a new winter coat - *now*! When he first popped up with his little car, she rushed off and bought a new jumper suit. You've seen it? Well, she tried going out with him in that and of course she was frozen stiff every time, leaving her old coat at home. So the other day she rushed round the shops and bought a new coat. And now she's so broke, broke to the world, she'll never have a thing for summer. And all for Mr Herbert - otherwise Bert - Dulver, otherwise Pink Egg.'

'I wondered,' mused Mrs Joe. 'That's why she's not bothering about future dates.'

'Can't think of anything but Egg or Pink Un.'

'It sounds to me like Touch-and-Go. She never had her heart in the Profession. Do you think she'll manage it this time?'

'She hasn't said much,' replied Susie, 'but it looks to me as if she's hoping to bring him to the boil.'

'He's no Egg, my dear, if she can't,' said Mrs Joe, majestically coy.

'But what a life if she does!' cried Susie. 'I ask you! Mrs Pink Egg! Just imagine - all your hopes on that! Horrors! I'd rather keep on, going to fifty Rawsleys, or having a resident season at Tewborough - '

Mrs Joe shuddered. 'Don't mention that Hole, please, my dear. Even to joke about it.'

'Yes, at Tewborough with a sniffy cold that never stops than be like poor Elsie. When I think of her Pink Egging it for all she's worth, I swear I won't ever grumble or feel so restless again.'

'Very nice,' said Mrs Joe, 'but you will.'

And of course she did.

IV

No one knew better than Miss Elsie Longstaff herself that, at that very moment, it was touch and go with the gentleman who has been somewhat unfairly introduced to us as Pink Egg. Mr Herbert Dulver was a gentleman friend of some two years' standing, though for the greater part of that time he had occupied a lowly place in the hierarchy of Elsie's gentlemen friends. Indeed, there had been periods when he had been as completely out of mind as he was out of sight. Shortly after The Good Companions had arrived at The Triangle, however, Mr Dulver had turned up again, for he was managing an hotel owned by his father, a substantial old place about fifteen miles out of Gatford and on the main London road. All the Dulvers - large, pink, and brassily cheerful persons - were landlords or book-makers of something convivial or sporting. Herbert had been managing an hotel at the seaside when Elsie had first made his acquaintance, and now, having acquired in a mysterious Dulverish manner a considerable sum of money, he proposed not only to manage but also to own another seaside hotel. He was a bachelor about forty who liked to clothe his pink plumpness in sporting tweeds, wore a fair clipped moustache, and looked at the world out of prominent light-blue eyes that had about them a kind of hard amiability. His manner and phraseology suggested the confidential, but his voice was loud and carried far and he made full use of it, so that he always gave the odd impression that he was bellowing out his innermost secrets. Actually, however, he had no difficulty in keeping to himself whatever was best known only to himself, and was in reality a far more astute man of business than he appeared to be, like all the Dulvers, who for several generations now had been ordering drinks all round and slapping everybody on the back and talking at the top of their voices while they quietly contrived to feather their nests. And this Mr Dulver had the traditional attitude towards women. Outside business, in which he demanded and took care to receive his money's worth, he was very chivalrous and gallant towards 'the Ladies', and both masterful and saucy with 'the Girls'. Elsie, who liked being one of the Ladies and one of the Girls too, understood and appreciated both these attitudes, but that did not prevent her from telling herself from the first that Mr Dulver would want watching. Not that this stood in his way at all, for in her heart of hearts Elsie admired a man who wanted watching.

Mr Dulver had run her out in his little car to the hotel for lunch, and now they had stopped on the way back, at a spot on the side of the road where a mound of hill and a little copse sheltered them from the tearing wind. There they lit their cigarettes and Elsie waited expectantly. She knew only too well that Mr Dulver had news for her and that this afternoon might decide everything. Miles of soft Midland landscape, brown fields, the glitter of water, the swirl of smoke, the grey distance, were spread before them, but she had no eyes for it all, for the real world had narrowed to those few square inches, pinker than ever, that represented the outward map of Mr Dulver's mind and where there might soon be seen the signals of victory or defeat.

'Well,' she cried, turning to look him full in the face and pouting a little, 'aren't you going to tell me? I've been thinking about how you were getting on down there all the week-end. Course, if you don't want to tell, it doesn't matter. I just wondered, that's all.' Elsie was cleared for action. Every sentence now would be a well-aimed shot from a different turret.

'I was waiting,' replied Mr Dulver. 'Didn't want to say anything in there. Between you and me, I'm thinking of taking it.'

'You are?' she exclaimed in glad surprise, very much the bright, friendly, interested woman. 'I'm glad, Bert; I really am.' Were her eyes shining, or were they just staring, bulging out, silly?

Bert looked pleased and important. 'It's a good little house, twenty bedrooms - might easily put in a few more, make an annexe, easy. Good smoke-room and bar trade too, though it wants working up a bit. Summer's money for dust, of course, but fair number staying in winter, specially week-ends. Golf, y'know, and fishing. Bang opposite the pier too - '

'Opposite the pier!' cried Elsie, reproachfully. 'Don't I know it is? Haven't I played Eastbeach, year before last, and on the very pier? What's the good of telling you anything, Bert? You never listen.' And she gave him a companionable tap.

'That's right,' he said apologetically. 'I'm that full of it, I'm forgetting you've been there, Elsie. Well, they want four thousand, lock, stock, and barrel, except the usual take-overs. As I say, it wants working up, mind you.'

'You could do that all right,' she told him.

'I could eat it,' he proclaimed. 'I tell you, I like the look of it, like the town too. Not far from London, either. Good road. Run up now and again and see what's doing.' He clicked his tongue appreciatively and looked doggish.

'You would!' cried Elsie, who knew her cues. 'You leave London alone. Time you behaved yourself, if you ask me.'

'Something in that,' he admitted, 'though we've all got to have a bit of fun, haven't we?'

"That's what I always tell them. We're a long time dead, I say.'

He looked at her admiringly and the arm resting on the back of the seat behind her came a little closer. 'You know what's what and you've been to Eastbeach,' he said. 'Honestly now, what d'you think of it, Elsie?'

'You don't want to know what I think of it.'

'Don't I? Well, what am I asking you for? Brought you out here to hear what you think about it. Come on, Elsie, let's have it, straight from the horse's mouth.'

'Who are you calling a horse!'

'Not you.' The arm was resting on her shoulders now. The little moustache came nearer. There was a kind of mistiness about Mr Dulver as he gazed at this fair ripeness, which was exactly his taste in feminine charm.

Elsie averted the kiss that she knew would inevitably have descended upon her a moment later, but she did it easily and quietly by drawing away ever so little and suddenly looking serious, businesslike. 'Well, I'll tell you what I think about it, Bert, if you'll only be sensible for a minute,' she began; and thereupon told him why she approved of Eastbeach and the hotel there, showing him quite plainly, if he only had the sense to see it, that she was a girl with her wits about her who knew what the hotel business was, even if she did happen to be on the stage. And all the time her imagination, dizzy as it was, still explored the possibility. She saw herself in that hotel, Mrs Dulver, telling the maids what to do; queening it for half an hour now and again in the saloon bar, hair always waved and good clothes; shopping in style - 'Good morning. Madam'; recognized by all the gentlemen in the town - 'Good afternoon, Mrs Dulver' - raising their hats; having a word with the girls who came to the pier pavilion - not stand-offish or rubbing it in but still - pitying them; taking little trips to London with Bert in the car - a bigger one by this time; going round the shops and doing a show - 'used to be in the profession myself, once, my dear'; the whole rich future. And a word or two could make it hers. 'Of course you know better than I do, Bert - a girl isn't much of a judge of these things, though I know a bit more than most - but that's my honest opinion. You go in and buy the place.'

'Going to,' said Mr Dulver complacently. 'Decided that first thing this morning, matter of fact, but just wanted to hear what you thought about it. And I'll tell you what it is, Elsie, old kid- '

'Old kid! What next!'

'You've got it where it's wanted,' he continued, tapping his forehead. 'Used to think you'd just got the looks and style and nothing else to it - '

'Thank you, sir, she said,' cried Elsie. 'Very good of you to admit the looks, I must say, *Mister* Dulver,' But she smiled at him very sweetly.

The arm tightened round her and the now amorous Bert tried to kiss her. To his surprise, however, for he had kissed her before she repulsed him, firmly if gently. 'Hello! Hel-low!' He drew back and looked at her. 'We aren't very matey today, are we? What have I done wrong?'

Knowing very well that the slightest chill would ruin all and yet realizing that now or never was the time when he must not have his own way too easily, Elsie felt as if she was walking on a tightrope. She smiled again; a little one this time, a bit mysterious. 'You never do anything wrong, do you?' she remarked lightly. 'But there isn't anything wrong. Honestly, there isn't. I'm enjoying myself. Aren't you?' And she looked at him archly.

'Not sure about that,' Mr Dulver muttered, not so certain of himself and everything else as he had been a few minutes before. 'Here, though' - and the arm tightened again - 'what about - '

'Going home?' she put in quickly. It was a terrible risk. If he said - and she could almost hear him saying it already, in a flash - 'All right, let's go home then,' then it was all over. Awful!

'I'm going to say something to you,' said Bert, severely and importantly. Bless him! - it didn't matter now how severe and important he liked to sound. 'Have you ever thought', he continued with great deliberation, 'of abandoning your stage career? Wait a minute. I mean, to get married.'

'Oh, I've been proposed to a good few times, I don't mind telling you,' cried Elsie, who didn't mind telling him.

'No doubt. Suppose you were asked now, though?'

'Depends on who did the asking.'

'I'm doing the asking.'

'You try me.'

'Go on then. What d'you say? Coming to Eastbeach as Mrs Dulver of the Black Horse?'

'Oh, Bert - ! Are you sure -?'

'Shouldn't be asking if I wasn't.'

Then Mr Dulver found himself being kissed. Into that kiss went a whole captured ecstatic vision of the future and a glorious farewell to cheap lodgings, bad meals, old clothes, cramped dressing-rooms, bored audiences, and long Sundays in the train; and it took his breath away, almost frightened him. But not for long. Bert was delighted. He may have been a Dulver - with something hard, brassy, behind those curving pink cheeks and prominent light-blue eyes - but nevertheless he was a member of the sentimental sex, and now he moaned over her like any lovesick lad. He must be in the Eastbeach hotel before the season began, and they must be married before he went to Eastbeach, even if it would be a rush. To all of this Elsie gave an instant and rapturous assent.

Then her mind went racing through all the possibilities and complications. 'But look here, Bert,' she said, looking very solemn, 'if it's going to be as soon as all that, it'll be awkward.'

'Not it,' he replied masterfully, holding her tight. 'You leave it to me. I'll fix it. We're used to these things in the hotel business.'

'That's all right, but' - she was genuinely troubled now - 'well, I've nothing ready, and - oh, you might as well know - I'm completely broke, will be for weeks.'

'Nothing in that. I knew you couldn't have much, from what you said. I'll fix that too - stand all the exes. You tell me what you want. Might as well do it properly while we're at it, what d'you say?'

What could she say - what were mere words - when she saw him shining there like a god? But when the car was headed for Gatford again, she never stopped talking, and he listened with a proud air of proprietorship. At Mohen's, the large jewellers' in Victoria Street, he pulled up, saying 'This is where you get the ring. Got to have a ring.' Seeing that their marriage was to take place almost at once, other men might have thought an engagement-ring unnecessary, but that was not the Dulvers' way; what there was to be done had to be done - in style. You never saw any Mrs Dulver without her full complement of rings. And Elsie, who was undoubtedly a born Mrs Dulver, admired her Bert all the more for this grand decision. 'You'll have to come in', he told her, 'to see what you fancy and try 'em on.'

'You go first, Bert,' she replied. 'Have a look round.' She had no idea what he would care 'to run to' in this matter of rings.

He disappeared into the shop, and she remained in the car for a moment, then got out, looking at the passers-by with the assured stare of an engaged woman.

'Eh, I've been looking for you,' said a familiar voice.

'Mr Oakroyd!' She smiled upon him. She even smiled upon his companion, a thick-set, bow-legged man, who wore an immense green cap.

'Ay,' said Mr Oakroyd. 'Miss Trant wants you to bring that there red dress wi' thingumbobs on - you knaw which it is - round to t'theater tonight.'

'All right,' replied Elsie indifferently. She had almost forgotten the existence of Miss Trant, the dress, and the theatre. 'You won't see me in that much longer, Mr Oakroyd. I'm giving Miss Trant my notice tonight. I'm getting married - quite soon."

'Nay, you don't say!' cried Mr Oakroyd. 'Well, well! I did hear you were doing a bit o' courting in t'district. I've seen him, haven't I? It's t'chap as comes round for you, him i' flight suits as keeps pub somewhere, isn't it?'

The chap himself put in an appearance at that very moment. 'Bert,' cried Elsie, 'this is Mr Oakroyd, our props man. I've just been telling him.'

'Hope to see you at the wedding, Mr Oakroyd, drinking our health,' cried Mr Dulver affably.

'Good enough! I'll be there,' Mr Oakroyd replied. 'This is a friend o' mine,' he added, rather proudly, indicating the thick-set, bow-legged, green-capped one. 'Mr Jock Campbell.'

'Hello! Know that name! Seen you before!' said Mr Dulver, who was very much at home in a situation of this kind. 'Saw you last Saturday.'

'That's right,' replied Mr Oakroyd, who appeared to think it was his duty to answer for his friend, apparently a very taciturn man.' 'Gainst Lincoln City here.'

'And played a good game too. If the forwards had only been as good as you backs,' Mr Dulver observed, 'the Triangle would have walked away with it. But your forward line's weak in my opinion.'

Mr Campbell, after swaying uneasily, now cleared his throat, preparatory to bursting into speech. 'Och!' he muttered, 'they're raw.'

'He means they're nobbut young lads, new to t'game,' his interpreter explained.' Don't you, Jock?'

'That's about it,' said Mr Dulver heartily. 'Well, pleased to have met you. Come in, Elsie. I bet you don't know what we're doing. Choosing the ring.' And he burst into a loud guffaw, which was answered by companionable if faint sardonic grins from Messrs Oakroyd and Campbell, who both did something rather vague to their caps and then moved away.

When Mr Oakroyd had discovered that he was lodging in the very same street as, indeed next door but one to, the famous Jock Campbell, now left back and captain of the recently formed Triangle United A.F.C., and formerly of Glasgow Celtic, Sheffield Wednesday - and Bruddersford United - he was very excited. Had he not spent many and many a happy Saturday afternoon at the Bruddersford ground cheering Jock's vast and miraculous clearance kicks? But when he also discovered that the great man was not only close at hand but was quite ready to make the acquaintance of an old admirer, to smoke a pipe with him, and take turn about paying for half-pints, Mr Oakroyd's excitement and gratification knew no bounds. Jock was forty now, and so a veteran, an ancient of days, among professional footballers; on the field he looked old, if only because he had met so many footballs with his head that he was almost completely bald in front; he was heavy and he was slow: but he was an unusually powerful man and his long experience, his guile, enabled him to play a good game even yet, so that though his best days, when fifty thousand spectators roared their approval at him, were over long ago, he was still an acquisition to such a junior club as the Triangle United. He had not been at Gatford long and was not a man to make friends easily, and it was not really surprising that he should take pleasure in Mr Oakroyd's company. They had a common theme in Bruddersford, where Jock had lived several years; they were both separated from their wives; and they both had a detached taste for football and tobacco and beer and a deep philosophical interest in the chances and changes of this life, though the older of the two, Mr Oakroyd, was the more eager and romantic. Such idealism as Mr Campbell had, centred about public-houses: his one ambition now was to do what so many of his successful fellow-gladiators had done, to find a nice little public-house, not too far from a football ground, and turn himself into the landlord of it. A good benefit match might do it. For the rest, he was a man of vast but comfortable silences. Mr Oakroyd, as we know, could hardly be called loquacious, but compared with his new friend he was a chatterbox.

'Yond's pleased wi' hersen nar,' Mr Oakroyd shouted, as they continued their walk down Victoria Street. He had to shout because the wind was making such a din. 'She's bin fair sick to get hersen off this long time - and nar she's gone an' roped him in. An' it'll just suit her lahdidahing it a bit i' t'saloon bar wi' all her best clothes on and her hair all frizzed up.'

'Ay.' said Mr Campbell.

'Not a bad sort o' chap she's gotten hold of,' Mr Oakroyd continued. 'Right landlord style, did you notice?'

'Ay,' said Mr Campbell. And then, two minutes afterwards he muttered something that Mr Oakroyd, who was now very clever at this kind of thing, interpreted to, mean that, in Mr Campbell's opinion, Mr Dulver was obviously in a big way of business and was not a man to serve pints himself.

They turned out of the main street into a quieter thorough-fare. Here Mr Oakroyd chuckled. 'Pink Egg! That's what Soosie - young lass o' troupe - calls him.' he explained, 'and if you nob-but tak a good look at him he's a bit like one, more still wi' his 'at off. Pink Egg! Eh, she's droll.'

This shocked Mr Campbell into speech. 'It's no name that, man, to gie a landlord in a big way o' business.' he said solemnly.

Mr Oakroyd, well acquainted with his companion's great desire and respecting such an ambition, one for heroes, made no reply, and they covered the next two hundred yards or so in silence.

'Hoo's the lass that's awa'?' Mr Campbell suddenly inquired. He had heard all about Lily in Canada.

'Nay, I haven't heard for a bit, not sin' I were telling yer,' replied Mr Oakroyd. 'Seemingly she's doing champion. Allus says so. But I'd like to see for mysen,' he added, a trifle wistfully.

'Ay.' said Mr Campbell. And then, growing reckless as a conversationalist, he said: 'An' the wife? Hoo's she?'

'I can't get to know owt. Neither she nor t'lad'll say. I wrote nobbut t'other day an' asked 'em right aht if she were poorly an' if I could do owt. Eh, it's damn silly going on like that! But it's my wife all over.'

'They gae their ain gate.' Mr Campbell brought out from the depths of his own experience.

Nothing more was said until they reached Crimean Road, where they both lodged, and then Mr Oakroyd, who had been looking vaguely troubled, returned to the subject of Elsie and her marriage. 'That's one going o' t'owd lot,' he said, as if The Good Companions had been together for six years instead of six months. 'Nar it's started, mark my word. Elsie's nobbut t'first. More to foller, or I'm a Dutchman! Happen you've noticed it yersen, Jock? Nowt changes at all for some time, and then - all of a sudden, afore you knaw where you are - they're going right and left, and it's all to bits.'

'Maybe.' Mr Campbell ventured.

'I'm down o' this, I am an' all,' Mr Oakroyd went on. 'I mun hear what t'others has to say. There's been a summat i' fair these two-three week.'

'Ay, a sicht too much wind,' replied Mr Campbell gravely. And we will allow him to have the last word - for once in his life.

CHAPTER TWO
A Chapter of Encounters

I

ELSIE finished with the show on the last Saturday at Mundley, when she had been given a most successful Benefit Night, concluding with genuine tears and bouquets. Jimmy had already slipped down to Birmingham to interview and book her successor, Miss Mamie Potter. This first week of their return to the Gatford Hippodrome was going to be exciting. The new soubrette was due to arrive on Monday morning, to rehearse in the afternoon, to appear at night. Then on Wednesday there was Elsie's wedding, which was to be celebrated out at the Dulver's hotel on the London Road. They were all going and the bus had already been ordered. Then on Saturday there was to be another Grand Benefit Night - you could see the bills plastered all over the town - this time for Miss Susie Dean, our popular comedienne. Next Saturday was Susie's twenty-first birthday. And she was giving a tea party first, and there was to be some sort of jollification, only vaguely outlined, as yet, after the show. Moreover, the Hippodrome would be packed out every night, as they all knew, with enthusiastic Gatfordians. Here was excitement enough for hard-working professionals. What a week!

Yet all was not well with them. The old members of the troupe, Jimmy and Mitcham and the Brundits, were still quietly in despair about the Bournemouth offer, not yet accepted. Miss Trant seemed so dreamy and remote these days that she was considered unapproachable for the time being. It was very odd, but there it was. Business was never better, and, on the other hand, nothing bolder had been attempted for years in the C. P. world than Miss Trant's present venture, the renting of the Hippodrome, on stiff terms, with some nasty clauses slipped in; and yet - so fantastic is the sex, as Jimmy and Mr Mitcham pointed out to one another - she did not seem to be bothering her head about it at all. But then all the young people were rather queer. Jerry Jerningham was more aloof and mysterious than usual, and was thought to be up to something, though nobody knew what. In spite of birthday and benefit - or because of them - Susie was still restless, rather snappy at times, and given to wriggling her pretty shoulders at people who asked the simplest and friendliest questions. She had snubbed poor Inigo so often lately that now he kept out of her way, stalked about with a new and purposeful air, and was understood to be hard at work revising the eight numbers he had written for them, which he called his *Tripe à la mode de Jazz* - to the entire mystification of his friend, Mr Oakroyd. Success had come at last, but all these young people seemed to be taking it the wrong way, which proved conclusively to Mr Mitcham that young people were not what they were when he had been a young person.

Mr Oakroyd was mystified by many things these days. He was as interested as any of the others in the events of the near future. In his own fashion he shared any excitement that was going. Nevertheless, he found himself brooding somewhat darkly on Canada and 51 Ogden Street and the destiny of The Good Companions. He had never been very fond of Elsie, but she was 'one o' t'owd lot', and the fact that she was going and another taking her place troubled him more than it did any of the others. Perhaps he alone, from out of the depths of his philosophy of Sudden Change, felt that this coming week would take them all much further than they ever imagined, that the exciting plans they had made for it were nothing compared with some other plans already being laid down for them by the old powers, the conspiracy of the wind and the stars. The thread we saw dangling before him - so long ago, it seems! - as he walked up Manchester Road, Bruddersford, after the match, that thread, its colour changing, deepening, is now running faster and faster; and perhaps he has heard - in a dream, through some Old Salt reverie - the rattle of its winding spool.

The first thing that happened, of course, was Miss Mamie Potter. Jimmy had said that she was young but experienced, had no voice to speak of but danced well, and would do. When pressed more closely, he always pointed out that people who were in a hurry could not pick and choose as long as they liked, and that for his part he did not pretend to be able to work miracles. There was thought to be something queer, fishy, about this. The arrival, the rehearsal, the appearance on the stage, of Miss Potter soon settled the question. Jimmy had no good solid reason for not engaging her, and so he had engaged her, but some instinct must have warned him that all was not well. On the stage she was adequate enough; as a matter of fact she was better than Elsie had ever been. But off the stage, Miss Mamie Potter was insufferable. Within less than twelve hours of her first arrival at Gatford station, she had put all their backs up; and it was clear that she was indeed a born putter-up of backs.

Miss Potter had a sleek, almost electro-plated, blonde head; no eyebrows; very round blue eyes; a button of a nose, so small and heavily powdered that it resembled the chalked end of a billiard cue; and a mouth that was a perpetual crimson circle of faint astonishment. The upper half of her, her neck and shoulders and the thin arms ending so curiously in little dumpy hands, was poor; but her legs were really beautiful. It was as if she were being carried about by two fine sonnets. Those two exquisite, twinkling silky calves of hers seemed to be always making charmingly witty and impudent comments on the world. If she had never done anything but walk a little way in front of depressed males, she would have been a notable public benefactor, distributing a sense of the joy of life. Unfortunately, she talked; and she talked in a kind of idle, staring voice, and the result was havoc. Her perpetual opening 'I say' was very soon a storm signal.

'I say,' she said to Mr Oakroyd, after she had known him about quarter of an hour, 'you seem to get a lot of your own way here, don't you? You're only the props, aren't you?' Mr Oakroyd regarded her with astonishment and rubbed his chin hard. 'Ay, that's all,' he replied finally. 'Nobbut a sort o' dog like. Just let me knaw if you hear me speaking out o' my turn. You mun just set us right as you go on. We knaw nowt.' This speech might have puzzled and possibly quietened some people, but Miss Potter merely gave it a little condescending nod and then strolled away. 'I say,' she said to the horrified Morton Mitcham, 'some of those card tricks of yours are pretty ancient, aren't they?' Equally ancient, in her opinion, were Jimmy's gags and Mrs Joe's ballads. 'I say,' she remarked to Susie, 'you seem to go down here very well, but they're letting you dig an awfully big hole in the programme, aren't they?' This was after the show on Monday night. It had been a rather queer performance. The house was crowded and as generally enthusiastic as ever, but from somewhere at the back of the pit (which was the cheapest part of the house, there being no gallery at the Hippodrome) there had come, at odd times, various loud jeers and hootings and cat-calls, obviously resented by most people in the audience, though now and then raising a laugh. This had never happened before, and they were all talking about it after the show. The furious Susie told Mrs Joe that it must be Mamie Potter, but this did not satisfy Mrs Joe or anybody else, not even Susie herself.

On Tuesday morning, the wind had dropped to a mild breeze and a little watery sunshine crept over the Midlands. Miss Trant, still unsettled by her visit to Hitherton, still haunted by the daffodils and the bursting crocuses of the Cottage garden, decided that she must have some light and air, and so took Susie and some sandwiches for a run in the car.

'It's heavenly to see the country again,' cried Miss Trant, when they had left the car factories and the Triangle trams a long way behind. 'I wish you could stay with me at Hitherton, some time, Susie. Do you think you would like the country?'

'Oh, I adore the country,' cried Susie in her turn. She had imagined herself saying that, more than once, in interviews. She asked for nothing better, she always told the imaginary journalist, a young man, very nice, very respectful, than to retire to her little country place

- just a cottage where she could do everything for herself (see photograph). But what she did not know, that morning, was that very soon, sooner than she expected, she really would be giving those interviews. 'I've never seen enough of it', she went on, 'because I've spent nearly every bit of my time in towns - usually awful holes. If the country only had theatres and shops and people, it would be perfect, wouldn't it?'

Miss Trant laughed, then took the car into the side of the road, and stopped, 'We can eat our sandwiches here, don't you think?'

Susie sniffed the air appreciatively. 'It feels quite strong, doesn't it? - the air, I mean. It's so funny not to get it second-hand, used up a bit. I've been brought up on that kind, and this sort makes me feel a bit tight. Really it does. I want to giggle.' She skipped out of the car and pirouetted a little on the shining grass. Then she looked down ruefully. 'Jolly wet, though. That's the nuisance about the country, though, isn't it? - It's so wet and muddy. When it does dry up, it suddenly gets dusty then, and if you go a walk you're absolutely choked and too thirsty to speak and your shoes are too tight all of a sudden.'

They ate sandwiches. 'I wonder what the very superior Miss Potter thinks about us all this morning,' Miss Trant remarked. 'You don't like her, do you?'

'Like her!' cried Susie. 'She made me feel like murder last night. She did everybody. And as for thinking this morning, she won't have started yet. I know. She'll be just getting up now, wiping the cold cream off her face. Honestly, she's poisonous. She'll have us all quarrelling like mad within a week. They always do, that kind. You just watch. Jimmy ought to have known, even if he was in a hurry and she sounded all right. A woman would have spotted what she was right off.'

'Perhaps she'll improve in a day or two,' said Miss Trant, rather indifferently. 'I must admit she was rather terrible yesterday.'

'Did she say anything to you?' Susie inquired. 'I'll bet she did.'

'Oh yes. I wasn't left out, I assure you, Susie. She strolled up to me and said: "I say, I don't quite see why you're doing this, you know. This isn't your line at all, is it?" '

'She would! The cheek! How that girl's come to live so long beats me.' Having relieved her feelings, Susie grew thoughtful, stole a glance or two at her companion, then said, finally: 'But it isn't your line, is it?'

'I never said it was,' Miss Trant replied.

'No, of course not,' Susie went on. 'Don't think I'm going to be cheeky now. Or if you do, stop me. And I can promise you now that I'm not going to say a word about Bournemouth, not going to mention the place.'

'Thank you, my dear,' said Miss Trant demurely. 'As a matter of fact, the others haven't mentioned it lately - '

'No, they just look it now,' cried Susie. 'I've noticed them. Their eyes go rolling "Bournemouth" at you. Honestly, don't they? I noticed Joe - poor darling! - yesterday staring at you, like a sick cow, and I really thought something was the matter with him until it dawned on me he was trying to stare you into telling him something about the Bournemouth offer. But what I was going to say was this - Aren't you really getting a bit tired of us?'

'Gracious no!'

'Honestly now?'

'Not a bit. I won't include Miss Mamie Potter - '

'Gosh! I should think not.'

'But I assure you I'm not in the least tired of the rest of you, of the party. I'm like you, Susie. I'm feeling restless, not knowing what I want to do but only knowing what I don't want to do. The thought of our spending a whole summer on the South Coast somehow doesn't attract me at all.'

'I know. But what does attract you?'

'I haven't the least idea,' Miss Trant replied, as lightly as possible, though it was quite obvious she was in earnest.

'That's me all over - up to a point,' Susie remarked. 'I do know what I want, though - and a fine fat chance I've got of getting it! Inigo *annoys* me. Doesn't he you?'

'No. Why should he?' Miss Trant was amused.

'Don't laugh; it's serious. Well, he could *do* something, and he just doesn't. He's so *feeble* - just the amah-teurrr, you know ab-so-lutely.' Here Susie gave a vindictive imitation of Inigo's careless tones. 'When he follows me round, looking like a dying duck - and yet won't do anything - and is so high-and-mighty about the bits of things he writes for papers - though no paper will ever have them - and won't bother about his songs, though they might get him anywhere - oh, I could beat him, I really could. And then if I say something nasty to him, instead of answering back or putting his tongue out or giving me a good shaking - '

'Which I'm sure you've deserved,' Miss Trant put in.

'He just looks at me - like the Norphan Child - and walks away, and then stays away, sulking. He makes me furious. Not that it really matters, of course, what he does. But just now, when I'm dying for a chance myself, it's enough to make me sick to see somebody who has a chance not doing anything. So that's that. And now you can laugh, if you like. Let's go, shall we?'

On the way back a curious thing happened. The side-road they were on joined the main road about ten miles out of Gatford, and it chanced that when they arrived at the turning the traffic on the main road, consisting for the most part of new cars from Gatford, was thicker than usual, so that they pulled up for a minute or two. Miss Trant was idly watching the procession of cars when suddenly she stared intently and gave a little gasp. The next moment she was standing up trying to obtain a last glimpse of a car that had gone past them, there on the main road, and in the opposite direction from Gatford. The moment after she was sitting down again, still wide-eyed and a trifle pale.

'What's the matter?' cried Susie.

'I thought I saw someone I know - or used to know,' Miss Trant replied shakily.

Susie looked at her. Then she burst out in triumph: 'It's that man you once told me about, isn't it? Doctor McIntyre or whatever his name is? The one on the boat.'

'Doctor McFarlane. Yes, I thought it was. But it was all so quick. Besides - oh, it's absurd!'

'Why is it absurd? I don't see it. Couldn't he be here as well as anywhere else? Haven't you ever tried to find out where he is?'

'No, I haven't,' Miss Trant replied not very firmly. 'Why should I?'

'Why should you!' Susie was both sympathetic and derisive. 'If it was me, I should know all about him. Doctors ought to be easy to find. Wouldn't it be marvellous if you didn't feel well and sent for a doctor, and then *he* came and said: " *What, you!*" You don't know. He may have been in Gatford or Mundley or Stort or somewhere round here all the time. Let's get back at once and find out. If you don't, I will.'

It was useless for Miss Trant to protest, and indeed she did not protest very much. Once back in Gatford, Susie made for the nearest telephone directory and was so excited that she could hardly turn the pages. Susie was always wildly romantic on other people's behalf, and is to this day. But no Dr Hugh McFarlane was to be found in the telephone directory, which cast a wide net in the district. This was rather a blow for Susie, but she was not daunted. She pestered Miss Trant until that embarrassed lady was compelled to admit there was such a thing as a Medical Directory, where any doctor might be found. She was also compelled to admit that she had never examined one. 'And how you couldn't beats me,' cried Susie. 'It's no use you saying you don't want to know, because you do.'

'But it's all so ridiculous,' the other protested. 'I haven't seen him for years. He's probably forgotten my existence.'

'And probably not,' Susie told her. 'The sort of man you'd like probably wouldn't, though I must say I wouldn't give most men six months. I believe', she added shrewdly and boldly, 'you're frightened.

I'm being really cheeky now, I know, but it's because I'm so fond of you. And I hate to think of you just looking after us and then sitting alone reading about the three musketeers or Robin Hood or whatever it is you do read about, when there may be, somewhere round the corner, a marvellous Scotch doctor who' - and here Susie became very dramatic - 'when he comes back to his lonely house, late at night, after performing all sorts of operations - and "Bless you, doc!" the poor people say - I got that from a film - sits in his chair and smokes a pipe and thinks of you - and already his hair is turning grey at the temples - '

'Oh, do be quiet, Susie,' cried Miss Trant, crimson, half-laughing, half-angry. 'I shall really be cross if you don't.'

'All right then, I will,' said Susie, preparing to depart. They were at Miss Trant's hotel now. 'But I shall go round to the Free Library and see if they've got that book with all the doctors in. You can't stop me doing that. Good-bye.'

And about three-quarters of an hour later Miss Trant was called to the telephone. It was Susie. 'I daren't come round, and I couldn't wait,' said Susie. 'I looked at that book. It's stiff with McFarlanes. They must all be doctors. Honestly, dozens of 'em. I'm not sure whether I found the right one.'

'He was born in 1885 and went to Edinburgh.' Miss Trant told the receiver, and then heard a little laugh come floating back to her.

'Well, anyhow he isn't here. Isn't it a shame? I got it down to three - and they were all miles off - one in India and another in Aberdeen - and I think the other was in London. I asked the Library man if the book wasn't out of date - and he got quite annoyed - but when he calmed down a bit, he admitted that lots of the doctors could have moved since it came out. And he's seen our show - and he recognized me after a bit and was quite sweet. So I think it probably was him, don't you?'

'No, I don't,' said Miss Trant. 'It couldn't have been. You shouldn't have bothered. It's all - nothing.'

And when she returned to her room, she reminded herself that it was all nothing. It is not much fun being so intimately concerned with nothing. The thought of it can even rob you of your legitimate pleasure in a good historical novel. Louis the Eleventh of France and the Duke of Burgundy made a poor show of capturing Miss Trant's interest for the rest of that afternoon. One sneered, the other stormed, but all in vain - poor shadows!

II

The next day, Elsie became a Dulver. From all parts of the country there came Dulvers to welcome her, the males all large, shining, pink, hoarse, and brassily convivial, the females all large, blonde, and elaborately coiffured and upholstered. It is difficult to imagine what the Dulvers would have made of a christening or a funeral, because it is difficult to imagine a Dulver either coming into this world or going out of it; but there could be no doubt they were designed by Nature to celebrate weddings. The customary festivities, all the eating and drinking, the healths and back-slappings, sledge-hammer compliments and naughty jokes, might have been invented for them. Elsie was inspected by all manner of Dulverish relatives, who looked as if they were quite capable of having her stripped and weighed, and of pinching her in sundry places to make sure she was a sound article. After being thus inspected, she was approved. The general opinion obviously was that, with her shape, colouring, and disposition, it was only a matter of time - with some further coiffuring, upholstering, and the sipping of small ports - before she became a very good specimen of the female Dulver, fit to queen it in any hotel. And Bert was proud of her. Bert's father and mother, two fine heavy Dulvers, were proud of Bert. All the relatives were proud of somebody or something, if only of their appetites - 'I'm sixty past,' one gigantic purple Dulver told everybody, 'and I can eat and drink with the best yet.' Thus they were all happy.

Mr Dulver senior, in the business himself and now the host of so many professionally convivial persons, had no alternative, could not have found one even if he had looked for it: the thing had to be done in style. The style he had chosen he called 'the slap-up', but it might also be described as the Late Roman, so great was the crowd of guests, so lavish the feast. The immense wedding breakfast that awaited them in the long room upstairs drew a tribute even from the old masters, the purple Dulvers. Mr Oakroyd, who was there with the rest of The Good Companions, told his friend Mr Jock Campbell that the commercial travellers of Bruddersford, a body of men famous for their mighty feasts, had never done better than this. 'That'll be champagne i' them gurt bottles, eh?' he whispered. Mr Campbell replied indifferently that it was, and that in his opinion champagne was poor stuff. 'Tak' notice o' the whisky, man,' he added. 'If a few o' them gaes in for the wines an' sweet drinks, it'll work oot tae a bo'le o' whisky a man. An' if I started on it, juist wetted ma lips, I couldna run the length o' the half-way line Saturday.' Mr Campbell did not sigh because he was not given to sighing, but he shook his head and looked as wistful as it is possible for a thirteen-stone full-back to look, as he thought what he might have done with all that good whisky if there had been no football field waiting for him on Saturday. But he was gravely happy to be in the presence of so many landlords in a big way. He had been greeted as an old acquaintance by many of the sporting Dulvers.

Miss Trant met some old acquaintances too. At first she was rather dazed among all this hand-shaking, back-slapping, guffawing, roaring press of people, and after she had shaken hands with the ecstatic Elsie and her Bert, before the wedding breakfast began, she retired into a corner and found herself wishing it was all over. The Dulvers were too large and loud for her, though she could not help being amused by them, for they were all so like one another and so unlike any other set of people she had ever known.

'Now you're Miss Trant, aren't you? That's right, that's right.'

This came, in a thick, husky voice, from a stout elderly man, who now stood before her with his head cocked on one side. 'And you don't remember me, do you? Knew you right across the room. Couldn't get the name at first - got the face all right, not the name - then it come back. Now stop a bit and think. Take your time. Remember me?'

She had seen that prominent, reddish nose, that damp forehead, those little humorous eyes, somewhere before. He had not looked so clean then. Sheffield. That funny little house. It was Elsie's uncle, the trombone player. Unkerlarthur, they had called him. She told him so.

'That's right. You've got it,' he said, shaking hands. 'I've heard all about you, through our Elsie. She doesn't write to me, you know, but our Effie hears from her regular, and she passes it on to me - some of it, anyhow. Been good to our Elsie, you have, Miss Trant. Oh, I know! Well, she's a good girl, isn't she? - I mean, fairly speaking and taking her all round, she is a good girl, isn't she? And' - here he became very confidential - 'she's done well for herself, hasn't she? He's a nice feller.'

Miss Trant agreed that he was, and said they both seemed very happy.

Unkerlarthur came nearer and was so confidential that his mouth seemed to slip round to the right side of his face and stay there. 'They said to me this morning, both of 'em, "Any time you want a holiday, little blow by the briny, you come and stay with us at where's it - Eastbeach." Well, I shan't go, 'cos people get you there, then find they don't wancher. "What's he come for?" they say. But I like to be asked, don't you? Course if it's something extra special, like this, I'd go. Only got here just in time this morning. I was playing at the theatre last night, and had to be up at five this morning to get here at all. Got a substitute for tonight - and God help 'em when he starts. He's got a note like riving oilcloth. Our Effie's here. Have you seen her?'

Miss Trant had hardly time to say she had not, before

Unkerlarthur dived into the through and reappeared in about two minutes, dragging Effie with him. Effie, looking like a larger and coarser edition of Elsie, almost hurled herself at Miss Trant, into whose mind there came leaping the oddest recollections of the hotel on the road from Derby, the Tipsteads, and the queer evening in Sheffield.

'Well, I don't know!' screamed Effie, who was obviously in the highest spirits. 'Fancy us meeting like this! Of course I knew we should. And aren't you looking well! Ten years younger, honest. I hardly knew you. How d'you think I'm looking?'

'Very well indeed,' said Miss Trant, who had just come to the conclusion that Effie resembled nothing so much as a tropical sunset accompanied by rumours of earthquake. 'You're a little thinner perhaps.'

'Think I am!' cried Effie triumphantly. 'Nearly a stone down, which is more than our Elsie can say. Now you've put a bit on, I should say, but then you could stand it, couldn't you? Theatricals suit you, Miss Trant, my word they do, the way you've come on this winter. Remember when I asked you to take some things to our Elsie? That started it, didn't it? If it hadn't been for that, you wouldn't be here, and Elsie wouldn't be here, and I shouldn't be here, not really, you know, if you think about it.' And Effie rattled on in this strain for another five minutes, after which she rushed away and joined some male Dulvers.

'By her palaver', Unkerlarthur observed sardonically, 'anybody'd think she was three brides rolled into one 'stead of the bride's sister. I always knew our Elsie'd go first. I'd have laid five to one on it. Our Effie tries too hard, that's what's matter with her. You've got to let 'em think it's their ideear, haven't you? - the fellers, I mean. But soon as our Effie meets 'em, she lets 'em hear the wedding bells - an' they don't like it, you know - it has to come gradual. This'll go to our Effie's head properly, this will. There'll be some trade on with her now. She'll never rest till she's got hold o' some poor chap.'

'Miss Trant!'

The voice was familiar. At first it did not seem to come from anywhere in particular, but after a moment or two, during which there was quite a commotion in that corner of the room, and large Dulvers appeared to be hurled right and left by some invisible force, there emerged from the crowd, shaken, gasping, but triumphant, little Miss Thong.

'Now isn't this a surprise?' she cried, so excited that she could hardly get the words out of her mouth.

'Take it easy,' Unkerlarthur put in severely.

'I should think it is,' said Miss Trant, smiling. 'And a very nice one too. I'm so glad to see you again.'

'There now!' cried Miss Thong, as if to some unseen audience that had been waiting for this moment. 'But I said to Elsie, in a letter of course, after she wrote to me and gave me the wonderful news and said "*Do try* and come", I said to her, "Well, if I *can* manage it - and that will depend on the work and Pa, but chiefly Pa - but if I can," I said to her, "don't tell Miss Trant and then it'll be such a surprise." But after I thought to myself, "Oh, she won't remember you, you silly little thing, seeing all the people she does and going from place to place all the time, fresh faces everywhere." But you did, didn't you?'

'I recognized your voice before I actually saw you,' Miss Trant told her.

'Did you really? Well, but you see, I saw you and called out and then couldn't get to you and had to push a bit.'

'I saw you knocking 'em about,' said Unkerlarthur solemnly.

'This is Elsie's - ' Miss Trant began.

Unkerlarthur held up his hand. 'We've been interjooced, Miss Thong and me. Haven't we?'

'Earlier this morning,' cried Miss Thong. 'And a treat it was too, you telling me all about the theatre. I had to push because everybody here's such a size, aren't they? I thought I was going to be lost and then they'd have to put a notice up: "Lost - Miss Thong. Finder Rewarded." ' She laughed, coughed, and laughed again. 'But did you ever see so many enormous people? I never did.'

'That's 'cos they're all in the public line o' business,' Unkerlarthur explained. 'They may not take a lot themselves - some of 'em'll hardly touch it - but the smell does it. Then some of 'em's bookies, and they've got to be fat - nobody's never give nothing to a thin un.'

'Would you believe it!' cried Miss Thong. 'But they're all nice, aren't they? One or two of them have spoken very nicely to me, although they don't know who or what I am, and when I came I never expected to be noticed. "Just let me see it," I told Elsie. And now I suppose it's nearly time to begin eating all this, though how anybody - and I don't care how big they are - will ever get through a quarter of it, I can't think.'

'I shall do my share,' said Unkerlarthur sturdily. 'I'm peckish.'

'If I get a mouthful down,' Miss Thong gasped, 'I shall be lucky, I'm that excited and silly. You know me of old, don't you, Miss Trant? Always the same with me. I go on and go on, sitting in my little room - you remember it, don't you, Miss Trant? - they're building now where they kept the hens, though it's not spoiling the view - and there I am, doing my work, seeing nobody but customers coming in - and Pa of course - unless there's something special on at the chapel. And then', she continued, after gasping for breath, 'when something does happen,

I'm all upset - just excitement and silliness, that's all. "Oh, stop it, you silly little thing," I say to myself many a time, and I could shake myself sometimes, I could really, though that wouldn't make it any better, would it?'

'Worse,' Unkerlarthur told her, 'make it worse. What you want to do is to take it easy. What's the matter with you is temperament, that's what it is. Our family's been just the same, except me. And there's men playing in bands now - men I've known, men I've played with; I could give you their names - and they won't take it easy. They'll rehearse all right - oh yes - quite all right. When it comes to the night, all of a dither. What happens? Say a wrong sheet o' music is slipped in - a wrong sheet, that's all.' He looked sternly down at Miss Thong.

'Well, fancy!' said Miss Thong, who evidently felt that something was expected of her.

'It's a thing', said Unkerlarthur, still looking stern, 'that happens many a time. Where are they? These fellers that won't take it easy, I mean. Where are they? They're lost, finished - can't find the right sheet - can't pick up the cues - and bang goes the part! And all 'cos they won't take it easy.'

'So there you are, Miss Thong,' said Miss Trant, smiling at her.

But Miss Thong did not stand rebuked. 'You've no idea', she told them both, 'what a treat it is to me to hear all these things about the theatre. And then seeing you all too, close to!'

'They're sitting down,' said Unkerlarthur, who promptly prepared to sit down himself.

'You must sit next to me', said Miss Trant, 'unless you've arranged to sit somewhere.'

'D'you think I could? Don't you think they'd mind?' Miss Thong's long witchlike nose flushed with pleasure. 'If I got between two of these big ones, they'd only see the top of my head, wouldn't they? Do you think they'd mind if we sat here?'

So Miss Trant and Miss Thong sat together, and the latter chattered, gasped, ate, drank, coughed, and laughed so much that it was a wonder she did not shake what remained of her entirely to pieces. The Good Companions were scattered round both sides of the long table. Mr Oakroyd sat with his friend, Mr Campbell, who was now looking very wary, as if something very strange might suddenly pop out of the great meat pie just in front of him. Mrs Joe was very stately, and looked well, flanked as she was by two reddish shining Dulvers. The tall figure of Mr Morton Mitcham was to be seen at one end of the table, among the important people. Two young female Dulvers, all gold and pink, were attending to Jerry Jerningham, whose accent was now so fantastic that many of the older guests were under the impression he was a foreigner.

Inigo had tried hard to find a place by the side of his adored Susie, having had quite enough of the barren policy of pretending to avoid her; but he had not been successful. A very dashing young Dulver had carried her off and safely wedged her between his attentive self and the gigantic purple Dulver. This fellow had been hanging round her ever since they arrived, and Susie did not seem to mind at all. Indeed, she seemed to like his society - a fellow of a type that Inigo had always detested - a loud, brainless, teethy, pink ass, absolutely. It was incredible that Susie should be amused for more than five minutes by such a grinning idiot. If she was not pretending, he concluded, then there must be a vulgar streak in her somewhere. Impossible that a man could really be in love with a girl if he could think about vulgar streaks in this way. If he could only hold on to that vulgar streak, he would soon feel wonderfully detached. Meanwhile, he would show her that it did not matter to him if she spent her time giggling with fifty appalling young Dulvers.

For some reason, which Mrs Joe and Susie said was known only to the deity, Miss Mamie Potter had been invited. Miss Potter was there at Inigo's elbow, and was only too pleased to keep him company throughout the feast. He did not dislike Miss Potter as heartily as most of the others did, but he had no great opinion of her and he could not understand why she seemed so anxious for his company. There were plenty of young Dulvers there eager to wait upon her, and why she should prefer him, as she so obviously did, was a mystery. But for the last day or two she had been very gracious to him. It was very odd. However, there it was, and now he tried hard to amuse her and to look as if he had no other object in life than to keep her amused. Miss Potter did not exactly smile upon his efforts because she hardly ever smiled; her features were so circular that smiling was difficult; but at least she contrived to modify that insufferable look of faint astonishment when she glanced his way. She also contrived, while appearing to taste one or two things merely for appearance' sake, to put away a good deal of food and several large glasses of the sweet champagne.

When they had all finished eating, the gigantic purple Dulver suddenly arose and held up his glass. 'Now then, ladies and gentlemen,' he boomed, 'I give you the 'appy pair. May they never regret this day. I've regretted mine sometimes.' Laughter, and a cry of 'Now then, Walter!' from an equally gigantic and almost as purple female. 'And so has the wife, though from what she just shouted at me, you mightn't think it. 'Owever, that's always blown over. When I 'ave regretted it, ladies and gentlemen, I've always found afterwards I was a bit below par at the time.' Laughter and applause. 'It was a 'appy day for me, and, if you ask me, this will be a 'appy day for Bert. Until today, Mrs Bert was a stranger to most of us, but we can see by the look of her she's going to make him 'appy. And if she hasn't got a good husband, then I don't know where you're going to find 'em, that's all I have to say. Here's the best to 'em both.' And the toast was drunk with enthusiasm.

Bert, called upon to reply, said that he had nothing to say, and by rights shouldn't be there at all. He was a married man now, and perhaps the less he said the better. (Cries of 'Shame!' and 'Quite right!') But he would just like to say this. He had not always been lucky picking out winners. (Laughter, and 'What about *Sporty Boy?*' from the dashing young Dulver who had attached himself to Susie.) But this time he was sure he had got a winner all right. (Applause, and 'Then put your shirt on it, my boy', from the purple Dulver, followed by screams of expostulation and laughter from the ladies.) And they knew, he hoped, they were all welcome to come and have a look at them down at Eastbeach.

It was evidently felt by the company that it was time now for somebody belonging to the bride's party to make a speech. As Unkerlarthur was the only male relative, people looked at him, and after pretending for a minute or two that he had not seen them, Unkerlarthur was compelled to struggle to his feet and address the company. 'Well, I don't know,' he remarked, feeling the end of his nose as if he were not sure it was still there. 'This is right out o' my line. I might play a bit of it if I'd the old trombone here. Anyhow, I'm only the bride's uncle, and it's a long while since she took any notice o' me. But our Elsie's always been a clever and - what's better still - a good girl. I can see she's got a good husband - as husbands go. And if she doesn't make him a good wife, then I don't know what he wants - and he doesn't, neither. So we'll just fill up again, and I'll say - here's to 'em.'

This was felt to be sound but not entirely adequate, and now Mr Morton Mitcham rose both to his feet and the occasion. Two-thirds of the people there had not the slightest idea who he was, but he looked so imposing that immediately an awed silence fell on the company. He began by announcing that he felt very diffident, though it was difficult for the keenest observer to detect the slightest signs of diffidence. He felt however, he went on to say, that it was his duty, as a fellow-artiste, to say something about Mrs Herbert Dulver, long known to the Profession as Miss Elsie Longstaff. They had been on the road together, a remark that brought an enthusiastic 'That's right', from Mr Oakroyd, who was beaming upon everybody. Mr Mitcham then proceded to develop this theme of comradeship upon the road. Like the born orator he was, he had the trick of making everything appear about ten times life-size, and very soon it seemed as if he and Elsie had been on the road together, the best of friends, for about half a century. You saw them traversing continents, deafened by the applause of whole nations. The fate of the English Stage was bound up, it appeared, with the history of The Good Companions, a history that was already a gigantic epic. Through his haze of sonorous words, the figures of Miss Trant and Inigo and the other Good Companions loomed titanically. The departure of Elsie was conjured into a thunderbolt from the malicious gods, and you felt the earth shaking beneath its impact. All was gloom for a short space, but then the heavens brightened again. Apparently this marriage was the only thing that could possibly have enabled Mr Mitcham to bear up under the sorrow of losing Elsie. You gathered that it was an event to which he had been looking forward for years. And Mr Dulver was the one man in the world, it appeared, worthy of playing the chief part in it. He had the highest opinion of Mr Dulver, whom he had known intimately - or so he made it seem - for at least ten years. And now, not only for himself, not only for his fellow-members of the troupe, not only for the whole Profession, but on behalf of all these and of the audiences here, there, and everywhere, that had taken Miss Elsie Longstaff to their hearts, he wished them every happiness and drank their very good health. This he did, amid applause and clinking of glasses, in what appeared to be about half a pint of almost neat whisky, which went to join a good deal more of the same liquor. It was this noble draught that inspired him to rise again and point out that these were the sentiments of a man who had been four times round the world.

Elsie, flushed with pride, happiness, and the sweet champagne, and already looking more of a Dulver, was compelled to respond. She told them she had had good times and bad times on the Stage, but mostly good times lately. At this point, her sister Effie suddenly and very dramatically burst into tears. When Effie had subsided a little, Elsie went on to say that she did not expect to have all good times now she was married, but felt sure she and Bert would be a happy pair, and she would do her best. And all of them had been very kind and nice, and she thanked them and hoped to see them all again before very long. All the presents, she added, were beautiful. ('And so they are!' from Miss Thong.) And now she and Bert would have to be going, because they were catching the afternoon train down to Eastbeach.

Then followed any amount of hand-shaking, back-slapping, and kissing. Everybody trooped below to give the pair a good send-off, and the final scene outside the hotel when the two drove away and the whole company gave three cheers, under the joint leadership of the gigantic purple Dulver and Mr Morton Mitcham, was so striking that Mrs Joe, tearful but enraptured, said she had seen nothing like it since the finale to the second act of The Rose of Belgravia in which she and Joe, as a chambermaid and an ostler respectively, had sung side-by-side for the first time. By this time little Miss Thong had had so much excitement that she looked blue and her teeth were chattering, so Miss Trant packed her into her car and took her back to Gatford, there to rest and have a quiet cup of tea, A few of the other guests also departed. The remainder went upstairs, some to talk, smoke, and finish the bottle, some to dance.

'Changes, ladies and gentlemen,' roared Mr Mitcham, as he reached the landing again. 'Bound to come, bound to come. I know. I've seen - eh - thousands of 'em. Very sad, but can't be helped - in-ev-it-able.'

'You've said it,' cried Jimmy.

'Thank you,' he replied, simply but with great dignity, and then lit a very large cigar that had been pressed upon him by an admiring Dulver. He and Jimmy and one or two others of vast experience formed a circle, while another was formed by several football-loving Dulvers and Joe, Mr Oakroyd, and Mr Jock Campbell, who obliged by demonstrating, with the aid of a bottle and two glasses and an ash-tray, exactly what happened when Everton scored that curious goal against Sheffield Wednesday and so won the Cup. And in various corners, the ladies, among whom Mrs Joe was prominent, discussed weddings they had seen and married couples they had known, and happily swapped reminiscences in which obstetrics, accidents, operations, various internal disorders, and deaths of every description, played their part.

There was dancing in the other room. This would not be worth mentioning if it were not for the fact that Susie and the dashing young Dulver danced together all the time. Inigo was left with Miss Mamie Potter, whose beautiful and extraordinarily intelligent legs enabled him to make a fair show of what was certainly not one of his major accomplishments. The dashing young Dulver could hardly be described as a good dancer - he threw himself about too much to be that - but he was at least energetic and knowing, and therefore better than Inigo. There was one awful moment when Inigo imagined he caught a smile of derision on the faces of Susie and her insufferable partner. They were grinning at him! After that he held Miss Potter so close and threw such energy into his dancing that she had hardly breath enough to bring out her usual 'I say'. When at last their bus came and it was time to go, Susie was not to be seen and neither was her cavalier, and it was reported that he had taken her back to Gatford. 'I say,' said Miss Potter, 'I don't admire her taste. I thought he was ghastly, didn't you?' And so he and Miss Potter sat in the back of the bus, close together, and Inigo, his head a multi-coloured whirl of drinks and dancing and gloom and gaiety, decided that he liked Mamie after all and that when they reached the end of the journey he would kiss her. But by the time they were back in Gatford, the gloom was spreading and his head ached a little and life seemed rather dreary and preposterous, and so instead of kissing Miss Potter he hurried away to his rooms, to rest for an hour or two before the show began. At the end of that hour or two he had decided that he must have it out with Susie.

'This can't go on,' he told himself - and her - sternly, as he brushed his hair and conjured his reflection into an image of a startled Susie. 'If you think I'm a man to be played with, you're wrong, absolutely.' No, that sounded ridiculous. Something cool and sneering might be better. 'I must congratulate you on your friends. I am beginning to wonder whether the honour of being considered one of them will not be too great a strain for me - ' No, that would not do, either. 'Look here, Susie, I've had enough of this,' with quiet but manly determination. Anyhow, he would have it out with her.

III

The time is a quarter to twelve on Thursday morning, the day after Elsie's wedding. The place is the little upstairs room (where there are plenty of cushions and you may smoke) of Ye Jollie Dutche Café, in Victoria Street, Gatford. In the far corner is a table that must be distinguished from all the others if only because it is the only one there on which any cups of Jollie Dutche coffee ('Our Speciality') have made their appearance this morning. Behind it, sometimes lolling and sometimes sitting bolt upright and looking very fierce, are two persons, a tallish loose-limbed youth, with a long wandering nose and a long wandering lock of hair, and dressed in baggy and indiscriminate clothes and a pretty dark girl, a compact and shapely girl, artfully tricked out in black and scarlet. The waitress who served the two coffees - she wears a sort of federated Dutch costume, but has Gatford, Mundley, or Stort written all over her - recognized these two at once, and by this time has told all the other waitresses downstairs that one of the girls from the Hippodrome, the funny dark one, and the piano-player are above, having big coffees just like ordinary people. And we recognize them too: Miss Susie Dean and Mr Inigo Jollifant.

'I never heard such cheek,' Susie is exclaiming. 'What's it got to do with you?'

'Oh, nothing, of course,' the gentleman replies loftily. 'Apologies for interfering in your private affairs.'

He is having it out with her, and so far it has come out badly, not at all according to plan. Now he pulls away at his absurdly large cherry-wood pipe, and tries to do that loftily too. Unfortunately, it will not draw properly. If he had fifty pipes, they would not draw properly. It is one of those mornings, not at all the time to have it out with anybody, and especially Miss Dean.

'However friendly we were,' Susie continued, 'you'd have no right to talk to me like that. If I chose to talk to a man and dance with him, it's no business of yours. Besides, you know nothing about him.'

'I don't want to. I know enough about him to see that he's poisonous. But - as you say - it's no business of mine. I'm disappointed, that's all. Some girls might like that type of chap, but for you - *you* - even to look at him, well, it sticks in my gullet, that's all! Why, even Mamie Potter - ' he was going on rashly.

'Mamie Potter! You're not going to tell me what she thinks, are you? That would be the last straw. And you talk about people being poisonous! But go on, go on. What did Mamie Potter say?'

'It doesn't matter what she said,' replied Inigo sulkily. The sooner Miss Potter was out of the conversation the better.

'Of course it does! Your friend, Miss Potter! You ought to have seen yourselves yesterday. And if we're going to tell one another who we ought to know, it's my turn now, and I say, keep away from that girl. She's dead rotten from the knees up. Everybody's fed up with her already - except you, of course. She'll wreck this show yet, if we're not jolly careful. I know the sort.'

'She may be all that. I don't know, and I don't care,' said Inigo, quite willing to sacrifice fifty Mamie Potters. 'But what I do know and care about is that you behaved rottenly, absolutely, yesterday. You just flirted with that bounder, that pink teethy barman - '

'He's not a barman. And even if he was, you needn't sneer at him. If I liked him, I wouldn't care if he was a bottle-washer. I'm not like you, I'm not a little Cambridge snob.'

'No one could ever call me a snob,' said Inigo heavily.

'Aw - aw - couldn't they?' said Susie, in a wild burlesque of his offended tone. 'Well, I'm calling you one, and I believe you are one. And if you're not one, then you're simply jealous.'

'All right then, I'm jealous.' Inigo sounded very sulky now.

'Then you shouldn't be jealous,' said Susie severely. But then she gave him a mischievous little glance. 'Anyhow you oughtn't to be horridly jealous. It's quite possible, I'm sure, to be nicely jealous.'

'No, it isn't. I hate it. But it wasn't so much jealousy as sheer dislike of seeing you make yourself so cheap with a bounder - '

'If you say another word, we shall quarrel properly,' cried Susie. 'That's the nastiest thing anybody's said to me for years. Apologize for "cheap" at once or I'll never speak to you again. I mean it.' And she really looked as if she meant it.

'I take it back then,' Inigo muttered. 'But you know what I mean.'

'No, I don't, except that you're stiff and green with jealousy. And why you should be, I don't know. It isn't as if we've been very good friends lately.'

'And whose fault's that?' he demanded.

'Yours. Of course, it's yours, Inigo,' and she gave him a wide innocent stare.

'You know very well it's not. Look here, Susie, you've been unbearable lately, absolutely. You know what I think and feel about you - '

'No, I don't,' she put in, immediately. 'Tell me.' And she leaned back and gave him a delicious smile.

'Oh, I think you're - ' he groaned. For a young man who intended to have it out, he was behaving very strangely.

'Go on, Inigo. Don't stop. Tell me.' She made a show of settling herself very comfortably in her seat.

He pushed back his lock of hair, and then looked at her, steadily, gravely. 'I'm not going to tell you any more, Susie,' he said at last. 'It's all just fun for you. You don't really care a damn. Well, it isn't fun for me, not just now, anyhow.'

There was silence for a few moments, then Susie said, in a small voice: 'Why don't you go on to the next part, Inigo?'

'What's that?'

'You ought to say now "If you think I'm the kind of man you can play with, you're wrong".'

Inigo looked confused, and, glancing at him, she laughed. Then she hummed a little tune.

'I'm going,' he announced savagely.

'No, don't go.' She laid her hand lightly on his. 'I hate quarrelling. And if you go off in a rage, like that, you'll make me feel sorry I came here instead of accepting that Dulver man's invitation to go out in his car today and have a fine fat lunch somewhere. Yes, he asked me, and was most pressing. And I refused. I saw quite enough of him yesterday.'

'I should think so,' cried Inigo, highly relieved.

'Not that being with you is much good, these days,' she went on.

'Why? What's the matter with me?' Then he suddenly changed his tone. 'I know there's nothing very wonderful about me - '

'I'm sure you don't,'she told him.

'I suppose you're sick of seeing me about,' he said, humbly. 'And the ironical thing is, I wouldn't be about here at all, if it weren't for you. That must be getting pretty obvious to other people too by now. Miss Trant pointed it out to me the other day. Because you're with the show, Susie, I couldn't drag myself away from it. If you went, I'm darned sure I couldn't stick it out another week.'

'That isn't saying much for the others,' she told him.

'Of course I like the others, at least most of 'em. It wouldn't break my heart to see the last of Jerry J. or the Potter girl, but I'm very fond of all the old ones now. But after all, I'm not in love with 'em.'

'Which means you are with me.'

'Absolutely.'

'Still?'

'Worse than ever. So there you are. And if anybody had told me a year ago I should be dithering like this, I should have wanted to give him one on the jaw. And yet I wouldn't change it now, though a jolly rotten dither it's been lately, I can tell you.'

'Sorry, Inigo. Sorry - absolutely.'

'Tell me, are you fed up with me? Does the sight of me mooning round make you feel sick these days? Or what is it?'

'Well,' said Susie slowly and earnestly, 'I've been in a queer sort of mood lately, I know. And you've been so heavy and serious lately, too, not half so amusing as you used to be. But it isn't just that. You - oh, you irritate me!'

'Why? What do I do?'

'Oh, you're so - so - I don't know - feeble.'

'Feeble!' It came out in a shout. He stared at her, amazed.

'Yes, feeble.'

'Oh, am I, by jingo!' With that, the outraged young man sat up, suddenly flung an arm round her, twisted her round towards him, and kissed her soundly and well before she could do or say a single thing. There are heavens that await only reckless men, and he spent a delirious minute in one of them. Then he found himself shot out of it, and back in Ye Jollie Dutche Café with all his courage evaporated. He waited, breathless, for some-thing momentous to happen now, and though this creature by his side had been for some time the very centre of his universe, he had not the least idea what would happen. He could almost feel himself cringing.

Susie was staring at him, her eyebrows raised, and breathing hard. 'Well - ' and then she suddenly laughed.

His bravado returned with a rush at the sound. 'And that's the kind of man I am,' he announced.

'Well, it's not the kind of girl I am,' she told him, 'especially at twelve in the morning in an imitation Dutch café. So don't try it again, that's all.'

'Didn't you like it?'

'It made me feel quite sick,' she said calmly, turning an impudent face, still rosy and brilliant, towards him. 'No, not again! Who do you think you are? Now listen.' She looked serious. 'When I said you were feeble, I didn't mean that. I meant you were feeble about work.'

'Work!' Inigo pronounced the word as if he had never heard it before.

'There you are, you see. You don't even know what I'm talking about. You're just a feeble amateur, that's all you are, Inigo. This C. P. business - the Stage, in fact - is just a bit of a game to you. Well, it isn't to me. I'm a Pro. I'm not doing this for fun, young feller. I haven't run away from school for a few months.'

'If you think I'm going back to that school or any school - ' Inigo began.

'Never mind about that. It's me we're talking about now. I want to get on and if I don't get on soon, I'll burst. Why, that Dulver man yesterday - '

Inigo groaned.

'One of the first things he told me', she continued, 'was that he'd heard how clever I was and was coming to see me because he knew young Jack Rozzy very well and young Rozzy is working with his father now, old Rozzy, who's the booking agent for the P. M. H. Syndicate - '

'Help!' cried Inigo.

'Don't be silly. Well, I didn't believe all he told me - the Dulver man, I mean - but still, it was something. You never know, something might come of it. And at any rate he did understand I wanted to move up a bit and not stick in this all my life.'

'But what do you want me to do? Have I to go to young Rozzy and tell him to tell old Rozzy - '

'Oh, shut up! You think this is all nothing, and that's just what makes you so irritating. It's serious. Of course I don't want you to go to any Rozzies. I don't want you to help me. I can look after myself. But if you'd only go and get something done for yourself - and you could easily, with those songs - I wouldn't mind. I hate to see chances thrown away. It makes me sick. It's the way you hang about and just don't do anything that irritates me. It's so - so amateurish and feeble.'

'So that's it, is it?' said Inigo softly.

'Yes, that's it,' she replied defiantly. At this moment, another customer arrived, a solitary man, who came in, as solitary men always do, very quietly. A few moments after, three men entered together, making as much noise as a little army, as three men always do. Apparently all four were amateurish and feeble, for Susie regarded them with contempt.

Inigo had been fingering a card in his pocket. He still looked a little agitated, but there was the ghost of a smile hovering on his face now. 'As a matter of fact - ' he began; but then he must have thought this matter of fact should not be introduced into the conversation, for he suddenly stopped short.

'Well? Go on.' Susie looked at him, not unkindly but not with any obvious signs of admiration.

'Nothing,' he replied lamely.

Susie's rather full lower lip made a tiny movement that said quite plainly: 'You are exceedingly feeble, this very minute, and not my idea of a man at all.' She flicked away some cigarette ash from her clothes, and then rose. 'I must go.'

Inigo returned to his lodgings, wondering whether he had 'had it out' or not. Certainly a great deal had come out, but very little of it had figured in his original programme. If it had not been for one thing, he would have felt miserable, crushed, about two feet high. That thing was the card in his pocket. It had been his original intention to tell Susie about that card. The moment she had shown herself repentant - perhaps a little tearful - he had decided to wave away all her apologies, and then to raise her at once from the depths of contrition by showing her the card and telling her what he had planned to do with it. That moment, as we have seen, had never arrived, and so the card stayed in his pocket.

It had found its way there only that very morning, half an hour before he had left his rooms to meet Susie. A young man with a masterful nose, wavy black hair, and a startling pink shirt and collar, had bustled in on the very heels of the landlady, and had announced himself as Mr Milbrau, Midland representative of Felder and Hunterman. 'And you can't say you don't know *them*, eh?' this visitor chuckled.

'Who?' Inigo was still rather dazed.

'Felder and Hunterman.'

'I don't,' said Inigo, looking at his visitor in astonishment, as well he might, for that gentleman, with all the dexterous rapidity of a conjurer, had put down his hat, taken a chair and drawn it nearer to the fire, sat down, lit a cigarette, crossed his legs, and rubbed his hands, all in one flash of activity.

'Ha-ha, 's a good one!' cried Mr Milbrau. 'Didden' think you'd be up - 'smatter of fact - but here y'are, up all ri' and having a dig at the old firm.' He rubbed his hands harder than ever.

'But who are they?' demanded Inigo, in all earnestness. 'I seem to have heard the name before.'

'Stop it now,' said Mr Milbrau. 'You can't grumble. I've bought it - consider I've bought it! Let's ge' down to business, and stop pulling my leg.'

'I'm not pulling it, no intention of doing, absolutely,' said Inigo, who could not see why a strange young man in an angry pink shirt should rush in and talk about pulling legs. 'All I say is that I seem to have heard the name of Whater and What's it before.'

Mr Milbrau stared and his mouth fell open, though the cigarette still remained hanging from one corner of it and calmly went on smoking itself, as if specially trained to do so. 'Seem to have heard the name!' he almost screamed. 'Felder and Hunterman, biggest people in the music-publishing trade today - *and* the oldest! And you a pianist! You mus' have played thousands of our numbers. Oh, you can't mean it! Here, have a cigarette.' And the very next second, there were two rows of cigarettes about six inches from Inigo's nose.

Inigo politely refused, and filled and lit a pipe while Mr Milbrau explained why he had called. 'I'm doing this Midland round d'you see - songs and dance stuff,' he began, 'and these two days I'm here, in the Triangle. Come here ev'ry two months. Went to your show las' night. Nothing else to do - and then it's business with me, d'you see, because we like to know how our numbers are going. And you surprised me, I'll tell you that now. You did! You surprised me. You've got a classy little show there, an' I know' cos I've seen hundreds – hundreds - anundreds. That comeediyenn - oh, clever kid, clever! Whasser name? Dean - that's it. And that boy doing your light comedy work and dancing - that boy's good - he is - he's good. A nice li'l show! Mindjew, some of the numbers' - here he raised both hands, then let them fall - 'dead - you couldn't kill 'em - they're dead. I'm travelling about twenty numbers now - both sentimen'als and comics - an' they'd juss make the diff'rence to that show of yours, they would, juss the diff'rence. No, no, wai' a minute, wai' a minute. Don't make a mistake. I'm not here to sell you anything.'

Inigo was relieved to hear it, though he did not say so. He waited for his visitor, who was now lighting another cigarette, to continue.

'Here we are,' said Mr Milbrau, looking with half-closed eyes through a cloud of smoke at a scrap of paper. 'Now you got one or two numbers in your show that were new to me - and they were - good.' He brought this last word with a shout. 'Tricky numbers, real tricky! They got me going all ri' and I'm in the business d'you see. I put 'em down on this bit o' paper. Don't say I got the titles ri' but you'll know. Now as a favour, juss as a favour, take a look at 'em.' He handed over the paper, and Inigo saw at a glance that all the five numbers, headed by *Slippin' round the Corner*, were the very ones he had composed himself.

'Now all those numbers you have there', Mr Milbrau went on, 'are new to me. And I'm in the business. And they're good, they're tricky, they're catchy. It's the chunes - words are nothing, written 'em myself before now - it's the chunes! Now juss as a favour, jewmind telling me where you got 'em from? You're the pianist and so you know 'em all, d'you see. That's why I come to you. Got your address las' night at the Hippodrome after the show. And I'm busy - I'm terribly busy, gotter get away this afternoon - but I had to know. Now jew-mind telling me where you picked 'em up?'

'Not a bit,' replied Inigo heartily. 'I wrote them myself - the music, you know.'

'You did?'

'I did. As a matter of fact I've just finished writing them out properly. There they are, on the table.'

Mr Milbrau jumped up, saying, 'Mind if I look?' and without waiting to know if Inigo minded or not, began to turn over the manuscript sheets and wag his head and hum now and again. When he had done, he put the sheets neatly together and gave the pile a smart slap. 'Who were you goin' to give 'em to?' he inquired very quietly but with a momentous air.

'Not the least idea,' Inigo told him. 'I hadn't thought about it.'

Mr Milbrau shook his head. 'Hadn't thought about it! Doesn't know Felder and Hunterman! And turns out this stuff! Don't tell me you're a reg'lar pro - you're not - and I knew it right off. Suppose you wouldn't like me to take these along?' he inquired.

Inigo told him he would not.

'No. Thought you wouldn't. All ri' - don't blame you. Now I'll tell you something. If I was you - if I'd written these - jew-now what I'd do? I'll tell you. I'd put them in a bag, take my hat and coat and walk right out of that door, take the nex' train up and be at Felder and Hunterman's with 'em, before they closed tonight. I would. An' I wouldn't play 'em another night, either. You don't know who's listening. I tell you, I'd be up in the Charing Cross Road with these numbers this afternoon, and I'd stay there, never mind about the job here. In a month you'd laugh at it. I'm excited about these numbers. I don't look it but I am. But I'm not trying to rush you into anything, am I? You listen to me, Mr Jollifant. Don't send these numbers anywhere. Take 'em. Go with 'em. Play 'em through yourself – once – thass all. An' if you go to Felder and Hunterman's – an' they're the biggest people in the trade today – once'll be enough. Take 'em to Felder and Hunterman's an' ass for Mr Pitsner – P-i-t-s-n-e-r an' say I told you. Here, I'll tell you wha' I'll do. I'll write to Mr Pitsner myself – an' tell him. I'll write tonight. Bedder le' him know your coming. Send him a wire. Busy man, Mr Pitsner. You'd never seen him if you hadn't had an intro, but when you do see him, 's'business. Here, I'll write on this card too as well's send a letter. You show 'em tha', you'll walk up withou' a wor'. Thus Mr Mibrau, who ended by gabbling so furiously that there was hardly a consonant left in his speech.

And that is how Inigo came to be in possession of the card that saved him from feeling absolutely crushed after his talk with Susie.

Back in his lodgings, he took it out of his pocket, put it on the table, and then smoked a pipe over it. Feeble, was he?

IV

The various encounters of that week may appear to be of little or no importance, but actually all of them, whether real or imaginary (for we do not know whether Miss Trant saw Dr Hugh McFarlane or only thought she did), were important to the people who took part in them, and indeed to many other people too. And the last encounter of them all is no exception. It happened on the Thursday evening, in the tap-room of the Market Tavern, the public-house that adjoins - as it should - the space just behind Victoria Street where Gatford still has a weekly open market. The day for that market is Thursday, so that the Market Tavern was fairly crowded when Mr Oakroyd visited it, a little after six, on this particular Thursday evening. Mr Oakroyd knew that it would be crowded, having been long enough in Gatford to know all about such things. It was his habit to enjoy a half-pint about this time every evening, before he began his night's work at the theatre. Sometimes he liked a quiet, peaceful, meditative half-pint, and at other times he preferred a noisy, gregarious half-pint. It depended upon his mood. When a glass of beer is one of a man's few pleasures and luxuries, he will not casually swill it down, not caring when or where he drinks it. He will exercise to the full his power of choice. That is why places like Bruddersford are full of public-houses. To the outsider, anybody who does not understand such matters, these public-houses look all alike, but to Mr Oakroyd and his friends they are as different from one another as the books in a bedside shelf are to an old reader, and a pint at one of them is entirely different from a pint at the next one.

On this Thursday evening then, Mr Oakroyd, alone, in need of noise, cheerfulness, company, possibly the company of other men who knew the road, decided for the Market Tavern. The tap-room was all a babble and a haze, so crowded that it took him nearly ten minutes to push his way through, order his half-pint, and finally receive it over the dripping bar-counter from Joss, the big barman there. During this anxious interval, he had nodded to a few habitues, and that was all: he had not time to have a look round the place, which was incidentally the largest tap-room in all Gatford. There seemed to be a lot of strangers about, but then there usually was on Thursdays, chaps in from the outer districts and the country, and chaps who sold things in the market - genuine men of the road, though not on the grand scale. Once he had edged away from the bar-counter, taken a pull at his half-pint, and seen that his pipe of Old Salt was going well, Mr Oakroyd began to look about him.

"'Ow do,' several acquaintances called out.

'Na then,' replied Mr Oakroyd affably, giving them a nod.

There were so many chaps standing in the middle of the room, a long narrow room, chaps arguing in groups, that Mr Oakroyd, who had not strayed very far from the bar-counter, could not see the other end. But there was no reason why he should see it, and so he stayed where he was, not feeling at all lonely now because he knew quite well he could join any of these groups if he wanted to and talk away as hard as the next man. He was content to muse a little, and take in, without making any effort to listen, the scraps of talk that came flying from every direction. 'So I says to 'em, I says," Well, what of it? 'Oo made you boss of the job?" And 'e says, "Clever, arncher?" And I says, "Clever, yer bloody self!" - 'Then, from the other side: 'I betcher 'e did, I betcher. Time me an' Jimmy went to Birmingham, 'e did. 'Ere, Jimmy, 'alf a minute!' Somewhere behind was the usual political reasoner: 'Government can't do it, I tell yer. It doesn't matter what you say, chum, they can't do it. They'd 'ave to pass a lor before they could do it. Don' chew believe Government can do what they like, chum.' And so it went on, and Mr Oakroyd, who had heard it - or some-thing like it - many times before, listened with a touch of complacency. These chaps were all right, but most of them would do better to talk less until they had seen something. He, who had seen a lot in his time and might now see a great deal more before he had finished, was saying nothing. Still, they could go on talking: it did them no harm.

A moment came, however, when most of the chaps who had been talking at the tops of their voices suddenly fell silent, and there followed one of those curious lulls common to all companies. It was then that Mr Oakroyd heard a voice coming from the far end of the room.' 'E came to the back o' the stall, see,' it said. 'Big feller - proper fifteen-stoner - but all blown out, all beer and wind, an' yeller blobs under 'is eyes like fried eggs - nuthin' to him. An' when 'e gets to the back o' the stall, 'e takes a good look at me. "That's right," I says, "'ave a ruddy good dekko, Mister Sexton Blake. An' bring Pedro the blood'ound nex' time." Oh, you should 'ave seen 'im! "That'll do," 'e says - usual style, see - ' And having heard so much, Mr Oakroyd immediately began threading his way through the crowd to that corner of the room. There could be no mistake about it. That was the voice - never to be forgotten - of his old companion of the road, Joby Jackson.

Mr Oakroyd found him in the farthest corner, the centre of a little admiring group. He wore the same red scarf and if the suit he had on was not the very same brown check he had worn before, it was twin-brother to it. His face was as red and his eyes as bright as ever, and if there was any change in him it was merely that he did not look quite so dashing as he had done last autumn. Winter, his lean period, had left some faint mark upon him. For a minute or two he was too busy concluding his story of the big puffy man, a story that demanded a wealth of illustrative gesture, to notice Mr Oakroyd, who stood a yard or two away, holding his half-pint and puffing away at his little pipe, too shy to interrupt but determined to be seen.

'Well,' said Joby, having dismissed the big puffy man, to everybody's admiration, 'what about some more pig's ear. 'Ere, I'm paying for this lot. Same again, boys?'

He jumped up, and caught sight of Mr Oakroyd. He stared; he frowned; then delighted recognition lit up his face. "Ello, I know you! It's George. George with the little straw basket!'

'That's right,' grinned Mr Oakroyd.

Joby pushed his way round the table and clapped Mr Oakroyd on the shoulder. 'You mended the old stall. 'Alf a minute, where was it? I know. Don't tell me. We went to Ribsden, didn't we? That time big Jim Summers started 'is bit o' bother. But you didn't live 'ere, did you? Up in Yorkshire, wasn't it? Good old George! 'Ere, I've wondered about you many a time, you an' your little straw basket - four days at Sunny Southport that ruddy little basket was - an' your bag o' tools. 'Strewth, George, fancy you turning up agen ! 'Ere, we must 'ave a gill or two an' then you can tell me the tale. Never mind them fellers, they can wait.'

'Ay, I will that,' said Mr Oakroyd, one vast delighted grin. 'I were fair capped when I heard you. "Eh," I says to mysen, "that's Joby." I'll just sup this off, then we'll ha' some more. Well, ar yer getting on, Joby lad? Is trade i' rubber dolls keeping up these days?'

"Aven't seen a rubber doll for months,' Joby replied. He began ordering two half-pints and kept on ordering them until he was served. 'No,' he said, wiping some of the froth off his face, ' I'm out o' that now. Did well at Nottingham Goose Fair, then Tommy Muss - remember Tommy, 'im an' the tart? - 'e sloped agen - an' then I started beer-shiftin', see. Got up Newcastle way and gets playin' pontoon back of a boozer up there an' loses the 'ole ruddy issue, stall and all - what a life!'

'What about motter-car?' Mr Oakroyd inquired sympathetically.

'Oh, poor old Liz! She was napoo before I got up to Newcastle, just after I cleared out o' Nottingham, blind to the world. She gets goin' down a ruddy 'ill, see, an' I can't stop 'er. Down the other side there's one o' these removin' vans big as a row of 'ouses coming. I give the old bus a turn at the bottom - an' wallop - we're into the wall with our guts droppin' out. The poor old bitch 'ad got all 'er front smashed in. "Finnee!" I says, an' gets the stuff out, waits for the first feller with a lorry to give me a lift for arf a dollar, an' leaves 'er there, proppin' the wall up.'

'Nowt else to be done, I can see that,' said Mr Oakroyd, nodding sagely. 'Cost you more ner it 'ud be worth. Eh, but it's a pity! I've thowt monny a time abart yon motter-car, all fixed up to live in. It were champion.'

'You wait a bit, George. I'll 'ave another before you can turn round. Any'ow, I'm properly in the cart after losing the lot in this boozer. I scrounges round a bit, an' then I meets a feller I know who's with Baroni's Continental Circus, goin' round to old skatin' rinks an' covered-over swimmin' baths with a lot o' cockatoos an' dancin' dogs an' mangy monkeys an' a couple of old trottin' ponies - see? You never saw such a piecan of a circus. I could make a better one out o' the market 'ere. But this feller - a feller called Johnny Dooley, a bit of a mug - 'e says, "I can get you in. It's better than nothin' " - so 'e gets me a job. An' what d'you think I was, when I wasn't feedin' the dogs an' shampooin' the cockatoos an' taking the tickets an' helpin' to move the how-d'you-do's? I'm Tonio the Famous Continental Clown. You oughter see me, my God! An' gettin' two pound five a week - when you got it! Everybody in that ruddy circus was dying of 'unger, honest they was. Even the ponies could 'ardly stand up. If you saved up and bought yourself a packet o' fags, it was as much as your life was worth. They'd 'ave murdered you for 'em. They tore 'em out of your 'and. When I'd been with 'em a month, I'd forgotten what a piece o' steak looked like. There was fellers that 'ud eat anything - they'd 'ave eaten you. "'Ere," I says, "I've 'ad enough of this. Time to give the Baronios and Tonios the soldier's farewell." Then I meets a feller I know who's running one o' these mug auctions, see.'

All this, and a great deal more, describing Joby's adventures during the winter, was poured into Mr Oakroyd's ear as they stood close together, at no great distance from the bar. Two more pints, procured this time by Mr Oakroyd, had been consumed by the time Joby had neared the end of his recital. He was now, once more, an independent trader with a little stall of his own, but only in a very modest way. 'I've gone back to an old line,' he concluded. 'You'll 'ave seen it. Joey in the Bottle. Little glass figgers - put 'em in a bottle full o' water - waggle the cork a bit an' these Joeys dance about, see. Old - but clever, amuses the kids! An' very cheap to buy. Money for dust if you've got a good pitch. Don't satisfy me, though. I'm 'elpin' a feller too when I'm not selling Joey - a feller that auctions oilcloth, smart feller. I 'old the pieces up an' give 'em a bang to show it'll last till you get 'ome. Workin' 'ard and savin' up, that's Joby just now, see. 'Ere, George, what you doin'? I'm tellin' all the ruddy tale.'

Mr Oakroyd stole a glance at the clock. By this time he was

usually at the theatre - he liked to be there early - and he would certainly have to leave in a minute or two to be there on time at all. So he explained briefly what had happened to him since the autumn. Even then, however, he was interrupted. A big man with an immense grey moustache pushed his way through the crowd and laid a hand on Joby's shoulder. 'Time to be off,' he remarked, and disappeared.

'That's the oilcloth feller,' Joby explained.' 'Ave to push off, George. 'Ere what did you say this 'ere show o' yours is called? Did you say they're 'ere this week?'

'That's right. "Good Companions", they call 'em.'

Joby's eyes widened and his mouth puckered up, to whistle soundlessly. Then he looked grave, confidential. 'You 'ad any bother there, George, lately?' he asked quickly, with a rapid glance to left and right.

'Ar d'you mean?'

'Any kind of bother?'

'Well, there's been a bit o' calling out o' t'back,' said Mr Oakroyd. 'And that's summat new to us. Giving t'bird they call it, but funny part is, all t'rest o' t'audience fair goes off their heads, they likes it so much. It's nobbut a few o' t'back.'

'You watch out, George,' said Joby, buttoning up his coat. 'You're in for a lot o' bother if you're not careful. Never mind 'ow I know. But I do know, see. You watch it, George. No, I can't stop. 'E's waitin'. Come in 'ere agen and look out for me.' And, without another word, he was gone.

And Mr Oakroyd did go in again and look out for him. He went in on Friday, and at dinner-time on Saturday, but Joby was not to be found. Curiously enough, there was no more 'bother' either on Thursday or Friday nights, and all the Good Companions, little knowing what was in store for them, congratulated themselves on being free at last of the few stamping and jeering hooligans in the audience. Mr Oakroyd himself, however, was not so sure. It was all very mysterious. Even Mr Jock Campbell, on being consulted, could make nothing of it, though it was his opinion, the result of long experience in arenas, that all crowds were partly composed of lunatics. And though this was all very well, the fact remained - and Mr Oakroyd could not ignore it - that he had been told to look out and watch it by Joby Jackson, who was sane enough, a philosopher of the road.

CHAPTER THREE
Inigo in Wonderland

I

INIGO noticed, without surprise, that the Gatford Hippodrome was elongating itself, swelling, soaring, conjuring out vast darkening sweeps of galleries. This made it all the more difficult to find Susie. It was like playing hide-and-seek in the Albert Hall. After he had walked about quarter of a mile round the back of one enormous empty gallery, he suddenly discovered Mr Milbrau of Messrs Felder and Hunterman standing by his side. "Scuse me,' Mr Milbrau was saying, 'but the Tarvins are here.' Somehow this frightened Inigo. He hurried away, ran down a colossal flight of steps, and entered a lower gallery. He must find Susie at once, and he knew that she was in one of these galleries. Half-way round he came upon Mr Milbrau again. 'Here he is,' Mr Milbrau shouted; and immediately a number of lights were turned on. The next moment, Mr Tarvin appeared, looking much smaller and fatter than he had ever done before. 'Ah, there you are, Jollifant,' he said. 'We're looking - chumha! - for you.' And there, hurrying up behind him, was Mrs Tarvin, a terrifying figure. Her head was so big. As big as a coal-scuttle and with eyes like flashing lamps! Horrible! He turned and ran, and then all the lights but one dim glow, high up on the roof, went out. He raced frantically through deep menacing shadows. Gallery after gallery, innumerable curved flights of steps were passed in this wild descent, but at last he arrived at the floor of the theatre. And it was packed with people. They were even standing in all the gangways. Now the place was brilliantly lit, and it was obvious that the performance was about to begin. He noticed for the first time that he was already in his stage costume. He would have to push his way through all these people. He pushed and pushed and finally reached the stage, where Jimmy was waiting for him. There was something faintly sinister about Jimmy. 'Come on, Inigo,' he croaked. 'You're late. We've got a new stunt. Duets at the piano, that's the idea. Got a new pianist.' And he hustled Inigo over to the piano. And there, waiting for him, was this horrible huge-headed Mrs Tarvin, nodding and grinning. 'I won't,' Inigo shrieked. But Jimmy's grip on his arm had tightened. "S all ri', quite all ri',' said Mr Milbrau, who appeared to be holding him now on the other side. Inigo struggled but he could not free himself.

'Hoy, justa minute, ju-ust a mi-in-ute!' This voice did not belong to either Jimmy or Mr Milbrau. It was a new voice. It had no part in the proceedings. It seemed to stop everything.

Inigo stared at the man opposite, stared at his big blue-veined nose, heavy cheeks, and gingerish moustache. These features, he remembered now, belonged to the man who had entered the carriage with him at Gatford station. Yes, he was in a railway carriage. That was all right - he ought to be in a railway carriage. But why? Then, as he shook himself, yawned and rubbed his eyes, it all came back. It was Saturday morning and he was on his way to see Mr Pitsner of Felder and Hunterman. He had wired Mr Pitsner yesterday, Friday morning, and that gentleman, who must have received Mr Milbrau's letter, had replied: *Yes come along can hear songs eleven and twelve tomorrow.* And then he had had to work it all out with a time-table. How to get to London and back between the end of Friday night's show and the beginning of Susie's birthday tea-party this very afternoon? - that had been the problem. It had meant catching a fiendishly early train from Gatford to Birmingham and then getting the express. And this was that early train. The mere snatch of sleep, the shivering wash and shave in the darkness, the scalding gulp of tea, the dash to the station through the queer dim streets. And here he was. And nobody knew anything about it, he reflected, hugging himself. Not a word about Mr Milbrau and Felder and Hunterman and this flying visit to London had escaped him. Ah! - that was deep. He meant to spring it on them as a surprise when he returned, that is, of course, if anything happened worth springing. If nothing happened, then nobody would be any the wiser. He was not going to let her think him feebler than ever.

He sat up and rubbed his hands. He felt cold and stiff and unpleasantly empty. It was too early in the day to be riding in trains, absolutely. The windows still showed a flash of angry red sky, and a chilly vapour hung about the flying fields. His eyes were hot and heavy, and somehow he had to stare hard at things to see them properly. Even then they did not seem very real. His dream hung about the fringes of his consciousness like the mist on the fields outside. This world of the cold railway carriage and the dawn breaking over an unknown landscape appeared to have little more solid reality than that other world of the long dark galleries, the ever-appearing Milbrau, and the monstrously-headed Mrs Tarvin. But this world, though it might have its minor discomforts, was infinitely the more pleasant. And warming, quickening, at the heart of it was his sense of adventure. These two feelings never really left him all that day. In the last little room, the inmost place, of his mind was a tiny Inigo hugging himself and crooning over the adventure. And because the day started, like a dream, in the darkness and hurried him at once into the unfamiliar, it never quite lost its unreality; it might be large and highly-coloured and crowded with moving shapes, but it always remained brittle, ready to be smashed into smithereens by a mere cry of 'No, you don't!'

"Aving a bit of a tussle, wasn't you?' the man opposite grunted amiably. 'Bootin' 'em a bit, eh? Gave my ankle a good old rap, I can tell yer.'

'Sorry!' said Inigo, and admitted he had been dreaming. The only other person in the compartment, one of those little old women who seem to be for ever travelling on unimaginable errands, whatever the hour or route, was dozing in her corner.

'Saw yer drop off just after we starts,' the man went on. 'I've caught this bleeder three times this last fortnight - 'ad to. My missus says we'd better go and live in Brum an' 'ave done with it. Doesn't like getting up an' making me my bit o' breakfast, an' yer can't blame 'er.' He brought out a small tin, selected a cigarette-end, which he contrived to light after it had been tucked away under his large moustache. 'I've offered to make my own breakfus' but that don't do for 'er,' he continued, complacently blowing out smoke. 'Muss 'ave a proper breakfas', she says, me goin' out like this, an' so she sees I 'as one.'

Inigo tried to imagine a deliriously domestic Susie insisting upon his having a proper breakfast on a morning like this, but he did not succeed in creating a convincing image of her in the part. Would she ever even share a breakfast with him? He had never thought of her having breakfast, but now that meal, hitherto regarded as a very prosaic business, a mere gobbling of eggs and bacon, became touched with wonder and romance. He heard her voice - he could always hear her voice though he could never call up her face - asking him to pass the marmalade. He saw himself as a delightful attentive breakfast companion, without stopping to reflect that never in his life so far had he given any signs of being any such thing.

The London express offered him breakfast as soon as it left Birmingham, and he accepted its offer with alacrity. It was full of people who appeared to be old friends. Even the ticket-collectors and dining-car attendants seemed to know everybody. Men leaned across Inigo to ask one another where old Smith was. He had hardly begun his porridge before the man sitting next to him suddenly turned and shouted: 'Hello! Wondered where you were. I say, is there any truth in that story about Bradbury and Torrence?' Inigo, startled, was about to stammer that he had not the least idea, when he discovered that his neighbour was not addressing him at all but a man busy chipping an egg at the other side of the aisle. And though the ticket-collector examined his ticket and the attendants brought him food, they did it impersonally, without any of those remarks about the weather and the number of people on the train that seemed to be offered to everybody else. At first he felt as if he had blundered into a party given by a complete stranger, perhaps the Lord

Mayor of Birmingham. After a time, however, he merely felt that he was not really there at all. The train and its passengers did not believe in him.

A chance remark might break the spell. He tried the experiment at the end of breakfast, when the man next to him was lighting a pipe.

'I say - er - what time do we get in?' said Inigo.

'Yes, rather,' the man replied, poking at his pipe. And then he looked across the table at the man opposite, and, raising his voice, said: 'I told Mason the other day that the Chamber of Commerce people were making a big mistake.'

'Mistake!' roared the man across the table. 'They're making the biggest bloomer I ever heard of.'

Inigo's neighbour nodded vigorously, gave another poke or two at his pipe, then turned sharply. 'What d'you think?' he inquired.

Inigo was quite ready to damn the Chamber of Commerce heartily, but once more it was the man at the other side of the aisle, the egg-chipper, the man who knew about Bradbury and Torrence, who was being addressed. And this fellow crossed over, put an arm at the back of Inigo's seat, leaned forward, so far forward indeed that Inigo could easily have set fire to his beard and thought once of doing it, and then replied: 'I'm not so sure about that, my boy. Remember what happened after the Stavely Commission? Well, it might easily happen again - in my opinion.'

It was very odd. Inigo did not seem to be there. They did not appear to believe he was a real person. But as he knew very well that he was there and that he was a real person, this only meant that that dreamlike sensation persisted, robbing even a London express of its substantiality and turning roaring tons of businessmen into flitting shadows. Even when they finally chuff-chuffed into the terminus, the sensation still remained. There was nothing about that gloomy phantasmagoria to suggest that reality was breaking through. The place looked as if it had been designed by the same mad architect who had built the colossal Gatford Hippodrome of dreamland. Inigo hurried out of it.

II

It was too early to go to Felder and Hunterman's, and Inigo was in no mood for exploring London. Besides, the streets were being slashed with cold rain. One minute a pale sun would creep out and set everything glittering, and the next minute the rain would come sweeping down, up would go overcoat collars and umbrellas, and the streets would be full of people running as if for their very lives. A lunatic city. Inigo went into a tea-shop not far from the station, and there ordered a cup of coffee he did not want. This tea-shop had the air of still being in the hands of charwomen. There were no charwomen to be seen but the place seemed to smell damply and cheerlessly of their labours, and Inigo felt that at any moment a number of them would come trooping back to dry it off. The waitresses looked as if they had not yet recovered from a bitter reveille that had dragged them out of their little bedrooms, miles away in East Ham and Barking, and brought them sniffing in cold buses and trams and tubes to this tea-shop. Every customer, every order, was to them an affront. Their day had not really begun; they had hardly washed themselves yet; and as a protest against being disturbed so early they banged down sugar-basins and cruets on the little damp marble-topped tables. At close range they used the sniff, and at a distance the yawn. Such patrons as they had, however, seemed completely indifferent, in no way affected by these marks of contempt. They sat lumpishly, unstirring, at their little tables, as stolid and incurious as the bags they had dumped down beside them. The one exception was Inigo, who found himself compelled to order, receive, and sip his coffee with an apologetic air. There was, however, an Inigo inside, the skipper on the bridge, who was already indignant and protesting. There appeared to be a general conspiracy to pretend that he was feeble, of no account. And this tiny bristling Inigo inside asked everybody and everything in this huge lunatic warren of a London to wait, that's all, just wait.

It is true that when he was actually on the way to Felder and Hunterman's he suddenly felt ridiculous. The whole enterprise lost its sanity, seemed daft and hollow. What was he doing here with his parcel of silly songs? He ought to be going to Newman and Watley, the scholastic agents. They were solid and sensible. Their talk of French, History, C.of E., some games, £150 Resident was reasonable, and not at odds with these offices and shops and buses and policemen. But Felder and Hunterman? Jingling songs? *Slippin' round the Comer?* Preposterous, absolutely! He was making a fool of himself. Everything he saw in the streets announced that there was probably no such person as Mr Pitsner. The very name shattered conviction. By the time Inigo had reached Charing Cross Road, he was troubled by a little hollow place somewhere in the region of his stomach. He did not want to go any further.

There was still plenty of time, so he allowed himself to loiter. He began to look at shops. That saved him. Mr Pitsner became real again. He had strolled into a little world in which the silliest jingle of a song was more important than Newman and Watley and all their clients. He had now no excuse for believing that his visit was ridiculous. Charing

Cross Road was bursting with songs. If the shops were not filled with sheets of music, then they were filled with gramophones and records and saxophones and drums and banjos. The place seemed to be a Jazz Exchange. Moreover, he saw rows of songs that he had already played himself and dismissed as poor stuff. He marched into one shop and glanced through about twenty of its newest songs, and most of them were so bad that he found himself gleefully whispering 'Tripe, tripe!' His self-confidence returned with a rush. These people thought day and night about these jingles, and even then they could only bring out this muck. He hesitated no longer, but marched upon Felder and Hunterman with all colours flying. He would show them.

'I want Mr Pitsner please,' he said sternly, handed over a card, and then without paying any more attention to the assistant, looked about him with a nonchalant, faintly contemptuous air. He refused to be impressed, though there could be no doubt that Mr Milbrau had been right when he had said that his firm was the biggest in the trade. The place was fantastic. It was a vast bustling warehouse of sugary sentiment and cheap cynicism. Lost sweethearts - in waltz time and the key of E flat - were handled here by the hundredweight. Bewildering rows of smiling Negroes implored you, in spite of the fact that they were clearing anything from two hundred pounds a week upward in London and occupying luxurious suites of rooms and riding about in gigantic cars, to take them back to their shack in Southland. 'Just Little Miss Latch-Key!' one wall screamed at you. 'S'Impossible!" another replied. 'She's a Blonde on Saturdays', one row sneered, only to be answered, two hundred times over, by a companion row that cried: 'She's All I've Got'. And these were not merely songs. The least of them were Gigantic Successes. They were Hits, Whirlwinds, Riots, Ear-Haunters, Red Hots, Stormers. Messrs Felder and Hunterman announced they were 'Handing You Another'. Mr Felder told you, in large crimson type, to 'Get It Now and Watch it Grow!' Mr Hunterman promised that it would be 'The Sensation This Season at Douglas and Blackpool!' And together they implored you to believe them when they said: 'It's the Big Hit They'll Ask to Have Plugged at Them!' They told you frankly they were compelling every dance band in the country to play it, they were sweeping the North, they were sending the West End crazy. And they were proud of it.

Inigo shrugged his shoulders. He still refused to be impressed. Oh, Mr Pitsner would see him, would he? Very well. He stalked after the assistant, down the corridor, into the lift. Mr Pitsner's room appeared to be at the top of the building and so he had ample time to imagine what Mr Pitsner would look like. He saw a sort of super Milbrau, older, fatter, and more Hebraic, with even blacker hair and pinker shirt. He braced himself to meet this loud, hearty, designing fellow.

He did not meet him, however. He met a thin grey man, very quiet in manner and dress, a man who looked as if nothing had surprised him for twenty years. He gave Inigo the impression that he was tired and that he knew a great deal. Possibly he was tired of knowing a great deal. There was no mistake, though. This was Mr Pitsner.

'I'm glad to see you, Mr Jollifant,' he said in a low and rather mournful voice. 'I'm not always here on Saturday. In fact, I'm nearly always at home. But this time you've caught me. People don't usually get into this room when they've just brought a few new numbers to us. If they did, I should never be able to get into it myself. But I had Milbrau's letter about your things, you see. And Milbrau's a very smart man.'

Inigo, who had accepted one of the fat Egyptian cigarettes that Mr Pitsner had silently offered him, agreed that Mr Milbrau was a very smart man.

'Yes,' Mr Pitsner continued sadly, 'he's one of our smartest young men. In fact, I'm thinking of taking him off the road. He's got something of a flair, something. I've backed his judgement once or twice and been rather fortunate. He seems to have been quite carried away by these things of yours. It's surprising,' he added, in exactly the same mournful low tone, 'but that doesn't happen once in five years, really new work coming from - well, if you don't mind my saying so - from an outsider. People think it's always happening, but it isn't. You're a pianist, aren't you?'

Inigo briefly explained what he was and what he had done, and Mr Pitsner listened politely but with a sort of quiet despair. When Inigo had done, Mr Pitsner touched a bell and told the girl who answered to send Mr Porry in. 'I'd like Porry to hear them,' he said, watching the smoke curl from his cigarette. 'He's our memory man. He never forgets a tune.'

Inigo was bold enough to say that he hoped Mr Porry would not remember these tunes too well. The moment he had spoken, he regretted having done so, but Mr Pitsner, though it had been hinted to him that he might be a possible thief, showed no signs of resentment. He merely shook his head. 'We shan't steal them, if that's what you mean,' he said. 'It wouldn't pay us. Some people would, people in a small way. But it wouldn't be worth our while. As a matter of fact, Porry's here to prevent you stealing. No old stuff, you see, with a note or two altered. That won't do. If we want anything like that, we can manufacture it here. Now would you like Porry to run through them on the piano or will you do it yourself?'

Inigo said he would do it himself, but he did not feel very cheerful about it. No worse audience than Mr Pitsner could possibly be imagined. It was incredible that he could be connected in any way with the rows of silly songs and the photographs and the screaming placards below. It did not look as if earthquakes and revolutions could arouse in him the least interest, let alone a few jingles. Mr Porry, a nondescript middle-aged man, arrived and accepted one of those cynical Egyptian cigarettes, and then Inigo dashed into one of his later numbers. Having got through one, he did not wait to hear any comment from the two sitting behind him, but went straight on to the next, keeping that *Going Home* number of Susie's and *Slippin' round the Corner* until the last. By the time he had come to these two, he had lost any feeling of diffidence, He was simply enjoying himself at the piano again, and if Messrs Pitsner and Porry did not like it, they could jolly well lump it. He slipped round the corner with all his old mischievous spirit. The music was in front of him, just as a matter of form; he never looked at it. He let the old tune rip, and as he played, odd little images of people and places, from Mrs Tarvin and Washbury Manor to Rawsley and Sandybay and Susie and Elsie, Miss Trant and Oakroyd, came glimmering and joggling through his mind.

'A-ha, a-ha!' a great voice roared in his ear. 'What have we here? Listen to this, Monte. *Tumpty-tum-tidee-dee*. Don't stop, ol' man, don't stop. Let her have it once more.'

Two other men were now in the room. The one who was imploring Inigo not to stop was a big fellow with a paunch, a swollen face, and a humorous eye. That was Mr Tanker. The other, Monte, was no other than Mr Monte Mortimer, whose name was known even to Inigo, who did not pretend to much knowledge of the theatre, as a producer of revues. Mr Mortimer was rather like a smallish, plump, and shaven Assyrian. He would have looked perfectly at home superintending the preparations for some gorgeous and possibly depraved entertainment at the Court of Nineveh. This life of big hits and gigantic successes had not left him so weary as it had Mr Pitsner, but on the other hand he had nothing of Mr Tanker's gusto and goodfellowship.

'I'd like to hear those things through,' said Mr Mortimer, after there had been introductions and explanations.

Mr Pitsner nodded. 'You ought to. I'd thought about you before you came in. I rather think they're what you're looking for,' he added, in his usual tones of quiet despair.

'Two sure winners there at least, if you ask me,' Mr Pony put in, with the air of a man who knows the value of his opinion even though it has not been sought.

'That last is one, Porry,' cried the genial Mr Tanker. 'It's tricky. It really is, by God it is. Tricky. You could plug that one till the roof went, Monte, and they wouldn't mind. Not like most of the bitchy stuff we have to keep playing. Have you got the words there, ol' man? Good. Well, when you come round to that one again, I'll sing it. I will, I'll sing it. And don't let anybody tell me after this that we baton-waggers are jealous. We don't know what jealousy is. Now then, ol' man, let her have it again.'

Inigo did let her have it, and Mr Tanker, who was Mortimer's musical director and a composer of these things himself, stood by the piano, humming and tapping and beating time, putting in some amusing little saxophone, banjo, and trombone parts. When they came to *Slippin' round the Corner*, he produced a husky little tenor voice that battled manfully with the song. Inigo, who by this time had decided that he did not give a damn for any of them, darted and flashed among the keys, in which antics he was finally assisted by Mr Tanker, who put in fantastic little variations, in the high treble. And now another voice was there, humming away. It had brought with it all the perfumes of Araby. Inigo was aware of a presence, somewhere near him, but until he had banged the final chord there was no time to make out what it was.

'Whoa!' cried Mr Tanker, mopping his brow. 'Hello, Ethel! Isn't that a beauty? They're all damned good, but the last two are real hell-busters.'

'Don't tell me you wrote that, Jimmy,' said the lady who had just arrived. She spoke in a strong metallic voice, and indeed she looked a strong metallic person. Inigo recognized her at once as Miss Ethel Georgia, the well-known revue and musical-comedy artiste. He had seen her on the stage once or twice, and had seen dozens of photographs of her. Behind the footlights she was a ravishing creature, but at close range everything about her, her face, her figure, her clothes, her voice, her whole personality, was overpowering, too stunning. Inigo felt as if he were being introduced to an amiable blonde tigress.

'He's just popped in from Little Woozlum or Puddleton-on-the-Slag,' Mr Tanker explained, 'and brought in a bunch of winners. That's one you've just heard.'

'What you have just heard, ladies and gentlemen,' Miss Georgia wheezed nasally, in a parody of those dance-band men who announce their tunes, 'is Ethel Georgia's new number, to be featured with sensational success in Mr Monte Mortimer's forthcoming revue *Who Did?*'

'I'm not so sure about that, Ethel,' Mr Mortimer called out.

'I am, Monte,' she retorted, with a flash of personality that was like a magnesium fire. 'I want it.'

'We'll see about that,' he replied easily. There was, however, a certain suggestion that he had tamed tigresses in his Assyrian days and could still do the trick, if necessary.

They all began talking at once, even the mournful Pitsner, who somehow contrived to hold his own with the others without raising his flat sad voice. Meanwhile, however, Inigo found himself talking to another new arrival who must have come in with Miss Georgia. He was a rotund fellow, most unwisely dressed in a plus-fours suit of glaring Harris tweed. As he peered at Inigo through a pair of horn-rimmed glasses, Inigo felt that there was something familar about this rather droll face.

'I'd like to have a look through those other numbers', he said, 'before Ethel grabs the lot.' Miss Georgia was now in the middle of the room, arguing with Mortimer and Tanker. 'If she gets her lily-white hand on 'em, no earthly chance for yours truly. She's a terror. I'll bet you're wondering what the devil I'm doing here in these clothes. Well, I'll tell you. I ought to be just laying one nicely on the green now, out at Esher, but she rings me up, not ten minutes before I was due to start. And did I get my golf? Be yourself! Drags me round here, round everywhere. And I've got a matinée this afternoon. I've to be funny from ten to three until five to five. She's all right, she's not working till Monte puts on his new show. But look at me. Still working, rehearsing Monte's show - or what there is of it - and then can't get a round of golf in. Oh, she's wicked! Here, even the wife's frightened of her. "Tell her you won't go," she says to me. "Tell her yourself," I says. And did she? What a hope! Now let's have a look at these songs.'

By this time Inigo thought he had recognized him. 'Aren't you Mr Alfred Nott?'

'I am. I'm the only man in England who is not not Mr Alfred Nott. Can you squeeze a laugh out of that? I thought not. Trouble about that gag is, if you're sober it doesn't amuse you and if you're canned, you can't work it out. Every time I used to meet old Billy Crutch when he was soaked, I used to tell him that one, and believe me or believe me not, it bothered him so much he always ordered a black coffee and then went home in a cab, to think it out. Here, this looks a good number. Just tiddle it quietly, will you, old boy?'

But Inigo was not allowed to do any quiet tiddling. The others pounced upon him, though even when they had him in their midst they still went on talking to one another. It is true they were talking about him. He could not help wondering what would happen if he quietly walked out.

'The point is, Pitsner, you've got to let me have the first cut,' said Mr Mortimer. 'And so long as the rights are tied up - '

'So long as they are,' said Mr Pitsner, out of the depths of his weary cynicism and Egyptian smoke.

'Well, you know that's all right so far as we're concerned. You can tie that string on the dog's tail now,' Mr Mortimer continued.

Miss Georgia yawned spectacularly at the lot of them. 'Hurry up, for God's sake, Monte, and buy that bunch, anyhow. You've got one number so far that's worth a damn, and I brought that one in.'

'Right, Ethel, quite right,' said Mr Tanker heartily. 'I know 'cos I wrote some of the duds myself. But then I'm not jealous. I'm not a comedienne.'

'Aren't you, Jimmy?' she cried. And then she let out a sudden hard peal of laughter. 'You never know till you've tried. A bit of *crêpe de Chine*, Jimmy, and some powder might work miracles. Come round and I'll see what I can do for you, sweetie.'

'Keep the big gags for the night, Miss Georgia,' said Mr Tanker with tremendous mock severity. 'And now let's get on with the business. I'm thirsty.'

Mr Pitsner held up his hand and looked at Inigo. 'We like these things of yours, Mr - er - Jollifant - '

'You've got it in you, old boy,' the irrepressible Mr Tanker put in, clapping Inigo on the shoulder. 'Your fortune's made - nearly.'

'The point is this.' It was Mr Mortimer's turn now. 'I can use all those numbers you've got there. And some more, if they're as good. And some more after that. Performing rights, sheet music, gramophone records - well, you know what happens or you ought to do. There's bags of money in it, as you know, bags and bags. And Mr Pitsner here and I can start you going. All right. Well, I understand you came up to see Felder and Hunterman. You're not tied up to anybody else, not even negotiating with 'em, is that right?'

'Correct, absolutely,' replied Ingio cheerfully. 'Nobody in London has heard these things, though I don't mind telling you they've been a colossal hit in all sorts of places you've never heard of. With my troupe, you know.'

'That's what Milbrau wrote to me,' said Mr Pitsner sadly. 'Getting over tremendously in - where is it? Gatford. He said they were eating it.'

'Good! I'll bet they were,' cried Mr Mortimer, who seemed to be in an excellent temper now. 'Well, my – Mr - er- Jollifant - you've come to the right firm, no doubt about that, and of course you'll be willing to publish here. That right?'

'I should think so.'

'And as you happen to be a lucky man,' Mr Mortimer continued smoothly, 'you've struck - this morning of all mornings - the one man who's looking for you. That's me. I could easily come the old game, discourage you, say we've plenty of stuff just as good, and so on, but that's not my style, and if it was, I shouldn't be Monte Mortimer - '

'So three cheers for the red, white, and blue,' cried Miss Georgia derisively. 'Band, please!'

'If you're solid with Felder and Hunterman, that'll do Mr Pitsner here. Now I come in. I use those numbers' - he paused impressively - 'and I use some more.'

'Bravo!' cried Mr Tanker.

'Now you're talking like a man, Monte,' said Miss Georgia, patting him on the shoulder. 'That's the kind of talk I like to hear. Give the boy his chance. And give this little girl one too. That number about slipping is mine from now on, eh?'

'So there you are,' said Mr Mortimer, smiling at Inigo. 'And now what do you say?'

This was when Inigo began. 'I've a good deal to say.' he announced, with a highly creditable appearance of complete calm.

'I know.' Mr Mortimer waved a hand. Messrs Pitsner, Tanker and Porry smiled in concert. 'Terms, of course. Don't you worry. The terms will be all right. They're going to surprise you.'

Inigo grinned. 'That's what we're going to talk about. I've got some terms too. I hope they won't surprise you. But they might.'

They all stared at him, and Miss Georgia pursed up her scarlet lips and produced a droll little whistle. Then Mr Mortimer looked at Mr Pitsner, and Mr Tanker looked at Mr Porry. If one of the arm-chairs had suddenly made a remark, had perhaps pointed out that it was getting rather tired of that room, they could hardly have been more astonished. Inigo walked over to where Mr Alfred Nott was still examining the manuscript music.

'I fancy this one,' said Mr Nott. 'Here, ol' man, you're not taking it away, are you?'

'For the time being,' replied Inigo firmly, 'I am.' And he gathered the sheets together and then put them in the small *attaché* case he had brought with him. He did this with great deliberation, and reminded himself that no man who could justifiably be called feeble would have been able to achieve such calm and poise.

Somebody coughed. Then Miss Georgia, who was clearly enjoying the situation, suddenly let out a harsh scream of laughter. There was a murmur of voices. Inigo turned and rejoined the group.

'I must say I don't quite - ' Mr Pitsner began.

Mr Mortimer interrupted him. 'Leave this to me, Pitsner,' he said. 'You're all right in this. Now then, Mr Jollifant - '

'What about a drink?' cried Mr Tanker jovially. 'That's what you mean, isn't it, Monte? For God's sake, let's have a drink before there's any more talking.'

'I'm agreeable,' said Mr Mortimer. 'We'll run round and have a look at Robert. He ought to be having an inspiration about now. Come on, Mr Jollifant. Bye-bye, Pitsner, that'll be all right.'

As they filed out, Inigo was rewarded with a huge friendly grimace from the redoubtable Miss Georgia. 'I don't know what you're pulling,' she whispered, 'but some of you nice boys from college have got a Nerve. You'd get away with murder.' She squeezed his arm. 'You freeze him a bit. It'll do Monte good.'

But Inigo could only stammer vaguely in reply to this. Faced with Miss Georgia, he had no nerve. She terrified him.

III

Robert proved to be a grave, white-coated American who stood behind a cocktail bar in the glittering basement of one of the West End hotels. Inigo did not know which hotel it was. He knew very little about these establishments, and then everything had happened so quickly. Leaving Messrs Pitsner and Porry behind, the four of them had rushed down and entered an enormous car; the car had shot them round several corners; and after that he found himself looking at Robert. The entry of Robert upon the scene did not make for clarity and a steady progression of events. After two of his cocktails, the very largest and strongest that Inigo had ever tasted, Inigo found the day tended to slip further and further into unreality. He himself was all right, solidly there in the centre and quite determined to do all that he had planned to do, but everything else, however bright and noisy it might be, was at some remove from himself and reality, all phantasmagoria. Throughout he realized that Mr Monte Mortimer was a personage of great power and influence, who had only to clap his hands and your name would be in all the papers and on all the hoardings, but he did not feel any respect for him because, after all, Mr Mortimer too was a figure in the phantasmagoria.

That is why Inigo, after being asked what the idea was, did not hesitate to speak out boldly. 'You like these things I've written, don't you?' he said. 'You want to use them, and you'd like me to write some more?'

'That's it. And you're lucky, as I told you before. Hello, Tommy! Yes, I want to talk to you, but you'll have to wait. All right, make it Tuesday.' These last remarks, of course, were not addressed to Inigo but to some stranger who wanted to join them. The place was filling with people, and most of them seemed to be anxious to talk to Mr Mortimer. 'Yes you're lucky.'

'No doubt you're right, absolutely,' said Inigo, speaking with great firmness and looking sternly at two people, a very large man and a very small woman, who threatened to break in. 'But I don't care much about that. In fact I don't give a damn.'

'What!' Mr Mortimer was horrified.

'Not really – not a damn. If you don't mind my putting it that way. I'm not trying to be offensive, you know, please understand that. Hello, is this for me?' For two more glasses, charged with the sorceries of the grave Robert, had suddenly appeared from nowhere.

'It is,' replied Mr Mortimer, a trifle grimly. Could this fantastic young man be drunk? The query, a hopeful one, was there in his quick glance at the glass.

'I want you,' Inigo continued, after smiling at Mr Nott, who intimated from a distance that the latest drink had been provided by him, 'I want you to see a friend of mine, one of the girls in our concert party.'

'Ah!' And Mr Mortimer put a great deal of meaning into this single syllable.

'I don't want you to engage her, naturally,' said Inigo with dignity. 'You haven't seen her. But once you see her you'll want to give her a part. She's a genius.'

Mr Mortimer smiled. Then he nodded to several people, presumably important people, people with names and careers in the profession, people who would only be too glad if he would give them even the smallest part. And then he smiled again.

'Genius,' said Inigo again. 'The real thing.'

The other was paternal. 'Don't you bother your head about your concert party, my boy. You've done with that. In a month or two, you'll laugh when you think of it. You will.'

'Because you've taken my songs, you mean?'

'That's right. You'll be too busy.'

'Can't be done,' said Inigo, who felt vaguely that this was a good hard business-like phrase. 'Can't be done, absolutely. Those are my terms. You've got to have a look at this girl – "see her working" as they say in *The Stage* advertisements. Otherwise, no songs. I don't want to be vulgar – though I feel it's all in the part – but take it or leave it.'

'But my dear chap,' the great man protested, 'it's absurd. It's all right standing by your friends – done it myself – but who d'you think I am? Of course I know there's always a certain amount of new talent knocking about in the provinces – I've gone down and spotted a few myself in my time – but really you can't expect me, Monte Mortimer, to go and have a look at a girl in a concert party I never heard of, you can't expect it, you can't really! No, damn it!'

'If you saw this girl - her name's Susie Dean, by the way,' Inigo added, with a little thrill of pleasure, 'you'd jump at her. Somebody will very soon, I can tell you that. And it might as well be you.'

Mr Mortimer shook his head and smiled like one who pities innocent and impressionable youth, ignorant as yet of this hard world.

This would not do for Inigo. 'You never heard of these songs of mine before, did you? Well, this girl's better than those songs. And as a matter of fact there's a fellow too in the party, a light comedian and dancer, who's first-class too. This is no ordinary concert party, I can tell you. Hang it, I ought to know. This girl's worth fifty of that Georgia woman. Take my word for it. Why, if somebody had told you yesterday about these songs of mine, you wouldn't have believed them.'

'That's all right,' said Mr Mortimer dubiously. 'But now I've heard the songs'

'And tonight you'll see this girl,' Inigo told him.

'Tonight! You're crazy.'

'The place is Gatford.'

'I never heard of it,' Mr Mortimer moaned. 'What d'you call it? Gatford? My God! Tonight at Gatford! Oh, come now, you've had your laugh - let's talk sense, let's get down to business.'

'I have got down to it,' Inigo pointed out. 'I'm up to the neck in it, absolutely. No Gatford, no songs.'

'It's blackmail, my dear chap, it really is. You can't dictate to me like that. You're cutting your own throat.'

'As to that,' Inigo told him, at once heartily and firmly, 'I don't give a damn. Have another of Robert's potions?'

'We must get a bit of food,' said Mr Mortimer. 'I ordered a table here. You must lunch with me.'

'Delighted! And, thank you. But I warn you', Inigo added, 'I shan't unbend. The more food and drink I have, the more iron goes into my will. Even now it's got a metallic sound.'

'Hang on a minute, my boy,' said Mr Mortimer, darting Assyrian glances to left and right. 'Hello, Jeff! 'Lo, Milly. Yes, in a minute.' And off he went.

Inigo found himself talking to Mr Alfred Nott, who popped up as quickly and quietly as a fish out of the sea. The place was very full now, and Robert and his assistants or acolytes were concocting and shaking and pouring out and handing over their liquid fire-and-ice as fast as they could. Everybody talked at once, at full speed, and at the top of his voice. Inigo was trying to tell Mr Nott, who was a friendly little man, all about The Good Companions, but other people's conversations or, rather, monologues were for ever getting in the way. He was compelled to learn that about twenty shows were rotten, their theatres full of paper every night; that various gentlemen of the profession had been touched for tenners; that various ladies had said once and for all that they were not going to have their salaries slashed like that and that if Mr Fenkel didn't like it he could do the other thing; that Queenie was at her old game, grabbing all the fat; that it was as much as your life was, worth at the Pall Mall to get a laugh when Tommy Mawson was on.

'Did you say you knew Jimmy Nunn?' roared Inigo.

'Know him well,' replied Mr Nott, in his wheezing voice. 'Me and Jimmy ... panto in Burnley in nineteen - let me see - it must have been -'

'What?'

'It died standing, believe me,' said a voice right in Inigo's ear.

He jumped and looked round. 'What? I beg your pardon.' he gasped.

'Granted,' said the owner of the voice, with grave politeness. 'I said it died standing. The remark was not addressed to you.'

'I know it wasn't, now,' said Inigo. 'I'm sorry.'

'But for your information, I may say it referred to the act of Kramer and Konley at the New York Palace,' the man continued bitterly. 'The act died standing and now they're through with Big Time. Isn't that so, Oby?'

'I'll say it is,' said a voice from the other side.

'Thanks very much,' said Inigo. He did not understand what they were talking about, but by this time it did not matter. This was not the ordinary sane world.

'Laugh,' cried Mr Nott, who was apparently just finishing a story, 'I thought I should never stop for weeks. You oughter seen him, ol' man.' And he laughed himself, and so Inigo laughed too, having no doubt at all that it had been very funny indeed.

Then Mr Mortimer arrived again, with various people swarming and crying in his wake, and said it was time they had a bit of food and led the way out of Robert's domain into a much larger room, more glittering and noisier still, a medley of little tables and hurrying waiters and popping corks and *Madame Butterfly* with full tremolo effects. Mr Nott went with them, and then Miss Georgia appeared again, bringing with her Mr Tanker and two other people whose names Inigo never caught, a Semitic youth with waved hair and a small dark girl with the whitest face and reddest lips Inigo had ever seen. The moment they had sat down, waiters descended upon them with oysters and caviare and champagne and other things that Inigo ate and drank in a dim sort of way. Everybody talked at once, and Miss Georgia and Mr Tanker, the Semitic youth and the small dark girl, all shouted to friends of theirs at other tables, and sometimes people stopped at the table because they 'just had to tell you' and then Miss Georgia or the Semitic youth 'just had to tell' them something back, so that it was like lunching in a painted and gilded pandemonium. Inigo, however, even when the champagne was still bubbling inside him, kept hold of the thread that had guided him from the real world into this sumptuous craziness, and though Mr Mortimer affected the utmost incredulity and dismay, Inigo held on and only repeated his 'terms'; a word he liked to bring out as often as possible because he felt it was a word of power. Mr Mortimer began looking at him with increasing respect. He condescended to ask questions, to which Inigo bellowed back (you had to bellow) the most enthusiastic replies. It was obvious that the great man was weakening. Inigo referred pointedly to the afternoon train he was catching, back to Gatford. The songs would be returning on that train too. Though of course they might come up to London again, those songs, quite soon.

'Get me a boy,' said Mr Mortimer to a waiter. Though the lunch was still going on, he took Inigo to one side, away from the table. A great man does not announce a decision when he is barely eighteen inches from a mixed grill. 'I'll do it,' he said impressively. 'It wrecks the rest of this day, but I can fix that. Tell me where I've got to go and don't forget to see I've got a decent seat. Better wire now. I can run you down myself in my car. No, I can't - shan't get down till about eight. How far is this place? About a hundred miles or so, eh? Do it under three hours and get back sometime tonight. You don't think so? You don't know my car, my boy. I'll eat it.' And when the page-boy arrived, he gave him instructions and messages innumerable, and among them was one from Inigo, a wire to the Gatford Hippodrome to reserve one stall. The great Monte Mortimer would see The Good Companions. Inigo did not say so in his wire; he sang it softly but triumphantly in his heart. And all the lights in the place seemed to grow brighter; the waiters suddenly began bringing nectar and ambrosia; the tables were crowded with the drollest good fellows and the prettiest women in London, such laughter, such wit; and the orchestra stopped making an irritating noise and decided to play the most delicious little tunes, to fiddle you into a happy trance.

'I should like to ask you a question,' said Inigo carefully, when he was taking leave of Mr Mortimer. 'You're a man of experience, you know the world. Do you honestly think I can be described as feeble?'

'As what?'

'Feeble is the word.'

'I could call you many things,' said Mr Mortimer, perhaps a trifle grimly. 'You're a young man who could be called many things. But not feeble. If you're feeble, most of the young men who work for me have been dead a long time. I don't know what you're like at pulling out the teeth of sharks, but in the ordinary way, just doing the ordinary sort of things, such as making a very busy and quite well-known theatrical producer go across England to see a pierrot show he's never heard of before, you're - er - well, you're not feeble. And - er - ' he paused, artfully.

'Well?'

'You can tell her that from me. And that's where I get one in, don't I? Thought so. See you tonight then, and my God, if this girl of yours is a frost, you'll hear something from me. And, don't forget, these numbers of yours have got to go with a bang. I'm banking on them, not the girl. Bye-bye.'

Inigo caught the 3.15. It sent him to sleep and then wakened him at Birmingham. The train from Birmingham to Gatford was crowded with young men who all seemed far more excited than Inigo was, though they had only been to a football match, whereas he had been - well, where had he been? Oh, he didn't know, it was all so absurd. Perhaps on the borders of a dream - by train, and at a reduced fare, namely a single fare and a third for the double journey - to a Charing Cross Road that might easily have begun swelling and quivering like a bubble. Felder and Hunterman, Pitsner and Porry - the Anthropophagi and men whose heads do grow beneath their shoulders. Gatford station, however, contrived to hint that it knew what was going on in his own head. 'Stuff and nonsense!' it said, platforms, porters, kiosks, and all.

IV

Susie's birthday tea-party, held in a large upstairs room in Miss Trant's hotel was just finishing when Inigo arrived. There were signs that Mr Morton Mitcham was about to make a speech over the ruins of the feast. Inigo, a little dazed and breathless, stammered something. Susie looked suddenly frozen; not a glimmer of welcome on her face. Miss Mamie Potter was not there because she had not been invited. But Jerry Jerningham was not there, either, though Inigo knew that he had been invited. All the others were present and were now looking at him reproachfully. No one knew where he had been.

'Nay, Inigo,' said Mr Oakroyd, who liked to speak his mind on all occasions, 'this is no time to turn up, lad. I thowt you'd ha' been t'first here, I did an' all.'

'That's right,' said Joe, with that complacent want of tact which made Mrs Joe, even yet, despair of him. 'Where in the name of goodness have you been to, young feller? We want an apology from you.'

'Oh, shut up, Joe,' cried Susie. 'We don't want anything of the kind. It doesn't matter. What were you saying, Jimmy?'

'I'm awfully sorry, Susie,' said Inigo. 'You see - '

'It doesn't matter,' she replied, coldly and wearily, and then she looked at Jimmy as if it were a pleasure to see a real human being.

Inigo sat down, and, though he knew his triumph was at hand, he could not help wishing that Mr Monte Mortimer was waiting outside. They all began talking again, and he felt out of it. 'Where's Jerningham?' he asked finally.

'Couldn't come, he said,' replied Mrs Joe, in a whisper that carried further than any ordinary tone. 'He sent a note and a present - very nice, too - I mean the present - a box of handkerchiefs, all in good taste, and very acceptable, upon my word, I was surprised. That young man is a Mystery to me, and I don't believe in making them - mysteries, you know. If he'd come and brought nothing, that wouldn't have surprised me. If he'd brought his present himself, that wouldn't have surprised me, either. But not coming himself and yet sending such a nice present, now that is surprising. He's a Mystery.'

But Inigo was not listening. He did not care whether Jerry Jerningham was a mystery or not. He was busy cursing himself because he had forgotten Susie's present. He had meant to buy it in London. They had all given Susie something - he could see the little parcels on the table - only he had forgotten. True there was Mr Monte Mortimer, who was really a large gift, but that was not the same thing. Here was Susie, twenty-one, never to be twenty-one again, though new solar systems should arise and new planets dawn in the blue, and he had not been here to wish her many happy returns and hand over something gloriously sumptuous and see her look at it, eager, excited, happy. She did not look a bit excited and happy now. Had her birthday party been a frost? Damn Felder and Hunterman and Monte Mortimer! He ought not to have bothered about them. And what did Jerningham, the little bounder, mean by not turning up, merely sending some snivelling handkerchiefs?

'Well, Miss Trant, boys and girls,' said Jimmy rising, 'time to go, if you ask me. We'll wish Susie all the good luck she deserves - and good health, that's a great thing in the profession, I give you my word - after the show tonight. We ought to go and have a bit of a rest. It's a big night tonight, house booked right up, and all for Susie here. Gatford's going to get the show of its life tonight, I say, so we'd better take it easy for an hour or so before we start. That's all right, isn't it, Susie?'

Susie nodded, smiling at him but not too cheerfully. They all drifted away from the table. There was a movement towards the door. Susie began gathering up her little packages. This was Inigo's opportunity.

'Look here, Susie, I'm awfully sorry,' he began.

'It doesn't matter,' she said, and turned away. The others were going now.

This would not do at all. He grabbed hold of her wrist. 'I'm awfully sorry I couldn't get here in time,' he added quickly, 'and I've gone and forgotten your present too. No, you must listen, you must.'

'I don't want to hear anything about it. Let me go.'

'I won't until you've heard what I have to say. You see, I had to go up to London today - '

'London!' There was a quick change of tone.

'Yes, London. I didn't tell anybody I was going. I had to see Felder and Hunterman, the music people - '

'Inigo, your songs! They've been hearing them. Have they taken them? Do tell me, quick!' She was excited enough now, and all her eagerness was for him and his songs; she was not thinking about herself at all. And this was a wonderful moment for him. He had sometimes thought she was selfish, and many a time, long after that day, he was to think so again, but the recollection of that moment in the hotel at Gatford always drove the thought out of his head.

'They want them all right,' he began slowly.

'Oh, go on, go on. You're so *slow*. Tell me all about it quick. If you don't I shall think you're feeble again.'

'Well, you see, that man Monte Mortimer heard them too and wants them for a new revue of his.'

Inigo!' She gave a little scream of delight. Then her face fell. 'You're pulling my leg. You never saw Monte Mortimer.'

'I did, I tell you, Susie.' And he told her what had happened in Mr Pitsner's room. She listened, breathless.

'You're made, my dear,' she cried. 'You'll be rolling soon. Marvellous! I am glad. And now the poor old Good Companions are busted. Yes, they are - bound to be.' Then, after a pause: 'But I'll tell you straight, I hate to think of Ethel Georgia singing those numbers. You ought to have told him about me,' she added wistfully.

'I did, woman, I did,' roared Inigo in triumph. 'I told him about nothing else.'

'You didn't, did you? Did he say anything? Laugh, I suppose?'

'Laugh be blowed! I'd have given him laugh. What he said doesn't matter. The point is he's coming to the show tonight.'

'What!' This time it was a scream. She shook him hard. 'Inigo, don't be so daft. He's not coming here.'

'He's coming here to see the show tonight,' he repeated with great deliberation and emphasis. 'As a matter of fact he's coming to see you.'

'Monte Mortimer!'

'The great chief himself - if he is a great chief.'

'But how? - why? - I mean, how did you do it? Oh, I don't believe it.'

'I just told him to come down, and he's coming down. I've reserved a seat for him. I may be feeble, but when I start - '

'Oh, shut up about being feeble! I never meant it anyhow. Let me think a minute. No, I can't think. Oh, I shall be all in bits. I've thought about something like this happening so many times that now I can't bear it. I feel funny already. I shall make a mess of it.'

Inigo was alarmed. 'Perhaps I ought not to have told you.'

'Of course you ought, silly. I'd never have forgiven you if you hadn't. I shall be all right when the time comes. If I'm not, then I'm no good. Gosh, what a chance!' She went twirling away, then just as suddenly came back to him, looking thoughtful. 'Suppose he doesn't like me. That'll be a ghastly wash-out, won't it?'

'He'll like you all right,' said Inigo. 'If he doesn't he's a fathead, absolutely. And he won't get any songs of mine. Under which king, Besonian, speak or die! That's what I shall say to him.'

'Darling! But look here, Inigo, I'm not going to let you tie those songs of yours to me like that - '

'Listen to me. Never mind about that.' He caught hold of her hands. 'I'm sorry I couldn't get back sooner for your party - '

'Don't rub it in. I couldn't help it, being furious, could I? You ought to have told me what you were going to do. Though it's more exciting like this, I must say, Inigo.'

'That's the point. If nothing had happened, you'd have been disappointed and your birthday would have been mucked up, absolutely. As it is, I forgot your present - '

'You didn't. The great Monte's my present. Marvellous present!'

'And I never wished you anything. It isn't too late, is it? Many happy returns of the day, Susie.'

'Thank you.' She said this quietly, demurely. But then, with a glorious rush: 'Oh - I'm an idiot - but I'm so happy. Inigo, you are a darling.' And her arms were about his neck and she had kissed him, all in a flash.

For a minute or two he held her there. No, not for a minute or two. These were not minutes, to be briskly ticked away by the marble clock on the mantelpiece and then lost for ever; the world of Time was far below, wrecked, a darkening ruin, forgotten; he had burst through into that enchanted upper air where suns and moons rise, stand still, and fall at the least whisper of the spirit. Let us leave him there. We must remember that he was a romantic and extravagant youth and very much in love - a young ass. Nor must we forget that such asses do have such moments. Isis still appears to them as she once appeared to that Golden Ass of the fable, and they still feed upon her roses and are transfigured.

CHAPTER FOUR
A Benefit Performance

I

THE last time we were actually present when The Good Companions began a performance was on a Saturday night, the first real Night they had, at Sandybay, months ago. That was a tremendous occasion - or so it seemed then - but it was nothing to this, a Saturday night at the Gatford Hippodrome. Susie's birthday, Susie's benefit, with Mr Monte Mortimer due to arrive almost any time, and every seat in the house taken - even the box. Yes, the Gatford Hippodrome had a box - not four boxes, not two boxes, but one solitary box. Its curtains were rather dingy, and it was difficult to make out whether its four little chairs were gilded or not, but nevertheless it was a proper box, ready to receive any great personage visiting the town who expressed a wish to attend a performance at the Hippodrome. And of course it could be booked, in the ordinary way. But as great personages rarely visited the Hippodrome and other people preferred to sit in comfort, this box was not often occupied, though professional friends of the manager would occasionally accept a seat in it for an odd hour. But now, on this great night, it had been taken. Nobody knew who had taken it, or at least nobody admitted having any knowledge. Thus, Jerry Jerningham might possibly have known something about it. He was not asked, partly because he was not there to be asked until there was barely time for him to change and make up for the opening chorus, and then again because no one imagined he would know anything about it. Mrs Joe might have asked him, because she was more pleased, excited, and curious about that box than anybody else. In her opinion, the box gave Tone to the whole evening. She looked forward to catching the gleam of a white dress front, to hurling a good chest note at a possible diamond tiara. And then again, as she pointed out, with a box you never never knew; anybody might be in that box, and anything - a solid contract for Bournemouth, for example - might come out of it. She was interested, excited, and made no secret of the fact. Perhaps the prophetic instinct was working in the depths of her mind - all conscientious contraltos, after all, sound prophetic - for it must be admitted that that box was important.

Indeed, everything is important now. The sands are running out, so that every grain has some significance.

That is why we must be there in time to see the curtain rise. We have done it before, but we must do it again because this is the last time the curtain will rise on The Good Companions. There will never be another opening chorus for them all after this one. That is what none of them knows, not even Mrs Joe, who has the deep notes of Cassandra herself. They are all eager to make this night a success, and the thought of the packed house recurs to them continually, warming them like wine. But most of them are still wondering about things. Miss Trant, having a word here, a word there, behind the scenes, still wonders what she is to do about it all, and now and then remembers the figure of a man in a car, a man so like the ghost that has long haunted the dim corridors of her mind. The older players are still wondering about the future, that Bournemouth offer. Inigo and Susie are troubled by thoughts of Mr Monte Mortimer. Jerry Jerningham obviously has concerns of his own, which he keeps to himself. Even Miss Mamie Potter keeps asking herself what these propose to do and whether she had better stick to them through the summer and then take a chance in town in the autumn. And Mr Oakroyd wonders what is going to happen to him, and what is happening in Canada, and what is happening in Bruddersford, for no news has trickled through from Ogden Street for some time. There they are then, all as eager and excited as you please but all busy wondering and wondering and planning a little. And not one of them guesses that this is the last time they will troop on together, that their semicircle is about to be broken for ever, that already the powder has been heaped and the train set and fired.

They have crowded in from Mundley and Stort as well as from Gatford itself, and many of them have seen the show before and know who Susie is and why she is having a benefit. Mechanics, fitters, electricians, clerks, and cashiers from the motor works, with their wives and sweethearts; typists and milliners and elementary-school teachers; women who might be anybody's wife or nobody's; men who might at any moment be awarded a medal or given five years' penal servitude, who might be heading for the town council or the gutter; lads who gape and nudge one another and guffaw; girls who wriggle their shoulders, slap their companions, and giggle; quiet girls whose lives are as yet only a vague dream; decent young men who slip in and out of the works and their lodgings, always near a crowd and yet as lonely as Crusoes; jovial middle-aged fellows who earn good money and can eat anything, and their tired wives, who have been fighting, right up to six o'clock this very evening, the week's long battle for cleanliness and respectability; wistful virgins who are eager to feast their eyes on the face of Jerry Jerningham, and amorous gentlemen who have a fancy for Miss Mamie Potter's legs; people who ought to be in hospital, people who ought to be in prison, people who ought to be attending the Victoria Street Wesleyan Chapel concert, the Triangle Girl Guides Rally, the debate at the Mundley Y.M.C.A., the Gatford Cycling Club Whist Drive, people who ought to be helping their father in the shop, people who ought to be in the Blessed Isles, so long and hard have they laboured in this unblessed island; they are all here, staring, chattering, eating chocolates, reading football scores in the paper, turning over their programmes. And now, just when they are all tired of amusing themselves, out go the lights above and up come the footlights illuminating the lower folds of the curtain in the old enchanting way. Is the curtain going up now? No, they will play something first; they always do. There it goes: *Rumpty-dee-tidee-dee, Rumpty-dee-tidee.* Some of the audience know this tune. It is a song called *Slippin' round the Corner,* and that good-looking young fellow, who dances, sings it. Iserntit lovely? And at this moment, as it comes softly twirling through the magically lighted curtain, the mischievous lilt of it working like leaven in the dark mass of the audience, it is lovely indeed, a rhapsody of love and idleness, news from another and brighter world than this in which we portion out our wages. It dances Gatford clean away; the streets, the factories and shops, the long rows of houses, the trams and lorries, the ugly little chapels and the furtive pubs, they tremble a little, they sway, they rock violently, and then off they go, jogging away into nothing, slipping for ever round some vast unimaginable corner. A little louder now, as if in triumph. Nothing remains but clean earth and a blue spangle of stars, and the lilt and the beat and the *Rumpty-dee-tidee* pulsating in the velvet darkness. Louder still now, more triumphant. And up it comes, shaped and coloured anew by the sorcery of the flying crotchets and quavers, this other Gatford, shining and fair, a suburb of Old Cockayne, with fountains sprouting the alternate black and gold of Guinness and Bass, gold-flake and honey-dew heaped in the streets, arcades of meat and pudding done to a turn, silk stockings and jumpers to be picked where you like, dances round every corner and a prize for everybody, goals to be scored at any hour of the day, girls like laughing and passionate queens, boys who would love you for ever and always in evening dress, and children, swarms of them, rosy and fat, with never a white drawn face or a twisted limb, scampering everywhere, running and tumbling out of the happy houses, out of the depths of memory, out of the very grave....

Ah, that was good, that was. Took you back, took you out of yourself, took you somewhere, you didn't know where. It deserves a clap. And tonight it's getting one. The piano by itself now. The curtain's going up. There they are, singing away, pretty as a picture. Give them another good clap. The two girls look lovely, don't they? You can't call that other one a girl; she's getting on, she is; but she's a fine singer for all that, a real good turn. But the two girls look lovely. That's the new one, the one in the blue. But the other's the one, her in the red, Susie Dean. It's her that's having the benefit. Make a cat laugh, the way she takes people off, but she's nice and pretty too. Look at her smiling. That red dress just suits her, dark eyes and dark hair. Well-made too, that girl. She'll be married though, they always are. If she isn't, she'll be marrying that nice-looking boy, Jerry they call him. Oh, he's a good turn. Just watch his feet. And there's the comic, the little one at the end, twisting his face about, Jimmy Nunn. He'll come on as a postman soon - and laugh, he'd make you die laughing! That tall one - no, the very long thin man, him with the eyebrows - he plays the banjo and then he does conjuring. They say he's played before the King and Queen or something like that. Quite a comic too, in his way, when he's conjuring. That other one, with the big shoulders on him, is a singer. He usually starts them off. That's right: 'Courtney Brundit will sing Number Twenty-seven on the programme.' That's him. And that young fellow at the piano can play all right, my word he can! It's a gift to be able to play like that. They say he's just married that new one, but of course you can't believe everything you hear.

The curtain is up, the show has begun. It is time we left the audience and went behind the scenes. We shall never find our way there again, after this night.

II

The trouble began when Joe was singing, at the very opening of the programme. It was a cloud no larger than a man's hand, but there it was. As usual, Joe was giving his audience, whom he apparently imagined to be a company of would-be navigators, some advice concerning the Deep, the Moi-oi-oighty Dee-ee-eep. Just as he was imploring them, for the fourth or fifth time, to Beeware (many Brave Hearts being asleep in this Deep), a horribly raucous and penetrating voice told him to 'pur a sock in it'. It came, this voice, from the back of the pit, which was the cheapest part of the house, there being no gallery. And it raised a loud and jeering laugh from that quarter, though the rest of the audience immediately made shushing noises. Joe himself seemed to pay no attention to this voice; he went on with his song; but Inigo at the piano noticed that his great fists were clenched and that certain veins in his forehead were swelling ominously. Joe, it was clear, was very annoyed, as he had every right to be. Besides, it was not the first time that voice had jeered at them. It had been heard one or two nights before.

When Joe had finished his first song, he was warmly applauded, the audience - bless them! - being as usual all the more enthusiastic because some of their number had been rude enough to interrupt. But from that same place at the back there came boos and groans and ironic cheers and they were so prolonged that they outlasted the applause. Joe was furious. 'Bloody swine!' he muttered to Inigo, across the piano. 'They're at it again.'

'Ladies and gentlemen,' he cried, 'by special request - *The Trumpeter.*'

'Shurr up!' the voice jeered, before anybody else could make a sound.

Some people laughed. The remainder indignantly shushed again and then clapped.

'If the gentleman at the back doesn't shut up,' roared Joe, his honest face inflamed even through the make-up, 'he'll be soon made to shut up.'

'Steady, Joe boy, steady!' whispered Jimmy, who was sitting just behind him. Most of the others had left the stage, as they usually did during an individual act.

The gentleman at the back and his friends signified their contempt for this threat, but other people in the audience, not having paid their money to listen to the town roughs, welcomed it. 'Turn him out,' they cried. For a minute or two there was quite an uproar in the place. Joe grimly waited until there was quiet again, and then began his series of apparently idiotic questions to a trumpeter.

Meanwhile, Mrs Joe, in the wings, was very agitated indeed. 'I'm convinced now,' she declared, 'that it's all a put-up affair. Before, I wasn't, though I had my suspicions. I know what you're going to say, Susie and you, Miss Trant, that some pros always think it's a put-up affair if there's ever a bit of booing or stamping. And so they do, and very silly too I call it. But there's a Limit.'

'It's disgusting,' said Miss Trant, 'and we've certainly had more than our share of it this week.'

'Perhaps it'll stop soon,' said Susie hopefully, still busy with thoughts of Mr Monte Mortimer. They may settle down when the show's got going.'

'And they may not,' retorted Mrs Joe, who perhaps did not like the suggestion that the show had not got going when her husband was actually on the stage. 'It sounds bad to me, and put-up. And whatever will those people in the box think! Booking it specially like that and coming in evening dress and then hearing such - such - Devilry!' For there were people in the box now, and Mrs Joe had caught sight of a white shirt front and a bare arm on the ledge.

'Well, if there's any more of it,' Miss Trant announced with decision, 'I'm going to have them turned out. It's vile and unpardonable, and I'm not going to have it.'

'If they spoil it for me tonight,' Susie said fiercely, 'I'll - I'll kill them, the beasts.'

'Don't say that, my dear,' said Mrs Joe. 'And if there's to be anything of that sort, Joe will do it. Just listen to that! The temper he'll be in now, it won't bear thinking of. It'll take me all my time to keep him quiet. You've no idea what Joe's like when he's thoroughly roused,' she added, with a droll mingling of shame and pride. 'Take a peep at him now, my dear. He's fairly bursting.'

Miss Mamie Potter strolled up. She was on next. 'I say,' she said, turning her round features from one to the other of them, 'what's up? They're not giving out the bird, are they? If they're starting that, I'm through. I shall just walk off. I will. I can't stand it.'

'If there is any trouble while you are on, Miss Potter,' Miss Trant told her, 'don't take any notice of it. I'll have it stopped somehow or other, if I've got to go and do it myself.'

'That's all right,' replied Mamie dubiously, 'but I'm not used to it.'

'Neither are we,' Susie put in, like lightning. 'And I'll tell you something for your own good. Monte Mortimer's going to be in front tonight.'

'Monte Mortimer! The big revue man! That's likely, isn't it? I've heard those yarns before, Miss Dean,' Mamie scoffed.

'All right then, don't believe me.' And then, in reply to the wondering glances of the other two, she went on: 'It's true. Inigo went up to town today, saw him, and persuaded him to come and see us tonight.'

'Well, I never did,' Mrs Joe gasped. 'Not that he's any use to me - or Joe, of course. But it's your Chance, Susie. What did I tell you, only the other day? You see, you never know.'

'I say, d'you mean it?' Miss Potter was apparently convinced now. 'Where's he sitting? Is he here now?'

'Fourth row of the stalls,' Susie replied shortly. 'I know because Inigo showed me the seat before we started. He's not come yet, but he's coming all right. Inigo got a wire after he had started.'

'And my God, I've got to go on now. That's a nice trick, anyhow,' cried Miss Potter, looking angrily at Susie. 'Why didn't you tell me before?'

'Because I hadn't a chance. Nobody's trying to crab you. He'll see plenty of you before the night's out. Lord, listen to that! Joe'll be furious.'

He was. They were applauding him loudly enough, but you could plainly hear the catcalls and booing from the back.

'Hear that?' he growled, as he joined them, and Miss Potter, looking very uneasy, got ready to take his place. 'There's somebody at the back there 'ud get such a pug in the lug - '

'It's bad and I don't doubt it's deliberate, put-up,' his wife interrupted, putting a hand on his arm, 'but don't let's us have vulgarities. We can be ladies and gentlemen, I say, even if they can't.'

'And I say they'd get such a pug in the lug if I could get at 'em. They'd better look out, that lot. I've a good mind to go and stand there when some of you are on, and keep 'em quiet one way or the other.'

'You've a good mind to do nothing of the sort,' cried Mrs Joe indignantly. 'Starting bother like that, Joe! You don't know how it might all end up. And Susie here with such a Chance!'

'Chance?'

'Of a Lifetime,' she told him, and then hastily explained why this was a night of nights.

Miss Mamie Potter was not faring any better than Joe. Indeed, it was worse for her. She had not much of a voice, and very soon this was pointed out to her by the back of the pit. By the time she had struggled through to the end of one feeble little song, Jimmy signalled to her not to sing any more but to do her dance and then finish the act. It is not easy to interrupt a dance but the roughs at the back did what they could. Miss Potter really could dance, and her beautiful flashing legs provoked a fine outburst of applause, but still the row at the back could not be drowned. And the audience was growing restless.

Jimmy dashed off while Miss Potter was taking her call. 'We'll do that Shopping concerted number next,' he cried. 'Must do something noisy. Can't you tell them to stop that row, Miss Trant, please?'

'I'm going to, now,' she replied. And she went, there and then. The manager was not to be found anywhere in the building, and nobody appeared to know where he was. There were only two men attendants for the auditorium, and neither of these was young, strong, and determined. The man in the pit, a decrepit fellow, protested that he was doing his best to stop the constant interruptions. 'But they're a tough lot, Miss,' he whispered. 'I give you my word. Don't know what they're doing here at all, I don't.'

'Send out for a policeman,' she said.

'Ought to be a bobby about,' he replied doubtfully. 'Usually looks in, but don't seem to have come this way tonight. However, there's one at the corner could look in, dare say. Keep 'em quiet, p'raps, if they saw him.'

Five minutes later, a policeman arrived and stood just behind the noisy fellows, after letting them know, by a familiar 'Now then, there! Give order!' that the Law itself in all its blue and silver majesty was taking charge. It happened though that there was little need of him. The concerted item they were giving now was a noisy rollicking affair that offered great scope to Susie and Jimmy for droll by-play. And they hardly begun singing the first verse, which was a mere excuse for the drolleries that came after, when Susie remarked a stir in front. Someone had just arrived, was finding his place in the fourth row, the end seat on the left of the gangway. It must be - could only be - the great Monte Mortimer. Susie flashed a glance at Inigo, who lifted an eyebrow in reply. For a minute or two, she felt horrible, wobbly on her legs and hot and dry in the mouth; everything went out of her head, words, business, everything; and she felt she could never be amusing on the stage again. Then a huge friendly laugh came over the footlights to her from the audience, tickled by some bit of business she had gone through quite mechanically. And then all her nervousness fell away from her, leaving her excited somewhere inside but feeling clear, masterful, full of wonderful tricks. She hurled herself into the little scene, became a laughing whirlwind of fun. She acted everybody, Jimmy included, clean off the stage. All the silly shopgirls she had ever seen, the girls who sniffed, the girls who were short, sagging, and wistful, the girls who were tall, haughty, and spoke through their noses, the girls who knew nothing and the girls who knew everything, were vividly present in her mind, and in a happy fury of inspiration she brought out the lot, created and destroyed them in a few seconds. The audience laughed; they roared; they leapt at her. Even those people in the box - and who were those people in the box? - seemed to be laughing, leaning forward; and once she thought she heard a voice she knew. As for Mr Monte Mortimer, she could not see him and did not know what was happening to him; but if he did not like this, he could do the other thing.

'Must keep it going now,' cried Jimmy, as they bustled off. 'You next, Jerry. Keep 'em going, boy. Show 'em what you can do.'

And Jerry did. He slipped round the corner for them. While he sang it, there was nothing there but a good little tune, but once he began dancing it was soon packed with meanings that had escaped both words and music. His long graceful legs and twinkling witty feet held the crowd in thrall. When finally he appeared to hurl away the last shreds of restraint, capering crazily and yet still keeping it all as deft and neat as surgery, and Inigo tossing his lock of hair over the piano was joined by Jimmy with his drums, Mitcham with his banjo, and the others as chorus, the house rose at him. A last double kick - *pom-pom* - and he was standing there, glittering a little and gasping, smiling at them. They pounded and thundered their approval. He bowed, flashed a smiling glance at the box, bowed again, then retired. Back he had to come, and for another delicious five minutes his feet told them how amusing life was. Another storm, and this time the girl attendant who looked after the stalls came forward and handed up some small parcels, one of which apparently demanded another smiling glance at the box, to say nothing of innumerable bows to the rest of the house. The others in the wings, clapping too, caught a glimpse of a gold cigarette-case. The other tributes were boxes of cigarettes and chocolates, customary offerings on the altar of hopeless passion. But that cigarette-case did not suggest Gatford. Even the most devoted typist or shopgirl could not have given him that lovely glittering thing. Jerry, however, who appeared to be becoming more mysterious every minute, rushed down to his dressing-room, and offered no explanations.

It had been arranged that Susie should go on next. She had begged Jimmy, whose original programme was now in ruins, for the next single act - 'while the going was good,' she said - and as this was her night, he could not refuse.

They clapped when they heard her name announced, and clapped still harder, cheered even, when she actually appeared. She gave them, with a wealth of by-play, that song of Inigo's about going home, and they loved every word and note and gesture of it all. Most of them had seen her before. She was the youngest, a favourite, and this was her night, so that there was every excuse for giving her a great reception. But if they had never set eyes on her before, it would have been just the same. This was indeed her night. She was entertaining them all at a birthday party. They were all old friends together, it seemed, and only because she happened to be the prettiest and gayest girl there, she was in the limelight and they were staring and listening in the dark. That first tight 'Now or never' feeling had left her long ago; she knew the great Monte was there, but she no longer bothered her head about him; and she carried everything before her, swept everything dull and heavy clean out of the world, with her gigantic rush of high spirits. Inigo, vamping idly at the piano, was amazed, almost frightened. This was Susie; everything - the adorable everything he knew so well - was there, but she was larger and brighter than life. The girl herself was lost in this public. Susie, this tremendous Susie-for-everybody, who was so obviously ready to take possession of any stage, any audience, to charge into the very centre of that daft wonderland of the morning and early afternoon, that world of vast electric signs and photographers and interviewers and press agents and enormous cars and expensive lunches for everybody in glittering noisy rooms. All of it seemed hers now by right. She had only to lift a finger and they would all be gathering round her and up would go the spangled lights, spelling her name in the crazed empyrean of Shaftesbury Avenue, In a flash he saw even the formidable Ethel Georgia slinking away, a little faded, tired, when she appeared. It seemed to him that that wonderlandish world was closing round her already. He did not know whether he liked it or not. Something hurt, though there was sweetness in the wound. One moment he felt he wanted to stop playing, to seize her by the arm and rush her away into the dark, just to sit in a tram with her, take her back to dingy lodgings, drop into the old round of Sunday trains and dry sandwiches and little halls and companionable shabbiness. The next moment he wanted to go on and on, to play and play until she had laughed and pirouetted herself into being everything she thought she wanted to be, and all the good things were heaped before her, and he was - well, dodging about somewhere in the background, looking on at the spectacle of her gigantic, her immortal happiness. But then again - but what then? Oh, he didn't know. He seemed to have been up and doing for several weeks without a break of comforting brute senselessness, good old sleep. He must be tired. But he didn't feel tired, he felt drunk, a trifle mad. *Tiddly-iddly-om-pom, tiddly-iddly-om.* Quite mad, in fact - absolutely. *Tom-pom.*

Susie gave one encore, she gave two encores, and even then the riot was not subdued. There were some little parcels for her too, and some flowers, including a bouquet - a real Grand Opera sort of bouquet, something undreamed of in the pierrot world - that was handed down from the mysterious box. She tried to say something, but was far too excited and breathless. Jimmy hustled the others on for a concerted number and left her happy and gasping in the wings, where she received the congratulations of Mr Oakroyd.

'I ought to go and sit down and be quiet in the dressing-room, Jess lad,' Susie told him, 'but I just can't. Look at this. Isn't it sweet? Oh! - I'm nearly bursting. What a night!'

'Champion!' cried Mr Oakroyd, rising to heights of enthusiasm hardly known in Bruddersford. 'Eh, that were a right treat, Soos lass. An' they tell me ther's one o' t'big men o' the the-ater business in t'house.'

'There is,' cried Susie. 'And I expect him to come round any minute and say, "Miss Dean, I've been looking for you for years. Open a week on Tuesday at two hundred and fifty pounds a week. If that's not enough, let me know." Something like that. What d'you say?' But before he could say anything, she waltzed him round a few times.

'So that's it, is it?' he said, when she had let him go. 'And what about poor owd Good Companions? We'll nivver see you ner more, unless we go up on a day trip and pay to go in. Never you mind, Soos lass,' he went on, when it appeared she was about to break in, 'you look after yersen and if yon feller does offer you ten pound a week to go up to London or owt like that, tak' it on. So long as there's nowt shameless about it, coming on naked and suchlike. You'll ha' to mind there, I'm thinking, for they're a bit of a foul lot i' London, they tell me. But if it's decent, tak' it. Eh, I'd right miss you if you went, I would an' all - '

'Darling!' cried Susie, who had been ready to laugh and cry all at once for some time, and now felt more like it than ever. She took hold of his arm and squeezed it hard. 'I think you're marvellous, Jess lad, and I'd miss you too. Let's run away to Canada together, shall we?'

'Eh' - a very long-drawn-out one this 'ime - 'ther's nowt I'd like better. We would have a do.' He stopped for a minute to contemplate rapturously the 'do' they would have, before returning to the world of fact. 'But listen here. Never you mind about t'Good Companions. Tak' what's offered if yer can benefit yersen. 'Cos ther's bound to be a bust-up i' t'party afore so long. Summat's going to happen. I can feel it coming. Ay, you can laugh, but I've a right knack that way. When t'United won t'Cup, I said they would right from t'start that year, and they all laughed at me at t'mill, but I wer right. An' I'll tell you another thing,' he added, taking breath.

'Go on, Mr Old Moore,' she said, laughing at him.

'I thowt ther wer going to be a right bit o' bother here tonight. An' I'm not so certain it's all ower yet, either.'

'You mean that lot at the back?'

'That's right. I've had a look at 'em and wer talking to t'owd chap that looks after t'pit, an' yon lot's game for owt. Ther's summat wrong there, let me tell yer. I can't mak' it out at all, I can't. Here, Jimmy's wanting you to join in, afore t'interval.'

So Susie went on again and helped to bring about a rousing curtain. Jimmy had cut the first half, perhaps in the hope that the roughs at the back of the pit would clear out at the interval and not come back, though for the last half-hour or more they had not made a sound. When the house lights went up, after the curtain had fallen, Inigo, peeping through with the excited Susie, had just time to see Mr Monte Mortimer leaving his seat. Was he coming round to see them? Or was he slipping out for a drink? As the minutes passed and he did not appear, Inigo came to the conclusion that Monte had wanted a drink, a cheerful conclusion compared with Susie's, which was that he had retired for good and all, in disgust. Just before it was time to begin again, however, they saw him back in his seat, and Susie was able to have a peep at his distinguished Assyrian features.

'He doesn't look bad,' she remarked. 'I'd like to scream at him "Well, what about it?" Wonder what he's thinking. Doesn't look as if he's thinking anything. Look, he's yawning. Oh, don't yawn. Fancy coming here and yawning!'

'Damn cheek, I call it,' said Inigo. 'He's probably eaten too much. He had enough lunch for five, and I'll bet he's been eating and drinking ever since.'

'Pig! No, I won't say that. You never know, he might sort of - what d'you call it? - know what I'm saying. Please, Mr Mortimer, I want a nice fat engagement. Thank you. Oh, this is awful! I feel sick. If he doesn't do anything about it, everything's spoilt, isn't it? I mean it'll be ghastly just going on in the old way. I wish it was time to begin again. I'm not going to look at him any more. There's nobody in that box now. I wonder who they are. Marvellous bouquet they gave me, and no name on it at all. It's a very handsome young millionaire - not too young, you know, not like you, Inigo - who's fallen madly in love with me. Hello, here we are.'

'Well,' said Jimmy, beaming at them all, 'I thought we were in for it, one time - '

'Thought somebody else was,' growled Joe. 'Just let me catch one of them fellows, that's all - '

'Those fellows, Joe, not them fellows,' his wife told him. 'And you'll do nothing of the kind.'

'It's all right now, though,' Jimmy continued. 'Got 'em all going in great style.'

'A riot,' Mr Morton Mitcham observed gravely.

And a riot it proved to be, though not the kind of riot mentioned in the columns of *The Stage*. When the lights went down again, all the people in the pit were back in their places, but the policeman was not there. He had seen nothing to worry about, and so he had majestically departed during the interval, leaving behind him - alas! - a fine chance of promotion.

'Shurr-up!'

'Oorder, *please!*'

'Sh-sh-sh.'

'Gerr-outcher!'

'Give order, *please!*'

'Send 'em out!'

'Sh-sh-sh.'

'Give order, gentlemen, *if you please!*'

'Ow! Ah-oo-er! Pur a sock in it!'

'... behalf of my fellow-artistes, like to appeal to those members of the audience at the back there to keep quiet (Hear, hear!), like them to remember that other people have paid their money and want to hear the show properly ... (Turn 'em out!) ... fair play ... British sportsmanship ... thanking you one and all...'

The audience loudly applauded this speech of Jimmy's, but the noise was even worse afterwards. Poor Mrs Joe, imploring the Red Sun to sink in-toe the West (just as if she thought it was uncertain in its movements for once, and feared some cosmic catastrophe), could hardly be heard, for the people who were indignant at the constant interruptions were as noisy as the people who interrupted. In vain she paused between verses, a figure erect and contemptuous, the Duchess of Dorking standing before a revolutionary tribunal. The silence she waited for never arrived. With a glance of despair not unmixed with pleading, addressed to the shirt front and bare arm in the box, she plunged into her second song. She was a Highland lassie now, a passionate tragic creature of the moors and the glens, waiting and watching for our old acquaintance, Angus MacDonald. Would he or would he not, she asked in her deepest chest notes, come from his camp o'er the sea? Did she hear the call of the pibroch? Apparently she did, though to everybody else it sounded like the last despairing bleat ('Order, gents, *please!*') of the aged attendant in the pit. She also heard the marching of men, but everybody else heard something like this too, a stamping of feet at the back. Yes, it was Angus Her Own coming home from the war. She asserted this triumphantly at the top of her voice, and even then she could hardly be heard. It seemed as if Angus was bringing the war home with him. Pale, trembling, she stalked off tragically at the end of her song, and did not return to face the uproar, though most of it was honest and admiring applause.

Meanwhile, it was taking Miss Trant and Mr Oakroyd all their time to restrain Joe in the wings from descending into the auditorium and 'knocking a few blasted heads together'. When Mrs Joe came off, however, he had to attend to her, for after smiling wildly and elaborately shrugging her shoulders and raising her hands, she suddenly burst into tears. 'I've not been so-so - so insulted since that awful time at Grimsby', she sobbed, 'when they were all drunk - and threw the fish.' Joe, muttering that somebody was going to get something worse than fish, gave her all the support of his stalwart person, and finally she was persuaded to rest in her dressing-room, where Miss Trant administered eau-de-Cologne and soothing words. Four of them were now struggling fairly successfully through a noisy quartette, full of comic 'business'. The attendant in the pit had given up his task of restoring order in despair. One or two members of the audience, pugnacious men, had attempted to take over his duties, with the result that there were loud arguments at the back for some time, and once or twice the sound of a slight scuffle. The remainder of the audience was becoming very restive indeed. One of the loudest and most indignant members was no other than our friend, Mr Monte Mortimer, whose professional sense of decorum was outraged by these constant interruptions, as well they might be, for he had heard nothing like it for years. If a few first-nighters in the gallery ventured a timid hiss or boo at Mr Mortimer's productions, he filled the papers next day with wild talks of conspiracies and terrible threats. Now, his was one of the loudest of the hushing voices, and every now and then he half rose from his seat and looked round, as if he were inclined to take charge of the proceedings himself.

'Leave it to me, Jimmy,' Mr Morton Mitcham whispered, with all the confidence of a man who has been four times round the world. 'I've managed tougher crowds than this. Let's put on my conjuring act, with you gagging in the house.'

There was something to be said for this. It meant that Jimmy would pretend to be a very rude member of the audience, who from the back of the pit would carry on an argument with Mr Mitcham who would finally ask him to step on to the stage, along with some other bona fide members of the audience, to 'watch him closely'. Mr Mitcham was an old hand, and was clever at getting laughs at the expense of his assistants from the audience. This might do the trick, creating order out of deliberate disorder. Jimmy had some misgivings, but thought it was worth trying, and off he went to change his costume and then sneak round to the back, leaving Mr Mitcham in possession of the stage. Mr Mitcham began by playing the banjo, but soon gave that up. Joe brought on his conjuring apparatus for him, and the two of them started gagging.

'I shall now require a few members of the audience,' Mr Mitcham announced, in his harsh deep drawl, 'to assist me and to prove to you, ladies and gentlemen, there is absolutely no deception.'

This was the cue for Jimmy, at the back, to open the comic dialogue. But something went wrong, apparently, for all that could be heard from the stage was a real argument. Then Jimmy's voice was raised in genuine protest: 'Here, half a minute, you chaps!' he was crying. 'Here, what are you doing? Let go.'

'A few members of the audience, please,' Mr Mitcham was repeating.

This was where chaos broke in, and an ordered narrative, even if it were possible, would no longer fit the occasion. There was a movement towards the stage, vague in the darkness. 'House lights!' Mr Mitcham hissed, but they did not come on. There was a door at the right of the proscenium that led directly through a short flight of stone steps bringing you into the wings. It seemed some people from the back were making for that door. There was also a central gangway running through both pit and stalls, there being no barrier, only a thick cord, between them, and down this gangway came several figures, now moving forward, now scuffling. And Jimmy's voice was heard from this group, still raised in protest. So far, so good, but now comes chaos, bewildering alternations of light and darkness, hurtling fragments of event.

'Let go, can't you!'

''Ere, what's the ruddy idea?'

'Turn 'em out.'

'Lights up, there, you fools!'

'Oh, will you!'

And shouts from some of the men and screams from some of the women. There seemed to be a struggle going on in the gang-way, not far from the stage now. Jimmy was in it.

Then a large figure sprang up from nowhere, charged into the scuffling group, and sent one or two men flying. It was Joe. 'Oh, you get out of it,' he was heard to bellow. And then somebody did get out of it. There was a crack; there was a thud; somebody had taken a full punch from the furious Joe. More shouts, screams, and cracks. That unconscious somebody, it seemed, was being lifted out of the way. Then the lights came on, uncertainly, as if they did not like it.

'My God!' cried Inigo, starting up from the piano. 'It's Monte Mortimer.' And it was. Mr Mortimer had interfered in the dark; he had got in the way; he had received Joe's punch; and he was now beyond those voices, where there was peace. We shall never meet him again. Farewell, Monte!

Somebody was shouting for the curtain to be dropped; twenty people were roaring for the police; and about a hundred more were shouting at random. Out went the house lights again, suddenly this time. Next minute, the stage lights vanished too. The whole place was in darkness, a black pandemonium.

'Hey!' Mr Oakroyd had cried, as three or four of them came clattering up the steps and round the corner. A rough lot they looked, too.' What you doing here?'

'Coming on the stage,' one of them had replied. But another had just put his lip out and growled 'Gairrr away!'

'Nar, tak' your hook,' he had told them, angrily.

Then he got a shove in the back that sent him banging against one of them, a big one. This fellow gave him another shove that sent him spinning. Then all the lights went out. Somebody had got at the switchboard. He jumped forward, bumped into a fellow, got a crack on the head, but was able to give somebody something to be getting on with. The stage-hand was shouting somewhere. So were a lot of other people. He charged at the switchboard, but people and things got in the way. Then he found himself grappling with somebody, got tripped up, went flying in the dark, with several people falling over him.

'Fire! Fire!' a voice shouted, not far away.

'Fire! Fire! Fire!' Innumerable voices took it up, voices rising to screams.

Desperately Mr Oakroyd picked himself up. 'There's no bloody fire,' he was yelling, in despair.

'No fire,' somebody was shouting on the stage. 'Keep your seats please!'

The uproar now was terrific, horrible. There were huge crashes all over the place. 'Get them lights on,' roared a voice. 'The lights, the lights!' And from further away: 'Fire! Fy-yer! Fy-yerr!'

Another dash for the switchboard. Somebody else making for it too. Joe. 'Come on, Joe, Joe lad,' cried Mr Oakroyd. Somebody there. Two of them. 'Tak' that, yer —,' from Mr Oakroyd, who landed one in first, this time. The other fellow gave a yell, his companion a grunt, and Mr Oakroyd grabbed a switch or two. The lights that came on now showed Joe leaping after one of the men; the other had dropped. Mr Oakroyd dashed on to the stage, to shout that there was no fire. The place was like a madhouse. Everybody was shouting and screaming, pushing and struggling. 'Keep your seats!' they shouted from the stage, he and Jimmy and Morton Mitcham and Inigo, with the women of the party beside them now, pale, amazed. But he had not been there a minute before all the lights but two or three, high up and giving the merest glimmer, went out again. That switchboard. He collided in the wings with a woman who had just dashed up the steps from the front, a large woman, screaming something - sounded like 'Jerry'. Must have been too, because the next moment, Jerry Jerningham appeared from nowhere, was immediately grabbed by this large woman, and whisked off, somewhere at the back. From somewhere too there came a series of crashes. Things were being overturned. Electric bulbs were going too. Chaps came jumping out of the big shadows, making off. They were still shouting 'Fire!' somewhere. Mr Oakroyd got some more lights on. There was a smell of burning too; it seemed to be coming over from the other side. He called to the others and hurried across. Plenty of smoke. It seemed to be coming from that pile of old curtain stuff there. He and Inigo got two extinguishers on it. No flame, but the smoke was worse, blinding and choking. Something rickety there too, wobbling a bit. Joe was shouting down from the top. He heard the swift rustle behind him. The curtain was coming down, moving by itself, it seemed, for he could not see anybody lowering it. A chap went tearing past. Wasn't that Joe coming down, still shouting? These big side pieces - part of the theatre's standard set, and very old - didn't seem any too safe. Here, they'd better look out. Something gave a nasty shake.

'Look out!' he yelled to them at the back. 'Get out of t'way, sharp!' Miss Trant, Jimmy, Susie, with her arms full of music, were still there. He shouted again, ran forward, waving his arms at them.

You would have thought the whole theatre had fallen in, it fell with such a crash, that piece of scenery. Susie and Mr Oakroyd were untouched. Jimmy was sitting on the stage, his head in his hands. But Miss Trant was lying there, white and still. The police were coming now, were actually here. There was the clamour of a fire-engine coming from somewhere outside. Miss Trant never moved as they bent over her, crying her name.

III

'Well, you've made a benefit of this all right,' said the Inspector grimly. His audience was composed of Inigo and Joe, still in their stage costumes, which were torn and filthy, Mr Oakroyd, all bruised and blackened, and two members of the staff of the Gatford Hippodrome. The rest had gone, most of them between half an hour and an hour ago. It was nearly an hour since Miss Trant had been taken away to the hospital, with Jimmy, still groaning, in attendance.

'What do they say at the hospital - about Miss Trant?' Inigo asked, shakily. He had never felt more tired in all his life. He could not stand on his feet any longer. He felt dizzy, sick.

'I'm getting that through for you,' replied the Inspector. 'I'll have a word in a minute or two. You chaps had better be getting along home now. You're played out, I can see that. Meantime, I've got to be making out my report.' He looked about him with a sardonic eye. The fire had not done very much damage; indeed, it was almost out when the fire-brigade arrived. Nevertheless, the Gatford Hippodrome looked a wreck. The stampede had left its traces on the body of the theatre; and the stage was a blackened and watery ruin. 'This part of it's nothing,' the Inspector went on, 'though I don't say it isn't bad enough. Nobody'll be giving a turn here for some time. It's life though, not property, that matters. There might have been dozens of lives lost - dozens, yes, scores - with people all trying to get out at once. Matter of fact, there isn't any so far, and doesn't look like being any. Lucky, I'll tell you, very lucky. Seven people injured, that's all the figure I've got - that's in the audience, not counting your two.'

'It 'ud ha' been all nowt, Inspector,' said Mr Oakroyd earnestly, 'if they hadn't ha' gone an' shouted "Fire!" like that. I knew what it 'ud be. We tried to stop 'em.'

'But there was a fire,' said the Inspector.

'Nay, ther wasn't, not when they were shouting. It come after, did t'fire, and it were nowt when it did come. Me an' him put most on it out oursens, easy.'

'That's true,' said Inigo wearily.

'Well, who started it all?' said the Inspector.

'I've told yer,' replied Mr Oakroyd. 'Chaps 'at came from back o' t'pit started it all. Turned t'lights off to begin wi', and it must ha' been them as shouted "Fire!"'

'Sure of it,' said Joe, and explained what happened to him when all the trouble first began.

'We'll have to look into this,' said the Inspector dubiously. 'Pity they got away, that's all. Nothing to work on at all.'

'Nay, you've got one on 'em, t'chap Joe an' me were sitting on so long,' said Mr Oakroyd. 'Hey, Sergeant, didn't you tak' yon chap wi' t'red scarf? He were one on 'em.'

'That's right, sir,' said the sergeant, coming up. 'We got him all right. It's Tulley.'

'Oh, it's Tulley, is it? We know him all right. An old friend of ours, Tulley is. What's he got to say?'

'Knows nothing about it, sir. Happened to be in the audience he says, and was getting out this way.'

'He's lyin',' Mr Oakroyd declared.

'We'll see about that,' replied the Inspector, who was still busy taking stock of the situation. He poked about for a few minutes and made some notes, while the tattered remnants of The Good Companions looked on listlessly. They said nothing, for there seemed to be nothing to say now until they had had news from the hospital. At last, however, a policeman arrived with the message, which he delivered into the Inspector's ear as if it were a state secret.

'Well, it's not so bad,' said the Inspector, turning to them. 'In fact, it's good. The lady's suffering from shock and a fractured arm, that's all. No need for anybody to worry - '

They gave huge sighs of relief.

'And your other friend - the little man, Nunn - only got a crack on the head. They're keeping him there overnight, but he'll probably be out tomorrow or the day after. He's all right, though there won't be any song-and-dance for him for a week or two, I should say.'

Inigo found himself giggling in a helpless sort of way. Everything had been rather crazy for some time now, of course, but still he didn't want to giggle about it.

'You change your clothes and get to bed, my boy,' said the Inspector. 'Have a bite of food and a drink of something and then turn in, quick. You chaps too. Off you go. You can't do any more here. And, I say, don't leave the town until I've seen you again. I've got your addresses, haven't I? All right then, pop off.'

They had changed and were just straggling off, like a little company of shipwrecked sailors, when they met Susie, who looked like a fantastic little ghost as she came through the stage door. She was still wearing her stage costume, though she had a big coat over it, and there were traces of make-up on her face, a pale ruin of rouge and tear stains.

'Have you heard?' she cried, and when they said they had, she explained she had just come from the hospital. 'It's not so bad, is it?' she said, smiling wanly.

'Better ner like,' Mr Oakroyd agreed.

'Mrs Joe's waiting for you at the digs, Joe,' she went on. 'She told me to tell you. And you'd to hurry up because she was going to see there was something hot for supper.'

'Ther should be a bit o' summat for me an' all,' remarked Mr Oakroyd contemplatively. 'I hadn't thowt owt about it, but I'm right peckish nar. Happen ther'll be a bit o' meat-and-tater pie warmed up. Yon landlady o' mine is great on meat-and-tater pie.'

'Let's keep out of the main street,' said Susie, first slipping a hand inside Joe's arm, then taking the expectant arm, Inigo's, on the other side, and squeezing them both a little. 'We don't want anybody to see us, do we?' They trudged on in silence down the gloomy side-street. Doors were being slammed with a kind of savage finality. Somewhere not far away, a hoarse reveller was shouting:

'E's a dee-ar old pal,
Ja-holly old pal,
But 'e opens 'is mouth tew wi-ide.'

It was Mr Oakroyd, who had just been considering for the first time in true perspective, the whole daft evening, who broke the silence. 'Well, by gow!' he began. 'Nar who'd ha' thowt - '

But he was not allowed to say any more. 'Don't start,' said Susie hastily. 'Just keep quiet, Jess lad. It's been a mess, an awful mess. I've cried enough tonight, I don't want to cry any more. And I don't want to talk about it now. There'll be plenty of time to talk about it all next week.'

'Absolutely,' said Inigo wearily.

'I dare say,' said Joe. 'Never mind, Susie. What's going to happen next week anyhow?'

'God knows!'

'I'm sorry, lass. I'll say ner more. I'll go on thinking about my bit o' meat-and-tater pie. We're not dead yet, though I seem to be stiff'ning a bit. Summat'll turn up.'

So they went trudging on, as quiet as the four shadows in their grotesque dance on the pavement, lengthening and dwindling between the street lamps.

CHAPTER FIVE
Long, and Full of Salvage Work

I

'WELL, well!' cried the voice, though softly. 'Well, well!'

'Is it the same?' asked the nurse.

'The very same,' the voice replied. It had lost some of the deep rough burr it had had years ago, this voice, but there was no mistaking it. 'No,' it went on now, 'I'll not do that. Let her have her sleep out.'

Miss Trant, however, had already had her sleep out. She was awake now, although her eyes were still closed and she had not stirred. The sound of that first quiet but startled 'Well!' had drawn her from some deep dreamless place into an upper region of flickering shadows, dreams, and voices. Where was she? The hotel? The hospital? No. The Mirland Nursing Home. And it was Tuesday afternoon. She was back now in full consciousness, though all it offered her at the moment was a quivering brownish space and these two voices. And one of them was his, hardly changed at all.

She opened her eyes, which discovered a world very bright, solid, looking as if it had just been made. He was standing by the door. She was not surprised to see him. She had not been surprised to hear his voice. It was as if she had spent years and years being surprised *not* to see him and hear his voice, and that that state of things had now quietly stopped.

'Hello!' she cried, feebly.

He came forward, smiling. He looked older, of course, but not strangely so. On the contrary, he looked more himself, as if this were the age he had been aiming at when she had known him, years ago. 'Miss Elizabeth Trant,' he said, with deliberation. Nobody else would have said it like that.

'Doctor Hugh McFarlane,' she replied, giving him her hand.

The nurse nodded brightly at the pair of them and departed.

'I thought you were asleep,' he said, sitting down beside her. 'And I didn't mean to disturb you.'

'You recognized me then?'

'I did,' and left it at that. He was just the same. He was capable of leaving the most gigantic gaps in conversation, never dreamt of filling them in with the nearest rubbish.

'How did you know I was here? Did you - read about us in the paper?' For the local paper had been very excited about last Saturday's doings at the Hippodrome.

'No, I never saw a word about it in the paper,' he replied. 'That would be the paper here though, wouldn't it? I only see *The Times* and *Glasgow Herald*, and there wasn't anything in them about it.'

'I should hope not.'

'But I did hear something about it,' he continued, thrashing the thing out in the same old way. 'Then I had to come here to see a patient of mine and saw your name, so I came to see if it was the Miss Elizabeth Trant I knew.'

She could not resist it. 'I thought you would have forgotten all about me by this time,' she murmured.

He shook his head gravely. 'Not at all. I hadn't forgotten you. I recognized you as soon as I came in. You haven't changed much, even with your little accident too. Subnormal now, aren't you? Yes, you would be.'

'I thought I saw you - in a car - the other day,' she told. him. 'One day last week it was, about ten miles out of Gatford. I came to the conclusion that it couldn't be you, but now I think it must have been.'

'Now exactly when was that? Last week, you say. What time of day would it be?' He brought out, quite solemnly, a little pocket-book.

'Afternoon, sometime,' she replied vaguely. 'It was - let me see - you were on the main road going out of Gatford - it seems ages ago now. Oh, it doesn't matter, does it?'

'It must have been last Tuesday, I think,' he said, frowning hard at his little book. 'Today week. I'd called here. Was I driving a red two-seater? I was? Then it was me you saw. Isn't that curious? I wish I'd known you were here.'

Miss Trant hesitated for a moment, evaded his level glance, then said hastily: 'As a matter of fact, we - I - tried to find out if you were here, just to make sure. But your name wasn't in the telephone book. And doctors are always in the telephone book, aren't they?'

'Not if they've just arrived,' he said, smiling at her. 'There hasn't been time to put me in the telephone directory yet. I've just entered into partnership with Doctor Heard - he's a man of some age and is giving up the practice soon - out there at Waterfield on the main road. I shouldn't have come here but I've been doing some work on the parathyroid glands, and that meant being near Masters in London or Hudson here in Gatford. So I came here to work with Hudson. You'll have heard of him?'

'I'm afraid I haven't,' she said, smiling back at him. 'It's terrible, but you people do the most wonderful things and we never hear anything about you.'

He stroked his long bony face. 'I suppose that is so, though I can't complain myself because I haven't done anything wonderful yet. But how did you come to be here? I never knew you had any inclinations towards the stage.'

She laughed. 'I hadn't and I haven't. It's all rather ridiculous, though I must say it doesn't seem very funny just now.' And she told him, briefly, what had happened since her father died. Sometimes he stared at her in blank amazement, and sometimes he gave a little low chuckle. It made her feel as if she were describing a visit to the moon.

'And now,' she concluded, 'don't ask me what I'm going to do, because I don't know.'

'I do. You're going to stay here until that arm's mended and you've had a nice rest and your nerves are quiet again.' He still called them 'nairrves'. He still brought out those huge vowels and smashing consonants, and when he turned his face towards the light there was still that glint of hair about his cheek-bones. 'And if there's anything that must be done, let me do it for you.'

'Oh, I can't worry you with my silly affairs. I'm sure you've plenty to do, too much, as it is.'

'Not at all. I don't say I haven't plenty to do - we're always busy you know - but still an old bachelor like me has time for anything.'

'You haven't married then?'

'No.' He stopped, and fingered his chin. 'Up to now, I seem to have been too busy. It's a thing that takes time, I suppose, getting married.'

'Well, you mustn't call yourself an old bachelor, not to me. You see, I happen to remember you're only two years older than I am, and I don't want to be told I'm old too.'

'Two years older! That's it exactly. Now who'd have thought you would have remembered that!' he cried, lighting up and altogether more animated now. 'You've as good a memory as I have.'

'I remember some things very well.'

'Och, so do I.' He was charging in quite recklessly now, without thinking where he might be going. 'I've never heard a mention of that old rock of Gibraltar without thinking of you - and the Colonel,' he added, hastily.

'Which of us reminds you of Gibraltar?' she inquired, laughing at him. 'Not me, I hope. It must have been my father. I think you were always rather frightened of him.'

'Of the Colonel! Not the least bit. It was you I was frightened of, if you must know.'

'Me!' This was too absurd. A memory of that large, masterful, dogmatic young Scot, setting her right about everything, suddenly invaded her mind. 'I'm sure that's not true. I never knew anybody who bullied me quite so much.'

'Ay, I was raw then, a raw lad.'

Tea came in at that moment. 'I've brought a cup for Doctor McFarlane,' the girl remarked, setting down her tray by the side of the bed.

'Thank you,' said Miss Trant. 'You will stay, won't you? You'll have to pour it out for both of us, I'm afraid. I can't manage it with this arm all tied up.'

If she imagined he would be very awkward and clumsy with the teapot, she was wrong. He did it all very deftly indeed, and she noticed now - and this was a new discovery - that his long bony hands were very finely controlled, sensitive. And then - it came in a flash while she was finishing her first piece of bread-and-butter - she suddenly felt how incredible it was that he should be actually there, the whole enormous lump of him, so tremendously like himself, quietly sharing her tea. And yet one part of her, so small and remote that it could not be said to have a voice, refused to see anything incredible in all this, would not even be faintly surprised, but settled itself down, as if this were the natural order of things. They talked easily now, chiefly about the present, Gatford and The Good Companions, and so forth. The afternoon, itself a pale flower of the early spring, filled the room with washed and delicate light, called out anew the scent of the daffodil and narcissus, and was ecstatically busy with rumours of a fragrant and budding world outside.

'And will you be going on with this - er - stage business?' he asked her. When he saw her smile a little ruefully and shake her head, his face cleared. 'There's nothing wrong with it, of course,' he continued, 'but it seems a daft sort of thing for somebody like yourself to be doing.'

'The moment they can get on without me, I shall give it up,' she confessed. 'It's been - well, fun, if you like. Anyhow, I wouldn't have missed it for anything. But for some time now I've been thinking I ought to give it up. You see, to begin with, it's impossible for me to take it seriously - '

'I should think not,' cried Dr McFarlane heartily, with the air of a man to whom a troupe of pierrots are no more than so many buzzing flies.

'But that's not fair to them, you see. It's their world, their life. I don't want to let them down now. It looked as if everything was going to be splendid. We were making money, and I was getting back all I'd lost. The clever young ones all thought they might get engagements in town, because some big revue man came down on Saturday to see them.'

'Was the row too much for him?'

'Oh no, worse than that. It's a miserable business for them, poor dears - but it's rather funny. I can't help laughing. It seems he came and got mixed up somehow in a dreadful scrimmage in the audience, and Joe, who didn't know who he was and probably didn't care, having thoroughly lost his temper, hit this man terribly hard, so hard that he had to be carried out.'

'Well, well! A knock-out, eh? I wouldn't have thought an actor-laddie could have done that.'

'Yes, but then Joe was once a heavy-weight boxer - in the Navy.'

'Ah!' said Dr McFarlane, who apparently knew something about heavy-weight boxers in the Navy. 'He might well do that then.'

'And now they're all heartbroken, though they pretend not to be when they come here to see me. The young ones feel they have lost their chance, and one of them, Jerningham, seems to have disappeared. Nobody has seen him since Saturday night. One of the older ones - Mr Nunn, the comedian - has his head bandaged up and won't be fit to act for a week or two. And the others don't know what is going to happen to them. We had taken the Hippodrome for another week, but of course we couldn't play in it even if it were fit to use.'

'It certainly isn't that, from what I hear,' he said grimly.

'That's the awful thing,' she told him. 'I'm responsible for all that damage.'

He stared at her in horror and dismay. 'You mean they'll come on to you to pay for all that?'

'I believe so. The Hippodrome people are going to claim it all from me. It's a wicked shame because it wasn't our fault at all, and we've already suffered for it. And just as I thought I should get back most of the money I'd lost, this comes along. Oh, it's a miserable business. And the others are absolutely heartbroken about it. They feel it's their fault, though it isn't at all, of course. It's mine, if it's anybody's - '

'Don't pay a penny piece,' he cried, rising from his chair. Because a man has been working hard on parathyroid glands, and in addition has contrived to remember a girl he once knew on a voyage years ago, that does not mean that he cannot be appalled at the thought of good money being paid out like that. It was a prospect to make hundreds of McFarlanes turn in their graves. It now made this McFarlane stride up and down the room. 'You've heard nothing definite yet?' he asked, finally.

'No, not yet,' she replied, smiling rather wanly. She suddenly felt tired now.

He stopped, looked at her, then quietly sat down again. 'You're tired now, Elizabeth?' he said, not taking his eyes off her face.

It coloured faintly. 'I believe I am.'

'Should I have said "Miss Trant"?'

'No, of course not,' returning his steady look with wide candid grey eyes.

'Too much talking. It's my fault.'

'Then I shall have to report you to Doctor Mason, Hugh. But don't go for a minute. Let me talk a little longer and then I shall feel better. What do you think I ought to do? I had thought of asking my brother-in-law - he's a solicitor in town - to come up and try and straighten it all out for me, but he and Hilda, my sister, are in the South of France. And even if they weren't, somehow I don't want the family here, crowing over me. Then I thought of asking Mr Truby, he's my own solicitor at Cheltenham, to see what he could do, but he's - well, I don't feel he'd be much good. He probably thinks I'm mad.'

'If it's a matter of taking to the law, I don't mean in court, but just being represented, then a local man is what you want, a man who knows what goes on in this town. I know a solicitor here - he's a patient of mine - of the name of Gooch, a fat fellow but sharp as a needle. I'll go and talk to him about it, and do what I can myself at the same time. And all you've got to do is to lie here quietly, not seeing your actor friends too often, just making your mind easy, reading a book or two -' He broke off, and regarded her quizzically. 'Do you still devote yourself to those romances and historical novels you used to like so well?'

'Yes. I don't read quite so many as I used to do - there aren't enough good ones to go on with - but I haven't tired yet.'

'Do you remember my telling you I thought them awful trash? I was raw then, if ever a lad was. I've been ploughing my way through Walter Scott whiles, and there's a great deal of human nature in those Waverley Novels of his. He'd have made a fine general practitioner, Sir Walter would.'

'There! You're coming on, Hugh.'

He gave a short confused laugh. 'No, I'm going on. I'll be looking in tomorrow if I can at all. If not, the next day for certain. That is, if you would like to see me.'

'Of course I should like to see you. I didn't think, though, you'd be able to get here again as early as that. Is - er - your patient here worse?'

'Ay,' he replied, with only the ghost of a twinkle to show that a joke was in progress, 'poor fellow, he seems to have taken a turn for the worse since this afternoon. So he'll need an early return visit.' He rose and took her hand. 'It's been a strange meeting this. I didn't think you'd have remembered.'

'It was clever of you to recognize me at once, like that, when I was asleep too.'

Having brought off one joke, there was no holding him now. 'I won't say I remembered your face, Miss Elizabeth Trant,' he said solemnly, 'but from the way you were lying, the sterno-mastoid muscle was prominent, and I thought I remembered the look of that.'

'What! Where? You don't - Oh, I see. You are absurd. Very well, Doctorrr H-ew McFarrrlane, it was your terrible accent - an' only that - ah remembered. Good-bye, Hugh. And if you can do anything to prevent me from having to throw all my money away here in Gatford, I shall be awfully grateful.'

Looking very grave again, at the thought of money being thrown away, he stood before her and declared with emphasis that he would do something about it. He was wearing a good suit - and was a far smarter figure than the bony young man she had known before - but it wanted brushing in places and there were one or two deplorable little stains and burns here and there. And his tie, of course, was monstrous. But greying hair suited him; he was almost handsome now.

'Fancy Doctor McFarlane being such an old friend!' cried the nurse afterwards. She was removing things very deftly, but as she spoke she kept an eye on her patient's face. Her duties compelled her to see life chiefly in terms of that rickety machine, the body, so it is not surprising that her hobby should have been human interest. Her next 'Fancy!', which was not long in coming, had quite a note of triumph in it. Evidently things were looking up in the Mirland Nursing Home.

II

'You've not had a reply?' cried Susie.

'I have,' Inigo replied, coming into the room. It was some time after eleven on the Wednesday morning. Susie had been dusting her sitting-room, which was also her landlady's parlour, in a fashion that fluctuated between the dreary and the dreamy. Ever since Saturday night, she had felt lost.

'It's not from Monte Mortimer himself,' Inigo went on, speaking rather carefully, as if he thought he was a solicitor or someone of that kind. 'It's from his secretary.'

'That's all the same. Hurry up, idiot, and tell me what he says. You're so *slow*, Inigo.' Then she plomped down into a chair. 'It's a washout, isn't it? I can see it is. Go on, though.'

'It's a letter and from the secretary,' said Inigo, sitting down and taking out the sheet of paper. 'This is what it says: Dear Sir, I have communicated your yesterday's wire to Mr Mortimer, who is away from the office at present, and he requests me, in reply, to tell you to go to the devil. He also requests me to add that any further communication from you or any other member of your troupe will be regarded as coming from there and will not receive any reply whatever. Yours truly, J. Hamilton Levy, Secretary. And that', Inigo added, with a poor attempt at nonchalance, 'is that.'

'Let me have a look at it,' Susie commanded, and then read it through herself. Having done that, she crumpled it fiercely and hurled it into the fire. 'And to think I've been sorry for that - that object - for the last three days! Mean beast! I hope Joe's punch knocked him silly. I don't care, I do.'

'Well, it did, my dear,' said Inigo, 'hence this colossal snub, absolutely. Looks to me as if he's still off duty.'

'I wouldn't have minded so much if he hadn't been so Smart Alecky about it. There's no need for him to try to be funny. His next revue'll need all the gags he can ever think of. Anyhow, he must be a rotten manager or he'd never let a thing like that stop him from getting in some good new talent. If I was running a show, I wouldn't care if I got fifty biffs, I'd engage people who could do something.'

'I'm awfully sorry, Susie,' he began.

'Don't be silly. It's not your fault. It isn't anybody's fault, really, and it certainly isn't yours. It's a washout, that's all, and the best thing I can do is to remember it's twice daily on the pier, or if fine at the pierhead and if wet in the shelter, that's my programme - if I'm lucky, because it's boiling down to that now, when you come to think of it. Hell! Give me a cigarette. No, don't, thanks. I don't want one.'

'You ought to smoke a pipe,' he said, lighting his. 'By the way, I saw Jimmy this morning - '

'Is he better?'

'Practically. Head still hums a bit, and says he's dizzy when he tries to walk about. He won't be fit for work for a week or two. But what I wanted to say was, Mamie Potter's gone.'

'Thank God! She wasn't much good anyhow, and she's brought us nothing but rotten luck. Thinks we're not good enough for her now, I suppose?'

'Something like that. Anyhow, she's gone. And nobody seems to know anything about Master Jerningham.'

'Oh, he's pushed off too, I expect,' said Susie, who was clearly anxious to relieve her feelings. 'He would! He'll look after himself all right - Ai give you mai ward.'

'I dunno. He may turn up again, babbling about his trousers as he did last time. Where was that? Tewborough, wasn't it? Gosh! the holes we've been in, Susie !'

'It's nothing to the hole we're in now, laddie,' she said darkly. 'We're in a mess, busted absolutely - as our sweet young pianist says. There's poor Miss Trant in a nursing home, and though she's sweet about it, she must be fed up to the teeth with the lot of us. They say she'll have to pay for all the damage too. Well, she's had enough of it, you can bet. No more Good Companions for her. That means we shan't have a cent to go on with. If she offered us any money, I wouldn't take it. Not after all she's done and had to pay out.'

'Well, I've got a spot, you know,' he remarked.

'Keep your spot, my child. I'm coming to your part in it soon. Then Potter's gone. That doesn't matter, but still it means we'll have to get another soubrette. Jerry's gone too, and that's really awkward. You wouldn't get another light comedian as good - not for C.P. work - if you advertised till all was blue. Then Jimmy's not fit for work yet. We'd have to put in old Jess as a Yorkshire comedian. Wouldn't he be marvellous! It's all right laughing, but - oh, it's murder. I saw myself up in town by this time, signing contracts like mad, looking for a flat. What a hope! And a week ago I was sniffing at Bournemouth. Bournemouth! It wouldn't look at us now. Two-night stands are all we're fit for, with a return visit to Rawsley the event of the season. Susie Dean. A riot of Sandybay! Front chairs one-and-ten-pence! Patronize the pierrots, girls and boys! Oh, hell - oh! - oh- '

'Susie!' He jumped out of his chair.

She shook her head fiercely, her thick dark bobbed hair swinging. Then she touched his hand for a moment and pushed him back. 'No, sit down, idiot. We're both idiots. I work myself up in the most ghastly way these days. It must be because I'm so excited inside all the time, have been for days.'

'I know,' said Inigo sympathetically. He was sitting down again now, but his hands were stretched out in front of him, as if it was impossible to restrain them from reaching out to her.

'You don't know. You don't know anything about it.' She was smiling mistily. 'O lord! where's my handkerchief? Wait a minute. Now then, I've not finished yet. There's you.'

'Me! What about me? I'm all right.'

'You're not. To begin with, you're absurd, and always will be. No, don't start saying you're not, because that's not what I'm going to talk about. You went up to Felder and Hunterman's on Saturday, they heard your stuff, and what's his name - you know - '

'Pitsner?'

'That's right. Well, Pitsner wanted your songs, didn't he, just as that ape Monte Mortimer did?'

'He did. I won't say he was keen, because I don't believe that man was ever keen about anything. He's got a sort of "But she is in her grave, and oh the difference to me!" look about him, Master Pitsner. Still, he wanted them all right.'

'Well, there you are. Pitsner didn't get a punch from Joe, you know.'

'True,' Inigo murmured. He knew what was coming and was hoping to dodge it. 'Pitsner didn't. But I've no doubt at all that something could be arranged, if you feel he ought to have one too. He could come down here for it, or perhaps one of us might go up there - '

'Don't be funny,' she told him wearily. 'You're not bad until you start being funny. Then you make me feel sick. Let's talk sense. You know he'll take those songs like a shot. And you know - or you ought to know, by this time - you can make bags of money up there turning out these things. Well, that's where you're going.'

'You mean - I ought to clear out too?'

'Of course! The sooner the better!'

'But I don't want to.'

'I dare say,' she cried. 'Because I'm not going, eh? I know your little game. You want to stay with us, going the old round, thumping out the old stuff, and looking at me over the top of the piano with the love-light in your eyes. For her sake alone he - thingumy-bobbed - renounced wealth and fame. Love was his guiding star. Came the dawn. Yeogh !' Here she gave a very un-ladylike imitation of acute sickness. 'What do you think you are - a little hero from Hollywood? Out you go, laddie. Honestly, you don't want to go trailing round another year - Rawsley, Dotworth, Sandybay, Winstead, Haxby, Middleford, and Tewborough - my God!'

'Oh, I don't know,' said Inigo, examining the bowl of his pipe with unnecessary interest. 'Seeing England and all that. On t'road - as our friend, Master Oakroyd, says. It's the sort of experience that might be very useful to a man of letters - '

'Man of letters!' Susie made a number of uncomplimentary noises.

Inigo flushed and kicked out a foot at nothing in particular. 'Shut up, Susie. I will write something decent some day, you see if I don't.'

Her dark eyes rested on his sulky boy's face for a moment, and lost their hard brilliance. 'Sorry! I don't know anything about it. I only know about silly songs, and you're marvellously clever at them. Anyhow, the point is - no self-sacrifice stuff. You've got to clear out of this mess.'

'But you see, there's no self-sacrifice stuff about it,' he explained quietly and slowly, while he examined, with what was apparently strong distaste, a large photogravure bearing the title *On the Road to Gretna Green*. 'I want to be where you are, as I've told you before.'

To this Susie made no reply. She looked into the fire, and they were both silent for a minute or two. 'But after all,' she said, finally, 'if you want to do something for me, you ought to clear out and get up to London. Look what you did last Saturday.'

'That's true,' he cried, brightening. 'That's the place to work it from.' He paused, thinking it over. 'I don't know, though. I'd have a pop at it, of course, but last Saturday's effort was gigantic cheek, absolutely, and I don't know if I could drag out any more Monte Mortimers. Still, you could slip up, couldn't you?'

She nodded, then frowned at the fire. 'It's a mess. Everything's got into a mess. I expect you must think sometimes I'm an awful little hard nut, always on the make. No, listen,' as he began to protest. 'But something nags at me inside telling me to get on quick. It's a sort of feeling I have about my father and mother. I've told you about it before, haven't I? As if it was because they had such a rotten time. And I feel I can't wait long. It's all right people saying "Oh, you're young. Plenty of time!" - that sounds all right - but there isn't. If nothing happens, I'll get stale soon. I know I will. I oughtn't to, but there you are. I expect I haven't the guts to keep on and keep it up.'

'That's rot. I see what you mean, absolutely, but it's rot about not having the guts. You've guts enough for ten.'

She laughed, came over to him, and twisted a finger in his lock of hair. 'Awful, isn't it? We sound like a butcher's shop. Let's talk about something else.'

'By the way,' he began. 'Ow! That hurts. Look here, creature, if you want to know what to do with your hands - '

'I don't, thank you,' letting him go.

'Pity,' he grumbled. 'However, I was going to say, I've just remembered that Saturday night was your benefit.'

'You don't mean to say you'd forgotten that?'

'No, not exactly. What I meant was, I'd forgotten you got the money. How much was it, and what have you done with it, and so on and so forth?'

'I haven't done anything with it, idiot. Matter of fact, I don't know exactly how much it all comes to yet, but anyhow I'm not taking it. Of course not, don't be silly! How can I? Here's Miss Trant going to be run in for hundreds and hundreds. I can't possibly take anything.'

'No, I suppose not,' he replied, poking his face meditatively with the stem of his pipe. 'Gosh! I'd forgotten about that.'

'You're lucky! That's all part of the hellish mess. I'm going to see Miss Trant this afternoon. I think I'll ask Mrs Joe to come too. At times like this, us girls must stick together, my child.'

They looked at one another, laughed, then carefully explained that they were really very miserable. And indeed they were about as depressed as it was possible for two such lively, youthful, optimistic souls to be. It was all the worse because there was nothing for them to do.

'Well,' said Inigo at length, after wandering vaguely about the room, 'I suppose I must be thinking about a spot of food. I'm having lunch out somewhere. Coming with me?'

'I don't feel like facing Ye Jollie Dutche,' she told him. 'I think I'll tea-and-egg it here. Hello, what's that?'

'That, my dear,' he replied, at the window, 'is a car. And it's stopping here.'

'Let me have a look. I knew it was. I felt it was. I've seen that car before somewhere. Something's going to happen, Inigo. It is, I know it is.'

'What?'

'I don't know. Come away from the window or you might spoil it. No, we must pretend now we don't care, else it might stop happening at the last minute. I've always felt that, haven't you? There you are, a knock.'

'Probably the doctor or somebody like that.'

'It can't be. I'm sure it isn't.'

And it wasn't. The landlady's head appeared and announced that a shover had called with a message for Miss Dean and for Mr Jollifant too if he was here, which he was as her own eyes could see for themselves, and she would send it in to give it to them.

Susie recognized the chauffeur at once, and we recognize him too, having met him once on the pier at Sandybay and then again, one Sunday afternoon, outside Hicklefield. Yes, it is Lawley, Lady Partlit's chauffeur.

'And you're to come round to the Victoria Midland Hotel for lunch, Miss,' he explained. 'And you, sir, too. I was going round to your rooms, but this has saved me the trouble. And I had to tell you that it was specially important, and they would be expecting you as soon as you could get round.'

'They?' cried Susie. 'Who are the others? Yes, we'll come, won't we, Inigo? But what's it all about?'

'Well,' said Lawley, grinning, 'it's a bit of a surprise, Miss. You'll soon see.'

Susie looked at him a moment with widening eyes, then flashed a glance that might have meant a thousand things at Inigo, and bolted, screaming as she went: 'Back in a minute!'

'Not so blowy as it has been,' remarked Lawley coolly to Inigo, 'but still on the cold side, if you ask me.'

III

They both jumped and spoke, but Susie's cry was a second quicker than Inigo's.

'Married!'

'Yes, quite a surprise, isn't it?' said the lady who had once been a Partlit. She glittered and jangled and flashed before their startled eyes; her little round mouth looked as if it would never be shut again; her big staring eyes were now dancing with happiness; and though she still resembled a cockatoo, neither cage nor jungle had ever seen a cockatoo so excited, so triumphant. 'And only this very morning. What a rush, my dear! I haven't breathed since Saturday, that horrible, horrible night. Yes, I've heard all about it, such a business! If I'd been a second later getting him away, I really think I should have died. At the time, of course, I could only think about him, but I've thought about you all since and felt so sorry. And poor Miss Trant too! But aren't you going to - or is that too late?'

'Of course we are,' cried Susie. 'It's lovely, and I'm sure you'll both be marvellously happy.'

'Absolutely,' muttered Inigo, who was still rather dazed.

'Now isn't that nice! Of course it's taken you completely by surprise. I knew it would,' the bride rattled on. 'And now, my dear, you must be ready for lunch. I think I'll ring the bell. He should be here any minute now. Telephoning, you know. We haven't had a single moment to spare since Monday morning, it's been such a rush. There he is, I think.' She flew to the door. 'Here we are, darling, and they were both so surprised - I knew they would be. Isn't it amusing?'

Susie was the first again. 'Marvellous, Jerry!' She was busy shaking his hand. 'I'm so glad. I hadn't any idea what was happening.'

For one wild moment, Inigo, who had not yet come to his senses, saw himself stepping forward to congratulate Jerningham on becoming Lord Partlit or something of that kind. It seemed incredible that Partlit should be merged into Jerningham. 'Many happy returns,' he stammered. 'I mean - you know - best wishes and all that.'

'Tharnks, Susie. Tharnks, Inigo,' said Jerningham gravely and without the flicker of an eyelid. He was more dignified, more beautiful, than ever, but his accent was also more fantastic. That alone had been unsettled by these momentous events; strange at any time, it was now wildly alien; and every sentence he spoke heaped up the mangled syllables. 'Glard you could cem on to lernch.'

'And we've got news for them, haven't we, darling?' cried his wife, who looked even more excited and happy now that he was here, as if there had been just a slight possibility before that he might never come back from the telephone.

'I should think you have news,' said Susie, smiling and being tremendously woman-to-woman.

'Oh, but that's not all, my dear, I assure you. Lots of surprises for you today. Isn't Mr Memsworth coming, darling? Lunch is ready.'

'Raight, he won't be lorng,' replied Jerry. 'He's jerst petting through a call to tawn.'

Susie glanced sharply at Inigo. 'What have we here?' this glance inquired, but did not stay for an answer. A waiter arrived with cocktails, and for the next few minutes they all sipped and chatted, with one eye on the door. The table was laid for five, so evidently Mr Memsworth was to be of the party. It had quite a festive appearance, though the room itself, the only small private dining-room in the hotel, seemed to have given up hope of provincial social life about 1892. But what the Victoria Midland Hotel could do, it was obviously about to do for Mr and Mrs Jerningham.

At last, Mr Memsworth made his entrance. It happened that there was a waiter on each side of the door when he appeared, but there ought to have been at least twenty, to say nothing of an orchestra. Mr Memsworth, however, contrived at once to create an atmosphere in which two waiters looked like twenty. The moment he stalked in, with his 'Sorry to keep you waiting' in a rich baritone that went straight to the back of the dress-circle, Susie realized in a flash it was the Memsworth, the great Memsworth, one greater than Monte Mortimer, and known in the profession as 'The Emperor' or, more familiarly, perhaps ironically, as 'The Emp.' This was partly a tribute to his managerial powers, for he was the greatest despot in the musical-comedy world, and partly a tribute to his actual presence, his terrific style. Unlike most manager-producers, Mr Memsworth had been an actor himself, having for years played 'leads' in musical comedy. Those were the days when the scene of every musical comedy was set in some vague Central European state, when every leading juvenile was a prince in hussar uniform and every principal comedian a baron with a red nose, a squeaky voice, and a passion for ladies' maids, when every stage was noisy with heel-clicking, hussar choruses, and stentorian announcements of 'His Highness, Prince Michael of Slavonia'. Night after night, year after year, Mr Memsworth had been some Highness or other, with the result that the manner had grown upon him; he could not divest himself of kingship. And now that he was a manager-producer - and a very successful one, having a sound knowledge of the public taste, an eye for talent, and a very good head for business - he still made princely exits and entrances, patted people on the back as if he were bestowing an order upon them, and laughed in that hearty manner only possible to great public personages. The fashion in musical comedy had changed - and he had been one of the first to recognize the fact - but Slavonia, with its soldiers and soubrettes, its waltz-time and impossible scenery, lived on in him. And now, as he came forward to the luncheon table, it seemed strange that he was not followed by two files of baritone dragoons.

Susie nearly choked when she was introduced - or rather, presented - to him. She knew all about him. The Emp. himself - here in Gatford! But then, of course, Lady Partlit - Mrs Jerningham - had something to do with West End theatres. She remembered that talk in the hotel outside Hicklefield. Those were Memsworth's theatres too. It was obvious now. Jerry had married her so that he could star in Memsworth's productions - something like that. 'And you're on in this, Susie,' she told herself, nearly bursting with excitement.

Inigo was quite cool, for the simple reason that he did not know who Memsworth was, except that he seemed the nearest thing one could ever get in this lower world to Prince Florizel of Bohemia.

They had not been sat down long when Mr Memsworth looked gravely from one to the other of them, and, raising a fork, commanded silence. 'Miss Dean, Mr Jollifant,' he began, in deep, solemn tones, 'the other night I had the pleasure of seeing your show here.'

'When?' gasped Susie.

'On Saturday night,' he told her.

'And I was there too,' the bride put in. 'Wasn't I, darling? And a terrible night it was too, my dear.'

'It was you in the box,' cried Susie.

'Of course it was. It was all going to be such a nice surprise. Mr Memsworth had to see me on business, and I said to him, "You must come and see these clever people," and he laughed - this was on the telephone - you did laugh, didn't you, Mr Memsworth?'

'I believe I was rather amused,' the Emperor admitted. 'But then who wouldn't have been, dear lady? I mean, in my position. New talent in Gatford is not an impossibility - there are no impossibilities in our profession - but it's - er - an improbability. I think you'll agree with me there.'

'Absolutely,' said Inigo heartily. He was enjoying Mr Memsworth and so thought that this was the least he could do.

'But though I laughed,' the great man continued, very impressively, 'I came, I saw - and I was conquered.'

Inigo gave a sudden gurgle. 'I'm sorry. But I couldn't help thinking about Monte Mortimer, who came and saw and was conquered too.'

'And I hope he's still feeling it,' said Susie.

The others stared at them.

'Mai dar Jollifant,' said Jerningham, raising his exquisite eyebrows, 'whort is all this about?'

'Ah, Monte,' the Emperor murmured. 'So you know Monte, do you? A very able fellow, very able - in his own line of business.'

'You see,' cried Susie, 'he was there on Saturday too - to have a look at us.'

'What!' Susie and Inigo began explaining together, and contrived to tumble out the story between them.

Mr Memsworth roared with laughter. It was as good as a baritone solo. 'But do you mean to say he was laid out?' he demanded. 'He was? Right under my nose too. My dear people, I'd have given pounds, pounds, to have seen it. Monte! On the jaw, I think you said?' The room shook with his imperial mirth. 'Waiter, the champagne. We must drink to this, we really must. Oh, why didn't I know at the time. You made him come up and then he was knocked out. Monte! What a story! Next time I see Monte at the club, I shall go up to him, look him in the eyes, and then simply say one word - Gatford. Monte will be at my mercy. Why, if this story got about - !' Mr Memsworth raised his eyes, his hands, towards Heaven, and then drank some champagne. 'But, Miss Dean, Mr Jollifant, this has its serious side,' he went on, solemn again now. 'Are you tied up with him in any way?'

'He told us to go to the devil,' said Susie. And Inigo explained about the letter they had received that very morning.

'What a rude man!' cried Mrs Jerningham.

'It's the Oriental,' said Mr Memsworth, 'the Oriental, dear lady. Monte is not a sportsman - never was, never will be. I know him well, in business and outside it. A very able fellow, as I said before - I don't know anybody who can put on a revue of the medium-class, semi-intimate, semi-spectacular - but not a gentleman.' He turned to Susie and Inigo. 'So that leaves you free. No more Monte! Well, I don't mind admitting that I think you're lucky. I don't say that Monte couldn't have done something for you. He could have done a great deal. He's made one or two good people. But I can do more - believe me, much more. I can put you - there.'

'And will, won't you, Mr Memsworth?' said Mrs Jerningham, who was evidently not only happy herself but anxious that everybody else should be happy. A bird of Paradise, not a cockatoo.

'I will try, if these - if your friends here - will allow me,' he replied majestically. 'As I say, I saw the show on Saturday, and to my astonishment, I discovered that here - playing in Gatford - in a troupe whose name is entirely unknown to me - are three young people of real, quite undoubted talent.' He paused, holding them with his eye. 'First, a young comedienne, who can sing, who can dance, who can act, who has - and this is the great thing - charm and personality. If she has ambition, as I'm told she has - '

'I'm bursting with it.' Susie told him breathlessly.

He bowed. 'So I believe. That's very important, more important every day. Must have ambition, must be ready to work hard, to put your profession first. Society and the journalists are ruining so many of our young ladies. They achieve a little success - and then, what happens? They go here, they go there; their names, their photographs, are in all the papers - very good publicity, of course - I don't object to it; but they don't work.'

'That's true, Mr Memsworth,' said Susie eagerly. 'But I'm ready to work till I drop, honestly I am. I'm not doing it for fun. I was - was born in the profession.'

'That's what we want,' he said. 'As a matter of fact, I was myself. Now, second - I found a juvenile lead.' He bowed to Jerningham, who blushed for once in his cool unblushing life. 'I know all about him now, so I needn't say any more. But third - I found a young composer who can write songs that get across and stay there,' He turned to Inigo. 'Do you think you can write some more like those numbers I heard?'

'I should think so,' replied Inigo carelessly. He was beginning to feel wonderlandish again, what with Mr Memsworth and the champagne. 'Any amount.'

The great man looked at him in grave astonishment, in which there was perhaps a touch of awe. Here was a very extraordinary young man, who was not at all impressed by the fact that he was about to be taken up by Memsworth. 'My word, my boy!' he ejaculated.

'He can too, Mr Memsworth,' cried Susie. 'Inigo's marvellous. He can just knock them off like anything.'

'Thart is so,' said Jerry, with lofty kindness. 'You can barnk on Jollifant, Mr Memsworth. You've nobody writing nambers for you to tech him.'

'And they eat them, even in the stupidest places,' Susie continued. 'You could see that the other night, couldn't you? But p'raps you couldn't. I was forgetting that wretched rotten business, busting up the show.'

'Ah yes. Curious, that, very curious. I've not seen anything like it for years.' Mr Memsworth looked thoughtful. 'No, nothing as bad for twenty years. I don't know what you people made of it, but to me it was obvious, quite obvious. Hooliganism, of course - but organized hooliganism. Somebody must have paid them to do that. The house in general was very enthusiastic. I saw that. Then why should these fellows kick up such a row, and go on doing it? Paid to do it. There for the purpose. I don't know who employed them, I don't know why they were employed, all I say is they were employed, paid to do it. I've seen it happen before, though not lately. I've had a lot of experience. You take my word for it. Organized rowdyism.'

'I'm beginning to think that, too,' said Susie, 'and I know that Mrs Joe does. I shall tell Miss Trant, don't you think so, Inigo, Jerry?'

'Meanwhile - to business,' said Mr Memsworth, looking as if he were about to give his loyal subjects a Constitution. 'I take it, then, Mr Jollifant, you're free to work for me?'

Inigo thought so, but put in a word about Felder and Hunterman.

'That can be arranged,' and Mr Memsworth waved a hand. 'Leave that to me. What I want you to do is to see Julian Jaffery, who's supposed to be doing the music for my new show or at least putting some new stuff into it. We should want those numbers I heard the other night and one or two others, and then you can set to work on another thing I'm planning. I've got most of the book. And I want you, Miss Dean, to rehearse a big part - in which you'll be playing opposite Mr Jerningham here, and you can work together - in this show that's nearly ready. You can take Mr Jollifant's numbers that you're doing now straight into it, though I may get one of my librettists to alter the words a bit.' He had in hand, it seemed, a splendid new musical comedy, that bore the provisional title *The Mascot Girl*. It had begun as a French farce, but had been taken to Vienna, where it was transformed into an operetta, which was entirely rewritten in New York as a song-and-dance show; and now, the last vestiges of the original plot having been removed, new words and music were being introduced so that it could blossom out again as an English comedy. Mr Memsworth told them all about it or at least contrived to suggest that he was telling them all about it, for there was not really much to tell. It was obvious that the thing would only begin to have a shape at the rehearsal. Nevertheless, it appeared that Susie and Jerry would have very important parts in it, and that Inigo's tunes would soon be delighting or worrying the whole country. In short, their fortunes were made, their ships almost in harbour.

'No,' cried Susie, her eyes dancing, 'I really couldn't eat or drink anything else. If I did I should be sick, I'm so excited.'

'Sweet!' murmured Mrs Jerningham, and patted her hand.

'But it's - it's - oh, golly! - it's marvellous. Isn't it, Inigo? Don't sit there, pretending you don't care tuppence. Isn't it marvellous? Aren't you dizzy?'

'Absolutely,' said Inigo, who was in fact a trifle dizzy.

'I don't mind saying it's jerst whort I've warnted,' Jerningham admitted. And he gave his wife such a sudden, unexpected and unasked for, altogether beautiful smile that no doubt she felt dizzy too. For smiles like that, she would have bought him whole theatres.

Mr Memsworth, whom the champagne had made more benevolent and regal than ever, so that he sat there like another Haroun al Raschid, smiled upon them all, and then explained to Susie and Inigo that they had better clear things up in Gatford and then report to him in town if possible in two days' time, and on Monday at the latest. Then he would have contracts ready and everything.

Susie stared at him in a happy dream: 'Oh, Mr Memsworth, don't disappear or anything, will you? I feel as if I'm sitting in my digs making this up, just to pass the afternoon. In a minute I shall wake up.'

'It's so very nice for you, isn't it?' Mrs Jerningham cooed.

'Nice! It's - oh, I can't begin. And you've done it, Lady - I mean, Mrs Jerningham, and I'm so glad you've married Jerry and I hope you'll both be happy for ever and ever.' And she flung out her hands, and Jerry shook one, with a solemn 'Tharnks, Susie,' while his bride squeezed the other, saying: 'You know, we've to go up to town tonight. All such a rush, isn't it? But I do adore a rush, don't you, my dear?'

'And this,' said Inigo, who had just accepted and lit a large cigar so that he felt almost vulgarly opulent already, 'is the end - the very end - of The Good Companions.'

Susie's face fell. 'Yes, it is, isn't it? I'd forgotten that. Yes, it's all right laughing, but it's rather sad, really. Why can't we have one nice thing without having to give up another nice thing?'

'That, my dear lady, is Life.' Mr Memsworth did this magnificently.

'I suppose it is, but it's beastly all the same,' said Susie. 'Oh, and what about the others, Jimmy and the Joes? What are they going to do now, poor darlings? Can't you do anything for them, Mr Memsworth? They're awfully good, really. You didn't get a chance to see them properly the other night.'

He shook his head. 'I don't doubt it. I wish I could do something for them. I'd like to oblige you, Miss Dean, and I like to see people in our profession sticking to their friends. But these others - sorry - not in my line. Too old, you know. Much too old even for the chorus. I might possibly find a very small part in something or other for the little comedian, but really I think he'd be far better off in his own concert-party work. And the others certainly would. Sorry, but still, they'll find work all right. Can't they carry on this present show?'

'Nathing left in it,' said Jerry. 'All the real tarlent gone.'

'No, that's not fair, Jerry,' Susie told him. 'But there wouldn't be enough of them to do anything with it. I mean, it couldn't be the same show, now that half of it has gone. Oh, it's a shame. They'll have to find work with another C. P. and it won't be easy getting into a good one 'cos the season's nearly beginning.'

Mr Memsworth looked thoughtful. 'The season - the season,' he mused. 'Now that reminds me of something that was said to me the other day. What was it? Ah, I have it. Bellerby, that's the man. Bellerby used to do a good deal of work for me at one time, and I ran across him the other day in town and he told me he was getting a resident concert party together for some resort or other, Eastbourne, Hastings, one of those places, you know. In fact, he asked me if I could recommend him a few decent people.'

'Oh, but that would be marvellous! Just what they want! Do you think this man would take them?' Susie asked.

'A word from me,' said Mr Memsworth, and a wave of his hand told them the rest.

'But how are you - I mean - will you write to him or something?'

'Mr Jollifant, just touch that bell, will you?' the great man commanded. This - his manner informed them - was his way of doing things, and they must now keep their eyes and ears open. The bell brought a waiter, and the waiter was told to bring Mr Nurris, who it appeared was Mr Memsworth's secretary. Mr Nurris was a pallid young man with darkish horn-rimmed spectacles. 'Look here, Nurris,' cried his employer. 'Can you remember Bellerby's address? You remember him? South coast somewhere. You can, eh? Then take a wire. Wait a minute, though. I must be out of this town by five. It's no use him wiring back to me. Who'll act for these four people?' he asked Susie and Inigo.

They gave him Jimmy's name and address. Thereupon, Mr Memsworth dictated a telegram of theatrical dimensions, recommending one comedian, one conjurer-banjoist, one baritone and feed, and contralto, all experienced C. P. artistes, and asking for terms, dates, and other details, to be wired to Jimmy Nunn. 'And if that doesn't bring a reply by tonight, you may take it from me that Bellerby is either drunk or missing or both. Get it off at once, Nurris.'

'And now,' said Susie to Inigo, after they had shaken hands all round and declared how splendid it all was and taken their leave, 'it looks as if we're all going to be fixed up. Aren't you excited? Honestly, I'm nearly ill. I want to rush up to everybody and tell them all about it. Just think of us sitting there this morning - me, anyhow - giving it all up as a bad job. And then this comes along. Wouldn't it be ghastly if I got run over or something now?' She squeezed his arm hard, then let it go and laughed.

'You've forgotten two people,' he told her, after she had finished happily babbling. 'One is Miss Trant.'

'I'm going to see her now, to tell her all the news. And I'm sure she won't mind a bit. I believe she'll be glad. And I shall tell her to keep all my benefit money, to help to pay the damages they say they're going to claim at the measly Hippodrome. It'll all help, won't it?'

'A spot,' he replied. 'Those damages are going to be a nasty piece of work. I don't like the idea of poor Miss Trant being left here, with a bad arm and a bill a mile long, while we trot off to town to make our fortunes.'

'If you put it like that - and I must say, Inigo, you've a nasty way of putting things - it sounds nearly as bad as murder. But it'll be all right. Everything's going to be all right for everybody, I feel sure it is. I've felt so all along. The trouble about you, my laddie, is you've no confidence - '

'Well, by gosh! I like that,' he protested, 'when it's only a few hours since you were moping away - '

'Don't talk such rot, Inigo. That's the worst of you. You talk such a lot of rot. It must be because you're - what is it? - an author - no, something worse than that - a man of let-ters. No, don't start being cross now, or you'll spoil everything. Who's the other one I've forgotten?'

'Our Mr Oakroyd.'

'Jess lad. So I had,' she cried. 'What a shame! I haven't seen him for days. Have you? Oh, something nice *must* happen to him, it really must. We can't all just leave him, alone with his bag of tools and his little basket thing. Do you remember his little basket trunk? Wasn't it sweet? He's been a bit broody lately too, so p'raps he wants a change like the rest of us. Well, I'm sure it'll be easy to find him a job. We could take him with us, or the others might be able to find him something if they get that resident job, or Miss Trant might want him to stay with her.'

'Why, what could she give him to do? What's she going to do herself anyhow?'

'Oh, I don't know. Don't be so silly and impatient, young man. Well, this is where we part. I'm going to see Miss Trant. I don't know what she'll think about me. Do I look all right, because honestly I feel tight, though I only had one glass of that champagne? And you run along and write another song or two, just to keep your hand in. No, run away. Isn't it marvellous? See you soon.'

'When?'

'Tonight - perhaps.'

He watched her dart across the road and then trip away down the other side, so eager, so happy, like a girl in a shining fairytale. It almost hurt him to see her like that. Something old, unreasonable, stirred apprehensively inside him - a little Inigo that had once looked up from his bone and his bride to see the trampling mastodon blotting out the sky. Then he grinned at himself and walked away.

IV

Once more we discover Mrs Joe in her sitting-room, surrounded by the brown cotton-woolly moors and glens that haunted the imagination of Mrs Pennyfeather's uncle. Mrs Joe is still knitting that mysterious garment, which is now more complicated and untidier than ever. She had knitted steadily through these dark idle days, and it looks as if there is a danger of her knitting herself inside this pink monster and having to be rescued with a pair of shears. We have never pretended that she was young but now, as she sits there, working away, she looks older than she did. In that mask of mingled dignity and simple foolishness, there has been a recent invasion of fine lines; her face begins to droop and sag. This past week she has suffered as an artiste, a wife, and a mother - for though George is safe on Denmark Hill, he has to be paid for, for his passion for playing football in side-streets with a little india-rubber ball is creating a terrible boot problem. No doubt she is thinking about these things, the bewildering mechanics of life, as she stares into the microscopic fire, itself evidence enough of the Brundit new economic policy. For a few minutes, during which we shall do well to look upon her with kindness, for very soon, this very night in fact, she is going her way and we are going ours and the acquaintance is at an end, she sits and stares and weaves the monstrous mesh. Then she starts up. Somebody has burst into the room. It is Susie.

Susie takes a deep breath, plucks off her hat, and flings it anywhere, takes another deep breath, and falls into a chair.

'You did give me a Start, my dear,' Mrs Joe tells her, reproachfully. 'I wondered what on earth it could be.'

And now Susie begins: 'Talk about news! My dear, I'm simply bursting with 'em. Jerry's married Lady Partlit, the woman I told you about, who sent the bouquet, and I've seen them both, had lunch with them, and Mr Memsworth, the Emperor, you know, the musical-comedy man, he was there too, and we're all going to London and Jerry and I are going to have parts, really fat parts, in a new show he's doing, and Inigo's going to write the music, and Mr Memsworth's wired to a man who's getting up a resident C.P. somewhere - '

'Stop it, child, stop it,' Mrs Joe shrieks. 'You're putting me in a Maze, with your Lady Partridges and Emperors. I don't know whether I'm sitting in this room or where I am. Now just calm yourself down and get your breath and begin at the beginning and let me take it all in.'

'Well, you see - '

'But, Susie, my dear, you're not teasing me, are you? I mean, you're not just making it all up. I couldn't bear that just now. Some other time, perhaps, it would be just a little fun and frolic between ourselves - nobody can say I don't like a little joking in a friendly way - but just now, what with all things being at Sixes and Sevens, no, worse than that, if you count in the injuries and loss of salaries, to say nothing of future engagements, that is, whether there'll be any at all and if so, where - I really couldn't bear it. So don't tell me anything you're making up, will you?'

'Making it up! I couldn't make it up. Nobody could. Just you listen and don't say a word.' After which, Mrs Joe does listen, entranced, to a very full account of the lunch.

'Did you ever!' cried Mrs Joe. 'I never did. There's your Chance, come at last, you might say, when hope had fled. Doesn't it show you? My words, it does.' She is almost aghast at this revelation of her prophetic powers. 'There was I, on Saturday, saying to you when you told me that Mortimer man was there, "What did I tell you? Here's your Chance, come to you, without asking, in Gatford." And then when nothing came of it and the things I've said to Joe about what he did that night really won't bear thinking of, not in cold blood - when nothing came of it, I could have slapped myself for Leading You On. "You've only gone and made it worse, you silly creature," I said to myself. And yet something told me. Try as I might, it still told me. And now here you are, with a Bigger Chance. And it had to come, even if it took a marriage no more expected than the Man in the Moon to do it, you might say. It - it - a thing like this -makes you ask yourself, Where Are We? - What Are We? - if you see what I mean.' She loses herself in these profundities for a moment or two. Then she throws aside all her knitting and needles and balls of wool. 'I'm glad. I'm very very glad, my dear. I know it means breaking up and starting afresh some - where else for us, with the season so near too, but I'm still glad, just for your own sake, my dear.' And she leans forward and kisses her young friend's flushed face.

'But, you stupid, I've news for you, too,' Susie points out.

'Anything I'm sure will be welcome,' Mrs Joe replies. Then she adds, a trifle wistfully: 'There hasn't been anything said about us, has there?'

'Of course there has. That's what I'm trying to tell you.' And out it comes, to delight Mrs Joe.

'Though,' she is careful to say, 'as things go in the ordinary way - and unless Luckiness has set in all round - it's only a Shot in the Dark so far. A manager says he wants artistes for a resident season at one of our best resorts. He says it once. Well and good! He may say it twice.

Twice is quite possible. But after that, he's not going to say it any more - and why? Because he's got the artistes. They flocked in, my dear, flocked. They don't need to be told twice. You do see what I mean, don't you? He told Mr Memsworth about this some days ago - perhaps a week ago, perhaps longer - and if he's told other people, he's already had the choice of a hundred. To ask for artistes for a good resident season,' she adds solemnly, 'is like - well, you might as well ask for haystacks for a needle.'

'Oh, he may not have booked anybody,' Susie remarks, rather carelessly. 'Anyhow, we'll soon see. He was told to wire a reply to Jimmy.'

'Joe's over there now. Went to discuss the situation, and so I told him, "Very well, but if it's to be a discussion, stay in the rooms and have something in. Send Out for a bottle or two of beer and leave it at that, and don't go discussing on licensed premises, because that's how the money goes." That's a thing to watch when you're married, my dear. Always get him to Send Out for something and do his discussing at home.'

Susie laughs. 'I'll remember that, though it doesn't matter because I don't intend ever to get married.'

'Don't tell me, because I know how you feel. I was just the same at your age. But then - all of a sudden, before you can say Jack Robinson - it comes over you.'

'I think I know somebody it's coming over now,' Susie tells her confidentially. 'And that's Miss Trant.'

'No!'

'Yes. I've just seen her. And I found him there, the great him. Didn't I ever tell you about that Scotch doctor she's been quietly in love with for ages?' To make sure of the matter, she tells her now. 'And there he was the day,' she concludes, employing what passes in theatrical circles for a good Scots accent, 'looking into herrr eyes and callin' herrr Eleezabeth. He's verra tall an' verra bony an' verra seerious, but wi' a nice kind face. An' if he's not proposin' marritch the morn's morn an' if she's no gladly acceptin' him, ah'll go an' eat ma best bonnet. Hoots, woman, its a - oh, I can't do any more, but anyhow there they are, falling in love all over again like billy-oh, and blushing away every time they look at one another. And Miss Trant pretends to be very worried about what we're all going to do, and about the show busting up, and about all this money she may have to pay out, but she doesn't care a damn, really. I could see it in her eye. What she's thinking about now is her Doctorr McFarlane, ye ken. And good luck to her, the darling, I say.'

'So do I, indeed I do,' Mrs Joe reflects for a moment. 'It's a noble profession, though I must say I could never fancy one of them. Don't you feel that too, my dear? I mean, as soon as you said anything to keep them in their place a bit, they'd Say, "Let me look at your tongue", and then where would you be? Besides, think of being married to a man who knew everything that was going on inside you, all about your liver and everything! You'd never be able to look him in the face. I remember a doctor - well, he wasn't quite a doctor but he was going to be one - a medical student, you know - and he was very attached to me, I couldn't keep him away - this was before I met Joe, long before, when I first went on the stage - and he was very good-looking and most amusing company, but one Sunday night, when he'd had a little too much - we'd been out to Richmond, I remember, and it was a very hot day - and he told me what he'd been doing to a rabbit - it was a dead rabbit, but still - well, I never fancied him after that. I didn't like the look in his eye. But Miss Trant, I dare say, is different. You feel - don't you, my dear? - she wouldn't care about a thing like that. It's all Temperament.'

But now there are noises off. Enter three gentlemen, carrying bottled ale.

'Has Susie told you?' Joe roars at his wife. 'Well, Jimmy's just had a wire. We've just left him.' He rubs his hands and shows her a long slow delighted grin.

'What does he say then?' Mrs Joe demands, impatiently. 'Don't stand there, without a word. Of all the aggravating men, Joe - !'

'Wants to see us on Monday,' Mr Morton Mitcham tells her. 'Terms are good. Open middle of April, clean run through until end of September. Rehearse beginning of April, on full pay. And if it's the same Bellerby I played with in Nought Six, he's a gentleman.'

'Bit of your doing, this, Susie,' Joe roars again. 'I've heard all about you. After this, up among the stars so high, eh? Shan't be allowed to talk to you after this week.'

'Don't be an idiot, Joe. But honestly, isn't it marvellous?'

'Slendiferous! And what do you say to me for giving that other fellow a tap on the jaw? Don't forget us, will you?'

'As if I should!'

He gives her a gigantic hug. Mrs Joe and Mr Mitcham explain to one another, with the ease and rapidity of veterans, the advantages of a resident season on the South coast. Inigo discovers some tumblers on the sideboard and opens the beer. The gentlemen immediately fall to drinking healths and Mrs Joe admits that at this moment she could do with 'something sharp'. Susie, perched on the edge of the table, exchanges smiles with Inigo, because the others seem so happy. Somebody wants to know where Mr Oakroyd is, and nobody is able to supply the information. Everybody, however, has so much to say and is so eager to say it that Mr Oakroyd, who after all has not disappeared into the blue, is soon forgotten. Susie has accepted a cigarette, Joe and Inigo have their pipes, Mr Mitcham has brought out one of his famous cheroots, so that now the room is full of smoke. Thus we see them through a blue haze: Mr Morton Mitcham, towering, fantastic, less like a broken-down senator than he was when we first met him at Dullingham Junction, but still the same conglomeration of creaking bone, bending brow, and retreating hair, the same traveller from unimaginable places; Mrs Joe, flushed, almost sparkling now, ten years younger than she was an hour ago, talking away and sipping her bottled beer but still ready at any moment to play the Duchess of Dorking; the great shoulders and honest beaming face of Joe himself, as he nods and grins and agrees with everybody; Inigo of the wandering nose and wandering lock of hair, at once clean and untidy in the pleasant undergraduate fashion that remains with some men; and Susie, swinging her legs at the table's edge, turning eagerly from one to another of her companions, talking, laughing, teasing, fooling, as if those dark eyes of hers would see ten thousand years of life undimmed. In another moment they will be nothing but names and news. We see them through this haze, which thickens, deepens, shredding away colour, blurring shape, like Time itself flowing mistily away, and then the curtain comes rustling down, and now we cannot see them at all and perhaps will never see them again.

V

And what was Mr Oakroyd doing all this time? What has kept him in the background? The answer is - a new part. For the first and last time in his life, Mr Oakroyd played the detective, a role for which - not being a reader of sensational fiction - he had no particular liking or aptitude. But the great catastrophe had left him darkly brooding, and after innumerable pipes of Old Salt and some talk with his friend, Mr Jock Campbell, a man compact of suspicion, he had begun to put two and two together. Thus it came about that he played the detective, and we shall soon discover to what purpose if we wait for him in Miss Trant's room at the nursing home, on the morning of the day when Susie and Inigo were due to depart to London, and even Mrs Joe and the others were thinking seriously about packing.

Miss Trant was still in the nursing home, but if she had been in a hurry to leave it, she could have done so. She preferred, however, to stay on until her arm was completely better, to the great content of her new medical adviser, Dr Hugh McFarlane, who contrived to visit her every day. He had now gone into the matter of the Hippodrome claims with Mr Gooch, and this meant, of course, that he had to see her as often as possible, whatever might happen to a good general practice and the parathyroid glands. Having completely recovered from the shock, Miss Trant was now able to get up, but for the time being she was keeping to her room. When Hugh called, on this particular morning, he found her sitting in an arm-chair.

'I telephoned to Gooch,' he explained, 'and he's coming along to see you. Something very special, he says. I don't know that I can stay for long, but he'll tell you all about it, Elizabeth.'

'It's a shame, your doing so much,' she told him. 'I'm sure you can't spare the time. You mustn't bother any more about it, Hugh.'

And he replied that it was no trouble at all, and she said she was sure it must be, and he replied again, quite gruffly, that it was a pleasure, and by this time their eyes had joined in the dialogue and were making the most reckless remarks to one another, so that though their tongues had framed only the most innocent friendly syllables, she was bright pink and he was brick-red. Shy people can engage in this commerce for quite a long time before anything decisive happens, and it is not a stage of the passion that has any interest at all for outsiders (though Miss Trant's nurse, who had followed every move, noted every blush, and taken the temperature of the affair each day, must be excepted), so that we can safely withdraw to await the arrival of Mr Gooch.

Mr Gooch was a solicitor with a very large practice and also a marked Midlands accent. These two things taken together indicate that he was an unusually astute man who knew a great deal about everybody in Gatford, Mundley, and Stort. Miss Trant's family solicitor, Mr Truby of Cheltenham, would not have approved of Mr Gooch at all, but then Mr Truby would have been afraid to contest claims that Mr Gooch regarded as mere whims, impudent triflings. Hugh's Scotch instinct for a good fighting lawyer had not been at fault when it had taken him to Mr Gooch. For the rest, it only remains to be said that Mr Gooch was not at all sharp, wizened, ferret-faced, but a stout rubicund man with an enormous flat face that suggested nothing but a sleepy good-humour.

Having bluntly told Miss Trant that he was pleased to meet her and glad to see she was sitting up, Mr Gooch came at once to business. 'Now, Miss Trant,' he began, 'I've looked into this matter. I thought at first it was a hopeless job. You can't deny your liability, you see. I've had a look at your agreement with the Hippodrome, and your liability's there all right. Of course you never thought of anything of this sort happening, did you?'

'Naturally not,' Miss Trant replied. 'Who would? I mean, it's not the kind of thing that does happen, you see.'

'Quite so,' said Mr Gooch, creasing his vast face. 'Only you've got to be prepared for anything in this world. That's what agreements and contracts are for. Ninety-nine times out of a hundred they're only time and money thrown away, but there's always the hundredth. This is it. It's a pity you put your name to that agreement, Miss Trant, if you don't mind me saying so. These theatrical lettings are out of my line - and I don't pretend to know a lot about 'em - but that one you signed doesn't look right to me, smells fishy, that one. And that's going to be worth looking into, I fancy - afterwards, just to make a bit of mischief. But it's watertight, no mistake about that. You're liable, and when they claim, you'll have to pay up.' Having said this, he looked at her in a manner that suggested he was quite pleased about it.

Miss Trant was not pleased and came to the conclusion that Mr Gooch was a fool. 'It's a shame,' she cried. 'I wouldn't care if it was my fault in any way. But it wasn't, as you know, and I've had to suffer anyhow. I and my party have lost money, you see, quite apart from anything I may have to pay. And then we've suffered in other ways too. And all because a few hooligans were determined to spoil our performance.'

Here Dr McFarlane muttered something that hinted what he would do to such fellows if he caught them. It may have concerned their parathyroid glands.

'Quite so,' said Mr Gooch again, still smiling good-humouredly. 'But though we might whittle the claim down a bit when it comes - it hasn't come yet, you know, but it's on its way, you might say - we can't contest it. I want to make you understand that, Miss Trant. That's clear, isn't it? All right, then that's settled.'

He still seemed very pleased with himself, and Miss Trant began to think that even poor Mr Truby, though he may have been thinking for months she was wrong in her head, could have done better than this. And what made it much worse was that he was Hugh's choice. Poor Hugh! - he had looked so knowing about his Mr Gooch.

'But there's another point,' Mr Gooch continued, with relish, 'and this is where we really come in. You're responsible to them, all right. But who's responsible to you? Who, in fact, is the guilty party?' He paused and looked at her expectantly.

She gave a mental if not an actual shrug. 'That's soon settled too,' she replied, not without irony, 'but it doesn't help much. A gang of roughs - from nowhere. If it hadn't been for them, nothing would have happened. But what good will that do us - I mean, knowing that? Oh - it's all stupid! I'm sorry, but it really is.'

'It might turn out stupid for somebody,' said Mr Gooch, who was quite unperturbed, 'but it's not half so stupid as it looks. Quite tricky up to a point, in fact - quite tricky. I didn't want to bother you just now with all this, but I thought you'd better know the line I'm taking. If you don't mind waiting a minute, I'll just see if he's here. I left a message for him to come along.' With that, he lumbered out, leaving Miss Trant staring at her companion.

'I don't understand what he's talking about,' she confessed, frowning. 'Is he - really - a reliable man?'

Hugh laughed. 'I've been watching you, Elizabeth. I saw you thought he wasn't going to be any use to you.'

'No, that's not fair. I didn't. Only - '

'Just wait. He's here.'

He was and there was somebody with him. It was Mr Oakroyd, tightly clutching his cap and looking very embarrassed. He gave her a very uneasy grin.

'Well, Mr Oakroyd,' and she smiled, 'this is very nice. I didn't expect to see you.'

Mr Oakroyd cleared his throat. 'Ar yer getting on, Miss Trant?'

'Very well, thank you. What have you been doing lately?'

'Well - er - I've been busy - like.' And he nodded towards Mr Gooch.

'Oh!' cried Miss Trant. 'I didn't understand. You've come here with Mr Gooch, have you?'

'That's right,' replied Mr Oakroyd, more at ease now. 'Any rate, he left word for me to come here. Said I'd better tell yer mysen.'

'And you got hold of the other chap,' Mr Gooch inquired, putting his head on one side in a droll fashion, 'made sure of him, did you?'

'He's here,' said Mr Oakroyd, jerking a thumb over his shoulder.

'He's here, is he?' Mr Gooch was quite lively. 'Where? Outside?'

'On t'mat,' replied Mr Oakroyd, grinning. 'D'you want him in?'

'If Miss Trant doesn't mind,' said Mr Gooch, glancing at her.

'Of course I don't mind,' said Miss Trant, staring at them. 'But what is it all about?' And she suddenly began to laugh.

'It's like this here, Miss Trant,' Mr Oakroyd began, earnestly; 'After that there do o' Saturday, I begins to put two an' two together. There'd been summat up all t'week, though it were nowt to Saturday. Saturday capped t'lot, as yer knaw very well. Nar there's one or two had said to me they thowt it were a put-up job, them chaps makking all that to-do. I didn't like look on it at all, I didn't. So I put my thinking cap on.'

'That's the way,' said Mr Gooch approvingly. 'Thinking cap.'

'Nar a friend o' mine that doesn't belong here but 'ud been here a bit, this chap 'ud dropped a remark to me when I saw him last week - it were in t'Market Tavern o' Thursday - an' when I towd him I was here wi' T'Good Companions, then he says, "You had any bother lately, 'cos you're going to have some right sharp?" Summat like that, he says. Well, I didn't tak' much notice on it at time, an' he were off afore I could say owt. So I lets it drop, you might say. But t'other day, o' Monday it wor, when I begins to puzzle it out a bit, I thowt, "Ar did he knaw we'd have some bother?" He'd said we would have and - by gow! - we'd had some bother an' all. So I puts two an' two together. I thowt to mysen, "He's in t'know, he is. If this here's a put-up job, he's been where they've been putting it up, as you might say." That's what I thowt.'

Mr Gooch wagged his huge head at Miss Trant. 'That's the way,' he said once more. 'Thinking cap again.'

Miss Trant was interested now. 'Go on, Mr Oakroyd. This is exciting.'

'So I sets off to look for him, this here friend o' mine. Any rate, I maks a few inquiries. Meantime, I goes to see Jimmy Nunn, an' he tells me what Soosie towd him about Doctor McFarlane here going to Mr Goodge about this here job, so I goes to Mr Goodge an' all an' tells him what I think about it an' he says there might be summat in it an' I'd better keep on looking for this friend o' mine, d'you see." I'll do what I can," he says," to help you to find him. What's he like?" he says. An' I tells him, an' off I goes again an' comes on one chap 'at 'ud seen him an' he puts me on to another chap. Eh, it were a business! But at finish up, I finds him.'

'Was he here in Gatford?' Miss Trant asked.

'Here! He wor fowty mile away an' just settin' off to go another fowty or fifty. He's allus on t'move,' he added, not without pride. 'I were wi' him one time - on t'road. If I hadn't been, he wouldn't ha' come back. He worn't set on it - 'cos he didn't want to be mixed up in t'job - but he come i' t'finish, being a pal o' mine.'

'Well, we'd better have him in now,' said Mr Gooch, 'unless Miss Trant doesn't want to be bothered. You can leave it all to me, you know, Miss Trant, but I thought you might like to hear what he has to say.'

'I should think so!' cried Miss Trant. 'Hurry up and bring him before he runs away.'

'Nay, he'll noan do that,' said Mr Oakroyd, almost reproachfully. 'I'll fetch him.' And off he went.

'And you really think there's something in this?' said Dr McFarlane, looking anxiously at Mr Gooch.

'I'm pretty sure there is,' that gentleman replied, smiling and half-closing his eyes. 'Pre-tty sure there is.' Then he opened his eyes, wide. 'But I can't tell you exactly what - not yet.'

'Well, whether there is or not,' cried Miss Trant excitedly, 'it's lovely. And I hope there is, just for Mr Oakroyd's sake. I've told you about him, haven't I, Hugh?'

'This is him,' said Mr Oakroyd, returning at that moment, 'Joby Jackson. Nar, Joby lad, yer can tell 'em yersen.'

Our old friend Mr Jackson looked from one to another of his audience and rubbed his chin dubiously. We see him for a moment robbed of that bright confidence which was part of his charm.

'Now then?' said Mr Gooch.

'It's like this,' said Joby hoarsely. 'Yer not making a police-court job o' this, are yer? If y'are, I want to keep out, see? Anything to oblige a pal - an' anyhow they did the dirty on yer - but I don't want to be put in a little box with a clever bloke on the other side saying, "And where were you on the fourteenth of July last?" No witnessing for me. Oh no! I'll tell yer what I know for George 'ere, but yer don't put me in the box, see?'

'There isn't going to be a box; don't worry,' said Mr Gooch. ' It isn't that sort of business at all.'

'Good enough then,' said Joby, hesitating no longer and speaking with more freedom. 'What yer want to know is 'ow did I come to know there might be a bit o' bother, that's it, isn't it? Right.' He paused, gave a sharp glance round, thoroughly enjoying the situation. 'Well, I'm 'ere in Gatford, see. One morning in a boozer - not the Market Tavern, lower class of 'ouse altogether - tell yer its moniker in a minute - the Black Bull, that's it. Know it?'

Mr Gooch pondered for a moment. 'Corner of Castle Street,' he said finally. 'Little place. Nearly got its licence taken away last year.'

'That's the place,' said Joby. 'Well, I'm in there, see - one morning, havin' one with some o' the lads. When I say some o' the lads, I don't mean they was pals o' mine. But I knew some of 'em. Matter o' fact, some of 'em was on the road, same as meself. They wasn't workin' just then, 'cos Gorley's place is near 'ere, see - an' Gorley's the feller that owns some o' them Cock'rels and Swishbacks - and they was 'ere, waitin' for the engines to be over'aulded, see. The other fellers I didn't know-local fellers, they was, all in a click, y'know, a gang, with about the price of a pint between the lot of 'em. Well there we are - when in comes a feller, a biggish bloke, all dressed up, smart feller. One or two o' the lads knows 'im, see, same as if they'd done a bit o' work for 'im one time, when they *did* work. This feller then looks us over, nods 'ere an' there, very friendly like, calls the landlord an' orders drinks all round. Sensation in court! Then when the landlord's gone and we're all well into the pig's ear, he sort o' gathers us round like an' says quietly, "Any o' you fellers like to earn some easy money?" "What's the idear?" we want to know. "Only a bit of a joke on my part," 'e says, "just payin' somebody off," 'e says, "an' money for nothing for some o' you lads." He didn't look a money-for-nothing bloke to me, I don't mind tellin' yer, an' when 'e says, "Before we go any further, who's game?", I didn't catch on, see. I thought, "I don't like the look of you, chum. Bit too careful about your joke. Too much lookin' over the shoulder." So me an' two or three more wasn't in it, see, an' we sits in the other corner, tryin' to look as if we wasn't still drinkin' the beer he paid for. 'E whispers for about ten minutes, then slings it. But I got a word or two, something about a show at the Hip. When 'e goes, the other fellers lets on then, see. "Why don't yer come in?" they says to us. "Quid each for sittin' at the back o' the Hip. an' giving 'em the bird, an' p'raps another quid for Saturday if it pans out all right," they says - 'And those were the men then,' Miss Trant gasped. 'But why? I don't understand. Who was this man?'

'Now we come to it,' said Mr Gooch. 'Who was he?'

'I 'eard 'is name,' Joby replied slowly,' 'cos, as I say, some of 'em knew 'im - '

'Good! And what was it?'

'That's it. I've forgotten it. Clean gone. An' me with a memory, my God! that's won me more pints o' beer in bets than you could swallow from now to - '

'Come along,' said Mr Gooch. 'This won't do, you know. You might as well give us the name now. It's just that we want.'

'It's no good yer coming along me,' cried Joby aggressively. 'Yer can come along till yer blue an' it won't make no difference. I've tried to remember that feller's moniker all day. 'Ere, George, you can tell 'em. Wasn't I tryin' to remember it all along the road'ere?'

'Ay, yer wor, Joby,' Mr Oakroyd replied mournfully. It began to look as if he had had all his trouble for nothing.

'Well, can't you remember anything about him?' said Mr Gooch, who looked neither sleepy nor good-humoured now.

'Let's see. 'Alf a minute. Biggish bloke. Clean-shaved. Reddish face. Baggy under the eyes, poached-egg style. Too much whisky.' But that did not seem to help much, for Gatford and district could boast of dozens of middle-aged gentlemen exactly like that. Then Joby remembered something else. ''Ere, 'alf a minute. Pitchers. Something to do with pitchers.'

'Pitchers?' Mr Gooch stared at him.

'That's ri'. Yer know, films, cinemas!'

'Ah!' Mr Gooch sounded triumphant. 'Was his name Ridvers?'

'You've got it, chum,' shouted Joby, in great excitement. 'You've got it in one. Ridvers, that's it. Now 'ow the - I mean - 'ow did I come to forget that? Ridvers. That's it all right an' no mistake. Do yer know'im, Mister?'

'I know Mr Ridvers,' Mr Gooch replied, a trifle grimly, 'and Mr

Ridvers knows me. I don't think I shall have a lot of trouble with Mr Ridvers. I happen to know he's trying to sell his three cinema halls to a big syndicate. In fact, I know a lot about Mr Ridvers. And now I know a bit more, don't I? Well, well! Hello!' He stared at Miss Trant, who was wrinkling her brow. 'Do you know him too?'

'I'm just trying to think. There was a man, a horrid man, pushed his way into my room at the hotel one afternoon, two or three weeks ago, and he said he had something to do with cinemas here. He was awfully rude and disagreeable - a beast of a man - and so I wouldn't listen to him, just told him to go. And I heard afterwards that some of the men in the party had some trouble with him after that, downstairs. I'm sure that must be the same man.'

'So am I,' said Mr Gooch.

'I've a mind to call on this Ridvers,' Dr McFarlane began, looking very fierce.

'Leave him to me, Doctor, leave him to me,' said Mr Gooch. 'I'll attend to him. He's had his little joke, and this is where he pays for it.' He turned to Joby. 'And don't you worry about courts of law. This won't get that far, if I know Mr Ridvers; But I tell you what you can do, my lad, and I'll see you don't lose by it. You can just give me as many names of those other fellows as you can remember. That'll help us to show Mr Ridvers we know all about his little games.' He whipped out paper and pencil and took Joby aside.

'Well done, Mr Oakroyd!' said Dr McFarlane, shaking him by the hand. 'That's fine.'

'Isn't it?' cried Miss Trant. 'Whatever happens, I'm very very grateful to you. You've been wonderful, finding all this out for us.'

'Nay, I've done nowt. It's Joby who'll ha' done t'trick.'

'No, it's you really, and I can't tell you how grateful I am. And listen, I've been wanting to talk to you, now that we've all broken up. Aren't you sorry?'

'Eh, I am, Miss Trant. I don't like thowt on us all leavin'' one another, I don't. Ther's Soos an' Inigo off this afternoon - I'm off to t'station wi' em if I can get - an' though I'm right glad they're doing so well, I'll be right sorry to see 'em go, I will that. Eh, we've had wer bit o' fun together, three on us.'

'But tell me,' said Miss Trant, looking at him very earnestly, 'what are you going to do? I've been wanting to talk to you about that.'

'Nay, I've been so throng wi' this business, I don't fairly knaw. Ther's been a bit o' talk about it. Soos wants me to go to London afore so long, 'cos she fancies she can get me summat to do there. An' Joe says if I went wi' them, p'raps ther'd be a job there - '

'And I don't know exactly what I'm going to do,' she said, 'but that's what I was going to say to you too. But look here, will you talk to the others seriously today, and then come to see me - let me see - tomorrow morning sometime, and then we can talk about it properly. Will you do that?'

'Ay, I will,' said Mr Oakroyd solemnly, and then awkwardly took his leave of her. But he did not talk it over with the others and he did not call upon her the next morning.

'Yer mun come an' have a bit o' dinner wi' me, Joby lad,' he said, as they left the nursing home in triumph. 'I towd t'landlady yer might - she's a right good sort is this, an' I've been there a time nar - an' she'll have it ready.'

'I'm with yer, George,' said Joby in great content. He had been promised a reward for his services by Mr Gooch, and, reward or no reward, had enjoyed his morning.

They had hardly set foot in the house, however, before the landlady rushed up and thrust something in Mr Oakroyd's face, just as if it had been there some time and she was anxious to get rid of it, fearing that it would explode at any moment. And indeed this is indeed exactly what she felt, for the thing she handed over was a telegram. At the sight of it Mr Oakroyd's triumphant morning crashed to smithereens. 'By gow!' he muttered, staring.

It was Joby's turn to read it now. *Come at once mother bad. Leonard.* He made a little clucking noise. 'That's ruddy 'ard lines, George,' he said, seriously, sympathetically. 'The old trouble-and-strife, eh? Bad, eh? Aw, that's rotten, George. 'Ope for the best, though.'

'I knew ther were summat. I did, I knew,' Mr Oakroyd was muttering. Then he looked at Joby. 'I mun be off soon as I can. When's t'next train up there, lad?'

Joby knew, for he was an authority on trains. There was one in the middle of the afternoon, and this gave him time after dinner to scrawl his Bruddersford address and a few words of explanation on a bit of paper, to be conveyed to Miss Trant by 't'landlady's little lad', to put his things together and settle his bill, to hurry round and say good-bye to Susie and Inigo. There was no time to see the others, but perhaps they would not be gone when he returned, if he did return. Joby went with him to the station, though his own train did not go until five o'clock.

'All the best, George. An' don't forget - Joby Jackson, *World's Fair* - finds me ev'ry time, see. Keep smilin'.'

'So long, Joby lad. See thee again some day. On t'road, eh?'

And then the train went roaring North.

CHAPTER SIX
Mr Oakroyd Goes Home

I

IT was deep dusk when Mr Oakroyd's train arrived at Black Moor Junction. He could see the street lamps twinkling on the hills, and here and there trams crawling up and down like golden beetles. The train stopped several minutes at Black Moor, as it always does, and then, having lost all its enthusiasm, it slowly chuff-chuffed into the gloom until at last it came to a standstill in Bruddersford Station. Mr Oakroyd stepped out, carrying the small suitcase that for some time had replaced the famous little basket trunk, and made his way to the exit with all the easy dispatch of a travelled man. He could dismiss railway stations with a glance now, having been so long and so far on the road, all the autumn and winter, from Sandybay as far up as Middleford. This was really the first time he had come back to Bruddersford since he began his travels, for though he had visited Ogden Street just after Christmas, he had only gone by tram from Luddenstall, and that did not count. He had often seen himself coming back like this, arriving by train and so on, having a bit of a holiday like, smoking a leisurely pipe in Woolgate long after everybody else had clattered off to work, slipping round to the Working Men's Club at night to tell some of the chaps where he had been and what he had seen. But now it was all different. This trip had a shaky and darkish look about it. As he crossed the end of Market Street to get into Woolgate, the great black tower of the Town Hall jerkly shook out the notes of *Tom Bowling*, a very melancholy tune on the chimes. Mr Oakroyd had never admired it, but now he suddenly decided he hated it. How folk put up with such a din was a mystery.

'Here, lad,' he cried, at the corner of Woolgate, "ave you got t'*Evening Express*?' Buying a paper made him feel a little more cheerful.

Walking up Woolgate, he had a shock. Buttershaw's, the tripe and music shop, was closed, empty, to let. Something must have happened there. When was it he had been talking to Mrs Buttershaw, something about Lily and how she used to go there for pantomime songs? Yes, on a tram, it was, one Saturday. And Joe Buttershaw had been there five-and-twenty year to his knowledge; everybody knew Joe's; and now it wasn't there. It made everything look uncertain, strange, as if half the street had gone.

Not a sign of anybody in at 51. It was hardly time for Leonard to be home, if he was still working at Gregson's, but it did not look as if anybody was there. He knocked, though he knew somehow before he put his hand to the door that it was useless, for the place had a real shut-up look about it.

'Eh, it's Mr Oakroyd!' Mrs Sugden was looking out of the house next door. 'Just a minute, Mr Oakroyd. I've got t'key.'

She opened the door and marched in with him. There was a bit of fire in the grate, and the table was laid for a late tea. Mrs Sugden, happily bustling about the room, talked with gusto. 'Did your Leonard send for yer? I told him he'd 'ave to send. And I've been doing a bit o' tidying up for him, an' getting him his tea. A lad like that can't look after hissen, can he? An' I've been right sorry for him, I'ave.'

Mr Oakroyd, very uneasy now, asked where his wife was.

'Eh, didn't your Leonard tell yer?' cried Mrs Sugden, staring at him. 'She's in t'Infirmary. They took her away - eh, when was it - Friday or Saturday - ay, it were Friday, 'cos I were just paying me insurance, I'd got t'book in me 'and, when they come for her. They 'ad t'operate right sharp - eh, she were that bad. She'd left it so long. She'd been badly for weeks and weeks. Got a pain 'ere.' Mrs Sugden put a hand on her ample side. 'I could see she were bad. "Eh," I says, "yer can't let it go like that, yer mun see t'doctor." "No doctors for me, Mrs Sugden," she says. "I can manage." Ay, that's just what she said. "I can manage." An' I could see wi' me own eyes she were bad. At t'upshot, I calls to your Leonard - that were t'beginning o' last week - an' I says to 'im, "Eh, Leonard, you'll ha' to mak' your mother see t'doctor. It's no way o' going on, this isn't. She's poorly." "I think she is," he says, "though she's said nowt to me." "I knaw she is," I says. "I'll get one," he says. But no doctor come that day nor t'day after. Next morning she couldn't get up out o' bed, she were that bad, an' I come in for a bit an' your Leonard fetched t'doctor to her, an' he said they'd 'ave t'operate soon as they could. It were owd Doctor Mackintosh - 'im 'at sees 'em at t'club - an' - eh! - he wor in a state about 'er. Nivver seen him in sich a stew. He were fairly boiling an' sweating.'

'What's it she's got?' asked Mr Oakroyd. His voice was so hoarse that he had to clear his throat and repeat the question.

'It's summat like appendis,' replied Mrs Sugden, 'only it's farther on like. Your Leonard said summat about perry - perry- totitis, but I couldn't quite mak' it out.'

'And what about this here operation, did it come off all right?'

'Oh, they operated, straight off. They 'ad to. Eh, I believe she's 'ad another sin' then, Mr Oakroyd. I believe she 'as,' Mrs Sugden added, with mournful gusto.

He stared at her in horror. 'She - she mun be bad then,' he stammered finally.

'Eh, she is, poor soul! Your Leonard's nobbut seen her once, an' I 'aven't set eyes on her sin' she were ta'en away, but Mrs Flather - her little lass is in - towed me she were in a bad way, one o' nurses 'ad said summat to her about it. But we mun hope for t'best, that's all. An' standin' here talkin'. Sit yer down, Mr Oakroyd, an' I'll mak' yer a bit o' tea. Your Leonard'll be here in a minute - it's his time - an' I allus mak' him a bit. I've been bakin' today. I'll fetch a curran' cake an' a piece o' fatty cake in, if you'll just watch t'kettle a minute.'

Ten minutes later, she had come and gone again, and Mr Oakroyd was sitting at the table with his son, Leonard, a very subdued Leonard indeed. The dandy huntsman who had marked and captured bright feminine prey in so many social-and-dance halls, cinemas, and cheap cafés, had vanished, and in his place was a troubled, frightened lad with a trembling lower lip, a lad who had caught a glimpse of another and dreadful huntsman. He could add very little to the information already supplied by Mrs Sugden.

Mr Oakroyd found relief in a sudden spurt of anger. 'Yer gurt fathead,' he cried, 'why didn't you let me know afore 'at your mother was so poorly? Haven't sense you were born wi'!'

'I couldn't,' Leonard mumbled miserably.

'Ar, d'you mean you couldn't? Course you could!'

'I couldn't. I told you, I didn't know at first, and then when Mar was taken so bad, she said, "Don't tell yer father." It's last thing she did say to me.'

Mr Oakroyd's anger fell away from him. He stared down at the table. 'What did she want to say that for?' he asked quietly, at last.

'Nay, I don't know,' his son muttered. 'Except she didn't want you to know.'

Mr Oakroyd pushed away his cap, and made a little sad clicking noise. 'When I come at Christmas, I knew she were poorly then, an' I towd her so. An' I towd our Lily she wor in a letter I wrote. Eh, dear!' For a moment he surveyed in silence the whole melancholy confusion of this life. 'Well, I'll go to t'Infirmary i' t'morning. Happen they'll let me see her. What did they say when you asked today?'

'Said she was just about the same. She's bad. Father; she is bad.' He got up from the table and turned away.

Mr Oakroyd automatically filled his pipe with Old Salt, but did not light it. He remained where he was at the table, flattening his cheek against his fist, and sank into a troubled reverie. Leonard went upstairs, came down again, smoked a cigarette over the fire.

'Me Aunt Alice came last night,' Leonard remarked, breaking the long silence.

'Ay, she did, did she?' Mr Oakroyd left the table now and lit his pipe. 'An' ar's she gettin' on then?' His wife's sister, this Alice, was married to a railwayman, and lived at the other side of Bruddersford. Mr

Oakroyd had not seen her for years. As a matter of fact, he disliked both her and her husband.

'All right,' said Leonard indifferently. 'Me cousin Mabel's gettin' married soon.'

'Well, well! Last time I saw Mabel she were nobbut a bit of a kid wi' a mucky pinafore, as you might say. And nar she's gettin'wed. Who's t'chap?'

'Johnson, they call him. He works in the railway office - penpusher. You might think he owned it, to hear him talk. Lot o' swank! And Mabel's no kid now. She's over a year older than me, nearly as old as our Lily.'

'You haven't said owt to our Lily yet, have you?' asked Mr Oakroyd anxiously.

Leonard shook his head. 'I haven't written her a letter for two months. She doesn't write to me. You'll be writing, won't you?'

What was he going to write? The thought chilled him, but warmth returned with the thought of Lily herself. If only she were here with him! But no, she was better out of it. He stared about him, then suddenly remembered something. 'Here,' he cried, 'where's Albert? I'd forgotten him.'

'Gone. Went a fortnight since.'

'Well, that's summat, anyhow. A bit o' yon Albert's talk nar 'ud just about put finishing touch on it. An' what's happened to him then?'

'Gettin' married this week.' And Leonard grinned sardonically. 'Got caught all right, Mr Tuggridge did. Told him he would, but he wouldn't leave her alone. They didn't give him any option, neither, when they knew. Her father come to see him. Poor old Albert!' Yes, his days as a wandering gallant were over. No more ogling and pursuing and picking up for him. He had picked up once too often. He had 'got caught' and would soon be seen with a perambulator.

'Poor owd nothing!' cried Mr Oakroyd scornfully. 'I'm sorry for t'lass as weds him. Gurt clever head - gas-bag! An' that's no way for you to talk, neither, lad,' he added severely. ' "Got caught"! It makes me fair shamed to hear a lad o' mine talking that way. If I'd said owt o' that sort in front o' my father, he'd ha' ta'en a stick to my back, he would that. D'yer think t'lasses is nobbut for you to go follerin' round an' laking wi'? What d'yer think they are - bits o' toys?' He regarded his son sternly for a moment. 'Ar yer doin' at yer work? Still wi' Gregson's?'

'Yes,' Leonard replied, rather sulkily. 'Doing all right. Got the second chair now and a lot of reg'lar customers. I'm making nearly four pounds a week.'

'That's the style. Well, happen you'll be better off when you "get caught" as you call it. Might knock a bit o' sense into you if a decent lass gets howd on you. You nivver knaw.'

'Chap offered me a job in Manchester the other day,' Leonard mumbled, 'and I'd like to have taken it. More money and a change. I'm getting sick of Bruddersford. If - if owt happens to me mother I shall go.' He swallowed hard.

Mr Oakroyd relaxed the severity of his expression. 'Ay, lad, you mun do whativver you think best. I've no call to be tellin' you what to do. An' whativver else you've done, you've noan been a bad lad to your mother.'

Having said this, he cleared his throat, and looked sternly at the evening paper, as if he knew very well he could not believe a word it said. Leonard, muttering something about 'a walk round', disappeared. Mr Oakroyd read the paper through carefully, unhopefully, smoked a pipe or two and stared solemnly at the fire, then went to bed.

II

The Bruddersford Infirmary could not be mistaken for one of the local factories because it has no tall chimney. Otherwise there is little difference. It is a rambling ugly building, all in blackened stone and surrounded first by an asphalt courtyard, where the smuts drizzle ceaselessly, and then by tall iron railings that would not seem out of place around a prison. Through these railings a nurse may be seen occasionally, and as she flits across those grim spaces of stone and soot she looks like a being from another world, incredibly immaculate. Here, out of the sunlight, far from green shades and blue distances, where no birds sing, but where the lorries and steam-wagons come thundering down and the trams go groaning up the hill, here behind this rusting iron and walls thickened with black grime, the Bruddersfordians have a bout or two, a tussle, or a fight to a finish, with Death.

The last time Mr Oakroyd had visited the Infirmary was to see a friend of his from Higden's, a good many years ago. He could hardly remember what it looked like inside. He was familiar enough with the outside, for the place was not quarter of a mile from Ogden Street and for years he had walked past it nearly every day. This morning, however, even the outside seemed strange. His wife was somewhere inside it, behind one of those dark windows.

'Is it special?' asked the porter, ''cos this isn't visiting time, yer knaw.'

'Well, I don't know fairly,' said Mr Oakroyd. 'I wer sent for, like, an' I've come a long way.'

'If yer'll howd on a minute, I'll see. What's t'name again? All right. Yer can wait in there.' And the porter, after pointing to a door, turned away.

There were several people in the bare little waiting-room. One of them was an enormously fat woman, wrapped in a shawl. The tears were streaming down her face, and she made no attempt to dry her eyes, but repeated over and over again, without any variation of tone: 'They nivver owt to ha' let him come in, nivver.'

On the other side was an oldish man, whose drooping face Mr Oakroyd dimly recognized. 'Fower operations in eighteen months, that's what she's had,' he was saying. 'Fower operations.' There was mournful pride in his voice. He looked round, nodded vaguely to Mr Oakroyd, and then began again: 'Ay, fower operations.'

The others there, including two children, said nothing at all. They just waited, and Mr Oakroyd had an obscure conviction that they had been waiting a long time. His heart sank. He wanted to go away.

The porter was standing at the door, beckoning to him. 'Oakroyd, isn't it? That's Num-ber Twen-ty-sev-en, List-er Ward. Well, t'sister says she's very sorry but yer can't see 'er now but will you come again this afternoon.'

'I see,' said Mr Oakroyd, and immediately found himself invaded by a feeling of relief. He tried to be disappointed, told himself he must see her as soon as he could, but nevertheless he could not help feeling relieved. He had been in there only a few minutes, had not really been inside, but even so it was comforting to be back again in the bustle of Woolgate. Something dogged him, however, throughout his stroll through the main streets. He was like a chap out on bail.

He called again in the early afternoon, only to be told to return later. Then at last he was admitted. He climbed up four flights of stone steps and then found Lister Ward. A nurse met him at the entrance. 'Let me see,' she said, 'you're for Number Seventeen - little Doris Smith - aren't you?'

When Mr Oakroyd told her he was wanting Number Twenty-seven, she seemed disappointed, and this made him all the more uncomfortable, as if he had no right to be there.

'Yes, I remember now,' she said, looking all round him but not at him. 'Sister said you could see her, didn't she? You're the husband, aren't you? She hasn't been asking for you. There's a son, isn't there? I thought I'd seen him. This way then, and don't make too much noise. This isn't the proper visiting day, and you mustn't disturb the others.'

He crept after her in a fashion that would not have disturbed a fly. He tiptoed so gently that his legs ached. They had to go almost the whole length of the ward, and though he tried to see as little of it as possible, he could not help noticing some things. All the women were in bed and they all seemed to have something blue on; some were old, some very young; some asleep, some staring fiercely; and there were strange things, pulley arrangements, on some of the beds; and one or two were completely surrounded by screens. No moaning and groaning; not a sound, it was all as quiet as a waxwork show; all tidy and polished and still; very queer, frightening.

The nurse suddenly stopped. She turned round, looking right at him this time. 'Your wife's very ill, you know,' she whispered. 'You must be very quiet with her. Don't mind if she's not very clear, wandering a little. Just a minute.' She walked forward to a bed, and he heard her say: 'Now, Twenty-seven, your husband's come to see you.' What else she said he did not know, but he saw her leaning over the bed, doing something, and then she stepped back and nodded to him. He tiptoed forward, feeling horribly clumsy, uncertain. One hand, held behind him, was tightening, tightening, until its nails were digging into the horny palm. Then he stood by the bedside, looking down into the face of Number Twenty-seven.

'Eh, lass,' he said huskily. He tried to smile, but could only make a grimace. 'Nay - nay.' And there seemed nothing more he could say.

Her face was all bone and sharp wrinkles and seemed as brittle as egg-shell. Her mouth was a short line, dark, bitter. But her eyes, though they wandered with an awful slowness, still gleamed in their hollows, and there looked out from those eyes the soul, stubborn, unflinching, ironic, of Mrs Oakroyd. He himself could feel this, though he had no words for it. But an inner voice was saying 'Eh, she'll nivver give in,' and he stared at her in mingled pity and awe.

Her eyes roamed over him. She stirred a little and there came a sickly sweet smell. A hand travelled slowly over the folded sheet, and as he sat down he grasped it. His face working desperately but to no purpose.

'Jess? What - what - you doing here?'

'Our Leonard sent.'

At the mention of Leonard those eyes changed, softened. They would not do that for anything else now, it seemed.

'I didn't tell him to.' Her voice was clear but slow, a voice speaking out of a dream.

'He thowt he'd better send word. He's been a good lad. I told him he's been a good lad to his mother.'

'Time you thowt so,' she said, with a flash of the old sharp spirit. 'Ay, ay, a good lad ... our Leonard. Is he coming soon?'

'Soon as he can or whenivver you want him,' he told her.

She nodded, very slowly, so that it hurt him to watch her doing it. Then she looked away, at nothing it seemed, as if he was no longer there. He waited through a shrinking and numbing silence. At last, however, she looked at him again, and it was as if she had returned from far away and was faintly surprised to find him still there. He tried to think of something to say, but there seemed to be nothing he could say and somehow his voice too had rusted away.

'I'm bad, Jess,' she said finally.

His voice came back. 'Eh, lass, why didn't you tell me afore?'

She did not seem to hear this. 'I wish they'd let me alone,' she muttered. 'They can do nowt.'

'Nay, they will,' he said, and tried to convince himself that they could do something though in his heart he knew they could not.

'Can't - can't I do owt?' he asked desperately.

To this she made no reply beyond looking at him searchingly, with a faint gleam of irony in her eyes. When it faded and she stirred again, it seemed as if he had been dismissed. Her hand crept out of his and moved uneasily over the sheet. When she spoke again, she began wandering. There was something about their Lily, about Higden's, about a peggy-tub she had borrowed; all a dreamy jumble. The nurse came up quietly and touched him on the shoulder. He stood up, looked on while she gave his wife something to drink.

'You'd better go now,' she told him. But she withdrew for a moment.

His wife looked at him, steadily now. 'Going, Jess, now, aren't yer? Yer managed all right for yersen when yer went away, didn't yer?'

'I nivver owt to ha' gone.'

'Nay, lad, I don't know. You've done nowt to be sorry for. Couldn't be helped. Are yer going on all right?'

He nodded.

'Better so, then,' she went on. 'And our Leonard's doing right well. Eh, he is - right well!' She closed her eyes for a moment, then looked at him again, with the wizened ghost of a smile. 'Yer mun go and see our Lily some time if yer can get. That's what you've allus wanted, isn't it? Nay, Jess, I know. Tell our Leonard to come tonight.'

This time, when he found himself outside in Woolgate again, he also found that he had not really left the Infirmary behind. It was the streets and shops, the trams and lorries, the whole noisy bustling business, that seemed grotesque, unreal now. Half of him still went tiptoeing in that long room of beds and blue-covered shoulders, of pulley things and screens. The quiet of it remained with him and conjured away all the solid reality from the traffic of the streets. What was all the commotion about? Mr Oakroyd did not say all these things to himself; he could not have found words for most of them; but nevertheless he felt them. You could have read them in his wondering glances as you passed him in the street.

When he went the next day, she was obviously weaker. Her eyes had a drugged look; she mumbled in her talk; and nearly everything she said was disconnected, wandering, the old wreckage of dreams and scattered memories. He sat there for an hour, staring sadly, squeezing his fingers, and then crept away, hurt, and frightened.

In the evening, he went again, with Leonard, and they were told they could go up to the ward. They were not admitted, however; the sister said it had been a mistake: Number Twenty-seven could not be seen just then. Perhaps it might be as well if they stayed some time in the waiting-room below. And they caught a glimpse through the door of screens round the bed. They waited an hour, two hours, turning over evening papers that seemed to say nothing, starting up every time the door was opened. It was late. They inquired again, and were told it was useless waiting any longer. There was no change; they must hope for the best; everything that could be done was being done. But next morning, before the earliest buzzers had sounded, Number Twenty-seven was dead.

After he had visited the cold little chapel, where the body would remain until the undertaker wanted it, they put into his hand a parcel wrapped in brown paper, and mechanically he accepted it and took it home, and mechanically he opened it there. Some clothes; a brush and comb; a little envelope, out of which rolled a wedding-ring. There was something else in the envelope. False teeth.

'Eh, well I don't know!' cried Mrs Sugden, who was for ever in the house now. 'What they want to bother yer with them things for? Poor soul! They've ner more sense than – nay, I don't know!'

But Mr Oakroyd only nodded and then stumped away.

III

He did what had to be done without protest. He helped Leonard to put something in the paper. He saw the undertaker and the insurance man. He sent a cable to Lily, and this alone of all his duties brought about a thaw inside his numbed self. When the man explained how it could be sent and when it would probably get there, he felt a sudden warmth and wanted to cry. For the rest, he did what he had to do, but was so quiet that his wife's relations, who came pouring in with her sister, Alice Bairstow, at their head, did not know what to make of him. Noisy and red-eyed but secretly rejoicing in their own immortality, they discussed him in corners. It was Mrs Sugden's opinion that he was 'taking it 'ard', but though her position as sympathetic neighbour and tea-brewer to the bereaved was recognized, it was held that her opinion on this matter was uncalled-for and therefore of no consequence. Mrs Bairstow was heard to say that what really troubled her brother-in-law was remorse, as well it might. He had gone off God knows where and left her to it, and this is what had come of it. But she did not go so far as to say this to him. All she did was to deal with him in a spirit of large but strained tolerance, and make a great fuss of Leonard. Once or twice Mr Oakroyd glowered at her and was obviously on the point of saying something sharp, but most of the time he simply humped about, looking grey and wooden, and nodded agreement to everything she said. What she did say chiefly concerned the funeral, which was to be in the best traditions of Ogden Street. She sent out a host of invitations, and pledged the forthcoming insurance money royally.

It was on the morning of the funeral that Mr Oakroyd received a letter. For a moment, he thought it must be from Lily, and his heart leaped up, but as soon as he saw it was not, he lost interest at once and stuffed it into his pocket without reading it. There would be plenty of time for that afterwards, when all the black fuss and bustle was over. This being a funeral in the grand tradition, it was a very lengthy affair. The assembly of the carriages and the mourners took some time. Then there was the long slow drive out to Dum Wood Cemetery, where serious Bruddersfordians go walking on fine Sunday afternoons, many a year before they are taken there to await the last trump. Then followed a service in the cemetery chapel, where the Rev. J. Hamilton Morris, B.A., of Woolgate Congregational Chapel, tried to dwell upon the virtues of the deceased and found it very difficult because he knew very little about her. He did what he could, however, looked manfully at the tear-stained or grim faces, and finally asked the grave where its victory was. And when all was done, there was the long drive back, not to 51 Ogden Street, but to Caddy's in Shuttle Street, where a funeral tea had been ordered. Caddy's, being old-fashioned, still made a speciality of these repasts, and on their business cards might be seen, sandwiched between *Catering* and *Wedding* Cakes the announcement: *Funeral Teas*. Mourners, mostly relations, still come considerable distances, and not only must they be refreshed but they must also be provided with an opportunity to exchange news, for many scattered families only meet at a funeral. It is not perhaps true to say that these teas are the most jovial functions known to elderly Bruddersfordians, but it must be admitted that they are generally a success, going with a swing that many social events in Bruddersford never know. Everybody has that pleasant feeling of having carried through a painful duty; after a sight of the open grave, it is good to return to life, to eat and drink and swop news with uncles and cousins; and, moreover, what with long rides, services, and standing about in cemeteries, to say nothing of the havoc wrought by the emotions, a mourner develops a real appetite and funeral teas are good solid meat teas. That is the reason why the comedian who plays the Dame in the Bruddersford pantomime never fails - has not failed these last thirty years - to bring down the house with the remark: 'I buried 'im with 'am'. On this occasion, Mrs Bairstow had ordered Caddy's to provide a sound specimen of their knife-and-fork tea, and they had disappointed neither her nor any of her hopeful guests.

Among those who did full justice to both the ham and the tongue was Mr Oakroyd's old friend and our old acquaintance, that independent craftsman and keeper of hens, Mr Sam Oglethorpe. Here was one person Mr Oakroyd could talk to, and though actually he did not do much talking, he kept close to Sam from the moment they all tramped up Caddy's stairs.

'Well, Jess,' said Mr Oglethorpe, 'I'll ha' to be off. I've getten t'hens to see to, tha knaws. Farls can't wait if fowk can.'

'Ay,' said Mr Oakroyd disconsolately. Then he brightened up. 'Here, Sam, I'm coming wi' yer.'

'Won't they want yer?' said Mr Oglethorpe. They had wandered away from the tables now.

'If they do, they mun want on. Ther's nowt I can do here nar.'

'Right, owd lad,' said Mr Oglethorpe cheerfully. 'We'll get t'tram.'

They said little or nothing, either on the tram or on the walk to Wabley from the terminus, but they smoked companionably all the way, and Mr Oakroyd did at least lose the feeling that he was wandering in an ugly dream. Sam might not be one of the brightest or have much to say for himself, but he was a comfortable sort of chap to be with at a time like this.

'I'll tell yer what,' Mr Oglethorpe suggested, when he had finished attending to his fowls, 'we'll ha' a sup o' beer. Tha doesn't want to go on to T'Anglers? I thowt not. Well, I'll fetch a sup and we'll car quiet a bit i' t'hen-hoil. Nay, don't you come; I'll fetch it mysen.'

This was that same combined hen-house and workshop where he had sat and talked to Sam and his nephew Ted, of the lorry, on a Sunday night that now seem years and years away. It was while he was waiting in there that he remembered the letter in his pocket. It was from Miss Trant:

Dear Mr Oakroyd,

I was so sorry to learn that your wife was ill and that you had to go home. I do hope that by this time you have better news of her. I have some news for you. Mr Gooch has seen this man Ridvers, and he has frightened him into agreeing to pay the claim for damages. I don't know whether this is a very legal thing to do - it doesn't seem like it - but it is only right he should pay for his stupidity. It will cost him a good deal too, which means that I have been saved a good deal - thanks to you. Please remember this when you hear from Mr Gooch, as you will very shortly. The other news is that Dr McFarlane and I are to be married very soon. We shall live just outside Gatford for a time. I'm afraid this means that a plan I had for offering you some work at Hitherton won't be possible now, though it was only vague. But will you please come and talk over your plans - unless you have already fixed something up for yourself? I have just had a very excited letter from Susie in London. She has begun rehearsing already and likes her part.

Yours sincerely,
Elizabeth Trant

He read this letter through twice, very carefully. He was glad that Miss Trant would not have to pay. He was also glad that she was marrying the big doctor chap. He told himself he was glad, yet he was conscious of feeling only a vague disappointment. The letter - a fine letter too - ought to have cheered him up, but it did not cheer him up. He was still numb, frozen, with just the tiniest bit of an ache somewhere.

There was a cosy gossiping look about Sam when he returned with his jugful. Mr Oakroyd wanted to feel like that too, but somehow he couldn't manage it.

'Well, Jess,' said Mr Oglethorpe, in his usual slow, meditative Jobbing Work style, 'an' ar yer've been finding things down South?'

'Nay,' said Mr Oakroyd, 'we've had a bit o' bother just lately, bit of a mix-up, you might say.' A week ago, he would have plunged at once into an account of the whole affair, but now he couldn't, not without an effort. It all seemed such a long way off, like a tale in a book.

'Ay, I dare say,' said Mr Oglethorpe, nodding and frowning judicially. Obviously it would not surprise him what happened down South. 'Been i' the-ater line, haven't yer, Jess? I did hear. An' what is there to do i' that line o' business? Be a change from Higden's, eh? Diff'rent altogether, I'll be barnd?'

Mr Oakroyd admitted that it was, and decribed briefly what he had been doing for the past six months. If he had been describing fairyland, his hearer could not have been more astonished and delighted, but though he felt a faint warmth at this reception of his news, a reception long anticipated, often imagined, he could not really be kindled. And it was just the same when they came to talk of his travels.

'An' Bristol an' Bedfordsheer, Jess,' cried Mr Oglethorpe, 'did yer ivver get theer?'

'Bristol and Bedfordshire?' he repeated, puzzled.

'Nay, lad, don't yer remember? I mind it as well as if it wor nobbut yesterda'. Yer come here, it wor t'last time yer ivver wor here, an' yer wanted to be off somewhere - down South - an' I says "Well, wheer d'yer want to go," an' yer says, "Bristol an' Bedfordsheer," an' I laughs. An' then - by gow! - afore I can turn rahnd - yer've gone. Eh, I've had monny a good laugh ower it. I've been dahn to Bruddersford, we'll say, an' one o' t'chaps o' the t'club has assed "Where's Jess Oakroyd, Sam?" an' I've towd them. "Bristol an' Bedfordsheer," I says. "Ar d'yer mean?" they says. "Well, he come here," I says, "an' he says to me he'd like to go to Bristol an' Bedfordsheer, an' t'next minute he wor off," I says. Don't tell me yer nivver went, Jess.'

'I remember,' said Mr Oakroyd slowly. 'Well, I nivver got to Bristol, Sam, though I've nivver given it a thowt. I may ha' seen Bedfordshire, but I don't knaw fairly. We've been all ower t'shop, up an' down an' across, on t'road, yer knaw. Ay, I've seen a deal.'

'Then yer owt to be satisfied nar, lad,' observed Mr Oglethorpe, with a suggestion of irony. 'Tell us wheer yer've been an' what yer've seen.'

Mr Oakroyd rubbed his chin. 'That's a big order, Sam,' he began doubtfully. 'When yer've been about, a bit, places - '

Mr Oglethorpe stopped him at once. He looked very reproachful, though waggish. 'Nar, Jess,' he cautioned, 'yer not goin' to tell me 'at places is all alike when yer come to know 'em.'

'Well, summat o' t'sort,' Mr Oakroyd muttered.

His friend instantly banged the table. 'Them's t'words, very words, 'at our Ted used i' this very place that Sunda',' he roared. 'Very words he said. An' yer said "Nay, I'll be damned if I'll ha' that." And I backed yer up. Our Ted wor only talking abart it t'other week here, when he wor wondering where yer'd got to. Well, well, well! That caps t'lot. We live an' we learn, we live an' we learn. Nay, Jess!'

'Howd thi noise, Sam!' Mr Oakroyd protested goodhumouredly. But he looked, and felt, confused. 'I don't mean all places is alike. Your Ted wor wrong. He went too far, too far bi half, he did. What I think is this - '

'Nay, Jess, leave it, lad, leave it nar. Say ner more. Here, have another sup o' beer. Bit better ner like, this beer. If they don't look aht, they'll be puttin' some malt an' hops in it agen, same as they used to, instead o' just colourin' t'reservoy watter an' fillin' t'barrels wi' that. Well, what's t'next job then, lad? Still in t'the-ater line?'

Mr Oakroyd did not know, and he hardly seemed to care. He had asked himself this question several times, but somehow had found it quite easy to leave it unanswered. It was as if something inside him had just snapped. 'I don't knaw,' he replied, blowing out his breath in what was recognized to be the Bruddersfordian equivalent of a sigh. 'I don't, Sam. There was a bit o' talk about me gettin' summat else i' t'same line, but I don't knaw what'll come of it. I haven't thowt about it. I suppose I mun be looking round.'

Mr Oglethorpe nodded sagely. Then he looked very grave. 'Keep aht o' t'Joinery an' Jobbing i' this neighbourhood, Jess, that's all. Way things is nar, it's nowt - nowt at all, it isn't. It's just like t'hens scrattin' for a bit o' summat.'

'Is it war ner it wor?' inquired Mr Oakroyd.

'Nay, trade's so bad and ther's so monny either stopped or on short time, they'll ha' nowt done, d'yer see, Jess? They'd let t'places go to rack an' ruin afore they'd have owt done. Sitha, I can't put me nose in onnywheer withart seeing hawf-a-dozen little jobs 'at wants doing. But fowk hasn't bit o' brass to spare. They can't thoil it, lad. I've nearly made as mich aht o' t'hens. I've been keepin' farls nar for fowerteen year, an' I shan't be capped if at finish t'farls is keepin' me. So don't set up for thysen on t'Joinery an' Jobbing i' these parts, Jess. Might be different dahn South, I dare say, but here - it's nowt. Keep to t'the-ater line, I say, 'cos fowk seems to ha' brass to spend on the-aters an' t'animated picters an' suchlike these days when they haven't a sixpence for owt beside. Has ta 'ad onny young actresses i' tow, Jess?'

'Nay, Sam, who d'yer think I am?' But Mr Oakroyd was not shocked. He had replied almost mechanically.

It occurred to Mr Oglethorpe then that this was hardly the time for such badinage - the clay of Dum Wood Cemetery being hardly dry on their boots yet - and hastily and awkwardly he changed the subject. But he could not change his friend's heavy and abstracted mood, and soon their talk dwindled to nothing; Mr Oakroyd returned home accompanied by a dark confusion of thoughts and memories, in which his adventures on the road, all the ups and downs of The Good Companions, had their place. Yet they were only like shadows flickering on a wall. He wanted to see them all again, these Good Companions; he could dwell affectionately on his thought of them; but nevertheless they were little figures, far away, and he realized, in his own dumb obscure fashion, that it was not they who had the power to wake him back to life. Nor was it anybody or anything in Bruddersford. He walked slowly through the familiar streets, a shrunken figure in an ill-fitting suit of black, solitary beneath the street lamps that only intensified the great dark above, a man alone. No, not entirely alone, for keeping step with him were immense vague shapes, so many configurations of mystery, pain, and death. 'Then we mun sell t'home up,' said Mr Oakroyd, early the next morning. He was looking disconsolately across the table at Leonard, who had just announced that he had decided to take the job he had been offered in Manchester.

'No good keepin' it if you're not going to stop in Bruddersford,' said Leonard.

'Well, I'm not,' his father remarked quietly.

'What are you going to do?'

'Wait a bit, lad, wait a bit. I'll see.' Mr Oakroyd was rather irritable now. 'We can't all be barbers wi' jobs i' Manchester round t'corner, can we?'

'I was only askin',' said Leonard, a sulky boy again.

'That's all right, lad. Tak' no notice. I'm glad you can look after yersen. Yer doin' right well, Leonard, an' if you'd nobbut settle a bit an' not go malackin' abart so much wi' t'girls - '

'I've 'ad enough of that,' said Leonard, who believed at the moment that he had.

'That's all right, then. You'll do champion,' said Mr Oakroyd, regarding his son for once with something like approval. 'Well, we'll ha' to sell up. Ar's it's got to be done, that's t'point? We're havin' no auctionin'.'

'Wouldn't be worth it anyway,' said Leonard, with a glance round the room. 'Not enough stuff here.'

'By gow! - we live an' learn. I thowt once upon a time I'd getten a good home together,' cried Mr Oakroyd, with some bitterness, 'but seemingly it's not worth sellin' up nar.'

'Best thing we can do', said Leonard, wisely disregarding this outburst, 'is to get one or two of these second-hand-furniture chaps in, and they'll offer a price. Albert'll tell me who's the best. I'll go and see him this morning if you like.'

'All right.' Mr Oakroyd looked about him now. 'I wonder if ther's owt our Lily 'ud like for hersen,' he mused.

'Dare say there might.' Leonard lit a cigarette. 'But she'll have a better place of her own now. Jack Clough gets good money out there.'

'I'll look abart a bit. Then if ther's owt I think she could do wi', I'll pack it up in a box.' He suddenly remembered something. 'Eh, whativver I do. I'll ha' to go back to Gatford! I left my tools.'

Leonard stared at him. 'Gor, you made me jump, Par! Is that all? Tools!'

'Ay, tools, lad, tools! It's enough an' all. I'm a tradesman, I am, an' I can't set mysen up wi' a pair o' scissors an a pair o' clippers an' a drop o' hair-oil. I want summat to work wi' when I start. An' I been using some o' them tools for twenty year, an' don't you forget it. I wouldn't be wi'out 'em for owt. I'm a tradesman, see - an' if you ask me, ther's noan so damn monny on us left.'

'Can you wonder,' said Leonard, with all the scorn of a younger and wiser generation, 'wages they pay?'

'Happen not,' said his father gloomily. 'For all that, a chap 'at's learnt his trade an' can use his hands - he isn't a machine an' he isn't a flippin' monkey - he's a man, lad, wages or no wages, a man.' And he gave the table a bang. It was immediately answered by another, at the door. 'Hello, who's this?'

'Postman. I'll go.' And when Leonard came back, he added: 'One for me and one for you.'

Mr Oakroyd had been told by Miss Trant that he would hear from Mr Gooch of Gatford, but nevertheless he was astonished. He was even more astonished when the following little bombshell had exploded under his nose:

Dear Sir,

Following the instructions of our client, Miss E. Trant, upon the satisfactory termination of our negotiations with Mr Ridvers, we have pleasure in handing you herewith our cheque, on behalf of Miss Trant, for £100 (one hundred pounds) receipt of which kindly acknowledge to us as well as to Miss Trant herself.

Yours faithfully,
Goring, Son, and Gooch

And there it was, with the letter, a little bit of blue and white paper: *Pay Mr J. Oakroyd or Order*. A hundred pounds. Nay!

'Here,' he shouted to Leonard, 'I've getten a hundred pounds. Eh, it's aht o' all reason. A hundred pound! That's right, isn't it?'

"Well I'll be blowed! What you got that for, Par? Let's have a look at it. That's right. It's a cheque, that is. But what you got it for?'

'Well, I did a bit o' puttin' two an' two together for this Miss Trant I been workin' for. Must ha' saved a good deal, I dare say, but this is aht o' all reason. Nay - a hundred pound!'

'Depends what you did, doesn't it?' said Leonard, looking very knowing.

Mr Oakroyd explained briefly what he had done.

'Well, that's it then,' said Leonard. 'You might have saved her a right lot - 'spect you did - wish I had it.' He inspected the cheque again. 'I know a bit about these things. You can't cash this, y'know, Par, 'cos it's got Company written on. You'll have to pay it into t'bank.'

'What bank? Haven't got a bank, though I once had a bit in t'Post Office. An' I'd some trade on gettin' owt aht on 'em an' all.'

'You goes to bank with this, and you pays it in,' Leonard

explained, proud of his knowledge of high finance, 'and then if you want it - money, y'know - you take it out again. That's way you do it.'

'Put it in an' tak it aht,' cried Mr Oakroyd, puzzled. 'I call that daft. Still, if that's t'way, I'll do it. An' I mun do some o' this kindly acknowledgin' too. Eh, but - a hundred pound!' And he stared at his son in bewilderment.

'Come in handy, that little lot,' said Leonard, who was now slipping into the part of the knowing young man. 'That and what you'll get from selling up here, it'll give you a good old start all right.'

'Nay, I can't keep all I get from selling t'home up,' Mr Oakroyd protested. 'You mun have half, Leonard. We might get summat for our Lily an' all. Onny road, we'll divide an' make a divvy on it.'

'Our Lily won't want anything. She's well off, she is. And I don't,' added Leonard, who, to give him his due, was not a grasping youth. 'Keep it yourself, Par. What there is, is yours all right. But we shan't get much, I can tell you now. I'll go and ask Albert.'

As soon as he was left alone, Mr Oakroyd began rummaging about to see if there was anything that Lily might like. He wandered upstairs, spending quite a time there, looking not at little old possessions but at the very past itself, so that times, seasons, occasions, events, he had almost entirely forgotten returned all clear and bright but very small, part of a melancholy enchantment.

A slight noise from downstairs called him into the immediate present again. He descended quietly, to discover in the living-room, just by the old sofa, what looked like a hillock of dirty blue serge. The next moment it turned itself into Mrs Sugden rising from her knees, panting, purple-faced, and a trifle confused.

'Mornin', Mrs Sugden,' he said, rather dryly, 'I couldn't think what it wor.'

'Eh, Mr Oakroyd, I 'ope yer don't mind,' she cried, puffing and blowing. 'I looked in to see if there was owt I could do for yer, an' your Leonard towed me as he was passin' yer were sellin' up an' I were just 'aving a look at t'sofa. I've been wantin' one for some time an' I thowt I might as well 'ave it, if it's goin', just as well as t'next.'

'Ay,' he said, wagging his head at her in a kind of half-mournful, half-humorous resignation. 'So you might, Mrs Sugden. Tak' a look while you've a chance. Here today and gone tomorrow, that's our motto.' And he left her to it, but now, when he looked round upstairs, there was only so much furniture and odds and ends all worse for wear, just old junk. He had to comfort himself with a pipe of Old Salt.

And then it happened.

'Mr Oakroyd, Mr Oakroyd,' she was screaming up the stairs, 'there's summat come for yer.' And when he hurried down, she added, holding something out to him: 'Looks like a sort o' telegram.'

It was a cable. Trembling, Mr Oakroyd put his pipe down on the table, and even then only opened the envelope with difficulty. He stared, breathing hard. *Very grieved all love if you come out here very welcome and good job any time Lily Jack.* Again and again he read it, making sure. And then it was as if a huge door had been opened and the sunlight was flooding in, warming him to life again.

'An' will yer go?' asked Mrs Sugden, when at last he had satisfied her curiosity. 'Eh, it's a long way off.'

'Long way! Long nowt! If it were from here to t'moon I'd go - '

And Mrs Sugden, hearing the terrible voice of love triumphant, was silenced. No doubt she knew that when this voice peals out, all other voices in the universe are nothing but reedy whispers, better silent. Perhaps she acquired the sofa as a reward for recognizing these authentic tones.

Another person heard them that morning. This was the young man at Torry's Shipping Agency in Shuttle Street. He looked up from his book to see a detestable, cheap, black suit, a mouth that was in earnest, and two blue eyes that blazed with excitement.

'Nar, lad,' said this caller, in the usual and regrettable Bruddersford manner, 'just tell me how I can get to Canada.'

The young man put away his book and took out a pencil. This sounded like business. 'Assisted passage, I suppose?'

'Ar d'you mean?'

The young man began to explain about emigration and government grants and forms to fill in, but he was quickly cut short.

'Nowt o' that,' said Mr Oakroyd. 'Ther's no government i' this. I'm payin' for mysen. I can manage third class nicely.'

'Then that's different,' said the young man, who now began to talk about the various routes and steamship lines. 'Of course it depends on where you want to go at the other end. But we might begin with this end first. You could go from either Liverpool or Southampton.'

'Champion !' cried Mr Oakroyd.

'Yes, either Liverpool or Southampton.'

'Good enough!' Then, after some thought, he went on: 'Nar I fancy Southampton, an' I'll tell yer for why. I'd like to call at a place i' t'Midlands - Gatford - an' then I'd like to go to London on t'way, 'cos ther's some friends o' mine there 'at I'd like to see afore I go. So we'll mak' it Southampton, lad.'

'Good! Southampton.' And the young man flourished his pencil. 'What part of Canada are you going to? We could probably arrange to book you right through.'

'Yer a smart young feller, I can see,' said Mr Oakroyd in great delight. 'Just get your map aht an' I'll show yer where I want to go. It's where my dowter lives an' I can put me finger on t'very place. Yer knaw abaht Canada, do yer? Ay, well, you an' me'ull mak' a right good job on it.'

For the next hour that young man of Tony's never returned to his book. On the other hand, he did not miss it. Life had walked into the shop.

V

It is Saturday afternoon again, and once more something queer is happening in that narrow thoroughfare to the west of the town, Manchester Road. A grey-green tide flows sluggishly down the road a tide of cloth caps, leaving the ground of 't'United', where Huddersfield have just been defeated by three goals to two. Somewhere in the middle of this thick stream of cloth caps is one that looks newer than most of its neighbours. It belongs to Mr Jesiah Oakroyd, who has contrived to attend this match before leaving Bruddersford for years, perhaps for ever. He is catching a train to Gatford, his first little halt on his long journey, this very evening, and already his suitcase and his big tin trunk are at the station, waiting for the 6.50. Casual talk is easy in such a slowly moving throng and is favoured because it helps to pass the time even when it does not also relieve the feelings. Mr Oakroyd is engaged in it. We can just overhear a sentence or two.

'Ay,' his neighbour observes, 'if they'd nobbut laked like this all t'season they'd ha' been somewhere at the top instead of being nearly at bottom. They're just wak'ning up nar it's nearly over.'

'Well, it's been a grand match today, it has,' says Mr Oakroyd dreamily. 'I nivver want to see a better. Eh, it were t'owd form all ower agen. Them last two goals - nay, by gow!'

'Ay, them wor a bit of all right.'

'All right! They wor grand!'

And then we hear no more. The tide of caps and men flows on, slowly but gradually gathering speed, like our years. It recedes, shrinks, until at last you do not notice it at all. Manchester Road is now only one of a hundred thoroughfares, for Bruddersford itself, the whole spread of it, has come into view. Holdsworth's giant mill looms there on the left; the Midland Railway's station glitters in the sun again, and there is an answering gleam from the glass roof of the Market Hall; a silver streak shows one of the canals; and in the centre of the tall chimneys, shaking the air with its *Lass of Richmond Hill*, is the tower of the Bruddersford Town Hall. It points a finger at us, and then is gone, lost in a faint smudge of smoke. Another moment and Bruddersford is only a grimy crack in the hills. The high moorland between Yorkshire and Lancashire rises steadily, clear in the pearly light of Spring. Once more, the miles and miles of ling and bog and black rock, and the curlews crying above the scattered jewellery of the little tarns. There are the Derbyshire hills, and there, away to the north, are the great fells of Cumberland, and now the whole darkening length of it, from the Peak to Cross Fell, is visible, for this is the Pennine Range, sometimes called the backbone of England.

Epilogue
BEING A MERE POSTSCRIPT ADDRESSED TO THOSE WHO INSIST UPON HAVING ALL THE LATEST NEWS

No, Susie has not married Inigo. On the other hand, she has not married anybody else. There have been times when rumours and little paragraphs in the gossip columns have sent Inigo flying round to see her (not that he is not always seeing her), but she has laughed and told him not to be silly. Once, it is true, there was real danger - for, after all, nobody can deny that Sir Douglas Heath-Watchett is an extremely attractive young man - and that was the time when poor Inigo, convinced that all was lost, fled to Norway and tried to fish. He returned, however, to find Susie still laughing and Sir Douglas booking a passage to Florida, where there are fish even larger than those in Norway. Susie says she is too young to marry yet and that life is too amusing. When she finds herself on the point of being relegated to minor parts or, alternatively, when there is no more fun in being a star comedienne with a huge and rapturous public of her own, then, she declares, she will grab the first nice man she sees and hurl him into the nearest registry office. No doubt Inigo will contrive to be that man.

He has the best chance, for he sees her almost every other day, and they go here, there, and everywhere together. Both of them - as everybody should realize by this time - make absurdly large sums of money. Susie talks gravely enough about her salary, being nothing if not a child of the theatre, but to Inigo the whole thing is still an elaborate joke. He watches with droll amazement the rising tide of performing fees, sheet music royalties, gramophone royalties, and so forth. Mr Pitsner still seems a quite unreal person, and Inigo would never be very surprised if the money Mr Pitsner hands over suddenly melted into thin air or turned, like fairy gold, into a heap of withered leaves on the bank counter. It is incredible that he should make so much money out of what seems to him a mere parlour trick. His writing, however, is a very serious business. He has published a volume of essays, so sternly literary that it is almost impossible to read them, entitled *The Last Knapsack and Other Papers*. The only copy ever seen is in Miss Dean's dressing-room. She pretends to laugh at it, but in secret she is rather proud of 'the fact that it is dedicated 'To Susie, the Best Companion', and she is determined to read it all through, one day. Inigo says that the book has had such a poor sale simply because he was foolish enough to publish it at his own expense. The next book, now in preparation, is to be brought out at the expense of the publisher, who will then be compelled, Inigo declares, to make everybody read it.

Sometimes, but chiefly in the way of business, they meet Jerry Jerningham, who is, perhaps, rather plumper than he was, in spite of diet and massage and exercises. He is, of course, one of the most successful young men on the light musical stage. Now that he has triumphantly acquired an American accent, a perpetual reminder of his season on Broadway, he is busy building his own theatre. The fact that it is to have no pit is desolating many of the outer suburbs. Mrs Jerningham is not a public figure, and, indeed, is rarely seen these days. Now and then, however, she lunches with Susie, who listens very sympathetically to an account of all her troubles. This account is always liberally punctuated with the cry: 'But don't think for a moment, my dear, that I'm sorry I married him.'

Jimmy Nunn, Joe, and Mrs Joe are still in concert-party work, and lately concluded a successful season with 'The Red Revellers' at either Rhyl or Llandudno. Jimmy's digestion is beginning to trouble him again, and he admits that he is not as young as he was, so that the sooner he is able to run a little show of his own, the better. There is some talk of his managing it this coming season. George is still something of a charge on his parents, being apprenticed to the motor trade, but very soon he will be earning his own living, and then Joe and Mrs Joe will - as they say - 'look about for something'. What that something will be they have not yet quite decided. Joe still favours a seaside hotel, and Elsie Dulver, who saw them at Eastbeach, has promised her assistance in finding one, and Inigo and Susie have both offered them a substantial loan. Mr Morton Mitcham is no longer a performer - he has gone into management - at least, that is how he puts it - though actually he is nothing more nor less than the manager of the pier at - where do you think? - why, of all places, Sandybay. He is now one of the figures of the town, and is for ever discovering old acquaintances from the East among the anglers who drink Scotch every morning and evening in the little bar at the end of the pier. He is regarded with something like awe by every younger member of a visiting troupe, because it appears it was he and no other who discovered Susie Dean and Jerry Jerningham, and those who doubt his word are invited to call at his lodgings and see for themselves certain bills, programmes, and photographs.

The McFarlanes have settled in Edinburgh, where Hugh has a fine practice and also lectures grimly at the University from time to time. He has published a very small book with an enormous title - it begins with *Some Observations on the Parathyroid Glands*, and then goes on and on, *With Special Reference*, and so forth - and Paris and Vienna think there is something in it, whereas Leipzig and Chicago are not very sure. Mrs McFarlane is even less certain, but, on the other hand, is positive that though Hugh is doing far too much, he is looking much better than he did, don't you think? I am sorry to say that Mrs McFarlane, though the wife of one of Edinburgh's most respected citizens and the delighted mother of two small and very fat boys, has a secret vice. Now and again she likes to sneak away, buy *The Stage*, and devour it in a corner. If you went in very quickly, you might easily catch her one day, smiling at the advertisements: 'Wanted Known....A Riot at Little Sandmouth, last ...' Sometimes Hugh has to go up to London, and then she tears herself away from the fat little boys and accompanies him, and then she sees Susie and Inigo and perhaps watches Jerry's beautiful capers from a stall. There are letters, too, of course. Incidentally, it is surprising what letters Mrs Joe can write. The matter is humble enough - the old stories of pier pavilion audiences, queer lodgings, and Sunday trains - but the penmanship is at once flowing and exquisite, and the style worthy of Lord Chesterfield himself. I do not say that Mrs Joe always writes like this, but those are the sort of letters Mrs McFarlane receives from her, once in a while.

Then there is Mr Oakroyd, far away in Canada, or, to be exact, at Pittford Falls, Ontario. Here we come to a difficulty. The trouble is that nobody has been out to Canada and that any news of him can only trickle through those craggy little letters of his. It is certain that he is a very proud grandfather, that he and his son-in-law, Jack Clough, are now running some good, solid tradesman-like business of their own, and that everybody there is very well, thank you. I know that Mr Oakroyd does not live with his daughter, but has a little place of his own just down the road, where he can smoke a pipe over his three-week-old copy of the Saturday sports edition of the *Bruddersford Evening Express*, which is sent out to him regularly by S. Oglethorpe, Town End, Wabley, Yorks. Moreover, I gather that Pittford Falls regard him as a man with vast theatrical experience and a topographical authority on the Mother Country. The photographs that Susie sent out, and the box of gramophone records, including *Slippin' round the Corner* sung and played in half a dozen different ways, that Inigo gave him, these things have only confirmed and increased his reputation. There is no doubt that he is enjoying life, but apparently there are drawbacks. Thus it seems that Pittford Falls has a nasty trick of being either too hot or too cold; there are no cosy little public-houses, and the club that he has joined is not really an adequate substitute; the tobacco is too sweet, not a patch on Old Salt; stoves are not up to much when you have been used to sitting in front of a kitchen range, where there has been a bit of baking going on, perhaps, during the day; and there is a queer, empty look about the place. For some time now, I hear, they have been planning a trip to the

Old Country, and Mr Oakroyd admits that he longs for a sight of good old Bruddersford. Whether he is as happy there as he thought he would be I do not know, though not for the world would he venture far from Lily and the two children, for they are all for ever having 'a bit o' fun'. We must leave it at that. In this place, whether we call it Bruddersford or Pittford Falls, perfection is not to be found, neither in men nor in the lot they are offered, to say nothing of the tales we tell of them, these hints and guesses, words in the air and gesticulating shadows, these stumbling chronicles of a dream of life.

The Good Companions
on Stage and Screen

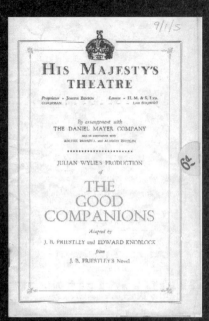

Top:
Programme
cover of the
first ever stage
adaptation of
the novel,
1931.
(Photographer
unknown)

Bottom left:
John Gielgud
as Inigo
Jollifant, 1931.
(Photographer
unknown)

Bottom right:
Gielgud and
Adele Dixon in
a scene from
the play, 1931.
(Photographer
unknown)

The Good Companions on Stage and Screen

Since 1929 *The Good Companions* has entertained and enthralled millions across the world. Its spectacular success and theatrical energy made it a prime target for adaptation from the outset; if it could draw so many readers then it was logical to suppose it would entertain theatre and cinema goers in exactly the same way. As it was the public didn't have long to wait. The first dramatisation came within two years of publication, the first film version within four and since then people have been pointing a camera at it, staging it and recording it for over 70 years. In all it has been adapted for the stage three times; radio several times; filmed twice and made into a nine-part television musical. It provided Priestley with his first excursion into the theatre; was the first ever 'talkie' to be screened publicly to the King and Queen; and has been played out and adapted by some of the worlds best-known actors, directors, actresses, writers, lyricists and composers.

Strangely, for such an English book, the first adaptation was part written by Edward Knoblock, an American author who spent just about all his professional life in Paris and London writing criticism, plays, novels and film scripts. When the rights were bought Priestley made it clear he wished to have a hand in the writing. As Knoblock was a friend the two men agreed to collaborate. Priestley had already written a dramatic version of Thomas Love Peacock's popular novel *Nightmare Abbey* that had failed to reach production so the opportunity to work with an established playwright like Knoblock was a means to enhance his technique and gain some reputation in the field – one he came to dominate over the next twenty years.

Once the script was complete a company was put together by the famous pantomime impresario Julian Wylie. His cast was impressive: rising stars John Gielgud and Adele Dixon (who appeared in the first ever BBC high definition service broadcast, 1936) played Inigo Jollifant and Susie Dean;

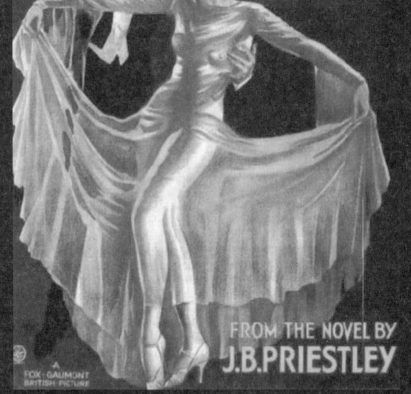

An original poster for the 1933 film. (Artist unknown)

Priestley toasts the cast of the 1931 production. John Gielgud, Edith Sharpe, Adele Dixon and Edward Chapman. (Photographer unknown)

Edward Chapman took the role of Jess Oakroyd, Edith Sharpe played Miss Trant and music was by the popular composer Noel Gay – best remembered now for his musical *Me and My Girl*.

Gielgud, who had just finished playing *King Lear* at the Old Vic saw *The Good Companions* as a new challenge and accepted without hesitation. His only reservation was that he believed himself to be almost the only man in England not to have read the book.

Apprehensive about this before meeting his new director (Wylie was a temperamental man infamous for outbursts of sudden rage) he sat up half the night skimming through and getting to know his part. Gielgud need not have worried, he found Wylie charming, broad-minded and thorough in his methods. Wylie admitted going to see *King Lear* with the view to getting him for the part of Jollifant. Gielgud was amazed to find that the self-proclaimed King of Panto was an enthusiastic aficionado of Shakespeare and of his Lear.

Production was not straightforward. Two weeks of reading in the Boardroom of the Dominion Theatre was followed by four long weeks of rehearsals and then three weeks of trial performances in the provinces. The adaptation called for a cast of more than 37 extras, 15 enormous sets, a vast orchestra and a stage Gielgud regarded as 'the size of a desert'. The crowd scenes and whole cast musical numbers were particularly awkward to direct and took all of Wylie's talent to perfect. The supers were divided into groups and numbered by Knoblock. Wylie then shouted them into shape from his position in the stalls like a sergeant-major. The effort was worth it and these scenes were later hailed as marvels of stage-craft by critics and audiences alike.

The opening night at His Majesty's Theatre in the West End came on the 14th May 1931. The run lasted for nine months and was followed by a national tour. In the autumn the play also opened on Broadway at the 49th Street Theatre with a Wylie assembled cast of Hugh Sinclair as Jollifant, Vera Lennox as Susie Dean, George Carney taking on Jess Oakroyd and Valerie Taylor as Miss Trant. Reviews were not kind. American critics found the play too unlike like the book and its characters. A mystified Priestley believed the production was every bit as good as London and was left to surmise that the critics had formed a different mental picture of

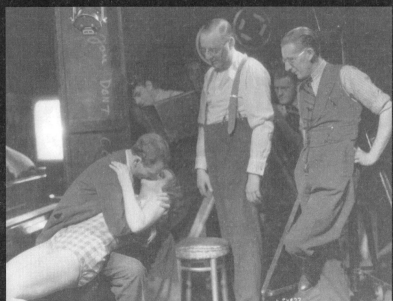

Top:
Victor Saville
(left) and his
assistant
William Dodds
overlook John
Gielgud and
Jessie
Matthews in a
scene from the
1933 film.
(Photographer
unknown)

Bottom:
Jess Oakroyd
and his
crooked
companions
arrive at the
Kirkworth Inn
after their
journey down
the Great
North Road
together. From
the set of the
1933 film.
(Photographer
unknown)

The cast of the 1933 film become Good Companions. (Photographer unknown)

Englishness from that of English people. American audiences turned out to be more appreciative than the press, but after 68 performances running at a loss the play was taken off.

Despite its inability to conquer Broadway this first adaptation's long West End run made it a qualified success. For John Gielgud it was his first taste of celebrity and the best regular money he had ever collected. 'Suppers at the Savoy were no longer a luxury, and sometimes I enjoyed hearing people say 'that's John Gielgud' as I passed.' Such familiarity was something he enjoyed for the rest of his long and remarkable career.

A theatrical hit was nearly always a guaranteed success at the cinema box-office and the play soon became a film. Michael Balcon, Head of Production at Gaumont-British, bought the rights and appointed his friend and long-time collaborator Victor Saville as director. The pair had already made a string of films together and eventually became the studio's most prolific and valued team.

The project was particularly appealing to Saville; he enjoyed the book's realism and saw it as representative of British class divisions in a society ravaged by economic depression – a situation common in many of his films and one he loved to explore.

Based closely on Knoblock and Priestley's stage play the film was the studios most ambitious effort to date with a record 72 sets and over 100 speaking parts.

Like Wylie before him Saville handled all this with consummate skill and the film is vintage British Cinema at its very best. It continues to interest critics, film-historians and cinema-goers to this day and is quite regularly screened at venues such as The National Film Theatre.

Saville and Balcon invited Gielgud to reprise his role as Inigo and take up his first major film role. Edmund Gwenn took on Oakroyd and Miss Trant was played charmingly by Mary Glynne. For the part of Susie Dean Saville tested hundreds of girls and then decided he wanted 'The Dancing Divinity', Jessie Matthews. Balcon didn't agree and only allowed Saville to have his way after some fierce arguing. In the end Saville's judgement was justified; the film was a huge breakthrough for Matthews and helped set her up as one

Top:
Filming scenes outside the Gatford Theatre. The scenes in which this theatre caught fire greatly impressed King George V at the premiere of the 1933 film. (Photographer unknown)

Bottom:
Mr. and Mrs. Oakroyd, Edmund Gwenne and Florence Gregson take a break from filming, 1933. (Photographer unknown)

Front cover of a 1957 Good Companions song sheet. All of the novel's major stage and screen adaptations had their own signature tunes and all had soundtracks released either on gramophone or LP. The soundtrack of the 1974 production was released on CD in the 1990s. (Artist unknown)

The cover of the original 45 single release from the 1957 film. (Artist unknown)

of the most popular and potent leading actresses of 1930s cinema.

The film was the first 'talkie' to be shown publicly to the King and Queen of England. The Royal Standard was hoisted over the New Victoria Cinema (now the Apollo Victoria Theatre) in London for the very first Royal Command Performance, an occasion that was to follow year after year. Unlike modern film premieres the screening was in the afternoon because King George V wanted to be back at Buckingham Palace in time for his tea. After the film the king met the cast and spoke at length to Victor Saville about the making of the climactic fire scene. As a divorcee Jessie Matthews was barred from the line up and not presented to the King and Queen, yet to her delight Queen Mary saw her from the Royal Box as she waited by her aisle-seat in the stalls. The Queen called the King's attention and he leaned over and acknowledged her, an event that made Matthews a faithful subject forever.

The 1933 film was remade in 1957 in full cinemascope colour by the Associated British Picture Corporation with direction by J. Lee Thompson who's best remembered now for such

films as, *Woman in a Dressing Gown, Ice Cold in Alex, Tiger Bay, The Guns of Navarone* and *Cape Fear*. Songs for the film were penned by Paddy Roberts, C. Alberto Rossi and Geoffrey Parsons, with musical direction by Louis Levy.

The film was Associated British's attempt to create an English version of the Hollywood musicals of the day and although it does retain the essential spirit of the novel it had the misfortune to be released just as rock and roll was taking off and its music and songs didn't really appeal to young audiences clamouring for Elvis Presley, Tommy Steele and Cliff Richard. Similarly, the updated Hollywood treatment failed to impress lovers of the book and people seeking the sombre realism that was prevalent in J. Lee Thompson's other films.

The picture's great strength is its cast with a host of minor roles being played out wonderfully by actors who subsequently went on to become much more famous. John Le Mesurier, Anthony Newley, Rachel Roberts, Thora Hird, Shirley Ann Field, Joyce Grenfell, and Melvyn Hayes, all provide great incidental pleasure to the modern watcher. In the lead roles Celia Johnson (the Jane Austen of British

Top:
Filming the 1933 scenes of the 'Sandybay Pavilion', Jessie Matthews on stage.
(Photographer unknown)

Bottom:
Victor Saville on the camera crane directs Jessie Matthews in the Gatford Theatre scenes, 1933.
(Photographer unknown)

cinema) and Eric Portman are perfect as Miss Trant and Jess Oakroyd and John Fraser and Janette Scott emerge as stars in their own right - both went on to become icons of 50s and 60s cinema.

I have very happy memories of making The Good Companions and the film was enormous fun from beginning to end. At the time I was a contract artist with Associated British Pictures and they were looking for something to launch my adult career. Expectations for the film and my role in it were enormously high and of course I was a great admirer of J.B. Priestley who was a highly prized and influential author able to capture and express what it was like to live in England at that time.

Six weeks before filming I met up with the choreographers Paddy Stone and Irving Davies and had a wonderful time learning the dance routines prior to filming. The cast was very strong, a wonderful array of talent that included my mother – Dame Thora Hird. We were all extremely enthusiastic and worked hard to make it a success. It was a happy set to be part of and I think that happiness comes across in the final film. Sadly it wasn't the triumph everyone hoped for and I think

now that expectations were too high. Associated British believed in it and pushed it all the way with no expense spared. Horrified I would miss the premiere in London because I was playing Peter Pan in a nationwide tour they flew me by helicopter to Elstree Studios and made a special film so I could welcome all the first night guests.

I think Associated British made several mistakes with the film. First of all they tried to imitate Hollywood style musicals and created a soundtrack that was out of keeping with the new music of the day. There was also a lack of imagination from the top. I remember the Head of Studio Robert Clark attending a pre-production meeting with the choreographers, set and costume designers where they discussed the big final scene where I as Suzie Dean would be lifted into flight and sent off around the world as a famous star. Clark's reaction was 'so she'll be travelling then, I suppose she'll need a jumper and skirt'. The expressions of the designers were a picture all of their own! Finally, I'm not sure J. Lee Thompson was the right sort of director for such a production. He had a talent and specialty for social realism and was quite experimental – a Hollywood style musical wasn't him at all and I found

Janette Scott and John Fraser as Inigo Jollifant and Susie Dean in a still from the 1957 film. The pair emerged from the production as genuine stars. (Canal+ Image UK)

him humourless and rather unmusical.
Nevertheless it was a wonderful
experience and if seen now the film has
a lot to offer especially some wonderful
cameo performances from the cast. It
certainly didn't harm my career and I
enjoyed every minute of it.
Janette Scott – Susie Dean

I had a wonderful time making The
Good Companions, *working with Bobby*
Howes, Eric Portman and the great
Celia Johnson - Rachel Roberts, Shirley
Anne Field, Paddy Stone and Irving
Davies, and of course dear Janette
Scott. With hindsight, I think we made a
big mistake emulating "Show-Biz"
American musicals of the time, since the
whole charm of the book is the utterly
English, provincial charm of it. The
result was glossy, but ersatz.
As a result of making it, however, I was
put on contract by PYE Nixa, and made
a few records, two of which got into the
top ten!
John Fraser – Inigo Jollifant

1974 saw the arrival of the next major
adaptation, this time the product of
collaboration between the lyricist
Johnny Mercer, writer Ronald Harwood
and the composer Sir André Previn.
Mercer had loved the book for over
forty years and had always wanted to
turn it into a musical. In 1973 a British
consortium headed by Bernard Delfont
approached Previn and asked him to
suggest possibilities for a new West End
musical. Previn also wanted The Good
Companions and when he approached
Mercer to write the lyrics the two men
happily took the idea back to Delfont
and Priestley. Everything was agreed
and Ronald Harwood was brought in to
write the libretto.

At Mercer and Previn's invitation
Priestley became involved in putting
the show together and spent several
mornings casting a parental eye over
rehearsals. He was particularly
impressed with the music which he
found to be just right and 'very
whistleable'. Previn was equally
impressed by Priestley's energy for a
man of eighty years and took pleasure
hearing about his future plans and how
the book had propelled him to fame
and fortune many years before. 'It
would be remarkable for a lad of twenty
at Oxford let alone a man of eighty.'

Sir André Previn here recalls the genesis
of the show:

I'd had an interest in British Music all
my life and along with it a fascination
with the literature of the first 30 years

Theatre poster for the 1974 West End production. (Artist Unknown)

HER MAJESTY'S THEATRE

Proprietors:
A.T.P. (London) Ltd.

Chairman:
SIR LEW GRADE

Managing Director:
TOBY ROWLAND

Deputy Chairman:
LOUIS BENJAMIN

General Manager: RAYMOND LANE
Box Office: 01-930 6606

Bernard Delfont, Richard M. Mills and Richard Pilbrow on behalf of the Bernard Delfont Organisation Ltd
present

John MILLS · The · Judi DENCH

GOOD COMPANIONS

The Musical of the Novel by **J.B. Priestley**

Christopher GABLE · Marti WEBB

Hope JACKMAN · Malcolm RENNIE
Roy SAMPSON · Jeannie HARRIS · Bernard MARTIN

Ray C. DAVIS

Music by
André PREVIN

Lyrics by
Johnny MERCER

Book by
Ronald HARWOOD

Choreography by
Jonathan TAYLOR

Orchestrations by
Herbert W. SPENCER & Angela MORLEY

Designed by
Malcolm PRIDE

Lighting by
John B. READ

Sound by
David COLLISON

Musical Supervision by
Marcus DODS

Production Associate Peter Rawley

Directed by **Braham MURRAY**

First performance at Her Majesty's Theatre, Thursday 11th July 1974 or so of the 20th century. I had always been fond of The Good Companions because there were so few picaresque novels of its type. Through the early 1970s I'd been thinking that I'd like to write another show for the commercial theatre – the first one I wrote, 'Coco,' was reasonably successful, but I wasn't really happy with it and wanted to try again. I tried getting hold of The Good Companions, but was told it was unavailable. Then a strange thing happened.

Back then my undisputed idol among lyric writers was Johnny Mercer. I wrote him a letter asking would he like to write a show with me? 'Yes,' he said, and 'what a fine idea, I'll come over next month.' When we met he suggested The Good Companions because it was his favourite book. The coincidence was so extraordinary that there and then I contacted Mr Priestley and this time he agreed.

I was very happy during the time we worked together. John's lyrics were inimitable. He had a particular blend of the deeply poetic and sweetly vernacular that no other lyricist had been able to approach. My favourite memory is making the demonstration records – Johnny singing and myself

accompanying. He was a dynamite singer: blessed with the immaculate time-keeping of a jazz instrumentalist. I think we created a very good musical – the ultimate in the theatre, it had everything.
André Previn

The playwright, author and film producer Ronald Harwood here gives some reflections on the production and Priestley.

I was brought up on Priestley in Cape Town, South Africa, where I was born and educated. I read many of his novels and was a devoted admirer. I first met him in 1968, Victor Saville, the film producer, had bought the rights to Priestley's novel, Lost Empires, and I had been employed to write the screenplay. The film was never made but Priestley, apparently, liked my script and years later when Johnny Mercer and André Previn had the idea to turn The Good Companions into a musical, he approved of my doing the book. I became friends with Priestley and through the 70s my wife and I spent several weekends at his house near Stratford.

Because his work was for the most part optimistic, he had the deprecating

HER MAJESTY'S
T H E A T R E

THE
GOOD
COMPANIONS

Top left:
The front cover
of the opening
night
programme
11th July
1974. (Artist
Unknown)

Top right:
Sir André
Previn during
rehearsals.
(Photographer
unknown)

Bottom:
Dame Judi
Dench, Sir
John Mills,
Christopher
Gable and
Malcolm
Rennie set off
together.
(Photographer
unknown)

nickname Jolly Jack Priestley. It was an unfair sobriquet. I never saw him jolly. He took pride in being a Yorkshireman, full of common-sense and in touch with the man-in-the-street. He was also intensely serious and sensitive; his love of music, both classical and popular, was profound and he had an original way of thinking which was never fanciful. He was and still is one of the great names of English letters; yet, somehow he gave the impression of being an outsider, up against the Establishment, disparaged by the literati in London, a man of contradictions.

After many weeks rehearsing the 1974 musical the day came when Mercer, Previn and I were to take J. B. through our production. We met in a studio at Chappel of Bond Street, Previn at the piano, Mercer singing the songs and I describing the action scene by scene. Wives were present, and other interested parties, more than a dozen of us. The presentation went well, J. B. was pleased and we all repaired to the Westbury Hotel for a sumptuous lunch. Just as we were sipping coffee, Previn and his then wife, Mia Farrow, were told that their car had arrived and they departed. Mercer, a generous man who had just sold his share in a record company for many millions, called for the bill. He then took out his credit card holder and flicked it open. The cards were contained in plastic envelopes, concertina fashion, and a long string of them unfolded. The elderly Italian waiter put on his reading glasses and started studying the cards, bowing lower and lower until eventually he reached the last card at the level of Mercer's knees. He straightened up and said, 'Sorry, we don't take any of these.' Mercer was aghast and an awkward silence followed. J. B. kept his eyes averted. My wife and I had a rather frantic, whispered conversation about our overdraft. I paid the bill. It drastically increased our borrowing. Two days later I received a letter from J. B.

Dear Ronald,

I was aware of your embarrassment yesterday when it came to paying the bill. I hope you realise there was nothing I could do to help since I was the Guest of Honour.

However, I trust you noticed that I had Boiled Beef and Carrots for my main course which happened to be the cheapest dish on the menu and which also happens to be my favourite.

Yours,
J. B.

Top:
Sir André Previn, J.B. Priestley, Ronald Harwood and Johnny Mercer pause on a London Street en-route to a sumptuous lunch at the Westbury Hotel, 1974. (Photographer Unknown)

Bottom:
The 1974 cast become Good Companions. (Photographer unknown)

Like the 1957 film this new adaptation had an exceptionally talented cast and starred John Mills as Jess Oakroyd, Judi Dench as Miss Trant, Christopher Gable as Inigo Jollifant and Marti Webb as Susie Dean. The musical premiered at Her Majesty's Theatre in the West End on the 11th July 1974 after a one week run in Manchester. There were some good reviews particuarly for the performances of the leading players. There was also the early hope of a transfer to Broadway, but this was rejected by American producers who felt it was too English to cross the Atlantic.

In the end the production ran for 252 performances. This was less than expected, not because of poor reviews, but due to some intense IRA attacks across the capital that summer. People just didn't feel comfortable coming into the West End. Despite its relatively short run this adaptation has become the definitive musical version of the novel and is still performed by numerous dramatic societies to this day. On the 11th August 2000 it even made its professional debut in the USA at The Eureka Theatre in San Francisco.

The final major adaptation of the book was aired on ITV in 1980 and was the most ambitious and lengthy of all extending to nine hour long episodes with an additional documentary to accompany the series. Produced by Yorkshire Television, written by Alan Plater, directed by Bill Hays and Leonard Lewis with music by David Fanshawe it became the most comprehensive of all the book's adaptations and also the most faithful to the storyline and characters of the original novel. It too had a cast bursting with brilliance, a healthy mixture of established stars and upcoming new faces. Many went on to become big television stars of the 80s and 90s and most are still delighting audiences to this day. Some of the main characters give their recollections of the show and Priestley here.

I think I had secretly always wanted to play the young soubrette Susie Dean in The Good Companions. *I had read the book many years before the ITV production was planned and seen the film with Gielgud and Jessie Matthews and had been enchanted by it. However, this was to be a 'television musical' and I would have to sing to quite a high standard which I had not done before. I worked incredibly hard at finding a high soprano voice and to my great joy got the part.*

Top:
The 1980 cast pose at the end of Sandybay Pier (actually Llandudno), the scene of Judy Cornwell's dancing ordeal and a series of calamitous events. From left to right, back row: Judy Cornwell, Jeremy Nicholas, Vivienne Martin, Bryan Pringle, Jo Kendal, John Blythe, and John Stratton. Front row: Frank Mills, Jan Francis and Simon Green. (Photographer unknown)

Bottom:
The 1980 Cast have their turn at becoming Good Companions. (Photographer unknown)

It was a huge and exciting project. The scripts by Alan Plater were excellent and David Toguri choreographed with flair, turning several unlikely actors into swans. I felt a slight worry about the music, which was technically extremely difficult and (I thought) not really of the period. However, we eventually got the hang of it and gave it all we could. As the show took 15 months to complete we became a real company just like the Dinky Doos in the book. I felt completely at home playing Susie Dean. Yes, she could be vain and annoying but she was young, ambitious and determined – a very modern girl in fact!

As an admirer of Priestley I was thrilled when one day whilst filming a few of us were taken to meet the great man. He was gentlemanly and charming and interested to see his characters come to life again, but for some reason I was slightly overcome by his gravely voiced presence and didn't ask him all the questions I wish I had. A missed opportunity but I still have a fast disintegrating Polaroid photo of the occasion which I treasure. Another of my favourite possessions is a pencil self-portrait Priestley sketched while waiting to deliver a lecture at St Pancras Town Hall in 1942. I found it in a junk shop a few years ago. He is of course characteristically in profile with pipe firmly clenched between his teeth. Even though his books have been somewhat out of favour in recent years I am delighted that they are to be reprinted and available again. His work is beautifully crafted, humorous and full of accurately observed characters. He deserves to be more widely read.

Jan Francis – Susie Dean

When word got round in early 1979 that Yorkshire Television was casting The Good Companions, I had never read the book but knew that Gielgud had played Inigo Jollifant on stage and film in the early part of his career and that it was a plumb part for an actor-pianist. I was determined to get it. On the very day before I was finally offered the role, I wandered into a second-hand bookshop in central London and, amazingly, spotted in the shelves a rare two-volume first American edition of the book – signed by Priestley. With his interest in synchronicity, it was the kind of strange coincidence he would have enjoyed.

Reading this 'cosy fairy-tale' (Priestley's own description) was my first encounter with his dry, wry humour, affectionate

Jeremy Nicholas and Jan Francis chat with Priestley and his wife Jacquetta Hawkes during a break in filming at Burford, summer 1980. (Courtesy of Jeremy Nicholas' personal collection)

characterisation, acute ear for dialogue and Dickensian powers of description. I loved it. When the scripts arrived, I found that the nine-part series we were to film was not, as I had assumed, a straight adaptation of the book but a musical for TV. Backstage musicals are rarely successful.

Exhilarating to work on, this mammoth undertaking somehow came together over fifteen months. The series was not the huge hoped-for hit with critics or audiences, but I went on reading Priestley – all the plays, novels, essays (especially Delight) and the autobiographical Margin Released which taught me how to find my voice as a writer. I read Lost Empires. It inspired me to compose a suite for a brass band with that title and I wrote to Priestley asking if I might dedicate the work to him. His affirmative reply is a treasured possession. Much later, I met Gielgud and plucked up courage to tell him that we had both played Inigo Jollifant. 'Hm,' he said dismissively and to my huge disappointment. 'I always thought he was rather a silly young puppy.'

Jeremy Nicholas – Inigo Jollifant

In the script I was supposed to dance down Llandudno pier. My song was By the Sea. The pier was long and I had been dreading it because of a bad back. When the day arrived Bill Hays had the idea we would do the whole number in one take, but there were the extras and all the dancers including the sailors with whom I had to do my high kicks and lifts. We started our rehearsals and then spotted a body floating by the side of the pier. The coastguard was called and we congregated like seagulls watching the gruesome scene of a bloated corpse being fished out of the water. When rehearsals started again Vivienne Martin got her handbag containing all her credit cards kicked over the side. Luckily the coastguards were still around to fish it out for her. By the end of the day the dancers dressed as sailors were groaning with each lift and my back was killing me. When we finally finished and I saw the scene later with all the singing in sync and smiling sailors, no one would have guessed the number of groans, blasphemies and expletives that had been part of the number.

During filming Priestley came to watch and we had lunch with him. I was thrilled. When the day came I had some

Publicity shot taken between filming at Keighley Railway Station, one of the most authentically preserved railway stations in the country and a common location for screen productions. (Photographer unknown)

of his books I hoped he would autograph, including Literature and Western Man. *I sat next to him at lunch. He was very old, about eighty-six, but his eyes, though rheumy and heavy-lidded, were observant. I wanted to know who had inspired him for his characters in* The Good Companions. *Who had he modelled Miss Trant on? Susie Dean? Over pudding I told him that I had just finished my first novel. His eyes opened and his expression softened. Now he was listening. He wanted to know what the book was about. All the questions I had asked him were now coming back to me! He signed all the books I had brought with me and wanted to know what I thought of* Literature and Western Man. *I am so pleased the book is coming back into print. He is an author who should be read.*

Judy Cornwell - Miss Trant. Judy Cornwell's autobiography Adventures of a Jelly Baby **is published by Pan Macmillan.**

It was the spring of 1979, I was in my final term at the London Academy of Music and Dramatic Art and I was called in to audition for the role of Jerry Jerningham. Six weeks later I began rehearsals for what was my first job. I had stepped out of my life as student and straight into the professional world of actors and actresses from whom I was to learn so much about acting and television technique over the next twelve months.

These were heady, exciting times full of hard work and a lot of laughter. I vividly remember our travel days when we would meet at King's Cross station and, just like the Good Companions themselves, spend the next couple of hours engaged in noisy anecdote and gossip. I watched, slightly removed – in those days I had nothing to add. Many of the actors were veterans of a bygone period in the theatre when mid-day drinking was quite the norm and it was too much fun not to join in. "So, this is what actors do - sit on trains, drinking a lot of gin and tonic in the middle of the day?" At Leeds station we would separate to our various hotels and bed and breakfasts. I would have to have an afternoon nap, exhausted by my new life as an actor.

Simon Green – Jerry Jerningham

In recent years the story has continued to draw interest from producers and writers. During 1995 it was adapted for the stage a final time, on this occasion by Sayan Kent and Bob Eaton. First performed at The New Victoria Theatre,

Wills's Cigarettes

J. B. Priestley

The Good Companions gave Priestley enormous fame. These two cigarette card images show just how popular he had become by the early thirties. Both are from a series featuring famous British Authors. (Artists unknown)

MITCHELL'S CIGARETTES

J. B. PRIESTLEY

Newcastle-under-Lyme on the 13th September 1995 the show also played professionally at The Theatre by the Lake Keswick in 2001 and at the New Wolsey Theatre, Ipswich in 2003. In between these productions Eric Pringle wrote a three part adaptation for BBC Radio 4 which had its first airing through August 2002 and was repeated on the BBC's new digital Radio 7 in 2006.

Like the book the adaptations explored here have entertained tens of thousands, and have also showcased a horde of highly talented and remarkable individuals. Because of their existence Priestley's novel has found a life far beyond its cover and each have given critics and audiences much to muse over. At the close of *The Good*

Companions Priestley wrote that 'perfection is not to be found, neither in men nor in the lot they are offered, to say nothing of the tales we tell of them, these hints and guesses, words in the air and gesticulating shadows, these stumbling chronicles of a dream of life'. These words drive to the heart of all artistic ventures and are especially pertinent when applied to book adaptations. Reading is a very personal activity and some readers can never separate a novel from a film or stage version. Nevertheless, the various films and stage productions the book has spawned have carried Priestley's most successful story into every corner of the world and have helped to ensure its permanence and durability.

Priestley tells us of characters and situations that we recognise, and by which we are excited. We all know his plays; now is the time to be re-introduced to his novels.

Timothy West

Last Word

'A Dream of Life with J.B. Priestley'

Alan Plater

Dramatising *The Good Companions* for Yorkshire Television was an excellent adventure in all kinds of ways. For one thing, it resulted in my one and only appearance onscreen as a television interviewer and presenter and a memorable meeting with the great man at his house near Stratford.

'Is this a nice place to live?' I asked him.
'Good enough for Shakespeare, good enough for me.'

I'm not sure how revelatory our interview was in relation to the novel itself. It had been written half-a-century earlier and I had been living with it for a year or more; consequently I knew more about it than he did. In any case he felt the runaway success of the book had resulted in other, arguably more important work, being overshadowed. But that is the inevitable consequence of becoming a bestseller.

The series itself had what we all learn to call 'a mixed reception' from the critics. In retrospect, it's astonishing what we were allowed to do. We turned it into a full-blooded television musical with original songs and music. David Fanshawe wrote the music and I wrote the lyrics, some of them maybe too clever for their own good; but I had just read a biography of Lorenz Hart and had fallen in love with triple-rhyming schemes.

We also played games with time – which seemed appropriate to the author's ideas on the subject. Each of the first three episodes took place in the same time-frame, focused on each of the central characters – Jess Oakroyd, Elizabeth Trant and Inigo Jollifant. They all meet up at the end of Episode Three and after that the story proceeded chronologically with – another bold stroke – the final act of Episode Nine told entirely in song with a coda spoken to camera by Priestley himself: '…these rambling chronicles of a dream of life.'

It's difficult to imagine getting away with stuff like that today.

We had a terrific cast and had lots of fun on the road. Indeed, the spirit of making the series was strikingly parallel to that of the concert party in the story – it's a celebration of the reckless but fundamentally innocent merriment of court jesters who (and we try to keep this a secret) have the best job in the court.